TWIN EXCHANGE – ONE WEEK IN EACH
OTHER'S LIFE ...

They dressed in each other's clothes: Stephanie
in Sabrina's dark blue suit with red piping,
Sabrina in Stephanie's brown suit with white
blouse. She left the top two buttons open but
Stephanie, with a faint smile, did them up.

'I forgot –' Stephanie tugged at her finger and
held out her wedding ring to Sabrina. Her hand
was trembling. 'This is the first time I've ever
taken it off.'

Sabrina touched her fingers as she took the ring.
'I'll take care of it.' She put it on, thinking how
many years it had been since she had worn one
of her own.

And in the sixth-floor room of the Furama
Inter-Continental Hotel in Hong Kong, Sabrina
Longworth and Stephanie Andersen handed to
each other the keys to their front doors, in
England and America. And then it was time to
go.

Deceptions

JUDITH MICHAEL

SPHERE BOOKS LIMITED
30-32 Gray's Inn Road, London WC1X 8JL

First published in Great Britain by
Sphere Books Ltd 1982
Copyright © 1982 by J M Productions Ltd

Reprinted 1983
Published in America by Poseidon Press, 1982

TRADE
MARK

Set in Pilgrim

Reproduced, printed and bound in Great Britain by
Collins, Glasgow.

For Cynthia, Andrew and Eric

Part I

Chapter 1

Sabrina Longworth stood at the window of the Quo Fu Antique Shop on Tian Jin Road and debated whether she should buy the fantastically carved jade chess set or the bronze dragon lamp. She could buy both, but she hadn't even seen what was inside the shop. If she bought everything that took her fancy on a two-week trip through China, she'd go home a pauper.

When Stephanie arrived, she'd ask her what she thought. Maybe she'd buy the lamp for Stephanie. If, for once, Stephanie would let her buy her something.

From the shadows inside the dim shop, Mr Su Guang watched the American lady, amazed at her beauty. Mr Su, an artist and curator of antiques, had studied in America and had loved a fair-haired girl who took him to her bed and taught him to appreciate Western as well as Oriental beauty. But never had Mr Su seen a lady as vividly beautiful as this one. Her deep auburn hair shone bronze and gold in the late afternoon sun and was held in a loose knot at the back of her neck by white enamel combs etched in gold. In the delicate oval of her face, her eyes were a dark midnight blue, wide-spaced, and her mouth was generous, with the faintest downward curve at the corners giving it a vulnerable look. Watching her, Mr Su wanted to offer his help. What man, he wondered, looking at that lovely mouth, whether laughing or weeping or in repose, would not feel the same way?

She was not tall, he saw, but she held herself like a queen, slender and graceful against the background of crowds of people walking and bicycling home, carrying live chickens or ducks for their dinner or pulling their purchases on makeshift carts. Occasionally the lady glanced at them, but mostly she studied his window display. And of all the objects

1

there, she had fastened on the two finest. Mr Su decided to invite her in and take from locked cases precious antiques he showed only to those who could appreciate them. Smiling in anticipation, he stepped forward. Then, abruptly, he stopped, his mouth open in astonishment at the vision in his window: the lady had become two.

In every way they were the same, even to the silk dresses that Mr Su recognized came from a shop not far from his. But he had no more time to wonder, for in the next minute the two ladies entered his shop.

Inside the door they hesitated, waiting for their eyes to adjust from sunshine to the half-light of candles and kerosene lamps. Mr Su stepped forward and bowed. 'Welcome. May I offer you tea?'

The first lady, who had led the way inside, held out her hand. 'Mr Su? I am Sabrina Longworth. I wrote to you about buying for Ambassadors, my antique gallery in London.'

'Lady Longworth! I have been expecting you. Yet now I find not one but two of you!'

She laughed. 'My sister, Stephanie Andersen, from America.'

'America!' Mr Su beamed. 'I studied in America, at the Art Institute of Chicago.'

Mrs Andersen looked at her sister. 'A small world,' she said, and turned to Mr Su. 'My home is just north of Chicago, in the town of Evanston.'

'Ah! I have been there also, visiting the university. Come, come, let us have tea.' Mr Su was excited by the luminous beauty of the ladies, brightening his shop as no candles could. Identical beauty, identical voices: low and soft, with a faint lilt he could not identify. How could one be from America and one from London when they both spoke with an accent vaguely European? They had been educated in Europe, Mr Su decided, and, as he bustled about the tea table, he asked about their tour through China and the antique dealers' groups sponsoring it. 'Lady Longworth,' he said, offering her a cup. She laughed and looked at her sister. Embarrassed, Mr Su looked from one lady to the other. 'I have made a mistake.' He bowed. 'Mrs Andersen. Forgive me.'

2

She smiled. 'There's nothing to forgive. Strangers often confuse us.' She looked again at her sister. 'The housewife from Evanston and the Lady from London.'

Mr Su did not understand, but he was relieved. They were not insulted. He resumed his chatter and, after they had drunk several cups of tea, he showed them his rarest treasures.

Lady Longworth, Mr Su noted with approval, handled antiques with reverence and appraised them expertly. She was also, he discovered, an experienced bargainer. She knew intuitively when he had gone as far as he could within the price range set by the government, and she wasted no time in deciding to buy or to go on to the next piece.

'Sabrina, look!' Mrs Andersen was kneeling before Mr Su's collection of antique magic equipment. She turned the intricate pieces in her hands. 'I'll buy one for Penny and Cliff. No, I'd better buy two, to keep peace in the house.'

Working his abacus with swift fingers, Mr Su added up Lady Longworth's purchases, including the jade chess set and bronze lamp from the window, plus the cost of shipment to London. Then he took from his magic cabinet an ivory carving and held it out to Mrs Andersen. 'With my compliments.' At her look of surprise, he said, 'You admired this but put it back when I told you the cost. Please accept it. You bought for your children; I would like you to have this for yourself.'

She smiled with such delight that Mr Su sighed for his lost youth. He bowed and held open the door as they thanked him, and he watched them until they disappeared around a corner in the narrow, twisting street.

'How do we get back to the hotel?' Stephanie asked. She was carrying the bronze lamp, and Sabrina had the chess set, trusting neither to the shipping company.

'I haven't the faintest idea,' Sabrina said cheerfully. 'I thought I remembered how we got here, but these streets are worse than the maze at Treveston. That'll teach us to escape our keepers and wander around Shanghai alone. We'll have to ask someone.'

Stephanie took from its box the carved ivory Mr Su had given her. 'Did you see this?'

Sabrina handed her the chess set and stood still to study the delicate piece. It was made up of dozens of tiny, fancifully carved figures, interlocked to form an openwork cube. One piece moved under her finger. 'It comes apart!' she exclaimed.

'I'm afraid to try,' said Stephanie. 'I'd never get it together again. But isn't it lovely? Ladies of the court, all intertwined.'

'Clever Mr Su, telling us he thought the two of us together are like one person. Where do you think we are?'

A bicyclist stopped beside them. 'May I help you?' he asked in careful English.

'We've lost the Heping Hotel,' Sabrina said.

'Lost? Ah, you have lost the way. It is indeed confusing. If you will follow me, I will lead you to NanJing Road East.'

'Does everyone in China speak English?' Stephanie asked.

'We study in school,' he said casually, and rode ahead slowly as they followed.

'You didn't buy anything for Garth,' said Sabrina.

'I probably will. I told you, I'm not feeling very generous toward him right now. Anyway, we have another week. Oh—!'

'What is it?'

'Only one more week. Such a little time. Before I left, two weeks seemed forever. Now I've gotten greedy. I wish ... Sabrina, did you ever wish you could just disappear for awhile?'

'Lately I wish it about once a day. But usually what I want to get away from is me, and wherever I went, I'd still be me.'

'Yes, that's what I meant. You always know what I mean.'

The bicyclist turned a corner, looking around to make sure they were following. 'Maybe China is the farthest we can disappear,' Sabrina said.

'Then perhaps I'll stay,' said Stephanie lightly. 'And really disappear. For awhile at least. No more Stephanie Andersen. I'll tell Mr Su I'm Lady Longworth, staying on for a few weeks, and since you're his best customer, he'll be delighted to help me. That is, if you don't mind my temporarily disappearing into your name and title.'

'Not at all, but if you're going to be me, I'd appreciate it if you'd go back to London and solve my problems.'

'Only if you go to Evanston and solve mine.'

They laughed. 'Wouldn't that be a lark?' Sabrina said, and then the bicyclist turned again, pointing. 'NanJing Road East,' he said.

Before they could thank him, he was gone, blending into the hundreds of bicyclists, cars and pedestrians jamming the wide road. Stephanie walked slowly, staring with unseeing eyes at the shop windows. 'It would be a fairy tale,' she said. 'Living your wonderful life. The only problem would be fighting off your Brazilian millionaire.'

Sabrina looked at her. 'I'd have to fight off your husband.'

'Oh, no; no, you wouldn't. Garth mostly sleeps in the study. We haven't made love in ... a long time. You wouldn't have any fighting to do at all.'

They fell silent, passing the bookstore and walking on to the artificial-flowers store. Stephanie paused, gazing at the petals and leaves of colored paper and silk. 'Do you suppose we could get away with it? I'll bet we could. Not for long, of course, but ... we could do it.'

Sabrina met her eyes in their reflected images overlaid with iridescent pink and red bouquets and nodded. 'Probably. For a few days.' She laughed. 'Remember, in Athens, when you—'

'We could look at ourselves from far away, from another life, and figure out what we want to do—well, I mean, I could figure out what I want; you always know exactly—'

'Not exactly, and you know it.'

'Well then, we'd both have a chance to think about—'

'Ah here you are!' Their guide, leading the tour group out of a nearby shop, began to scold them for wandering off on their own.

'Let's talk about it later,' Stephanie had time to say before they were swept up and taken back to the hotel for dinner and a four-hour acrobatic show.

But it was the next afternoon before they had a chance to

5

talk. Stephanie wanted to window-shop on the rest of NanJing Road East. 'I keep thinking about it,' she said. 'Do you? Last night I was too tired to talk, but I thought about it, and this morning I haven't been able to think about anything else.'

'I know.' Since the day before, the idea had clung to the edge of Sabrina's thoughts. 'It's one of those crazy ideas that won't go away.'

'Not that crazy. Sabrina, I'm serious about it.'

Sabrina looked at her. 'It wouldn't solve anything—'

'How do we know? The main thing is that we'd get away from what we are now.'

They were silent. Sabrina felt her blood quicken. Stephanie always knew what would strike home: to get away . . .

'And we could do it,' Stephanie went on. 'We know so much about each other's lives. We've talked about them and we think the same way—'

They did. They both knew it; they always had.

'Everything would be new, and we'd be able to think about ourselves in different ways. . . .' Her words tumbled out. 'You can't do that when you're in the middle of a life that has no time for thinking. And you've said so often you'd like a taste of my life, it's so different from yours. . . . Listen, what do you have to do the first week you're home?'

'Not much.' The idea had caught hold, and Sabrina's thoughts flew ahead. 'I didn't schedule anything in case I needed to recover from China. There's nothing that really needs doing. Ambassadors could even stay closed for another week.'

'And there's not much to do at my house, either,' Stephanie said eagerly. 'Penny and Cliff go their own way. You can call in sick at the office – Oriental dysentery or something. They all know about China; I had to get special permission to be gone for two weeks. Oh – but you'd have to cook for everybody at home.'

Sabrina laughed. Her eyes were bright. 'I'm a good cook. How do you think I eat when Mrs Thirkell is on vacation?'

'They don't know what they're eating, anyway,' Stephanie raced on. 'They're always in such a hurry to be somewhere else. You'd really be alone most of the time.'

They stopped at the paper-cuts store where intricate flowers, dragons, boats and hundreds of other folded creations were displayed. Sabrina could feel a familiar excitement building inside her, gathering itself, preparing to leap. She had felt it so often in the past, since she was a little girl: the pull of a challenge, the joy of a dare, the excitement of winning – gathering itself, preparing to leap. 'To be someone else . . . ' she murmured.

'To live another life,' Stephanie said. 'An adventure, Sabrina!'

They smiled, remembering – twenty years ago, Sabrina thought. They were eleven, living in Athens. Their first great adventure.

They walked on. 'A week,' Stephanie said. 'Just one incredible week.'

'You might get greedy again,' Sabrina said lightly.

'So might you.'

A block from their hotel, in front of the Shanghai Cakes and Pastries Store, Nicholas Blackford bumped into them as he navigated with a stack of wrapped pastries. He smiled guiltily. 'It seems so difficult to diet away from home. I should have brought Amelia. You must scold me, Sabrina, as you used to when you worked in my shop and monitored my bad habits. Or am I speaking to Stephanie? Do you know, I am ashamed to say this, and I assure you it is no reflection on either of you, but Sabrina – Stephanie – I really cannot tell you apart.'

Sabrina and Stephanie looked at each other behind the bald and bouncing figure of Nicholas Blackford. Strangers often confused them, but Nicholas had known Sabrina for ten years. Her eyes dancing, Sabrina swept a low curtsy to Stephanie. 'Lady Longworth,' she said in a clear voice. 'Welcome to Shanghai.'

Stephanie stretched out her hand to help her up. 'Mrs Andersen,' she said. 'How glad I am to be here.'

Chapter 2

They were always moving. It seemed barely the blink of an eye from the time they settled in a house and arranged their furniture and hung up their clothes to the time when the servants would begin packing everything into cartons for the trip to a new city with a different language and a school full of strangers. It started when they were two years old in Washington, D.C., and from then on they moved every two years: Norway, Sweden, Portugal, Spain – and now they were moving again.

'Not already!' Sabrina groaned when she came in from horseback riding and found her mother wrapping a fragile vase in a blanket. 'We just got here!'

'Two years ago,' said her mother. 'And Daddy and I told you last spring we'd be moving to Athens in August.'

'I don't want to go to Athens,' Stephanie wailed. 'I like Madrid. I like my friends. And we were going to get the best sixth-grade teacher in the school!'

'You'll make new friends in Athens,' her mother said calmly. 'The American school will have good teachers. And Athens is full of wonderful things.'

'Athens is full of ruins,' Sabrina grumbled.

'Which we will explore,' said her mother, fitting the wrapped vase in a carton and stuffing crumpled newspapers around it. 'I'm sorry, girls, I know you don't like it, but we don't either. It's just something we have to—'

'Daddy likes it,' Sabrina said stubbornly. 'Every time we move he gets more puffed up and important.'

'That's enough, Sabrina,' her mother said sharply. 'The two of you go upstairs and start sorting your clothes and books. You know how.'

'We've had enough practice,' Sabrina muttered to Stephanie as they went upstairs.

In fact, she was already beginning to be excited about Athens, but she couldn't admit it because Stephanie was so miserable. Stephanie wanted to stay in one house and one school with one set of friends for years and years; she hated it when things kept changing around her.

But even if Sabrina was silent, Stephanie knew how she felt; they almost always knew what the other was thinking. 'I get excited by new things, too,' Stephanie said, throwing sweaters onto the bed. 'But wouldn't it be wonderful to have a real home for awhile?'

'I don't know,' Sabrina said honestly. 'Since we've never had one.'

She didn't think the rented houses had been so bad; Mother would walk in like a magician and make them beautiful and comfortable and soon they could hardly remember their old house. And that was exactly what happened when they moved to Athens in August. In a two-story white house that sparkled in the sun, with a garden and separate rooms for Sabrina and Stephanie, Mother filled the rooms with their furniture and rugs, putting everything in just the right places. Then, while their father went to the embassy to meet the staff and move into his new office, the three of them were driven in a limousine around Athens and its suburbs.

As they drove, the city crept through the windows of the car, making Sabrina quiver with anticipation. Everything was spread out, waiting to be discovered: strange smells and sights and sounds, new words to be learned and new songs to sing, folk tales to hear from the servants their mother would hire, new friends to trade stories with. She could hardly wait.

But Stephanie's unhappiness kept her quiet and even made her excitement fade away. She drooped and picked at her dinner their first week in Athens, just as Stephanie did, until their father put down his fork with a clatter, saying, 'I have had enough of this. Laura, I thought you talked to them.'

She nodded. 'I did, Gordon. Several times.'

'Evidently not enough.' He turned to face them. 'We're going to get a lecture,' Sabrina whispered to Stephanie. 'I will explain this one more time,' Gordon began. 'Our State Department rotates members of the diplomatic service to a new post every two years. We do not question that policy. Do you understand?'

'It's stupid,' Sabrina said. 'You're always starting over and then you can't do a good job.'

'I hardly think,' her father said dryly, 'that an eleven-year-old girl is in a position to pronounce the US State Department "stupid". Or to say that her father cannot do a good job. I've told you before that rotation prevents our getting personally involved in the affairs of other countries. Our first loyalty must always be to America.' He looked seriously at Sabrina and Stephanie. 'I might add that it is good for you, too. How else would you get to know so many countries?'

'You mean,' said Sabrina, as seriously as her father, 'it's good for your career, so we'd better decide it's good for us, too.'

'Sabrina!' Laura snapped, and held Sabrina's eyes with her own until Sabrina looked away.

'I'm sorry,' she said.

Laura picked up her wine glass. 'Tell us about your new school. You too, Stephanie. No more pouting.'

As Sabrina obediently described their maths and science teachers and Stephanie listed the books they would read in literature and history, Laura watched them, frowning. They were becoming difficult to control. She was proud of them – her vibrant, spirited daughters, already beautiful and quick-witted – but too often they were also impudent and secretive, banding together in their struggle for independence. She had no idea what was the best way to handle them.

The problem was, she didn't have time. Her time belonged to the diplomatic career of Gordon Hartwell. She had vowed silently at their wedding to push him and help him until he became an ambassador, perhaps even Secretary of State, and nothing in the years that followed had stopped her, not even the unplanned birth of twin girls.

She was Gordon's partner, taking his place at meetings and receptions he was too busy or bored to attend; being at his side night after night at intimate dinners, banquets, tours for American senators, and entertaining American businessmen; and sitting with him in his study when he was thinking out loud to solve a problem.

He needed her. Once he had been poor and anonymous, a

history professor in a small college in Maine. She had brought him her beauty and style, which added to his prestige, and also her wealth and sophistication, which eased him into the presence of the rich and powerful. Even now, when he had developed the smooth skills of a polished diplomat and had forged his own reputation as an expert on European cultural and political agreements, he needed her. They still had a long way to go, and he knew she would not let anything stop them.

Nothing ever stopped Laura when she made up her mind. She managed Gordon's career, their nomadic life in Europe, their social life and her daughters' upbringing. She concentrated on Gordon, but she made sure that competent servants cared for Sabrina and Stephanie and whenever possible took a few hours to guide their growing up herself.

From the first, she insisted they be brought up as separate individuals. Why should they be peas in a pod simply because they were identical twins? So their bedrooms were furnished in different styles, they dressed differently from each other and were given different presents to help them develop separate interests.

And once again Laura got what she wanted: her girls were different. She thought Sabrina was most like her, always eager to tackle the unknown, while Stephanie resembled Gordon: calmer and more cautious. Gordon saw that, too, and though he didn't spend much time with them, when he did it was Stephanie who got most of his attention while Sabrina watched with dark, somber eyes.

But they were not quite as different as Laura liked to believe. Even she could not deny that their minds worked together, often in startling ways, and the instinctive bond between them was so strong she knew no one could break it unless they did it themselves.

But that made their restlessness even more difficult to handle: two adolescents, not one, pushing for independence.

'Why can't we explore the city by ourselves?' Sabrina asked. 'We've hardly seen any of it.'

'You've had those school field trips,' Laura said. She was

11

brushing her hair at her dressing table and red glints flashed in the mirror.

'Ugh.' Sabrina made a face. 'We've seen every statue and church between here and heaven, but in a whole year we haven't met one real live person except at school – and they're Americans! Just let us go for a little walk. Just around the embassy. We never get to do anything!'

'No,' Gordon said. He was adjusting his black tie at the triple mirror. They were going to dinner at the king's palace.

'Why not?' Sabrina wailed.

'Sabrina,' Gordon said sharply. 'Keep your voice down.'

Stephanie stood beside her father. 'Why not, Daddy?'

'Because there are dangers,' he said, ruffling her hair. 'For young girls, and especially for American girls whose father is a member of the embassy.'

'What kind of dangers?' asked Sabrina. 'Mother goes out alone; she's a girl and she's related to you. Is she in danger? Why can't—?'

'Sabrina!' Gordon warned again. 'If I tell you there are dangers, you will trust my word. I can tolerate the refusal of the premier of Greece to take my word for something, but I will not tolerate it in my daughter.'

'But what can we do around here?' Sabrina ignored Stephanie's cautioning hand on her arm. 'You go out and leave us stuck with the servants, you get to see Athens and meet people and have fun . . . Everybody gets to be with you but us!'

Laura fastened jeweled combs in her hair. 'We do spend time together—'

'We don't!' Sabrina burst out. 'Mostly it's just when you're showing us off to old people from America!' Before Laura could make an angry response, Stephanie drew her attention away.

'Most of the time you're with Daddy or doing your own shopping. And Daddy's always working. Other families aren't like that. They have weekends together and they eat together and have a real family.'

'The only family we have is us,' Sabrina finished. 'Stephanie and me – we're our whole family!'

'Silence, both of you!' Filling his pipe, Gordon spoke to their reflections in the mirror. 'Some professions take the cooperation of a whole family. We work for our country. It would be selfish to think of ourselves first.'

'You think of getting promoted,' Sabrina flashed, and then shrank back from her father's look.

'You know nothing about what I think and you will not comment on it here or anywhere else. Is that clear?'

Sabrina met her father's look. 'If you talked to the Russians like you talk to us we'd have a war.'

Laura stifled a laugh. Gordon flung down his tobacco pouch and Sabrina watched the shreds of tobacco fall like skinny worms all over the rug. 'Leave the room,' her father said.

'Just a minute, Gordon.' Laura stood, tall and magnificent in black silk and long white strands of pearls. Sabrina hated her for being so beautiful and distant, and at the same time she wanted to crawl into her arms and be loved. But the only person who ever hugged her was Stephanie. Sabrina wondered if her parents ever hugged and kissed. Probably not. They'd wrinkle their beautiful clothes. But then her mother surprised her. 'The girls do need more attention,' she said. 'I'm going to take them on some of my shopping expeditions.'

'Oh—!' cried Stephanie.

But Gordon shook his head. 'I think not.'

Laura sighed deeply. 'Gordon, I am doing the best I can. I know you don't approve of the places I go, but I assure you they are simple working-class neighborhoods, not dens of terrorists. And I have to go there to find the best buys.'

'What terrorists?' Sabrina asked.

'There are no terrorists,' said Gordon in exasperation, but he looked at his watch, and Sabrina knew that meant he had lost interest in them. 'Take them if you insist, but use the limousine.'

'Of course.' Laura fastened her silk cloak. 'Shall we go?'

The shopping expeditions began the next day after school. Trailed by neighbourhood children who called them the three beautiful American ladies, they hunted for antiques and works of art in shops, markets and private homes. Laura

13

called it her hobby, but it had long since become her passion. She studied in libraries, talked with museum curators, attended auctions and watched furniture and art restorers at work. Over the years their rented houses became showplaces of her purchases: gleaming woods and mosaics, sculptures and paintings, leaded glass and finely woven fabrics. By the time she began taking Sabrina and Stephanie with her, Laura had become an expert appraiser and bargainer, supreme in her own world, where Gordon never came.

She also had become an advisor to friends and the international set that mingled socially with diplomats. They called on her so often that, had she not been Gordon Hartwell's wife, she could have made a different life on her own. But she loved the glittering social life Gordon gave her, so she kept both her passions and taught them to her daughters.

Sabrina and Stephanie, eleven years old, for the first time became friends with their mother. They shared her private world; they spoke her private language. She poured out her knowledge and they absorbed it hungrily, as if it were love.

The three of them browsed in dingy shops where old people gossiped in corners and dust tickled their noses, and they visited homes where whole families gathered to show them rugs and paintings that had been theirs for generations. But best of all were the open-air markets, with row after row of stalls hung with rugs, baskets, tapestries, vases, even furniture, and standing in front of each someone shouting, 'Buy this! Buy here! Such a bargain!' Sabrina and Stephanie wanted to buy everything, but their mother ruthlessly separated the fake from the genuine, brushing aside protestations from vendors who expected Americans to be gullible. Laura was in control, absolutely confident, and Sabrina and Stephanie watched her with wide-eyed wonder: this was a different woman from the one they knew at home, where she was Gordon's wife.

But those afternoons came only once or twice a week, and by spring Sabrina was chafing to see more of Athens. 'Let's ask if today we can shop somewhere new,' she said as they climbed into the embassy limousine after school.

Theo, the chauffeur, spoke to the rear-view mirror. 'No shopping today, miss. Your mother told me to bring you to the embassy.'

'Oh, no!' Stephanie cried.

Sabrina struck her schoolbooks in frustration. 'Daddy probably wants to show us off again. Well, I won't do it. I'm going to do my buck-teeth smile.'

Stephanie brightened. 'And I'll cross my eyes.'

Grinning grotesquely, Sabrina hunched her right shoulder to her ear.

Eyes crossed, Stephanie stuck out her tongue and licked her chin.

They studied each other's demonic poses and imagined their father, tall and proper, saying to solemn visitors, 'Meet my daughters,' and they collapsed on the back seat in a fit of giggles.

'Damn, damn,' grumbled Theo, and they looked up; what did they do wrong? But he was cursing a traffic jam caused by an automobile accident ahead. 'We'll be here an hour,' he said, throwing up his hands.

Sabrina and Stephanie looked at each other with the same wild, wonderful idea. Each of them reached out to a door handle and, without a word, pushed down, swung open the doors, slammed them shut and sped down the street, ducking around corners and pushing past shoppers. Theo, lumbering after them and shouting their names, was left far behind.

'We did it, oh, we did it,' Sabrina sang. 'Now we can explore by ourselves.' The earth felt light and airy beneath her feet. 'Oh, Stephanie, isn't it wonderful?'

'Wonderful,' echoed Stephanie.

Hand in hand, they strolled through shops and crowded squares, chewing on sticky *baklava* they bought from a street vendor, reading Greek signs aloud to practice their vocabulary and pausing at butchers' stalls, where they listened in fascination to the gruesome sound of air whistling through sheeps' lungs frying in oil. Finally Sabrina looked at her watch and sighed. 'Well, it's been half an hour; we'd better get back before Theo gets unstuck.' But before they could turn, they heard shouts and a clatter of running feet, and

Stephanie ducked as a stone struck the building near her head.

'Terrorists!' Sabrina exclaimed. She looked around, grabbed Stephanie's hand and pulled her down a flight of stairs to a heavy door that was partly open. They slipped inside, shutting it tightly behind them. The room was dark after the bright sun and it took them a minute to see three children huddled in a corner. When Sabrina came close, the baby began to cry. 'Oh, don't,' Sabrina said. She turned to the oldest, a thin boy about their age with straight eyebrows and a shock of curly hair, and said in Greek, 'Can we stay here a little while? Some men are fighting in the street.'

The boy and his sister spoke rapidly in Greek and Sabrina and Stephanie looked at each other helplessly; it was too fast for them to follow. But they recognized the boy's intent look as he stared at them; they had seen it many times. He smiled broadly, pointing at each of them. 'You are a mirror,' he said slowly in Greek, and they all laughed.

From the street above came loud crashes and men's voices shouting to each other. An acrid smell drifted into the room. Sabrina and Stephanie twined their fingers tightly together. They were all silent, listening. The smell burned in their noses, and then they heard gunshots.

The boy moved, herding his sister and the baby to a cot and covering them with a blanket. He was scowling in an effort to look brave. When Stephanie whispered, 'What should we do?' he pointed to the door.

Sabrina became angry. 'You know we can't go out there,' she said in Greek. The shouts were louder. 'Those are terrorists.'

The boy looked at her defiantly. 'It is a war of independence.' Sabrina looked bewildered and he shrugged at her ignorance.

She ran to the high window and climbed on a box to look out, but the boy ran after her and pushed her away. She fell to the floor. Stephanie cried out, but Sabrina scrambled to her feet. 'He's right. Somebody might have seen me. I just wanted to know what was making the smell.'

'Burning cars,' said the boy.

'Burning—? Why would they burn cars?'

'To block the street.' He muttered, 'Stupid American girl.'

'How do you know we're Americans?' Sabrina asked. The boy threw up his hands in despair, and then they heard banging on the doors up and down the street.

'We've got to hide!' Stephanie said wildly. 'They mustn't find us!'

'Where can we go?' Sabrina asked the boy urgently. 'Please, we shouldn't be here. You could be in trouble if they find us. Is there another room?'

He hesitated, then pointed under the cot. They pushed it aside with the little girls still on it and saw a trapdoor in the floor. The boy put his fingers in a notch on one side and pulled it up. Taking a deep breath, Sabrina slid through the opening, holding out a hand for Stephanie to follow. The door slammed in place above them and they heard the cot scrape the floor as the boy pushed it back.

It was so dark they could not see each other or what was around them. The air was damp, with a cloying odor. A cellar, Sabrina thought, but the ceiling was too low; they banged their heads when they tried to stand up. There was knocking on the door of the room above and they stayed still, crouching in the damp blackness. Stephanie's fingernails dug into Sabrina's hand. With her free hand Sabrina swept back and forth in the darkness for a place to sit. She felt the hard-packed dirt of the floor and then something like burlap. Burlap with lumps. A sack of potatoes. That was the rotting smell: they were in a vegetable cellar.

They sat together, arms around each other, heads touching. A few inches above them boots clumped back and forth, and rough voices asked rapid questions. Sabrina heard the word "guns" and the boy's "No." But then she heard drawers being pulled out and crashing to the floor.

Shudders ran through Stephanie's body as she gasped for breath. Sabrina tightened her arm around her shoulders. 'Wait,' she breathed close to her ear. 'They'll be gone soon. Hold on to me.' She closed her eyes; it was less scary than not being able to see anything.

'My stomach hurts,' Stephanie whispered. Sabrina nodded. So did hers. The smell of rotting vegetables stuck inside her nose and she could taste it deep in her throat. It made her gag. She buried her nose against her jacket and took a deep breath. That helped. Above them the men were arguing. The baby began to cry. And in the blackness Sabrina felt something crawling up her leg.

She jerked back just as Stephanie felt it, too, and gave a little scream, trying to stand up. Sabrina pulled her down. 'Don't,' she whispered. She thought the baby's crying had covered Stephanie's scream but she couldn't be sure. She brushed Stephanie's legs and her own. Spiders. One clung to her fingers and she crushed it against the dirt floor.

She was shaking all over. She'd tried so hard to be brave, but Stephanie's fear had seeped into her. Now with each footstep above them she felt herself being dragged into the open. They'd be raped. They'd be killed or held for ransom. They'd be cut up in little pieces and sent back to their parents one piece at a time and Mother would cry. They had never seen their mother cry, and thinking about it made Sabrina start crying, as if the full terror of the afternoon only became real when she thought of her mother crying over them.

Then suddenly it was over. The boy said loudly, 'My father.' A man asked, 'Where?' and the boy answered, 'On Cyprus.' The men's voices changed; one of them laughed and said, 'A patriot.' The footsteps moved out the door and up the steps to the street. The door closed. Only the thin wailing of the baby could be heard.

Sabrina was steadily brushing her legs and Stephanie's, holding Stephanie tightly with her other arm and breathing into her jacket. In the sudden silence she had a new fear: What if the boy kept them there? He probably hated them for hiding while he faced the men alone. What if he put something heavy on the door so they couldn't get out? She sprang up, hitting her head so hard it made her dizzy, but she pushed at the ceiling, trying to find the trapdoor. 'Where are you?' Stephanie whispered frantically, but Sabrina was desperately moving her hands back and forth on the ceiling. Something sharp jabbed her fingers, and just as she realized it was a nail in the trapdoor the boy opened it. She blinked in the light, limp with relief and shame. He was as young and afraid as they were; how could she have thought he would hurt them?

When the boy had pulled them up, Sabrina and Stephanie stared at each other. They were filthy, their skirts torn, their faces streaked with tears and dirt. Sabrina's fingers were scraped and bloody, and when she moved a spider fell out of her hair. Seeing it, Stephanie violently ran her hands through her own hair. The boy was replacing the drawers the men had flung to the floor. On the cot, the little girl and the baby lay still, their eyes wide and blank.

Now that it was over, Sabrina became curious again. 'What did they want?' she asked.

'Guns,' said the boy. 'They are Greek patriots fighting for independence in Cyprus.'

Sabrina remembered something about it from school. 'Why are they fighting here?'

'To get rid of the Turks.' The boy spat out the word.

'But are the Turks here?'

'No: In Cyprus. Fighting Greeks. My father is there. I should be with him, fighting the Turks.'

'Then who is in the street?' Sabrina demanded, stamping her foot in frustration.

'Greeks and Turks and police,' the boy said, as if it were obvious.

Stephanie was feeling better. She knew Sabrina was ashamed because they had hidden, and she began to feel ashamed too. 'Where is your mother?' she asked the boy.

'Dead. My aunt was to be here, but she is late.'

'Dead! Oh, Sabrina, we should—'

But Sabrina was looking at the boy intently. 'Would you really fight?' she asked.

'If I had a gun,' he answered, 'I would kill.'

Sabrina's eyes were dark with wonder. 'What's your name?'

'Dmitri Karras.' They stared at each other.

The room was quiet; outside, the noise had faded, leaving only the crackling flames of the burning cars.

'Sabrina,' Stephanie said. 'It's late. Shouldn't we go? And maybe – if their mother is dead – we could—'

'—take them with us,' Sabrina finished.

Dmitri drew himself up. 'I take care of my sisters.'

'Yes,' Sabrina said. 'But come for awhile. Come for dinner,' she added as graciously as her mother in the embassy reception room. 'Our chauffeur will bring you back whenever you want.'

Dmitri could not take his eyes off her: so proud and beautiful. Like a queen. He hated her and he loved her. 'Okay,' he said at last.

And so it was that firemen arriving a few moments later came upon five children walking down the street – a Greek girl carrying a baby, and a Greek boy with eyes riveted on two identical American girls, scruffy with dirt but real beauties, their faces framed in auburn curls. The firemen took them to the police, who drove them to the address they gave, which the police knew was the American Embassy, and there was going to be hell to pay.

One of the policemen had telephoned ahead, and a crowd was waiting on the embassy porch. Laura flew down the walk to gather Sabrina and Stephanie to her, exclaiming in dismay at their torn, dirty clothes and the blood on Sabrina's hands. Gordon followed, his face like stone. As he reached them flashbulbs exploded on all sides from the cameras of thirty reporters who, like everyone else, had thought Cypriots had kidnapped the twin daughters of the American chargé d'affaires.

Sabrina leaned against her mother in the wonderful warmth of her arms. Everything was all right. They were home. Then, remembering Dmitri, she looked around and caught a glimpse of him through the crowd of jostling reporters.

'Wait!' she commanded loudly. She and Stephanie pulled away from Laura and went to Dmitri. 'These are our friends. They saved us. I've invited them to dinner.'

'Sabrina!' Her father's voice lashed her. 'Not another word. You have done enough damage with your recklessness and impudence. How many times must I warn you—?'

Sabrina stared, open-mouthed and stunned. They were home. Why was Daddy scolding her? He hadn't even hugged them. She was hurt all over and she was so tired and she had felt so safe when they saw the embassy and then Mother had held them ... Why was Daddy making her feel so awful? Tears filled her eyes and spilled over. She tried to stop them, but they ran down her cheeks and she tasted them on her lips.

'—a self-indulgence that shows you have no regard for my career. This time you have dragged your sister into it and these children, too, whoever they are. You are to go inside this instant; I will decide your punishment when—'

'That's not Sabrina! You've mixed us up!' Through her tears Sabrina saw Stephanie hammering on Gordon's arm. Stephanie was crying, too. 'That's Stephanie, not Sabrina, you've mixed us up, you can't blame her in front of everybody, she didn't do anything and, anyway, we both had the idea, we got out of the car at the same time. Theo will tell you, and then the fighting started and we hid, and you can't blame Sabrina – Stephanie – either of us, it's not her fault!'

The reporters moved in, taking pictures. 'Sir, if the young ladies – Sabrina? or Stephanie? – would tell us what happened—'

Gordon, struck dumb, was looking from Sabrina to Stephanie and back again. Sabrina heard him mutter, 'How the hell am I supposed to—?' but Laura took over, stepping in front of him.

'No interviews, please,' she said. 'The girls are exhausted from their ordeal, and not well.' She was not well herself, still gripped by the paralysing fears and guilt she had felt all afternoon: she had never done enough for her children, and now they might be dead. But the clamoring reporters and the danger of a scandal touching Gordon aroused her to her duty, and she pushed her anguish down, out of sight. It would wait. Later, she would recover, in private.

'Sabrina, Stephanie, take these children inside. Get some food and wait for me in your father's office. Now!' she said, and they ran up the walk with lights flashing in their faces. Behind them, a recovered, suave Gordon promised the reporters a statement the next day.

But sensational stories appeared in the morning papers without Gordon's official version, each one featuring large pictures of Sabrina and Stephanie with the Greek children.

By then the girls were locked in their separate bedrooms, but a Greek maid brought the newspapers with their breakfasts and later, when Gordon and Laura were out, unlocked their doors. Sabrina danced into Stephanie's bedroom, holding the paper. 'I've never had my picture in the newspaper before. On the front page, just like Mother and Daddy! And it says they found Dmitri's aunt! Oh, Stephanie, isn't it amazing, so many things happening at once?'

Stephanie sat by the window. She was confused; everything seemed upside down. 'Daddy fired Theo,' she said.

Sabrina stopped in midflight. 'I know.' She sat in the window seat. 'That wasn't fair. Daddy knows it wasn't his fault. I wish he hadn't fired him. But everything else is so exciting—'

'But what about the bad things?' Stephanie cried. 'Mother and Daddy are furious and the ambassador told Mother we're uncontrollable and Americans aren't supposed to get involved in street fighting—'

'We weren't,' Sabrina interrupted.

'And then it was our fault that Theo got fired and I feel bad.'

'So do I.' Sabrina looked out the window. The cuts on her fingertips hurt, and she pressed them against the cool glass. 'Everybody's mad at everybody. We really made a mess. But, still, it was exciting, wasn't it? All shivery and – oh, I don't know – important. More real than school and books and movies. Dmitri cared about things so much. So did those men. It was an adventure, Stephanie!'

'I know . . . and it *was* exciting – now that it's over—'

'Everybody at school will see it in the paper—'

'—and be so jealous—'

'I'll bet they never had an adventure like that—'

'Even if they did, they'd be scared, not as brave as you.'

'I was scared, and you know it. Every time they walked above us—'

'But you were brave, too, Sabrina. You always are. I wish I was.'

'Don't be silly, of course you are. You told Daddy you were me.'

'Oh, I had to do that, after I was such an awful coward in

that cellar. At least now we're both being punished, instead of just you.'

'Did you see Daddy's face? Was he confused!'

'Mother knew.'

'She knows what clothes you wear.'

'But Daddy hardly ever looks at us.'

They fell silent, thinking about their father.

'Stephanie,' Sabrina said slowly. 'What if you couldn't have adventures without bad things and good things both? Would you want to give them up?'

'Oh, I don't know. I suppose not. I just wish I had some way of knowing ahead of time—'

'But we don't.' They watched a bird light on a tree branch near the window, so close they could see each feather. Sabrina loved to sit like this, next to Stephanie, comfortable and peaceful. Sometimes she wished she was as calm as Stephanie and didn't talk back to her parents and teachers, or think danger was exciting. But she was so restless, and there were so many tantalizing things to try, that she couldn't sit still for long. And, strangely, she thought Mother secretly liked her best that way. So sometimes she talked back or tried something risky in gymnastics (with teachers yelling at her not to, which made it even more fun) just so Mother or other people would admire her and love her.

But mostly she got excited about doing different things because there was so much to discover. 'What I think,' she said to Stephanie, who was sitting quietly, waiting for her to go on, 'is that I'd rather have some bad things happen than not have any adventures at all.'

Stephanie thought about it. 'Well,' she said finally. 'It's a good thing you're here. Because if you weren't, I probably wouldn't have any adventures. Ever. And I wouldn't like that, either.'

Later that year, they read about the settlement of the war in Cyprus. Dmitri and his sisters had gone away with their aunt, and Sabrina and Stephanie devoured stories in Greek newspapers and magazines, hoping to find news of anyone named Karras. But there was nothing, and in the fall they moved to Paris without knowing what had happened to them.

Gordon Hartwell was appointed chargé d'affaires of the US Embassy in Paris in the summer of 1960, the year President Makarios took office on the independent island of Cyprus and John F. Kennedy was elected President of the United States. But whatever changes occurred in the world, life for Sabrina and Stephanie was the same as in Athens. Their rented house was in an enclave of Americans; they attended the American school; they shopped in the famous flea markets on the edge of Paris only with their mother, never alone.

But Laura knew that explosive pressures were building in Sabrina and when the girls were fourteen she let them go to social events for the sons and daughters of diplomats from other embassies. There were picnics and swimming parties, dances, tours of the wine country, excursions to soccer games, horse races, tennis and bicycle races and ski holidays. They made friends from a dozen countries, and their speech soon blended the accents and vocabulary of all of them. It was if they had their own country, separate from the rest of the world.

But then, once again, everything changed. At dinner one winter night their parents told them the great news that Gordon had been nominated by the President, and confirmed by the Senate, as ambassador to Algeria. But, Laura added, there was a problem. Speaking quickly so the girls could not interrupt, she reminded them that Algeria had just won its independence from France and it was still unsettled; possibly even dangerous for foreigners. It was certainly no place for teenage American girls.

'But there is a boarding school in Switzerland,' she went on, 'that we have looked into.'

They had selected it from a dozen recommended schools. Juliette Institut International de Jeunes Filles was a high school of impeccable reputation. Under the amiable dictatorship of Professor L. E. Bossard, wealthy young women became cultured, superbly trained in sports and educated to the entrance standards of any French, American or English university. Its rules were strict, its students closely supervised. Professor Bossard would make sure that no scandal would attach to Juliette – or the parents of its girls.

Gordon would take up his new post in the spring, Laura told Sabrina and Stephanie. She would stay with them in Paris until the school year ended. Then Gordon would join them and they would drive to Switzerland to see the girls safely ensconced under Professor Bossard's wing.

Sabrina looked somberly at her parents. This was what her mother had worked for all these years: Gordon as an ambassador. And now that she had succeeded, she was sending them away. 'It's not Algeria,' she said. 'It's because Daddy's an ambassador and you're sort of one, too, and you don't want to worry about us maybe doing something embarrassing to such very important people.'

Laura slapped her face. It was the only time she had ever hit her, and she was ashamed immediately afterward. 'Forgive me,' she said to Sabrina. 'But for you to talk to me that way—'

'She didn't mean it,' Stephanie said quickly. 'It's just that we don't want to go away.'

'I meant it,' Sabrina said. 'And I do want to go away. I don't want to be with people who don't want me.'

Laura's eyes flashed, but she said smoothly and emotionally, 'Of course we want you; we'll miss you both terribly. But we can't turn down this appointment because of you. Algiers is a city still in turmoil, the schools are not—'

'It's all right,' Sabrina said. 'I understand.' Her stomach was churning and she hated her mother, and her father, too – looking out the window as if he weren't involved at all. 'It sounds like a wonderful school. We'll have a wonderful time, won't we, Stephanie? I guess we ought to practise our French some more; it is a French school, isn't it? We ought to start now, I guess. Stephanie, do you want to come upstairs with me and begin to practise our French?'

There was a long silence. The Hartwell family sat unmoving around the dinner table in the beautiful home that Laura had made for them in Paris. They were suspended on a breath of air, waiting to be carried in different directions.

Then Sabrina stood, followed by Stephanie, and the two of them went upstairs, to be together.

Chapter 3

At exactly 10:00 PM, the mahogany doors of the grand ballroom in the Hotel Geneva swung open on a Venetian palace of papiermâché and paint. Marbled columns supported a vaulted ceiling, and arched windows looked out on painted canals with gondolas and poling boatmen. The varnished ballroom floor was surrounded by a hundred round tables, each set with an orchid centerpiece and china and silver for four. As the doors opened the room became a kaleidoscope of four hundred young men and women in tuxedos and ball gowns crowding in for their graduation ball.

They came from ten select men's and women's schools on the shore of Lake Geneva, and they knew each other from years of chaperoned social events, trips to the great cities of Europe and sports competitions. Only that morning, they had competed in the annual Lake Geneva Sports Festival, their last chance before graduation to win trophies for their schools, their names etched impressively in brass or silver for victories in archery, sailing, fencing, swimming, horsemanship and soccer. From early morning until mid-afternoon, they struggled, hair slicked back, skin streaked with sweat and dust, muscles taut with the lust for victory. Now, polished and sophisticated, they mingled in the other kind of sports festival sponsored by their schools: finding a suitable partner for marriage.

Stephanie, in a froth of lemon yellow chiffon, her hair falling in heavy waves down her back, sat with Dena and Annie in the gilt armchairs at their table and watched for Sabrina to come in. She had to talk to her; so much had happened, so many new feelings danced inside her, and there was no one else she could share them with, not even her two closest friends.

It wasn't that she needed Sabri.
they had made separate lives, with
beginning, when they arrived and dr
shore of Lake Geneva, they had huddl
the road climb through vineyards of
edged with red and then, at the crest of th
an iron gate into a park and on to the squar
was Institut Juliette. Stephanie was assigne   .ne
fourth floor with Dena Cardozo, Sabrina on   .rd with
Gabrielle de Martel, where they lived and studied, along
with one hundred and twenty other young women, for three
years. It was the longest time they had ever lived in one
place.

Where before Sabrina and Stephanie had been together all
the time, at Juliette they began to go in different directions.
They took art classes together and they both had joined the
fencing team, but in their junior year Sabrina turned to
sailing and captained her crew to first place in four Alliance
races. Stephanie stayed with fencing and, on a team with
Dena and Annie MacGregor, brought Juliette four trophies
before the end of her senior year.

They studied and took up sports with different groups, but
they always felt each other nearby, like a ribbon woven
through their days. Whenever they could they snatched an
afternoon or a holiday to go off together, apart from everyone
else. 'To make sense of things,' Sabrina would say and settle
back with a happy sigh to talk and listen.

'Hey,' Dena said as a waiter filled their glasses with
champagne. 'You're dreaming again. Come back; I'm making a toast.' She raised her glass. 'To college, and the hell
with it.'

'Don't be silly, Dena,' Stephanie said, turning her attention from watching for Sabrina. 'You don't want to stay in
high school.'

'I want us to go on being roommates.'

'Then come to Paris with Sabrina and me.'

'You come to Bryn Mawr with me.'

'I want to go to Paris, Dena – to the Sorbonne.'

'Your parents enrolled you at Bryn Mawr.'

rolled ourselves at the Sorbonne. One of these
y ll understand that we mean what we say.'
a's eyebrows went up. 'Tough talk.'

Stephanie shook her head. Sabrina's determination had
done it; alone, she would have given in to her parents, even
though the money was theirs, left in a trust by their
grandfather. Laura and Gordon wanted them at Bryn Mawr
because Laura had gone there and because it was time, they
said, the girls lived in America. But Sabrina and Stephanie
wanted Paris; for years they had dreamed of Paris.

'Have you seen Sabrina?' Stephanie asked, becoming
impatient. Soon the dancing would begin and then they
would have no chance to talk.

'Not since the fencing match,' Annie said. 'But there is
your Charles.' She paused. 'He has a nice face.' She paused
again so Stephanie could confide in them. When she was
silent, Annie asked outright, 'Where did you go this
afternoon, after the match?'

'For a walk,' Stephanie said vaguely, catching glimpses
through the crowd of Charles, sitting with his senior class.
She felt a pang of longing as his thin, serious face smiled at
a friend, the way he had smiled at her that afternoon when
he put his arm around her and led her out of the gymnasium,
away from her disastrous fencing match.

They had gone to lunch in Lausanne. In a tiny café with
red tablecloths and white curtains where they were all alone
and, at last, away from spectators, she wept over a lost
championship.

'Too *timid*,' she said through her sobs. 'Putting everything
I had into one attack to win a point and then when I needed
one more – just one – to win the trophy, I couldn't follow
through. I don't know why. Sabrina would have—'

But Charles told her how wonderful she was, and how he
admired her grace and skill. 'Everyone knows that technique
is more important than strength,' he said. 'You don't have
to be aggressive. Remember how they cheered you.' He
talked on and on until her sobs quieted and she began to feel
less hopeless. She leaned against him, happy and trusting,
thinking she was falling in love, and then his voice changed
as he began to stumble over his words. Stephanie knew he

was trying to ask her to come with him to the small hotel next door, but it was his first time and he could not manage it and Stephanie, as inexperienced as he, had no idea how to help him. In all late-night talk with her friends about sex, hours were spent on how to say yes or no, but not one minute on how to lead the way.

Looking at him through the crowd in the ballroom, Stephanie remembered his arm around her while they talked for hours and thought about the hotel next door until they had to separate to get ready for the graduation ball that night. I love Charles, she thought, and smiled to herself.

'Ah,' said Annie expectantly, seeing the smile. 'A very good walk.' But still Stephanie was silent. The only one she could talk to about Charles was Sabrina. But Sabrina was nowhere to be seen.

With a flourish of trumpets, the directors of the ten Alliance schools were introduced to loyal applause. As the orchestra played the traditional medley of school anthems and then the first waltz, the lights slowly dimmed to a blue evening haze with hundreds of candles flickering like tiny stars. The ballroom swirled with color and young men crowded about Stephanie, claiming dance after dance. She glided about the room, dreaming, waiting for Charles.

'Too bad about the match,' one of her partners said, bringing her to earth. She nodded shortly, 'You're good to watch, though,' he added soothingly. 'Girls usually aren't interesting, but you're so beautiful I really enjoyed it.'

Stephanie stopped dancing. 'What an amazingly stupid remark.'

'Hey,' he said defensively, 'I only meant—'

'I know what you meant.' She wasn't interested in him; she wanted Charles. Where was he? Why hadn't he asked her to dance? 'Excuse me,' she said, and walked away, moving like a shadow between swaying couples, searching the room. And then she saw him. He was in a shielded nook, talking animatedly to a young woman. She stood with her back to Stephanie, wearing a shimmering ice-blue gown, her heavy auburn hair caught loosely at the back of her neck by a matching ribbon. Sabrina! Stephanie thought, and started forward eagerly. How amazing to find them both—She

29

stopped as she saw Charles's expression – eager, fascinated, adoring. In their whole afternoon together, not once had he looked at her like that.

The music stopped and a young man approached Stephanie. She did not turn her head. All she saw was Charles and Sabrina.

' . . . this dance?' he asked, and reached for her. Still without looking at him, she shook her head.

'Why not?' he cried. 'Stephanie, what's wrong?'

His plaintive voice calling her name rang out in the quiet moment before the conductor brought down his baton for the next dance. Charles swung about. For an instant Stephanie's eyes met his and then she fled, holding up her skirt and weaving between the whirling couples out of the ballroom.

Sabrina ran after her. Ignoring Charles's frantic questions, she pushed her way past curious dancers and through the mahogany doors. She caught a glimpse of Stephanie's yellow dress in the closing elevator and sped down the corridor to take the next one to the floor where the Juliette seniors were staying for the night of the dance.

'Stephanie?' She knocked on the door of Stephanie's and Dena's room. There was no answer. She waited, catching her breath. Her heart was pounding at the memory of the awful despair on Stephanie's face. I didn't know, she thought. I didn't know. But I would have, if I weren't so selfish. 'Stephanie, please.'

'It's open,' Stephanie said.

She was curled on the couch, crying, and Sabrina ran to her, kneeling on the carpet to take her hands. 'I'm sorry, I'm sorry. Why do I hurt you when I love you more than anyone in the world?' Stephanie tried to pull her hands back, but Sabrina clutched them. 'Please, Stephanie, I didn't mean to hurt you. I wasn't flirting. He just came up to me—'

Stephanie jerked her hands away. 'They're always "just coming up to you",' she said furiously. 'Have you ever thought of saying no?'

Sabrina stared at her. 'I do. But this was different. Charles—'

'Don't lie about it! It was just another—'

'Stephanie, stop. It *was* different. He thought I was you.'

'That's not true,' Stephanie said swiftly.

'It is. I got there late, I was alone, and when he came up I didn't recognize him. I'd never seen him before this morning, at your match, and that was only for a minute, when the two of you were leaving. And he didn't say my name at first; we just started talking, and then all of a sudden he called me Stephanie, but I couldn't stop him—'

'You could have stopped him before then. You knew what was happening.'

Sabrina's shoulders slumped. 'Of course I did.' She looked down at her beautiful dress and thought how wrong it was to look so pretty and feel so terrible underneath. She needed Stephanie; she'd come to the ball looking for her, desperate to talk about what had happened that afternoon, and now she'd hurt her and they were quarreling. 'I guess I didn't want to stop him.'

'Why not? Do you always have to show everyone you're better than me?'

'Stephanie!'

'Well, you are better, aren't you? Everyone knows it. You won the sailing championship this morning. You would have won my fencing match. You wouldn't lose a boyfriend. You never lose anything.'

With a sinking feeling, Sabrina saw how wide the gulf was between them. 'I didn't know he was your boyfriend,' she said helplessly.

'You knew I left the gym with him. That was a clue.' Stephanie's eyes were flat. 'Why didn't you tell him who you were?'

Sabrina spread her hands. 'Something happened today . . . I was looking for you, to talk about it, but you were dancing and then . . . '

In spite of herself, Stephanie was caught by the unhappiness in Sabrina's voice. 'What happened?'

'Marco came in from Paris.'

'I thought he couldn't come until tomorrow.'

'He was anxious.'

Stephanie heard the contemptuous note. 'For what?'

'Some . . . games he thought I should play now that I'm grown up.'

They looked at each other. 'What did you do?'

'Threw a paperweight at him and told him to get out.'

Stephanie laughed in reluctant admiration. 'Did he?'

'All the way back to Paris, I guess.'

'You don't think you'll see him again?'

'I know I won't. He called me a fool. Maybe I am.'

Stephanie was about to ask what games Marco had suggested when the thought came that once again Sabrina had beaten her; *she* had been desired and pursued, while Stephanie couldn't even get Charles to take her to a hotel. 'But why did you take it out on me?' she cried, and Sabrina felt as she had once when the calm eye of a hurricane passed and the furious winds returned.

She jumped up and began walking back and forth, rubbing her arms to warm them. She was ashamed of her trick on Charles and frightened by Stephanie's eyes. But worst of all was the gulf between them. How had they pulled so far apart?

'I didn't take it out on you. I'd never do that. I really didn't know he was important, and when I realized he'd mixed us up it was like a game. But it was only a few minutes; I was about to tell him when we heard your name. Stephanie, I would never hurt you—'

'It doesn't matter,' Stephanie said wearily. 'He liked you better than me, anyway. Whatever I try to do, you do it better.'

'That isn't true.'

'Then tell me why you left the fencing team.'

'Why I—? That was a year ago. It has nothing to do with—'

'Because you were so much better than I was.'

'I wasn't better, I was different.'

'More aggressive, more formidable. Everyone knew it.'

Sabrina stopped pacing. Stephanie's pain cut into her. 'I wanted to sail. And I knew I could be captain.'

'You knew nobody paid attention to me when you were fencing. That's why you left the team.'

'No. I like sailing better than fencing. That was the only reason.' She had never lied to Stephanie before. I'm sorry, she said silently. I just don't know what else to do. 'Anyway,

32

what difference does it make, it's all past. Unless you want us to fence together at the Sorbonne; why don't we do that—'

'It's easier for you to get good grades, too.'

Sabrina shook her head. She felt sick. How long had Stephanie been hiding these feelings?

'Oh, yes, it is. You never study or cram and then you get A's, and I'm always studying.'

'And getting A's.'

'Yes, but everything comes to you, Sabrina, like grades and fencing and Charles, but I have to work at them and then hold tight or they'll get away.' She was crying, and Sabrina knelt beside her again.

'Please, Stephanie, stop, please stop, I can't stand it if you cry because of me. I'm sorry about Charles, I'm sorry about fencing, but you're more important than anything.' She was crying, too, for Stephanie and for herself, because she'd done everything wrong and Stephanie's anger was shutting her out. 'I don't know what you want me to do, but I'll do whatever—'

'There isn't anything.' Stephanie sat straight. 'Sabrina, I've decided to go to Bryn Mawr instead of the Sorbonne.'

Stunned, Sabrina stared at her, 'Bryn Mawr?'

'It's a good school, and since I'm already enrolled there, thanks to Mother and Daddy, that's where I'll go.'

'But we were going to Paris together.'

'Sabrina, don't look so—lost! What are you worried about? You'll be fine. I'm thinking of me. I have to find out who I am separate from you. You're so bright and exciting, I just fade away when you're around. Nobody would notice me at all if you didn't step aside sometimes.'

'No, no, no.' Vehemently, Sabrina shook her head. 'Of course people notice you, what are you talking about?' But Stephanie was silent, and Sabrina jumped up and began to pace again. Why hadn't they ever talked about these things? We're changing, she thought; we're talking in different ways. And so she told Stephanie something she had never even admitted to herself. 'Stephanie, when I do exciting things, or crazy things, it's because everybody expects it. They tell me how wonderful I am and then I look for more things to do . . . ' She paused. 'I'm afraid if I don't, they'll stop loving me and thinking I'm wonderful. You're the only one I'm sure of who loves me just because I'm me. Everybody else talks about how beautiful I am, or how exciting it is that I win races and contests, how spectacular I am.' She hesitated again, then burst out, 'I need to be the center of attention. I wish I didn't.'

Stephanie had stopped crying. 'You'll have the attention all to yourself in Paris.'

Sabrina stood still and gave her sister a long look. 'I don't deserve that, I was trying to be honest.'

'I'm sorry. I meant we'll each have our own attention. For the first time.' Her eyes were bright. 'It'll be an adventure, Sabrina. You always told me I should want them, remember?'

Sabrina searched those bright eyes for malice but found none. 'I never tried to overshadow you,' she said helplessly.

'Maybe not. But I still feel like I'm just Sabrina Hartwell's twin sister.' She looked down at her hands. 'We'll write to each other instead of talking.'

Sabrina heard a new note in Stephanie's voice; she was beginning to waver. I could change her mind, she thought. If I pushed, if I reminded her of how often we needed each other the last three years, she'd come to Paris. We'd be close again. Once she had told her mother and father, 'Stephanie and I are the only family we have.' It was still true. I could convince her to come with me, she thought.

But she couldn't do it. Because Stephanie was right; she had to get away. Sabrina shrank from that awful fact – my sister doesn't want to be with me – but she couldn't deny it. She gloried in her own brightness and Stephanie had to escape, to find her own. I won't stop her from doing that, she thought. I won't make it any harder than it already is. I've done enough tonight to hurt her.

So she sat beside Stephanie on the couch and swallowed the tears welling in her throat. 'What a lot of talking we'll do on summer vacations!' she said brightly. They sat together, not touching, their hands in their laps like proper young ladies. I love you, Sabrina said silently to Stephanie, and began that moment to live her life alone.

Chapter 4

The audience in the opera house stilled as the lights dimmed. Spotlights came up on heavy gold curtain, the conductor swung down his baton and the sensual Spanish music of the overture wove through the hall, its gypsy lilt making Stephanie want to dance. She looked at Dena. 'Thank you,' she whispered, grateful for everything: New York at Christmas, shopping, theaters and the Cardozos' box for her favorite opera. Sighing happily, she let the music catch her up as the curtain majestically parted on a crowded scene of brilliantly dressed dancers and soldiers in bright red uniforms.

A commotion broke the spell; behind them, someone pulled open the door of the box, then stumbled against a chair. Stephanie and Dena swung about. 'Sorry,' a voice said. In the shadows Stephanie saw a tall man with dark hair trying to close the door and tug off his coat at the same time.

'Are you in the right box?' Dena asked.

He nodded and sat in the armchair behind Stephanie. Dena waited, but he said nothing more. She studied him for a moment, then looked at Stephanie, shrugged and turned back to the stage, 'Rumpled,' she murmured.

Stephanie gave a small laugh at Dena's swift judgment. Whoever he was, he was respectable, even though his jacket needed pressing. And he was self-confident enough to offer a single apology and then stop.

In the next minute she forgot him. On the stage, Carmen was singing with slow, taunting sexuality to the infatuated young soldier, Don José, and the song flowed through the audience like molten gold. Stephanie leaned forward, feeling its power. But she was distracted, aware of something besides the music. She turned around and met the eyes of the stranger, watching her.

She was the one who turned away, flushed from the steadiness of his gaze. He was older than she, with a strong face and a more direct look than she was used to in the men at colleges near Bryn Mawr. Turning her head slightly, as if she were looking at the side of the stage, she saw from the corner of her eye that he was still looking at her. He's missing the whole opera, she thought, and felt her lips curve in a smile. For the first time she wondered who he was and how he had a ticket for the Cardozos' box.

'Excuse me,' he said. 'Did you drop this?' Stephanie turned to look at the program in his outstretched hand and shook her head, her lips curving again. He knew she hadn't dropped it; he could see her program on her lap. Their eyes held for a moment and then she turned away again. But for the remainder of the first act, she could see him at the edge of her field of vision, watching her.

'Garth Andersen,' he said, holding out his hand as the lights came up at intermission. Dena reached out quickly to take it.

'Dena Cardozo. Are you a friend of the Bartons?'

He chuckled at Dena's protectiveness, making her feel young and uncertain. He shouldn't do that, Stephanie thought, and as if he realized it himself he said quickly, 'We're old friends. And I apologize for my noisy entrance. The Bartons neglected to tell me they shared the box and then I was late; I forgot the time at work and was afraid I'd miss the overture.' He held out his hand to Stephanie. 'We haven't met.'

'Stephanie Hartwell.' She fit her slender hand to his long, thin one. A musician, she thought. Or an artist.

'What work?' Dena asked. 'Research,' he answered briefly and invited them to the lobby for a drink. He wondered why Dena asked all the questions. Did she always ask, and was Stephanie always silent? Or was Stephanie not interested?

As they drank their wine, Garth answered Dena's questions, telling them he was a molecular biologist, a professor at Columbia University, a researcher. 'In what?' Dena asked, but he said it was too complicated for intermission talk. That was true, but he never talked about his work to strangers, fearing they would turn away, bored and uncomprehending. He didn't want to talk about himself, anyway; he wanted to ask his own questions about Stephanie Hartwell.

In the crowded lobby, reverberating with high-pitched laughter and rapid tongues, she was a quiet island, her body very still, her movements small and controlled. As Garth talked, he memorized her deep blue eyes, the delicate lines of her cheekbones and her wonderful mouth, wide and generous, surprisingly vulnerable, asking for protection.

Dena watched him, but not with jealousy. She was pleased he was interested in Stephanie because it was clear that Stephanie was interested in him. Lucky Stephanie, Garth thought, to have such a friend. And at the final curtain he asked if he could take them home. 'We have a limousine,' said Dena. She looked up suddenly, as if remembering. 'Stephanie, I promised I'd call Mother before we left for home. I'll be right back.'

When they were alone, Garth met Stephanie's smile with his own. 'A nice thing to do.'

'Dena is always doing nice things.'

'I want to see you. Tomorrow?' She shook her head. 'Then the next day.'

'No. I'm sorry.' Her eyes were clear and honest. 'I'd like to. But I'm staying with Dena's family for the holidays and they've made plans for us. They're so wonderful to me that I can't just disappear and leave them with tickets and schedules. I'm sorry.'

'And after the holidays?'

'I go back to Bryn Mawr.'

'To graduate?'

She laughed. 'Hardly. I'm in my second year.'

He frowned. 'You look . . . how old are you?'

'Nineteen.'

'You look older.'

'Isn't nineteen old enough?'

'I wouldn't have thought so,' he mused. 'But it will have to be.'

Dena came back and they gathered their coats from the back of the box, friendly in their goodbyes. Garth stood in the shadows, feeling like a bumpkin at the side of the road as the royal carriage passed by. They had wealth, sophistication, style and all the world waiting for them. He looked at the opera stage where three hours of passion had just been sung and saw a vulnerable mouth and clear, honest eyes. He pulled on his coat and smiled to himself. This bumpkin was going to follow the carriage all the way to the castle.

Bryn Mawr College is tucked amid the hills and leafy splendor of Pennsylvania, an hour's train ride from New York. Stephanie had barely arrived and begun unpacking when Garth called.

'I'm going to be in your neighborhood this weekend,' he said casually. 'I thought I might drop by, if you'll be home.'

She laughed. 'What will you be doing in my neighborhood?'

'Spending the day with you.'

They met at Pembroke Arch, the campus rendezvous, and shook hands formally. 'Where are you taking me?' he asked, as they began to walk.

'I have to stop at the library for a few minutes and then I thought we'd have breakfast at Wyndham House. If that's all right? It's so early, I thought—'

'Too early for you?'

'No, I'm glad you're here.' Snow had fallen during the night and they walked on shoveled paths, the dark lines bisecting sparkling white expanses dotted with gray, Gothic stone buildings.

Garth followed Stephanie through the library and down a staircase to the basement loading dock. 'No one else could be here today,' she said, 'and they're delivering some furniture for the antique auction upstairs. As soon as I sign for it, we can leave.'

A truck was backed up to the wide doorway and Garth watched as Stephanie talked to the driver. In a minute she came to him with a gesture of uncertainty. 'He says his forklift won't work so he can't unload the crates. Do you want to go to breakfast while I hunt up a maintenance man? I don't know how long I'll be.'

'I grew up with forklifts,' Garth said. 'Shall I have a look?'

She tilted her head to look at him. 'Do scientists do research with forklifts?'

He laughed and went through the loading door to the flatbed of the truck. 'Minnesota farm boys use forklifts. And fix them regularly.' He conferred briefly with the driver, who found a toolbox in the cab of the truck, and then turned to Stephanie. 'How long is breakfast served?'

'For three hours.'

'I'll have an impressive appetite.' He bent over the motor, working quickly and easily. 'Try it,' he said to the driver after a few minutes, and when the engine started he walked back, smiling, to Stephanie. 'Science is wonderful.'

'So are Minnesota farm boys.' Reaching up, she ran her finger along his forehead and brought it away covered with grease.

He smiled ruefully and spread his blackened hands. 'I never could work on an engine without carrying away half its grease. My mother used to comment on that. Where can I wash up?'

'Through there and down the hall.'

'Don't go away.'

'I won't.'

He went off with long strides, still feeling her touch. And when he returned, he found her in the same place, signing the delivery slip.

For breakfast, Stephanie had gotten permission to take Garth to the dining room of Wyndham House, the best on campus, usually reserved, with the upstairs bedrooms, for visiting alumnae and parents. As they studied their menus beside a large window overlooking the campus, she snatched glimpses of him, taking pleasure in the strong lines of his face. His brown eyes were deep-set above prominent cheekbones, his mouth was wide, his strong chin marked with a cleft. When he smiled, fine lines radiated from the corners of his eyes, disappearing into his thick black hair. Everything about him was clearly defined; nothing was blurred or soft. Even his voice, deep and resonant, could reach the back of the largest lecture hall without straining.

'Do you still have your farm?' she asked when they had ordered.

'No. I gave it to my sister and her husband.' Now that she was asking the questions, he talked easily, telling her about the farm carved out by his grandfather – wheat glistening gold beneath the sun, the feel of the earth when he worked it, the solitary hours he spent as a boy, dreaming of being a famous scientist, and the hours of close companionship with his father, learning all he knew so that when he retired, Garth could manage the farm.

'A peaceful, secure childhood,' he told Stephanie as the waitress brought pancakes and sausages and filled their coffee cups. 'A loving one. Everything in its place; no doubts about the future.'

'But it all changed?' she asked when he fell silent.

'It all changed.' He paused, remembering. 'When I was eighteen I had a scholarship to college – I would have been the first of our clan to go. But I had to give it up to manage the farm when my parents were killed in an automobile accident.'

Stephanie drew in her breath. 'You say it so calmly—'

'I didn't at the time. It destroyed almost everything I believed in. But it was eight years ago,' he added gently.

Eight years ago, she thought. He was eighteen, his parents were dead and he was running a farm. No wonder he thought I was young; I haven't done anything. 'Did you run the farm?' she asked.

'For a year. My sister was still in high school, and I stayed with her; I was the only family she had. When sh_ married right after graduation, I gave her the farm as a wedding present.' He paused again, looking out at the snow-covered campus. 'And then I came to New York, looking for another world where everything was in its place and there was a chance of predicting the future.'

'Science,' Stephanie ventured.

He nodded, smiling at her. She listened so carefully he thought she might hear all the unspoken words – about his poverty in New York, and his isolation, so different from that on the farm. He had no time for friends, holding three jobs while taking extra courses so he could graduate early and begin to teach. And lately, when he could go out, he didn't, because he was afraid of taking time from research, from preparation for his lectures, from anything that might slow down his progress in his field. Except for an occasional evening with a few close friends, he never went anywhere.

Until now.

He finished his coffee and sat back. 'My turn. I don't know anything about you.'

'But you haven't finished. Did you find a world where everything was in its place?'

'Almost everything. Where are you from? I can't place your accent.'

'I grew up in Europe. But what is it you find? I don't know what a molecular biologist does.'

Garth laughed, discovering the pleasure of having a beautiful woman insist that he talk about himself. 'All right,' he said. 'We study the structure and behavior of molecules in living things. I specialize in the structure of genes and how we might alter them to eliminate genetic diseases.'

Stephanie rested her chin on her hand, watching his eyes and his mouth. 'If you change the structure of genes,' she said hesitantly, 'aren't you changing life?'

He looked at her curiously, like her professors when she asked a good question. 'What does that mean?'

'Wouldn't you be tampering with – what makes life?'

'Well, I don't call it tampering; that sounds as if I'm screwing up the works. Look, those antiques you signed for; didn't craftsmen change the wood in making them? Doesn't a sculptor change marble?'

'But artists don't have power. A marble statue can't change the world. But you could, couldn't you, by changing genes?'

'Possibly.'

'Well, somebody ought to control that.'

'Who?'

She looked at him over her coffee cup. 'The government?'

'Petty, untrustworthy, plodding, narrow-minded, no vision.'

'Scientists, then.'

41

'Probably just as bad. Most of us are a little crazy. The fact is, you can't limit research; it pops up every time you try to cut it down.'

'I guess I have to think about that. What do you want out of your research?'

Back to the personal, he thought, admiring her tenacity. But the answer would take too long for today. He put it off. 'To make a pile of money by inventing a boysenberry syrup for eternal youth.'

She laughed. 'What's wrong with cherry?'

'Run of the mill. No drama.'

'Garth, you don't really want to make a pile of money.'

'Oh, don't I?'

'But do you expect to?'

'Oh, if you put it that way, no. Not in university research. Private companies pay well, but they're not my style.'

She looked a question.

'I don't like commercial pressure. In a university, no one peers over my shoulder to see how close I am to discovering something that will make a profit. I like research for its own sake, being free to follow leads that might help—'

'Humanity.'

'Something like that. You're right, though. It's unlikely I'll ever be able to afford you. Are we leaving?'

'Yes.' Stephanie was taking bills from her wallet. 'That is the silliest remark I've ever heard. I think it's wonderful that you care about research, about people, that you're willing to earn less so you can do what you believe in. That was a silly remark.'

He caught her arm as she stood up. 'Wait. Now wait a minute. First, I'm paying for breakfast.'

'You're my guest. I invited you.'

'I invited myself for the day. I may be only a lowly assistant professor who cares about humanity, but I can afford to take my friends to breakfast. Aside from my silly remark, why are we leaving?'

'I have to get back to the library to see if they need help setting up for the auction. It's less than a week away, and so many people have been sick that we're behind schedule.

I'm sorry, because I promised you the whole day, but I have to do it – it's my job.'

'Your job.'

'I work for the art department and we run the auction.'

'Why do you work for the art department?'

'To earn money.'

'I thought—'

'Yes, I know you did.'

Garth had paid for breakfast, and as they walked across campus he felt suddenly lighthearted, filled with energy. She doesn't live in a castle, he said to himself and, packing a snowball, threw an exuberant pitch at a gnarled tree, where it clung like a white star to the black trunk. He looked at Stephanie's bright face. 'Tell me about the antique show. Do you know, I've always had a secret desire to fondle a nude statue. Could this be my chance? Will you have any nude statues?'

Stephanie laughed. What a wonderful day they were going to have. 'We will have statues of nudes. If you want nude statues, you will have to undress them.' It was his turn to laugh, and he took her hand securely in his as they walked up the steps of the library.

Garth had plenty of time to ponder the contradictions in Stephanie Hartwell before she visited his laboratory in New York. He spent nine Saturdays in Bryn Mawr through the winter and spring and learned about her twin sister and the break between them, still unhealed, and about her parents in Algeria, who would soon move to Washington when her father took up his new position as Under Secretary of State for European Affairs. He heard all about her posh, ridiculously expensive Swiss school, and he learned that her sophistication came in patches from a crazy upbringing that taught her enough about Europe to fill an encyclopedia but not enough about sex or men to fill one page of a diary. He knew about her quick intelligence, her quiet beauty and friends like Dena who clustered around her, offering places to stay over vacations; everyone wanted to give Stephanie a home. And so did Garth. Because he had fallen in love with her.

'I'll meet you at your office,' Stephanie said when he called her at the Cardozos' apartment. 'It's silly for you to pick me up. How do I get there?' He gave her directions and she skipped to her room to dress. Spring vacation in New York: a whole week with Garth, since the Cardozos knew about him and hadn't made plans for her. A week with Garth. She sang it to herself on the subway.

But as she walked to the university, the noise of a crowd cut across her thoughts. It seemed to come from all directions until, turning a corner, Stephanie found herself engulfed in it: the shouts of young people massed together, waving signs and cheering a freckle-faced boy who stood on a truck, yelling hoarsely through a bullhorn. A wall of policemen with linked arms stood between Stephanie and a four-story building whose windows and windowsills were crowded with shouting, gesturing men and women. Uncertain, she looked about, trying to find an address. She started to ask a policeman, but the noise drowned out her voice. Then, suddenly, Garth was there, his arm around her, walking her quickly past the occupied building and into the one next door.

They rode the elevator to the fourth floor. 'Quite an introduction to my home-sweet-home,' said Garth ruefully. 'If I'd known beforehand, I wouldn't have let you come. But it seems to be a stalemate, so we'll have a quick tour and then get out.'

'I've never been close to a demonstration; Bryn Mawr is so quiet—'

'We've been blessed with them like clockwork. They've almost become part of university life.' He unlocked a door. 'Come into my parlor.'

The laboratory was partitioned down the middle by tall steel cabinets, and as they walked to one side Garth stood back to watch Stephanie's reaction. At first she was puzzled, then disappointed, then intrigued. It was a strange room, with no shiny equipment, no test tubes or flames or bubbling liquids, not even a microscope. Instead, crowded on a long soapstone bench were children's Tinkertoys: constructions of sticks, wires, balls, bits of plastic, string and paper, in all shapes, sizes and colors. On the floor, boxes overflowed with more material. Photographs of constructions covered the walls, and a large blackboard, gray with erasures, was filled with labeled diagrams of others. In the corner a desk and a battered typewriter were barely visible beneath piles of books and papers.

Garth grinned. 'I am known in these parts as the Tinkertoy man.'

'I'm not surprised,' Stephanie said. 'Garth, what is all this?'

He swung his arm to encompass the room. 'My models. Works of art, each made by hand—'

'Garth. Be serious.'

'You know, I am serious. These cockeyed models are my works of art.'

'Tell me.'

He smiled at her serious face. 'Each model is a different kind of molecule. The balls are atoms, the sticks are the forces that hold them in their different arrangements. You do know what molecules are.'

She nodded. 'They have them in Switzerland, too.'

'Sorry, was I talking down?'

'A little. But I really don't know very much.'

'Here.' He erased the blackboard and sketched as he talked. 'This is the cell, and inside it, the nucleus. Inside that, these ribbons are the chromosomes, made up of long strands of a particular molecule.' He reached down to pick up a model, but just then a roar surged from the crowd below and he looked impatiently at the window. 'We can come back another time.'

'No, tell me now.' She felt close to him in the silent laboratory; outside there was danger, but inside, with Garth, was safety.

'I'll make it short. The molecule that makes up the chromosomes is DNA. This is a model of it: something like a ladder twisted into a corkscrew. DNA is the molecule that controls heredity. It's a blueprint; the different kinds of rungs on the ladder are organized in special ways that make up a code, with all the information needed for the duplication of life. That's where I come in: trying to understand how this molecule, this ladder, is made.'

45

'And when you do?'

'Then I might learn how to repair it when it's damaged.' He returned the DNA model to the bench. 'Kids are being born now with diseases we can't cure, because somewhere on their DNA ladder something went wrong with one or more of the rungs. If we knew how—'

He broke off. The shouting was louder; a girl's voice came through the bullhorn. 'There's more to it, but that's the meat and potatoes. We'll get to the rest on a quieter day. Shall we go?'

As they were leaving Stephanie glanced at the other side of the laboratory. It was more familiar, with microscopes, test tubes, beakers, syringes, a sink. On one wall, beside a large window, dozens of white mice scampered in small cages. Looking over her shoulder, Garth said, 'Bill and I trade information; he's working on inherited diseases in mice.'

Stephanie smiled. 'Tinkertoys and pet mice. Modern science—' Abruptly she screamed as an explosion threw her against him and fragments of glass shattered at their feet.

Garth cursed. 'Don't talk,' he said roughly. 'And try to hold your breath.'

'Why?' she asked, but his arm was muffling her face as he half-carried her into the hall and up a stairway. Suddenly she was violently ill: her eyes stung, tears streamed from under their swollen lids and her chest felt crushed as harsh gasps tore through her burning throat.

Then there was cool air and sunlight on her face, and Garth's strong arm steadying her. 'I can't stop crying,' she said. 'I can't open my eyes.'

His other arm came up to cradle her. 'You'll be all right in a few minutes. It's only tear gas.'

'Only—!'

'Not permanently damaging. Can you stay here alone? I'll get some water.'

'Where are we?'

'On the roof. Be right back.'

The burning lingered, but within ten minutes Stephanie could open her eyes and look over the parapet at the police dragging coughing, crying students into paddy wagons. 'Why did the police throw one at us?'

46

'Not exactly at us; somebody had lousy aim. You'd think with all their practice they'd be in better form. Stephanie, I've got to go back and cover that broken window. Do you want to wait here?'

'I'll come with you.'

But in the laboratory she shrank back from his rage. It welled up as he stood in the room, his face rigid, the veins standing out in his neck. 'Bastards.' The word ripped from him. 'Goddamn bastards.' She followed his gaze to the wire cages where, a short time before, she had laughed at the scampering mice. But none scampered now. They lay in limp piles, a breeze from the broken window gently stirring their flat white fur.

With a vicious kick Garth sent the empty tear-gas canister sailing through the air, scattering papers that lay in disarray on the floor. Glass crunched under his feet. 'A year of Bill's work, a year of experiments and study—' His voice rose. 'Remember those kids I told you about, born with diseases we can't cure? They're at the end of a road that begins here. Do you see what this means? Do you see that this university thinks it's more important to clear out a bunch of students than to protect the work of its scientists?'

'I don't think you mean that,' Stephanie said quietly. She was trembling, not from the tear gas but from Garth's anguish, the depth of his caring. He knew what was important; he knew what he wanted and where he was going. His world was far larger than hers.

Kneeling on the floor, she began to pick up the scattered papers, putting them in a box she found on the desk. Garth studied her bent head, the heavy auburn hair falling forward around her face. Wonderful, calm Stephanie. Wise beyond her years one minute; a young girl the next. Waiting. And who was he to think he could give her what she was waiting for? Beside her, he still felt like a bumpkin.

She stood up. 'I think I've cut myself.'

Blood ran down her hand. 'All that glass,' he said angrily. 'Let me see.'

She held out her hand like a child. Carefully he drew out a long sliver, found a gauze pad in a drawer and pressed it to the cut. She flinched. 'Something still in there,' he said.

It was her turn to look at his bent head as he rummaged in the drawer again and found tweezers. 'All the comforts,' he murmured. 'Always cut yourself in a biologist's lab.' He looked up and caught her watching him. 'Do you know,' he said conversationally, 'you are probably the only woman in the world who can look beautiful after being tear-gassed? You have just passed the Andersen beauty test. We administer one canister of tear gas, and those whose beauty is only skin deep are transformed immediately into hiccuping toads. Why do you laugh? I am telling you that I love you and I want to marry you and I think I have found the splinter so if you will hold very still I will remove it.'

He bent over her hand and probed in the wound. 'Sorry,' he said when she flinched again. 'I would also like to take you home and make love to you, a desire I have had for several weeks in the less conducive atmosphere of Bryn Mawr. There. Done.' Without looking at her he reached for more gauze and wrapped her hand in a neat bandage. 'Boy Scout training in the wilds of Minnesota. What do you think?'

'About what?' she asked faintly.

'One or both of the above.'

She moved forward confidently, knowing already the shape his body would take in enclosing hers. 'Yes,' she said. 'To both of the above.'

In May the bushes on Bryn Mawr's campus bloom densely pink and white and the ground is a carpet of petals that drop as new ones appear. A hot sun burns away the April rains and birds cluster in ancient trees. It is the season of weddings.

In the courtyard of Thomas Library, Laura stood beside Stephanie, casting a critical eye on the circular pond with its placid ducks, the neat rows of chairs beside it and the long tables set with food and drink. 'It's not so much a wedding,' she said thoughtfully, 'as a garden party. Didn't you want something more formal, darling?'

'I wanted this,' Stephanie said dreamily, watching her friends and Garth's gather in small groups, waiting for the ceremony to begin.

'Stand still, both of you,' commanded Gordon and clicked his camera.

'And leaving school,' Laura went on. 'Are you sure, Stephanie?'

'Mother, if Garth is in Illinois, how can I stay here?'

'He could have waited two years.'

'No, he couldn't. The job at Midwestern is too good.' She kissed Laura's cheek. 'We'll buy a big house with lots of bedrooms and you'll visit us. You've never been to Evanston, have you? Or Chicago?'

'Neither one.'

'Well, now you will.'

Stephanie saw Sabrina come into the courtyard and join Judge Fairfax and the Cardozos. 'Excuse me,' she said and crossed over to take her hands. 'You look wonderful!'

'No, you're the one . . . is it possible to be as happy as you look?'

'When I come to your wedding I'll ask you that.'

Sabrina smiled. 'Judge Fairfax says he bounced us on his knee when we were babies in Washington.'

'And predicted I'd preside at your weddings,' said the judge. 'I'm waiting for Sabrina's to give me an excuse to come to Europe.'

Sabrina raised her eyebrows and once again changed the subject. She never talked about herself, Stephanie thought; not even in her letters. She wrote like a good friend, describing her days, asking interested questions, but always a little remote, just as she was last summer when they were in Scotland with their parents. Then she had been quiet and withdrawn, reluctant to let others draw her into conversation, as if she were afraid someone would accuse her of attempting to outshine her sister. Stephanie understood, but she refused to make things easier. It evened things out, she thought, if Sabrina felt awkward for once. She was ashamed of being mean, but she did nothing to make Sabrina feel better and for the whole month neither of them had had a good time.

Once each of us was half of the other, she thought, watching Sabrina talk to the Cardozos. Now I don't know

49

anything about her – whom she loves or what she dreams about. And she doesn't know me.

'Sabrina,' she said, touching her sister's arm. They walked together, bending their heads to each other. Gordon caught them with his camera – his glorious daughters, identical but elusively more and more different: Sabrina strangely cool and quiet in a slim dress of dusty rose that subtly traced her body, her hair hidden beneath a matching cloche; Stephanie glowing in a white embossed gown edged in embroidered lace, a camellia nestled like carved ivory in the dark auburn of her hair. 'I've got to apologize,' she said.

'Don't,' said Sabrina. 'I think I understand.'

'How can you? You left school early so we'd have a few days together, and I've done all the talking; you haven't told me anything about yourself.'

'It doesn't matter. You look so happy; I've never seen you look so happy. Stephanie, I love you. Just enjoy your day.'

'You do like Garth, don't you?'

'Of course I do. He's charming and he's in love with you. Stephanie, I'm happy for you. I'll talk about myself some other time. Not today.'

Stephanie put her hands on Sabrina's shoulders and pressed her cheek to hers. She was glad Sabrina wouldn't talk about herself, that was the terrible truth. She didn't want to discover that behind Sabrina's casual letters was a life more exciting than hers. She had Garth, she didn't need Sabrina. 'Thank you,' she said to Sabrina, then stepped back as Garth came up. 'You two never had a chance to get acquainted.'

Sabrina and Garth exchanged a quick glance. 'I'm sorry,' he said. 'I thought I could get here sooner. Too much to do. The end of the school year, the end of my teaching at Columbia. All that nostalgia to deal with. We'll get acquainted later.'

Stephanie shook her head. 'Not unless Sabrina leaves Paris and settles down in Illinois.'

Sabrina smiled involuntarily at the idea, and Garth was struck by the imp that broke through her cool, remote lips. But she snatched it back; the imp disappeared. 'We'll visit,' she said. 'Don't professors come to Europe for research and – whatever else they do?'

'Children,' said Gordon. 'The judge is ready.'

Judge Fairfax stood before a bank of high bushes, Stephanie and Garth before him, with a friend from Columbia on Garth's left and Sabrina on Stephanie's right. As they arranged themselves, Garth whispered in Stephanie's ear. 'She's cold. You're far more alive than she is. And much more beautiful.'

In a sudden moment of illumination, Stephanie saw what her sister had done. Sabrina's wedding present, she thought: to diminish her beauty and subdue the vitality that makes her the center of attention. To stand in the shadows and leave the sunlight to me. She felt a wave of love and then of guilt. But I can't help it, she thought, if we're not close and she doesn't confide in me. We're making our own lives; we don't need each other anymore.

How do you know? a small voice asked. Have you asked her if she needs you?

Judge Fairfax began to speak and Stephanie pushed away her thoughts and her guilt. She only had time to think how amazing it was that just when she and Sabrina were farthest apart she had found Garth to love her, and then she concentrated on becoming his wife.

Chapter 5

The castle rose up from the green hills of Hampshire, its battlements and towers worn by the centuries to a pale gray, its windows cut deep into stone walls. Beyond, a forest of copper beeches loomed, like a gleaming bronze curtain rustling in the June breeze.

'Treveston Castle,' Stephanie read in awestruck tones from Sabrina's letter. 'Eighty rooms, twelve hundred acres of farms and parks ... Garth, look!' she cried, glancing up. 'Peacocks!'

Garth slowed the car and looked at the two peacocks, the castle and the silver-blue lake that curved behind it, taking in what was once the moat. 'A cozy cottage,' he said ironically, but in spite of himself he was impressed. Straight out of a fairy tale, he thought; Minnesota farm boys and Midwestern professors have trouble believing such a thing is real. And, of course, it is ridiculous; it doesn't belong in the twentieth century. But still, it casts a spell: magnificent, beautifully proportioned, larger than life.

'Can you imagine Sabrina living here after the wedding?' Stephanie asked. 'I'd feel . . . dwarfed. As if I'd intruded in a house built for giants. I don't know how she'll do it.'

'Ask her,' Garth suggested, and stopped the car as a servant came up to open the doors and take their luggage inside.

Stephanie brought it up later as they took a tour of the grounds. 'I think about the people,' Sabrina said. 'Not four hundred years of wars and knights and royal processions, but the family. Especially the black sheep.'

The three of them walked on paths that wound among a thousand rose bushes as Sabrina told stories of the black sheep of the Longworth family. 'I think they invented one every generation, partly to liven things up, but mainly so they could be as eccentric as they liked and still have someone more disgraceful to point to.'

Stephanie laughed. 'Is there one now?'

'Not that I know of. I think Denton would like to be one, but his father and the board of directors frown on publicity, much less scandal.'

'I didn't know he worked. How does he – and have so much time to travel and be with you?'

'He works when the mood strikes. It seems he has a system . . .'

They walked on, talking, as Garth lingered behind, turning aside to look at the high hedges of the famous Treveston maze.

'Garth, we're going in,' Stephanie called. 'Do you want a tour of the house?'

'I'll catch up to you,' he said. Stephanie had shown him a letter of Sabrina's that described the maze: a triangle two hundred feet long on each side, planted in 1775 by Staunton Longworth in a labyrinth of hedges where visitors could be lost for hours. Garth peered through the opening, pondering geometric patterns Staunton Longworth might have used.

I'll try it later, he thought. Or tomorrow, after the wedding.

Inside the house, he followed the sound of his wife's voice. But, disconcertingly, he found it was Sabrina who was talking as he met them in the library. Odd, that over the years their voices remained identical even though they lived in different countries.

' ... restored the ceiling,' Sabrina said, gesturing, and Garth began to pay attention, admitting to himself once again that even though it was an anachronism, more museum than home, it was as splendid as anything he had ever seen.

The rooms led one to another in stately grandeur, hugely proportioned and fabulously detailed, from parquetry and carved lintels to mullioned windows framed in ivory damask drapes with fringed velvet ties. The castle dated from 1575, when Sir William Longworth, member of Queen Elizabeth's Privy Council, built it in Treveston Village on land granted him for loyal service. Fifty years later his grandson hired England's greatest architect, Inigo Jones, to remodel the south front and add three state rooms and a Grand Staircase. Other descendants made more additions to a total of eighty rooms, and in the twentieth century the farms and parks were improved, including the addition of a narrow-gauge steam railway crisscrossing the estate.

Shakespeare's troupe entertained in Treveston's Great Hall, and generations of farsighted Longworths filled the castle with a priceless collection of Titians, Rembrandts and Gainsboroughs, rare books and prints and seventeenth-century tapestries and furniture.

'Of course, you can't just hang a picture or buy a new rug when you want to,' Sabrina told Stephanie later as they sat on the balcony of her sitting room and bedroom. They were having tea while Garth tackled the maze. 'That's the first rule. But isn't it exciting anyway?'

'You look so happy,' Stephanie said. 'Is it possible for anyone to be as happy as you look?'

They laughed in remembrance. Four years ago, Stephanie thought. Four years of being apart. In that time, while she was settling down in Evanston, Sabrina graduated from the

Sorbonne, moved to London and went to work in Nicholas Blackford's antique gallery on Lowndes Street. She lived alone in a small flat, made new friends, helped organize two charity auctions. And in her letters to Stephanie she never mentioned her feelings. But now she might, Stephanie thought; because suddenly, it was so wonderful being together. She recalled Sabrina's look when they arrived. Love. And gratitude. 'You are happy, aren't you?' she asked.

'Happy or excited,' Sabrina said. 'I think with Denton they're the same. He's so incredible – he strolls through the world as if it's one of his Treveston gardens. You can't believe how overwhelming it is.'

'Oh, yes, I can,' Stephanie said dryly, taking in the canopied bed covered with Sabrina's clothes, the maid folding and packing them for the honeymoon, the Regency dressing table and wardrobe, the French doors leading to the balcony where they sat.

'No, it's not money,' Sabrina said. 'I mean, of course the money is wonderful – I've been living beyond my salary ever since I came to London. And it's not that Denton's father is a viscount, though that's part of it. Mostly it's the way Denton assumes he belongs wherever he goes. And he loves me, so by now I'm almost as confident as he is.'

'You don't need Denton to make you confident.'

'But I do, that's the trouble. You know how I've always tried to impress people so they'd like me ... well, look at Mother, how pleased she is with me and my spectacular marriage.'

'Mother didn't need that to love you.'

'Probably not, but have you ever seen her so affectionate?'

'No,' Stephanie admitted.

But the next day, watching Sabrina after the wedding ceremony, Stephanie thought she had never seen anyone more sure of herself and in command. A queen, she thought. I'll never look like that. Or have a castle. She felt a quick flash of envy, and then it was gone as Sabrina looked her way and their eyes met. I just want her to be happy, she thought.

Sabrina's lips sent her a silent thank-you before Denton nudged her to turn back to the guests in the reception line.

'My dear Sabrina, you have taken London by storm,' the Duchess of Westford said as she reached them. She beamed with the admiration only the very secure give to those younger and more beautiful than themselves, and Sabrina accepted it with a smile, in her gown of white silk and chiffon. Her slender neck rose above the triple strand of pearls and diamonds that was her husband's wedding gift; a matching strand glimmered like stars woven through her dark auburn hair. The duchess kissed her. 'I don't blame Iris for capturing you for her son. I wish I'd found you first, for mine.'

'But I captured her, you know,' said Denton. 'Mother only found her. She was looking for a desk and she found Sabrina.'

'She found the desk, too,' Sabrina said gaily. 'I sold it to her and then she invited me to tea.'

'Superb taste,' said Lady Iris Longworth to the duchess. 'Sabrina helped her mother furnish their home in Washington – of course, you've met her father, the under secretary of—?'

'Um,' the duchess nodded, less concerned than her friend Iris with Sabrina's credentials.

'Duchess,' said an impatient voice. 'Can I kiss my old Juliette roommate?' And in a flurry, Gabrielle de Martel moved forward to kiss Sabrina's cheeks. 'You look like a woman who has been swept off your feet by a handsome, debonair world traveler and bon vivant who quite properly adores you and has promised to give you a piece of the world for each birthday and Christmas.'

'If I can't find anything better,' Denton added.

'But what can I give you, then, except the moon?' asked Sabrina.

'Oh, forget the moon. I wanted it once, but now I have you.' He held her hand, and Sabrina smiled at his cheerful round face and rosy cheeks and trim black mustache. His shrewd black eyes were often hard, but when he looked at her they softened and became eager. 'I can't really believe even now that you belong to me.'

The line moved on. 'Sabrina, you'll both spend a week with us at Ranstead; do say you will, I'm counting on you. We'll just be a small group, twenty or thirty, so we can really get acquainted.'

'But we expect you at Harleton House in August, Sabrina, don't forget.'

'Sabrina, did Denton tell you we arranged for two weeks at Colburn Abbey in September?'

'Sabrina, have you hired a secretary yet? I can recommend—'

'When will your London house be ready, Sabrina? I've heard such wonderful things about it.'

'Never.'

'I beg your pardon?'

'We're going to be houseguests for the rest of our lives, swooping down on great homes and castles and perching awhile and then swooping on. We have so many nests to choose from, we don't need our own.'

Iris Longworth tapped her arm, smiling in spite of herself at Sabrina's mischievous eyes. 'You will be criticized if you jest about our friends' invitations. They take them very seriously.'

Sabrina nodded. 'Thank you.' She knew her voice was not penitent, but at least she hadn't smiled, even though her laughter kept bubbling up because she was having such fun. She looked down the receiving line to catch Stephanie's eye again, but Laura was between them, nodding her approval as she saw Sabrina looking her way. I've given Mother the ultimate antique, Sabrina thought; an in-law with four hundred years of lineage. Gordon was less enthusiastic; he preferred Garth to Denton. 'More solid,' he said, 'more serious.' More like himself, he meant, but he was friendly to Denton, and Sabrina felt she had finally pleased both her parents at once.

And Stephanie? She stepped back to see her: calm, quietly friendly, as six hundred strangers greeted her and commented on her remarkable likeness to her sister. Gabrielle had reported that she was chatting comfortably with some of England's richest women about her two babies, life in a Chicago suburb and her husband's latest research grant.

Beyond Stephanie, Sabrina saw Garth watching her with a curiosity he made no effort to hide. She knew what he was thinking and gave a little smile, as if to apologize, before turning back to the guests.

Garth moved back from the receiving line to lean against a window. He was trying to fit his memories of Sabrina with this stunning, vibrant woman, shimmering in the mist of her gown, her warmth and vitality the center around which the party revolved. Where was the cold, distant woman who had attended his wedding four years earlier at Bryn Mawr, and the reserved sister-in-law who had made two brief visits, spent mostly with Stephanie, when their children were born?

Garth knew he had never met this woman. Either something had transformed her – or the Sabrina he had met in the past had been hiding her true self.

He looked at his wife. In a long, pink dress Sabrina had bought her in Paris, she was softly beautiful, a pastel portrait in the slanting afternoon sunlight. She said she'd gained weight, though Garth had not noticed, and she no longer had the regal posture drilled into them at Juliette, but she outshone every woman there except Sabrina, and she was holding her own with the aristocracy of England. Garth was proud of her.

'Clever man, to escape,' Sabrina said with a low laugh, suddenly beside him. The reception line had wound to an end. 'I wish I'd been able to. Let's get Stephanie and hide somewhere.'

'And your husband?'

'Denton is discussing racing cars; he's investing in one for the Grand Prix. Do you know anything about the Grand Prix? Neither do I, but I have a strong suspicion I will soon learn. For now, though, I deeply desire a hiding place where I may remove my shoes.'

He chuckled as they rescued Stephanie from a plump earl 'who kept talking about spaniels,' Stephanie exclaimed, as they slipped into a small study. 'He said the wedding reminded him of his last dog show!'

They laughed together. Sabrina pulled off her shoes and curled up on the couch with a happy sigh. 'Oh, how I've missed you. Nobody else always laughs at the same things I do. Stephanie, how can you keep your shoes on? Two hours in that line—!'

At the other end of the couch, Stephanie shook her head ruefully. 'I can't take them off. Not in a castle. I can talk to your lords and ladies and feast at your table, but I cannot take off my shoes. It's all right,' she added quickly. 'I think what you have is wonderful. It's just that I'm more comfortable in my own home, I'm happy to say.'

Sabrina relaxed. 'I'm so glad. I was afraid—'

'I'd be jealous?'

'Not exactly. That you'd think I'd grabbed a bigger spotlight.'

'Oh. No, I don't. Isn't that strange? Maybe because I have my own now and I like it.'

'No more being shoved in the shade?'

Stephanie thought about it. 'Seems it's gone.'

Garth looked at them with patient curiosity. 'A code?' he guessed.

Stephanie started. She'd forgotten he was there. For a minute it had been just her and Sabrina, alone, as they used to be, their thoughts and words weaving together. She turned to him. 'Once I told Sabrina her spotlight put me in the shade where no one noticed me.'

'And then she went off to America,' Sabrina said. 'Leaving me alone with my spotlight.'

Stephanie gazed out the window at guests drifting like flower petals through the gardens, accepting champagne and hors d'oeuvres that waiters presented on silver trays. Four years ago, standing before Judge Fairfax in a different garden, she'd brushed aside the thought that Sabrina might need her; she hadn't really wanted to know.

Well, now she knew. She heard the echo of Sabrina's voice: 'Leaving me alone with my spotlight.' So Sabrina had missed her. Sabrina had needed her. Maybe as much as she had missed and needed Sabrina, even though, with Garth and the excitement of getting settled in Evanston, it had taken her a long time to realize it.

On the lawn, the guests were beginning to congregate near the tent. Sabrina sighed. 'If I don't get back, Denton's mother will say I'll be criticized.' Groaning, she pulled on her shoes. 'Weddings should be held in bed. That's where most of them begin these days anyway.'

Garth chuckled. Stephanie turned from the window. 'Sabrina, when are you and Denton coming to visit us? We have so much to talk about, so much time to make up—'

Something stirred in Sabrina. Stephanie's eyes, clear and shining, met hers without envy. Sabrina felt like singing. So much love to make up. 'I'd come tomorrow if I could. I'll see what Denton has scheduled. He's full of plans to show me all his favorite places. But as soon as I can . . . ' She held out her hands. Stephanie took them in hers and they held each other close, for a long moment, as they had in the far-off days when they were all the family they had. 'As soon as I can,' Sabrina whispered. 'I'll be there. I promise.'

Denton Longworth worked now and then in his family's shipping company, where he was vice president of finance and a member of the board of directors. To a point, he had done what his father expected of him, graduating from the university and immediately joining the company. But he had no intention of spending the decade between his twenty-fifth and thirty-fifth birthdays at a desk. Later he would settle in, but first there was a large world to enjoy. So he devoted one year to the office, building a dedicated staff capable of carrying on efficiently in his absence, and then he took off for the playgrounds of the world.

He worked when he felt like it. Rounding the corner of his thirtieth birthday, he discovered in himself a talent for reorganizing small, struggling companies his father acquired at bargain prices, and since that gave him pleasure – the yardstick by which he measured all his pursuits – he spent a few days a month at it.

Now, halfway through his thirtieth year, he assigned himself the happier chore of introducing his bride to his playgrounds and put his considerable energies to work on a grand tour. Within a few months, at Biarritz and Cannes, Wimbledon and Buenos Aires, Minorca and Zermatt, jaded members of the international set were falling over themselves to entertain Sabrina Longworth and bask in her irresistible combination of beauty, sophistication, open delight in new discoveries and warm gratitude. For when had anyone in their circles last expressed the simple emotions of delight and gratitude? No one could remember.

Wherever they went, invitations awaited them, sent on by Denton's secretary in London. Denton would fan through them, letting some drop to the floor and handing the rest to Sabrina. 'Pick out the ones that appeal to you, sweets. And toss out the rest.' But he would watch her. 'You're not throwing out Cora's invitation, are you? Wonderful hostess; no one misses her parties. And why did you—?'

So by the time they reached Monaco in May, almost a year after their wedding, Sabrina simply glanced at the invitations and handed them back to Denton. 'You decide. I still don't know everyone.'

He spread them on the coffee table in their suite, arranging them like a poker hand to fill the afternoons and evenings when they were not gambling in the Casino or watching the Grand Prix. 'Well done,' he told himself, having fit everyone in. 'We'll even have time for Max.'

'Who?'

'Max Stuyvesant. Amazing you haven't met him yet; he's all over the place. Pleasant fellow, something of a mystery, you'll like him. He wants us for a cruise on his yacht, four days, just after the race. Good idea; totally new experience for you.'

'Why is he a mystery?'

'Because no one knows how he makes his money.'

It was not that everyone hadn't tried to find out; they had. But no one got beyond Maxim Stuyvesant's own answer: he was 'in art,' which could mean anything. Some guessed he owned galleries in Latin America and Europe; others that he was an agent for wealthy clients. There was a rumor that he supported young artists, hiring people to bid on their paintings at auction to drive up the price and create excitement, then pocketing most of the inflated prices collectors paid for them. Cynics said he was a grave robber in the tombs of Egyptian kings.

However he made it, he spent his wealth lavishly, flying guests in his private plane high above Monte Carlo's fireworks displays, taking thirty friends for week-long African safaris, transporting two hundred people by train across Europe to a Yugoslavian dance festival. Sabrina hated him. He loomed above her, broad-shouldered, with a frizzled halo of red hair and flat gray eyes that guarded his secrets. Denton was surprised. 'How can you not like him? You haven't talked to him; all you've done is say hello and make yourself at home on his boat.'

'He's arrogant and brutal and I'll bet he doesn't know the first thing about art.'

'How can you possibly—?'

'I feel sorry for his wife, too. She's like a puppy, waiting for him to pet her.'

Denton was silent. Sabrina slipped on her evening gown of blue-black silk that settled about her like a delicate moth's wing, baring her shoulders and back. 'You'd better dress, darling. Cocktails are at eight, and if we aren't prompt he'll stare at us with those awful eyes and turn us into statues. That's the kind of art he's in! He casts a spell on people and then sells them to their grieving families as mementos.'

'Sabrina! Max is our host!'

'I'm sorry, Denton.'

'I hope so. Where are my cuff links?'

Their stateroom was hung with a French tapestry over the king-size bed. The carpet was deep, the furniture pale ash with ebony handles, the bath blue and silver with a whirlpool in the tub. The *Lafitte*, 104 feet long, had six such staterooms and five crew rooms. Its decks were teak. In its salon thirty people could move about comfortably beneath a teardrop chandelier. Its chef and wine cellar were famous. Sabrina had learned never to ask the cost of anything, but Denton, planning to buy one like it, said the price, with furnishings, was two million dollars.

Five couples were the Stuyvesants' guests on the *Lafitte*. Over cocktails, Betsy Stuyvesant, Maxim's third wife, small and soft in cashmere and silk, her blond curls trailing wistfully about her ears, told them she was not allowed to interfere in the ship's operations. If they needed anything, Kirst, the head steward, was at their service. For going ashore, Maxim made all arrangements. She fell silent and did not speak again that evening.

They dined on fish soup with saffron and orange peel, followed by baby octopus in champagne sauce; the wine was chilled white Palette from the hills above Marseilles. Max proposed a toast. 'To a successful cruise.' He smiled lazily at his dinner partner, a willowy blonde he had introduced as Princess Alexandra, from a country no one had heard of. Across the table, her husband, Prince Martova, looked fixedly at his plate.

Beside the Prince, a tanned, sleepy-eyed woman asked, 'And where do we go tomorrow?'

'East,' said Max, still looking at Alexandra. 'Along the Italian Riviera di Ponente to Alassio and Genoa and back. Four days. A lifetime.' Alexandra smiled.

Sabrina glanced at Denton and saw him smile lazily at Betsy Stuyvesant, as if he were trying to look like Max.

In the morning they found fruit, croissants and coffee in the small dining room. Max was their maestro. 'Sunbathing on the afterdeck for those who want. Waterskiing at four. Games and stimulants in the salon at all times. Movies in the small theater; Kirst will run them if you wish. We lunch at one. Enjoy yourselves, *mes amis.*'

Denton stretched. 'The salon first, I think. Then sunbathing. All right with you, sweets?'

Five people were in the salon, sifting through the cocaine and hashish and varicolored capsules in a corner cabinet. 'Max is a lovely host,' the sleepy-eyed woman said, and asked Sabrina, 'What's yours?'

Denton stepped in. 'Good of you, but I'll take care of my wife.' He tapped a small amount of white powder into an empty vial and pocketed it. Watching, Sabrina tried to separate this Denton from the one who lived with her in London. That one hardly took a drink, never smoked or used drugs, never looked at women as he had looked at Betsy Stuyvesant last night. On their travels she had seen hints of this other Denton; now he was in the open. Preoccupied, she followed him from the salon and along the deck to the cluster of reclining chairs and chaise longues used for sunbathing by day and for drinks and snacks at night. Alexandra was there with her husband and two other couples, all offering their beautifully tanned nude bodies to the molten Mediterranean sun.

Denton barely glanced at them. 'Come on, sweets,' he said, dropping his robe. Sabrina felt foolish and clumsy in her reluctance. There was only one Denton, her husband, and he was showing her how he expected his wife to behave. 'Totally new experience for you,' he'd said of Max's invitation. And when had she been afraid of new experiences? She looked at the magnificent women's bodies spread out before her, oiled and glistening. Hers was better. She dropped her robe and lay beside Denton, letting his large hand oil her back.

But she shook her head when he took some of the white powder on his finger and offered it to her. One thing at a time, she thought, and he did not insist. He sniffed the powder into each nostril as the others sniffed theirs or smoked hashish. The sun beat down on the quiet deck and Sabrina drifted in it until a shadow crossed her eyes. She opened them to see Max standing above her. Her muscles instinctively tightened, but he was looking past her at Alexandra. And in a long languorous movement, Alexandra stood and went with him toward the staterooms.

As if she had been waiting, Betsy took Alexandra's place. Denton watched her stretch and pat oil on her white skin. She caressed her breasts, humming to herself, then lay back and in another minute was asleep, her hands clasped as if in prayer.

He turned and found Sabrina's eyes on him. 'You're right,' he said, smiling indulgently. 'She's like a kitten. Cuddly. But not important.'

Sabrina had said Betsy was like a puppy, but she let it pass.

At lunch in the port of Alassio, Alexandra maneuvered to sit beside her. 'Honey,' she murmured. 'Relax. You're getting yourself all upset. They make the rules; we follow them. Everything's easier when you accept that.' Sabrina toyed with her appetizer, bending her head to listen. 'You see your Denton thinking about spreading little Betsy's legs, or doing

63

it, you just close your eyes and soak up the sun or learn to snort coke or go off with a good book.'

'How did you know—?'

'Now, see, that's something else you have to learn. Nothing is secret on this little canoe. You can do what you want – no limits – but whatever you decide, Max will know about it almost as soon as you do.'

Sabrina wrapped a slice of pink prosciutto ham around a wedge of pale green honeydew melon. 'Are you really a princess?'

Alexandra laughed heartily. 'That's another lesson, honey. Everything around here is only partly true. You remember that when you're watching your husband watch someone else.'

In the afternoon, as the *Lafitte* sailed east, they water-skied behind the high-powered speedboat that the yacht carried in place of one of its lifeboats. Sabrina and Alexandra skied side by side, skimming the water in a blue and gold mist. Sabrina felt young and strong and beautiful. I can do anything, she thought.

On the yacht, wrapped in bath sheets and drinking wine on the sundeck, Alexandra said, 'You're a hell of a skier. Where'd you learn?'

'At school in Switzerland.'

'Boarding school?'

'Yes.'

'The privileged life. I went to high school in Los Angeles.' She laughed at Sabrina's surprise. 'My mother was a two-bit actress who taught me how to move up in the world. She made me a better actress than she was. Speaking of which, you've perked up. Is that an act?'

'I don't know. I just decided, out there on the water, that I could do anything. Even live like the rest of you.'

'Honey, you said that as if it were a dose of arsenic. If you think we're poison, what are you doing here?'

Sabrina shivered in the breeze and pulled the bath sheet tighter.

'I didn't mean you. I like you. But I don't like watching Denton ... being expected to watch ... damn, I sound stupid, don't I?'

'Just unprepared. Didn't he tell you beforehand? Everybody knows about Max's cruises.'

'I didn't. And Denton never told me.'

'And he's different in London? Cozy by the fire, tucked in by ten?'

Sabrina hesitated, watching the Italian shore come into view. 'No. But I always know where he is when we go out separately.'

'Do you, now.'

Sabrina ignored her disbelief. 'The trouble is, it doesn't really matter to Denton whether I like something or not.'

'It doesn't matter to any of them, honey. That's the first rule.'

'So I don't know whether I have a choice.'

Alexandra nodded. 'You're catching on. As long as you want what they provide, you haven't got one small goddamned choice. Now go make yourself glamorous. Dinner in Genoa tonight. Wonderful food.'

As if he had heard their talk, Max organized the evening to demonstrate the life he and Denton could provide. Limousines whisked them along the highway far above Genoa to a restaurant with a sweeping view of the seacoast. After a leisurely dinner served by the chef and maître d', with a small orchestra playing in the background, they drove to a private party in a glass and wood home jutting out over the ocean, where they drank smooth ruby wines and gambled until three in the morning, when they returned to the yacht. Max took Sabrina's hand as she was going to her stateroom. 'You honor us by being our guest. We will have many cruises together. Pleasant dreams, my dear.'

Denton was in bed, keyed up, pleased with her. 'You were smashing; they all loved you. And I won at *Trente-et-Quarante*; haven't done that for a long time. Come to bed, sweets; I'm waiting.'

He pulled her to him, hastily stroking her body, straining and urgent with the excitement of winning and Sabrina's shining success. 'They'll be talking about us for months,' he murmured with satisfaction as he climbed on top of her. He centered himself and plunged in. 'Mmmmm, nice and tight,'

65

he murmured with the same satisfaction, and closed his eyes.

Sabrina lay beneath him, moving as he liked her to move. He was in a hurry, so she knew this time would be like all the others; she was partially aroused and she would end up partially satisfied, rubbed and pounded to numbness. She had tried to talk to him about their lovemaking, but he had had so many women before her, grateful women, that he considered his technique a subject for applause, not discussion. Sabrina thought of telling him that women were grateful because he allowed them to be near – in fact, underneath – the future Viscount Treveston, but she was silent. Because he really believed he wanted to make her happy. 'I never enjoy sex unless my woman enjoys it, too,' he told her the first time they were in bed. And he meant it. As he meant it when he said he never enjoyed parties or hunting trips unless his companions and opponents also enjoyed what he had planned for his own pleasure.

And because he was generous when he got his way, and cruelly silent if he was disappointed, almost everyone lied and told him they were happy. Everyone fakes something with Denton, Sabrina thought as she deliberately quickened her breathing, tensed her legs for a minute and then grew limp. 'That's my fine girl,' Denton said, his satisfaction intact. And then he plunged deeply and forcefully to achieve the final satisfaction of his day.

When Denton was asleep, she went on deck and let her thoughts float on the cool air. It was four-thirty. The yacht had slowed and was rolling slightly as it sailed west; they were returning to Monte Carlo. Sabrina heard the muffled sound of a boat with its motor cut, and then in the light from the yacht she saw Max's speedboat, piloted by his secretary, Ivan Lazlo. She watched from the darkness as he and a crew member hoisted it on the yacht, then disappeared down the forward stairs to the crew's quarters. Odd, she thought, this far from shore, where could he have been? She toyed with it a moment, then shrugged. Ivan Lazlo had nothing to do with her. Nothing about Max had anything to do with her; she just wanted the cruise to end. Two more days. She let the breeze cool her until she was sleepy and then went back to lie beside Denton and fall asleep.

The next day they slept late and had breakfast in bed. Denton kissed her and Sabrina smiled at him, cozy and warm. He smiled back. 'Sweets, I'm going to spend the day with Betsy. You can do what you want, but you ought to spend some time with Aldo Derona. He's interested in you, and he's a pleasant chap—'

She flung herself from the bed, putting space between them. 'I am not available for loaning out.'

'Now, sweets, that's a little harsh. You can't be surprised; you've known what was going on. I waited, but you didn't say a word, you adjusted beautifully. I'm proud of you. I hardly think I deserve harsh words.'

She was stunned, as helpless as if they spoke different languages. She looked at Denton: he seemed to be speeding backward, away from her, receding to a small figure in the distance. 'Sabrina?' said Denton uncertainly. His amiable eyes were worried as his wife looked at him in icy silence. He held out his hands. 'Sweets, you're getting too excited, as if you think I don't love you. Of course I love you, I always love you.' He waited. 'None of this means anything, you know; it's not important, it's a game, something we do because – well, damn it, because it's different, but actually it's not, you know, you mustn't think it's different or special, it's not, it's no different really from bridge or waterskiing or any of the friendly things we all do together. Oh, thank heavens,' he added, for she had begun to laugh, shaking her head and calling him a fool, but still she was his laughing wife again. 'Waterskiing,' she said. 'Friendly things,' and repeated them, putting her hands to her forehead. And because he was Denton, he did not hear or acknowledge the despair in her laughter.

For the remainder of the cruise Sabrina avoided Denton. She never knew whether he took Betsy to bed or not. Mealtimes were peaceful, and on the last night Max led a toast to Sabrina and Denton's first anniversary, which they would celebrate in America while visiting Sabrina's sister. Denton leaned over and kissed his bride, and Sabrina thought of their being alone finally to talk and work everything out.

She put her hand on the back of his head to hold the kiss, and that made it easier to ignore the lingering thought that, after all, they were still playing by Denton's rules.

Chapter 6

Stephanie handed Denton a long, two-pronged fork and asked him to check the meat. He gripped the handle as if it was his golf club and sent a frantic prayer over the heads of the other guests to Sabrina, at the far end of the backyard. But she was talking to some professor, leaving Denton with two slabs of flank steak sizzling contemptuously at him from the Weber grill. How did one check meat? He poked tentatively at the slabs, then a bit harder, gathering courage, and finally plunged the fork through the meat, all the way to the handle.

'Voila!' said Stephanie at his elbow. 'I used to know fencers who had that technique.'

'Have I totally destroyed it? I'll buy more at the market if—'

She laughed. 'You haven't destroyed anything. And you don't have to run away; I won't ask you to work again.'

'It's just that I'm not very good at it, you know.'

'Lack of practice. I'll take care of it, Denton.'

'Well, then, I'll just find my wife.' He wandered off.

Sabrina, glancing up, thought he looked like a tourist badly in need of a toilet, searching for someone who spoke his language. Stephanie was watching him, too; she met Sabrina's eye and they smiled together.

'The differences are cultural, perceptual and situational,' Professor Martin Talvia was saying, sliding the words around his pipe. 'Comparing your features one by one, you and Stephanie are identical. As whole individuals reflecting singular environments, you are quite separate and your being twins teases rather than shocks.'

Sabrina nodded gravely. 'You might say we look different because our lives are different.'

He curved forward like a crane, peering into her eyes, deep blue, shining with honesty or gentle mockery. Of course she was making fun of him but what a delight she was. 'You might say that. But if you were a professor of sociology you would be ashamed to speak so simply.'

She was laughing as Denton came up. He put his arm around her shoulders and squeezed. 'What's the joke, sweets?'

Sabrina's muscles tightened. The yard was full of people Denton could talk to; why did he hover and clamp her against him whenever she was having a good time? Because he's not happy, she thought, as Martin asked a question about England and Denton answered with the jovial charm that meant he was bored. He's a stranger, and suburban barbecues aren't part of his life. But she was a stranger, too, she reminded herself. She'd lived in Europe since she was two, and she'd met Stephanie and Garth's friends only briefly when their children were born. Why was she having a good time?

Because she loved meeting new people, but Denton was always bored away from his own crowd.

'Aunt Sabrina?' She looked down into the small, wise face of four-year-old Clifford Andersen. 'I'm supposed to tell everyone dinner is ready.'

Sabrina bent down. 'An important assignment.'

He nodded seriously. 'That's what Mommy said. But she said to hurry, and there are too many people. So would you pick me up, and if I'm tall everybody can hear me at the same time.'

Sabrina laughed and lifted him in her arms. 'As practical as your father. Ready?'

He took a deep breath and in a piercing voice shouted, 'Dinner's ready! On the patio!'

At his son's raucous cry, Garth looked up to see Sabrina's vivid laughing face beside Cliff's small one, red with effort and self-importance. It was a picture he remembered, of Stephanie with Cliff when he was born.

'Aunt Sabrina, why didn't you let me tell them?' came a wailing cry from the yard, and Penny Andersen flung herself with the anguish of a disappointed three-year-old on the ground at Sabrina's feet.

'Can't anyone control these children?' Denton asked. Sabrina gave him a swift look and knelt with her arms around Cliff and his sister.

'How would it be if you announce dessert?' she asked Penny. A smile broke through and the little girl nodded vigorously. 'Well, then, I'm starving. Who's going to sit with me at dinner?'

'I am!' they both cried, and led her to the patio.

On the patio and the lawn, small groups sat in nylon-webbed aluminum chairs, eating marinated flank steak, potato salad and thick slices of French bread, and drinking the red wine the guests had contributed. They talked about the coming political conventions that probably would nominate Richard Nixon and Hubert Humphrey, and they discussed their children's schools, crabgrass, food prices and the university, where most of them taught.

Darkness was falling, and Garth lit kerosene lanterns. Dolores Goldner leaned toward Denton. 'Stephanie's told us so much about you both, but not the little things, like what you eat at home or where you shop. We really know so little about royalty.'

'The nobility,' Denton said stiffly.

'Oh, of course. I'm afraid we Americans don't take the class system as seriously as you do.'

'Denton,' Stephanie said hastily. 'Tell us about Treveston, especially the history of your family and the castle.'

'Aunt Sabrina sent me a picture,' Penny said.

'Me, too; I'll get it,' said Cliff and jumped up, knocking his plate off his lap and scattering his dinner to left and right. 'Cliff!' Stephanie called, but he dodged through the door into the house. 'That's not fair!' Penny cried. 'I said it first!' She scrambled to her feet, tripped over Sabrina's foot and ran after her brother.

'Penny!' Stephanie's voice rose sharply, and she clenched her hands.

Sabrina stood. 'Shall I calm them down?'

'It's all right,' Stephanie said. 'I told them they could stay up until after dinner. It is now after dinner as far as they're concerned. Go on without me; I'll get them started on the long road to bed.'

She was trembling. Sabrina watched her go into the house. 'Excuse me,' she said, and followed her through the kitchen door.

Stephanie was already upstairs, and she waited in the kitchen. It was a wonderful old-fashioned room with a high ceiling, maple cabinets and countertops, and a Delft chandelier suspended over a worn sofa and low coffee table where the children often played. There was a large pantry next to a breakfast room with a round maple table and chairs and a maple corner cabinet filled with dishes. The furniture had been old and scarred when Stephanie bought it and restored each piece to its silken, honey-colored finish. 'I wouldn't sit anywhere else,' Sabrina said when she first saw the breakfast room. 'I don't' Stephanie answered. 'At least, this is where I sit when I have time to sit.'

Sabrina was standing beside the round table when Stephanie came downstairs. She watched her stop in the kitchen to put something in the refrigerator and thought again, with the surprise she had felt when they arrived the week before, that she was not taking care of herself. She was heavier and had a faded look, the edges of her beauty smudged and dulled. Sabrina, slender and vivid in a red Italian peasant skirt and soft white blouse with full pleated sleeves, knew she was outshining her sister, but Stephanie seemed unaware of it. Or unconcerned. In her own home, with family and friends, what was most important to Stephanie?

'Can we sit for a minute?' Sabrina asked. 'I could easily miss another rendition of Treveston history. I'll tell it to you if you like.'

Stephanie sat down with a little smile. 'Denton's mother told me at your wedding. I thought Denton would like a chance—'

'To have people listen to him.'

'He does like it, doesn't he?'

'He does like it.' They smiled together. Sabrina reached out her hand and Stephanie clasped it. 'I'm sorry it took us a whole year to get here. I had a terrible time getting Denton

71

to give up his international playgrounds for a week in an American suburb.'

'And now that he's here, he's bored.'

'Don't blame yourself, Stephanie. It's not your fault.'

'Garth took him through the lab, but—'

'No, science isn't Denton's thing. He likes other kinds of experiments.' Stephanie looked quizzical at the bitter twist in Sabrina's voice, but Sabrina went on. 'Anyway, being apart isn't as bad as it used to be. Do you feel that? Just knowing we can write or call and understand each other after all those years when it seemed we couldn't—' She gave herself a little shake. 'Tell me about you. Is there anything you haven't told me? About you and Garth? And the kids?'

'Nothing important. I've got what I always wanted, a home and a family. Permanence. When did we ever have that for more than the blink of an eye?' They laughed softly, thinking back 'Are *you* all right? I've felt all week that something was wrong.'

'Oh, there was something, on the cruise, and we haven't talked about it yet. Denton overloads the schedule and we never have time to talk. I'll work it out. You were pretty upset just now with the kids.'

'Was I awfully shrill? I wish I didn't get so excited. But Garth works day and night in the lab, and I'm alone with them so much my patience wears out. I didn't want them ruining the party for you.'

'How could they ruin it? I'm having a wonderful time. I teased Martin about his awful academic sentences.'

'They are awful, aren't they?'

'Yes, but funny. I like your friends.'

'I'll trade them for your castle and that yacht you've been on.'

'Stephanie, you don't mean that.'

'No, of course not. I wouldn't know what to do with your life; it's so unreal to me. And I have everything I want. Except money; I do get tired of scrimping. No,' she said quickly, seeing Sabrina's face. 'You can't help us; Garth would be hurt. Anyway the real problem is that he's not here, helping me. But that's not fair; he works so hard and everything really is fine. I don't know what's wrong with me tonight.'

My red skirt, Sabrina thought; cruises you don't know anything about; my letters to you from fourteen countries in the last year; the issue of *Town and Country* on your night table that says Denton spends a hundred thousand dollars a year on clothes for each of us and that I spent half a million dollars furnishing our London house.

But she said none of that aloud. Instead, she let Stephanie know that she understood by saying lightly, 'It's the strain of having Denton as a houseguest. He simply can't remember he has no servants at his beck and call. It's in his genes; I think Garth should study him. I made him hang up his towels this morning, and he called me a revolutionary out to overthrow the nobility.'

Stephanie smiled. 'Most of the time he's charming. And he takes care of you; you look marvelous.'

'The Mediterranean sun. You could use some.'

'I know. And I should lose weight. Maybe this summer. Is the sun the only reason you look beautiful and glamorous and happy?'

Sabrina looked thoughtfully at their clasped hands. 'Do you know, in the last year I have met about nine thousand people, give or take a thousand, and haven't had a personal conversation with one of them?' Except, oddly enough, she thought, Alexandra, but she couldn't talk about Alexandra or the cruise to anyone, not even Stephanie. She was ashamed of it, as if she were to blame for the guests and their games. 'I'm not used to talking about whether I'm happy.'

'But you aren't talking. You're evading.'

'I know.' She sighed. 'Remember once I told you I couldn't tell the difference between love and excitement with Denton? I still can't. And I have trouble talking about it.' Because you love your husband, she added silently, and you have a place where you belong. And I can't admit that I envy you. I've only been married a year. I have to try harder. Maybe next year will be different. 'But when I'm ready to talk, the best thing in the world is knowing you're here.'

Stephanie's eyes were bright. 'It is the best thing.' She stood up and peered at her image in the darkened window, combing her hair with her fingers. 'Time to hostess again, Sabrina,' she said, leaning down to kiss the top of her sister's head. 'I'm glad we're back.'

Voices murmured on the patio; lanterns flickered over shadowed faces, red wine and black coffee, climbing roses and beds of snapdragons. Sabrina felt she was on a quiet island: a loving, relaxed, uncomplicated life. I have to remember it, she thought, until I come home again. And it did not seem at all strange that she called it home.

At midnight, Stephanie saw the last guest out. She came back to the jumble of food and dishes on the patio and shook her head wryly. 'Does anyone know the magic words for making elves appear?'

'Those are the words,' Sabrina said. 'And we are your elves. Denton and I will clean up.'

At the expression on Denton's face, Garth grinned. 'There sits a terrified man. Don't worry, Denton; you're unskilled labor. I'll do it.'

'Not by yourself.' Sabrina began to stack plates. 'I have to do something useful.'

'You're unskilled, too,' Garth said.

Stephanie stifled a yawn. 'Well, I'm not. I can do it twice as fast as both of you. Anyway, Sabrina's a guest. Everybody go to bed.'

Sabrina kissed Stephanie on the cheek and gently pushed her towards the door. 'You worked all day; Garth and I will finish up. Go on. You can criticize our efficiency tomorrow. If you have the courage.'

Denton watched with calm interest as Sabrina and Garth silently scraped plates and piled them on trays. He stepped lightly forward and kissed Sabrina's forehead. 'I'll wait for you upstairs, sweets.' She nodded, absorbed in stacking cups.

Garth eyed the pile appraisingly. 'Risky.'

She ignored him and lifted the tray. At the kitchen door the tall stack bulged in the middle and the cups toppled, shattering on the flagstone patio. Sabrina bit her lip and walked into the kitchen to find a broom. Garth followed with his tray of dishes and returned with a dustpan. They swept up the pieces in silence.

In the kitchen, Sabrina ran water in the sink. 'I proved your point, didn't I? Unskilled labor.'

'It was an unkind remark. I apologize.'

'Why? You don't approve of me – of either of us, in fact. I've watched your face when we talk about our travels—'

'My fatal flaw. A wide-open face.' He picked up a clean towel. 'Sabrina, it isn't that I don't approve. I don't understand you. Your way of life, the things of your life, what you're looking for. They're so different from mine that I can't make sense of them. That is, no doubt, another flaw in my character.'

Sabrina moved her hands in the warm soapy water, remembering student days in a tiny apartment near the Sorbonne and working days in London before she married Denton. She hadn't washed a dish since then. She and Garth worked quietly, their voices low. Behind them, the honey-colored kitchen was in shadows and the house was dark and silent. She felt peaceful. 'How do you know so much about our life?' she asked.

'Full reports from Stephanie, describing everything in rich detail. The key word there is rich. Let me ask you something.' He dried a platter with careful attention. 'Is Stephanie unhappy because I spend so much time at the lab, or because I don't give her your kind of life?'

'But she isn't unhappy, you're wrong—'

'I don't think so. Look, I'm asking for help. You know Stephanie better than anyone else. You'd know her real feelings—' He saw her face change. 'I'm not asking you to betray any secrets, you know, I'm her husband. I love her. All right. We'll forget you're her twin. How about this? Pretend you're a scientist looking for explanations. The fact is: Stephanie is unhappy. What's the explanation?'

'Your work.'

He picked up another platter. 'Three in a row. You, Nat Goldner and Marty Talvia. They scold me regularly. I know it's hard on Stephanie; every day I vow to reform. But then the questions pull me back, the mysteries, the fascination—' He stopped. 'Sorry; you wouldn't understand.'

Sabrina let it pass. 'You're a lucky man.'

'Because of Stephanie? You don't have to tell me—'

'No. Well, of course because of Stephanie, but I meant – you have good friends who help you know who you are.'

Intrigued, Garth stopped drying. Sabrina gazed unseeingly at the dark window. 'Denton chases himself around the world to find out who he is, and he can't do it. Or even admit he's trying. People fawn over him because he's heir to Treveston, but a lot of them don't like him and he doesn't know why. He's bored a lot and he doesn't know why that is, either. He just escalates his fun. He won't listen to me because when I don't like something he does he says I'm unsympathetic. But if he had friends he might see himself through their eyes, what kind of a person he is, what he wants to do with his life. The way you do. That's what close friends do, isn't it? They value you and care about who you are instead of what you are. They help you discover your own worth.'

His face was startled. 'Well said.'

She submerged a frying pan. 'How nice that I've impressed you.'

'I'm sorry. I didn't mean to insult you. But how did I know you have a head full of ideas? Your husband doesn't, and in your kind of life—'

'Why do you keep talking about our kind of life? You've already admitted you can't make sense of it. Parts of it are wonderful.'

'And the other parts?'

'Some things we'll change. That happens in any marriage.' Who am I, she thought, to lecture on marriage? 'We won't keep running around the world forever; when we have children we'll stay at home in London. I want to meet different people, and work with art and antiques; I've been asked to help organize a new museum of primitive art . . . so many things I want to do. And I want to entertain. You wait; we'll invite you and Stephanie and the kids to a barbecue on our terrace.'

Garth smiled absently. 'Sabrina, I don't think you should count too heavily on Denton's settling down.'

She let the water out of the sink. 'Why not?'

'Because I don't think he can.'

'What are you talking about? You don't know Denton—'

'I know him better than you think; I've been his host for a week, remember? And the kind of life he makes you lead—'

'Oh, don't be so stuffy!' She stood with her back to the sink and glared at him. How dare he pass judgment on her! He was so solemn – no spark, no fire, and he didn't know how to laugh. He had a wonderful face, strong and sure, with warm deep eyes, but still he was dull. And smug. A smug, narrow-minded professor. 'What makes you think I'm suffering? I have the most wonderful life in the world. You seem to have trouble understanding it, in your sterile laboratory, but to me it's exciting. It has crowds of people and new cities and scenery, parties, dances, different kinds of food, wonderful shops and markets, new clothes, books from all over the world, theaters—'

'Stop! You've convinced me. Sabrina, I admire you. I'm sorry I was stuffy and tried to knock down your castle.'

She gave him a quick look before turning back to wipe the counter. 'But you still don't think Denton is about to settle down.'

Garth folded his arms and leaned against the refrigerator. 'Sabrina, has Denton ever told you he thinks perfecting a life of pleasure is an art?'

'Oh, he talks like that—'

'An art that requires full-time attention, and as much involvement and careful planning as any job. If you pin him down, he'll say it *is* a job. Few men give up a job for a family. I don't think Denton is one of them. Many men assume their job comes before their families. I think Denton is one of them.'

The room was silent, broken only by the soft swish of Sabrina's cloth as she wiped out the sink and then polished the faucet. 'You're wrong.'

'I hope I am.'

He hung up his towels. Sabrina's eyes were dark. These were the doubts she couldn't talk about to Stephanie, doubts she'd thought were locked within her. And now they'd been put into words by the unlikeliest person, one who had never seemed interested in her or Denton.

Garth went into the pantry to turn out the light. When he

came back she asked, 'Do you mean he might want to give it up but something keeps him from it?' Garth nodded. 'Well, what something is it?'

'I'd call it passion.'

'Oh, for heaven's sake, Garth, Denton isn't passionate about anything. ' She caught her breath. Now she'd given that away, too.

'Except his pleasure,' Garth said. 'His way of life. That's his passion. And he's consumed by it. I suppose he could conquer it, but it would be a struggle. Denton doesn't strike me as a man who welcomes struggle.'

'Is that a scientific guess?'

'It's more than that.' His voice roughened. 'I looked at his eyes. There are many kinds of passion, Sabrina, but they recognize each other. Denton's eyes have the same look I see every time I look in my mirror. I knew it as soon as I saw him. Odd, but he's a kindred spirit.'

Sabrina heard the painful honesty in his voice and thought of the glittering fixedness of Denton's eyes that she had tried to call eagerness. She turned her wedding ring on her finger, the circle of diamonds catching the light and throwing it back in flashes of color. 'Thank you,' she said quietly, and smiled. 'I apologize for calling you dull. You're not.'

'You called me stuffy. Dull, too?'

A laugh escaped her. 'If I can't remember my insults, I shouldn't use them. I apologize for all my unkind words. You're not dull and you're not stuffy.'

'And you're not empty-headed or unskilled.'

They laughed.

'Shall I turn out this light?'

'I'll do it after I lock up. Good night, Sabrina.'

'Good night, Garth.'

She walked from the warm kitchen through the dark dining room and living room, feeling her way around the furniture. At the foot of the stairs she turned and looked down the length of the house to the lighted kitchen. His head bent in thought, Garth was at the back door, making his house secure for the night. Then he put his hand to the switch, and, as the room went dark, Sabrina slowly climbed the stairs to go to bed.

In the empty storefront, stripped to its bare walls, Sabrina held open the door as the carpenters carried in stacks of lumber. Her life had been stripped as clean as this empty space she was renting – and I'll build them both up together, she thought, smiling to herself at the idea. Fresh and new after I failed with Denton.

At the back of the shop, where the carpenters had set up their sawhorse, Laura was examining blueprints. Sabrina stood at the front door, watching rain beat down on the high black taxicabs crowding Brompton Road. Three years. That's all we could make it last. And then it took me another year to discover that nothing would ever be the same again.

'My lady,' a carpenter called, his voice echoing off the walls. As Sabrina walked back to him, he drew a chalk line on the dusty floor. 'Is this where you want the door, my lady?'

'That's fine,' she said, and smiled ruefully at her mother. 'I feel like an impostor; it isn't my title any more.'

'Oh, use it,' said Laura. 'It will help you. Even Americans love to roll titles on their tongues. Last month I gave a talk in a high school and someone called me Mrs Madame Under Secretary of State.'

'Much more impressive than mine.'

'But yours is legitimate. Does Denton want you back?'

'I don't know. What difference does it make?'

'I thought you might be lonely.'

'Oh.' Sabrina picked up a blueprint and pretended to study it. Of course she was lonely. Lonely and scared. But she'd been that way for a whole year, beginning when she left Denton.

She had moved into a small ground-floor flat, seeing no one except when she was at work in Nicholas Blackford's antique gallery, where she had worked before her marriage. For six months she lived alone, besieged with telephone calls from Denton, his family, her parents, all telling her what a fool she was. Gabrielle called from Paris.

'Sabrina, he'll settle down now that his father's dead and he has the title and the estate.'

'His father died a year ago,' she said. 'And he's still the same.'

Other friends called. 'He adores you, Sabrina. His playing around is just working off excess energy. He'll get over it. How many men adore their wives? You don't know how lucky you are.'

I'm tired of his excess energy, she thought. I'm tired of living on a roller coaster with nothing solid beneath it. I want a home, children, a place to belong. But all she said was, 'There are things I want to do with my life, and there's no room for them on Denton's social calendar.'

Stephanie called. 'Do you want me to come to London?'

'Not now,' Sabrina said. 'It's scary but manageable. I'll let you know. And Mother said she might come. Isn't that amazing?'

Laura had come, stayed awhile and returned to Washington. In November Sabrina and Denton had agreed on a settlement, and she had moved back to the house on Cadogan Square that she had restored and decorated with such excitement when they were married. Now it was hers. And then, from November to April, one whole London season, she had not seen or heard from anyone in Denton's circle – her circle, she once thought. She spent long hours working in Nicholas Blackford's shop and long nights alone in her exquisite, empty house. London had become cold and foreign; she had no one to talk to. Except Stephanie. But talking to Stephanie had become a luxury because she was worried about money: for upkeep on the house, for the shop she was planning to open, for living from day to day until the shop began to support her.

Yes, Mother, she thought, I have considered going back to Denton. To the protection of his family, to his circle. These days I never know what lies ahead. At least with Denton I always knew what he had planned. I even knew, most of the time, whom he was sleeping with.

'When you were here last winter,' she said aloud, 'before the property settlement, I felt like I was twelve years old, wanting to go shopping with you and Stephanie.'

'You didn't tell me that.'

'I know. If I'd talked about it I might have curled up on your lap and asked to be comforted. Wouldn't that have been awkward?'

'My lady, excuse me,' said the carpenter. 'Are the plans correct, that this wall is not to reach the ceiling?'

'Yes,' Sabrina answered, looking at the blueprint he held.

'But you'll hear sounds from the showroom even if you close your office door.'

'I hope the sounds are customers and I hope very much to hear them.'

'Ah. Of course. I hope so, too, my lady.'

'Why would it have been awkward?' Laura asked.

'Because you never let me sit on your lap when I was a child. Why start now, when I'm grown up and can take care of myself?'

There was a long silence. Sabrina glanced at the lines in her mother's face and wished she had not spoken. Why recall the past when they were learning to be friends in the present? Laura was as proud and beautiful as ever, and Sabrina was happy with her – a beautiful woman with her beautiful mother. It was another step in growing up.

She broke the silence. 'What do you think I should do with the new wall? Shelves or paintings?'

'Oh – perhaps both? Paintings mounted here and shelves in the corner? And maybe an easel or two in front, for other paintings.'

'Easels. A marvelous idea. On a small rug. If the budget allows.'

'Sabrina, why didn't you demand more money from Denton? By the time you finish here, you won't have much left.'

'Enough for about six months if I'm careful. I couldn't ask him for more. He told me so often I belonged to him that I wanted to snap my fingers and walk away. Dramatic but not very practical. So I took just what I thought would get me started. You mustn't worry, Mother. I've given free decorating advice to Denton's friends and relatives for years, they know what I can do. How can I be anything but a smashing success?'

If they come, she thought. She hadn't told Laura she'd been ignored for six months; she was ashamed of it, as if somehow it was her fault. And she didn't want Laura worrying over her. I'll make them come, she vowed.

'Of course you'll be a success,' Laura agreed. She ran her hand over the paneled wall. 'Do you know, this was always my dream? A shop of my own, instead of picking things up on the fly.'

'But you can have one now. You're in Washington for good.'

'Oh, it's too late. I can't start from scratch; I haven't got your energy. I must have lost it somewhere between embassies. I'll just help now and then with Ambassadors. I was touched that you chose that name.'

Sabrina put her arm around her mother and they watched the carpenters put up the office wall at the rear of the shop. The showroom was long and narrow, fronted with a square, paned window. The walls had dark oak wainscoting; the ceiling was molded in plaster octagons. Sabrina felt a shiver of delight and astonishment every time she walked in the door – that it was hers, that she was turning her dreams into reality, fitting her life to her own patterns and rhythms. I've never done that, she thought. I went from my parents to Juliette to the university to working for Nicholas and then to Denton. I've never made my own rules. Impulsively she spread her arms wide. 'Isn't it wonderful!' she cried.

Laura smiled, and Sabrina again put her arm around her shoulders. It felt good to both of them. We need more touching, Sabrina thought, as we get older. And more love: giving it and finding it. 'Mother, thank you for coming. You've made it more exciting. And less frightening.'

'Thank you for asking me,' Laura said. 'Giving me a chance, after all these years, to make a shop. I guess if we wait long enough, we get most of the things we want. Sabrina, why don't you move to America? We would all be so glad. There's nothing keeping you in London.'

'Yes, there is. Right now it's my home. And I know it better than any other city. The wealthy people, the markets, the competition. And the old people. Especially the sick ones. The ghoulish truth is that the only way to grab the best antiques and art is to know who's dying so you can have cash ready when their estates are auctioned. And I have friends in London.'

'You have a sister and parents in America.'

'Mother, please understand. I love all of you, and I miss you, but this is where I failed with Denton and this is where I have to succeed on my own. I want to find out what I can make of myself. Can't you understand that?'

'Yes,' said Laura. She paused. 'I think I may be envious.' And, for the first time since Sabrina was fifteen and leaving home for boarding school, she put both arms around her daughter and kissed her. 'I am so proud of you,' she said. 'And I love you.'

Chapter 7

Lady Andrea Vernon had made Alderley House famous for its grand balls and when Sabrina stood in the doorway beside Nicholas and Amelia Blackford, she drank in the light and color and music as if she could never get enough. When a tanned young man with a lean face asked her to dance and they swept down the length of the wine and gold room, she felt young and carefree for the first time in months. Her taffeta gown swirled in an amber cloud as she turned and turned to the music, looking about her at the ballroom. It had been redecorated in the year since she had seen it last, and she admired the restoration of the gilded ceiling. But she stared in disbelief at the hundreds of light fixtures on the walls; they resembled the veined noses of alcoholics. Where in heaven's name had Andrea's designer dug them up? She shook her head, her fingers itching to sweep the walls bare and decorate them with a simple elegance to match the ceiling. 'You don't agree?' the young man asked.

'Oh, forgive me, I was daydreaming. What did you say?'

She listened while he spoke, and listened to the man who cut in on him, but her thoughts kept drifting to Andrea Vernon's walls and other walls, other rooms she had thought once she would be called on to decorate.

'I heard someone say you'd opened a shop,' her partner was saying. 'What do you call it?'

'Ambassadors,' she said.

'Good name,' he said casually. 'Doing well?'

'Doing well?' She steadied her voice. 'Of course.'

'Good,' he said, and she knew he had not really listened to her, or he was ignoring the trembling in her voice to avoid asking if she was having problems. No one at a ball wanted to hear that a beautiful young woman had problems.

The truth was, no one anywhere wanted to hear; so no one did. Sabrina kept to herself the fact that her shop had no customers.

All around her were the aristocracy and business elite she had counted on. Once they had been her friends. She had gambled on that friendship. But in eight months, she had been proven wrong again and again. No one had come.

She had sent announcements to everyone she knew. Nicholas had said to watch especially for Olivia Chasson. 'Where she goes, others follow. If you get her favor, you have nothing to worry about.' Each day, eagerly, excitedly, Sabrina unlocked the shop door and waited in her office for Olivia Chasson and her friends to walk into the tapestry-hung room she and Laura had designed after the eighteenth-century salons of the great homes and castles of England. The eagerness and excitement faded; the feeling of adventure disappeared while she waited for the noise the carpenter had said she would hear from the showroom. Oh, for some noise, she prayed day after silent day, even the tiniest noise, like the tiptoe of a cautious duke. But only a few tourists came, wandering in off the street to browse but seldom to buy.

By now her money was gone. She had borrowed from the bank, and soon she would have to mortgage her house. After that . . . But she refused to think of that.

'Dinner,' said her partner, who had been describing his polo game. 'Shall we have something?'

They filled their plates at the buffet and sat on a couch in an alcove of drapes. They ate in silence. Sabrina wished for Stephanie. She wished for a friend to break up the long days and evenings and laugh with her and sometimes let her cry.

She even wished for a few of the invitations she'd turned down when she was Denton's wife.

'But if she married Denton for his money,' a woman's voice said on the other side of the drapery, 'why didn't she take a bigger settlement?'

Sabrina grew very still. When her partner began to speak, she put her finger to her lips.

A second voice answered, high and indignant. 'How do you know what she took? Denton is too much of a gentleman to talk, but I know for a fact she demanded three million pounds and Treveston and the new yacht. Her own solicitor said that was outrageous. But you know how Denton adored her, so of course she got a fortune. He'd have given her everything he owned.'

'Except Treveston,' the first voice said dryly. It was puzzlingly familiar, but Sabrina could not place it.

'Well, my dear, he couldn't give away a national treasure like Treveston. You do know that she grabbed the London house.'

'My sweet ballroom gossip,' said a man's voice, joining them. 'May I guess the subject of your sharp tongue? Could it be the beautiful Lady Sabrina Longworth, or have I stabbed more completely in the dark than you have stabbed her in the back?'

'Peter, that is grossly unfair,' said the indignant voice. 'We were simply discussing the settlement poor Denton had to make.'

'Poor Denton,' the first voice coolly mimicked, 'gave up so little he probably charged it off to "miscellaneous". Sabrina didn't make a dent in his playtime.'

'Then how did she get that shop on Brompton Road?' demanded the indignant voice. 'I walked past it the other day, and she has an armoire in the window that I know for a fact is worth two thousand pounds at the very least.'

'Rose! You walked past and didn't go in?'

'My sweet Rose wouldn't go in,' the man's voice said, 'unless everyone did. And the pack has decided Sabrina is a pariah, all of you who cozied up to her when she was Denton's wife—'

'Peter, don't be crude. If you looked past her face you'd

know why she married Denton. She didn't even try to disguise it; she deserted him less than a year after his father died and he became viscount. But Americans are always obvious, aren't they?'

Sabrina sat rigidly in the corner of the couch, her eyes lowered, as she tried to think about what she was going to do, tomorrow and the day after and the day after that.

She heard a chair scrape and the first voice came from a different location. 'She's never played by your rules and you've never forgiven her. I think I may do something about that.'

Sabrina tilted her head. She knew who the voice reminded her of: someone who'd told her long ago that she had to play by "their" rules.

Her partner touched her arm. 'Would you like me to take you home?'

She looked up, her eyes very bright. 'That doesn't seem like a good idea.' Her voice became stronger. 'I think I'd like to dance some more.' And think of how I'll fight them, she thought, now that I know what is happening. Why didn't I figure it out long ago?

His eyes admired her. 'Brave lady. They're a bit vulgar, the Raddisons, especially Rose, but—'

'Well, now, fancy meeting you here, isn't life curious,' said the cool voice that had been behind the drapery, and Sabrina turned to meet the lazy smile of Princess Alexandra Martova. 'Will your friend forgive us?' asked the princess. 'I'm about to take you under my wing.'

Alexandra Martova was the owner of four floors of chic rubble. She had come to London alone, with nothing in the world but the proceeds from her divorce: a Swiss bank account, a house on the island of Minorca off the Spanish coast, an apartment in Paris, alimony of ten thousand dollars a month and a Great Dane she called Maxim, after an old friend. Tall, willowy, with light blue eyes turning up at the corners and blonde hair falling sleekly to her shoulders, she had a decisive air she had not had when Sabrina met her on Max Stuyvesant's yacht. 'I decided to make my own rules,' she told Sabrina. 'Looks like you did the same.' She had come to London because she was bored. 'Nobody knows how to give a good party. So I decided to show them how it's done. Honey, I am about to become the most famous hostess in Europe.'

But first she needed a house. She found one in Belgravia, tall and narrow with high windows, like a Victorian lady with eyebrows raised in surprise. It had a red door with a lion's-head knocker. Alexandra loved the outside but hated the dim, cramped interior, so she had everything ripped out, leaving only the shell. 'I want you to redo it for me,' she said to Sabrina. 'Top to bottom. Have some more wine.'

She blew plaster dust from the bottle and refilled the cut-crystal glasses she had brought in a picnic basket. Sabrina sat on a packing crate, sipping the light fruity Beaujolais and surveying the rubble-strewn expanse that was Alexandra's second floor. With the interior walls gone, she had a straight view from front to back. All that remained of the original rooms was a marble fireplace with a chipped mantel. Streaks of sunlight, dancing with dust, cut across exposed beams and fragments of wood and marble that reminded Sabrina of the antiques her mother once bought, knowing they would shine with beauty when she polished them. Sabrina felt the same tingling desire she had had in those days when she watched her mother's sure hands with awe and envy. I can make this beautiful, she thought. Eyes shining, she turned to Alexandra. 'Thank you.'

Alexandra raised her glass. 'I'm planning on us helping each other. You need a commission, but I need more: a house and respectability. I know everybody in London town, but, sad to say, they know me, too. After all those years and all those beds in Monte Carlo and points west, being a princess is not enough. I need to be launched, is what I need.'

Sabrina shook her head ruefully. 'I'm not the one to launch anybody. You ought to know that, after last night.'

'Honey, you've learned more than that since you were tagging along behind Denton; you're just shook up by that little eavesdropping and you're not thinking straight. Now, you sit there and listen to me while I lecture at you. You are going to launch me as soon as I launch you. Didn't you hear me say I was taking you under my wing? You will do my house. We will present it to society with a grand party. And it will be such a sensation that within a week people will be saying that if Lady Sabrina Longworth won't lower herself to be your design consultant, you are nobody. And that will include the high and mighty Olivia Chasson.'

Alexandra drained her glass and strode about the room, leaving footprints on the dusty floor as she skirted piles of plaster and wood. 'And when your rocket goes off, mine does, too, right into respectable society, which by then is snuggling up to you again. Because I'll tell you, Sabrina, what you don't seem to understand is that people have always raved about you. You're absolutely gorgeous – more than me, which I'd never admit to anybody else – you're fun and nobody can predict what you're going to say or do. There's never been a breath of scandal about you and people who hate each other love you. Do you know when I started hearing about you? Right after you were married. Wherever I went – Rio, Cannes, Majorca – people talked about you. For a whole year I kept waiting to meet you so I could kill you. Then on Max's little boat you were so damned innocent and unhappy I couldn't believe it, and then I started to like you. Craziest thing.'

She sat down on her crate and stretched her long legs. 'Look, the only reason they're mad at you now is that nobody knows why you and Denton split and what you took him for. You ought to tell them – don't shake your head like that, I'm only saying I think you should. What they believe is that you appeared from nowhere and married one of them and took him for his title and God-knows-how-much money, and then opened a fancy shop as a hobby subsidized by poor Denton; and poor Denton is talking about his broken heart in every bed he can find his way into. I know what you got because it so happens you and I used the same solicitor for our divorces, and he was moaning about how much you gave up. It's your story, I'm not telling anybody, but most of them are waiting for you to prove them wrong because they're crazy about you. Sabrina, listen.'

Alexandra poured the rest of the wine into their glasses. The sunlight had faded into late afternoon, and in the pale gray chill she looked like a marble statue. 'You are the perfect person for me. You have class and style and independence. I give you this house to design; you stand at my side when I give my first party in it. What do you say?'

Sabrina had a faraway look. She had heard everything Alexandra said, but at the same time she was miles ahead, already designing the house, estimating dimensions and wall locations, furniture styles and arrangements, art works, draperies, rugs. She couldn't wait to begin. But she had to be sure of one thing. 'Carte blanche?' she asked calmly.

Alexandra's eyebrows shot up in mock surprise. 'Ho, what have we here?'

The grateful Sabrina of a few minutes before was gone; so was the bewildered one of last night. This Sabrina, professional and self-assured, looked beyond Alexandra at the shell of the house and asked, 'How much are you willing to spend?'

'Whatever it takes to do it right.'

Sabrina nodded. 'Tell me the effect you want and I'll create it.'

'Yes, ma'am.' Alexandra grinned in admiration. 'At your service, ma'am.' They laughed and lightly touched glasses before drinking the last of the wine. 'When can you start?' Alexandra asked.

Sabrina slipped into her coat. 'I already have,' she said.

They met for lunch and dinner and so many hours of talk that Alexandra finally moved from her suite at the Connaught Hotel into one of Sabrina's guest rooms. They talked about Alexandra, and as they talked Sabrina sketched rooms that would fit themselves to her. She hired the contractor who had remodeled Ambassadors to supervise the electricians and plumbers and plasterers. Specialists installed the intricate parquet floors she designed. In a few weeks the furnishings arrived: an eclectic unorthodox mixture far more daring than Alexandra realized.

There were neo-Rococo pieces from the 1850s in flowing curves and curlicues with mother-of-pearl inlays, gilt and painted flowers on a black lacquer background. This was the willowy, frivolous Alexandra of jewelry and parties. Sabrina alternated them with George Jack furniture from the 1890s:

89

deceptively simple chests with inlaid designs of sycamore and other woods shading into each other. This was the Alexandra who talked wistfully of the 'someday' when she could drop the act she put on for everyone, including herself. And finally Sabrina added a few striking modern Soriana chaises and ottomans by Scarpa: flat to the floor, made of soft leather squished into shape by chrome-plated steel tubing. 'The Alexandra who is soft and hard at once,' she said as the last chaise was moved into place. 'Calculating and loving, earthy, sexy, holding back, but oh-so-comfortable once she relaxes with you.'

Alexandra whirled through the rooms, up and down the stairs, touching and sitting and leaping up to run again. 'I love it, I love it, I want to move in, I want to have a party. Can I move in today?'

Ceremoniously, Sabrina handed her the key she had been using for four months and the guest list for the party she had drawn up the night before. The next day they began to plan Alexandra's launching.

It was a May Day ball, beginning at 10:00 P.M. on the first of May and ending with breakfast on the morning of the second. It was also the triumph of the 1976 season, the only social event given equal coverage on the society and architecture/home-furnishings pages of newspapers and international magazines.

'The educated eye finds the Martova house outrageous and chaotic,' wrote Europe's most influential interior-design critic. 'But only at first. In its remarkable ambiance, the eye soon discovers a design refreshing, enchanting, and uniquely the mark of a strong individual who knows herself and her client.'

'As for the ball itself,' wrote a society reporter whose story wound around photographs of the more prominent of the two hundred guests, 'the orchestra was delightful, as were the love songs of the costumed singers and dancers in the salon. The clothes worn by the women were a galaxy of the world's great designers, and the tables were never empty of exotic food. Princess Alexandra was a statuesque goddess all in white with a necklace of emeralds. The star of the evening was Lady Sabrina Longworth, stunning in cloth of gold, a favorite of London society ever since her marriage to her former husband, Lord Denton Longworth, Viscount Treveston (who was not at the ball). Lady Longworth was responsible for the brilliant design of the princess' Belgravia abode. Among the guests were Peter and Rose Raddison of the automobile Raddisons, Lady Olivia Chasson and Gabrielle de Martel, daughter of the finance minister of France, who says she soon will be looking for her own London flat.'

Sabrina moved from room to room in the house she had created. She forgot the reporters and barely noticed the guests clamoring to congratulate her on her design. She heard eager voices talk about 'getting together soon' and knew that the evening was a triumph, but she moved on, not wanting to talk, just looking at the house, alive with light and talk and laughter, exactly as she had envisioned it. She had designed other places – the house Denton bought her on Cadogan Square, and Ambassadors – but they were done to her own desires. This was the first time she had created for someone else a place to live and love and grow.

Stephanie would be proud of her, she thought; that afternoon she had sent her photographs of each room. One of them, a close-up, showed a small, personal touch, a gesture she could not resist. In a dim corner of the first-floor salon, she had lifted out five tiny sections of the parquet floor and replaced them in a new arrangement, a distinctive S, the only one in the house. No one would ever notice. But she had left her mark.

Sunday was a day of recovery. And on Monday morning, as she dusted the furniture in the showroom, Sabrina heard the small oriental chime that rang when the front door was opened. She looked up and then moved forward with a smile to welcome Lady Olivia Chasson to Ambassadors.

Chapter 8

Sabrina and Stephanie stood together on Cadogan Square in the chill October morning, near the end of a long row of five-story red brick Victorian mansions. Across the street was a locked park belonging to the owners of the mansions overlooking it. Sabrina's was one of them, embellished, like the others, with Gothic turrets and gables, balconies, pavilion roofs and pointed stained-glass windows.

Mrs Thirkell took Stephanie's suitcases upstairs. 'Do you want the grand tour now?' Sabrina asked, and Stephanie nodded, already feeling the cool elegance wrap itself about her as they walked through the ground-floor reception hall, dining room and kitchen. The drawing room took up the second floor; on the third floor a study and billiard room were separated by a bookshelf wall that swung open to make one large room; the bedrooms were on the fourth floor. Stephanie lingered in each room, in the harmonious balance Sabrina had achieved between sunlight and shadow, soft hues and brilliant colors, loose weaves, shimmering silks and sensual velvets, polished woods, muted wallpaper and glowing veined marble. 'I could live here,' she sighed. 'My fantasy house come to life.'

On the fourth floor she looked into Sabrina's bedroom suite, brown and gold when Denton was there, now peacock and ivory, and the two guest rooms. 'Choose yours,' Sabrina said, and Stephanie walked unhesitantly into a room that was a spring garden in pale pinks and greens.

'The fifth floor is Mrs Thirkell's apartment, and storage,' Sabrina said, helping Stephanie unpack. 'Now, how about lunch? It's so wonderful that you're here at last . . . what is it? What's wrong?'

Stephanie was standing before the tall pier glass, shocks of dismay running through her as she watched Sabrina bend and move. Once she had looked like that. But no longer. 'Not even nicely rounded,' she said with desperate honesty. 'Just plain dumpy. And stoop-shouldered. At Juliette they'd say I don't look like a lady. And they'd be right. But they never taught me how to stand straight while I'm scrubbing floors or watching for stray crayons and hockey pucks that could kill me if I tripped over them.' But there were other things, too. 'My hair,' she said mournfully. 'My nails, my hands . . . well, I don't have the time you have to soak and steam in beauty salons.'

It wasn't fair and she knew it. For three years, ever since designing Alexandra Martova's house, Sabrina had worked harder than anyone Stephanie knew, managing Ambassadors, buying at auctions all over Europe, visiting estates to design new rooms, even flying to New York, where Stephanie had met her twice for brief visits while she was buying for clients. And through it all she stayed vibrant and lovely while Stephanie, at home in Evanston, grew faded and worn.

Sabrina put her arm around her. 'Can't you take some time? Don't you and Garth play tennis any more?'

'Not for ages. He used to ask, but I was always busy in the house or with the kids, so finally he got up some regular games with friends.'

They were silent, looking at their images. 'How did it happen so suddenly?' Sabrina asked.

'It wasn't sudden. It's been downhill since I saw you last year.'

'But you didn't tell me you were having a bad year.'

'I didn't know what to say.' Her world had seemed so precarious; she had been afraid that if she talked about it, everything would collapse. Penny and Cliff were growing up and she hardly saw them; Garth was deep in his work. She had started her own business, organizing estate sales in the North Shore suburbs. For a while it had grown so fast she could barely keep up with it, but then it slowed down, and she didn't know why.

'How's the estate business?' Sabrina asked, and Stephanie jumped. 'I was just thinking . . . not as good as it was.' She turned to finish unpacking, and Sabrina sat on the arm of a chair.

'But you're good. You know what you're doing.'

'With everything in a house except the people who live there. I keep thinking how good you'd be, telling Mrs Somebody her soup ladle isn't Georgian, it's early Woolworth, and you're tagging it at one-ninety-five instead of a hundred and a quarter. Have I time to change before lunch?'

Sabrina nodded. 'Well, I don't feel comfortable enough to tell people they haven't got the fortune they thought they had. I hedge and tell them I'll get a second opinion, and after awhile I guess they think I don't know my business. Is this sweater and skirt all right? I feel so dowdy.'

'You look fine. We're not going anywhere until tonight.'

'Tonight?'

'There's a play and then a party to meet the author and the cast.'

'Sabrina, I can't go; I haven't anything to wear.'

'You can borrow one of—'

'Not any more. Once I could, but now I'm two sizes too big.'

'We'll find something. I thought you'd like to meet my friends and see some of London.'

'Oh, I would. But—'

'Stephanie, we'll do whatever you want. Let's eat and then we'll talk about it. But first, tell me more about last year; what else happened?'

They walked downstairs. 'It was an odd year. Nothing felt right and I guess I just let go. I didn't realize how far, though, until now.'

Sabrina hesitated. 'And Garth?'

Stephanie shrugged. 'What about him? He's all wrapped up in his lab, he's on some kind of faculty committee, he counsels students and at night he goes back to the lab.'

In the drawing room, on a round table beside a window, Mrs Thirkell had set out oyster bisque and salad, white wine and winter pears. 'You don't need Garth for tennis,' Sabrina said as they sat down. 'Or to have your hair done or just to take time for yourself. Can't you think about yourself more?'

'What difference does it make? I mean, of course I don't like the way I look, but we never go anywhere that I need to dress up for – just to friends' houses or sometimes a movie.

And if you really want to know about Garth, I can't remember when he last looked at me. And Penny and Cliff – oh, ten- and eleven-year-olds are so wrapped up in themselves. I'm like a piece of furniture they dodge around when they're dashing out to see their friends. What do they care whether I'm overweight? I'm sorry, I shouldn't whine; I've got a family I love and a home that's a lot happier than most. We almost never fight. But as far as how I look, Sabrina, the truth is, nobody cares. And it doesn't seem worth the effort of diet and exercise and new clothes.'

'I care,' Sabrina said. 'Because you're not being fair to yourself. If Garth is crazy enough to ignore you, shouldn't you pay twice as much attention to yourself?'

Stephanie looked at her sister and shook her head wonderingly. 'I get so involved at home I forget how wonderful it is to be with you. Why did I wait so long to come to London?'

'Money, you said, and you wouldn't let me buy your ticket.'

'No, I could slip into the habit of letting you buy me things, and that would be bad all around. But if Garth would accept more invitations to European conferences, I'd be here all the time, tagging along at half-fare. In fact, I just might move in. I did tell you, didn't I, that you've brought my fantasy house to life?'

'Excuse me,' Sabrina said to Michel Bernard as Brian handed her a list of messages. She skimmed it. 'Yes to Olivia Chasson; no to Peter and Rose Raddison; yes to the duchess, but tell her I can't begin the job until next month, possibly not until August; no to Nicholas and Amelia Blackford, but say I'd love to come for a weekend next month when things calm down. And Antonio says eight instead of eight-thirty? All right. After you take care of these, why don't you go home? I'll lock up.'

She turned back to Michel. 'Where were we?'

'Talking about my one newspaper story. You make me feel like a sloth. Do you always have a dozen projects going at once?'

'Lately. Incredible, isn't it?'

'You're incredible. You know, we've been researching this story all over Europe, and we hear about you and Ambassadors wherever we go.'

Sabrina took a deep breath. Dear Michel, to tell her that. A good friend, going back to college when he and Jolie Fantome, already living together, made her part of their small family whenever she was lonely. Now they wrote together and drifted in and out of Sabrina's life as they roamed the world for stories. She had not heard from them in months until Michel called to ask for background information on their investigation into the recent international wave of art forgeries involving small galleries.

Jolie and Michel were Sabrina's only friends who had to work for a living, as she did, and she relaxed with them, letting her enthusiasm show as she could not with wealthy customers and friends who expected her to be as casual about money as they were. 'You've really heard about Ambassadors in other countries? I wondered; I had calls last week from Paris and Brussels. Oh, Michel, what do you do when all your dreams start to come true at once?'

'Revel in it. You've earned it. You did it all yourself.'

'But sometimes I'm afraid it's happening too fast. Do you know there's an old Chinese superstition that if you look directly at something beautiful it will disappear? You can sneak a sideways glance but you mustn't stare, because beautiful things are fragile and fleeting and a hard look could destroy them. I feel that way about my life. If I talk about it, or look too closely, everything might collapse.'

Michel shrugged. Superstition had no place in modern journalism. 'You've made yourself one of the most successful, talked-of women in London. That isn't likely to collapse. Who's Antonio?'

'What?'

'Antonio. Eight o'clock instead of eight-thirty. Or am I prying?'

'Oh. A friend.'

'Ah. I am prying. Well, leaving aside romance, you have success, fame and, no doubt, a handsome income. What more could you want?'

'Work. And I've got that, too. My own work that I love, and that I'm good at. That's the best thing.'

'The best thing,' said Jolie, coming into the office, 'is independence. Especially after being led around by that little dictator you married.'

'The best thing is money,' said Michel. 'Try buying groceries with independence.'

'Oh, God, here we go a—'

'Don't let me stop you,' Sabrina said, getting up as the doorbell chimed. 'Just don't throw things until my customer leaves.'

In the soft lights of the showroom, Rory Carr was admiring a tapered French pedestal clock, its round face surrounded by porcelain angels. 'Very fine, my lady,' he said, bowing low over her hand. 'From the Comtesse du Verne's estate, perhaps?'

Sabrina smiled. 'You always impress me, Mr Carr. I did not see you at the auction.'

'I have known the family for years, my lady. In fact I saw them last week in Paris, and the young Count sends you his regards. But today I am here on business, to show you something very special. If I may?' As Sabrina nodded, he lifted a leather case to the table and opened it. Lifting out a large parcel, he unwrapped it with slow, sweeping gestures. Sabrina admired his sense of drama. Impeccably dressed, with silver hair and soft pouches beneath his eyes, he was a showman, but he knew art, and in the past year he had sold her six superb eighteenth-century porcelains. Unlike some works that lingered in her shop, they had sold almost immediately.

Reverently Carr stood a chinoiserie group on the table: a pagoda-like summerhouse with a curved staircase and four young boys wearing straw hats and carrying butterfly nets and baskets of berries. The boys were dressed in white and yellow; the pagoda, with latticework and beading on the roof, was in brilliant primary colors. 'Lück,' Sabrina murmured. Long ago, in a Berlin museum, Laura had shown her and Stephanie groups made by Lück and other artists for the Frankenthal porcelain factory in the 1750s. Sabrina lifted the

97

group to see the Frankenthal mark, a crown above a Gothic *F*, baked into the underside.

'The owners?' she asked. Carr handed her a rolled-up document and she skimmed it. 'Only three?'

'So it seems, my lady. I would imagine it was sold only in dire circumstances. As you see, it is extremely fine.'

Sabrina studied the group. 'How much?'

'It's a bit dear. Four thousand pounds.'

Not a muscle moved in Sabrina's face. 'Three thousand.'

'Oh, my lady, I really ... Well, for you, thirty-five hundred.'

'I'll send you a check tomorrow,' she said.

He bowed. 'Admirable Lady Longworth. Would that everyone made decisions so decisively! I wish you good day.'

'Sabrina,' Michel said as the door closed behind Carr. 'Do you deal with him often?'

She turned. 'A few times in the past year. Do you know him?'

'Rory Carr, right?'

'You know him.'

'We've come across him.'

'Lately?'

He nodded. A chill touched Sabrina. She ran a finger over the cold porcelain: superb color, fine shading in the delicate construction of the little house. 'How have you come across him?'

'His company. Westbridge Imports. High-class stuff from all over the world, new and antique, sold through small galleries like Ambassadors. And, it turns out, some bad apples in the barrel.'

'Forgeries?'

'Seven so far that connect at some point to Westbridge – that's confidential, by the way.'

'But that doesn't mean Rory Carr—'

'Right. He could have been taken in. But he's no fool, and he's the liaison with galleries. We'll know more when we find the moneyman behind Westbridge and some other import firms we're watching in America and Europe. All we

98

know now is that Westbridge is owned on paper by a guy named Ivan Lazlo.'

Sabrina repeated the name. 'I've heard it, but it was a long time ago. France? Italy? I can't remember.'

'Well, if you remember, let us know. And keep an eye on what Carr brings you. What about the stuff he's brought so far?'

She closed her eyes. 'They had certificates of ownership. The ceramic marks were genuine. I always – as you put it – "keep an eye" on what I carry. I wouldn't survive a week if my customers doubted my judgment.'

'Hey, I didn't mean—'

'My lady.' Brian stood in the office doorway. 'Señor Molena is on the telephone.'

'The friend.' Michel kissed Sabrina's cheek. 'We'll be off.'

Antonio Molena made dozens of telephone calls a day – in Brazil, running his businesses, or in London, talking to his managers in Brazil and arranging meetings in Europe with financiers, friends and mistresses. A self-made millionaire with the ruthlessness of his Portuguese father and the mysticism of his Indian mother, he had waited fifty-one years to find the right woman to grace his empire. When he met Sabrina at a New Year's party at Olivia Chasson's country home, he made up his mind in ten minutes as 1978 gave way to 1979 – the year, he decided, in which he would marry and have his first son.

He banished his mistresses with appropriate gifts and swooped upon Sabrina like the great bird of prey he resembled, pursuing her for five months with the single-mindedness that had made him master of vast coffee plantations in Bahia province and cattle ranches in the interior province of Serro de Amambai. By now he had expected to be married, with Sabrina running their home in Rio de Janeiro and awaiting the birth of their son. Instead, he was forced to tarry in London and fit himself to her schedule until he could compel her to accept him.

Because she could not make up her mind.

Her friends said he was everything a woman could want: enormously wealthy and powerful, a modern prince who flew his own plane, but scattered through his conversation ancient folktales from the tribe of his mother and grandmother. 'It is better that you do not love me yet,' he told Sabrina. 'The Guarani gods say love is the last thing, not the first. It grows slowly through sharing and creating. When you live together and build a family, love will come.'

Society was waiting for Sabrina to marry again. At every party she was paired with someone new in the tireless round robin of matchmaking. Antonio stood above them all with his determined courtship, his certainty about their future, his powerful and mercurial personality – mystic and practical, businessman and playboy. He and Sabrina were seen at many of the playgrounds Denton had proudly shown her, but he worked as hard as he played. Between film festivals and auto races, balls, derbies, hunts and country weekends, he would fly to Brazil to work twenty-hour days, or shut himself in his London apartment to make marathon telephone calls and dictate long documents for his staff of secretaries in Rio.

And each day he called, to remind Sabrina he was waiting.

But she was wary. 'After all,' she told Alexandra, 'I thought marrying Denton was a good idea.'

Alexandra snorted. 'You were young and innocent. Dependent. Now you're on your own, with a business, a house and me to advise you.'

'All right, advise me. Why should I marry Antonio?'

'Because, like all of us, you're happiest with a man around.'

'Any man?'

'Honey, Sabrina Longworth doesn't have to settle for any man. Your Antonio is a very rare bird.'

He was working on a plan to build villages, hospitals and schools for the peasants in the Brazilian provinces he dominated. His purpose was to keep them from organizing against himself and the other landowners, but publicly he said only that he wished to give dignity and comforts to the poor. It was important work that Sabrina would share. In addition to supervising the raising of their children and acting as his hostess, she would help him improve the lives of thousands of people.

'King Antonio the First,' Sabrina joked to Alexandra, but not to Antonio. He was so serious, and how did she know those thousands of peasants wouldn't be better off with him arranging their lives?

'It's just that I don't want him to arrange mine,' she said to Alexandra.

The first time she went to his bed, in his apartment in London, he surprised her with his gentle hands, caressing slowly, steadily, in a sensual rhythm as insistent as his courtship, until she was so open and longing she pulled him inside her. And when he let her lead him with her body, instead of forcing her to follow as Denton had done, he finally satisfied the arousal Denton had numbed. For the first time Sabrina understood what sexual gratitude meant.

'But if I marry again,' she told Alexandra, 'it won't be for gratitude. It will be for love.'

She knew what love was: it was sharing. She had learned that with Stephanie. In her years of living alone, she had looked for someone who desired a companion, not a beautiful ornament; who would soothe her fears, not simply applaud her skills; who wanted caring, not the status of her poise and position in society; who would cherish her, not demand that she mold her life to his. She knew what sharing was, and it didn't seem to fit Antonio.

Then, just as Michel warned her about Rory Carr, Antonio telephoned. Maybe those Guarani Indians had something after all; maybe it was an omen. How did she know Antonio wouldn't share a problem and help her solve it? It was time she found out. With an eager step she went to take his call.

Garth opened his office window to the lake breeze as the morning sun climbed in the sky. Already it was hotter than usual for the end of May, and a few students dangled bare feet from the rocks along the shore, yelping as their toes met the forty-five-degree water. Frisbees sailed over huddled groups studying for finals, bicyclists passed lovers strolling beneath the trees, fingers tucked in the back pockets of each other's jeans. The air smelled of summer; a time to be outside. But Garth had an appointment. He rummaged for his file on Vivian Goodman. If he was lucky, he might get in a short walk before his two o'clock class. He was halfway to the door when the telephone rang.

'Garth,' Stephanie said. 'I have to talk to you about Cliff.'

'I'm meeting with the dean. I'll call you back in—'

'No, this is my only time alone in the office, everybody went to lunch early. Please, Garth.'

'Well, if it can't wait until tonight. What's he been up to?'

'I think he's been stealing things.'

'Stealing—? I don't believe it. Why do you think so?'

'I found a radio and two calculators in his closet this morning, under a pile of clothes. I was going to wash them—'

'Under the clothes?'

'Yes. Still in their boxes. They've never been opened.'

'I can't believe . . . He didn't steal them.'

'Then how did they get there?'

'Maybe they belong to his friends.'

'Garth, he *hid* them.'

'Well, what do you think happened?'

'Someone in my office says kids are stealing things and selling them.'

'What for? He has an allowance, and he's earned extra money all year cleaning basements and attics. Why would a sixth-grade kid need money, anyway? I thought even his richest friends have to wait until seventh grade for their first Mercedes.'

'Garth, don't joke; it's not funny.'

'It's not funny at all. Stephanie, Cliff is a solid, straight boy; he's not a thief. But it occurs to me that he could be envious of all the wealthy kids in his school. Or maybe ashamed. If some of his friends have taken up shoplifting as a hobby, they might have talked him into going along. Have you asked him how he feels about his classmates buying whatever their spoiled hearts desire?'

'Have *you* asked him?'

'If I had, I'd know the answer. Stephanie, I'm sorry, but I'm late for my appointment. We'll talk tonight.'

'I want you to come home early and talk to Cliff. It *just*

occurred to you he might be envious? It occurred to me a long time ago. You don't talk to him; you don't even know what he's thinking.'

'Not always, but he should have secrets. I did, at his age; I thought parents were nosy intruders. Does Cliff know you go into his room?'

'No, and don't tell him. He's told me not to.'

'Then how do I talk to him about the goods?'

'You'll think of something. We can't ignore it, Garth. When will you be home?'

'About six.'

He raced up the stairs. William Webster, Dean of Sciences, was waiting for him, floating in a haze of pipe smoke behind his desk. Garth opened his file and sat down. 'Bill, I'm asking you to reverse the tenure committee decision on Vivian Goodman.'

'I figured.' Webster leaned back, his chair creaking beneath his bulk. A happy man with a contented paunch and a bald head shining with satisfaction, he disliked controversy. For a week he had tried to deflect Garth to his assistant, but eleven years in a university had taught Garth its political maneuverings. Now he waited on the edge of Webster's protective smoke screen for the dean to talk about Vivian Goodman. 'You held two meetings on her? You read her papers and her book on research techniques? You read the evaluations from other biochemists?' Garth nodded. 'So you followed procedure. And the vote was eleven to nine to deny tenure, thus dismissing her from the faculty. Garth, you know that granting tenure is like a marriage: giving a professor a lifetime job, inviting him into your professional family forever. You have to be mighty sure of him to do that.'

'Or her.'

'I am told,' Webster went on, ignoring the interruption, 'that Mrs Goodman's published papers are a bit sloppy and her book does not blaze new trails. Her most enthusiastic supporters seem to be her students. Which, of course, means very little. Dear me, nobody was more popular with students than you, my boy, but you would never have gotten tenure if your research and scholarship hadn't been first-rate. We're proud you're one of us. And students still like you and so does the faculty. Why, if you were ambitious, you might knock me out of my seat.' He laughed heartily. 'Lucky for me you prefer your laboratory. Well, I'm glad we had this chat; it's a pity Mrs Goodman has to leave, but she'll find another job and we'll muddle along without her. Glad you came in, Garth.'

Garth sat still as Webster rose through his smoke to escort him to the door. 'Please sit down, Bill,' he said quietly. Webster hesitated, frowned and sat down. 'Vivian is as good a biochemist as most of those in the department. Her work isn't sloppy, it's meticulous. It's true that she's not a trailblazer, but how many in the department are? Most of the faculty that you tell me I am in some mystical way married to spend their time snipping away at old ideas, not whacking trails after new ones. The truth is, Vivian was voted out because she's a woman.'

'Oh, come now, oh, shame on you, my boy, you know I do not tolerate prejudice; I will not be accused of it. Mrs Goodman was treated like any other faculty member and the vote went against her. I will not be intimidated into granting tenure to someone just because she is a woman, ignoring her work—'

'I've told you her work is quite satisfactory.'

'So you say. But others—'

'The evaluations from other universities agree.'

'But your committee, Garth, your own committee voted. How could I overrule it? Now, I myself have not read Mrs Goodman's work, but in my experience anyone with a home, a husband and two children to care for cannot possibly do the kind of work men produce with one hundred percent effort. This is not a criticism; I've met Mrs Goodman, and she is attractive and seemingly intelligent. But we cannot ignore the many demands on her time. We have a responsibility to science.'

Garth kept his voice even. 'Bill, eleven men voted against the promotion of one woman who is as good a scientist as most of them and a better teacher. I can't pretend that's standard procedure. I am making a formal request that you reverse the decision.' He held out the folder. 'I've written the minority report, signed by all nine of us. It includes a list of women denied tenure in the last twelve years, with descriptions of their scholarship. I'll leave it with you and call back in a week to talk about it.'

Webster kept his hands folded. 'Ah, Garth, I won't be able to read it. I am truly sorry, but I leave tomorrow on a business trip.'

After a moment, Garth drew back his hand. 'I'll have to take this to the vice president, Bill, you understand that.'

'Garth, what's gotten into you? Why are you playing cowboy on a white horse? Don't tell me you've got a thing going with this woman? You'll make a fool of yourself, going over my head; and if it comes to a battle, I can line up quite a force against you.'

Garth stood, towering over the dean. His dark eyes were burning, but his voice was low. 'You've called me a cowboy, a fool, a liar and an adulterer, all in less than a minute. That must be some kind of record, Bill. Enjoy your trip.'

Webster called out 'My boy—!' but Garth was gone, striding down the corridor, down a stairway, down another corridor to his office. In the corner beside his desk was his tennis racket, and he picked it up, slamming an invisible ball with furious strokes. 'Damned idiot. Ass. Braying his monumental stupidity—'

'Oh, excuse me,' said a startled voice, and he turned to see the rosy face of Rita McMillan, a senior in his two o'clock genetics class.

He grinned and lowered his racket. 'It beats warfare. What can I do for you, Rita? Sit down; I'm harmless.'

She sat on the edge of a chair. 'It's ... our final paper.'

'You chose the paper instead of the exam?'

'Well, I thought I'd do better 'cause I sort of ... freeze up in exams?' He nodded, wondering why students so often turned statements into questions, as if asking if they really meant what they were saying. 'But now I'm having problems with the paper.'

'Then take the exam. You can change your mind.'

Tears filled her wide eyes. 'I don't think I can do either one.'

'You mean you want an incomplete so you can finish up this summer.'

'No, then I wouldn't graduate, and my parents . . . ' Tears rolled from her eyes in round droplets and she dabbed them with a tiny handkerchief.

Garth frowned. 'What do you want to do, then?'

She looked at him carefully through her tears. 'You know those times we had coffee and talked about my research project? I was thinking about them; they were, you know, just about the best nights I ever had. And then that time, you know, we had tea at the student union? We talked and talked and I could tell, you know, how much you liked me and . . . well, anyway, you know, some of the girls told me—not, you know, in this department, but in some . . . well, they're—I mean, their professors are . . . well, you know, we could have coffee again, is what I mean, at my apartment this time . . . and we could . . . and then I could . . . show you my paper? I mean, it's not finished, but you could give me—like, a C and, you know, I could graduate and . . . oh, don't look like that—!'

All the coiled anger Garth had carried from the dean's office exploded inside him. 'You stupid little fool. You . . . whore.' He paced to his window and back. 'Selling yourself for a grade when there are women knocking themselves out for a degree, a job, a good salary, tenure . . . and getting trampled by self-righteous men. But you know how to get what you want, don't you? You don't need brains, just tears and a cunt—oh, my God.' He took a long breath and flung himself past her to stand at the door. 'You'd better leave. I'll give you an incomplete if you can't finish your paper or take the exam, but that's all I'll do. Now get out. Just get out of here.'

She scurried around him, wide-eyed, but from astonishment, he noted, not fear. She had expected a different reaction. Had he really given her a reason to think—? His telephone rang and he snatched it up. 'Andersen,' he barked.

'Professor Andersen? One moment please for Mr Kallen.'

Kallen? Who the hell was—? 'Professor Andersen, this is Horace Kallen, president of Foster Laboratories, in Stamford,

Connecticut. You participated in a seminar we sponsored a year ago in Chicago.'

'Mr Kallen, I have a class in five minutes.'

'Then I won't keep you. I'm going to be in Chicago next week, and I wondered if we could have lunch together.'

Garth began to pay attention. Presidents of international companies did not call professors for lunch dates; their secretaries did that. 'I suppose so,' he said. 'But if it's another seminar—'

'Oh, no.' A chuckle came over the wires. 'We'd like to talk to you about your joining us here in Stamford as director of our new research facility. We're interviewing several candidates, but you are definitely our first choice.'

The bell in the administration building tolled twice. 'When will you be here?' Garth asked.

'Tuesday. Shall we say one o'clock at the Ritz-Carlton?'

'Yes.'

Later, sitting on the couch in the kitchen while Stephanie made dinner, he told her about it. 'A year ago I wouldn't have considered it. But after Bill threatened me with a battle—'

'How much would it pay?' Stephanie asked. Her back was to him as she sliced vegetables.

'I don't know. Would you really want to move to Connecticut?'

'I'd move tomorrow.'

He was taken aback by the vehemence in her voice. 'You like Evanston. Our friends, the kids' school, your job—'

'The job is dull, we'd make new friends, I'm sure Stamford has fine schools.' Opening the refrigerator, she took out lettuce, a red onion, cherry tomatoes. She looked at him. 'It would be wonderful to have money. And be close to New York. Some excitement for a change.'

Garth was beginning to feel uncomfortable. He had only made the lunch date because of his anger at Webster, fueled by the encounter with Rita McMillan; he had no reason to leave the university. But Stephanie had jumped at it. They knew nothing about the job, but already she was finding reasons to accept it while Garth, having cooled off from

Webster, was losing interest even in the lunch. But of course he would go, if only to satisfy Stephanie.

'We'll see what Kallen says.' He watched Stephanie turn back to the counter. 'I didn't tell you about Rita McMillan. Damnedest thing—'

'Are you going to accept the job?'

'It hasn't been offered.'

'If it's offered.'

'I don't know. I told you I'd see what Kallen says. I started to tell you about Rita—'

'Mom!' Penny cried, running in. 'We're starved!'

'Have you set the table?'

'It's Cliff's turn.'

'Well, has Cliff set it?'

'He's doing it now.'

'Make sure he remembers the napkins. And have both of you washed your hands?'

Stephanie took potatoes from the oven. The kitchen was silent. Garth waited, then shrugged and picked up the newspaper.

'Mom—!' Penny said.

'All right, Penny. Garth,' Stephanie said. 'Come to dinner.'

'Stephanie—'

'Sabrina! I've been calling and calling—'

'I was in the country, and I gave Mrs Thirkell all of July for her vacation.'

'I've been worried that you might be in trouble.'

'My bad dreams reached all the way to Evanston?'

'You are in trouble.'

'No, but I thought I was. A couple of weeks ago I was afraid I might have bought a forged porcelain, but I checked it and it's genuine. No more bad dreams. How's your estate business? Have you found some wonderful antiques for me?'

'I . . . haven't done any for awhile.'

'Oh, Stephanie, why not? You love it.'

'Yes, but I didn't have any business. I'm working at the university now. Not as much fun, but it helps pay the mortgage. Maybe I'll get back into estates if we move. Sabrina, Garth's been offered a job. Director of Research at a pharmaceutical company in Connecticut.'

'Garth is leaving the university?'

'I want him to. It pays ninety thousand a year.'

'Oh, Stephanie, how wonderful for you! No more worries about money; you can work at whatever you like. Why don't you open an American Ambassadors? We could trade customers across the ocean. And we can see each other more often! We'll take turns flying back and forth. It's the first time we'll both have enough money. Is Garth excited?'

'I think he's going to turn it down.'

'But—why?'

'I don't know. He had lunch with the president of the company a couple of weeks ago, and he says he's thinking it over and we'll talk about it later. But he's not very enthusiastic. They want us to come to Stamford – I have to pass inspection, too – but Garth says he's too busy.'

'He wouldn't be committing himself, would he?'

'No. Just visiting, talking to people, having a weekend with his wife. He might even look at me then and notice that I've lost weight.'

'Have you really?'

'You'd be proud of me. After your lecture in London I turned a new leaf. Diet and exercise, and then I splurged at a place on Michigan Avenue that looks like a bordello. They used all the mud of the Mississippi on my face and styled my hair. Nobody noticed at home, but I was having such a good time I didn't care. If we looked in your mirror now, you'd wonder which is the famous European designer and which is the dull university housewife.'

'Don't say that; it's not fair. You shouldn't make fun of your life; you don't know how often I wish I could have a taste of it.'

'But not the whole meal.'

'Stephanie, what else is wrong?'

'Oh, problems with Cliff that Garth somehow avoids discussing with him. And Penny wants special art classes and she's good, she deserves them, but they're awfully expensive, and that brings me right back to Garth's job offer, and I feel so . . . helpless. Pinned down and trying to get away. Do you know what I did?'

'What?'

'Don't laugh. I applied for a visa to China. There's a tour in September sponsored by the International Antique Dealers, and I thought—'

'But so did I! It sounded so wonderfully far away that I—'

'You applied for a visa?'

'I had to. It takes—'

'Sixty days to get one.'

'Oh, this is wonderful; we'll go together! Can you afford it? I would have asked you to go, but—'

'Of course I can't afford it. I mean, we have money in the savings account, but not for trips to China. I didn't tell Garth.'

'Then you don't think you'll go.'

'Probably not. I just felt very adventurous filling out the application, and it's fun to think about.'

'I'm not sure I can go, either. September could be a busy time for me. But if we could figure out a way . . . '

'Oh, if we could – what a crazy, beautiful dream!'

After she hung up the phone, Sabrina sat in the stillness of midnight, curled in the deep cushions of the love seat in her bedroom, and thought about herself and Stephanie. Their lives were so different, yet somehow, miraculously, they were closer than ever. Alexandra and a few others were good friends, but Stephanie's was the only voice that sounded like her own.

The telephone rang. 'My Sabrina, forgive me,' said Antonio. 'I knew you were not sleeping, for your telephone has been busy.'

She felt a sharp dismay. 'I thought you left for Brazil today.'

'So I did. I am in New York. In two days I go to Rio. I am calling to wish you pleasant dreams. And when I return on August 15, you will give me your answer so we may plan our future.'

She sighed with relief. He was really gone. For four weeks

she could think about what she wanted to do without his smothering pressure.

But the weeks flew by, and Sabrina was just getting used to the freedom of his absence when he telephoned that he would be with her in two days. She was looking mournfully at her calendar when Michel and Jolie came to say goodbye. 'We'll be in Berlin and New York,' Jolie said. 'The story grows bigger. We came to warn you about Rory Carr.'

Sabrina shook her head. 'That Lück summerhouse was genuine. I know you mean well, but try to understand. He could take his pieces to Adams or any other big porcelain dealer and perhaps get more for them, but he likes to help small galleries and I'm grateful to him. I don't believe he would sell a forged piece, and I know he hasn't tried it with me. I don't think he's involved at all.'

'He's involved up to the pouches under his eyes,' Michel said bluntly. 'How many pieces have you bought from him?'

'Seven. And I've sold all of them but the summerhouse.'

'Sabrina,' said Jolie, 'we've got to catch a plane, so we haven't much time, but please listen, we're trying to help you. We've traced five forgeries to Carr and Lazlo and Westbridge Imports, all sold through small elite galleries like Ambassadors.'

'Five?' Sabrina repeated it. 'You're sure?'

'Looks like. And what's more, it seems that some of the galleries may be collaborating with Westbridge to make a hell of a profit. They pay less because the pieces are forged; then they charge the going rate as if they were genuine. That's as far as we've gone, but it's a messy story. Since you've dealt with Carr, please check again the stuff he's sold you. Will you please do that? Look, we have to run. Here's our number in Paris. Why don't you call us there tonight? Sabrina?'

'What? I'm sorry, I didn't hear you.' She felt sick and wished they would leave. Some of her wealthiest, most influential customers had bought the porcelains she'd purchased from Carr. Her head was pounding. 'What did you say?'

'We'll call tonight to see how you are. And Sabrina? You'll check them out? And let us know what you find?'

She walked with them to the door. 'I'll try. I'm not sure how I'll do it, but I'll try.'

On the sidewalk, as Jolie hailed a cab, Michel asked idly, 'By the way, did you ever remember where you came across Ivan Lazlo?'

'Oh, yes, but it was ages ago – seven years, I think. He was Max Stuyvesant's secretary. I met him on a cruise on Max's yacht.'

Michel tilted his head. 'Stuyvesant.'

'That's ancient history,' said Jolie as a cab pulled up. 'His secretary is Dennis something. I met him when I photographed Max's sculpture collection for *Art World*.'

'Oh, well,' Michel said casually. 'Probably nothing in it. Call you tonight, my dear.' They waved goodbye as Sabrina walked from the blinding August sun into the dim coolness of her shop. Six porcelains to worry about and Antonio coming back. She looked at her calendar. Dinners, picnics, concerts, house parties. August was supposed to be the dull month when everyone went away. How could she think if she had no quiet time?

She sat at her cherry table. The telephone rang, and Brian came to the door. 'My lady, Señor Molena—'

'No,' she said. Not Antonio until she had to deal with him in person. 'No calls for awhile. Take a message, please, Brian.' She stared at her clasped hands until he reappeared.

'Señor Molena regrets that he cannot return for another week, my lady. He will see you on August 22 or 23 and will call you tonight.'

A reprieve. 'Thank you, Brian.' How could she think of marrying a man who gave her the most pleasure by staying away an extra week?

But she would think about Antonio later; now she had time to check on the porcelains. Except that she had no idea how to begin. She couldn't go to Olivia Chasson and ask to borrow a porcelain figurine she had sold her without some explanation. She could be honest with Alexandra, but there would still be the other five to worry about. 'Brian,' she said suddenly, 'let's lock up. It's summer and it's Friday and your vacation starts tomorrow. I'll see you in two weeks.'

She walked home. The sun pressed down on her throbbing head and she shaded her eyes. Usually she loved this walk, but today she was hardly aware of it. The small, elegant shops and boutiques of Beauchamp Place, slumbering in the heat, did not tempt her, and even the outdoor fruit and vegetable stands that she loved failed to slow her pace. She was dizzy from the heat and suddenly very tired, but she walked more quickly, turning into the shade of Cadogan Square. In a few minutes she stood at her door.

Mrs Thirkell opened it before she could use her key. 'My lady! You didn't walk! In this heat!' But Sabrina barely heard her. She was looking at her polished brass door knocker in the shape of a hand holding a scroll. The certificates. She had copies of the certificates of ownership Rory Carr had provided with each porcelain; she could verify them. She had all next week, while Brian was away.

'My lady! You should rest!'

She smiled at Mrs Thirkell. 'A bath, I think. And then a light supper. I'm going to be working tonight.'

Mrs Thirkell sent Sabrina's regrets for the dinner party she was to attend that night while Sabrina went back to Ambassadors for the certificates. She spent the evening looking up telephone numbers in her office directories for Paris, Bonn, Geneva, Milan and Brussels, and the next morning she began making calls.

It took a long time; everyone seemed to be away. Sabrina thought of Europe in August as a huge chessboard, with populations moving from square to square. But servants and secretaries gave her forwarding numbers, and soon she was getting through.

In five days she had verified the ownership of four porcelains. On Wednesday she confirmed the ownership of the next figurine through six families. And on Thursday morning she turned to the last certificate, listing previous owners of a rare Meissen porcelain stork, and found they were names of people who did not exist.

For the next three days, in her silent office, she made

dozens of calls, her heart racing, but there were no errors in spelling, no mistaken addresses. Every name was false.

And, therefore, so was the porcelain stork.

She stared blankly at a small landscape on the opposite wall. She had been careless. Five superb porcelain figures, the impeccable presence of Rory Carr and his friendships with the titled families of Europe, her customers' demand for fine objects – and she grew careless. Her success depended on her sharp eye and her knowledge, but somehow she had bought and then sold a porcelain without properly examining it.

When that became public knowledge, the sterling reputation that set her above so many design galleries would be tarnished. Customers who gave her open-ended commissions would look for different designers. A few might give her another chance, but most, even acknowledging that everyone makes a mistake now and then, would turn their backs on her. Failure was seldom tolerated by those with the luxury of unlimited choice.

Sabrina shivered. She would have to buy back the stork at its current market value. If she didn't have enough cash, Alexandra would probably help her. But money wasn't the problem. Exposure was the problem. She could not buy it back without telling the owner the truth.

Who was the owner? She read the invoice stapled to the certificate. Lady Olivia Chasson. 'Why not?' she murmured. The best and the worst. Lady Olivia was Sabrina's best customer, spending fifty thousand pounds a year on redecorating her homes and on gifts. Frequently she sent new customers to Ambassadors, including foreigners who shopped by mail or telephone. She was one of Sabrina's most ardent supporters.

And she could destroy someone overnight if she felt she had been cheated.

But we know each other so well, Sabrina thought. I can talk to her. She is one of the few people with enough confidence in herself to keep the story quiet after I buy back the stork or replace it with another piece. I think it will be all right. We know each other so well. I think I can make it come out all right.

When the telephone rang she answered without thinking, her voice light and a little breathless with the effort to dispel her fear.

It was Antonio, back three days earlier than he had expected, telling her he would pick her up at eight o'clock for dinner.

Some people, Sabrina thought wryly, lead simple lives. But then, she added honestly, I didn't want a simple life. I wanted excitement, whirlwinds, adventures. Now all I have to do is cope with them.

Antonio first. And then Olivia. She could delay giving Antonio an answer, and as for Olivia, this wasn't three years ago; people knew and trusted her now; she had her own place in society – not a reflection of Denton's but one she had made for herself. Whatever happened, she could handle it.

For the evening, she chose a dress bare enough for August but not seductive and put up her hair with mother-of-pearl combs. She was surprised to discover that she was looking forward to seeing Antonio. His presence was so overwhelming that when he was gone he left an empty space in her life: something like an excavation for a building. She didn't want to fall in, but it was too big to ignore.

The trouble was, even when he was there, filling his space, he did not give her what she needed. She thought of the time, months before, when she had tried to tell him about Michel's suspicions of Rory Carr. He deliberately led the conversation to other subjects until Sabrina gave up and did not try to confide in him again.

But tonight she would. Share with me, she murmured to his photograph on her dressing table. He knew Olivia; he might have an idea how to approach her. Sabrina was so glad she was going to see him, she thought perhaps she was falling in love with him after all.

But by the time they sat opposite each other at Antonio's favorite table at Le Gavroche, and Sabrina had listened to his problems with bankers, clerks, the postal service of eight different countries, coffee-pickers in Brazil, ship-loaders in New Orleans and United States government regulations on imported beef, she had lost all desire to talk about anything but the weather.

'Yes, yes, it may rain, my Sabrina,' Antonio said impatiently, adding as an inspired afterthought, 'It does not rain much in Rio.'

That made her laugh, and for a moment she felt better.

'Ah, you are lovely,' he said softly. 'Like a queen. I have come back for your answer, Sabrina, to be my queen – so I may spread the world at your feet—'

A memory streaked past Sabrina: Denton saying he would buy her a piece of the world for each birthday. Why did the men she knew offer her things instead of feelings?

In the act of spearing veal and dipping it in three different mustards, Antonio saw Sabrina's frown. He put down his fork. 'You cannot be surprised. I told you I would expect your answer tonight.'

'Antonio, I want to talk to you.' Rapidly, before he could stop her, she told him about Jolie and Michel's suspicions of Rory Carr and her discovery of the forgery. She ignored his deepening scowl. 'Of course I'll buy it back from Olivia and tell her the truth. I'm sure she won't broadcast it; why should she? If you could help me decide how to tell her—'

'Sabrina.' She waited. 'Your friends say there have been five forgeries? And it appears that some galleries are collaborating with this Westbridge?' She nodded. 'And your friends will publish their story in the newspaper. Exposing this Westbridge. And its book-keeping.'

Around her the softly lit room dimmed as the fears of the past week returned. 'Of course,' she said slowly. 'Descriptions of every piece sold to every gallery, including Ambassadors.'

'Ah, you are a child,' he said. 'You think you will ask Olivia to keep silent, but what you will be asking her to do is lie when all her friends read descriptions of her Meissen stork in a story on forged art. Why should she lie for you?'

Sabrina looked at the discreet crowd dining on the restaurant's famous veal and duck and spicy gossip. They would lie for their own protection, but few would lie for another. Some friends would lie to protect me, she thought: Alexandra, Antonio, a few others. No, she added with bitter humor; there's a limit to the number of times Alexandra can rescue me.

'My Sabrina,' Antonio said, signaling the waiters to remove their plates and bring coffee. 'I am glad you finally told me of these problems. I admire your strength and spirit, but there are limits to what any woman can do alone in the world of commerce. I will not allow you to suffer. I will hire solicitors to deal with this Westbridge, I will help you close your little shop and then I will take you far away, where you will have no more difficulties.'

'Where you buy off the clouds so it will not rain.'

'I beg your pardon? Is this some of your humor, my Sabrina?'

'No. I apologize.' She could do it; she could marry him and let him carry her off to live where he was indeed like a king and she would be safe at his side. But always in his enormous shadow, and without her "little shop".

It wasn't enough. She held her glass of cognac to the light and looked into its amber glow. I want more than a protective shadow. I want someone who knows that that "little shop" is a very big part of me, something I built, something I'm proud of. I want someone who will put his arms around me at night, in the quiet time when I wake up frightened about tomorrow or next week or next year, and hold me, and tell me I'm not alone. I don't know if Antonio would ever let me admit to fears when I am under his protection.

She put down her glass. She couldn't make a decision now; she refused to be forced into one when she was being pulled in so many directions. Antonio would have to be patient a while longer. And if he refused, then she would face that fact alone.

He was waiting for her to speak. She changed the subject, finishing her dinner with the poise and light conversation that had carried her through a number of complicated affairs, and then quietly told him that she was very tired and wished to go home.

He stood abruptly and reached for the chiffon scarf she had worn around her shoulders as the waiters, caught by surprise, rushed to help. 'You make difficulties for me, my Sabrina. I wish only to help you.' When they reached her front door, he said brusquely, 'I will telephone you tomorrow.'

In the quiet beauty of her drawing room, she sat beside a window reliving that long day, from the time she discovered the forged porcelain to the moment when she refused to answer Antonio, however bad the future might seem. She tucked her legs under her and put her head back against the chair.

Everything piled up. She was always running, as she had told Michel, afraid her life would get away from her. It took all her time and energy to keep her business going while keeping up with her crowd of friends, who were also her customers – wearing the right clothes, entertaining, taking time from Ambassadors for house parties and cruises. She loved it all – the brilliant, glamorous life of Sabrina Longworth, photographed and described in magazines around the world: aristocratic friends, luxurious homes, exotic foods, travel, clothes, her famous Ambassadors – a spinning world she could keep balanced as long as she was in control. But now she felt she was losing control.

She was so exhausted she ached all over. She felt hollow and alone. The clock on the landing struck ten-thirty. She hadn't been home this early in months. Now that she had time to think, she was too tired. All she really wanted to do was cry.

But that was for later. If she needed it. Because she wasn't alone. She calculated quickly – ten-thirty in London; four-thirty in Evanston. Stephanie would be home from work; Penny and Cliff would be outside playing. A good time to call. She reached for the telephone.

On her way to work, Stephanie stopped at the bulletin board to read the notice, dated August 18, that the office would be on a full schedule through September, even though classes would not start until the end of the month. Another reason she couldn't go to China. As if kids and house and money weren't enough. If she were a professor, the university would pay her way. Unlocking her desk in the room she shared with two other women, her anger flared as it did every time she thought of Garth spending a month in Berkeley and San Francisco.

He got a vacation while she stayed home and worked. He had a month near the ocean, an exciting city to explore; she had Lake Michigan, Evanston, two children, a house, a job. 'It's not a vacation,' he said. 'I'll be at the university, working. No time for romping through the city or degenerating in its nightspots.'

He joked about it, but he flew off and left her behind. And at the end of the summer session, worn down by office work and the humid August heat, Stephanie didn't think she could greet him with a cheerful face when he returned the next day. How could she keep her resentment from bursting out and ruining his homecoming for all of them? Well, she just wouldn't talk. Let the rest of them make conversation.

'Stephanie,' said one of the secretaries. 'Coffee?'

'No, thank you,' she said. 'I want to finish and leave early.'

She organized her desk as secretaries from six deans' offices traded tidbits on the latest campus scandal. This one was nastier than most, accusing women students and professors of trading sex for grades. Whispers had floated around campus all summer, but lately their volume and ferocity had increased and Stephanie had begun hearing names mentioned by groups huddling in corridors. One of the names was their friend Martin Talvia. She would have to tell Garth when he got back.

Stephanie began to type up notes made by guidance counselors in sessions with students. But in a few minutes she stopped; the women were glancing at her furtively.

'What?' she asked. 'What's happened?'

'Stephanie,' said William Webster's secretary, 'would anyone want to make trouble for you and Garth?'

'I can't imagine—' She stopped. 'What is it?'

The secretary held out a piece of paper. 'This was on my desk this morning. With Dean Webster's mail.'

Stephanie took it. A letter, typed on pink stationery: 'If you really want to know who gives grades for work between the sheets instead of in the classroom, take a good look at the famous Professor Garth Andersen, who talks like a monk but fucks like a monkey.'

She read the words over and over. Childish, but ugly and very effective. Bile welled in her throat. She swallowed, feeling it burn. Not Garth. No one was more decent and honest than Garth.

But Garth stayed away most nights, 'working,' he said, and on those nights he slept in the study 'to avoid disturbing' her. He never looked at her anymore; he hadn't noticed when she lost weight and changed her hairstyle and bought new clothes. He wouldn't take her to Stamford. How long had it been since they had a real marriage?

Carefully Stephanie folded the note and put it in the pocket of her sundress. 'Stephanie,' the secretary said. 'It isn't true. Everybody knows Garth—'

'Thank you,' she said and turned blindly back to her typewriter. She sat for a moment until her stomach settled and then worked steadily through lunch, until three o'clock, when she went home.

Penny and Cliff were visiting friends in Highland Park; she would pick them up the next day before going to the airport to get Garth. Alone in the rambling, quiet house, she rehearsed her argument with Garth, leaving out no detail of their courtship and marriage, reliving all that was good and all that was wrong with the past twelve years.

And she forgot most of it the next afternoon when they faced each other in their bedroom, while Penny and Cliff were playing. 'I don't believe it. If I ever have, I'm sorry, but when was the last time you listened to what I was saying?'

'What should I listen to? Talk about the university? Did it ever occur to you that I'm sick of the university? But it's all you care about. You don't care about me. When did you last even look at me? We talk in the kitchen, we eat at the same table, we get dressed to go out, and you never once look straight at me. Or if you do, you look through me, thinking of something else – probably the university. If you closed your eyes, would you know what I look like? Would you know what your children look like? Do you have any idea what we think about? Do you remember how we used to make love, before it got to be a kind of routine exercise you perform when you do me a favor and sleep in here instead of

in the study? You know one thing, you care about one thing
– the university, and whatever it is you do there—'

'You know what I do. I tell you every—'

'And whoever you do it with.'

'What does that mean?'

'You know what it means.'

'I don't and I don't give a damn. What I do know is, you
sit there and complain that I don't care about you, but you
haven't once asked me about Berkeley, and when I try to tell
you about it, to share one of the most important times in my
life with you, you won't let me.'

'How could I know it was so important? You never told
me—'

'I told you a hundred times this last year, and then again
and again, every phone call from Berkeley—'

'Talking about yourself all the time, not once asking about
Cliff.'

'Cliff?'

'You were going to talk to him – remember? Weeks ago
when I told you I found some things in his room – a radio and
– I forget what—'

'I meant to. Stephanie, I'm sorry, I really meant to, but the
last few weeks, getting ready for this seminar—'

'You keep talking about it as if it were something you
never did before. You could do it in your sleep.'

'I have tried to tell you in every way I could that this was
different. Stephanie, please listen. I worked for two solid
years for this. I know I neglected all of you, but there was
so much to do to be ready to stand up in front of this group
– the top geneticists in the world, Stephanie – and give the
major paper of the seminar. I put together everything I've
done for the last twelve years and then took a flying leap into
the future, telling them what we should be doing in the years
ahead. And then those eminent scientists dissected my every
word so we could spend the rest of the month talking shop
based on the conclusions of my paper. All that kept me going
was that I learned to chant molecular formulas to calm my
nervous stomach. The hotel staff thought they'd been
invaded by mathematical Krishnas.'

121

She laughed reluctantly. 'Well? It went all right, you said.'

'A little better than all right. It was, in fact, a triumph. Everything I ever hoped for—'

'That's wonderful. And it means you've finished your work here. You can take the job in Stamford.'

Garth stared at her. 'Is that job all you think about?'

'It's important to me. And it would be to you if you cared about what I want.'

He moved from the window to stand behind a deep armchair where Stephanie curled up at night to read. He rested his hands on the back of the chair and looked at them. 'I do care. But I can't wipe out my needs, even to give you what you want. I'm torn, Stephanie; I wish you could understand that it isn't an easy choice. There's the money – I know what it means to you; it means something to me, too; do you know what a budget I'd have for research and staff? But there's the other side – the freedom of the university, my teaching, which I love; you know how I feel about those things.'

'We talked about those same things before we were married. Don't you think it's time you grew up and wanted other things?'

'Yes, by God, it is. And one of the things I'd like is a wife who gives a damn for my needs and provides some support when—'

'Don't you dare accuse me of not caring about your needs! I spend most of my life – when I'm not earning money to help pay for the house you live in – ironing your shirts, cooking your meals, cleaning your bathroom, making sure you have the kind of soap you like for your tender skin—'

'Damn it, that's not support, that's maid service. Stephanie, we used to talk about my dreams, and you encouraged me to hold onto them.'

'That was a long time ago. I've given you twelve years; now you might give me a few. I want to get out of the Midwest and meet new people and live a different way. I want the excitement of New York—'

'For God's sake, you've been talking to your sister.'

'What?'

'My Lady Sabrina, who dines at castles and dances until dawn. Every time she calls she gets you more dissatisfied. You never expected me to be a rich lord until Sabrina married one, and now you nag me to be something I'm not just so you can have the kind of pampered, parasitic life she has.'

'She's not like that! You have no right – you don't know her—!'

'Well, whose fault is that? She hardly ever comes here; you run to meet her in New York or go off to London – by God, this crazy China thing is her idea, isn't it? She put you up to it.'

'No, no, no!' Stephanie clasped and unclasped her hands as she walked around the room. 'It was my idea. Sabrina doesn't know anything about it – it was because of Cliff and—'

'I've apologized for that. I will talk to him, I promise—'

'Oh, you and your promises. Well, when you do, you might ask him about cuff links and tie tacks and Cross pen sets.'

'Good Lord. All in his room?'

'All under his dirty clothes. I suppose I should be grateful; a confirmed criminal would think of other hiding places.'

'Stephanie, I am sorry. I'll talk to him tomorrow. It sounds as if he wants to be caught; he knows you'll find what's underneath those clothes when you do the wash. Have you talked to anyone else about this?'

'How could I? I tried to talk to Cliff, but he got hostile; and I don't want anyone else to know until we decide what to do.'

'So you've carried it around by yourself.'

'Oh, has that finally occurred to you? Has it finally penetrated your biologist's brain that I am lonely?'

'Now, wait a minute, you have close friends who—'

'I'm not talking about friends. I'm talking about someone who can put his arms around me at night, in the quiet time when I wake up frightened about tomorrow or next week or next year. I'm talking about someone to hold me and tell me I'm not alone.'

Garth gave her a long look. 'Don't you think I might want that, too? But you turn your back in bed, you move away when I put my arm around you, you turn your head when I try to kiss you.'

'When have you last done any of those things?'

'Not for a long time. And I miss them. But I got sick and tired of being rejected.'

'Well, you found another place for them, didn't you? Big scientists don't stay rejected long. They know where to go for fun and games, don't they, professor?'

'What the hell are you talking about?'

'About those sweet young things you make love to. Students!' She spat out the word. 'Did you think you could keep it a secret? You and all the others, big men who don't need cash like those poor ordinary guys who find their prostitutes on the street; all you have to do is promise a passing grade—'

'Shut up!'

'Don't you dare talk to me that—'

'I'll talk to you any way I want. We've lived together twelve years and you actually believe that I would – oh, the hell with it.'

He was trembling, his breath coming in short gasps. He folded his arms, holding himself in, then swung about and strode out of the room. Stephanie shrank back, frightened by his face and his rigid jaw. She heard him hesitate in the hall outside the bedroom door, and she waited for him to come back so she could find out the truth. She was confused. They had so many loose ends; they hadn't come to any conclusion. But in a moment she heard his footsteps running down the stairs, and after another pause the front door opened and slammed shut.

She looked around the room frantically. This was not happening; she and Garth would never do this to each other. They hadn't resolved anything, she couldn't see ahead, and that was terrifying.

But she could see one thing. She was going on her trip. She had to get away, and she'd told Garth she was going. He would take care of his children; she could count on him for that even if he had become a stranger in other ways. And when she got back they would work things out. She looked at her watch. Four-thirty. Ten-thirty in London. She was reaching for the telephone when, beneath her hand, it rang.

Chapter 9

A block from their hotel, in front of the Shanghai Cakes and Pastries Store, Nicholas Blackford bumped into them as he navigated with a stack of wrapped pastries. He smiled guiltily. 'It is so difficult to diet away from home. I should have brought Amelia. You must scold me, Sabrina, as you used to when you worked in my shop and monitored my bad habits. Or am I speaking to Stephanie? Do you know, I am ashamed to say this, and I assure you it is no reflection on either of you, but Sabrina – Stephanie – I really cannot tell you apart.'

Sabrina and Stephanie looked at each other behind the bald and bouncing figure of Nicholas Blackford. Her eyes dancing, Sabrina swept a low curtsy to Stephanie. 'Lady Longworth,' she said in a clear voice. 'Welcome to Shanghai.'

Stephanie stretched out her hand to help her up. 'Mrs Andersen,' she said. 'How glad I am to be here.'

At the bubbling laughter in their voices, Nicholas strained to see over his packages and sent pastries flying. 'Oh,' Stephanie said, feeling somehow at fault, 'let us help.' She and Sabrina gathered up the packages and carried them to his hotel room, where he insisted they take a few 'for being good Samaritans.'

Stephanie shook her head, but Sabrina accepted them. 'The Guarani Indians would say they're an omen that our idea is sweet. Or something like that. Thank you, Nicholas.'

'Who are the Guarani Indians?' Stephanie asked as they walked down the hall to their room.

'A tribe in Brazil. Antonio's ancestors. He says. More likely he comes from a long line of Portuguese pirates, but he likes to quote Indians and it does lend a certain piquancy to country weekends in Derbyshire. You won't meet him because he's in Brazil for the month, but you might as well learn about the Guaranis while you're learning everything else.'

Inside the room they looked at each other, touching their fingers, as if each were looking in a mirror. 'Are we really going to trade places?' Stephanie asked.

'Do you really want to?'

'Oh ... more than you, I'm afraid. To stop being me for awhile, to play at being you in your wonderful life, to live a kind of dream – I can't believe it's possible.'

'Then let's do it. As long as you don't think you'll come home like the three bears and growl, "Somebody's been sleeping in my bed."'

'There wouldn't be anything to growl about. Sex just isn't a big part of our marriage anymore. Otherwise I wouldn't even think of – well, I know you wouldn't make love to Garth, he's my husband, and he isn't your type at all – I can't imagine anyone farther from a Brazilian millionaire than Garth – but there won't be any problem.'

'After you've been apart for two weeks?'

'I don't think that would make any difference. Even if it did, you can say you have your period.'

'Does that mean hands off?'

'Yes, of course. But it's not only then. There's never much hands-on in our house. I told you, Garth usually sleeps in the study.'

'Stephanie, usually isn't always.'

'Well, then, you just turn your back.'

'Is that what you do?'

There was a pause. Stephanie walked around the ornate nineteenth-century beds and stood at the window, looking at the rippling water of the river below. 'I get angry when he doesn't come near me for two weeks, three weeks, and when he walks into the bedroom, all I can think of is that he has no right to be in there. Or in me. He accused me of that when—' She stopped.

'When what?'

'Oh, we had a fight a couple of weeks ago, right after he got back from California, but it didn't last long. We smoothed it out. It wasn't anything unusual, just a quarrel; you and Denton must have had your share of them.'

'A few,' Sabrina said dryly. Stephanie was clasping and unclasping her hands, and Sabrina knew she was nervous because she wasn't being honest. She was afraid that, if she told the whole story, Sabrina would refuse to change places and walk into – what? A quarrel? Garth's refusal to take a trip to Stamford or decide about the job? It didn't seem very serious, at least from an observer's point of view, and that's all Sabrina was going to be for a few days: an observer. And then she'd leave.

'It's no good,' Stephanie said abruptly. 'I have no right to ask you to leave your wonderful life and step into mine; they're too different. I don't know why I let myself get so excited . . . we'll just forget the whole idea. It was crazy from the beginning.'

Sabrina walked swiftly to her and put an arm around her waist. 'Don't say that; don't sound so sad. Of course it's crazy, but we've done crazy things before. We said it would be a lark.'

'But you can't really want to do it, Sabrina – you have a fairy tale and everything I have is ordinary. And there are things I haven't told you.'

'Well, don't. Unless I absolutely have to know them to get through a week without giving myself away. I meant it, you know, when I told you I wanted a taste of your life. My life may look like a fairy tale from the outside, but it has its own dragons.'

'Fire-breathing?'

'Fire-breathing.'

'Well, I guess I don't want to know about them. Unless I have to.'

'I don't think you do. I closed Ambassadors and gave Brian an extra holiday while I was gone; we'll just extend it a week. Antonio went to Brazil for the month to give me a chance to miss him, because I wouldn't let him arrange my life and I wouldn't give him a yes or no on marriage. He said he wouldn't even telephone. Which, knowing Antonio, is the greatest miracle of all. My calendar is clear; I wanted time to recover from China. Mrs Thirkell is at the house, but she hardly ever looks up from whatever she's stirring on the stove. It will be a quiet week; all yours and all London to choose from.'

'And a closetful of clothes. You don't mind?'

'Of course not. I'll be wearing yours.'

'Blue jeans and shirts.'

'A novelty. I haven't worn jeans in years. Stephanie, stop feeling ashamed of your life. Don't worry about me. We're talking about a one-week caper, not a lifetime.'

'If you really want to ... I don't want you to lie about it.'

'I'm not lying. Stephanie, don't you think I might want the same things you want? To stop being me for awhile? To live a different kind of life? I want the experience of a home, a family, a community where people know each other, a chance to slow down, to be alone, to think – I don't have any of those. And you and I are so close that I can have them with your family in a way I couldn't anywhere else. It's a fantastic idea. In fact, it's probably everybody's secret wish. For one glorious week we'll leave everything behind and discover strange and wonderful things by living a completely different life. And at the end of the week we'll turn up our coat collars, steal away to a mysterious rendezvous, whisper the secret password and trade places again. You'll go home and I'll fly back to London. *And no one but the two of us will ever know.* What could be simpler? What could be more fun?'

'Oh, Sabrina!' Stephanie threw her arms around her sister and hugged her. 'Thank you. I love you.'

Once again Sabrina felt the ripples of secrets in Stephanie's life, but she ignored them. Stephanie wanted this so badly, and it was something she could do for her. And it would be fun. The challenge had caught her imagination, and already she saw herself in her sister's world, blending into her family, settling into the rooms of her rambling old house. 'Have you changed the furniture?' she asked. 'Let's start there. We only have a week.'

They left Shanghai the next morning and flew to Sian, where their small group stood on the edge of the great tomb of China's first emperor, who had died two thousand years before. Only recently discovered, the tomb was still being excavated, inch by inch, revealing an army of more than seven thousand larger-than-life terra-cotta warriors and horses the emperor had commanded to be made to accompany him to the afterlife.

In the Sian Museum they saw, close up, some of the giant figures from the tomb: noble, perfectly proportioned, serene. 'Grand visions,' murmured Stephanie. 'I don't know anyone who has them today. Except perhaps Garth.' She seemed surprised at her own words.

Sabrina looked at her quickly. 'But that's wonderful.'

'I suppose so. It's hard to live with.'

The next day they drove through the magnificent countryside around Guilin. Limestone mountains thrust straight up from flat green plains, their craggy peaks hidden by swirling mists, their sides eroded by water into caverns and needle-sharp points. Water buffalo grazed between fields of sugarcane and grapefruit trees, and on the blue-green Li River floated hundreds of boats, from tiny rafts with single fishermen using rice as bait to crowded houseboats rocking beneath huge square sails.

Sabrina felt as if she were intruding on a painted scroll or an illustration in a book. But she was fascinated by the dreamlike beauty and peaceful, misty scenes of farmers, fishermen and small neat houses. 'Do you think people are happier when they're surrounded by beauty?' she asked.

'If they have enough to eat,' their guide answered, smiling, and led the group to a porcelain factory.

Sabrina and Stephanie stayed behind. 'It's either the fourteenth or fifteenth of the tour,' Sabrina said. 'Whichever it is, we'll skip it.'

They walked instead along the river. 'What haven't we covered?' Stephanie asked. 'Friends, time schedules, grocery stores, the office – you are going to call in sick, aren't you?'

'I'd better. I don't know how to type.'

'But you shouldn't work anyway. A job in the dean's office of Midwestern University is nobody's definition of a great adventure. Ask for Ted Morrow, he's the dean, and tell him whatever strikes your fancy. He won't be happy, but ignore what he says; he's nicer than he sounds. If Penny asks about the art classes, tell her we haven't decided yet. I think Cliff has a soccer game that week, but he won't mind if you don't go.'

'Why shouldn't I go? I've never seen Cliff play. I'd like to.'

'Actually, he'd like it, too; one of us always tries to be there. The house will probably be filthy, because I can't imagine Garth and the kids cleaning, but if you can stand it, don't worry about it. I'll do it when I get back.'

'I can clean a house.'

'When did you last clean a house?'

'In the year one. But it's like bicycle-riding; once you learn, you never forget.'

Stephanie laughed. 'I didn't mean to sound as if you can't manage a house, only that it's not your responsibility.'

'Stephanie, I'd like to do whatever feels right. How else can I have the experience of living your life?'

'I'm sorry. Of course you'll do what you want. You should. I don't know why I'm being so silly. I think I'm nervous. Two more days—'

'I know. I'm all tied up inside, too.'

That evening they were in the crowded industrial city of Canton and the next day they went to its famous zoo. In that tropical paradise, an oasis in the dingy city, Sabrina had the dizzying sensation of being cut off from everything. She lagged behind and sat on a bench in the botanical orchid garden, surrounded by the riotous colours of exotic flowers. For two weeks she had been locked in a land and a society completely different from her own. For two weeks she had seen nothing familiar; even the flowers were different. And now, instead of going home, she was going to another strange place: a different land, a different society, a different house. She would live with strangers – for how well did she really know Garth or the children? She would have nothing to hold onto. But that's foolish, she thought. I'll only be gone a week longer than I'd planned, and then I'll be home. I've been away longer than that before.

Stephanie came looking for her, and they walked through the rest of the zoo, admiring the rare giant pandas. The next morning they boarded the train to Hong Kong. The tour of China was over.

Later, Sabrina regretted that she had been so tense with anticipation she hadn't been able to appreciate the Victorian grandeur of the train: an old-fashioned steam engine with enormous red wheels and a red cowcatcher, rolling on a track so smooth their tea had not a ripple. They sat on cushioned seats with white embroidered cloths behind their heads, a carpet beneath their feet and velvet curtains on the windows as they sped through a lush tropical countryside of heavy trees and dense vegetation. But they barely looked at it. They were absorbed in their game, repeating, memorizing, recalling people and places from past visits to each other. Stephanie clasped and unclasped her hands and Sabrina found herself doing the same.

'Money,' Sabrina said. She opened her purse. 'This is my Check Card; you can cash a check anywhere with it. And my checkbook; there's plenty in the account for a week. If you have an emergency, call Mr. Eccles at the bank; he'll transfer as much as you need. Write my name.'

'What?'

'Write my name. As if you're signing a check.'

'Sabrina, I'm not going to spend your money.'

'Of course you are. I have only fifty pounds cash; you'll need more before the week is out. What will you do? I'll have all your dollars.'

'There aren't many.'

'We'll settle accounts later. Stephanie, don't worry about money; you can't have any fun if you do. I promise I will demand repayment of every pence after we're home again. Now sign my name.'

Stephanie wrote, her lip caught between her teeth as she concentrated. 'What do you think?'

'Lovely. Start a little higher on the L and make the final stroke of the h a little longer and you've got it. Now how about me? Do I cash checks?'

'At the grocery. I usually do it when I shop. I have about thirty dollars with me. You just cash more as you need it.' She rummaged in her purse. 'This is the card for Dominick's; this is for the Jewel. I keep them in the checkbook.'

Sabrina confidently wrote Stephanie's name, and as the train followed a river through the rich, rolling country they talked about the Evanston post office, pharmacy, hardware store, self-service dry cleaner and Stephanie's house: a broken valve on the pressure cooker, garment bags with extra sweaters, bologna sandwiches, a bent latch on the washing machine, two overdue library books.

As the train approached Hong Kong, they talked of London: restaurants and pubs in Belgravia and Knightsbridge, Chelsea shops and boutiques, the Tate Gallery, Westminster Abbey, Portobello Road, Mrs Thirkell's day off, emergency telephone numbers. Sabrina wrote down a name and telephone number and gave it to Stephanie. 'If you have a real emergency, something so urgent it won't help to call me in Evanston, call this number.'

Stephanie read it. 'Alexandra Martova.'

'You didn't meet her when you were in London because she was out of town, but I've told you about her. If you have to, you can tell her what we've done; you can trust her with anything.'

'Thank you. I was thinking I'd be awfully alone.'

'Not with Alexandra there.'

Off the train the quiet trading of their lives went on in the midst of the chaos and noise of Hong Kong: streets so crowded they had to walk sideways, buildings climbing the mountains in vertical concrete slabs with windows reflecting the densely packed boats in the harbor, their masts a tangled forest swaying in the breeze. After dinner Sabrina and Stephanie walked from the Jade Gardens restaurant to their hotel. A crowd trailed behind them as they passed fortune-tellers, shoemakers, cooking stalls, salesmen with open valises of blue jeans and dealers behind folding tables spread with jade carvings and jewelry.

'Garth,' said Sabrina.

'What?' Stephanie asked

'Did you buy him anything?'

'Oh. No.'

'Well, for peace in the family—' Sabrina looked at the jewelry displayed on one of the tables. 'Excellent!' enthused the dealer in crisp English. She shook her head. 'Very excellent stuff!' he insisted. She shrugged and turned. 'Wait,' he said. Bending down to a box between his feet, he brought out a small tray. 'These?' She looked closely and pointed to a round tie tack that glowed softly under the garish streetlights. For the next ten minutes they bargained rapidly, bouncing prices back and forth like tennis balls. Finally Sabrina nodded and paid. The crowd applauded.

'Mother used to do that,' Stephanie said.

'It's fun once in a while. It's a game. This seems to be my week for games, doesn't it?'

'I should have thought of buying Garth something.'

Sabrina was thoughtful. 'Isn't it strange? It's as if we've already traded places.'

That night they slept fitfully and woke feeling still tired. 'My heart is pounding,' Stephanie said. 'Like mine,' said Sabrina. They dressed in each other's clothes: Stephanie in Sabrina's dark blue suit with red piping, Sabrina in Stephanie's brown suit with white blouse. She left the top two buttons open but Stephanie, with a faint smile, did them up.

They went again through each other's purses and wallets, checking passports and airline tickets. They stood a last time before the mirror. 'How strange I feel!' Stephanie said. Sabrina could only nod, caught between anticipation and the strange sense of loss she had felt in the orchid garden in Canton.

They turned to pick up their suitcases. 'Oh!' Stephanie exclaimed. 'I forgot—' She tugged at her finger and held out her wedding ring to Sabrina. Her hand was trembling. 'This is the first time I've ever taken it off.'

Sabrina touched her fingers as she took the ring. 'I'll take care of it.' She put it on, thinking how many years it had been since she had worn one of her own.

There was a knock on the door. 'The bellboy,' she said.

As he came in they picked up their shoulder bags. 'One more thing,' Sabrina said. 'I've been saving it.' She reached into her pocket and held something out to Stephanie.

Stephanie smiled. 'So have I.'

And in a sixth-floor room of the Furama Inter-Continental Hotel in Hong Kong, Sabrina Longworth and Stephanie Andersen handed to each other the keys to their front doors, in England and America. And then it was time to go.

Part II

Chapter 10

From the depths of the warm bed, Sabrina heard a door open, the rustle of clothes, the door gently shut. She frowned, coming out of her dark sleep: why was Mrs Thirkell in her room so early? A drawer was pulled out, slowly, quietly. Sabrina opened her eyes and tensed in shock, her fist against her mouth. A tall man wearing pajama pants, his naked back to her, black hair tousled from sleep, trousers over his arm, a folded shirt in his hand.

Garth.

She closed her eyes again. Not Mrs Thirkell. Not her own bedroom; not her own bed. Her sister's house, four thousand miles from London, a lifetime from—

'There's no bologna!' The indignant cry pierced the bedroom quiet.

Garth took two long strides to the door. His voice was low and muffled as he called down the back stairs. 'Cliff, I told you to keep your voice down. I'll help you make your lunch in a few minutes. You are not to wake your mother.'

Your mother.

Sabrina felt imprisoned in the bed. It was a lie. It was supposed to be an adventure, but it was all a lie. She felt ashamed and a little afraid. *I have no right to be here; I don't belong. These are real people and I'm a fraud.*

The night before, it had seemed like a game, careless and exciting, from the moment when she left the plane and saw, waiting for her—

The dresser drawer closed. Silence. Then the brushing sound of bare feet on the carpet, a shadow across her sunlit eyelids, the warmth of a kiss on her cheek. She fought back panic, willing herself to lie still and breathe deeply and slowly. Last night he had slept in his study, but now—

The shadow moved away from her face. The bathroom door opened and closed, a light switch clicked, water sprayed from the shower. Sabrina burrowed into the protective cave of the bed. *I won't get up. I'll stay here the whole week, until Stephanie comes back. This is her life, not mine. What am I doing here?*

The night before, she had been so keyed up, so tense and watchful, that she never stopped to question what she was doing. It had not been difficult. Perhaps that was the trouble. Everything had seemed almost too easy, a little joke on all of them, until this morning, when Garth, the husband, came toward the bed. His bed, his house, his life.

They had been waiting at the airport when her plane arrived. Dinner time in Chicago, six-fifteen, and they were all there, standing on the glass-enclosed balcony above her as she inched ahead in the customs line. Penny and Cliff fidgeted and mouthed exaggerated hellos while Garth stood quietly, watching her. They were like an audience, waiting for her performance. Sabrina's hand shook as she moved slowly forward. I have stage fright, she thought.

But when, at last, she left customs, she forgot it in the midst of the family. Penny clung to her, arms around her waist, and even Cliff, tall for his twelve years, with flaming red hair, a pugnacious nose, and a pretense of cool disdain, kept touching her arm to assure himself she was really there. Behind them, Garth bent to kiss her, but she turned slightly as Penny spoke and his lips only brushed the edge of her mouth. 'Welcome home,' he said. His eyes were searching hers as she turned to Cliff and Penny, who were eyeing the box she had carried off the plane. 'Is it a present?' Penny asked. She looked up at Sabrina with dark blue eyes; Stephanie's eyes, Sabrina's eyes. Her small face, framed in black curls like her father's, already had the vivid beauty that Sabrina and Stephanie had had at eleven. To Sabrina, it was like looking in a mirror that erased time.

'A present for the house,' she answered. 'A beautiful bronze lamp. I bought it in Shanghai from a little man named Mr Su, who once lived in Chicago.'

'For the house,' said Penny, crestfallen.

'And,' Sabrina went on casually, 'Mr Su had an amazing

cabinet in his shop, filled with magic tricks. Somehow, probably by magic, two of them got into my suitcase.'

Cliff's eyes brightened. 'Chinese magic? What does it do?'

'It makes curious boys disappear,' she said, bending to kiss the top of his head. 'How can it be a surprise if I tell you about it now? Wait 'til we get home.'

In the station wagon, the two of them perched on the edge of the back seat and fired questions at her about China. Garth drove silently; Sabrina could not tell if he was listening to the three of them or not. But in the twilight closeness of the car, excitement churned inside her: it felt so good to have a family waiting when she arrived; it felt good to be with them now, talking and laughing. And no one had noticed a thing. It's working, she thought. It's going to work.

'We wanted to order out Chinese food,' Cliff said as Garth brought the luggage from the car. 'But we thought maybe you'd had enough in China, so we changed it to pizza.'

'And I'm cooking it!' Penny announced, turning on the oven.

'Finishing it,' said Cliff.

'Cooking it!' She pulled two boxes from the freezer. 'And since I'm the cook, Cliff does the dishes.'

'You're not cooking, you're just putting them in the oven. And I cut up the salad stuff this afternoon, so I did more than you, so you're doing the dishes!'

'I'm not doing the dishes! I want to talk to Mommy.'

'You can talk later.'

'No I can't.'

'You can too.'

'You will both do the dishes,' Garth said firmly. 'I want to talk to your mother. Is the table set?'

'Yes,' Cliff grumbled.

Sabrina knelt beside her suitcase. 'How about presents before dinner?'

In the clamour – how do two children manage to sound like a dozen? she wondered – Sabrina pulled the wrapped gifts from the sweaters Stephanie had used to cushion them. She gave Penny and Cliff theirs and, standing up, held out the third to Garth. He looked at her extended hand. 'For me,' he murmured as if to himself and met Sabrina's eyes. 'Thank you.'

'Take it,' she said, puzzled by the strange note in his voice, and at last he reached for the small box and began to unwrap it. While Penny and Cliff were absorbed in their gifts, reading the instructions Stephanie had written in the hotel in Hong Kong, Sabrina watched Garth. He had aged in the three years since her last visit; the lines radiating from the corners of his eyes had deepened; his face was thinner, and his black hair was mixed with gray. But his eyes had a boyish eagerness, like Cliff's, as he unwrapped his gift, and then, as she watched, he grew thoughtful and a little sad, looking at the lustrous sphere of jade in his palm. He cupped his fingers around it. 'A beautiful thing.' He moved toward her. 'I didn't think you—'

Confused by the expression in his eyes, Sabrina felt a spurt of anxiety. 'The pizza!' she said quickly, and ducked away before he could kiss her. Opening the oven with one hand, she reached with the other to pull out the drawer beside it. Waxed paper and foil. She opened the next one down: towels. She opened the next.

'What are you looking for?' Garth asked.

'Where do you keep your potholders?' she asked absently.

There was a moment of silence. Sabrina held her breath. *Fool. Fool.*

'Where we always keep them,' Garth said.

'You mean you haven't reorganized the kitchen while my back was turned in Asia?' she asked gaily, and with a brief prayer opened the bottom drawer to find a neat stack of potholders and oven mitts.

'All these knots come untied at once, right?' Cliff said at her elbow. 'And then sort of tie themselves up again? But I can't get them to do it. Did Mr Su show you how?'

'I can't make my little man disappear,' said Penny on her other side. 'I pressed where the instructions said, but nothing happened.'

'Mom, if you'd hold one end of the string—' said Cliff.

'No, first show me where to press on the box,' Penny interrupted.

Feeling hemmed in and shaken by her slip over the

potholders, Sabrina gripped the edge of the stove. 'The line forms to the right,' she said, trying to keep her voice low and steady. 'But not until we've eaten. I am not available until I've had my pizza.'

Their mouths open, Cliff and Penny stared at her, and then at each other. What had she done? Sabrina was trying to think of something to say when Garth, after a quick glance at her face, said easily, 'Now why didn't we think of that? Your drooping mother stands here starving and exhausted from traveling eighteen hours to get back to us from the wilds of Asia, and we don't even give her a chance to eat.'

Gently moving Sabrina aside, he took the pizzas from the oven. 'Penny, put the salad on the table; Cliff, pour milk or cider for the two of you. I'm going to open a bottle of wine to celebrate our traveler's return. Go on, now; I'll help you figure out your magic tricks later.'

But the real magic, Sabrina thought, was Garth taking over. He moved them all to the dining room and brought everyone into the conversation.

When Sabrina described the rows and rows of men and women exercising in streets and factory yards before going to work, Garth asked Cliff and Penny to compare their school exercises. When Sabrina talked about the classes most people attended after work to study and improve their behavior, Garth said he knew of a few professors he'd like to send there, and Cliff said that was how they went over mistakes after soccer practice. When Sabrina told about a family in Canton living in two rooms – a grandfather, a mother and father and their three children – Garth led Penny and Cliff to imagine cutting down their ten-room house to two, bringing in their grandfather from Washington and another brother or sister, throwing out possessions to make room for everyone and then getting through a day's routine.

Sabrina was grateful to him; he made the talk easy, almost a game. How nice this is, she thought. The family. Sitting on four sides of a table, listening, talking, sharing the fun and strangeness of everything she told them, and in that way stretching out her trip, making it somehow larger. She was used to coming home to an empty house, sharing fragments of her experiences with friends. She sighed. This was nicer.

139

Then, in the space of a minute, exhaustion swept over her. 'I'm sorry,' she said after the tenth yawn. 'I guess the traveling has caught up with me. Does anyone mind if I go to bed?'

Garth stood up. 'Of course you should go to bed. By tomorrow you'll be yourself again.'

And just who is that? Sabrina wondered wryly as he brought her two suitcases from the kitchen. She kissed Penny and Cliff good night. 'We'll spend lots of time together tomorrow,' she promised, and then she and Garth walked upstairs.

He put the bags inside the bedroom door. 'I suppose—' he said with a strange diffidence. 'Since you're so tired, I'll sleep in my study. Unless you've changed your mind—'

About what? she thought. About his coming to bed? Frowning, she remembered Stephanie saying, 'We quarreled, but we made it up the next day.' Did they? Or did they only agree on a truce – civility but no sex? If so, it made things easy for her; she'd simply assure him she hadn't changed her mind. But she did not even have to do that. Garth saw her frown and moved away. 'We'll have to talk about this, you know,' he said quietly. 'We never went back to that quarrel before you left for China. It's still unfinished. Tomorrow, when you're rested—'

Oh, no, she thought. I can't finish your quarrel; you'll have to wait a week. And I'll have to find a way to stall.

'Good night, Garth,' she said. 'Thank you for the pizza.'

He looked startled. 'You're welcome.' He kissed her quickly. 'And you are more than welcome home. We missed you. Sleep well.'

As soon as he was gone, she dropped her clothes where she stood, and slipped into bed. She barely had time to turn over before she was asleep.

And the next morning she listened to the sounds of a family getting ready for the day: water running, the rattle of dishes and silverware, Cliff and Penny alternately friendly and squabbling as they made their lunches, Garth's deep voice, their laughter. Then the slam of the back door, the turn of a key, and silence. They were gone.

Sabrina lay still, listening to the silence. Beyond the open window a dog barked, a woman called a child to breakfast, a distant driver honked his horn. But within the house nothing stirred. She had it all to herself.

Her panic was fading and, as it did, her confidence returned. There was nothing to worry about; Garth had behaved just as Stephanie had said he would. And last night she had slipped into the family as smoothly as she had planned. Now, for a week, she would play her part and then slip out, smoothly and silently, without leaving a mark. Anticipation began to bubble within her. It was time to begin.

First a shower. Then breakfast. She was starved; she'd been too tired to eat much the night before. And then an exploration of the house to make sure there were no more potholder mistakes. She had to call Stephanie's office, water the plants, pick the ripe tomatoes in the garden and think about dinner, which probably meant grocery shopping . . . She leaped out of bed; how could she waste time with a new life to learn?

She luxuriated in the shower, washing away the last of her fatigue, and dried herself in the folds of a velvety bath sheet she had bought at Harrods and sent to Stephanie last Christmas. As she combed her wet hair, she made a quick inspection of the linen closet and bathroom, pausing when she found a vial of sleeping pills prescribed for Stephanie. *Does she take them on nights when Garth isn't home, or when he is?* Then she went to the clothes closet in the bedroom.

Quiet colors; casual clothes. Blue jeans, linen pantsuits, shirtwaist dresses. Skirts, blouses, oxford-cloth shirts. The dress Stephanie had worn at the backyard barbecue for Sabrina and Denton seven years ago. The suit she had worn two years ago on a weekend trip to meet Sabrina in New York. Nothing had been thrown out or given away; each year Stephanie added one or two carefully chosen blouses, a dress or sweater, occasionally a suit, to her wardrobe. Always simple and always of superb quality; Laura had taught them how to shop on a diplomat's limited budget.

Pulling on blue jeans and a white cotton turtleneck shirt, Sabrina pictured Stephanie on Cadogan Square, dipping into her closet and bureaus filled with bright, frivolous designer clothes. She smiled to herself. What different weeks they had before them.

Downstairs, drinking tea, munching on the half-stale remains of a coffee cake, she explored the large kitchen, memorizing the contents of cabinets and drawers: mixer and blender, brightly enameled castiron pots and pans from France, wooden utensils from Portugal, clay roasters from Germany, glass pitchers, ironstone dishes from England, Swedish stainless silverware and small gadgets Sabrina had never seen and had no idea how to use. She shut the drawer on them. If she didn't know what they were for, she didn't need them. She refilled her mug and took it with her on an exploration of the rest of the house.

It was ninety years old, creaking and shabby; Stephanie often fretted about the repairs they could not afford to make. The walls looked like old porcelain, webbed with tiny cracks; in some rooms a single crack ran like a flash of lightning from ceiling to floor. The oak floors were dull and scratched. The walls and window frames needed paint, there were chipped tiles in the bathrooms, the carved moldings at the ceilings and on the walls at chair height needed restoring, the furniture needed new slipcovers.

And it was a warm, welcoming house that fitted itself snugly around Sabrina as she moved from floor to floor.

Stephanie had furnished the rooms in autumn colors, faded now to softness, as if touched by the slanting rays of a late-afternoon sun. She had found antique lamps at garage sales and flea markets and, after polishing and repairing them, had placed them everywhere – on end tables, suspended from the ceiling, standing beside chairs and couches – so that circles of light overlapped on the worn Oriental rugs, brightening their ancient flowers and designs.

It was nothing like Cadogan Square, yet Stephanie had made of it the same kind of sheltered retreat, serene and comforting, that Sabrina had made in London. 'A home,' Sabrina murmured, standing beside the curved radiator in Stephanie and Garth's bedroom. She looked through the wide curving window at the front yard below, where beds of bronze and yellow chrysanthemums bloomed in the shade of huge oak trees. Still, it was odd, she thought, that she felt so comfortable in a shabby house that was slightly rumpled, like a suit someone had slept in, when she was used to the gleaming òrder and elegance of her Victorian house in London.

The telephone rang.

She wasn't ready for telephone calls; she hadn't had time to think about them. It was only nine-thirty; who would call so early?

'Hello?' she said, but nothing came out. She cleared her throat. 'Hello?'

'Am I speaking to the lady of the house? This is Lady Longworth in London, and I wish to speak to—'

'Stephanie!' At her sister's voice, lilting and mischievous, Sabrina laughed with relief and pleasure. 'How wonderful! I was so busy memorizing your kitchen cabinets I forgot you were going to call this morning. Is everything all right?'

'Oh, I can't begin to tell you. Strange and wonderful. Unbelievable. Like a dream. But what about you? Does Garth suspect anything?'

'Nothing. Of course, we hardly talked . . . and he slept in his study. Penny and Cliff are fine, full of energy. They loved the magic tricks. Oh, I said the bronze lamp was a birthday present from you. Happy birthday tomorrow, Stephanie.'

Stephanie laughed. 'Happy birthday, Sabrina. What a strange way we're celebrating. You really didn't have any trouble?'

'Not a bit. They knew I was exhausted, and when I did something really stupid—'

'What?'

'Asked Garth where he kept his potholders.'

'Oh, no.'

'It was all right; I slid around it. Stephanie, we don't have to worry; it's amazingly easy. They have no reason to suspect anything, and I can handle little mistakes. I can handle all of it. When you come back everything will be waiting as if I hadn't been here at all.'

'What does Garth . . . I mean, does he seem . . . What did he say about the tie tack?'

'He loved it.'

'And you didn't have any problem with the office?'

'The office. Oh, damn, I forgot all about it. I'll do it right away. I'll say I've had Asiatic hiccups and couldn't talk until now.'

'Where are you?'

'What?'

'Where are you sitting?'

'Oh. Your bedroom. I've been exploring, and I'm about to go grocery shopping. Your family ate everything in sight and didn't replace it.'

'They never do. Be sure you buy—'

'Stephanie.'

'Yes?'

'Don't worry about me or your family. You're too far away to change anything. Just enjoy your week. Now tell me what you've been doing. Have you gone to Ambassadors or called Brian for messages?'

Sabrina listened to Stephanie. Mostly she had just browsed in London; she'd run into Gabrielle and Brooks, who told her they were going to live together; Mrs Thirkell was worried about – Sabrina grew impatient; it all seemed far away, and she had so much to do. Finally Stephanie said, 'Well, then, unless something comes up I won't talk to you again until I see you in Chicago on Monday. At the airport.'

'Have a wonderful week,' Sabrina said, and was on her feet before she had finished saying goodbye. She hurried to the third-floor stairs to finish her tour. But she turned back. It could wait; she had to make a grocery list and call the office. She went downstairs and was walking into the kitchen when the telephone rang again.

She could ignore it, but that would only delay things. And after all, she thought, if I can fool the family, I can fool friends. She answered on the fifth ring. 'Hello?'

'Hi, welcome home. Did I wake you? If you're still sleeping off your trip you can call me back.'

Silence. *Close friends don't identify themselves on the telephone. We forgot about that. So what do I do now?*

'Stephanie? Are you there?'

Fake it. It's only the first of many.

144

'Yes, sorry, I was finishing some stale coffee cake. How are you?'

'We're all fine. Breakfast so late? Did China turn you into a lady of leisure?'

'Oh, everyone let me sleep this morning. I suppose it won't last.'

'I suppose not. Was it a glorious trip?'

It was almost ten; she had to call the office. 'What?'

'I said, was it a glorious trip? You *are* still asleep.'

'No. I just remembered I haven't called the office about not going in today.'

'Well, go ahead and call me back.'

'No!' *How can I call her back when I haven't the faintest idea who she is?* 'I mean, I've waited this long, I can wait a few more minutes. Tell me what's happened while I've been gone.'

'Not much. School started, so the house is peaceful; Nat is at a conference in Minneapolis until tomorrow; and I've decided to overthrow the Evanston City Council for not putting a stoplight at the corner. Piddling stuff compared to China.'

Sabrina laughed. Nat was Nat Goldner, so she was talking to Dolores Goldner and everything was fine.

'Oh, and you're coming to dinner tomorrow night,' Dolores added. 'Did Garth remember to tell you?'

'No. You're not having a party—?'

'In the middle of the week? Just the six of us. To celebrate your birthday and provide an audience for your exotic tales. Six-thirty?'

'Fine. I'll look forward to it.'

There was a brief pause. 'I should hope so,' Dolores answered. 'See you then.'

A mistake: she had been too formal. But it wasn't serious. On the whole, a pretty good job.

Job. She dialed the number on her checklist for Stephanie's office and left a message at the switchboard that she was ill. Then, surveying the pantry and refrigerator, she made a grocery list, thinking up menus and snacks, becoming more and more ambitious. She was filled with energy and confidence, as if she had stepped into an adventure story and

145

found everything she wanted – a home, a family, friends – and knew she could make them hers. For awhile.

The confidence carried her through the first roughness with the car – why couldn't governments agree which side of the road to drive on? – and the cavernous supermarket that would have held ten of the markets she frequented in London. She had never shopped for four people and, fearful of buying too little, bought four times what she ordinarily would. Her shopping cart looked as if she were supplying an army.

Driving from store to store, she used Stephanie's list as a guide to buy for a house and a family. Sabrina Longworth carrying bags of groceries, turtle food, toilet paper, detergent, Ortho Spray for the roses. She laughed to herself. What would Olivia think of her now?

The streets were full of cars driven by women doing the same errands. It did not seem to matter whether the stores were two or three blocks from each other, or two or three miles apart; everyone drove. And everyone bought so much. In Europe, shoppers carried string bags with enough food for the day. Here, every shopper was laden with what seemed to be enough for a month. Well, so am I, she thought. But surely everyone else hasn't just returned from two weeks in China? No. The difference is that these women have freezers. They can buy two or three of everything without worrying about spoilage.

The car was full of brown paper bags. Sabrina felt the thrill of victory. No one had questioned her signature on a check; the butcher smiled at her when she asked him to trim the steaks; at the dry cleaners they had given her Garth's sport jacket without hesitation, the clerk in the camera shop greeted her by name as she gave him her rolls of film, and said of course the pictures would be ready tomorrow; she must be anxious to show them off; it's not every day that people go to China. She had done it all.

At three o'clock Garth called. 'I just wanted to make sure you were all right.'

'Did you think I wasn't?'

'I thought you were tense last night, almost as if you weren't sure how to behave.'

Some of her confidence ebbed away. *Stephanie didn't tell me he was a mind reader.* 'Did I really act like that?'

'A little. Did you sleep well?'

'Yes, I feel better. I keep thinking I'm still a tourist, but I'll settle down. What time will you be home?'

'Five-thirty. You are all right?'

'Yes, of course. I'll see you then.'

Cliff rushed in from school and Sabrina prepared to sit down and talk about his day. 'Hi, Mom,' he said, tearing open a bag of potato chips. 'Penny says to tell you she has gymnastics and she'll be home at five-thirty. I'll be back later.' He was halfway out the door before Sabrina caught her breath.

'Hold on!' Obviously friendly, parental, after-school chats were not part of the family routine. 'Five-thirty for you, too,' she said and Cliff nodded, slamming the screen door after him.

But it was all right, she thought; at least she would be alone and unobserved while she cooked her first meal for a family in a strange kitchen.

Garth was early and found her peppering the steaks. He had come through the house quietly and watched her from the dining room doorway. Slender as a young girl, in jeans and close-fitting pullover, she stood at the counter, her back to the door, murmuring to herself. 'Mortar and pestle. There must be one somewhere.'

Garth was puzzled. There it was again – that playacting: as if she'd been away much longer than two weeks and was seeing her house and her family for the first time. As if she no longer took anything for granted.

'No mortar and pestle,' she murmured. 'Well, a grinder, then.'

Garth moved forward and Sabrina whirled about. 'I didn't hear you.'

'I just came in. What requires a mortar and pestle?'

'Peppercorns. But I can grind them.'

'I have some at the lab, you know.'

'Peppercorns?'

'Mortars and pestles.'

'What do you do with them?'

'Crush peppercorns, of course.'

'To study their genes?'

'To modify their genes so they grow on trees in little square cans with plastic lids.'

'A peppercan tree.'

'So far a peppercan't. It's a difficult project.'

They laughed softly together. How beautiful she is, thought Garth. Has she always been this beautiful – or has something happened to change her? His eyes holding hers, laughter still on their lips, he moved toward her. Sabrina turned quickly back to the counter. 'Did you have a good day?'

He stopped as if struck. 'What?'

'I asked about your day.'

Laughter one minute, her back to him the next, without rhyme or reason. He looked at her, but she was absorbed in pressing ground pepper into the steaks with the heel of her hand. He shrugged and sat on the couch, opening the newspaper. 'Did you buy wine today?'

'Yes, I'll get it. Just a minute.' She laid the steaks on a platter and covered them with waxed paper. From the pantry she brought a bottle of red wine, a corkscrew and two glasses. Garth looked at the glasses and his eyebrows went up, but Sabrina did not notice. 'You didn't tell me about your day.'

'You didn't tell me about yours. Dull and routine after your trip?'

'No. Peaceful and pleasant. I took a tour of the house and decided China has nothing to equal it, cracks and all. Shall we sit on the patio? It's a magnificent evening and I've hardly been outside all day.'

Garth put down the paper. 'Good idea. I haven't either.' He led the way outside and opened the bottle. 'It's been a long time since we sat together before dinner.' He smiled at her as they sat at a small round table. Even if she was still angry from their quarrel before her trip, she was obviously trying to change their routine. Well, so was he, though she didn't seem to have noticed how early he'd come home and that he hadn't mentioned going back to the lab after dinner.

Sabrina gazed at the backyard. The late-afternoon sun, low in the sky, shone through tall honeysuckles at the far end. Its gold-flecked light spread over bronze chrysanthemums, rose bushes of deep red Mirandies and yellow Teas and the vegetable garden where glossy red tomatoes tangled with thorny raspberry stalks and yellowing cucumbers. No one had picked them while Stephanie was away.

The air was fresh and sweet; the sun lay like honey on Sabrina's face, and she felt at ease. 'I've done all the talking, about my trip. You haven't told me what happened while I was gone.'

'We missed you.' He poured the wine and examined the bottle. 'The house echoed and teetered on the edge of chaos. This is a new wine; are you experimenting?'

There was none in the house and Stephanie said you liked reds, so I bought one of my favorites. 'Someone on the trip mentioned it. You don't mind trying something new?'

'Of course I don't mind.' He sipped it and looked again at the label. 'It's very fine. What else did you buy?'

'Just groceries. And I put petrol in the car. It was almost empty.'

'Petrol?'

Sabrina gripped her wine glass. 'Am I still doing it? There was an Englishman on the trip, an antique dealer named Nicholas Blackford, and we talked shop a lot and I started using his British terms. In Hong Kong I called our hotel elevator a lift, and Nicholas said that made me an honorary English citizen. I don't know why I picked up his phrases instead of his picking up mine—' *Stop babbling. You'll make things worse.* '—anyway, I guess I'm still doing it.'

'Mom?' Penny was calling from inside the house.

Thank God for children. 'We're out here,' Sabrina called, and in a minute Penny rushed through the door and flung herself on the chair next to Sabrina.

'Barbara says she's going to make the puppets.'

'Oh?' said Sabrina cautiously. 'How come?'

'Mrs Casey told her she could.' Tears filled Penny's eyes. 'It's not fair!'

'Why did Mrs Casey tell her that?'

'I don't know! You talked to her last year, at the end of school – didn't she say I could make them? Isn't that what she said?'

'I think so. Did she tell Barbara she'd changed her mind?'

'Barbara says she just told her to get started on them. But I already started and the puppet show is for Christmas so we don't have much time and I have so many good ideas and it's my project!' She burst into tears and Sabrina leaned close to her.

'Maybe Mrs Casey just told Barbara to help you because she thought one person shouldn't do all of them.'

'I've got three helpers – you know that! I told you a long time ago! Will you go talk to her?'

'Well ... Mrs Casey never talked to you about changing her plans?'

'No!'

'Well, I'll think about it. It certainly doesn't seem fair that she didn't talk to you about it, whatever her reasons.'

'What are you doing out here?' Cliff asked, coming through the kitchen door.

'Having a quiet glass of wine before dinner,' Garth said dryly. 'Can I have cider?' Cliff asked.

'Pour some for both of you,' said Sabrina. 'We'll eat soon.'

'It's almost six-thirty,' said Cliff. 'I'm starved.'

'Six-thirty?' Sabrina was surprised. 'Weren't you supposed to be home at five-thirty? Both of you?'

'I was with Barbara,' said Penny, sniffling.

'I was talking to Hal,' said Cliff. 'It was very important. I meant to call, but—'

'Sloppy time-keeping,' said Sabrina. 'You might improve on it in the future. Starting tomorrow. Now how about setting the table? We'll eat about seven.'

Cliff and Penny looked at each other and turned and ran into the house. Sabrina heard them whispering furiously together.

'No lecture?' Garth asked.

'Oh, it's too beautiful out here to lecture anyone.' *I am not a good mother; not strict enough.* 'Did I tell you about the

150

weather in China? It was as if we were in three different countries, from cool highlands to the tropics.' She talked rapidly, gesturing with her hands, making Garth laugh with tales of their Chinese guide. Then she stood up. 'Dinner in just a few minutes. Shall we finish the wine with the steak?'

He nodded, and she went into the kitchen and breathed deeply. *Not too bad.*

At the table, his mouth full, Cliff made a face. 'What happened to the steak?'

Sabrina's heart sank. 'You don't like it.'

'A new recipe?' Garth asked. 'To go with the new wine?'

'I'm sorry,' she said. 'I found it in a cookbook—'

'Why are you sorry? It's excellent. Cliff, be daring and take another bite. Life is full of adventures. Penny, don't let him scare you; give it a try.' He turned to Sabrina. 'Does it have a name?'

'*Steak au poivre.* Steak with pepper.'

'And what else?'

'Butter. Madeira. That's all. It's very simple.'

'It tickles my tongue,' said Penny. 'I like it.'

'It's all right,' Cliff said. 'Not as good as hamburger. I'll get it!' he added, scrambling from his chair as the telephone rang. In a minute he called from the kitchen, 'Dad! For you!'

Garth left, and came back frowning. 'I have to take over a seminar tonight; one of our bacteriologists has the flu.'

'Poor fellow,' said Sabrina. 'Took his research home with him.'

Garth smiled, but he was annoyed. 'I didn't want to go out tonight.' How would she know he was trying to do things differently, just as she was, if he spent another evening away from home? 'If I can find someone else?'

'No, they need you,' Sabrina said. This would take care of tonight, and tomorrow night they were going to the Goldners'. 'Will you be late?'

'Probably about eleven. You'll be up, won't you?'

'I think so.'

But she was not. She played Scrabble with Penny and Cliff, then watched television in the living room while they did their homework. At ten o'clock she checked the front door, the patio door and the side door to make sure they were locked. Upstairs, after undressing and washing up, she slipped into one of the nightgowns folded in the top dresser drawer and pulled on the seersucker robe hanging in the closet. Then, curling up in the deep chair near the curved bedroom window, she took one of the books from the table beside it and began to read.

On the third page she looked up, as if suddenly awakened. What had she done? She had checked the doors, but no one had told her to. She had put on a nightgown, though she had not worn one in twenty years; she always slept nude. She had reached without looking to take the seersucker robe from its hook, but she couldn't remember noticing it when she looked through the closet that morning. And, without planning, she had come straight to this chair to read.

Stephanie must have told her these things. They'd described so many details to each other that last week in China, these must have been among them. Or, she thought, after a day of playing Stephanie, living in Stephanie's house, I'm becoming – just a little bit – my sister.

A wave of sleepiness swept over her. I'll think about both of me tomorrow, she thought, and then as she pulled back the covers and slid into bed, she smiled drowsily. *Both of me. What an extraordinary idea.* And then she fell asleep.

She woke at seven. The house was still. Sunlight flooded the room. Sabrina turned her head to the smooth sheet and pillow beside her. Had Garth come in last night and kissed her, as he had kissed her in the morning while she slept? She had heard nothing, felt nothing. She could not even remember if she had dreamed.

But it was a new day – Wednesday, her birthday, she suddenly remembered – a day when, in London, she might have felt melancholy at being thirty-two years old and alone, wondering what lay ahead. But today, in the midst of an adventure and a family, she was excited and full of energy. She sprang up, showered and was in the kitchen studying Stephanie's morning checklist when she heard the rest of the family beginning to stir.

But before she knew it they were in the kitchen, and her carefully planned procedures fell apart. Everything had to be done at once: fixing breakfast, making lunches, finding schoolbooks and lost pencils, quizzing Cliff for his daily spelling test, helping Penny sew on a button. Sabrina felt she was stumbling over herself, searching for dishes and utensils, forgetting to put jam on the table, leaving napkins out of the lunch boxes.

'Didn't the paper come?' Garth asked.

'I don't know,' Sabrina said, spreading mustard on Penny's sandwich.

'Mommy! You know I hate mustard!' cried Penny. 'I won't eat it!'

'You didn't look outside?' asked Garth.

'No.' *I didn't know about the paper. Stephanie told me about the mustard, but I forgot.* She tried to scrape the bread clean, then gave up and took a fresh slice.

Garth brought the paper from the front porch and began to read. Sabrina thought he was angry because she hadn't waited up for him last night, but there was no time or privacy to bring it up. In a hectic half hour they were all gone – Garth with his briefcase, Penny and Cliff with books and lunches – and the house settled with a sigh into peaceful stillness.

Sabrina felt triumphant. She had done it: gotten them fed, organized and out of the house on schedule without arousing suspicion. She was bursting to tell someone: look what I did; I took care of a family, and I've never done it before. But there was no one to tell, not even Stephanie. 'You're proud of *what*?' Stephanie would ask. 'I do that every morning of the year without giving it a thought.'

But still Sabrina was proud of it. Even though no one in the family cared what she did. They hadn't even remembered her birthday. How could three people all forget a birthday? It doesn't matter, she thought. I'll make my own celebration. Sight-seeing in Chicago. And I'll buy myself a present.

She cleaned up the kitchen and decided with a glance at the downstairs rooms that they could wait a day for dusting. Upstairs, she made the beds. In the study, Garth had folded his bed back into a couch. Sabrina opened it. The sheets and blanket were neatly tucked in. He plans to sleep here again, she thought, and felt a flash of pique; didn't he find her desirable at all? She laughed at herself. Evidently not. For whatever reason — that quarrel Stephanie assured her they'd settled? — he didn't want her. And a good thing, too.

Ignoring the mess in Cliff's room, she dressed to go out. She put on a navy linen skirt, rummaged through the closet until she found a bright yellow silk blouse and then chose from Stephanie's jewelry box a stunning necklace of opaque amber glass in large, roughcut chunks, so different from the rest of Stephanie's jewelry that she wondered where it came from. It was the kind of necklace she would buy for herself, and against the silk blouse it glowed like an autumn day. Pulling on a cream-colored linen blazer, she left the house.

In the glove compartment of the car she found a map and followed it to Lake Shore Drive and south to Chicago. She drove slowly, admiring the gardens of Lincoln Park on her right and the wide beaches and blue-green water of Lake Michigan on her left. The skyscrapers of the city appeared ahead, stark against the blue sky, and when she pulled into a parking lot they loomed above her, a mixture of the sculptured façades of the past and the sleek glass and steel of the present.

More than a thousand years younger than London, Chicago was loud and brash, everywhere selling itself. Sabrina felt homesick for London's privacy, its secretive closed-in mews and quiet storefronts, the careful distance maintained by people on the street.

But she liked Chicago for the aggressiveness that forced itself on visitors, insisting, 'If you don't like me now, I'll make you like me.' London welcomed visitors with civility and friendliness but also said clearly, 'If you like me, fine; if not, I'll survive nicely, thank you.'

I like them both, Sabrina thought. And I feel comfortable here. But why not? I live in Evanston. She walked on until she came to Grant Park and the Art Institute, where she climbed the broad steps between the two great lions guarding the glass entrance, to look for the exhibits Stephanie had urged her to see.

'Stephanie! What good luck to meet you here! I didn't know you were back from China!'

A tall woman, slouching, probably from trying to look shorter, with chestnut hair, large brown eyes behind round tortoiseshell glasses, pale lips. Wearing a plain brown suit and brown lizard shoes. Too much brown, Sabrina thought. She should wear red. At least a touch of red. She gave a friendly half-smile. 'I got back Monday night.'

'You look marvelous! Was it a great trip?'

'Wonderful.' She paused. 'How are you?'

'Better than when you last saw me. I've had a reprieve; they postponed the execution.' Sabrina looked blank. 'Sorry. Ghoulish humor; I use it to stave off despair. I meant I'm still on the faculty. Didn't Garth tell you? After he went over Webster's head, the vice president decided my case needed study, so I can stay for another year.'

'I'm glad,' Sabrina said. Another year? Why would they fire her? And why did Garth go over Webster's head, whoever Webster was?

'Glad is one word. Ecstatic is another. Hans just quit his job, which means I'm the only breadwinner on the premises. Still, to be safe, I'm applying at other schools for next fall.' Her voice suddenly dipped on the last two words. 'I don't want to leave, you know. We just bought the house, the children are settled in school and I've been so happy teaching here—'

Impulsively, Sabrina put her hand on the woman's arm. 'Why don't we have lunch together? You can talk about—'

'No, no. I'm trying not to talk. I'll become a bore and my friends will run the other way when I appear. Anyway, I'm due back for a meeting at four. I'll call; may I? Perhaps we will have lunch one day. I've always wanted to know you better.'

'I'd like that.'

'Then I will.' She turned to go, a brown, drooping figure. 'One thing,' she said, turning back. 'I don't need to tell you, because of course you know, but I want to anyway, how wonderful Garth is. He's supportive and encouraging, and he listens in a way that makes others feel special. I don't know where I'd be without him. Will you tell him how grateful I am? Whenever I try he cuts me off. I'll call soon about lunch. You're a lot like Garth: a good listener.'

Wandering through the exhibits, Sabrina thought about Garth. *He listens in a way that makes others feel special.*

On the ground floor she found a room of Early American quilts; some of them had a small but distinct initial in a corner of the design. She smiled, remembering her *S* on the floor of Alexandra's house, and thought of Garth. Supportive, the woman had said, and encouraging.

In the Art Institute store, she bought herself a birthday present, a lavishly illustrated book on Venice. Then, still thinking about Garth, she drove home, stopping on the way to pick up the pictures she had taken in China.

Garth. Three Garths: the indifferent husband Stephanie had described, a professional who would go over someone's head for a colleague, and the warm, humorous, companionable man Sabrina had lived with since Monday night. Which Garth was real? She didn't know. And she wouldn't have time to find out.

At home, Penny and Cliff buzzed conspiratorially while she made hamburgers and french fries for their dinner before she and Garth went to the Goldners'. Garth came home carrying a white box, which he placed like a mysterious centerpiece on the breakfast-room table. When he kissed Sabrina's cheek he touched her necklace, smiling with pleasure.

They all sat together as Penny and Cliff ate. 'You haven't talked to Mrs Casey,' Penny said to Sabrina.

'I'll make an appointment,' Sabrina promised.

Garth put up his hand for silence, and, more or less together, he and Penny and Cliff broke into a lusty, off-key 'Happy Birthday'. Sabrina felt a rush of happiness: they hadn't forgotten. She felt the family close about her. It was a new feeling. When she was growing up, her father's career had fragmented the family; later, Denton had refused to settle into one. On Cadogan Square she lived alone, luxuriously but without the embrace of people loving her, being part of her. Her face flushed and she was smiling. Until an inner voice whipped across her thoughts. *They're singing to Stephanie, not you.*

'Open the box!' cried Penny, bouncing in her chair.

Untying the ribbon, Sabrina found three boxes inside the

outer one. The largest held a cake with an elaborately flowered heart surrounding a rosy S. The second, imperfectly wrapped, contained two round, smooth stones, one painted with her portrait, the other with a baggy clown.

She held the cool stones in her hands. The portrait was remarkably fine, the clown a rough caricature, both lovingly painted, varnished, wrapped in tissue paper and tied with gold cord. I wish they were for me, Sabrina thought.

'They're paperweights,' said Cliff worriedly. 'Don't you like them?'

Sabrina pulled the children to her and held them close. 'They're wonderful and I thank you. I'm going to show them off to everyone.'

Penny beamed. 'I could make more, if people wanted them. Like at your office.'

'So could I,' Cliff said. 'But Penny's is better.'

'It's more artistic,' Sabrina agreed. 'But yours would be a fine gift for puffed-up lords and ladies who don't know what silly clowns they often seem to the rest of us.'

Penny and Cliff laughed.

'Lords and ladies?' Garth asked.

'Aren't you going to open Dad's present?' asked Cliff.

Thinking quickly as she unwrapped the slender box, Sabrina said, 'Some of the rich people I met when I was doing estate sales reminded me of those lords and ladies we met in England at – at Sabrina's wedding. Not all of them; just the ones who think money makes them better than other people.' Opening the box, she lifted out a porcelain bluejay about five inches high. She stared at it. Meissen. But how could Garth afford—? She turned it over and saw the mark on the underside: one of Meissen's own copies of his eighteenth-century originals.

'It's for your collection!' Penny said. 'To go with the ones Aunt Sabrina sent you. Isn't it beautiful? We helped pick it out.'

'Very beautiful,' Sabrina said to Garth. 'And very special. Thank you.' No one could know that a porcelain bird reminded her of problems waiting to be solved; they were Sabrina Longworth's problems, not Stephanie Andersen's, and for Stephanie, Garth, like the children, had chosen a gift

157

with love. I wish it were really for me, she thought again, and then it was time to go to the Goldners' for dinner.

On the white leather couch in the Goldners' living room, Sabrina handed around her Chinese photographs and talked about her trip. She was wound as tightly as a spring, trying to act at home with the Goldners and Martin and Linda Talvia – Stephanie and Garth's friends for twelve years – who had hugged her and welcomed her back and wished her a happy birthday, and who were closer than many families. She had given Dolores and Linda the silk scarves Stephanie had bought for them in Shanghai, and now she watched herself as she talked, and she watched the others watching her. As if she were at a play.

And that's just what it is, she thought, hearing herself describe porcelain factories and the jagged mountains of Guilin, shrouded in mist. It had been a play from her first stage fright in the airport. But now, strangely, though she was still on stage, she was also in the audience.

She was both Stephanie and Sabrina. One, sitting with her husband and friends in the Goldners' starkly modern living room, all leather, chrome and glass; the other, coolly, critically observing from a distance everything the other woman did.

'Wonderful pictures,' Martin Talvia said, leaning forward, reminding her, as he had done at that long-ago backyard barbecue, of a tall, thin, pipe-smoking crane. 'Did you take them all yourself?'

'We took turns,' she murmured, leafing through the ones in her hand.

'Who took turns?' asked Linda.

'Oh, a few of us,' Sabrina said quickly, but then she froze as she came upon three pictures Nicholas Blackford had taken in Hong Kong of her and Stephanie in their matching Shanghai silk dresses. Identical faces, identical figures. If Garth found out they had been together, how long would it be before he began to wonder about her mistakes and come to an obvious conclusion?

'What else?' cried Linda gaily, and reached for the pictures in her hand. Sabrina snatched them back. 'Hey!' Linda said. She laughed uncomfortably. 'What did I do?'

Sabrina's knuckles were white from clenching the pictures, and her face grew hot with embarrassment. 'I'm sorry. These are . . . they're pictures I took that aren't any good. I'm ashamed of them, I guess.'

'You're too sensitive, Stephanie,' Dolores said. 'We could forgive you a bad photograph or two.'

'But there were three,' Sabrina said, making her voice light. 'Linda, I'm sorry. Sometime when I'm feeling less sensitive, I'll show you my failures.' But you just saw one, she thought. She was trembling. She had to think faster, be better prepared, never let herself relax; there were too many ways she could be caught – and ruin everything.

'Let's eat,' said Dolores, and led the way to the dining room, ablaze with flowers from her garden. Sabrina stood in the doorway, overwhelmed by the magnificence of the displays, each a work of art, from the delicate centerpiece of frail branches of mountain ash heavy with orange berries to huge baskets on the floor and sideboard bursting with chrysanthemums, late snapdragons and sprays of glossy red maple leaves. Olivia Chasson had always boasted of her flower arranger; she'd fire him in a minute and steal Dolores if she saw these. Sabrina turned to her. 'They're the most incredible—'

'She won another prize with them,' Nathan Goldner interrupted. 'While you were gone. She's too modest to say so herself.'

Sabrina breathed a silent *thank you* and changed her sentence. '—the most incredible you've ever done. Which prize did you win?'

'First place in the Midwest Fall Competition,' said Dolores, serving baked chicken and rice. 'I thought I told you I was entering.'

'A wonderful pastime,' Martin Talvia said. He turned to his wife beside him, small and neat, her dark hair cut close like a cap, her mouth pouting beneath a little pug nose. 'You could do something like that. You're wonderfully creative when you try.'

Linda looked at him coldly. 'And when I don't try?'

159

'Then the house goes to pieces,' he said amiably.

'There's nothing creative about cleaning house. It bores me.'

'The way marriage bores you?'

She shrugged.

'More wine?' Nathan asked.

'Please,' said Sabrina. She was uncomfortable.

He moved about the table, refilling their glasses. 'Did I tell you—'

'The way I bore you?' Martin pressed on.

Linda shrugged again. 'How lively is somebody who writes books on corporations?'

'How would you know? You never listen when I talk about them.'

'I am not interested in corporations.'

'Ah, but if you listened. . . . Today, for instance, I collated survey results on adultery among executives' wives. Wouldn't that be right up your alley? You do know about alleys, at least.'

'Of all the filthy remarks! Why don't you just accuse me of something instead of hiding behind your textbooks?'

'Would you like that? Would you like me to spell it out?'

'Hey,' said Nathan. 'You're embarrassing us. Especially Stephanie, who's had two weeks to forget how you go on. I am changing the subject. Not to orthopedics, since I assume that fascinates no one but me, but to my hobbies. Which shall it be? My recent hike in the treacherous forests of southern Wisconsin, or the newest Venetian goblet in my glass collection?'

'The goblet,' Sabrina said quickly, grateful to him for cutting off the wretched quarrel – though everyone else, she noted, seemed to take it in stride, as if it were a regular occurrence.

'A good choice,' said Nathan, 'considering your wondrous necklace. I've never seen it before. Where did it come from?'

Sabrina's eyes widened. 'I don't know—'

'Sweden,' Garth said quietly.

Oh. A present from Garth. Which, for some reason,

Stephanie has never worn. So now Garth is pleased. Does he think I wore it for him?

'Where'd you find it, Garth?' Nathan asked.

'In Stockholm, when I was at the Genetics conference a couple of years ago.'

Two years. Why hadn't Stephanie worn it? They were looking at her. 'I never realized it was so beautiful,' she said. 'But this morning it looked like pieces of autumn sunlight, all golden and glorious like the day, and I felt so happy . . . I just decided to wear it.'

Garth's face softened as he watched her. She looked away. Dolores and Linda were clearing plates, and in a minute, catching on, Sabrina pushed back her chair. 'No,' said Dolores. 'It's your birthday. You don't work tonight.'

They sang 'Happy Birthday,' presenting her with a Cuisinart food processor from all of them. 'Use with caution,' said Linda. 'Or everything becomes baby food. You should see what I did to onions the first time.'

'The idea was to chop them,' Martin said. 'Which took two seconds. One more and they were diced. In the flicker of an eyelash, they were minced, mangled, pureed and juiced. Fumes filled the house. We wept for a week.'

He and Linda laughed with the others, their storm over. Sabrina cut the birthday cake, Dolores poured coffee and the talk turned to the neighborhood fight for a stoplight near the school.

Sabrina looked around the table. A quiet evening with simple food, friendship, shared experiences, even acceptance of a private quarrel. Nothing unusual. No suspicion, among a husband and four close longtime friends, that she was not Stephanie Andersen. How could that be? She made slips of the tongue; she couldn't answer some of their questions; her timing was off. Why didn't anyone see that something was wrong?

Because people see what they expect to see. No one has any reason not to expect me to be Stephanie. Whatever I do, they'll find a way to explain it or ignore it because otherwise it doesn't make sense. When people believe something is true, they work hard to make it seem true.

'You were so quiet over coffee,' Garth said later as they walked home. 'Was something bothering you?'

'Oh, no. I was just being comfortable. It was a nice evening.'

He looked at her strangely but said nothing more until they reached their front porch. He put his hand on her arm. 'I wanted to tell you—' She stiffened and he dropped it immediately, but she felt the force of his will, holding back words.

'I'm sorry,' she said. 'It's just that I'm not settled down yet. In a few days—'

He put out his hand and touched her necklace. 'It meant a great deal to me that you wore this tonight. Stephanie, I want to understand you, what you're trying to do. If you can't talk about it now, I'll wait until you can. I won't push you, I'll stay away from our bed, if that's necessary for you now. But at some point we have to talk about where we are and where we're going. There are too many questions, too many unresolved angers. ... What is it, why are you crying?'

'I'm not.' But there were tears in her eyes. 'I'm sorry,' she said again. 'Please just give me a few days—'

He kissed her forehead. 'I think I'll stay out here for a few minutes. Why don't you go on upstairs? I'll lock up.'

She nodded. 'Good night, Garth.' Briefly she touched his hand. 'Thank you for a wonderful birthday.'

Thursday morning, after everyone had left, Sabrina climbed the stairs to explore the third floor. There were three rooms, each with an angled ceiling beneath the sloping roof. One was a storage room; the second, simply furnished with twin beds and a dresser, might have been a maid's room or a hideaway for Penny or Cliff when friends spent the night. But the third room tugged at her and she went in.

It was a sad room, empty except for a small desk and chair and some cardboard cartons covered with dust. Someone had cleaned it, hidden every sign of activity and left, a long time ago. Sabrina sat at the desk and opened the top drawer. Neat stacks of paper lay side by side, each labeled with the name of a North Shore suburb: detailed records of Stephanie's estate sales in the two years she had kept her business going. There were itemized inventories of the contents of her clients' houses, everything from paring knives to canopied beds, with the price she had assigned each item, the amount it had brought at the sale and her commission.

In the next drawer, Sabrina found color photographs Stephanie had taken of each client's house, inside and out, and of the rare and valuable silver, crystal, furniture and antiques in the sale. Leafing through them, Sabrina knew she could have found buyers for most of them among her customers in England and Europe. What a wonderful team she and Stephanie could have made! But when she had suggested it once, on the telephone, Stephanie had changed the subject. Perhaps she knew her business was failing and was already preparing to pack it away.

Sabrina touched the open drawers. She felt in her fingertips the tenderness with which her sister had neatly squared each stack of papers and photographs and placed it perfectly in line with the others. *And at the same time my bad years were ending and I was beginning to succeed. Stephanie, why didn't you tell me? We could have worked together and saved your business. Instead, you kept asking about Ambassadors and I kept telling you all my triumphs. How awful for you, to hear about my success while your own business was already failing. I should have known. I should have kept asking until you told me everything. I let you down.*

Downstairs, the doorbell rang. She jumped up and then realized she was crying. She wiped her eyes on the back of her hand. *As soon as I get home, we'll talk about working together. We need each other.* She wiped her eyes again and ran downstairs.

When she opened the door, Dolores Goldner walked casually through the house to the kitchen. Sabrina followed, astonished at the intrusion. But was it an intrusion? Dolores must do this all the time, she thought. As Stephanie probably does in her house.

In England, the closest friends wait to be invited inside. In America, where even strangers call each other by their first names, friends walk in without asking.

'We have to talk about Linda,' Dolores said, sitting at the

163

table in the breakfast room. She turned, looking for something.

'I was about to make tea,' Sabrina said.

'The Chinese converted you to tea-drinking? That's why I see no coffeepot?'

Morning coffee. Sabrina remembered. She turned her back to make a fresh pot and her mouth curved in a small, wicked smile as she played with the truth. 'You can't believe how strange coffee seems to me. I feel as if I've been drinking nothing but tea for years.'

'Well, at least you didn't come back in blue trousers and jacket, or whatever it is they're wearing these days.'

'No, but everything I put on feels strange, too. As if I'm wearing it for the first time.'

'You're too impressionable. If you traveled more you'd get over that. Look what one trip did for you – drinking tea, hiding photographs ... you even look different somehow. Are you doing something new with your hair?'

'No, does it look new? I'm sure it's just what you said: I'm feeling different about who I am.'

'Yes, well, let's talk about Linda. She and Marty are in trouble. We must do something.'

Sabrina poured coffee into two mugs and sat down. 'For example?'

'No cream? Good heavens, Stephanie, aren't you carrying this too far?'

'Sorry, I was thinking about Linda.' At the refrigerator she hesitated, then decided against a pitcher and brought the carton to the table.

As Dolores talked about Linda, Sabrina's other self, the cool observer, watched: two women in a sun-filled breakfast room, drinking coffee, talking about their friend who was unhappy. The observer felt ashamed of herself, playing a reckless game of being Sabrina while Dolores was concerned about Linda. Sabrina disliked people who tried to arrange other people's lives – fleetingly, she thought of Antonio – but it was hard to dislike Dolores; she really cared about her friends. If she tried to manage them, it was because she wanted them to be happy.

'Stephanie? Are you with me? You look like you're a million miles away.'

'No, I heard you. I was just thinking how nice it is that people care about each other.'

Dolores looked surprised. 'I should think so. Now how about it? Lunch next week with Linda and then the crystal exhibit at the Palmer House. She needs a chance to talk. Can you get off work one day?'

I won't be here. But Stephanie would want to do it. 'I think so. Can I let you know on Monday?'

'Of course. We won't go without you.' She got up and walked back through the house as casually as she had come in. 'Will I see you at the soccer game this afternoon?'

'Yes.'

Sabrina had promised Cliff she would be there, and she found the school athletic field a few minutes before the game began. Cliff was slouching nonchalantly with his team, but his face lit up as he saw her and ran over. 'We're playing Lakeside. They're in third place. We'll win. The only one to worry about is the tall guy; he's their best forward.'

Behind Sabrina, about forty women and a few men watched the play, the women tense and silent, the men shouting instructions or criticism at their sons. Dolores came to sit with her, but Sabrina barely noticed. She and Stephanie had grown up with soccer in Europe, and she had kept up with it in the last ten years; some of the men in her circle were top amateur players. She knew the game as well as most Americans knew baseball, and within a few minutes she was caught up in the action.

Cliff was good, she saw; he was alert and fast, and his teammates trusted him. 'Go!' she breathed when another forward passed him the ball, and he moved it skillfully in short kicks towards the goal, twisting and darting around the Lakeside defenders. Sabrina jumped to her feet as if she ran with him, feeling the joy and excitement of the chase. Seconds later, with a thundering kick, Cliff sent the ball flying past the goalie to score for his cheering, shouting team.

'A prouder parent could not be found,' said Garth, beside her.

She turned quickly. 'I didn't know you were coming.'

'Neither did I. But I recalled your just criticism of my missing past games. What's the score?'

'One to nothing. Cliff's point.'

'I could tell that by looking at you.'

A proud parent. She felt like one. 'I'm glad you came,' she said to Garth. 'Cliff will be so pleased.'

He was; Sabrina saw his grin from across the field as he ran to them at halftime. By then he had made a second goal. 'Next half I'll do even better,' he said. 'Did you watch Pat Ryan? The tall guy? Is he mad! He made a bet with his team that he'd score more than me.'

Pat Ryan made three goals in the second half. One of Cliff's teammates scored, but Cliff had been guarded fiercely and had not gotten near the goal. A few minutes from the end of the game, with his team tied three to three, he was angry and frustrated. Seeing the desperation in his face, Sabrina shook her head. 'He's lost sight of the game.' Garth started to say something when a shout came from the field.

'Cliff! Here!' A forward on his team was yelling at him, but Cliff, taking the ball down the field along the sideline, ignored him. The forward had broken free of the Lakeside defenders and had a clear shot at the goal. 'Pass! Pass!' he screamed. No one from Lakeside was between them; it was a perfect play. Cliff looked up briefly and saw the play, but he also saw a small opening in his own path to the goal. 'Pass!' This time his coach shouted it – an order. Cliff scowled, hesitated, then, keeping the ball in his control, feinted to the left to maneuver through the opening.

'Oh, he's good,' Sabrina said. 'He has wonderful control. But he can't . . . he's going to lose the ball.'

Lakeside defenders had moved in to close Cliff's path to the goal, and one of them slid feet first into him, knocking the ball away. 'Got it!' cried a teammate, and kicked it to the waiting Pat Ryan, who ran it down field, with none of Cliff's grace but with the lumbering determination of an eleven-year-old about to win a bet. And in the last seconds of the game, with a triumphant howl, he kicked the ball past the goalie, making the winning score for his team.

At first Cliff would not talk about it. 'Coach chewed me

out,' he said once they were home. He sulked in his room while Penny set the table. Sabrina made a salad and took out the stew she had had cooking slowly in the oven all afternoon. Garth thought of asking when she had begun to enjoy soccer as a game instead of a duty, but he knew she could say bitingly, as in the past, that if he spent time with his family he might notice changes in them. So he let it go.

Cliff's sulking was a cloud over the dinner table. 'Punishment or reprimand?' Garth asked, ready to sympathize.

'None of your business,' Cliff said sullenly, his eyes on his plate.

'Clifford!' Sabrina was outraged. 'How dare you! Look at me. Look at me, I said!' Startled, he looked up. 'Who do you think you are to talk to your father like that? I thought we could talk about the game, what happens when you forget you're part of a team, but we won't talk about anything until you apologize. Now!'

'I didn't forget!' Cliff said hotly. 'I was trying—'

'I'm waiting for your apology.'

'Look, Mom, I had an opening to the goal—'

'Cliff!'

She stared him down. From the corner of her eye she saw Garth watching her. Apparently she had gone too far and wasn't behaving like Stephanie. But for the moment she didn't care. Garth had flinched at Cliff's rudeness, and she had reacted instantly. She would not have him hurt, not after last night, on their front porch, when he had given her understanding and affection, privacy – and time.

'Sorry,' Cliff mumbled.

'I couldn't quite make that out,' she said calmly.

'I'm sorry!' Cliff shouted. 'I'm benched for the next game.'

'Too rough,' said Garth. 'Half a game would have been sufficient.'

'Yeah, sure, tell that to the coach.'

'Maybe I will.'

'No, thanks anyway, Dad, he'd just give me more shit if you did.'

'Cliff!' said Sabrina.

Garth held back a smile. 'Some words are better for the locker room than the dinner table.'

'Yeah, okay, sorry.' He turned to Sabrina. 'What did you mean, I forgot I was part of a team?'

'You wanted to make Pat Ryan lose his bet, so you made a grandstand play, which a good team player wouldn't do.'

'I did *not*—'

'You had a teammate with a clear shot at the goal. But all you cared about was scoring the winning goal yourself.'

'But I thought I could. There was an opening—'

'With the whole other team closing in on it. And you knew it.'

'I had a chance.'

'With a miracle.'

'So what? At least it was a chance. Aren't I ever supposed to take chances?'

'Of course you should.' Sabrina smiled, almost to herself. 'Taking chances can be wonderful. But you have to evaluate the risks. Know what you're getting into. Otherwise, you're just being foolhardy.' She looked at him thoughtfully. 'You're a fine player, Cliff. You move well; you have good control and timing. But if you act like a one-man team, you're sunk, no matter how good you are.'

Cliff looked puzzled. 'How come you know so much about soccer? I thought you didn't like it.'

'I read a book. I felt silly not knowing what was happening.' Quickly Sabrina turned to ask Penny about the history test she had quizzed her on at breakfast.

Garth watched his wife as she talked. How lively and animated she was, as she had been last night at the Goldners'. Lively and animated with everyone, in fact – except her husband. Probably she'd been that way for a long time, but he didn't think it had been so obvious before her trip. He felt diminished, not important enough for her liveliness, not even important enough anymore for her to pretend.

Sabrina glanced at him as she poured coffee. What was he glowering at? Which of her mistakes?

'What did you do today?' he asked.

'Oh – Dolores came over for coffee.'

'Something special? Or just to talk?'

'She's mapping a campaign to make Linda happy. Isn't it curious how Dolores tries to arrange us the same way she arranges her flowers? Do you suppose one day she'll enter all of us in some contest like Midwest Marriages Fall Competition?'

He laughed. 'Would we win?'

'Does Dolores ever lose?' she countered. 'I did do something special today. I went upstairs to my old office.'

'And what did you find?'

'Dust. Memories. But it was exciting to go through the records, and I was thinking maybe I could start up in business again. I read the *Evanston Review*, and there are estate sales all over the North Shore. I suppose it's inflation, and people moving back to the city, or into smaller places when their children go to college . . . '

Her voice trailed away. Garth was looking past her, his face smooth and uninterested. He had glanced at her once, long enough to see her bright eyes that matched the excitement in her voice; long enough to think to himself that she had more enthusiasm for a defunct business than she had for him. 'If that's what you want,' he said distantly. 'It seems risky, though, unless you know why you failed before.'

A wave of fury swept Sabrina. She had cared enough about his feelings to risk giving herself away when Cliff was rude to him, but as soon as she mentioned the estate business he turned cold. He hadn't asked how she might make it succeed this time, or if he could help her. He reminded her of Antonio talking about her 'little shop'. Now she knew why Stephanie was angry at him; he cared for nothing but himself. She was surprised at how hurt and disappointed she was.

'I'm going to the lab,' he said, pushing back his chair. 'If you're up, I'll stop in later to say good night.'

She nodded. Just what she wanted: a quiet evening at home. But still she had a sense of loss, and as the front door clicked shut, the house loomed around her and she felt very much alone.

The atmosphere was strained at breakfast; even Penny and Cliff were subdued. Sabrina quizzed Cliff for his daily spelling test, longer than usual since the Friday list included words from all week. Penny asked again about Mrs Casey, and Sabrina said she would be seeing her next week. 'Early dinner tonight, Mom, okay?' asked Cliff. 'We both have parties to go to.' Then they were gone and she and Garth were alone.

He opened and shut his briefcase. 'I'm sorry about last night. I have no right to criticize you for lack of interest in my work if I show none in yours.'

What lack of interest? she thought. Of course Stephanie is interested in your work. But she didn't want to quarrel; she missed the comfort of Garth's smile. 'Thank you,' she said.

'If you want to talk about it now—'

'It can wait.' She looked at his briefcase. 'Should you be going?'

He kissed her cheek. 'Department meeting in half an hour. See you tonight.'

At dinner Garth was restless. Penny and Cliff charged in and out, getting ready to go to separate parties, and as soon as they left he stood and went to the window. 'How about a walk? I've been sitting in my office all day, watching students frolic by the lake. Do you recall why I decided to graduate those many years ago instead of remaining a perpetual student? I've forgotten.'

'So you could *give* exams instead of having to take them.'

He nodded. 'I was a practical youth. Which reminds me, I brought you something.' He left the room and came back with a paper bag. 'Compliments of the university. Which asks only that you make that excellent steak often.'

She pulled out a porcelain mortar and pestle. 'Wonderful; of course I will. What is it used for in the lab?'

'I have no idea. I stole it from the chemists. You might boil it for two or three days before using it.' Laughing, she took it to the kitchen. Garth followed, carrying their cups and the coffeepot. 'How about that walk?'

'I should clean up; Penny and Cliff left in such a hurry—'

'It can wait. Please.'

'You're not going back to the lab?'

'No, did you expect me to? Do you have other plans for the evening?'

'Of course not. I'd like to take a walk.'

The sun was low on the horizon and the air was soft and warm, with the fresh smell of the lake and the dusky fragrance of fall flowers. As they crossed the park, the water stretched before them, calm and densely blue beneath the fading sky. Far out, a few sailboats gleamed sharply white against the dark waves. Silent joggers ran past groups of boys playing touch football, and a small dog ran through the bushes, charging squirrels. Beneath the trees, lovers walked.

Garth took Sabrina's hand as they turned to follow the shore. In the slanting rays of the sun, their shadows stretched far over the water, mingling and separating. Sabrina leaned down to tie her shoe, and when she stood up she stepped to the side, a little distance from Garth. They walked that way, not touching.

'Vivian told me she saw you the other day,' said Garth.

'Who?'

'Vivian Goodman. She said you met at the Art Institute.'

'Oh. Vivian. I forgot to tell you. She said you'd been wonderful to her, but she's still worried. Can you do anything more or is it all up to the vice president now?'

He slowed and looked at her. 'Did Vivian tell you the story?'

'Well' – *Stephanie didn't know about it? Why not?* – 'she could tell that I was interested—'

'You pretended to be interested.'

'I *was* interested.' Her hands were cold. 'She's very strong, but a lot of things are getting to her – she might have to move, her children would have to change schools, and' – *What was her husband's name?* – 'and Hans just quit his job. I admire her and I like her. Of course I was interested.' She plunged ahead, taking a chance. 'If I didn't seem interested before, probably it was because it was different, hearing about it from you and hearing it from her.'

'You didn't hear it from me. You weren't interested enough to listen.'

'That's what I mean.'

171

She knew that made no sense, but Garth let it pass. 'I haven't talked to the vice president yet. Next week, I think.' He began to describe the members of the tenure committee he headed. Sabrina listened and at the same time considered her sister's marriage.

Last night she had been furious at Garth's lack of interest in her estate business. But *was* Stephanie interested in Garth's work? She didn't know. If Stephanie wasn't interested, she must have good reasons. But I don't need to know them, Sabrina thought; they're between Stephanie and Garth. I won't even think about it. She concentrated on what Garth was saying; when he described William Webster she laughed at his pungent words and understood Vivian's admiration.

It grew dark, and they walked leisurely in the pale glow of the Victorian lampposts lining the lake-shore path. They were silent, but it was a comfortable silence. Sabrina felt the quiet strength of the man beside her, his undemanding presence. He was a companion. She was not alone, but still she was a separate person, allowed to be herself.

And just who is that? She smiled in the darkness. *For a little while longer, both of us.*

'Daddy says yes,' Penny reported on Saturday morning, 'if you say yes. A bike ride and a picnic. Please, can we go? I can collect leaves for my science class and Cliff wants to find a toad.'

'Why not? It sounds like fun.' I haven't ridden in years, she thought. But no one ever forgets how to ride a bike. They packed bread and cold meat, cheese and apples, and chilled cans of ginger ale.

'What about dessert?' Penny asked.

'We'll buy donuts on the way.'

'You didn't forget! Cliff said you'd forget, but you didn't!'

Forget what? 'Why should I forget?'

''Cause you've been forgetting things lately and Cliff said you'd forget that we always get donuts on picnics, but I said you wouldn't and I was right, so can we go now?'

'Yes.' Sabrina handed her the baskets. 'Will you and Cliff help your Dad fasten these on the bikes?'

'Aren't you coming?'

'As soon as I finish cleaning up.'

As she put away the leftovers and wiped the counter, Sabrina mused about donuts. Had Stephanie told her? Or was it simply one more thing she couldn't explain?

'Mom!' Cliff bellowed, and she joined the three of them to begin her first bicycle trip in almost fifteen years.

She hadn't forgotten. And her legs were strong from playing tennis. Within a few blocks she knew she could ride as far and as hard as the rest of her family. Riding behind the others, she put her face up to the blue and gold sky and let her body find its own rhythm, muscles in harmony, while her mind drifted.

No one had told her about the donuts. Or the nightgown and bathrobe, or settling down to read in the bedroom armchair. Curious certainties. Was it because they were twins? She and Stephanie always read new studies and reports on twins, laughing at some because they were so foolish, recognizing the truth in others. But no one had ever tried the experiment of having twins take each other's place and live each other's lives. If they had, would one twin suddenly say, as she had on her second night here, 'I'll think about both of me tomorrow'?

She wondered if Stephanie had felt the same in London. We'll talk about it, she thought, when we meet at the airport on Monday.

Monday. Day after tomorrow. The week was slipping away. It wasn't enough, really. She'd barely had a chance to get to know Penny and Cliff and feel part of a family. And she hadn't had a minute to look at her London life from this distance, to try to sort it out. Wasn't that the main reason she'd agreed to the switch? To slow down her roller coaster life—

'Stephanie! Watch out!'

'Mom! There's a—!'

'Mommy!'

Sabrina heard their shouts, and the squeal of tires, and swung her head to the right to see a pickup truck bearing down on her. She swerved, cutting her wheel sharply to the left, skidding in the dry dirt on the road. As she tried to straighten out, the truck nicked her back wheel, knocking the bike against the curb. She was flung through the air against a tree, her left hand twisted beneath her head. She heard something snap, heard Garth call her name, and then the golden day went black.

In the darkness of pain and shock, Sabrina caught a word, a question, a cry. She tried to tell everything to slow down and wait for her, but the pieces rushed past. Garth was holding her, whispering her name – not her name, her sister's, but she was shivering and couldn't tell him he had the wrong name. Strangers were telling Garth to wait in the other room – but she needed him; didn't they know that? She was lying on a cot, rolling along a smooth floor; then someone moved her left wrist and a stab of pain wrenched her whole body. 'Don't!' she cried.

'Only be a minute, Stephanie; just hold on.'

Nat Goldner's voice, then his smiling face. Blinding lights, her arm strapped down below a square black box. X rays. But Nat had her name wrong, just as Garth had. 'Wait.' It came out in a whisper. Shivering, she cleared her throat. 'Have to tell you—'

'Hold on, my dear,' said Nat. 'Better if you don't talk; just relax.' She felt a needle in her right arm, and in a minute the shivering eased. And then she was too drowsy to worry about what they said.

'Mild concussion,' Nat was saying to Garth when Sabrina began to pay attention again. She was on a cot in a small cubicle enclosed in light green curtains. And her left arm felt peculiar. She reached over with her right hand and touched a plaster cast. 'Awake?' asked Nat. He and Garth looked down at her, Nat smiling, Garth's eyes dark with worry. Where were the children?

'Penny . . . Cliff,' she said through dry lips.

'In the waiting room,' said Nat. 'I've told them you're fine. You can see them in a minute. In fact, you can go home soon if you follow orders. Here, drink this.'

He put an arm beneath her shoulders and eased her up so she could drink. She had a terrible headache. 'Now listen, Stephanie, I've told Garth what you need to do—'

'Wait.' Why did they keep calling her by her sister's name?

'Just listen. You've got a fractured wrist and a mild concussion. No permanent damage; not even a scar. Now I've told this to Garth, but I'll tell you, too; take it easy for a few days. No work – office or home; let your family cook and clean house. You can shower if you keep the cast dry; wrap it in a plastic bag. Talk as little as possible for the next twenty-four hours. Drink six glasses of water a day and snack between meals. There's no medical reason for that, but it'll give you something to think about besides your headache. Which should be much better by tomorrow night. We'll X-ray the wrist again in four weeks; if it's mended we'll take the cast off then. Any questions?'

'Why do you call me Stephanie?'

'Because I've always called you Stephanie. Should I call you Mrs Andersen just because you're my patient? I'll give you a few tranquilizers, enough for a week. You'll be all right; maybe disoriented for awhile, but nothing serious. Don't worry. Now rest for a few minutes. We'll be right back.'

She lay quietly, looking at the cracks in the ceiling. Mrs Andersen. Stephanie. Garth. She raised her head and looked at the blue jeans and shirt she was wearing.

Stephanie's.

Stephanie in London. Without a broken wrist.

Oh, my God, I've got to call Stephanie.

Chapter 11

When Stephanie's plane landed at Heathrow Airport and she took a taxi to Cadogan Square, it was almost ten o'clock at night. For sixteen hours she had traveled across continents and time zones while her imagination spun into a whirlwind around the week ahead, and by the time she moved through customs and settled into a taxi, she was in a trance of exhaustion. Resting her head against the seat, she watched the lights flashing past. She had seen them from the air: a sprawling mosaic that filled her vision as the plane came in to land. Now she saw them separately: shops, lampposts, the windows of apartments. The lights of London.

She had been here the year before, visiting her sister. Sabrina had met her plane and taken her to Cadogan Square, where she had unlocked the door of her wonderful house and welcomed Stephanie inside. Now, in the dark taxi, Stephanie opened the soft leather purse in her lap and took out a set of keys. This time she was not a visitor. This time she would unlock the door. This time she was going home.

But the door swung open just as she reached it. 'Welcome home, my lady!' Mrs Thirkell beamed. 'You *have* been missed!' She had coins ready and tipped the cabbie before picking up the luggage he had dropped inside the door. 'You'll find a small repast in the dining room; I made your favorite trifle, and a few other dishes to tempt you, though I'm sure you don't need tempting after all that foreign food. You must be starved for home cooking. I was sure you'd be skin and bones, but I must admit you do look fine. Oh, my lady, I am glad you're back. Will you go up first, or straight to the dining room?'

My lady. Through her exhaustion, Stephanie thrilled to it and what it meant. A house organized around her comfort, everything taken care of, everything in order. But she was so tired. Tomorrow she would be able to appreciate it.

'I'll go up,' she said. 'I'm really too tired to eat.' She began to wish Mrs Thirkell good night, but stopped at the stricken look on her face. She saw in it the hours of preparation that had gone into her 'small repast,' her affection for Sabrina, her happy anticipation of seeing my lady's gratitude for good English food after wandering in foreign lands. Stephanie had never had a maid or a housekeeper. Sabrina would have known immediately that Mrs Thirkell's beaming face was more important than her own exhaustion.

'On second thought,' she said softly, turning toward the dining room, 'the trifle sounds wonderful. The Chinese have nothing to compare with it. I'll have something now, Mrs Thirkell, and then perhaps tomorrow morning you'll indulge me with breakfast in my room.'

176

'Oh, my lady, exactly what I planned. You go ahead now; everything is ready for you. I'll just take these bags upstairs.'

The jelly and the custard of the trifle drifted through her dreams that night, between Nicholas Blackford's pastries scattered on a Shanghai street and the roast she had cooked for her family the night before she left for China. Above the food floated Mrs Thirkell's rosy smile, surrounded by the bright lights of London and the bronze door knocker, shaped like a hand holding a scroll, that led the way into Sabrina's house.

The images clung to Stephanie's memory, so that when she awoke in the morning she knew instantly where she was. She woke slowly, stretching like a cat between smooth sheets of Egyptian cotton as fine as silk. She had not been able to find any nightgowns when she undressed the night before and now, with the cool sheets caressing her skin, she was aware of her nude body as if for the first time. She stretched again and at last opened her eyes.

The bedroom was large and L-shaped, the walls covered in striped silk of pale blue and ivory, a peacock-blue carpet on the floor. The high Louis XIV bed and night tables were in the small part of the room; a sitting room took up the large part, with a love seat and chaise before the fireplace, two French bureaux along one wall and a matching dressing table nearby. A round table with a floor-length damask cloth and two upholstered chairs were placed beside high windows overlooking the walled backyard and terrace four floors below. It was an exquisite room, at once soft and vivid, spacious and snug.

Stephanie walked nude about the room, surprising herself. How easy it was, how free and confident she felt. Brushing her fingers across silks and polished woods, the marble fireplace and velvet chaise, she came to the tall mirror beside the dressing table and stood on tiptoe before it, spreading her arms wide. 'My lady,' she said to her reflection, and smiled at the brightness in her eyes.

Excitement was spreading through her like a flower opening wide. She looked about the luxurious room and listened to the silence. No one was calling for breakfast to be made or a button to be sewed on; no dirty clothes were piled up behind doors, waiting to be washed; the office staff did not expect her. She was alone. She was free. She was Lady Sabrina Longworth.

She rang for Mrs Thirkell and asked for breakfast in half an hour. What time was it? It didn't matter.

In the carpeted bath and dressing room, she turned on the shower and stepped into the triangular pale yellow tub bordered on one side by trailing green plants and on the other by a recessed shelf of oils, soaps, brushes and shampoos. Debating among the unfamiliar names, she chose one at random. As the perfumed steam swirled around her, she thought with a sigh of pleasure that she had a week to try them all.

But suddenly, as she sat at the small table in the window, wearing a flowered silk robe, her hair drying in the sun, watching Mrs Thirkell arrange the breakfast dishes and morning newspaper before her, everything changed – as if a door had been opened, letting an icy wind cut through the cozy room.

'What will you be wanting this week, my lady?' Mrs Thirkell was asking. 'I'll arrange to have Doris come in if you'll be entertaining, and I think Frank should give us an extra day; that was a halfhearted job he did on the windows last time. Princess Alexandra called last night after you'd gone to sleep; she said she would call back today unless you care to call her. I'll be going to the market this morning, so if you will tell me your plans . . . '

Stephanie looked out the window, feeling helpless. She wasn't Sabrina Longworth; how could she pretend to be? Mrs Thirkell knew more about this kind of life than she did. She had none of her sister's sophistication and confidence with servants; she was ill at ease in the world of wealth. She was exactly what she had called herself in Mr Su's antique shop; a suburban housewife. About to make a laughingstock of both herself and her sister.

Mrs Thirkell was waiting for instructions. Stephanie shivered in the icy wind that had shattered her excitement. There was nothing she could do with her week of freedom but

178

hide in the house, where no one could see her and point a scornful finger.

'My lady, are you ill? Shall I close the window?'

'No.' Stephanie shook herself. 'It's all right, Mrs Thirkell; the air is warm. But I think I did catch something in China – maybe an Oriental flu – so I'll be staying in for a few days. And no entertaining. I'll leave the shopping up to you; the usual things.'

Worried lines creased Mrs Thirkell's forehead. 'Dr Farr could come over this morning, my lady—'

'No, no . . . I'll call if I don't get better. But I'm sure I'll be fine. In a few days, a week, I'll be back to normal.'

'And you won't be going to Ambassadors, my lady?'

'Not for a few days.'

'Well, then, if you have everything you need—'

'Yes, thank you, Mrs Thirkell; this all looks lovely.'

'Then I'll leave you with your breakfast. Though it's probably cold by now; I can warm it up in a minute—'

'Mrs Thirkell. Everything is fine.'

'All right, my lady. If you say so. I'll be going then.'

Stephanie picked up her spoon. If she had to be imprisoned, what more comfortable place, complete with a mother? Who feeds the prisoner well, she thought wryly as she ate sliced melon and strawberries. The coddled eggs and croissants were cool, but she was so hungry that she ate everything. By the time she finished the tea, still hot in its insulated server, she felt better. I can go sight-seeing, she thought. That would be safe.

But first there were the closets, and the two bureaus. The night before, she'd had a glimpse at the clothes inside them, a whiff of scent clinging to soft fabrics. She planned to try on a few each day, over the whole week, but once she began she could not stop. It was like having free run of a designer shop: silk and lace underthings, cashmere sweaters and silk blouses, suits, dresses, evening gowns, shoes and shawls. And jewelry, tucked into a velvet-lined Russian chest.

She was trying on a dinner dress when, once again, without warning, her mood changed. The dress was of lilac silk, closely following her body from narrow shoulder straps to a flaring hem at her ankles. Holding the matching jacket

179

trimmed in purple braid, Stephanie walked to the mirror and looked at her reflection.

Sabrina gazed back at her.

How had it happened? She stood with Sabrina's regal poise, balanced lightly on her feet, head high, eyes bright, lips curved expectantly. Slipping her feet into wisps of black high-heeled shoes and holding the jacket over her shoulder with one finger, she tilted her head, smiled exultantly and made a deep curtsy to Lady Sabrina Longworth.

There is nothing, she thought, that I cannot do.

Filled with energy, she looked at the checklist Sabrina had written and called Ambassadors. 'I'll be in to check the mail. Brian, but not much more; I'm a bit under the weather, and if there's nothing urgent, I'll stay home for a few days. What day would you like to take off?'

'Thursday, my lady, if that is satisfactory.'

'Perfectly.'

She listened to her voice. Smooth and controlled. She had never had an employee; never learned to talk to one. But to Brian it was a voice he knew. And on Thursday she would go in to check Sabrina's mail.

Mrs Thirkell returned, full of worry, and found Stephanie emptying one purse and filling another. 'I'm going to take a walk, Mrs Thirkell. Your wonderful breakfast almost cured me. I'll want a quiet week, however, so you can expect me for dinner every night. Do you see my watch anywhere? I can't seem to find it.'

'Wouldn't you have put it in its regular place, my lady?'

Stephanie paused. 'I have no idea. I was so tired last night I hardly knew my own name. I remember that excellent trifle, but—'

'And here it is' said Mrs Thirkell triumphantly. 'You may have been tired, but you put it exactly where it belongs.'

Stephanie looked at the watch nestled in a small lucite box on the dressing table. 'Amazing,' she murmured.

'Well, there,' said Mrs Thirkell comfortably. 'Habit does wonderful things for us. Here you are, my lady.'

Stephanie put on the watch and glanced at the time. Almost three-thirty. She was stunned. Where had the day gone? Penny and Cliff would be home any – no, of course they wouldn't – at least, not here. In Evanston. Sabrina would be waiting – Sabrina! She was supposed to call at – what time was it in Evanston? Nine-thirty in the morning. It was all right, then; she'd remembered in time.

But she'd almost forgotten. Guilt swept through her. How could she forget her family? How could she let almost a whole day go by without thinking of her own family?

'When would you like dinner, my lady?' asked Mrs Thirkell.

'Oh. At . . . the usual time. I won't be out long.'

She shut the bedroom door. Sitting on the chaise, the telephone in her lap, she closed her eyes. There was her house, speckled with shade from the oak trees in the yard. There was the kitchen, honey-colored in the sunlight, and her children, grabbing books and lunch boxes as they left for school. And there was her husband's back as he walked to the campus. Where was Sabrina? Alone by now; probably exploring the house. This might be her first telephone call. Stephanie smiled mischievously as she gave the operator her number in Evanston.

'Am I speaking to the lady of the house? This is Lady Longworth in London, and I wish to speak to—'

'Stephanie!' cried Sabrina, an ocean away. 'How wonderful!'

Stephanie tucked her legs under her, as she always did when they had a long talk, and began to ask about Garth and the children and answer Sabrina's questions. 'Sabrina,' she asked. 'Did you ever tell me about the box on your dressing table where you put your watch at night?'

'I might have. I don't remember. Why?'

'You probably did; I put it there last night when I was wandering around totally exhausted, and stuffed with Mrs Thirkell's trifle.'

Sabrina laughed. 'She's so proud of her trifle. And she knows I love it. She'll probably make another one for your birthday.'

'Should I call you then? You always call me, and Garth might wonder—'

'Why don't I just tell him we talked when you called to ask

about my trip? Enjoy your week; don't worry about telephone calls.'

Stephanie heard impatience in Sabrina's voice. 'Yes, he'll believe that. Are you in a hurry?'

'Oh, it's just that I have so much to do – the house and grocery shopping—'

Stephanie knew; errands, chores, the daily routine. After they said goodbye, she pictured Sabrina moving about her rooms, cooking in her kitchen, talking to her family, eating breakfast with Garth, sitting across the dinner table from Garth . . .

She wanted to call back and talk some more, but Sabrina had been impatient. And, after all, thought Stephanie, it's her house right now; I shouldn't interfere. She's not interfering with me. She jumped up and ran down the three flights of stairs to the front door. The week would pass all too quickly; it was time she got acquainted with her neighborhood.

Skirting the park, she walked to Sloane Square, smiling at its contrasts: the old Royal Court Theatre opposite the modern Peter Jones department store, and in the center a fountain with reliefs of Charles II and his mistress, Nell Gwynne, in happy dalliance. Respectable London, she thought; racy London. Letting visitors think what they like. Chicago tries harder to impress us.

She was looking for differences to make the week more of an adventure. Walking up the other side of Sloane Street, she admired the sleek window displays of art and antiques, fashion, shoes, jewelry and books. No shopping today, she told herself sternly, determined to watch her money – and then, unable to resist, bought a sampling of handmade candies at Bendicks, and a small vial of perfume at Taylor of London.

Nibbling on a candy, Stephanie strolled unhurriedly. She felt light and untethered, as if she were floating. How odd to feel that way, she thought, but then, passing Children's Bazaar, she knew why. *No one knew where she was.* No one was expecting her. She was alone; she was anonymous; she was free.

She passed strangers, some with closed, private faces, some

openly admiring her beauty, most simply absorbed in their own lives. No one looked at her as if she were an outsider, and suddenly she did not feel like one. She bought a magazine, handling the unfamiliar coins speedily enough to satisfy the clerk. Watching for landmarks, she easily found her way home. Her key worked smoothly in her front door the first time she tried it. Mrs Thirkell, telling her the mail was on the desk in the study, peered closely into her face as she asked if her flu was really better and showed no suspicion that she was not three inches from Lady Longworth.

Stephanie hugged her delight to herself as she climbed to the third-floor study. There is nothing I cannot do, she thought again. And silently she thanked Sabrina.

'My lady, I forgot to tell you,' said Mrs Thirkell on the house phone. 'Now that you're back the flowers are coming again.'

'Flowers,' she said cautiously.

'I put them in the drawing room, as usual.'

'I see. Thank you.' Stephanie walked down one flight and there they were, dominating the room, overwhelming, absurd, magnificent: three dozen red roses rising from a crystal globe. And nestled among them, like bits of luminous moonlight, a dozen great white orchids.

She had never seen anything like it. The scent of the roses reached her down the length of the room, and she walked toward them, thinking how ridiculous to do anything on such a scale, what a flagrant waste of money – and how impressive. She read the card.

> Welcome home, my lovely Sabrina. You have asked me not to call, so I do not call. But I return to London next week, and I rely on your goodness and the pleasant hours we have spent together to move you to give me an evening and then, at last, your hand as my wife.
>
> Antonio.

'My lady,' said Mrs Thirkell, as Stephanie tucked the card back among the flowers. 'Princess Alexandra.'

Alexandra walked in behind her, tall, blonde, striking. Stephanie had never met her; when she had visited Sabrina the year before, Alexandra was in France. But, seeing her walk in, Stephanie recognized her as a character come to life from the pages of Sabrina's letters – the daughter of a bit player in Hollywood who lived out all her mother's dreams by marrying a prince and moving easily among European nobility. She made a mock curtsy to Stephanie. 'Couldn't resist the chance to greet the returned traveler. Did it do the trick?'

'The trick?'

'Finding new ways of handling old dilemmas. Wasn't that what you said you were going off to China for?'

'I'm trying something new; I'm not sure yet it will do any good.'

'Well, in the meantime, you can revel at my house tomorrow night. A small do in your honor.'

'A small—?'

'Birthday party. Honey, I apologize. I wrote you about it, honest to God I did, but it just never got mailed. I don't know how these things happen in a house full of servants – they never happen to you, do they? Anyway, it doesn't matter, because you told me you weren't making plans for the week, so of course you're free and you know I wouldn't let your birthday pass without a celebration. Some of your friends are coming, I think about sixteen, and we'll call it a welcome-home party if you've stopped counting birthdays, so don't argue with me, just show up in casual finery at eight. I'm counting on you.'

'I think I have some kind of flu; I shouldn't—'

'The best cure for flu is a party. Ask any sensible doctor.'

'Well . . . I'll let you know.'

Alexandra blew her a kiss. 'See you tomorrow,' she said, and was gone. But before Stephanie could think about the party, the phone calls began, each one announced by Mrs Thirkell in a voice sternly disapproving of anyone who would force my lady to talk when she had the flu. Michel Bernard called from Paris to ask if Alexandra's party was still on; he and Jolie would be there. Andrea Vernon thrilled that her ballroom, redecorated by Sabrina with a hundred new lamps, was being featured in an Italian magazine, and the editor wanted Sabrina in the pictures they would be taking in two weeks. 'I'll let you know,' Stephanie said. Amelia Blackford called to ask if Sabrina would care to accompany Nicholas to the Chilton auction next week. 'I'll let you know,' Stephanie said.

Between calls, she opened the mail – a cornucopia of invitations. House parties, tennis matches, dinners, a fox hunt in Derbyshire, a luncheon in honor of a Comtesse in Paris, a dozen charity balls between October and May. To Stephanie they were as overwhelming as Antonio's flowers: too much – yet wonderful. And just as she had caught the fragrance of the roses from far off, she could imagine the brilliance and gaiety promised by the heavy parchment and elaborate lettering of each invitation.

Piling them neatly for Sabrina, she realized wistfully that, between telephone calls and the mail, Sabrina's calendar for months ahead was more crowded than her own for this one week. All she had was – she looked at the calendar – a hairdresser appointment and a fitting with the dressmaker. And Alexandra's party.

But was she going to the party? The idea terrified and tantalized her. She didn't want to go and make a fool of herself; but after seeing Sabrina's photographs, she wanted to see Alexandra's house. And how wonderful to be the guest of honor at one of her parties.

After dinner, curled up on the chaise in the bedroom with books on London from Sabrina's library, Stephanie thought about Alexandra's party. She thought about it as she fell asleep, she woke up thinking about it. I'll decide later, she told herself. After I do some sight-seeing.

But first, reluctantly, she telephoned Sabrina's hairdresser to cancel her appointment. He would know instantly that her hair had been cut by someone else. We can fool a husband, she thought wryly, but not a hairdresser. But I will go to the dressmaker; I've always wanted one, and this is my chance.

And Alexandra's invitation is my chance for a party this week. One party. To balance all those invitations. Why not? Climbing the steps of Mrs Pemberley's flat on a warm September morning, Stephanie held her head high. I'll celebrate Lady Sabrina Longworth's thirty-second birthday in style, and no one will know I'm really celebrating the birthday of a suburban housewife who never even had a dressmaker.

Mrs Pemberley adjusted the three-way mirror. 'Madame perhaps gained a pound or two on her Chinese excursion,' she said through a mouthful of pins.

Stephanie looked down at her bent head and said nothing.

'But, of course,' she added hastily, 'madame's figure is so superb it does not matter.' Her fingers, pinning a dart in the suede dress, trembled.

She's afraid, Stephanie thought, afraid I'll be offended and find another dressmaker. It was the first time she had ever felt the power that influential people have over those who serve them.

'Now if madame will look,' said Mrs Pemberley, getting to her feet. 'I made a small change at the shoulder, here, so the sleeve moves more gracefully, but otherwise it is as madame wished. As you see—' She opened a glossy French magazine to a photograph of a model in a suede dress. And suddenly Stephanie understood the high fashion in her sister's closet – thousands of dollars worth of designer clothes costing a fraction of that because she had found a dressmaker who could copy photographs down to the smallest seam, modified to suit Sabrina's flair.

She looked from the magazine to her reflected image. 'Marvelous,' she murmured, and Mrs Pemberley's face relaxed into a smile. She brought out another dress and then another, followed by an evening gown, two suits sleek enough to wear to dinner after a day of work, a floor-length wool paisley skirt with a velvet cloak and a pair of pants with a hacking jacket. As Stephanie tried them on, Mrs Pemberley made adjustments and chatted about other customers, many of them obviously sent to her by Sabrina.

'—and Princess Alexandra tells me it is your birthday today, madame; my very best wishes. The party sounds quite festive.'

'I beg your pardon?' Stephanie was startled. If she made a mistake tonight, how long would it be before everyone knew it?

Mrs Pemberley's fear returned; she clamped her lips so that no further personal remarks would slip through. Stephanie felt sorry for her but said nothing, and the fitting ended in silence. 'The garments will be ready in a week, madame,' said Mrs Pemberley as she was leaving.

Stephanie nodded. She felt guilty for causing her worry. 'I'm very pleased with them,' she said, and left quickly. She wasn't sure she liked having the power that Sabrina and her friends took for granted.

As soon as she left Mrs Pemberley, Stephanie became anonymous again. Riding double-decker buses and the underground, with its clean-swept cars and velvet seats, she explored from Kensington Church Street to Brook's Mews in Bond Street. The buildings were not as tall as American skyscrapers, the shops smaller but more numerous, making Stephanie think of rooms in a vast museum filled with fabulous objects – antique furniture, porcelain, chandeliers, cut glass, clocks, dolls, jewelry and paintings. Gazing and dreaming, she felt like a young girl again, shopping with Sabrina and her mother in the enchanted world of open markets and small dusty shops. How simple everything had seemed when they were children! No complicated marriage, no worries about money, no search for a different kind of life.

But we ran away from the chauffeur, she remembered with a smile. Wanting to be free.

The statue of King George I in Grosvenor Square looked blankly past her as she remembered Athens. I've done it again, she thought. Run away to be free. Across the square stretched the block-long American Embassy where they had visited occasionally with their father. She walked toward it. First I ran away from my father, and then from Garth. She walked past it. But of course I'm going back to Garth.

She joined the crowds strolling on Park Lane along the green expanse of Hyde Park, nannies pushing baby carriages, dowdy dowagers, free-skirted young girls talking of discos, businessmen in derby hats, businesswomen in suits and white blouses. Harrods and then home, she decided, and quickened her walk until she saw the distinctive round awnings with scalloped edges and the store's name in bold handwriting – the largest department store in Europe and one of the most luxurious anywhere in the world, even boasting its own uniformed doorman.

She wandered happily through the aisles, looking for a gift she could leave behind for Sabrina when she went back to Evanston, and was in the Wedgwood room when, behind her, someone cried, 'Sabrina!'

'Sabrina, isn't this amazing?' She was hugged and kissed on the cheek by an exquisite young woman, small and delicate, with a halo of ash-blond hair and wide gray eyes. 'We're going to see you tonight and now here you are. Happy birthday!'

Stephanie stared. 'Gabrielle! You haven't changed a bit!'

'In two weeks? I hope not. Unless you mean . . . have you already heard? Who from? We were waiting to tell you first.'

'Heard what?' Stephanie's heart was racing; what a stupid thing to say. But she had been so surprised – Gabrielle de Martel, Sabrina's roommate at Juliette, here in the middle of Harrods. Stephanie hadn't seen her in almost fifteen years, but she looked just the same, though Sabrina had written that she was divorced and living in London, modeling for a cosmetics firm. Her voice was the same too: light and a little breathless.

'Oh, good, you haven't heard. Here's my news.'

Stephanie looked up as Gabrielle put her hand on the arm of a man standing behind her and brought him forward. He towered over her, handsome, broad-shouldered, muscular, with thick blond hair and impatient brown eyes, exactly as Sabrina had described him. Brooks Westermarck, president of Westermarck Cosmetics; wealthy, hardworking, a favorite of society reporters and photographers, always accompanied by a different beautiful woman

'Welcome home, Sabrina,' he said pleasantly. 'Did you bring me my Chinese dancer?'

Dancer. Now what? Stephanie despaired. I can't keep up; there are too many—Then she remembered the carved jade figures Sabrina had bought in Peking. Which was Brooks's dancer? She didn't know. 'Of course,' she said easily. She could put off giving it to him for the week. 'But I still don't know your news.'

'We're living together,' said Gabrielle. 'You wouldn't advise me, so I made up my own mind. Now tell me, what would your advice have been?'

'To live with Brooks,' said Stephanie instantly.

Brooks laughed. 'Wise woman. Will you have dinner with us tomorrow night, Sabrina?'

'To celebrate,' Gabrielle added. 'At Annabel's. Brooks has been a member for years, but I've never been there. Do come.'

'Oh, not this week; I really planned to stay home the whole—'

'Because Antonio is out of town? He wouldn't mind; we're quite respectable. And I've been waiting to celebrate until you got back. Please, I want you to.'

'And what is more important than what Gaby wants?' asked Brooks, amused.

Well, why not? Stephanie thought. If Sabrina can have a full calendar, so can I. 'I will, then; thank you. But since it's your celebration, I'll expect you to do all the talking.'

'Wonderfully tactful, Lady Longworth.' said Brooks, still amused. 'You'll make Gaby the happiest woman at Annabel's.'

The honeymoon, Stephanie thought, surprising herself with her bitterness. Just beginning. Once Garth and I were like that, our faces shining with happiness, as if we had a wonderful secret. And we did: we were in love. How long ago that seems. I don't even remember how it feels.

At home, Mrs Thirkell brought her tea to the study as she went through the mail and telephone messages. And then she began to get ready for Alexandra's party.

In the bath, bubbles rising languorously about her, she heard the telephone and then Mrs Thirkell coming upstairs to stand outside the bathroom door. 'Princess Alexandra called, my lady. Her chauffeur will come for you at eight. What dress shall I put out?'

'I'll take care of it, Mrs Thirkell,' Stephanie said, wondering if she could ask her for a suggestion. She shook her head. Sabrina wouldn't do that. Sabrina would decide for herself.

And whatever she chose would be right. Because if you are Lady Sabrina Longworth, who will tell you that you have on the wrong dress? Or that you are not clever enough to keep up with the people you meet?

And when she walked into Alexandra's salon, she knew she was right. She stood in the center of the room, poised, slender, as simple and elegant as a jewel in a full-length emerald-green taffeta skirt and a white satin blouse with tiny rhinestone buttons. Guests surrounded her with a confusion of smiles, kisses and birthday greetings; she saw Gabrielle and Brooks and was trying to match the other faces with Sabrina's descriptions when one lively voice rose above the others.

'And do you know, they bought identical Chinese dresses and I could not tell them apart? You would not have believed my bafflement! Now tell me,' said Nicholas Blackford, smiling with genial wickedness at Stephanie as the other guests looked on. 'Which one are you, really? 'Fess up! You're Stephanie, come to fool us all; isn't that right?'

Stephanie was stunned, the center of attention with nothing to say. She felt sick. Sabrina was successfully deceiving a husband and children, but she couldn't even fool casual friends. She lowered her eyes and caught the light flashing from her rhinestone buttons. In an instant her head came up. She knew she looked exactly like Sabrina; no one suspected anything, Nicholas was playing a game. I can play, too, she thought.

She had hesitated only a few seconds. Looking at Nicholas's small figure bouncing on the balls of his feet, she put on a worried frown. 'Nicholas, you've confused me so much I'm not sure myself. But I've always trusted your judgment, so I put myself in your hands. You tell me who I am, and that's who I'll be.'

Everyone burst into laughter and applause. 'She's got you, Nicky,' said Alexandra. 'Who is she?'

Nicholas bowed over Stephanie's hand and kissed it. 'Who else but our magnificent Sabrina? I never had a moment's doubt, my dear. In China I was confused because of that dreadful diet I was on. You know, I was starving the entire time I was there.'

Stephanie smiled, the knot of tension unraveling inside her. 'As I recall, the pastry-shop clerks heard all about your diet. Many times.'

Amid the laughter, Alexandra led them to a buffet of hors d'oeuvres. Stephanie's breathing returned to normal. It was going to be all right. She was going to be all right.

'I wish I'd met your sister last year,' Alexandra said. 'Is she really your double?'

'No, of course not. We caught Nicholas with an armload of pastries, and he was so embarrassed he made up the first excuse he could think of.' Stephanie listened to herself in amazement. How easily she lied. But she knew why it was easy. These people heard what they wanted to hear. Whatever she said, they would make it fit what they expected her to say or wanted her to say. Did they really listen to her? Did they really look at her? Only as much as they wanted to. As she and Alexandra laughed together, she felt herself slide smoothly into place. The week was finally hers.

'Nicholas and his games,' said Alexandra.

Stephanie, envying her statuesque beauty and flamboyant gypsy dress, had been trying not to stare; now, with her new confidence, she looked boldly at her. 'You look magnificent. A gypsy queen.'

'It was your idea, honey. And you were right, as always. Now look, you're not eating and it's your party. Fill up your plate: grape leaves, spinach something with pine nuts, flaming Saganaki – where's Arnold with the match?'

'Arnold?'

'The caterer, honey. Why can't you ever remember his name?'

'Maybe I don't like the way he combs his hair,' Stephanie said, thinking: How incredible to have a caterer for only sixteen people. She'd given dinners for twenty or more with only Garth to help her clean up afterwards.

Arnold came from the kitchen with a long match and set aflame the squares of Saganaki cheese, fried in butter and surrounded with brandy. Stephanie looked at his hair, combed forward so that he looked like a sheep dog. How had she known? Had Sabrina mentioned a caterer named Arnold with sheep-dog hair?

'Sabrina, you look wonderful,' someone said in a low voice. 'No worries in China?'

She turned and met bright eyes in a pleasant face; a small man, ordinary looking; she would never notice him in a crowd. That was exactly the way Sabrina had described him: Michel Bernard.

'What should I worry about in China?' she asked

'Nothing; you're absolutely right. But when we got your letter we were afraid your news might spoil the trip.'

'Oh. Well, there wasn't time to think; our tour guide organized every minute—' She felt her way cautiously, with no idea what he was talking about. 'What – what did you think of my letter?'

'We thought it was wonderful, of course; and you were wonderful to have the courage to write it'. His voice dropped even lower. 'Not many experts would admit they'd been taken in by a forgery. But I want you to know it helped us. Oddly enough, not the stork as much as the names on the certificate you sent. Some of those names have been used more than once – would you believe it?'

She shook her head.

'It seems to be their first real mistake. You'd think they'd be smart enough to make up different names for each fake certificate.'

He paused, waiting for Stephanie to say something. She nodded.

'But the story's delayed by all this new information. We won't be ready to publish before November, middle or end of the month. That could help you, don't you think?'

'I think so . . . '

'Especially if you're going to try to get the stork back. Have you decided? Or don't you think the grand Olivia will keep your secret?'

'I don't know.'

'If we can do anything to help—'

Stephanie was dizzy. 'You could tell me what you've found,' she said desperately.

'Since we talked last? Not much; mostly confirmation of

what we already told you. But it's not a bad idea to go over the whole story; how about Monday? We'll be out of town until then.'

'Not Monday.' Monday morning she would be on her way to meet Sabrina in Chicago. Monday afternoon Sabrina would be flying back to London. 'Can't we talk this weekend?'

'Maybe. We'll call you from Paris on Thursday or Friday when we know our schedule. What do I hear?'

Stephanie heard it,too, softly but growing louder: a lilting Greek melody strummed on a bouzouki. As the guests grew quiet, listening, Alexandra pulled aside a curtain at one end of the room to reveal a small orchestra with the bouzouki player in front, sitting cross-legged on the floor. At his signal the orchestra picked up the melody, following the tunes his quick fingers wove together.

The lights dimmed. Like silent shadows, waiters set up a low table surrounded with large tasseled cushions, and set it with gold plates and goblets, baskets of pita bread, steaming platters of lamb and onion kebabs, shrimp in wine sauce, cod with tomatoes and currants, lemon chicken, bowls of fresh fruit and bottles of red and white wines from the Island of Rhodes, all illuminated by flickering candles set in saucers of floating camellias.

Alexandra took Stephanie's hand and led her to the cushion at the head of the table. 'The guest of honor.'

Wide-eyed, Stephanie felt like an awestruck girl from the country. How would Sabrina act? Pleased, but not overwhelmed; this was her world. She let herself look delighted and turned to Alexandra on her left. 'It's marvelous. You've become an expert on Greece.'

'Not me. Arnold has a Greek wife. I took her ideas and added a few of my own.'

'But,' said Stephanie, looking around the table, 'where are the sheeps' lungs fried in oil?'

'I vetoed them. How do you know about such things?'

'A long time ago we lived in Athens . . .' Stephanie told the story of the day she and Sabrina had escaped from their chauffeured limousine and walked into a street battle over Cyprus. Everyone fell silent, listening, and for a brief, clear moment she saw, as if from far off, the lavish table with its guests, and the small ghosts of two sisters huddled in a cellar, holding each other, while heavy boots tramped overhead. And in that moment she was both sisters: Stephanie living Sabrina's life; Sabrina describing a time when she and her sister Stephanie were frightened children, clinging together for protection.

'Poor things,' said Amelia Blackford. 'How terrifying for you.'

'Sabrina gave me courage,' said Stephanie softly. 'She always—'

'*Who?*'said Jolie and Michel together.

Stephanie laughed slightly. 'We gave each other courage.'

'Well,' said Amelia. 'Nothing that exciting ever happened to me.'

The spell was broken. The conversations resumed until the last of the baklava and thick black coffee was gone and Alexandra announced it was time for presents.

Everyone had brought something: Nicholas and Amelia, a nineteenth-century Saint Gobain hand mirror with a carved ivory handle; Michel and Jolie, a book of Greek art; Gabrielle and Brooks, a cashmere shawl from India; Alexandra, a set of crystal candlesticks. The other guests brought books, jeweled hair clasps, framed prints and a miniature porcelain dancer.

'And this,' said Alexandra, handing her a slender, silver-wrapped box. 'Antonio had it delivered. Do you want to open it now or at home?'

'Oh, now,' said Gabrielle. 'Do open it now.'

Stephanie was uncertain. 'Perhaps I'd better wait—' But the gift was already public. She tore off the paper and silently lifted from the box a gleaming strand of perfect star sapphires and diamonds. A note lay in the bottom of the box. She ignored it. There was a kind of brutality in Antonio's sending the gift to Alexandra's house, knowing it would likely be opened before a group of people – as if he had flung it in Sabrina's face, daring her to deny in public that he had the right to drape her in such jewels. Stephanie let the necklace

194

drop into the box. The others felt her embarrassment and said nothing.

Alexandra clapped her hands once. Dancers appeared, the lights were turned up and waiters moved about the table with after-dinner drinks. Stephanie excused herself to Alexandra. She wanted to be alone, and to see the house. 'I won't be long.'

'Take your time, honey. You know your way around.'

She didn't, but she remembered Sabrina's photographs. As the others watched the gyrations of a spectacular belly dancer, she slipped away and walked up the open staircase to the floor above.

She wandered from room to room in delight and pride. Sabrina had created an air of playfulness and exuberance that most designers, heavy-handed and pompous, never achieved, and now Stepanie could understand why the house was still being photographed for design magazines in America and Europe.

What luck, she thought enviously, to have such a chance – to take an empty house and create a home, an atmosphere, a place for parties and privacy and love ... oh, what a chance.

She stood before a whimsical Miro painting and gazed at the thick, childlike strokes, strong and full of purpose. What I wouldn't give for such a chance, she thought.

'Honey, you all right?'

She turned. 'Yes, I've been rude. I'm sorry.'

'It's your party and almost your house. If you want to be alone, don't apologize. What's he really like, your Antonio?'

'Occasionally crude.'

'That I know. That we just saw. And?'

'Occasionally pleasant.'

'How else could he keep you interested for almost a year? Okay, you'd rather not talk about him. Want me to show you something I discovered recently? You'll recognize it.' She led Stephanie downstairs to a dim corner of the salon and pointed to the floor. 'Isn't that amazing? Who do you suppose thought of such a thing?'

Stephanie bent down and looked at the small distinct S in

195

the design of the parquet floor. 'Clever,' she murmured, smiling. Sabrina had sent her a photograph of it, thinking no one else would ever know.

'Clever, indeed. You know, honey. I'm so thrilled with this place, you could have carved it six feet high over the front door. You didn't have to hide it.'

Still smiling, flushed with the pride and sense of ownership Sabrina had felt in completing the house, Stephanie touched the small letter with the toe of her shoe. 'It's big enough,' she said softly. 'It was enough that I knew I had left my mark.'

The next morning, haunted by her sister's mark in the floor, Stephanie went to Ambassadors. It was Brian's day off, and the shop was closed. She tried the keys on her ring until one of them opened the door.

She had been here before with Sabrina. Now she raised the shades on the front window and walked down the long narrow showroom modeled after an eighteenth-century salon. It was uncrowded and elegant, with a few fine pieces arranged in twos and threes, brightened by sunlight or the diffuse light of shaded lamps. At the back of the room, through a doorway, was Sabrina's office with the cherry table she used as a desk.

Stephanie sat at the table, taking in the long, low, crowded book-shelves, windows draped in antique velvet, oriental rugs and deep armchairs for visitors. Success and accomplishment were here, along with self-confidence, money, even power. She felt as small as her reflection in the silver tea service on a side table as she recaptured her feelings of the night before: pride, envy, ownership – and longing.

'I have to do something,' she said to her reflection. 'I've only done one thing, really: be a housewife. I've had one home for twelve years, one failed business, one man ... ' Wait, she told herself. Think about something to do, about getting back my own business. That's enough for now. Don't think about other failures. Only that one.

The chimes at the front door startled her. I forgot to lock it, she thought, and went to the showroom to explain that the shop was closed

'Aha, someone home after all,' said a heavyset man

hunched on a Regency armchair. He was taking off his shoes and massaging his feet. 'Lucky for you; you almost lost a sale. You work here? Well, of course you do, what a question. And you are one beautiful girl, which I'm sure you don't mind my saying. You have what Betty – my wife, that is – calls an English complexion. The wife says one thing about me: I can spot a foreigner even before they open their mouth, and I would know you for English anywhere. I see you're looking at your little chair here. I had to sit down, the wife's been dragging me in and out of antique shops all day. Couldn't even see the changing of the guard at Buckingham Palace, I thought my feet would fall off. She's somewhere, I came in here, your door was unlocked. I won't break your chair, if that's what's worrying you.'

'And what may I show you?' asked Stephanie, keeping her eyes lowered to hide the laughter in them. 'You could surprise your wife with something quite remarkable. For instance' – she went to a back shelf and returned with a French beaded evening bag and a magnifying glass – 'this dates from about 1690, a stunning piece of work – here, use the glass to look at it. Do you see the individual beads? And the stitching?'

He looked closely. The beads were no bigger than grains of sand, the stitches between them even tinier. Without the magnifying glass the floral design looked like a painting; under the glass it became a mosaic of wondrous delicacy.

'Not bad,' the man said admiringly. 'How the hell d'they do that?'

'I believe children made them. They probably suffered eyestrain, but the great ladies of the royal court had to have their evening bags.'

'Not bad.' he repeated. 'Betty'd like to be a great lady. How much?'

'Six hundred pounds,' said Stephanie, guessing from French bags she had seen in Bond Street.

'Don't give me pounds, give me dollars.'

'Twelve hundred dollars.'

He whistled. 'You've got a nerve, little lady. Two hundred, and that's probably too much.'

Stephanie was furious. How dare he try to bargain with her

as if Ambassadors was a stall in a flea market? She wanted to make this sale; it was suddenly very important that she sell something from Ambassadors, but she would make it on her terms, not those of some crude bargainer. She smiled gently. 'Where are you from, Mr—?'

'Pullem. Omaha. I'm in meat.'

Stephanie pictured him up to his chin in ground beef. 'And you go to Chicago on occasion? San Francisco? New York? New Orleans?' He nodded each time. 'And you take Betty.'

'Course. Kids are grown, nothing for her to do at home.'

'Do you know, Mr Pullem, in all those cities, and in every other city in America, Betty will be the only woman with an evening bag like this one? Everyone will beg to look at it. Every woman will want one. But there is no other exactly like it anywhere in the world.'

There was a pause. He turned the bag in his hands. 'Six hundred.'

'Is that in pounds?'

'Dollars! Dollars! Pounds are for meat, not money.'

Gently, Stephanie took the bag from him. 'I'm sorry, Mr Pullem. I would have been pleased to help you make your Betty a great lady.' She walked to the back of the store.

'Seven hundred!' he said. 'Make it seven-fifty and that's it.'

Stephanie turned. 'Mr Pullem. We do not bargain at Ambassadors.' She was arranging the bag on the shelf when she heard him stand up.

'You drive a hard bargain. Shoulda been an American.' He laid twelve one-hundred dollar bills on the table beside him. 'Betty doesn't like it I can return it, right?'

Stephanie wrapped the bag in tissue and a small box she found in Brian's office. 'Of course. I think you need not worry, however.'

He put on his shoes and reached for the box. As Stephanie gave it to him, with a receipt, he held onto her hand. 'You're one beautiful girl, you know. Hard bargains and all. Maybe I'll bring the wife in some day. When I make my second fortune.' He winked as he left.

Jubilantly, Stephanie let out her breath in a long sigh. I did it, she sang to herself; I can do anything. She locked the front door and put the money with a note in Brian's desk and twirled from his office to the cherry table. Standing there, she looked with a different air around the office and into the showroom. Now she belonged here. Like her sister, she had left her mark.

Annabel's only seems noisy to those who want a quiet evening. For most, the music and talk mean excitement: marriages begun or ended, affairs budding or withering, agreements concluded, acquaintances struck. The membership of Annabel's is distinguished, and so is the menu. In any season diners can order raspberries, asparagus, truffles or snails, flown in from private sources and elegantly served. Annabel's is a place to dine and dance, but more important, to see the ebb and flow of one's social world.

Maxim Stuyvesant often used Annabel's as a meeting place. The chatter and dim lights gave him more privacy than his office, and the staff would save his corner table for hours if they knew he was coming. In all the cities of the world where he conducted business and sought pleasure, Max looked for such a place. Annabel's, on Berkeley Square, was his favorite.

On Thursday night he arrived at nine with his guest, a small bearded man with piercing eyes magnified by round glasses and a cultivated air of boredom. As they settled themselves at Max's table, their waiter brought from the wine cellar a bottle of Chardonnay and opened it. Max sniffed the cork. 'The fish tonight?'

'Swordfish in sea urchin sauce. Very delicate. Very fine.'

He looked at his guest, who nodded. 'For both of us,' Max said. 'Let Louis select the rest of the meal. Bring some paté now, and give us half an hour before you serve the soup.'

'Louis?' asked his guest.

'The chef. He provides an excellent meal.'

'With half an hour for business.'

'With half an hour for pleasant conversation to put us in a proper mood for dining. Our business should take no more than a few minutes.' He filled their wine glasses. 'To the glories of the past.'

Ronald Dowling nodded, sipped, raised his eyebrows at the

quality of the wine and sipped again. 'The vase is all you claimed. I am impressed. Even in your dingy warehouse—'

'Not mine. Westbridge Imports.'

'They're the ones who brought it out? Across the Mediterranean to – where? France? Or directly on to Britain?'

Max smiled. 'Annabel's is noisy tonight; I didn't hear you. The Etruscan vase you saw comes from the collection of a noble English family forced to sell one of its estates to raise money. Westbridge Imports handled the estate sale; when they saw the vase they called me, knowing my clients are interested in ancient treasures and can afford to pay for them.'

Dowling smiled thinly. 'I saw the listing in the catalogue you sent me. You may tell that story to others, Stuyvesant, but I flew in from Toronto especially to see this vase. I'm paying you a million and a half dollars for it, and in return I expect the truth, not a fairy tale.'

'In art and sex one is never sure of the truth.'

'I'm not joking, Stuyvesant.'

'Ronald, if I told you an item was smuggled out of Turkey and listed as part of a duke's estate sale; that the duke was paid twenty thousand pounds to swear, if asked, that the item had been in his family for generations; and that the item will be smuggled into the country where its purchaser lives – would you not say that that sounds more like a fairy tale than my first story?'

Dowling's eyes gleamed. 'I'd say it sounds like more fun than drilling for oil and gas in western Canada – and a damn sight more dangerous.'

Max shrugged. 'Life is full of dangers. Try getting safely across Fifth Avenue in New York. Or the Via Veneto in Rome.'

They chuckled.

'All right,' Dowling said. 'Tomorrow I will deposit to your account in Switzerland ten percent of the purchase price in gold. When you deliver the vase to my home in Toronto, you'll receive the balance.'

'Not quite, Ronald. When the vase reaches Canada, approximately four weeks after the deposit of the gold, you will be notified. You will wish to examine it. When you are satisfied, you will arrange for the balance to be paid. And then you take possession.'

Dowling nodded. 'I was told you were a careful man. I like that. I'll call my agent in the morning.'

Max signaled to the waiter with his hand. 'Another bottle,' he said, and sat back, surveying the crowd. His survey stopped at a group of three people being shown to a table across the room. He gazed at one of them thoughtfully.

'—your other activities,' Dowling was saying. 'Real estate, you said? And art galleries? With so many legitimate—'

Max stood. 'Excuse me one moment; I must speak to someone.'

He moved smoothly between the tables and brass-covered pillars and was speaking as he reached the group. 'My dear Brooks, good to see you again after all these years. And Sabrina.' He lifted her hand to his lips. 'I had heard you were in South America. A malicious rumor?'

Looking up, Stephanie saw only the man, his bulk blocking her view of the room. His dark suit was superbly cut and his bearing assured, even arrogant. Red hair shot with gray frizzled in a mock halo around his head, and his flat eyes reflected her image, revealing nothing of himself. Her hand closely held in his, Stephanie was conscious of his power, and excitement flared within her. She lowered her eyes to hide it, but his face subtly changed and she knew he had seen. She had no idea who he was and glanced at Brooks, who was introducing Gabrielle.

'Max Stuyvesant, Gaby. Max. Gabrielle de Martel.'

Max deftly switched from Stephanie's hand to Gabrielle's, but the kiss he gave it was perfunctory. 'I believe you came to London about the time I left for New York.'

'Three years ago,' said Gabrielle, examining him with open curiosity. 'I've heard so much about you.'

He smiled amiably and turned back to Sabrina. 'Was it a malicious rumor that you were in Brazil?'

'Malicious or hopeful,' she said. 'Depending on who began it.'

He laughed. 'Your wit has not diminished. Later, after we have dined, will you dance with me?'

'I haven't—' she stopped. She hadn't danced in years, but had Sabrina? 'I'm sorry; I don't think so.'

'It would be a favor; I am assuming you would not criticize my lack of practice.'

She looked up at him, at the small smile on his lips, the flat gray eyes, watching. 'All right, I'd like to.'

'Until then. Brooks, Gabrielle; a pleasant dinner.' He bowed slightly and left.

'How odd,' said Gabrielle as the waiter poured their wine. 'You hear so many rumors about someone you feel you know him, and then he turns out to be completely different. You knew him years ago, didn't you, Sabrina? When you and Denton were married?'

'Yes,' Stephanie said cautiously. Had Sabrina liked him? Loved him? She had never mentioned his name. 'What rumors have you heard?'

'None that you haven't heard. He certainly seems more civilized than they make him out to be. But Brooks doesn't like him.'

Brooks gazed at her. 'You never fail to astonish me, Gabrielle. Was I impolite?'

'No. Impassive. The way you are when you disapprove of something I say or do, but you'll wait until later to spank me in private.'

'And have I ever spanked you?'

'Only with words.'

There was a pause. Brooks put his hand over Gabrielle's. 'I apologize. I never thought of a spanking. And I promise I will not spank Max Stuyvesant, in public or in private.'

Gabrielle laughed. 'I hope not. He might turn the tables.'

'Was there really an Annabel?' asked Stephanie. They were making her uncomfortable – childlike Gabrielle, who, surely, had been more grown-up long ago at Juliette, and Brooks, acting like a teacher, amused, critical, surprised when his student said something intelligent.

'I never met Annabel,' said Brooks as the waiter served their soup. 'But if you want to know the story of the club—'

'Where does he get his money?' asked Gabrielle.

Brooks sighed. 'The fascinating Max Stuyvesant. No one

really knows. He owns art galleries in Europe and the Americas, and he may be an agent, but none of that would account for his wealth. He's seen at auctions, and his private collection is considered one of the finest in the world. Beyond that, everything is rumor. He doesn't talk. And he's been gone for three years, so the rumors are no doubt even less reliable than usual.'

'Will you, Sabrina? Brian can manage Ambassadors another day, can't he? He did the whole time you were in China. And we'll be back Sunday evening. Sabrina? Have you been listening?'

'No, I'm sorry; I seem to have—'

'Drifted away. Now listen: Will you come with us to Switzerland?'

'Switzerland?'

'I repeat, since you were not listening. Tomorrow Brooks is flying to Bern on business, and I'm tagging along. I shall be dreadfully bored while he is working, so I'm asking you to join us. There's plenty of room in the plane, and Brooks will take care of your hotel room. We'll be back on Sunday. Yes?'

Stephanie did not hesitate. 'Yes.'

Gabrielle clapped her hands. A waiter cleared their plates, another poured coffee, a third divided a sugared Grand Marnier soufflé among them as they talked together like old friends. Stephanie smiled with pleasure. And her smile met the answering smile of Max Stuyvesant as he made his way once more to her table.

The dance floor was crowded, and they moved in a narrow space. The rhythm of the music, slow with a steady heartbeat in the bass, slid into Stephanie's blood, and her body swayed as she followed Max's lead.

'How is it we have never danced?' he asked.

'How is it we have never talked?' she responded recklessly. She felt young and unfettered, and she saw in his smile that she was beautiful and that he desired her.

'Talked,' he repeated. 'For some time I had the impression that you would have found cozy chats with me distasteful.'

'Which explains why we have never danced.'

'My impression or your distaste?'

'Both.'

'Very quick, Sabrina. Will you have dinner with me tomorrow night?'

'No.'

'How abrupt. Not even an excuse? The South American, for example?'

'I'm sorry. I'll be away until Sunday.'

'Sunday night, then.'

'Late Sunday.'

'I am free on Monday.'

'On Monday I'll ... be away again, for the day and evening.'

The dance ended. He still held her. 'We will find an evening. May I call you next week?'

Stephanie nodded, and they walked back to her table. She was shaken by her thoughts. She wanted him. A stranger – mysterious, arrogant, with cold eyes and an air of absolute assurance. So different from Garth, who was content to fill his own place in the world without demanding a larger one. How could she desire him? She had never desired anyone but Garth, and not even Garth, in this trembling way, for years. She breathed a sigh of thanks that she would be away for the next three days.

Which meant she would never see Max Stuyvesant again.

They reached the table. Gaby and Brooks were dancing and Stephanie hesitated. Well, then, she would never see him again. That was the best way to handle the feelings churning within her. 'Goodbye,' she said, unable to keep a regretful note from her voice.

He kissed her hand. 'Until next week.'

Stephanie watched him return to the table where his friend waited. She picked up her wine glass and a waiter rushed to fill it. The best way, she repeated to herself. She tasted the pale gold of her wine. Tomorrow they would leave for Bern.

The Lear jet was furnished with a built-in, curved leather couch, two armchairs and a long teak table used as a desk and for eating the Fortnum and Mason box lunches Brooks ordered for his trips. On the hour-and-a-half flight to Bern, Gabrielle and Stephanie feasted on French cheeses, bread and fruit, while Brooks read the reports of his managers in Bern.

'They're introducing a new line of cosmetics,' said Gabrielle. 'Or maybe an old line with new names. Brooks refuses to talk about it; you wouldn't believe the games they play with lipsticks and moisturizers and all the rest: passwords, codes, secret formulas, spies from other companies. It is big, big business.'

Stephanie rested her arm along the back of the soft leather couch, and looked through the window at the small, neat fields below, far different from the sprawling landscapes of America. But everything is different from America, she thought. Here is Stephanie Andersen, dashing off for a quick trip to Switzerland in a friend's private jet while her housekeeper tends her five-story town house and plans a tempting snack for Sunday night when my lady returns. 'Nice,' she said.

'What, the view? I like the Alps better. Do you know what I thought we might do? Visit Juliette. I haven't been back since we graduated, and it's less than an hour by train. What do you think?'

'I think I'd love it.'

But when they were there, standing in the park and looking up at the school's balconies and red tiled roof, they were dismayed. Nothing had changed, but – 'How small everything is!' they said. Professor Bossard's castle was just a large, handsome building in a pleasant park, neither as awesome nor as grand as it had seemed when they were students. 'And look how young the girls are,' Gabrielle marveled. 'Not nearly as sophisticated as we were.'

Stephanie smiled. 'Maybe we weren't.'

'Of course we were.'

'I don't know. We sat up there on the fourth floor and dreamed about growing up—'

'Third.'

'What?'

'We lived on the third floor. Your sister lived on the fourth, remember, with that girl, what was her name? The one from New York.'

'Dena Cardozo. You're right.' They wandered through the building — 'feeling older every minute,' Stephanie murmured. Professor Bossard was dead, his place taken by a rotund, white-bearded Santa whom they found in the gymnasium discussing tournaments with the fencing instructor.

Stephanie walked to the center of the room, imagining the foil in her hand, remembering a match she had lost, and a quarrel with Sabrina.

'Gaby,' she said abruptly, 'I'm starved. Let's go into town for something to eat.'

They walked down the hill, through the vineyards. 'I had a good time there,' said Gabrielle. 'But I was always disappointing people who expected too much of me. You knew you wanted to do something in art and antiques, but all I wanted was to find somebody to take care of me. To stand between me and the world and cherish me. Do you know what I mean?'

Stephanie nodded, her eyes on the choppy blue of Lake Geneva and the jagged Alps beyond the far shore. Wasn't that exactly what she had wanted with Garth? 'And now you have Brooks,' she said.

'Now I have Brooks. As long as I can walk the line that keeps him happy.'

In the town, they found the small café that had been their favorite when they were students. They sat outside in the sun and ordered lunch. 'Walk what line?' asked Stephanie.

'The one you warned me about.'

They were silent. 'And was I right?'

'You were always right about Brooks. He wants a child-bride he can mold and be proud of and be adored by. And he also wants someone who can fuck like a professional and make smart conversation at dinner.'

Taken aback, Stephanie said, 'Did I really say that?'

'Not exactly. But close. And I didn't believe you and now I do. So I play act: One minute I'm a little girl, and then I'm a demimonde who's had a hundred lovers, and then I switch

206

to the sharp lady who sees, for example, that he doesn't like Max Stuyvesant, even though he's trying to cover it up.'

'Not easy.'

'No. And I don't even know who I'm deceiving – him or me. But Sabrina, what can I do? I love him so much that I can't forget it for a minute; all I want is to sink into him and live there forever. And I'll do whatever I have to do to stay there.'

With her finger, Stephanie traced the red checks on the tablecloth, thinking of Garth, remembering New York before they were married, and their early years when everything was new and wonderful. He had loved her for what she was, not for what she could pretend to be.

They ought to be able to find that love again; it couldn't have disappeared completely. If she went home and told him she wanted to go back to the beginning ... but she couldn't go back. Not now, not today. How could she walk into her house and say, 'Hi, everybody, I'm home!' – and come face to face with Sabrina cooking dinner? But it's only three more days, she thought. Then I'll be back with Garth and my family. Not even a full three days. Just the weekend. And then I'll be home.

And what will be waiting for me?

A filthy anonymous letter about my husband, worries about money, Penny wanting art lessons, Cliff's shoplifting, and trying to start a business again.

All of it. Waiting for me. But I don't want to think about it now; there's nothing I can do, and it would just spoil the rest of my week. There's plenty of time to think about it when I'm home again. Plenty of time to take care of everything.

Gabrielle talked steadily on the train back to Bern, giving Stephanie new information about Sabrina and her life, the kind of details people take for granted. It's too bad I'm about to leave, she thought wryly. With these facts I could play Sabrina for weeks.

Still, she was nervous when Brooks shepherded them to the Kursaal after dinner; she had never gambled, and she didn't want to learn on Sabrina's money. But Brooks and Gabrielle took it for granted that he would buy chips for the three of them. So all I have to worry about now, Stephanie thought, is pretending I know how to play *boule*.

But it was so easy – a simplified form of roulette – that within a few minutes she was betting cautiously with the chips Brooks had stacked in front of her. Gabrielle leaned close. 'Brooks thinks you're being careful because you didn't buy your own chips. If you don't start being extravagant he'll be insulted. And very difficult to get along with.'

'No,' Stephanie said. 'It's just that it doesn't make sense to—'

Brooks interrupted. 'Of course, you're right; it can't compare with Monte Carlo, but it's the best Bern has to offer. We'll play for an hour or so and then Gaby wants to dance. Bet enough to make it interesting; all profits go to that new museum you're helping raise money for.'

Profits, Stephanie thought. When I've never gambled in my life.

But she began to win, thinking all the while how foolish it was to bet money on where a tiny bouncing ball would come to rest among nine slots. Surrounded by serious players, she bet whimsically on the first digit of her telephone number in Evanston, and won. She bet on the first number of her address, the first number of Penny's birthday, and the first number of Cliff's, and won all three times.

Gabrielle's eyes sparkled. 'What's your system?'

'Birthdays, addresses, telephone numbers.'

'Whose?'

'It doesn't seem to matter.'

'Sabrina, that's not a system; that's witchcraft.'

'You're probably right. Next thing you know, I'll turn into someone else.'

She bet the first digit of her London address. And she lost. It was so unexpected that she stopped short and stared at the little white ball that had betrayed her. She put a modest number of chips on the first digit of her London telephone number – and lost.

'Systems tend to do that,' said Brooks. 'So does witchcraft.'

Gabrielle, who had won once and lost twice on Stephanie's system, stood up and swept her remaining chips into her hand. 'These are for your museum, Sabrina. And I am for dancing.'

When they cashed in their chips, Stephanie had won a little over a thousand dollars. 'The system did well for the museum,' she said casually and followed Brooks and Gabrielle to a table near the orchestra.

It hit her as she was dancing with Brooks. The system did well for the museum? A week ago a thousand dollars would have seemed a miraculous windfall for groceries, paying bills, sending Penny to art classes, perhaps buying a new dress for herself. I'm becoming Sabrina, she thought. Thinking like the rest of them in this fairytale world.

'Sabrina,' said Gabrielle as they walked back to the hotel. 'This has been so wonderful I don't want it to end.'

'Neither do I.'

But tomorrow was Sunday. Her last day.

'Come home with me,' she suggested. 'I'll call Mrs Thirkell and tell her to expect us. She's only had me to feed this week, and she's happiest when she can show off for discriminating guests.'

Did she really know that about Mrs Thirkell? Of course she did. Because Sabrina knew it. And when they flew back Sunday evening and Stephanie led Gabrielle and Brooks upstairs into the drawing room, Mrs Thirkell's smile was so delighted, and her buffet supper so ample, that Stephanie knew she had chosen the perfect way to end her week: entertaining in her Cadogan Square home – before she had to leave it for good.

Chapter 12

From the time Garth brought her home from the hospital, Sabrina had not a moment alone. All she could think of was calling Stephanie, but Garth hovered over her, and Penny and Cliff danced about trying to be useful and admiring the cast that extended from her palm almost to her elbow. They brought her tea, ice cream and toasted English muffins, but all she wanted was to be alone for five minutes with the telephone. She lay on the couch, feeling trapped, her head pounding, as her family bustled about, being helpful.

By eight o'clock her eyes were closing. She tried to stay awake, but her headache and the medication were like heavy, muffling blankets and the house faded away as she sank into sleep.

'Let's get you to bed,' Garth said.

She jerked awake. 'No, I can manage——'

'Tomorrow you'll manage.' He lifted her and carried her upstairs to the bedroom, sitting her down on the bed. 'Leave everything to me.' He unbuttoned her blouse and slid the right sleeve off her arm, then eased the other over the cast. Half asleep, Sabrina closed her eyes. *I couldn't stop him even if I knew how. And it doesn't make any difference anyway.*

Supporting her with one arm, Garth pulled down her blue jeans and underpants, then unhooked her brassiere. He drew in his breath sharply as he saw the bruises covering the left side of her body. 'Poor love, you must feel as if that truck ran over you.' She opened her eyes, but he had moved to the bureau to take out a clean nightgown.

'I'm going to raise your arm; tell me if I hurt you.' He slipped the nightgown over her head. Like a child, she put her other arm through the strap as he held it. 'Now, stand up for a minute.' He pulled back the blanket and sheet, helped her into bed and covered her. For a moment he stood quietly looking down at her. 'If you're in pain, or need anything tonight, I'll be here. Just poke me and I'll wake up.'

Unexpectedly, tears came to her eyes. *You are so good. And I do want you near me. I hurt all over and I wish you would hold me and comfort me. But you're Stephanie's husband. I can't even tell you I'm glad you're close by.*

'Good night,' she said, and in a moment was asleep.

Garth was up and dressed before she awoke on Sunday morning. She had not heard him come to bed, had not been aware of him sleeping beside her, but when she opened her eyes he was there to help her dress, and he and the children stayed nearby for the rest of the day. Sabrina thought wryly of how she had told Stephanie she wanted the experience of a family. Well, she had it. But she wished she could have a few precious minutes of the aloneness of her London house.

In the afternoon Garth helped her upstairs to take a nap. As soon as he left the room she reached for the telephone, but it rang beneath her hand. Someone answered it downstairs, and before she could try again she fell asleep.

'Dolores called,' Garth said, coming in as she awoke. 'She's bringing dinner about six. And Linda has volunteered for Monday. If I go through town with my notebook, I may be able to sign up enough cooks for a year of dinners.' He paused, but she only smiled. 'Do you want to see Dolores when she comes?'

'Not today. Maybe I will tomorrow.' She felt defeated, making plans for tomorrow. Monday. The day she was supposed to meet Stephanie at the airport and go back to London, to pick up her own life. Our adventure is over, she thought. But how do I end it?

At the dinner table she was quiet as Garth served Dolores's casserole and pumpkin pie and made conversation with the children. He was baffled by his wife's behavior. She never gave in easily to pain or illness. But now she not only showed pain, she showed fear? – even something like panic. What was she afraid of? When he asked her, she shrank from him, shaking her head, so he dropped it. He felt helpless and angry. Why wouldn't she let him help her, let him be her husband instead of someone she feared or distrusted?

After dinner she refused his offer of a sponge bath and his helping hand to climb the stairs. 'I can manage. But thank you.'

She had stopped worrying about what Garth thought of her behavior; he would soon know the truth anyway. The problem was Stephanie. She would be leaving for the airport in a few hours. *I have to warn her, give her time to think about how she'll handle the mess I've made.*

She lay in bed, her mind spinning. She dozed, slept, woke when Garth came to bed, then forced herself to stay awake, watching the clock. One A.M., one-thirty, two. Eight A.M. in London. Garth's breathing was deep and regular. She slipped out of bed and crept down the stairs into the breakfast room, where she found the telephone in the dark and at last, in a low voice, gave the operator her own number.

The telephone rang in London; Sabrina could picture Mrs Thirkell when she answered, and her bedroom when Stephanie came on the line.

'Sabrina! I was just getting ready to leave. Is anything wrong?'

Rapidly, Sabrina told her about her accident.

'Are you badly hurt?'

'Nothing serious. I look a mess, bruised and battered, and I have an awful headache – a mild concussion, Nat says. But the real problem is my wrist. I ... fractured it. It's in a cast.'

Stephanie said nothing. Sabrina, her head pounding, closed her eyes. 'I had to warn you so you could think about it on the plane.'

Stephanie's voice was faint. 'Think about it?'

'How to tell Garth. Stephanie, I'm sorry, it's all my fault. At first I thought I could tell him and pave the way before you got here, but I can't, Stephanie; I'd only make things worse.'

There was no answer. 'Stephanie, don't you see, if you tell him right away, if the two of you talk about it together so he doesn't brood about it alone, you could work it out.'

The static of the telephone line stretched between them. In the peacock and ivory bedroom Stephanie listened to it, hunched over on the chaise, one arm held tightly across her stomach. 'Sabrina, you've lived with him for a week, do you honestly think he'd go on as if nothing had happened?'

'No, things would be different, but that doesn't mean they'd be worse. If you love each other—'

'Love has nothing to do with it. He'll say we've made a fool of him—'

'Well, we have, haven't we? He isn't a fool, but we fooled him.'

'*You* fooled him. And how do I make that all right? It's not like a quarrel—'

'No.' In a quarrel, Sabrina thought, two people are equal. In a deception, one person knows everything and the other knows nothing. When Garth discovers that he's been trying

212

to patch the problems of his marriage with a woman who is not his wife but his sister-in-law; that his wife and sister-in-law have played a monstrous joke on him . . . She slumped in her chair. 'I thought I was giving you a gift. A week for yourself. But all I've brought is destruction.'

'It's my fault. He's my husband. I didn't let myself think what would happen if he found out.' Stephanie closed her eyes. He'd never understand why I did it, she thought, never forgive me. It would be the end of everything for us. 'I can't tell him,' she said.

'But if I do it—'

'No, that would be worse. Oh, I don't know what to do. If only we could . . . Sabrina! Why couldn't we fake it?'

'Fake—?'

'Tell Nat what we've done. I'll wear a cast and he could pretend to take care of me and no one would know the difference.'

'I thought of that. But if you could see me . . . Stephanie, my whole side is black and blue and I have a cut on my forehead—'

'Oh.' Stephanie suddenly felt very sleepy. All she wanted was to curl up and forget everything. 'Just a minute,' she said to Sabrina, and, putting the telephone in her lap, she rubbed her eyes with her fists like a child trying not to cry. Garth, I'm sorry, she said silently. I didn't realize what I was doing. And I'm afraid. I don't know what's going to happen. She looked at the telephone in her lap, connecting her to Sabrina, and through her to Garth. There was nothing else to do. She picked it up. 'Will you be at the airport?'

Sabrina hesitated. 'All right. Of course.'

'What is it? Can't you drive?'

'Nat said I shouldn't, but there's no reason—'

'No, it's all right. I guess I can meet you at home. But what about Penny and Cliff?'

'Cliff has soccer practice, and Penny can go to Barbara Goodman's. I'll take care of it.'

'I'll see you in a few hours.' Stephanie hung up before either of them could say anything else.

Sabrina covered her face with her hands. In the dark

silence the minutes passed. *Garth, I care about you. Forgive me. Stephanie, I love you, I wanted to give you—*

The telephone began to ring and she grabbed it. 'Stephanie?'

'Sabrina, I can't do it, I can't do it. Please help me. I can't face him, I can't tell him. I can't do it!'

'All right.' Sabrina took a deep breath. 'I'll talk to him this morning, as soon as Penny and Cliff—'

'No!'

'But what do you want me to do, then?'

'Stay there. Could you do that? Would it be too terrible for you to stay until the cast comes off, or whatever happens next? Would it be very long? A couple of weeks? How long would it be?'

'Nat said four weeks.' Sabrina sat up, her thoughts racing. *Stay here. But how can I? I have Ambassadors, my home, my friends, a future that I have to make. This is not my life.*

'What happens in four weeks?' Stephanie asked. Her voice was growing stronger.

'More X rays. And, if my wrist is healed, Nat takes off the cast.'

'Well, I could come back then. No one would ever know. Sabrina ... ' Stephanie's voice was still stronger, pleading but excited. 'Everything is fine here; I can even take care of Ambassadors for you. I sold the French beaded bag – I'll tell you about it later. And you could manage, I know you could. We'd just go on doing the same things we've been doing, more of the same. Doesn't it make sense to keep on? Sabrina? Just four more weeks? Then no one would be hurt.'

'Wait.' Sabrina said. Her headache was pressing against her eyes, and she tried to think. She probably could do it. The week had gone so quickly; four weeks wasn't a long time, and there still were things she wanted to do here. In fact, she liked it here. And it was Stephanie's decision. But—'Stephanie, I don't know if I can manage for four weeks ... with Garth.'

Stephanie sucked in her breath. The bedroom dimmed as clouds moved across the tall windows, broken here and there by a pale silver sun. 'He's gone longer than four weeks without making love to me.'

'Stephanie. Two weeks in China. One week just ended. And four more. Seven weeks. Do you really think—?'

'You can manage. I know you can. It means so much to me – to my marriage.'

'What about later?'

'What about it?'

'If Garth finds out later, what will you tell him? The longer it lasts, the more impossible it is to defend. Stephanie, you could explain one week and go on from there, but would you have a marriage if he found out we'd played this joke on him for five weeks?'

The clouds scudded past the window, playing hide and seek with the sun. 'I wouldn't have a marriage. But I don't think I'd have one now, either, if I came home this afternoon and told him. So what difference does it make? Sabrina, I'm *begging* you—'

A knot unraveled inside Sabrina, and a thought sprang full-blown within her: *I'll have a family for a while longer.* 'All right. But we have to talk; there are so many things to talk about. Ambassadors, Antonio – will you call me later, when I'm alone?'

'Of course, whenever you want. Sabrina, I wish I knew how to thank you. I know it isn't your kind of life, it's dull and—'

'Stephanie?'

Garth's voice.

Sabrina cupped her hand over the phone. 'I have to go; Garth is awake. Call me later, about ten my time.'

'Yes, I will. Sabrina, thank—'

She hung up and was standing at the refrigerator when Garth came into the kitchen.

'Is anything wrong?' he asked.

'I was suddenly ravenous. Which probably means I've recovered.'

'I wish you'd wakened me.'

She smiled to ease the worry in his eyes. 'I wanted to let you sleep. But now that you're here, shall we finish Dolores's pumpkin pie?'

'At the risk of Clifford's wrath,' he said with a chuckle. And in the honey-coloured breakfast room, with the house dark and silent around them, they sat together and ate from one plate.

Chapter 13

Garth looked at his Monday morning genetics class and saw instead the sleeping face of Stephanie. Alabaster skin flushed with rose, auburn hair tumbled against the white pillow, eyelids fluttering as she dreamed.

A student asked a complicated question and he answered briefly. Smartass, he thought, trying to impress the professor with a question that could fill a book. The professor is not impressed. Anyway, he's groggy from 3:00AM pumpkin pie with his wife.

He dismissed the class early.

He'd call her, see how she was, then finish his paperwork so he could get to the lab before his next class. He took the stairs two at a time to his office. New gold lettering had appeared on the door: *Garth Andersen, Ph D Department Chairman*. He opened the door to tell his secretary to have it removed, then changed his mind. She had done it for him. For a year he'd resisted advertising himself while she argued that it was important for students and visitors to know he was chairman of the Department of Molecular Biology. Today, it seemed, she had ended the discussion by ordering the lettering on her own. He shrugged. It might make him seem more important to her and others; to him, the title simply meant more administrative work and less time in the lab.

He dialed his home number, but the line was busy. Beside the telephone was a reminder: 'Call Ted Morrow.' Damn, he'd forgotten.

He called and told him about the accident, and that Stephanie could not work for a week. 'And she won't be able to type for about four weeks, so if you hire someone else she says she'll understand.'

'Not to worry, Garth; we'll wait for her.'

Garth dialed his number again, but the line was still busy. He leafed through his mail. A bill for overdue books from the library, letters from biologists in Amsterdam and Stockholm, an advertisement for laboratory equipment, notice of a meeting with the vice president to discuss Vivian Goodman. If they kept going at this snail's pace, Vivian might get a life contract on her ninetieth birthday. And at the bottom of the stack, an airline ticket to San Francisco with his schedule for a week-long genetics conference in Berkeley beginning October 6. Less than two weeks away. Something else he'd forgotten.

He dialed Stephanie again. Busy. Probably everyone calling to see how she was. He looked through the conference schedule. There was no problem with his going to California. In two weeks Stephanie would be able to manage easily without him. But still, he shouldn't be gone for a week – not with everything between them so precarious. He picked up the phone and tried again to call her. Still busy. For the first time he thought something could be wrong. He looked at his watch. Plenty of time to go home and get back for his one-thirty class.

He found Stephanie in the breakfast room, talking on the telephone. 'I'll call if I need you,' she was saying, 'and you should call anytime you want. I think we've covered the important things—'

Her body became very still. Garth thought of the squirrels in their backyard who froze, alert and ready to flee, when they sensed movement nearby. He came up and put his hand on her shoulder, feeling the muscles tense beneath his fingers. 'When you're through,' he said casually. 'I was worried when I couldn't reach you on the phone.'

'—and if anything else comes up, we'll talk about it,' she said, finishing her sentence as if there had been no break in its smooth flow. 'Take care of yourself and don't worry about me; I'll manage.' She hung up and slowly turned around. Her eyes were shadowed. 'I'm sorry; I didn't think you'd try to call.'

'It didn't occur to you that I might be concerned?' He paused. 'Never mind. Who were you talking to?'

'My sister.'

'All morning? Did she invite you to London to recuperate?'

'No, she—'

'Then no doubt she is sending over her maid to do the housework.'

'No, Dolores is doing that.'

'What?'

'Dolores is sending Juanita, her maid, for a couple of days this week. All paid for. Why are you angry at Sabrina?'

'I'm not angry. I shouldn't have said anything; of course you'd want to talk to her after your accident. Did it make you feel better? Do you feel better?'

'Yes, I do. Are you playing hookey from your classes?'

'Dignified professors never play hookey. They are called away on urgent matters – a golf game, a dentist appointment, a love affair. Or a wife who might need help. Is Dolores really sending you her maid? I wish I'd thought of it.'

'You don't have a maid to send.'

'I could have kidnapped Juanita and brought her to you wrapped in a red ribbon. When is she coming?'

'Tomorrow.'

'Then how can I help you today? Grocery shopping?'

She laughed and opened the refrigerator. 'Look.' It was crammed with food. 'From Dolores and Linda and a parade of good samaritans. Even Ted Morrow's wife. How does news get around so fast?'

'Small town.' He searched the refrigerator, sniffing under lids and pulling out packages. 'Salmon salad, cheddar cheese, olives. Did anyone bring bread? Yes. And we have butter. Why don't you sit down and let me serve you? And then you should rest; you look pale.'

'I might do that.'

Garth filled a platter and put dishes and silver on the table. 'What important things did you and your sister cover?'

Absently rubbing the cast on her arm, Sabrina watched his hands as he filled their plates. 'Some ... problems. About Ambassadors. It seems fake porcelains are being sold to small galleries. We talked about checking for authenticity – that sort of thing.'

'It sounds like she bought one and discovered it was a fake after she'd sold it to a customer.'

She gave him a swift glance. 'Yes. If she asked your advice, what would you suggest she do?'

'Tell the customer the truth and buy it back as soon as she can. The longer she waits, the harder it will be to convince anyone, if the real story comes out, that she really meant to do the right thing.'

She bit her lip. 'Of course. The salmon is good, isn't it? Is there more?'

That was twice, Garth thought, that she'd changed the subject from her sister. Usually she related every detail of the glamorous London life that was a kind of endless fairy tale in her imagination. But now, instead of London, she was talking about the women who had come to the house all morning, bearing food.

'—and Vivian hadn't been here for ten minutes when Dolores turned into a pelican, quite haughty, with her neck growing longer every second. Vivian was completely bewildered, and she hadn't done anything, of course, except talk about people Dolores doesn't know. As soon as she left, Dolores unbent and became her other self, managerial but affectionate. Amazing how she puts up barriers when she's uncomfortable with someone.'

'And who else was here?'

'Linda, with some kind of Italian casserole all round and rosy and bubbling. They looked so much alike I couldn't tell them apart, but Linda bubbled with gossip, not tomatoes, so I knew which one to talk to—'

Garth was chuckling as he cleared the table. Dolores as a haughty pelican and Linda as one of her casseroles. He couldn't remember Stephanie ever being so sharp, observing their friends in fresh ways, witty but not cruel. And she looked different this morning – more vivid and excited. More beautiful. But then, how often had she accused him in the past of not really looking at her? What strangers they had become.

But it occurred to him that she was putting on some kind of performance, to entertain him, distract him from something. The phone call with her sister? Something else she

219

didn't want him to know? New ideas about herself, her marriage, that made her tense, worried, perhaps frightened, unpredictable. 'A few more days,' she said after their dinner at the Goldners'. But then she'd had the accident. Well, he could wait until she was ready to talk to him, and, meanwhile, she was trying to change their routine – a glass of wine together before dinner, showing interest in Vivian and the university, even cooking steak a new way.

He bent down to kiss her forehead. 'Take a nap. You'll need all your strength for dinner tonight; Penny and Cliff insist on cooking it.'

She looked alarmed. 'Can't they heat up Linda's casserole?'

'I'll recommend it. Call me if you need anything.'

'When will you be home?'

'As soon as I can. I hope by four or four-thirty.'

All through that afternoon and the next two days of meetings with graduate students, organizing his campus schedule and helping out at home, Garth thought about his wife. He had not thought about her this much in years – but then she had not puzzled him this much in years. He found himself hurrying home eagerly at the end of the day to be with her, and then he could not stop watching her. She would turn around and catch his steady gaze, and he would ask, quickly, how she was feeling.

'I'm much better,' she said with some impatience as they sat at dinner on Wednesday night. 'I shouldn't get so much attention. This is an excellent pot roast. Which of our benefactors made it?'

'Vivian brought it to the office this afternoon. She said she talked to you today.'

'Yes, we made a lunch date for next week. And she brought me the new issue of *Newsweek*. Why didn't you tell us you're in it?'

'A few paragraphs in a long article.'

'Dad's in *Newsweek*?' Cliff shouted. 'Where is it?' He bolted from his chair.

'The living room,' Sabrina called after him. 'Even a few paragraphs,' she said to Garth. 'They're part of something so important. And incredible.'

He looked at her curiously. 'You read the whole article?'

'Well, of course. You were in it, even your picture. But I would have read it anyway; it's a fantastic story.'

Cliff came back with the magazine folded to a page with photographs of three genetic engineering researchers: a blond woman at Harvard, a gray-haired professor from England and Garth in shirtsleeves in his laboratory. 'So stern,' Sabrina said, looking over Cliff's shoulder. 'As if you're about to flunk the whole university.'

Penny and Cliff giggled. 'What's it about, Dad?' Cliff asked.

'Read it. It's not too complicated.'

'Okay; but what's it *about*?'

As Garth took the magazine from Cliff and leafed through the article, Sabrina studied his face. Once, a long time ago, she had thought him stuffy and dull. Now, suddenly, he fascinated her. When she read the article that described him as one of the leading scientists in the field of genetic research, when she thought of him in the center of miraculous discoveries, he seemed to her like a being from another planet, mysterious and powerful, who knew things and did things she had never dreamed of. We're complete strangers, she thought. And without knowing why, she felt it was terribly important that she understand him.

'Yes, tell us,' she said. 'It isn't so simple. It's like a mystery with a new clue every time you turn the page.'

'Well put.' He smiled at her and she smiled back. 'It's been a long time since you felt that way.' Her smile faded, but Garth did not notice; he was pouring coffee. He looked up at his family and began to talk about his work.

When Garth had begun teaching, scientists had known little more than the structure of DNA and how it worked. But in the 1960s there was an explosion of knowledge in genetics and he found himself in the center of it. His calm manner and careful work, combined with daring leaps in his published papers, led to the invitation to participate in the month-long international seminar in Berkeley the August before Stephanie's trip to China. With that, he joined the ranks of the world's leading geneticists.

By now they were learning how to cut apart the DNA

molecule, ten-thousandths of an inch long, and replace a missing or damaged part by splicing in a healthy part from another DNA molecule. *Gene splicing*, *genetic engineering*, *recombinant DNA* – the phrases were dry and dull, but as he described them Garth's voice lifted, ringing with excitement at the marvels behind them.

And his family listened, absolutely still, absorbed in his words. As he looked at them sitting around the table, the blood coursed through Garth's veins; he felt alive and powerful and hugely happy. A man needed to talk about his work, to share it with his family. If he couldn't, no matter how important it might be to the rest of the world, it became somehow insignificant – a part of his life that filled hours of every day but still could not attract the interest of the most important people in his life.

Garth put his hand over his wife's and smiled at her, grateful because she had done this for him. And then he went on to tell them what was happening in laboratories all over the world, the subjects of the conferences he attended and the seminars he taught.

First there was research into genetic disease. In hemophilia, for example, the instructions for making blood-clotting chemicals are absent or not complete in the DNA. Scientists would isolate one cell with the damaged DNA and one from a healthy person, remove the part from the healthy DNA that carried the instructions for clotting and fuse it to the damaged DNA. Then they would put the repaired cell into a culture to reproduce until there were enough cells to inject into the hemophiliac, where they would continue to reproduce. And that person would no longer be in danger of bleeding to death with every cut.

At the same time, they were learning to make vaccines against disease. They would remove from a cell certain genes whose function was to make antibodies against a particular disease and splice those genes into bacteria. In a culture, this new strain of bacteria would multiply by the billions, becoming a factory for the production of those antibodies. And the antibodies could then be used to make a vaccine against that particular disease. For example: interferon, ready for testing to fight viral infections and cancer.

222

Or they would splice genes that control hormone-making into bacteria. And when the bacteria multiplied and the hormones were removed, they were used to fight disease. For example: insulin, being produced for use against diabetes.

Sabrina looked puzzled. 'I haven't read that hemophilia and diabetes have been cured.'

'They haven't. What I've told you is what we will be able to do soon, when we answer the questions still remaining.'

Sabrina looked at Garth's eyes, burning, intense, far-seeing, and heard in his voice the lure of limitless horizons. 'Not easy to come home,' she said lightly, 'and cut the grass or change a broken faucet, after you've been cutting DNA and changing forms of life.'

He gave her a long look. 'Thank you.' His voice was husky. 'That means more to me than anything you might have said.' He paused and looked around the table. 'But I note with astonishment that the dishes have not been washed.'

'We were listening to you,' Cliff said indignantly. 'Do we still have to clean up?'

'Have you created a new bacteria to do it?'

'You know I haven't.'

'Then I regret to say that leaves only you and Penny. Go on, now, both of you. It's late.'

It's late, he thought, leaning back with a sigh of pleasure. When did we last sit around the table, talking, being a family? I can't remember. But how hard have I tried lately to make it happen? He smiled at his wife. She had made it happen. 'All clear to you now?'

'I want to read more about it. It seems a little scary.'

'Awesome is more like it. The wonder of it, the leaps forward, the hope for people who never had hope before . . . But, at the moment, the best part for me is that you read the article and got us talking, shared my work for once, so you could understand why I get caught up in it and sometimes forget my family. Though right now I find it impossible to believe I could ever forget you.'

He went to her chair. Standing behind it, he put his hands on her shoulders and slid them down to enclose her breasts. Leaning down, he moved his lips along her hair, brushing it back from her ear. 'I think—'

'No,' she said tightly, and broke out of the circle of his arms to stand a little distance away.

She was very pale, her eyes averted, her face closed and frozen. 'Not now, not yet, at least not—'

Garth was stunned, and furious. He had been teased, then slapped down and dismissed. His wife indulging her whims. He strode to the door to get out, to get away from her, but her voice caught him.

'I'm sorry. I am sorry.' The words trembled, but she would not look at him. 'It hurts when I move ... my bruises ... I thought you knew how much it hurts me—'

'Bullshit.' He stood in the archway to the living room. 'Dolores isn't the only one who puts up barriers, is she, when the situation gets uncomfortable? She could take lessons from you.' His voice cut like steel. 'You needn't worry; I won't trouble you again. Force doesn't amuse me. Or arouse me. I'll take care that you don't, either.'

He slammed the front door and walked to the lake, breathing hard, damning his wife, and himself for allowing her to fool him. What the hell did she want from him? If she didn't want him at all, why didn't she just say so?

He walked for miles, coming home late to a sleeping house with lights burning in the living room and kitchen. Someone had put a plate of cookies for him on the counter. He left it untouched and went to the study, worn out from his seething anger. He slept on the couch without bothering to open it into a bed.

The anger was still deep and harsh when he woke the next morning, early, before anyone was up. He left without breakfast and went to the cafeteria in the student union for coffee.

'Tennis is what you need,' said Nat Goldner, startling him out of his thoughts. 'Anything that furrows the brow so menacingly can be exorcised only by demolishing a ball or an opponent. I offer myself. Unless you'd rather talk.'

'No, I'd rather demolish something. Good idea.'

They were equally matched and played a fast game. After an hour Garth began to relax. Nat was admiring. 'Good game. One of our best. Just think what we might have done if I'd been as furious as you. Do you have time for a second breakfast?'

'Lots of time; no classes today. But I want to get to the lab by ten.'

At the Faculty Club, a Victorian frame house near the campus, they sat beside a bay window overlooking the lake. A freighter was on the horizon, riding low in the water. 'Loaded with cargo,' Nat said, attacking his eggs Benedict. 'Coal for the coming winter. Hard to believe in winter on a day like this. How is Stephanie?'

Garth spread butter on his rye toast. 'She's fine.'

'No aches or pains or megrims?'

Garth looked up. 'An old-fashioned word from a modern doctor.'

'I like it. How else would I describe, in one word, depressed and irritable, with erratic behavior?'

'From just a broken wrist?'

'From trauma, or shock. Did Stephanie talk to you about the maid Dolores sent over? Juanita?'

'Only that she did a good job – when was it? Day before yesterday, Tuesday. It was good of Dolores to loan her out. Was there something else for her to tell me?'

'According to Dolores, who is quoting Juanita, "That lady certainly know what she want; she give orders like royalty."'

'Stephanie? Nonsense. She's uncomfortable ordering anyone around.'

'I'm only quoting Dolores.'

'Who is quoting Juanita. Who is probably exaggerating.'

'Garth, relax. No one is attacking Stephanie.'

'What else did reliable Juanita say via Dolores?'

'That Stephanie had her lunch on the patio while Juanita ate in the kitchen.'

'So?'

'It seems the women eat with the maids around here. I never knew that, but I'm never home.'

'Why should they eat together?'

'How do I know? Maybe the women want their maids to feel loved. Anyway, Stephanie didn't do it.'

'She's not used to having a maid.'

'Okay, I told you, I'm not attacking her. But, as her doctor, I ought to know about it if she's not acting like herself. She had one hell of a crack on the head, Garth, and she was frightened by it. Sometimes the fear lingers; patients think they're seriously hurt and the doctor is lying to them, having secret conferences with their family. All of which can make them act in tense, erratic, unpredictable ways. We can't deal with that if we don't know about it. So, does she?'

Garth left his toast unfinished and poured a second cup of coffee. 'No. She says her bruises hurt, that's all.'

Nat sighed. 'If she did behave like that, it would likely disappear within a short time as she got better.' Garth nodded. 'If you need to talk, anytime, you know where I am.'

'Nat, you're the one I'd come to. I value your sharp eye and your honest tongue. Even more, I value your friendship. And, of course, your tennis. When do our boys have their next soccer game? I forgot to ask Cliff this morning.'

'Tomorrow. And next Tuesday ends the season. I don't like the way the coach handles them, but there's not much we can do about it—'

And, talking about their sons and soccer, they finished their coffee and left, looking, Garth thought, like two respectable professors with model families, secure reputations and no problems that couldn't be dealt with by a fast game of tennis and a friendly chat over coffee.

He looked at his reflection in the glass door of his laboratory. Am I that man, he wondered, with that family? How can I be, if I don't understand my wife and she can't seem to make up her mind whether to hold our marriage together or tear it apart? Or maybe something is happening to both of us and we are somehow changing – almost as if we are becoming different people.

Cliff dawdled on his way home from school. If Penny got there first, maybe she'd have the breakfast dishes washed before he arrived. He wished Mom would get her cast off so she could do things like she used to; though, come to think of it, he had a funny feeling that maybe she wasn't ever going to do things the way she used to, not exactly. It was kind of weird, because Mom used to do everything. Now they never knew what she'd do and what she'd tell *them* to do and what she'd just sort of forget.

But she didn't get mad as much as before. Actually, she didn't pay as much attention to him and Penny as she used to. Sometimes he kind of wished she would. But probably her wrist hurt. Or something.

At least she was cooking again, with Dad's help, which just proved she could do other things, too. It wasn't fair that he had to work in the house after school and soccer practice. Maybe he'd talk to Mom about it; these days she talked to him almost like a grown-up.

'Mom!' he shouted, slamming the screen door and dropping his books in the living room. He found her in the kitchen sitting on the couch with Penny.

'We're having a private talk!' Penny said.

'You didn't do the dishes,' he growled with a disgusted glance at the sink.

'You're supposed to do them, too.'

'I want to talk to Mom.'

'I'm talking to her.'

'Mom—' Cliff said.

'I could sell tickets,' she suggested. Cliff was confused; he'd expected a scolding for arguing with Penny, but Mom didn't look mad at all; in fact, she looked happy. 'Cliff, how about taking some cookies and milk to the backyard? It'll be your turn in a few minutes.'

Penny watched him maneuver through the door with cookies and milk and a box of pretzels and then turned back to Sabrina. 'The thing is, they make me feel so dumb – and kind of scared.'

'Scared of what?' Sabrina asked.

'What they all talk about. At recess. You know.'

'I'm not sure. What things do they talk about?'

'Well ... oh ... you know ... fucking and screwing and masturbating and—'

'Penny!'

She shrank back. 'I knew you'd be mad. Everybody says you can't talk to your mother. But I didn't know who else to talk to. Barbara's no help; she doesn't know any more than

227

I do. And I can't ask a *teacher* – if anybody found out, I'd die!'

Sabrina nodded, remembering. You couldn't go to a teacher; that would betray the conversations of the other girls, and you couldn't ask the other girls because that would give away your ignorance. But Penny could wait a few days, couldn't she? Until Stephanie got home? It was a mother's job, after all. She looked at the embarrassment and worry on Penny's face and knew she could not.

'Hold on a minute.' Sabrina went to the sink and ran a glass of water to gain time. What do I know about young girls? When we were Penny's age we didn't know anything. How come eleven-year-olds are talking about fucking and masturbating? Why aren't they thinking about ice cream sodas and swimming lessons?

She came back to the couch. 'Penny, don't you have classes in health or something where you talk about your body and growing up?'

'There's sex ed, but that isn't the problem. All that talk about sperm and eggs and menstruating and venereal disease – everybody knows all that! That's not the problem!'

Sabrina gazed at Penny blankly. 'What *is* the problem?'

'I don't want to do any of it.'

In sixth grade? 'Of course you don't. Why should you? No one has intercourse in sixth grade.'

'But when they talk about it – what boys like best and what it would be like to screw with them – they make me feel dumb, like there's something wrong with me because *I don't want to do it!* Ever! It sounds awful. I don't want boys touching me there and sticking their penises in me. But when I said that, these girls laughed at me—'

'Which girls?' Sabrina asked.

'These girls in my class. They're menstruating and they wear bras and you wouldn't buy me one—'

'Well, but Penny,' Sabrina said, looking at her flat chest.

'I know, but in the gym locker room I feel like a baby! And then they whisper and giggle and talk about—'

Sabrina listened, appalled, as Penny's artless chatter described a generation she knew nothing about. At eleven she and Stephanie had felt daring because they'd run away from a chauffeur. What did these children have to look forward to if they did everything in grammar school? Would they, at forty, take up hopscotch?

She sighed. It wasn't a joke. Penny was bewildered and forlorn, and looking for help.

'See,' Penny said, 'I don't care what they do. I mean, if that's what they want, it's okay, but I'd rather draw or work on puppet costumes or things like that. Does that mean there's something wrong with me? Am I abnormal or something?'

'No,' Sabrina said quietly. 'I think you're the most normal one of all.'

'Really? Normal? Everything I said?'

'Not quite, because when you're older you'll change your mind about wanting to have intercourse—'

'You mean fucking.'

'That's one word for it; it's not mine. I'll tell you why. You know, don't you, that intercourse is also called making love?'

'Oh, sure, everybody knows that.'

'Really? But they prefer to call it fucking. Why do you suppose that is?'

'I don't know. I guess they just like it better.'

'Penny, why is intercourse called making love?'

'Because . . . you love somebody and you do it.'

'What if you do it with somebody you don't love?'

Penny frowned and then shrugged.

'You see, you can experiment with sex, and if you're lucky and things go well, it feels very good. You can do that with lots of boys and lots of times you'll feel good – like scratching a mosquito bite or eating a big meal when you're hungry. Or you can use sex only when you want to show a very special person how you feel. That's when it's called making love.'

She looked through the window at a climbing rose, heavy with late blooms. 'Making love is a way to show someone that you love him so much you want to be part of him. There are lots of ways to show you *like* someone: you talk and share private jokes; you smile at each other across a room; you hold hands and spend time together. But intercourse is more than all those things; it's the only way you can be as close to another person with your body as you can be with your mind.'

Sabrina twined her fingers with Penny's. 'Like this. Thoughts and bodies. And that's when you know you're in love. Do you think those girls in your class know the first thing about this? Or care about it?'

Penny looked at their hands and slowly shook her head.

'Penny, please listen. Wait for this. Whatever others do, don't let them shame you into trying to keep up with them. Don't turn lovemaking into fucking; don't make it as ordinary as a handshake. Wait until someone is so important in your life, so wonderful and special, that you want to share the things you are and the things you feel in this one way that is like no other way. Intercourse isn't an after-school sport or a way of scratching an itch. Intercourse is a language, Penny; it's using your body to say "I love you." Wait for that. Wait until you find somebody so wonderful you want to tell him you love him with your eyes and your mouth and then with your whole body.'

Meeting Penny's eyes, wide with wonder at her intensity, Sabrina heard the echo of her words. Within her something fell away; she felt empty and desolate. *I haven't followed my own advice. I wish—*

'But, if it's so good, how come you and Daddy hardly ever do it?'

In the silence, Cliff's ball thumped rhythmically against the side of the house.

'Why do you think we don't?' Sabrina asked.

'Well, he hardly ever sleeps in your room anymore. Does that mean you don't love each other?'

'No,' she said quickly, to smooth this new anxiety from Penny's face. 'Sometimes grown-ups get complicated feelings that aren't easy to explain. They can love each other and still want to be apart now and then ... sort of take a vacation from each other and think about themselves separately.'

'Is that why you went to China?'

'That was one of the reasons.'

'Lots of kids at school – their parents are getting divorced.'

'Well, we're not.' Too defensive, she thought, and added more quietly, 'We're not going to, Penny.'

'When you went to China, Cliff and I thought you were. 'Cause you went alone and Daddy was sad.'

Sabrina put her arms around her and Penny nuzzled her nose against Sabrina's breast. 'I love you, Mommy. Don't go away again.' Sabrina kissed the top of her head – black curly hair, like Garth's – and felt a rush of love and protectiveness she had never known before. *Don't be afraid, Penny. I won't let you be hurt.*

'I love you, Penny,' she said.

Outside, the thump of Cliff's ball was like a heartbeat. The thump stopped. 'Hey,' he said, appearing at the door. 'Isn't it my turn?'

I'd like a five-minute break, Sabrina thought, but Cliff was peering through the screen like a refugee. 'Yes, it is. Come on in.'

'Can I stay?' asked Penny.

Sabrina looked at Cliff. 'Is this a private talk?'

'I guess not.' Cliff took the place of his sister, while Penny sat on the floor and began to draw in her sketch pad. 'I . . . uh . . . it's about working in the house.'

'Yes?' Sabrina smiled at him serenely.

'I don't like it,' he blurted. 'And I don't think I should have to do it. I already go to school and practice soccer, and I have homework.'

'Yes?'

'Well . . . that's three jobs.'

'Two, if you really call them jobs. Student and soccer forward.'

'Well, two. But if I work around here, that's three, and nobody has three jobs.'

'What about me?'

'You? You're just a . . . a mother.'

'Just a mother. Well, think about this. I clean house; that makes me a maid – hardly as much fun as soccer. I'm a cook; job number two. I drive you around, so I'm a chauffeur; job number three. I'm a laundress; that's four. A gardener; that's five. I refinish furniture and arrange it, so I'm a decorator, that's six. I'm a hostess for our friends; that's seven. I nurse you when you're sick, that's eight. I work at the university; that's nine.' *Does Stephanie really do all this?* 'And, of course, I am, as you say, a mother, which makes ten, and a wife, which makes eleven. I may have left out a few. How many jobs did you say you have?'

He stared. 'But . . . you're supposed to do those things.'

'Who says?'

He thought about it, mentally weighing answers. 'The Bible?'

She laughed. 'The Bible has women warriors who whack off men's heads with their swords. Shall I be like them?'

'No, but . . . well, maybe it's not in a book or a law, but everybody knows what mothers are supposed to do – what they've always done. Family things don't change.'

She nodded seriously. 'And what are sons supposed to do?'

'Go to school.'

'Only in this century. All but the rich ones used to work twelve or fourteen hours a day in factories and coal mines. Earning money to help out their parents.'

'But that's all changed—!'

She made a face of mock surprise. 'A family thing changed?'

After a long moment Cliff grinned. 'Oh,' he said, and they began to laugh together. Sabrina, wanting to hug him, reached out to tousle his hair as their laughter grew, and that was how Garth found them a moment later when he walked into the kitchen.

Sabrina's laughter stopped. 'Cliff, we've talked away the afternoon, and what have we done for dinner?'

'We haven't done the dishes,' he said, sliding off the couch. 'Hi, Dad. Make any clones today?'

'I'm working on one for a respectful son,' Garth said, but he was looking at Sabrina. 'I brought a steak. If you'll tell me what you did last week, I'll do it this time.'

'I can do it,' she said, starting to get up.

'But I want to.' He liked doing things for his wife, who had always doggedly done for everyone else, no matter how sick she felt. He liked being needed by her, for a change.

Sabrina sat back. Garth poured two glasses of wine and put

them on the table in front of her. Then, following her directions, he crushed peppercorns with the new mortar and pestle and pressed them into both sides of the steak. Beside him, Cliff washed the breakfast dishes and talked about his science class. Sabrina watched them, father and son, working side by side. On the floor beside her, Penny hummed as she sketched, locked in her own world, unaware of the family. But Sabrina was keenly aware of it. She was not doing very well with Garth, but in spite of that she felt the force of the family holding her close, and she was content to be there, part of them, even though Garth's explosive anger of the night before hung unresolved in the air.

Garth sat beside her, and automatically she moved away from him. He ignored it, handing her a glass of wine. 'I owe you an apology for last night. I talked myself into something simply because I wanted it. It was thoughtless and I'm sorry. Especially since it was such a wonderful evening until then. At least for me.'

'For all of us. I should apologize, too—'

'There's no reason. It will take you a while to get back your equilibrium, and I should have known that. Instead, I was about as sensitive as a teenager on a back road.'

Sabrina frowned. 'Who said anything about my equilibrium?'

'Nat. Talking about the aftereffects of shock and concussion. We don't have to go into it; he simply made me aware that I'd been thinking of myself, not of you.' He held out his hand, palm up, and after a moment's hesitation she put hers in it. 'I don't like to think of myself as crude. I do apologize.'

'Thank you.' Gently she pulled back her hand. 'I think I'd better do something about dinner.'

'No, your job is to give orders and supervise. That way the responsibility for possible failure is shared. What do I do now?'

He enlisted Cliff and Penny, and they all worked while Sabrina, curled up on the couch, gave directions and let her thoughts wander. The days were settling into routine, but she was left in a strange limbo. Her brief adventure had collapsed, and she was no longer simply a visitor; this was home, this was her family. She was involved in the things they did today and planned for tomorrow, next week, two weeks from now.

But how could she make plans? She could not change the house or its routine; they weren't hers. She would begin things she would not have time to finish; she would make mistakes that could expose her at any minute; she would love Penny and Cliff and leave them; and Garth—

Garth. The biggest part of the future. The part she had to keep her distance from.

'Dinner,' he said, smiling, and reached out a hand to help her up.

On Friday, Juanita came again. Dolores called first. 'Go easy with her; she doesn't like to take orders.'

'Dolores, I have to tell her what I want done.'

'Don't. Just let her do what she wants. That's when she does best. You can make a suggestion now and then. As for lunch—'

'There's the doorbell. I'll talk to you later.'

Silently, Juanita cleaned the rooms and changed the beds while Sabrina began some of the jobs Stephanie had told her she always did at the end of September: putting away summer clothes, bringing out winter ones from the garment bags in the hall closet. At noon Juanita came up to her. 'What's for lunch?'

Oh, for Mrs Thirkell.

'Anything in the refrigerator that appeals to you,' she said, folding sweaters. Her cast made her clumsy, and she knocked two of them to the floor. Juanita picked them up.

'Mrs Goldner and the other ladies fix something for me.'

Sabrina took the sweaters from her. 'Thank you. Do you cook for yourself in your own home, Juanita?'

After a pause, Juanita said, 'Yes, ma'am,' and went downstairs. An hour later, when Sabrina went down for her own lunch, she found on the breakfast-room table a plate of cold sliced roast beef, tomatoes and French bread, silverware wrapped in a napkin, and a glass of cider. As she looked at it, Juanita came in from the living room. 'I thought you might have trouble fixing something, with your arm and all.'

'That was kind of you. It looks lovely. Did you have enough to eat?'

'Yes'm.' She went back to the living room.

Later, she found Sabrina in the backyard, pruning roses. 'I have a free day every other Wednesday. If you want, I could come here.'

'What do you charge, Juanita?'

'Thirty dollars plus carfare.'

Could they afford it? She didn't know. Stephanie always did her own housework. But why should I do it? Sabrina thought. After all, I gave up Mrs Thirkell. And it's only for the few weeks I'm here. Stephanie can decide what she wants to do when she returns. 'All right. Next Wednesday or the one after?'

'Next.'

'I'll see you then.' She turned back to the roses. They had had a small contest of wills, she and Juanita, and both had won. Juanita cleaned house her own way; Sabrina managed lunch in her way. Except . . . who had the last word? Juanita. She decided what Sabrina would eat and drink. Sabrina began to laugh. Wait until I tell Garth, she thought.

At dinner, the last of the donated meals, she listened as Garth and Cliff talked about the soccer game he had played that afternoon, the first since he was benched. He had scored twice. 'You shoulda seen it, Mom, it was great. You'll come next week to the last one, won't you? I like it best when you and Dad are both there.'

'Of course,' she said. 'I think Penny might want to come, too.' Then she sat back again, letting the others talk. Every few minutes Garth looked at her quizzically, waiting for her to join them or lead the conversation, as she had on other nights; but she was quiet. Let them be the family; she would watch.

'Headache still bad?' he asked after dinner.

'Only once in a while. Mostly it's like background noise; always there, but I get used to it.'

'But you're so quiet. Wasn't it a good day?'

'Oh, it was. Something amusing—' Penny brought a carton

of ice cream to the table, and while Garth scooped it into dishes and poured their coffee, she told about her contest of wills with Juanita. He chuckled, but he was surprised.

'You've always said you were uncomfortable giving orders; that was why you didn't want a maid.'

'Oh. Well, it's amazing how a broken wrist and pounding head make it easy to give orders and get used to having a maid. As a matter of fact, that was the other way Juanita had the last word. After she chose my lunch, she got me to hire her.'

Garth's eyebrows went up. 'You hired her?'

'Only one day every other week.' Sabrina was annoyed to find herself becoming defensive. She wasn't used to that. In London she never had to explain her decisions; she answered to no one but herself. Did Stephanie have to consult Garth whenever she wanted to spend money?

'Well, that's fine,' he said. 'You know how many times I've suggested it. I just assumed we'd discuss it first.'

I don't discuss my plans with anyone.

But suddenly she thought of Antonio, sitting across from her at Le Gavroche, casually dismissing her problems, saying he would get rid of her 'little shop' for her. Was it a luxury that she did not have to discuss her plans with anyone – or was it a burden, that she had no one to discuss them with?

'I'm sorry,' she said to Garth. 'The idea came up—'

The telephone rang and Cliff ran to get it, calling from the kitchen, 'Mom! It's Aunt Sabrina!'

In the breakfast room, Sabrina tried to hear Stephanie through a bad connection and the clatter of Penny and Cliff clearing the table. Something about Antonio; Stephanie sounded upset. 'I'll call you back,' Sabrina said. 'This weekend?'

'No.' Stephanie's voice faded. ' . . . away in the country.'

'Monday, then,' said Sabrina, adding, 'Don't worry about Antonio.' Whatever it was, it seemed far off and not very important.

Over the weekend, she almost forgot it. Imperceptibly, she had slipped completely into the family routine. She and Garth shared the house and yard work with the children, talking casually about family matters, and she was cooking again, choosing what she assumed were favorite recipes from spattered pages in Stephanie's cookbooks. She could not resist a few touches of her own, but she thought no one noticed until, over coffee on Sunday night, Garth said she made a more delicious meal with one good arm than most chefs did with two.

It was surprising how good that made her feel.

She thought about it later, when she and Garth were alone in the living room. They had watched a television show and then they read, sitting near each other in overlapping circles of light. Around them the house slumbered; music came softly from the record player. Sabrina looked up from her book and found Garth watching her. They smiled at each other – the only two people awake in the world. Abruptly she returned to her book, to break the spell.

At midnight, Garth said he was going to sleep – 'Early meeting tomorrow with the vice president.' And a little later, when she turned out the lights and went upstairs, she found him on the far side of the bed, eyes shut, breathing deeply. Holding her breath, trying to be invisible and weightless, she slipped into the near side. He did not stir, and before she could decide whether he was feigning sleep or not, she fell asleep herself.

On Monday Garth suggested she take a few more days off from her job. 'I'll call Ted and explain,' he said, and she let him. Coward, she thought. You'll have to go in sooner or later.

But some things could not be put off any longer. Sabrina finally had made an appointment with Penny's teacher, and after lunch she went to the school to meet her. 'Intimidating,' Stephanie had described her, and after one look at the small woman with perfectly waved gray hair, uncompromising mouth and rigid neck, Sabrina understood why.

'Do sit down, Mrs Andersen. Penny told me about your accident; I'm so sorry. How is the wrist?'

'I hope it is healing.'

'Of course, one cannot know what is happening beneath a cast. One can only hope. I want you to know, Mrs Andersen, as I told you last year, I enjoy Penny. She's a lovely child and a fine student. She is, however, a bit willful; you must watch that in her.'

Sabrina gazed calmly at Mrs Casey. 'Willful,' she repeated.

'She likes her own way. Of course, all youngsters do, but Penny is too sure of herself. She needs to be taken down a notch or two.'

'In what way?' asked Sabrina with interest.

'She must learn humility. Without it, Mrs Andersen, children are uncontrollable. Penny, like all of them, must be taught to respect authority, to take her place in the orderly progression of authority. It is a simple fact that adults know more than children. If children begin to think their opinion is as valuable as ours, how can we keep them in their place? How can we teach them? Of course, you understand all this, but I bring it up because Penny tends to be ... ah ... assertive. I encourage independence, to a degree, Mrs Andersen, but I do not encourage sedition.'

Sabrina nodded impassively. 'And the puppet show?'

'A good example. The show dramatizes westward expansion, the Mexican war, the gold rush. It is a teaching tool, not a game. Last spring I granted Penny's request to handle the costumes. When school began this fall she had already drawn a complete set of sketches, which showed admirable energy; but when I suggested certain changes she argued with me, and when I ordered her to make them, she refused, claiming the project was hers. Clearly, I could not tolerate that. There must be one central authority in a classroom or you have chaos. So I turned the costumes over to Barbara Goodman, who is—'

'Without discussing it with Penny.'

'Ah. Yes, I grant you, that was a mistake. I meant to tell her, but something came up and by the next day it had slipped my mind. I can understand that the child is upset about that, and I will make a note to apologize to her. It sets children a good example when adults apologize for their mistakes. But I might add that if Penny had altered her sketches she still would have her little project and I would have no need to apologize.'

'Mrs Casey.'

For the first time the teacher looked directly at Sabrina and saw the glint in her eyes. 'Mrs Andersen, this is a small matter. It will pass—'

'Please. It is now my turn.' Sabrina let a long moment go by. 'You are a tyrant,' she said pleasantly. 'Tyrants always have very definite ideas about the orderly progression of authority and keeping people in their place.' She was so angry she was trembling, but she kept her voice even and good-natured. 'If you were running your little show with adults I would ignore you. But you are lording it over sixth-grade children who haven't learned to defend themselves when someone in authority tries to stamp all confidence and independence out of them.'

'You cannot speak to me this—'

'My taxes pay your salary, Mrs Casey; you work for me. Please let me finish. As long as I am Penny's mother, I intend to do all I can to help her feel good about herself. I want her to feel confident that she can do things on her own, though not ashamed to ask for help when she needs it. I will not have her squashed into the subservient lump of humility you seem to require in order to feel powerful.'

'How dare—'

'I am not quite finished. I give you two choices. I can have Penny transferred to another sixth-grade class and give a full explanation of my reasons to your principal. Or I will allow Penny to stay if you can convince me you will concentrate on teaching instead of tyranizing.'

Mrs Casey was silent, twisting her hands in her lap. The rigid muscles of her neck had given way and her head trembled like a dried flower on a bent stalk. Sabrina, in the midst of her anger, felt pity. She had guessed that complaints already had been made about Mrs Casey, and as the silence dragged on she knew she was right.

On impulse, she said, 'Why don't we talk about this over a cup of coffee? Is there a place in the school—?'

Mrs Casey looked up. 'You know there is. The faculty lounge where you helped with our Christmas party last year.'

'Of course. I meant a more private place.'

'No one will bother us.' She took a breath. 'Mrs Andersen. I have been a teacher for thirty years. Teaching is all I have. It is my only family; I have nothing else in the world. Of course, you cannot understand that; what do you know about being completely alone? We all need something to believe in. I believe in order and authority. But I have always wanted to be a good teacher. If I am not, then I have nothing at all.'

Sabrina's anger vanished. Only pity was left. *I believe in myself,* she thought. *Mrs Casey has never been able to do that.* She stood up. 'Coffee? I think we can find a lot to talk about.'

When Penny danced home from school on Tuesday afternoon she threw her arms around Sabrina, bubbling with the news that Mrs Casey had put her in charge of the puppet costumes once again, with Barbara Goodman as her assistant. 'And she said she was sorry and even smiled!'

'And what did Barbara say?'

'Oh, she was glad; she doesn't know anything about costumes. Why are you sitting by the telephone? Is somebody going to call?'

'I was calling someone. But she wasn't home.'

'Then come and see my drawings. Mrs Casey says I can use all of them, but I have to change General Santa Anna. She showed me his picture in a book, so I know how to do it. Are you coming?'

Sabrina went upstairs slowly. She had been calling Stephanie to find out what she had been trying to tell her on Friday, but no one was home, not even Mrs Thirkell. *I'll call later,* she thought; *from the bedroom. No one will bother me.*

At dinner Garth looked at her quizzically. 'I heard a fascinating story today about my wife.'

She tensed. 'Oh?'

'From Vivian Goodman.'

Vivian doesn't know anything. There's nothing to worry about.

'She told me she went yesterday to talk to her daughter's

240

teacher about a project that had her daughter terrified – she couldn't do it and didn't have the courage to say so. When she got there, another mother was talking about the same project. It was so interesting she eavesdropped. You didn't tell me you called Mrs Casey a tyrant.'

Sabrina shook her head. She had decided not to tell Garth about that talk because she didn't know how Stephanie would have handled it.

'According to Vivian, you were cool, collected and devastating. I wish I'd been there. Usually your emotions run high about the kids.'

Of course. Stephanie's anger would have overflowed. But it's easy to be cool and collected, Sabrina thought, when dealing with someone else's child. I can't take credit for being less involved than a mother would be.

'Why are you shaking your head?' Garth asked. 'Didn't you call her a tyrant?'

'What? Oh. Yes. I ... it just came out; she really was talking and acting like one—'

'Don't apologize. Vivian tells me Mrs Casey has been terrifying her students for years. You're an amazing woman; I'm proud of you.'

She flushed with pleasure, then felt a little tremor of alarm. She was beginning to depend on Garth for praise.

'I didn't realize Barbara was Vivian's daughter,' she said, to shift the conversation. 'I didn't connect the names.'

'I thought you met them both at the class picnic last year.'

'Did I? I don't remember.'

And I'm getting tired of pretending, with no one to relax with, no one to talk to and just be myself. No one except Stephanie.

And why isn't Stephanie home? Or Mrs Thirkell?

Later, as she sat in the living room with Garth, reading and talking, the telephone broke the silence. 'Long distance for you,' Garth said, and she ran to the kitchen. *Stephanie. Finally.*

'Stephanie?' said her mother. 'We just got back to Washington. How are you? And how was the adventure in China? I haven't been able to reach Sabrina in London, so you'll have to give me all the news.'

Sabrina adjusted her thoughts from her sister to her mother. 'I thought you were in Paris. Or Geneva. Or somewhere.'

'Moscow, dear. Your father had a conference. But it ended early, so we came home. Now tell me about China.'

Sabrina talked briefly about China, once more describing Mr Su, the bronze lamp, the chess set, the intricate ivory carving Mr Su had given her of ladies of the court.

How can I do this? How can I fool my mother? Doesn't she have any suspicion at all?

'You sound tired, Stephanie. Is everything all right?'

Don't mention a broken wrist; she might want to come and help with the housework. And I don't know if I could fool her close up.

'I'm fine, Mother, just busy. You know how much there is to do after you've been away.'

'You're sure that's all? Are you and Garth . . . getting along all right?'

'Yes, of course. Why shouldn't we be?'

'You don't have to be so defensive. I detected vibrations in your last letter that caused your father and me some concern.'

'Everything is fine, Mother. I hate housework and love the house.'

Laura gave a surprised laugh. 'Is that new?'

'Maybe it just seems new, coming back from China.' Sabrina plunged ahead, letting the truth pour out; she hadn't had anyone to talk to for such a long time. 'I hate the laundry and I love the garden. I've hired a maid one day every two weeks and I'm considering letting the house go to pieces in between.'

'Stephanie, this is not like you.'

'Probably not. I've felt different since the trip. I like the quiet rhythm of this life; I like not having to keep up with a social circle—'

'Is that a criticism of us, my dear?'

Sabrina paused. 'No. I never even thought of you. Are you worried about keeping up?'

'We always worry about keeping up. You knew that from the time you were born. Sabrina understood it better than you, which is why she does so well in London. You could never have handled that pace.'

'No. Where was I? Oh, yes. I like the people I know in Evanston and the way they're connected with the university and the town. I like the comfort of the shabby rooms in this big, wonderful house. I like my family around me. Lots of noise but lots of life. They keep me from drifting off.'

'Stephanie, have you and Garth taken up drugs?'

'Mother!'

'Well, you certainly don't sound like yourself. Why am I getting this list of likes and dislikes?'

'Because I can talk to you, Mother. And I thought you would want to know how happy I am. And that Garth and I aren't getting a divorce.'

'My dear, I never suggested—'

'That wasn't what you were worried about in my letter?'

'It may have been. In these days, one does worry about divorce. Look at Sabrina. I'm not sure which was her mistake – marrying Denton or divorcing him – but I don't think she's a very happy woman. Do you?'

Sabrina was silent.

'Stephanie? Do you?'

'Probably not. At least not a lot of the time.'

'So you see, I worry. Well, my dear, your father is calling me. We'll be at your house for Thanksgiving, as usual. Do you suppose we could get Sabrina to join us this year?'

'I doubt it.'

'I'll ask her anyway.'

Sabrina lingered in the breakfast room after hanging up. *What I didn't say, Mother, what I left out about my life, was this: I like being part of a community that accepts me for myself, not because of my looks and my sophisticated small talk, my elite shop, my social connections or my former marriage.*

Oh, come on, a small voice jeered. Who's the community accepting for being herself? Sabrina Longworth? Or Stephanie Andersen?

She didn't need to answer.

On Wednesday Sabrina tried again to call Stephanie. 'Lady Longworth is out,' said Mrs Thirkell. 'Shall I ask her to return your call, Mrs Andersen?'

'Yes. I've been trying to reach her.'

'Oh, I'm so sorry, Mrs Andersen. I was visiting a sick sister in Scotland, and I believe Lady Longworth is redecorating a house on Eaton Square. But I shall make sure she returns your call.'

A wave of depression swept Sabrina as she hung up. A door had slammed in her face. Lady Longworth working on Eaton Square. Mrs Thirkell calling her Mrs Andersen. As if she had lost her place in that life. *But I can't. I won't. Just because I like being here doesn't mean this is what I want. I'll talk to Stephanie tomorrow. Find out what is going on there.*

And remind myself of where I belong.

But the next morning Penny woke with a fever and a hacking cough that terrified Sabrina. It's my fault, she thought; I didn't pay attention to how they dressed when they went outside. She called the pediatrician on Stephanie's list. 'Bring her in,' said the nurse. 'We'll take a look.'

Sabrina looked again at the list. Cos Building on Ridge Avenue. 'How do I get there?'

There was a puzzled silence. 'Oh, is something wrong with your car?' the nurse asked. 'Perhaps one of your friends—'

'Yes. Yes, of course. We'll be right there.' Frantically she searched the map she had been using for three weeks and memorized the route to the medical center across the street from the hospital.

'Not like you to get so upset,' the pediatrician said. She looked keenly at Sabrina. 'You look like you're under a lot of strain. The wrist? Or something else?'

'Could we talk about Penny?' Sabrina asked.

'Sure. Penny, you've got bronchitis; not severe, but it could get nasty if you don't take it easy. Bed for a couple of days, a vaporizer in your room and a lousy-tasting syrup to keep your cough loose. You and your mom should call on Saturday to let me know how you're doing. Any questions?'

Penny shook her head.

'I'm sorry,' said Sabrina, embarrassed by her rudeness. 'A lot has been going on. We'll call on Saturday.'

'Or before, if you need me. And relax. Penny's a tough little lady; she'll be well in no time.'

In the car, Sabrina shook her head. A bad case of overreacting. Stephanie would have taken it in stride. But I've never had a sick child before.

That night she and Garth went to the Talvias' for dinner, leaving Penny cheerfully propped up in bed, sharing dinner on a tray with Cliff.

'We bought you a present,' Linda said as they walked in.

'Another birthday?'

'Nope.' Linda laughed. 'But Dolores and I thought you needed cheering up, so we bought you this. It's cheerful.'

It was a robe of smooth polished cotton splashed with brilliant flowers: brighter than anything in Stephanie's closet; the kind Sabrina loved best. Her face lit in a delighted smile that made Garth draw in his breath as she thanked Linda. 'I think I'll wear it to work. It's too lovely to hide in a closet all day.'

'You really like it? Dolores thought you'd say it's too loud.'

'It's not loud, it's beautiful. What wonderful taste you have.'

Linda beamed. 'How did you know I picked it out?'

'Because Dolores thought it was too loud.'

She wore the robe the next night, feeling more cheerful about everything. Penny's fever was down and her cough seemed better. Linda and Dolores had bought the robe for her, not Stephanie. In the past three weeks they had talked almost every day on the telephone and often met in one of their kitchens for afternoon coffee. Whatever name they called her, *she* was their friend. She still hadn't talked to Stephanie on the telephone, but it didn't seem so important now; if anything were wrong, Stephanie would have called.

'A lovely robe,' Garth said. 'It almost does you justice.'

She flushed. 'Thank you.'

'You look much better.'

'I feel better. And Penny is getting well.'

'No more headaches?'

'Not a one. And the bruises look bad but I hardly notice—'
She stopped.

'Good,' he said easily. 'I was going to sit out the
conference, but I think, since you're doing so well, I'll go
after all.'

'Conference?'

'I told you about . . . I did tell you, didn't I?'

'I don't think so.'

'October 6. Tomorrow. Berkeley for a week. Good Lord, did
I really forget to tell you? That's unforgivable, how could
I—'

'It's all right, don't be upset. You probably told me and I
forgot it.' But I wouldn't have forgotten, she thought. A
whole wonderful week. No need for excuses in bed after I was
stupid enough to say I'm feeling fine. 'I'm glad you're going,'
she added.

'A week to yourself.'

She looked startled. How often did he know what she was
thinking? 'No, I meant, if it's something you want to do, I'm
glad you don't have to worry about us. We'll be fine. We are
fine.'

'Are you going to the office on Monday?'

'I think so. Yes, of course. Why?'

'You'd rather not go at all.'

'I didn't say that.'

'You've thought it.'

'I'll do what I have to do,' she said almost angrily.
'Anyway, I'll be socializing, too: I have a lunch date with
Vivian. I meant to ask you: what's happening with Vivian's
job?'

'Did I ever tell you my Theory of Universities? Like most
institutions, each one is similar to a vat of molasses – slow
and sluggish. If something goes wrong in one part, it spreads
out and covers it up; if you try to make a dent in it, it oozes
into the mark you think you've made. If you try to wade
through it too quickly, you collapse from exhaustion; and if
you try to beat it by plunging in and flailing away, you
drown.'

She was laughing. 'But if you heat molasses it gets thin and
moves quickly.'

246

'Exactly. So we lit a small fire under the vice president. Lloyd Strauss. You've met him.'

'And is he moving more quickly?'

'Like a tidal wave. In one week he has discovered that half the human race is female and has asked William Webster, whose paunch makes a formidable roadblock, to explain why our ivory tower resembles a club for men only.'

'You'd like to get rid of Webster.'

'Is it that obvious? I hope no one else sees that. It could look as if I want his job.'

'But you don't.'

'Lord, no. I want more time in the lab, not behind a desk.'

'Would Foster Labs give you what you want?'

'I've been wondering when you'd bring that up again.'

'I wasn't starting a debate; I only asked if it would satisfy you.'

He gave her a long, thoughtful look. 'I'm not sure.'

'How will you find out?'

'I suppose I'll have to go there and look around.'

She nodded.

'No comment?'

'What would you like me to say?'

'Damned if I know. You never lacked for something to say in the past. If I go for a look, will you come with me?'

'I don't think so. You should have a chance to think about it by yourself.'

'That's new. Until now—'

She stood and shook out the folds of her robe. 'I think I'll go up. I want to call my sister before I go to sleep.'

'Since when is she awake at five-thirty in the morning?'

'It's not morning; it's late in the—No, how silly of me, you're right, I got it backwards. Of course she won't be up. I'll call tomorrow. I'll just go to sleep now.'

'Without any more talk of Foster Labs?'

'I'd rather not. Not tonight.'

He waited. 'All right. I'll be up soon.'

'Good night.'

She climbed the stairs slowly, wondering how she could confuse the times in Chicago and London after she'd been here almost three weeks. She'd been uncomfortable with Garth – that was the reason. The easy intimacy of their talk troubled her. How did she know him so well that she knew what he was thinking? I don't want that, she thought.

But what did she want?

She wanted to keep distance between them – but she wanted his smile and praise.

She tried to think of him as her sister's dull husband – but they laughed together and his work made him fascinating and powerful.

She reminded herself that Stephanie called him withdrawn and neglectful – but she warmed to the feeling he gave her of being protected and cherished.

Lying in bed, thinking about him, she heard him come upstairs. He was in the bedroom doorway when Penny began to cough.

Sabrina threw back the covers.

'I'll go,' said Garth. He found Penny sitting up in bed, small and white-faced in the light from the hall. He poured a spoonful of cough medicine and she made a face as she swallowed it.

'Why is it so awful?'

'The worse it tastes, the faster you get well so you don't have to take any more. Snuggle down, now, and I'll tuck you in.'

'Daddy, could you stay a few minutes?'

He put his hand on her forehead. No fever. 'What, sweetheart?'

'I asked Mommy about art lessons. She said I could take them if it was all right with you.'

'Did she? Well, I think we can manage it. When do they begin?'

'Right after Christmas. But—'

'But?'

'I need paints and brushes and charcoal and canvas. And they cost lots of money.'

'Well, I don't know. I thought you could draw with sticks and mud on paper napkins. But if you insist on the same equipment Michelangelo used, we could make it an early Christmas present and get you everything you need.'

'Oh, Daddy!' She struggled out of the blankets to throw her arms around him.

He held her close. 'Now to sleep, don't you think? It's hard to paint a masterpiece if you're hacking away with a cough.'

'Daddy?'

'Something else?'

'Why is Mommy so different lately?'

Garth sat down again. 'How is she different?'

'Oh, you know. *Different*. Like she hugs us more than she used to, but she hardly ever scolds us. Sometimes it's like she doesn't even notice what we're doing. And sometimes she smiles at *you* and other times it's like she doesn't want to be close to you. And lots of times she looks far away and just ... thinks. Like ... like she's here and someplace else at the same time.'

Garth smoothed back her hair. There was no sense in pretending. Children were oblivious to much that their parents did, but what they did see they saw with uncanny clarity and insight. 'I think she's got a lot of things on her mind that she's trying to sort out. When you get to a certain age, usually in your thirties, you begin to wonder if you're doing what you really want to do, in the way you want to do it. So sometimes you stand back a little bit—'

'Like taking a vacation from everybody and thinking about yourself separately?'

He was surprised. 'Yes. What made you think of that?'

'That's what Mommy said when I asked her.'

'Did she. And what else did she say?'

'That you weren't going to get a divorce.'

'That we weren't—'

'But I think maybe she's still thinking about it.'

Garth sat very still, staring unseeingly at the light from the hall. Stupid ass. You stupid ass not to see it, to have to wait for your eleven-year-old daughter to tell you the obvious. His hand clenched an imaginary tennis racket; his muscles tensed to smash a ball across the room. Goddamned blind, stupid ass not to know that she's wanted to divorce you for – how long? Since her trip? Since before the trip? How long?

Penny knew. Penny had known for a long time, had even

talked to her mother about it. 'She's still thinking about it.' Of course she was thinking about it. And who else knew, besides Penny? Who else saw his wife more clearly than he did? How many were not afraid, as he was, to see her clearly?

Because of course he'd known, in some part of him that he pushed out of sight whenever it poked its obscene head out, that she wanted to leave. Everything pointed to it, from running off to China to ignoring the laundry. Even when he tried to tell her that he'd talked to Cliff, as she'd nagged him to, about the loot stashed in his closet, she'd seemed indifferent. Worse; as if she didn't even know what he was talking about. As if she didn't care what he did. Everything pointed to it: she wanted to leave.

Except that she was still here. And wanted to stay. He had to believe that, too; how else could he explain the effort she was making to change, to be more lively and curious, more interested in all of them, more exciting? It wasn't just a shared glass of wine before dinner, or admitting she felt ill and letting him take care of her; it wasn't even a dinner table conversation about his work. She was trying to act differently in every way, forcing him to do the same. So they could begin again.

Sometimes. She acted like that sometimes. Other times she withdrew. As if her thoughts were pulling her to and away from him, hour by hour, day by day. She was thinking about divorce. But she hadn't decided.

He felt tenderness and admiration for her. He had not realized she was so strong, forcing him to court her again, forcing herself to court him, even while she wasn't sure what lay ahead, whether she would still have to leave him, to be – whatever she wanted to be. Whatever she thought she couldn't be as his wife.

He had to show her he understood, that he knew now he'd almost let her slip away from him in his absorption in his work, and that, with her, he would begin again if she would stay and give them a chance.

That was all he had to do.

'Daddy?'

'It's all right, sweetheart. Your mother and I are not going to get a divorce. Lots of married people think about divorce, and sometimes, when they have very serious problems, they have to separate. But not always. And do you know something?'

'What?' Her voice was warm and sleepy.

'I love your mother and you and Cliff more than anybody in the world. Do you think I'd be silly enough to let us all break apart, with so much love?'

'I love you, Daddy,' Penny sighed, and slept.

Garth leaned down and kissed her forehead. Sometimes all the love in the world isn't enough, he said silently. But I'll do my best.

Lying beside his wife in the dark, he said quietly, 'I don't want to go to this conference.. The past week has been so good; I've felt we were learning to know each other after being a long way apart. I know that was my fault far more than yours, and I've wanted to talk about it, but then it seemed that, lately, we were, in a real way, beginning again. Have you felt that? Stephanie? I know you're not asleep. Has it been a good week?'

Hidden by the dark, she gripped her hands. 'Yes,' she said reluctantly. The quiet evenings, his praise for things she did, the closeness of their talk and laughter, the way their eyes met when Cliff or Penny said something amusing, sharing the work of the house, her sense of being connected to him, to a family. . . . 'Yes.'

He slid his arm along the pillow, beneath her neck, and pulled her to him. 'I want to know you again; begin again.' His lips brushed her cheek and closed eyes. 'Hold fast our good times and build on them. My love,' he said, and his mouth covered hers.

She lay, taut and frantic, her mind in a turmoil, swept by the waves of happiness and depression that had battered her for days. As his hands slid the nightgown from her shoulders, her thoughts shouted at her, echoing and contradicting each other.

Stop him . . . tell him . . . what? Get out of bed. Push him away. Tell him . . . what? That he can't do this?

He is a husband in his own bed.

His hands and mouth moved on her body; his lips

whispered on her breasts in slow kisses that shuddered through her. With her fingers she felt the bone and muscle of his shoulders, the smooth skin of his back, and realized she was embracing him. She tore her arms away. His body stilled, as if caught in flight, then bent to her again; he held her breasts and kissed the hollow of her throat.

Sabrina heard the small moan that tore from her and struggled against it. *We can't, we can't*— But his body moved against hers, demanding and already familiar, and beneath his insistent hands she felt herself letting go into dark languor and the desire that swept in heavy waves through the hunger of her body.

You must not do this. The cold voice slashed through the soft darkness and she winced. Thinking he had hurt her, Garth pulled back, but her body, quite separate from the tumult in her mind, helped him move onto her and when he entered her, she was open to him, wet and smooth. In a sudden rush of joy that burst like a flame before she could smother it, she rose to meet him with such a passionate force that he, so long abstinent, could not hold back. With a low cry he came, deep inside her, and then lay still, pressing her beneath him into the bed.

She stretched the moment out, the feel of his strength upon her, then put her hands on his arms to push him away.

He lifted his head. 'I'm sorry, my love.' He slid his hand down. 'Let me—'

'No,' she whispered, torn by the pain of loss and guilt. She longed for him and was ashamed, and she turned her head away.

He lifted himself and lay beside her. Sabrina shivered, feeling bereft.

'I'll stay home this week,' he said.

'No. I want you to go.'

'Then I'll try to cut it short. We have so much to talk about, so much time to make up.'

She heard a new note in his voice and tried to make it out. Not triumph; not satisfaction.

Anticipation.

'Good night, my love,' he said.

'Good night.' Her voice was barely audible. 'Sleep well.'

He reached out and took her hand, holding it tightly. And that was how they fell asleep.

Chapter 14

Stephanie and Max Stuyvesant walked together into the enormous white tent in the grounds of Chilton House. Holding her arm, he guided her through the crowd and they found seats near Nicholas Blackford and Alexandra just as the auctioneer mounted the rostrum. The chairs were closely packed, and Stephanie felt the pressure of his arm against hers as forcefully as she felt his commanding presence and his eyes on her face. She looked away as the auctioneer began a graceful speech of welcome.

The Chilton auction. The first highlight of the new social season. Three hundred bidders from Britain and the continent: wealthy, polite, dressed in country tweeds, seated in the carpeted tent and standing four deep along the sides. Outside, a hundred more watched through a raised flap of the tent, sitting on the smooth lawn or perched on walking sticks that opened at one end into a small seat. Sunlight filtered through high, thin clouds; the mild air smelled of cut grass and trimmed hedges.

The Chilton auction. The kind of high-flying, distant social event Stephanie always read about in newspapers.

And Max Stuyvesant. Whom she had met unexpectedly in the park outside the tent, and whose arm now pressed against hers, a constant reminder, even as she began to concentrate on the auction.

The auctioneer finished his history of Chilton house, built in the reign of Queen Anne, and a brief biography of its late owner, a renowned painter who had died without heirs. The executors were selling the house and its contents, as well as a separate studio, greenhouse, four garages, and ten acres of park. 'I shall open the bidding on the house,' said the auctioneer genially, 'at two hundred thousand pounds.'

A flurry of whispers rose from a group at the side of the

tent. 'The townspeople,' said Max. 'Worried about being saddled with an unacceptable neighbor. A momentous problem in a village of two hundred.'

'Done,' said the auctioneer, and a surprised murmur went through the crowd. In less than two minutes, the bidding had ended at two hundred and fifteen thousand pounds. Stephanie heard Alexandra say disgustedly, 'If I'd known it would go for nothing I would have grabbed it.'

'The Earl of Wexon,' someone whispered. 'Bought it for his mother.' A sigh of relief came from the townspeople, and many of them left as the real estate auctioneer stepped down and an auctioneer from Christie's of London took his place.

'Now the numbers will go up,' Max murmured. 'The contents always do better than the houses themselves. What are you bidding on?'

'The Meissen vases,' Stephanie said, marveling at the calmness of her voice. In Sabrina's suede skirt and tweed jacket, a cashmere sweater caressing her skin, and the confident bulk of Max Stuyvesant beside her, she blended with the crowd; she belonged. She turned the pages of her catalogue. 'The Louis XVI tulipwood bureau and the George III side table. Lord and Lady Raddison want the Regency breakfront, but I don't think we'll get it; they won't go above thirty-five hundred.'

'You're buying for Peter and Rose? Did they come on hands and knees, or is this your season for forgiveness?'

Stephanie frowned. What was he talking about? Had Sabrina quarreled with Peter and Rose Raddison?

'An impudent question,' Max said smoothly. 'Allow me to change the subject. I will be bidding on the three fruitwood statues, which means you and I are not opponents. And I am delighted that I found you this morning.'

She nodded, pretending to study the catalogue. She almost had not come. When Nicholas called her at Ambassadors yesterday, offering to pick her up, she had been slow and stupid. 'What auction?'

'My dear Sabrina, the Chilton auction! Amelia called you about it, and, of course, Christie's sent you the catalogue. You must come; how could I venture into the depths of Wiltshire alone?'

254

She laughed. The blind leading the blind; she had never been in Wiltshire. She'd have to get a map and study it. 'Of course, Nicholas; what time do we leave?'

'Eight, I fear. Absurd time, but what can one do?'

She found the catalogue and soon was swept up in its glossy pages, savoring the color photographs as she did whenever she read about items beyond her means. And then in a rush it came to her: she had the means. Ambassadors had a special bank account for auctions – and she had Ambassadors. In their long talk on Monday, Sabrina had told her to draw money for the shop as she needed it. For once she would participate in an auction instead of watching and dreaming like an outsider, or a child standing silently beside her sister as her mother bid.

Sabrina had told her to ask Brian anything about the shop. 'We discuss most things and compare notes, so he won't suspect anything if you have questions.' She had hesitated. 'One thing he doesn't know. Don't buy anything from a slick gentleman named Rory Carr or his firm, Westbridge Imports. Tell Brian, will you? They may be playing around with forgeries; stay away from them until we're sure. Everything else, just ask Brian.'

'Did you have any thoughts,' Stephanie asked Brian, 'about what we might want at the Chilton auction?'

They went through the catalogue together, and Brian suggested Meissen vases, a Louis XVI bureau and a George III side table. 'Yes,' Stephanie agreed. 'Thank you. Would you bring me the auction records?'

She spread the thick books on the table, looking up the prices paid for those items and similar ones in previous auctions. Taking notes, she soon had a list of the highest figures she could bid on each piece and still give Sabrina a profit when she sold them. She felt buoyed up. For the first time since that incredible moment two days ago when Sabrina called to tell her about her broken wrist, she could think of this life as her own.

All day Monday and late into the night she had sat alone in Ambassadors, going through files and catalogues, learning about Sabrina's business and finding books on the shelves to fill gaps in her knowledge of antiques. I don't know half as much as Sabrina, she thought; but as she read, she found details coming back from studying for her estate sale business. It wasn't a complete failure, she thought wryly. It was preparation for becoming my sister.

In the stillness of Sabrina's office at midnight, she breathed the mingled odors of furniture polish, dusky velvets and brocades, and the carnations Brian had put on her desk that morning in a crystal vase. She touched the glass, her fingertips tingling. Four weeks. Ambassadors, Cadogan Square, Mrs Thirkell. The shops and ancient streets of London. Theaters, restaurants, dinner parties; the tantalizing friendship of Alexandra and Gabrielle. Freedom.

The tingling stopped. She plunged into guilt, feeling as cold and hard as the glass vase. She was a wife and mother; what right did she have to freedom? Responsibilities pulled at her, and attachments. What had happened to them? Why wasn't she lonely, worried, anxious to get back where she belonged?

'Because I have no choice,' she said aloud in the midnight quiet. 'I can't go back. Everything would be destroyed if I went back now.'

And you're *very* unhappy about it, jeered a small inner voice.

No, I'm not, she thought defiantly. I miss the children, but I know they'll be fine; they have Sabrina. I would have gone back, but now I've been given the time and I want to fill it with everything I've ever imagined. I'll never have another chance. Is it so terrible to want that? I'll go home soon and pick up the pieces and be everything I'm supposed to be. But not yet. Not yet.

On Tuesday, she gave Brian the list of purchases Sabrina had made in China. 'The ones checked off are for display in the showroom; the others should be delivered as soon as they arrive to the customers listed on the back. You have addresses for all of them.'

'Yes, my lady. I'll take care of it.'

'And, Brian, I can't find the deposits for September.'

'Oh, my lady, I'm sorry; the ledger is in my desk. Lady Vernon sent her check last week . . . ' He waited. What for?

Some response. Surprise. Lady Vernon, perhaps, was not known for prompt payment.

'Did she indeed?'

'She did. And this time only six months late.'

'An improvement.'

'Considerably, my lady. It was eight months the last time.'

'If we live long enough, Brian, we may see Lady Vernon pay on time.'

He smiled. 'I will have checks ready for you to sign the day after tomorrow, my lady.'

And then Rose Raddison had come in to ask about the Regency breakfront at Chilton.

It occurred to Stephanie, sitting beside Max in the auction tent, that she could try to find out what he knew about a quarrel with the Raddisons – he must have heard the story since returning from New York. But she gave up the idea. His secretive eyes and faintly smiling mouth made her feel young and ingenuous, and she knew he could outwit her and get more information than he gave.

The bidding was rapid, and a number of lots had been sold. Stephanie studied the bidders, especially Alexandra, who had made the trip with them at the last minute. She bid gracefully and boldly, without the gesticulations and twitchings of others, but it soon came to Stephanie that the real skill in bidding was to be unobtrusive; to keep others from knowing whom they were up against. Not knowing the wealth of other bidders, they had no idea how high they would have to go and might drop out. She remembered Garth and Nat Goldner talking about poker and smiled to herself. The Chilton auction was a high-class poker game.

When the Louis XVI commode was presented, the auctioneer described its provenance, or history of ownership, and opened the bidding at eighteen hundred pounds. He paused, his face alert, his eyes sweeping the tent. When his glance reached her, Stephanie lifted her chin. 'Two thousand,' he said.

She felt a surge of triumph. He had understood. 'Any advance on two thousand?' he queried, and his dispassionate voice reeled off higher and higher sums at signals from other bidders. Then, in a delicate pause, as his glance again met hers, Stephanie touched the pin in her lapel. 'Six thousand,' he said, and added quickly as Stephanie touched it again, 'I beg your pardon; seven thousand.' There was a moment of confusion in the tent, and then two other bids. Stephanie heard the auctioneer's monotone announce 'Eight thousand' and 'Eight thousand five hundred,' and she became angry. She would not be beaten on her first try.

Again the auctioneer scanned the crowd. When he came to her, Stephanie turned her head slightly to the right and then back. 'Nine thousand,' he said, but she was already turning to the left and back. 'Ten thousand.' He waited. There was a buzzing in Stephanie's ears; she was terrified.

'Sold,' said the auctioneer, 'to Lady Longworth for ten thousand pounds.'

The crowd applauded. Stephanie stared at his bland face, too stunned to move. Ten thousand pounds. Over twenty thousand dollars. Twice what she earned in a whole year in her job at the university. Sabrina would never forgive her.

'Extraordinary, Lady Longworth,' said Max, his flat gray eyes showing admiration. 'Skillful, subtle and prudent. I hope never to find myself bidding against you.'

She looked at him somberly. If he was making fun of her, everyone would soon know it.

'I should have guessed Sabrina Longworth was bidding,' someone said nearby. 'I saw her pull that trick before: making a bid, then raising herself before anyone else has a chance. Wonderful, how it knocks out other bidders.'

How did I know? Stephanie wondered. She trembled. How did I know?

Max stood. 'Will you have lunch with me?'

Instinctively she turned toward Alexandra and Nicholas, who were standing as the crowd began an exodus from the tent. 'We can eat together,' Nicholas said. 'Amelia packed enough for all of Wiltshire.'

He brought a picnic hamper from his car and spread the food on one of the dozens of tables set on the lawn with white paper tablecloths and green paper napkins. At a bar run by the owner of the town pub, Max bought ale for the four of them. They sat on folding chairs eating Amelia Blackford's smoked turkey, chutney, bread and cheese.

'Amelia wanted to come,' Nicholas said between bites, 'but she's at the shop. It's amazing, you know, the way she's taken hold there. Like a professional. Never knew she had it in her.' He stood and began to bounce lightly on his feet. 'Sabrina, my dear, I've been thinking. What would you say to a partnership? I don't have enough to do. Once Amelia was unleashed – oh dear, an unfortunate way of putting it, but, in fact, she went considerably further than I anticipated on taking command. The truth is, I have very little to do. But I'm too old, or perhaps too comfortable, to start a new business, and I thought we might collaborate. You could handle interior design; I would manage the business end of Blackford's and Ambassadors.'

No one will take Ambassadors from me, Stephanie thought, and aloud she said flatly, 'No.'

Nicholas' face crumpled, like a child who has been slapped when he expected praise. Alexandra looked surprised and Stephanie's heart sank. Sabrina wouldn't have been so clumsy; she would have handled the offer with grace and friendship.

Max put his hand under her elbow. 'Some clarification is needed, Nicholas,' he said smoothly. 'Sabrina has—'

'Been very rude,' Stephanie said, moving away. She didn't need Max Stuyvesant to cover for her. 'Nicholas, I beg your pardon. My thoughts were elsewhere and I answered too quickly and impolitely. May I think about this for a few days? We can talk about it again later, if you still have kindly thoughts about me—'

'Kindly—! My dear Sabrina, I adore you! Take as long as you wish; I make the offer to no one else. Are we ready to go back in? I think the bidding is about to resume.'

'I'm not ready to sit again,' said Alexandra. 'Sabrina, shall we let the gentlemen find us seats while we explore the grounds?'

Bless you, Stephanie thought, and they walked off across the smooth lawn, wending their way through groups of picnickers packing up lunch hampers and returning their dogs to their automobiles, where they would stay for the rest of the afternoon, watched over by tuxedoed car attendants. Everyone was dressed in tweeds that blended with the pale green grass and the aged red brick of the house beneath dark oaks, and Stephanie felt she was walking through a muted painting from some distant time. It seemed gentle and beautiful and perfect: a place without anxiety or unhappiness. How strange that Sabrina had wanted to get away from it.

'You all right, honey?' Alexandra asked.

'A little jumpy, for some reason.'

'Delayed reaction from your trip. Maybe you need another one, to recover.'

Stephanie laughed. 'Not for awhile.'

'Where's the Brazilian lover?'

'In Brazil, as far as I know.'

'And Max?'

'What about him?'

'I wondered what you thought about his new look.'

Max. The force of his presence struck her even when he was far off. 'Have you known him long?' she asked absently.

'Honey, come back to earth; you haven't forgotten that famous cruise! If for no other reason than that's where you and I met.'

'You know, I did forget for a minute. Now why would I do that?'

'Well, I hope not for me. I don't mind remembering it. Max has a lot of enemies, I guess, and maybe he deserves them – I don't know and I don't want to know. He and I had fun, we were good to each other, and we're still friends. Anyway, it was a long time ago and we've all changed, so I don't mind remembering.'

They came to the small brick studio where the late owner had worked, and then to a row of garages. 'Lady Longworth!' said a delighted voice, and Stephanie turned to see an impeccably dressed man with silver hair and soft pouches beneath his eyes. He bowed and kissed her hand. 'I was hoping to see you here. You were in China, I understand.'

Stephanie waited for a clue so she could introduce him to Alexandra.

'Were you buying for your fine gallery?'

He had glanced twice at Alexandra. Stephanie was embarrassed and angry; he was not helping at all. She looked at him coldly. 'In part.'

'Successfully, I hope,' he said. 'But may I hope, too, that you did not find all the porcelains you need? I expect to have some items in a few days that I think will impress you. May I bring them in?'

A salesman. Or a dealer. 'Certainly,' she said, relaxed now because she would have no reason to introduce a salesman to Alexandra. 'I'll be glad to look at them.' She nodded a dismissal and turned with Alexandra to walk on as he made another, smaller bow.

'Do all salesmen dress like French counts?' Alexandra asked.

'Only in England. In France they dress like English lords.'

'And in Germany?'

'Like Italian dukes.'

Alexandra laughed. 'You mean they're all fakes.'

'Probably,' Stephanie said lightly. She felt daring; everything she did today was turning out well. 'Do you really think Max has changed?' she asked casually.

'Mellowed. Like a pear: sweeter, smoother, maybe softer, but probably just as tough at the core, where it counts. If I didn't know him so well I'd think he was just what I'm looking for.'

'Which is?'

'Oh, you know. Somebody who'll build me a castle, but let me be myself inside it. That doesn't mean fucking around; I don't have any trouble being faithful to one man; in fact, I like it. Men aren't all that different, you know; when you've fucked one, you've fucked them all, with minor and unremarkable differences. I see by your eyebrows you don't agree.'

I have slept with one man in my entire life. 'It might be debatable.'

'I suppose. If you want to spend the time. Anyway, what I want is something to do besides fuck and be beautiful. I just don't know what that might be. So I'm waiting for somebody to show me a direction without ordering me to take it. Possible, do you think? Probably not. Perfection isn't around every corner.' They had reached the tent. 'I see our gallant men beckoning to us. What's Max bidding on?'

'The fruitwood statues.'

'Probably for his new house. Watch his face when he bids; he always looks like he'd murder his opponents if he could.'

As the crowd settled down with murmurs and the rustling of catalogues, the statues were offered. Stephanie unobtrusively watched Max. With each succeeding bid, his eyes grew darker and his high cheekbones sharpened like ridges in his bleak face. He made it a contest of wills, and two or three other bidders fought him until he wrestled them out by paying more than he or anyone else expected. If he had let her bid for him, Stephanie thought, she might have saved him thousands of pounds.

'So you think you could have done better,' he said when the statues were his.

Caught by surprise, she laughed. 'Was I so obvious?'

'You are never obvious, my dear Sabrina. But we both know you could have done better. Next time I will let you bid for me.'

He watched with amusement and approval as she bought the George III side table for less than she thought she would have to pay. And then the Regency breakfront was offered, and Stephanie realized that was the piece she wanted the most. The Raddisons had done some harm to Sabrina – otherwise, why would she have quarreled with them? – and Stephanie did not want to go back in defeat.

The auctioneer began the bidding at two thousand pounds. At twenty-five hundred, Stephanie caught his attention. She repeated her signals of the morning, varying them slightly, more subtle because she was more confident. But she was also more combative and tried to hold herself back from bidding too high when she did not have to.

'Sold,' said the auctioneer at last. 'To Lady Longworth, for three thousand one hundred pounds.'

Applause surrounded her as it had in the morning, and

Max nodded, as if in confirmation. 'Masterful,' he murmured.

I beat them, Stephanie thought with triumph. If they thought they could give Sabrina trouble by limiting the price, I beat them. Wait 'til I tell ... She looked around, bursting with pride, but in that entire throng there was not one person in whom she could confide. I'll call Sabrina tonight; wait until she hears what I did.

But she couldn't do that, either. How could she tell Sabrina, trapped in Evanston to protect Stephanie, about the excitement she was missing? She felt the glow of her triumph fade. She would have to savor it alone.

'My compliments once more, Sabrina,' Max said. 'Perhaps you will give me lessons some day.'

She smiled. Max would enjoy the story of the deception; she wished she could tell him.

Why did she think that? Because there was an air of danger about him; as if he enjoyed taking risks himself and appreciated risk-taking in others. I probably wouldn't have liked that in a man, she thought, any other time but now. When I'm taking risks myself. And discovering how successful I can be.

'I have a new house,' Max was saying. 'On Eaton Square. Eighteenth century, once magnificent, but botched by owners who thought it needed improving.' On the back of his catalogue, he sketched the rooms with bold lines, describing each one. 'In the last three months half a dozen decorators have pranced through the house. One gouged a piece from an overmantle; another damaged a chandelier; a third suggested replacing the oak banisters with wrought iron. The others were equally asinine. Will you rescue the house and me from these idiots?'

Stephanie looked at the sketches. A house to decorate. Since the birthday party at Alexandra's, she had been envying Sabrina's luck, longing for her own chance to do the same. Now here it was.

'I have the furniture,' he went on. 'Too much furniture. Too much art. Too many rugs, drapes, lamps. Everything from my old London house and my New York town house. I have a crew of workers. I need someone to tell them what to do; I need someone to tell me which furniture to keep and how to arrange it, which to give away, which to sell. I need you.'

'No.' She shook her head. 'I'm sorry, but I can't do it.'

'You can. I pay very well.'

'Money has nothing to do with it.' She clasped her hands tightly in her lap. At first she thought she was turning it down to keep her distance from Max, but that wasn't why. The real reason was that she was afraid of failing.

For years she had told herself she would be just as successful as Sabrina if she had her kind of life, with the same chances. Now Max offered her a chance, and she felt the fear rising in her throat. She shook her head and pushed the chance away. Let me keep my illusions, she thought.

'This is absurd,' said Max. 'I've seen Alexandra's house and Olivia Chasson's London house. You are the only one I want.'

'But I am the seventh one you ask.'

'Ah, you are insulted. That I can understand. The others were sent by incompetent friends. Forget them; they do not exist.'

She laughed. 'That's not the reason.'

'Then what the devil is the reason?'

'I don't have time,' she said a little wildly. And told the truth. 'All I have is about four weeks.'

'And then? You melt? You dissolve? You disintegrate?' She was laughing again. 'If you have other commitments, you will do as much as possible in the time you have. I want you to do it. You will have a free hand and no limit on what you spend.'

Stephanie finally could not resist. Studying his sketches, she pictured the rooms he had described, ideas already filling the spaces between his bold lines. 'All right,' she said, as the auction ended and they began to move out of the tent.

And I won't fail, she vowed silently. Any more than I failed today. Why should I? I can do as well as Sabrina. All I need is a chance.

As for Max, she would see only as much of him as she had to in order to remodel his house. And whenever she felt like it she could withdraw from the project, turn it over to someone else and never see him again.

'When can you start?' he asked as they said goodbye.

'I already have,' she said.

The next morning Stephanie found a pile of checks on the cherry table, waiting for her signature. They were for expenditures Sabrina had approved before she went to China, and Stephanie memorized each of them so she could handle expenses in the coming month. She felt reckless, spending so much money. Not her money, but still – her signature on thousands of pounds' worth of checks in one morning.

She was on the last check when the telphone rang. In a moment Brian was in the doorway. 'Señor Molena, my lady.'

Stephanie's pen stopped moving. Sabrina had said Antonio would be away until the first week in October – at least another week. She grimaced; she would have to find a way to put him off until Sabrina was back.

'If my lady would like me to make an excuse—' Brian began.

'No,' she said, reaching for the telephone. 'But thank you, Brian.'

'My Sabrina,' Antonio said, his voice dark and intimate. 'I finished my work in São Paulo and hurried back to see you. You will forgive my impatience? And this evening we will have dinner.'

'No—'

'You have plans for this evening?'

She hesitated. This was absurd. She was always saying *no* as if she would be leaving in a few days. But that was no longer true. This was her home now, and she had to deal with it; she had nowhere else to go. 'Dinner will be fine,' she said.

'Eight o'clock, my Sabrina. It has been too long.'

He picked her up in his car and they drove through twisting streets to Fulham Road. While Antonio spoke amusingly of someone he met on the flight from Brazil, Stephanie watched the neighborhood change. Antonio looked at her puzzled face as they turned right along Brompton Cemetery. 'A surprise,' he said, smiling, and parked the car. Following him down a flight of stairs, Stephanie looked at his dark face and hawklike nose. From Sabrina's descriptions she had expected a difficult, demanding man and an elegant dinner. What she seemed to have instead was a pleasant companion and a basement restaurant on a dingy cemetery road.

But inside, La Croisette was all she had imagined, and Antonio a charming host. His eyes gleamed when he saw that she wore the sapphire necklace, and his voice was possessive when he introduced her to Monsieur Martin, who had dared to open his restaurant on unfashionable Ifield Road and, within a few months, had made it one of the most fashionable and expensive in London. Then, ignoring Stephanie, they launched into a serious discussion of the best fish for their dinner.

Stephanie listened dreamily; neither of them seemed interested in what she wanted, and she did not care. She was content to settle back in the spell of the room: soft lights and fine fabrics, ubiquitous waiters holding her chair and helping her slip off the loose satin jacket she wore over a satin sheath, the discreet hum of wealthy men and women who believed that the world existed to give them pleasure. My world, she thought, and when the maître d' poured her wine she smiled, not because he did it but because he did it well.

Antonio talked of São Paulo and Rio de Janeiro, of costume balls and dinner parties, of the hospitals and schools being planned for the villages he was building. He was trying to impress her, and succeeding. He would have impressed Sabrina, Stephanie thought. However he had behaved in the past, if he had been like this she might have married him.

'I can't marry him,' Sabrina had said in their long telephone call on Monday. 'Everything would be easier if I could, but it wouldn't work; I can't be what he wants. But I'll tell him myself when I get back. Just tell him you need more time; I've kept him waiting so long.'

'Could you write to him?' Stephanie had asked. 'I'm not clever enough to keep him waiting patiently for four more weeks.'

'I might . . . yes, why not? I'll send the letter to you so you can mail it from there. I'll do it today; you should have it the first of next week. If he calls before then, just say you need a few more days. I think he'll accept that and not push you.'

It was too soon for her to have Sabrina's letter, but Antonio seemed content to make casual conversation and look at her; he had not even pushed her to talk. When he did ask about her trip, Stephanie talked lightly and gracefully about Mr Su, the terra-cotta warriors buried in the emperor's tomb at Sian, the houseboats on the River Li and the orchids in the zoo at Canton. Antonio asked about farm workers, and she told him about the little she had seen, not enough to satisfy his curiosity.

'Go yourself,' she suggested. 'You'd have a wonderful time.'

'*We* will go,' he said. 'It will be wonderful if we go together.'

He signaled to the waiter to bring both of them a cognac, and then he related a long Guarani legend about a search for rare jewels that seemed to have something to do with the search for love. But Stephanie listened only to the deep flow of his voice, relaxed in his easy companionship.

In the close darkness of the car she sighed and rested her head against the seat. 'And your shop?' he asked. 'Everything goes well?'

'Yes,' she murmured. 'Everything goes very well.'

'With your newspaper friends, too?'

'What?'

'They have not published their story. I left word with friends to send it to me in Brazil, but it was not published. Have they changed their mind?'

'No.' Jolted out of her dreaminess, Stephanie grew cautious, not knowing whether he knew more or less than she did. 'It's been postponed for two months.'

'Ah. Excellent. Then while Olivia still thinks her Meissen stork is genuine, there is time for me to help you.'

'No,' she said quickly, storing away the new information to think about later. Then, because he was being kind and she did not want to hurt him, she added, 'Not for a few weeks.'

'When you are ready, my Sabrina. But do not wait too long. I am concerned only for your welfare.'

'Thank you,' she said warmly, wondering how Sabrina could dismiss him so casually.

She turned her head to look at the shops and buildings they were passing. None of them were familiar. He was taking her home by a different route, but she could not ask him about it; Sabrina Longworth, at home in London, would know where they were.

She was framing a way to tell him, as soon as they reached Cadogan Square, not to call until he heard from her, when he pulled into a circular driveway and stopped the car in front of a sleek modern building. A uniformed doorman greeted him.

'You can put the car away,' Antonio said.

'Yes, sir,' said the doorman, walking around the car to open Stephanie's door.

She did not move. His apartment. His bed. Why hadn't she realized that was where he was going? Because she hadn't thought of going to bed with him. Because they weren't lovers. Sabrina and Antonio were lovers. Stephanie Andersen had never been to bed with any man but her husband.

'Sabrina,' Antonio said, an edge of impatience in his voice.

'I thought you were taking me home,' she said, feeling foolish as the doorman waited, his hand outstretched to help her.

Striding to her side of the car, Antonio reached past the doorman to grasp her arm and pull her out. 'You saw where I was driving and you did not stop me. What is this game you are playing?'

'Not a game,' she gasped, infuriated at the grip of his hand, at being pulled from the car, at her own stupidity. 'I did not think I had to monitor your driving,' she said icily. 'That you would dare assume I would come here, without asking me—'

She stopped, conscious of the open interest on the doorman's face. Beyond him, across the street, was a small park. 'Shall we walk for a few minutes?' Without waiting for an answer, she turned to the doorman. 'Please don't put the car away.'

'*Caramba!*' Antonio muttered, and moved off, still gripping her arm. 'Leave the car here,' he flung over his shoulder to the doorman.

In the park, Stephanie pulled her arm away. 'Never have you done such a thing,' Antonio fumed. 'I do not expect such behavior from you. The woman who is to be my wife does not behave in this fashion. We had an arrangement—'

'Our only arrangement was that we would not see each other for a month. You returned before that time and I agreed to see you. I agreed to nothing else.'

'You wore my jewels, you smiled, you were warm, soft, delicious. You were pleased with me and with our evening, and you behaved in ways that would please me. You will kindly remember that you said tonight I could soon get you out of this mess you have made for yourself in your little shop—'

'Little shop!' she blazed. She stopped walking. 'The mess I have made? You are unforgivably insulting.'

Astonished, Stephanie listened to herself. She ought to be careful; what if Sabrina changed her mind and didn't write the letter – decided to think about Antonio some more – perhaps even decided to marry him while Stephanie was driving him away? But anger over-rode her caution. Stephanie and Sabrina were angry and insulted. Sabrina would not marry him, and Stephanie would tell him why.

'You treat me like a child. I will not tolerate that. I do what I want to do. No one forces me into anything.'

'My Sabrina, I do not force you, I want only to care for you—'

'In your way, as you decide.'

'What else? You foolish girl, are you doing so well by yourself? You would not be in trouble in your little – in this shop of yours if you had allowed me to manage your affairs. You are in danger of losing everything. I offer you security, position, wealth. And you fling at me some foolish idea of independence.'

'Antonio, please take me home.'

'What does that mean?'

'That my foolish idea of independence is very important to me and I will not give it up.'

'You will not marry me?'

'No.'

'You will. I would not have waited all these months if I was not sure of that.'

'Will you take me home or must I take a taxi?'

'I will call you tomorrow.'

'I will not be home.'

'You will be home. By then you will be calm and reasonable.'

Thank goodness for Mrs Thirkell, she thought as they drove to Cadogan Square; someone to answer the telephone. This weekend I'll be away, and by next week Sabrina's letter will end it for good.

But, feeling guilty about what she had done, she called Sabrina that night. The connection was bad and they did not talk long; Sabrina seemed remote and uninterested. 'Don't worry about Antonio,' she said. Still, the next day, when Stephanie left for Olivia Chasson's weekend house party, she felt adrift, without guidelines or anyone to advise her.

Olivia, whom she was meeting for the first time, was a good antidote, shrewd and sharp-tongued. 'No Antonio?' she asked when Stephanie arrived alone.

'Not at the moment.'

Olivia nodded sagely. 'I thought that would end. An overbearing man. I have observed that self-made men, not content with making themselves, are grandly determined to make everyone else as well to their own specifications. Men who are born to wealth seldom have that problem.'

'Why is that?' Stephanie asked, laughing.

'Because growing up with wealth leaves them so bored they're satisfied only with large projects, such as saving the world. Look at the Rockefellers, for example. Oh, hell, I must greet the Raddisons; why do I invite them when I detest Rose?'

'Perhaps a thorny rose makes your other flowers seem sweeter.'

Olivia threw back her head and laughed. The guests in the

270

large salon turned and smiled with her. 'You're a gem, Sabrina. How dull life would be without you. I would like you on my right at dinner.'

'Of course,' Stephanie said carelessly, and then saw, in Olivia's face, how important that was. 'I'd be honored,' she added quickly.

She watched Olivia cross the room and smiled as Rose Raddison waved gleefully in her direction. A waiter gave her a glass of champagne. Lights from chandeliers danced in the sparkling wine, scattering like jewels as Stephanie moved about, accepted and admired by everyone. Not one of the polished guests in that room challenged her right to be part of their world, where no one thought about the mortgage or grocery bills or whether the garbage had been taken out for the night. An enchanted place, she thought, where I belong.

The Chasson country house in Kent had large, square rooms and tall windows overlooking gardens, a croquet lawn and a small lake. The salon where Lord and Lady Chasson entertained before dinner was known for its painted ceiling and heavy chandeliers. The year before, Sabrina had redecorated it, upholstering the chairs in creamy suede and the couches in pale green velvet. She stained the parquet floor a rich, dark oak that reflected the chandeliers, so guests seemed to float between shimmering pools of light. A long, gleaming Chippendale commode held a collection of nineteenth-century porcelain dancers, and on a small console table at the far end of the room, reflected in its matching mirror, stood a tall, pure white Meissen stork.

Looking thoughtfully at the stork, Stephanie drifted down the room toward it, smiling serenely at the strangers who greeted her. She felt at ease. A letter had come from Sabrina and everything was fine at home; Dolores had even sent Juanita to help in the house. No problems, Sabrina wrote, adding, 'I'm so bruised and stiff there's no question of doing anything in bed but sleeping.'

Surrounded by brilliant lights and soft murmurs, Stephanie imagined Sabrina in Evanston, guarding her marriage so she could return to it without any harm being done. She looked down at Sabrina's white wool challis dress with its pattern of silver threads in the skirt and pictured her closet in Evanston. Sabrina in blue jeans cooking dinner. I owe her everything, she thought.

She picked up the stork and ran her fingers over the smooth glaze, the delicate lines of wings, feathers, talons, the small fish in its beak. Olivia thought the Meissen stork was genuine, Antonio had said. At Alexandra's party, Michel had talked about a forgery. About 'getting the stork back.' Sabrina had told her not to buy from someone named Rory Carr because it seemed he dealt in forgeries.

Stephanie felt excitement rising within her. Sabrina had bought porcelains from Rory Carr, and at least one of them was a forged Meissen stork. Sold to Olivia Chasson. The stork she was holding was a Meissen; probably made by Kandler. She turned it over to see the mark on its underside. Yes. And it was superb; so perfect the wings seemed to flutter as she touched them. No wonder Sabrina had been fooled.

There is time to get back the Meissen stork, Antonio had said. She could do that for Sabrina; she held it in her hand. But how was she to get it back? She couldn't tell Olivia it was a forgery – only Sabrina could divulge that. She couldn't say it needed repair, because obviously it didn't. She couldn't sneak it out, because it was too big, and, anyway, the house was full of people. But somehow, before the end of the weekend—

'Sabrina, I'm so glad you're here!' Stephanie jumped. Rose Raddison had glided up behind her, braying directly in her ear. She was as thin as her nasal voice, with a narrow slice of a nose and a sharp, quivering chin. Her eyes were her best feature, and, to emphasize them, she made them up heavily. Stephanie thought she looked like an emaciated panda. 'When you told me about the breakfront the other day, I was amazed, I confess it, and didn't properly thank you. Now I'm sure that silly rumor that you didn't like us isn't true.'

'A strange rumor for someone to start,' Stephanie said, thinking – Go on, go on, tell me why.

'Well, some people like to make trouble.'

'But not little Rose,' said a pleasant, colorless man appearing beside them. 'My sweet wife dispenses only love and kindness. Did I say that correctly, my love?'

'Peter finds himself amusing,' hissed Rose.

'And so she wonders, Sabrina,' he went on, 'why you avoid her. Could it be that after four years you still remember overhearing her slandering your good name at Andrea Vernon's ball?'

'Overhearing,' Stephanie repeated neutrally.

'Peter is totally irresponsible,' cried Rose. 'Dear Sabrina, we would never accuse you of eavesdropping. Your friend Alexandra did mention recently that you happened to be nearby that night – *so long ago* – when we were saying how sad it was that you and Denton—'

'When you were saying,' Peter interrupted, 'that Sabrina took Denton for everything he had. But, of course, Sabrina wouldn't remember something like that, would she, dear Rose?'

Rose stretched her neck. 'Sabrina has manners, Peter. Your crudeness is quite foreign to her. If she believed that lie she would not have done so fabulously for me at the auction. However did you do it?'

Stephanie's eyebrows went up. Sabrina had never told her that story; how terrible it must have been. But now, talking about the auction, why was Rose Raddison's voice trembling with anger? 'However did I do what?' she asked coolly.

'Get it, of course, at that incredible price. You are a wonder!'

Stephanie understood. Rose had set her up to fail, just as she had thought. Feeling properly malicious for Sabrina's sake, she said, 'I wanted to save you the pain of being unhappy if I failed.'

Laughter burst from Peter Raddison. 'A direct hit, dear Rose.'

Ignoring him, Rose met Stephanie's calm smile. 'You've always been arrogant, for an outsider—'

And, at that moment, Stephanie knew what she was going to do with the stork, still resting cool and fragile in her hand.

'I beg your pardon?' she said softly. 'I couldn't make out—'

Rose thrust her face forward. 'I said you're an outsider—'

Stephanie took a step backward and Rose followed—'and if you think you fool anyone—'

'Oh!' Stephanie cried. Stepping back, she had caught her heel in the fringe of the Persian rug. Off balance, falling, she reached out wildly to catch herself and the Meissen stork flew from her hand, falling to the parquet floor with a shattering crash.

'Oh, my God,' breathed Rose. Stephanie, rubbing her ankle, looked calmly at the shards of white porcelain at her feet. Guests crowded about them. Peter Raddison backed away from his wife. Two servants materialized with brooms and dustpans. Olivia came up and Stephanie turned to her.

'I'm terribly sorry, I don't know what made me so clumsy—'

'You were on the defensive, my dear,' said Olivia. 'Any closer and Rose would have devoured you.'

'We were having a conversation,' Rose said through tight lips. 'But if I was in any way responsible for Lady Longworth's becoming overexcited, you must send me a bill for the – it was a bird of some kind, wasn't it?'

'Olivia,' Stephanie said quietly, 'I will replace the stork. I may know of another Meissen quite similar—'

'You will do no such thing, my dear. We carry enough insurance to replace the British Isles if someone should lose them. Find me another, by all means, and we'll take care of the cost. Is your ankle badly hurt? Shall I call a doctor?'

'No, thank you, it's only twisted.'

'Well, come and sit down.'

'Olivia,' said Peter Raddison in a carrying voice, 'Rose is feeling ill. Will you forgive us if I return her to London? You know she gets such dreadful headaches. If she can manage at home, I may return alone, if that would not upset the symmetry of your party.'

'As you please,' Olivia said indifferently. 'I'll see you out. Sabrina, sit down and rest.'

Stephanie sat peacefully on a couch while voices swirled about her, dissecting the Raddisons, talking about the Chasson art collection in the upstairs gallery, a new play in London, a charity ball at Barchester Towers in December. Olivia disappeared through the double doors with Peter and

Rose. The servants finished sweeping up the last of the Meissen stork.

I have become an expert at deception, Stephanie thought.

There was, she soon discovered, no routine in Sabrina's life. Ambassadors was a focal point for business and much of her social life, but Brian took care of the everyday running of the shop, leaving Lady Longworth free to attend auctions, visit homes she was decorating, go on week-long cruises, or work in the shop. After the fixed schedules of her life in Evanston, Stephanie felt, for awhile, at loose ends, always looking at her watch to be home on time, to begin dinner on time, to get to the grocery before it closed. Now when she looked at her watch, it was to plan the rest of her day or think about the evening. There was only one deadline, and it was on her calendar: Nat Goldner's X ray of Sabrina's wrist in three weeks.

On Monday morning, the first day of October, she woke planning her meeting with the contractor at Max's house to check on his progress. That afternoon she and Max were going to the warehouse to look at his furniture. If they could keep to her work schedule, she would begin furnishing the top floors in two weeks.

Successive owners had long since demolished the original interior of the house, altering fixtures and walls, boarding up some windows, removing a chimney. During the past few years, when it had been used as a private school, students had covered the walls and ceilings of the fourth floor bedrooms with colorfully obscene limericks.

'Mr Stuyvesant says they add a touch of humanity,' said the contractor. 'And not to paint them over.'

Stephanie smiled. 'I'll make a note of it.'

They went through the house, checking the work against Stephanie's drawings. Each day she saw her ideas closer to completion, restoring the balance of walls and windows, using the angles of sun and shadow to bring the house to life. She felt she had never been happier.

It was in her face. 'Pure happiness,' Max observed that

afternoon as they walked through the cavernous warehouse. 'Always, with a new project? Or is this one special?'

'Always.'

'Now I am disappointed.'

'But not surprised,' she laughed. She was glad to see him. Among the gossiping people of Sabrina's world, he was confident and casual, intriguing, private. He fended off personal questions, and his flat gray eyes were empty of emotion. There could be nothing personal between them, Stephanie thought. She was safe for the brief time she was here.

They were walking down an aisle lined with wooden lifts stacked to the ceiling, each six feet high, six feet deep, six feet wide, packed with furnishings. A lift truck lowered twenty-two of them, one at a time, to the concrete floor, and workers pried them open with crowbars. As they brought out the furnishings and Max checked them against his list of contents, Stephanie watched, trying not to gawk.

It was not easy; she had never seen anything like it. Ranging through all the great periods of art and furnishings, from Russian samovars to William Morris chairs to Art Deco lamps, even including a disassembled fifteen-foot-high Jacobean canopied bed, Max's collection turned the dingy aisles into a dazzling palace.

'Did you rob a museum?' she asked lightly to hide her awe.

A light flickered in his eyes as he glanced up from his lists. 'A dozen. Do you see anything you can use?'

That was carrying nonchalance too far. 'Don't be absurd, Max. It's magnificent and you know it; much more than we'll be able to use.'

'Good. And now I'm sorry, Sabrina, but I must go; I couldn't put off another appointment for this afternoon. I'll leave you to make your choices, and my chauffeur will return for you in half an hour; is that all right? He'll wait as long as necessary to take you home.'

She turned away to hide her disappointment and took from a packing crate a porcelain canary perched on a spray of flowers. 'Copenhagen,' she murmured, remembering the day her mother had brought one home in triumph from a flea market in Paris. 'Yes, of course,' she said. 'But I'll be here for hours. Your chauffeur shouldn't have to wait—'

'He is paid to wait. Will you have dinner with me Thursday night?'

'Yes.'

He kissed her fingertips. 'Until then.'

The vast collection fired Stephanie's imagination, adding to her excitement. The house filled her thoughts, and she spent more and more time there, working closely with the contractor, whom Max was paying an exorbitant fee to meet her schedule. I have to see it finished, she thought; I can't leave without finishing it.

Max paved the way, too, for delivery of flooring, cabinetry, wallpaper, light fixtures.

'Is there anyone you don't know?' Stephanie asked when, with a telephone call, he assured delivery of handcrafted Swedish rugs for the bedrooms.

'I don't know you. Yet.'

On Friday, Stephanie stopped at Ambassadors to go through the mail and reflect for a few moments on her dinner the night before with Max: friendly, casual, bantering, almost impersonal. Not once had they relaxed their guard in hours of conversation. I've taken up fencing again, she thought wryly. The chimes over the front door broke her thoughts, and she looked up to see the elegantly dressed elderly man who had greeted her at the Chilton auction. But he was not as smooth as he had been; Stephanie was puzzled to see that he was watching her closely, studying her. She held out her hand.

'My lady.' He bowed. 'I bring you something very special.'

Dramatically, he opened a parcel and unwrapped a porcelain statue of two figures: a regal Venus watching a small, mischievous Cupid, wings folded back, face bent over his arrows. The statue was made of biscuit porcelain in the pale rose pink called *rose pompadour*; with the thrill of discovery Stephanie recognized it as Sèvres, from the late 1700s, of enormous value.

He was watching her, and she kept her face smooth, hands

clasped before her. More poker, she thought; just like the auction. 'Very fine,' she said calmly.

'My lady,' he murmured reproachfully. 'It is quite extraordinary. Sold privately in Germany last week; I was told in advance it would be offered. As soon as I saw it I thought of you.'

Don't buy it. Stephanie tilted her head. Where had the thought come from? She looked past the statue through the front window, at the overcast sky and busy street, and let the silence stretch out.

The salesman adjusted his foulard, a small movement that betrayed nervousness. 'We haven't discussed price, my lady, but of course you know the value.' She slid her gaze slowly from the window to his face. He cleared his throat. 'Perhaps you wish to think about it. I can leave it here; we trust each other ... ' She continued to look at him and saw him swallow, and swallow again. 'I understand,' he said, glancing around the shop, 'that you had a sad accident at Lady Chasson's. A strange coincidence, breaking a piece you sold her yourself.'

And suddenly Stephanie knew who he was. Rory Carr. He had come to find out about the stork – whether it had really been an accident.

'Mr Carr,' she said, testing it.

'My lady?'

Right on the button, she thought triumphantly. And you're the one who sold Sabrina that stork.

'I have no need for porcelains now.' She let a note of genuine regret slip into her voice. 'I must refuse this one, as fine as it is.'

'But my lady, this is unexpected. We have dealt with each other for such a long and pleasant time—'

'Yes,' she said firmly, feeling more confident as cracks appeared in his suave speech. 'But not today. I bought many porcelains in China, and until I go through my inventory I will buy nothing more.'

'My lady!'

'Nothing, Mr Carr. And now, if you will excuse me—'

She saw a quick gleam of fear in his eyes. 'My lady, perhaps I can change your mind.'

'You can tell me nothing I don't already know,' Stephanie said. That was probably rash, but she was swept along by a sense of adventure. By herself, she had solved the problem of the stork; now she was getting back at Rory Carr for cheating Sabrina. It served him right if he was afraid. Sabrina would have been afraid when she discovered the forgery. If only Sabrina had told her about it when it happened; she would have known enough not to encourage him at the auction.

But it didn't matter. It was over. He was leaving, and that would be the last of him.

'I will hold the Venus, my lady, and call in a few days.'

'If I want to buy from you, Mr Carr, I will call you.'

When he was gone she went into her office, closed the door and called Sabrina. There was no answer. Ten o'clock on Friday morning in Evanston. She could be anywhere. Grocery store. Hardware store. Dry cleaner. Or at work. Was she going to the office this week? Stephanie couldn't remember. She closed her eyes, thinking back to their last phone call. What had they talked about? She couldn't remember. She was losing touch with her other life, her real life, her home.

I can't do that, she thought; I can't lose touch. It's the only real thing I've got. Behind her closed eyes she pictured the house, the porch, the living room. There's the new lamp, she thought; Penny's charcoal pencil, the tear on the couch that I meant to fix before I left for China. And in the kitchen, the new rack for mugs and – what's that on the counter? Oh, the Cuisinart I got for my birthday; Sabrina told me about it. And upstairs in the bedroom, the quilt on the bed and the striped wallpaper ... No, no, the striped wallpaper is here, on Cadogan Square, with the blue carpet and ... and what? In her mind the two bedrooms wavered and merged. Which was which? Which was real?

The trouble was, she was too tired to think. Trying to do everything, she was not getting enough sleep. Every night she went out to the dinner parties, theater parties and concerts that made up Sabrina's social life. She was collecting them, as if in a scrapbook – the elegance and color, the varied foods and entertainment that filled the hours. But she soon found it was as exhausting as it was exhilarating to keep up with the rapid-fire gossip, knowing glances and shared recollections of different groups of people whom she had trouble keeping separate. By the time she got home she was so keyed up that she slept restlessly, and the next day she had trouble distinguishing her dreams from her London life and both of them from her real life.

If it was real. 'Which is my home?' she asked out loud.

'My lady?' Brian opened the door of his cubicle and stood, waiting.

Stephanie pushed back her thoughts. 'Brian,' she said, 'I just told Rory Carr we would not be buying from him for awhile. Will you note that, please? There is some question about his honesty.'

'In what respect, my lady?'

'He may deal in forgeries. Until we are sure, we will avoid him.'

Brian restrained his curiosity, and Stephanie gathered her drawings and left for Max's house.

That night, Gabrielle telephoned. She and Brooks were having trouble, and fragments of quarrels and suspicions trailed through her talk. Each night, as Stephanie unlocked her door, the telephone was ringing, and she answered it to hear Gabrielle pour out new fears.

'He's changed,' Gabrielle said a week after her first call. 'He's cold and . . . I think . . . suspicious. He watches me; if I write a letter he looks over my shoulder. If I get a telephone call he has to know who it is. And now he's started going to the office at night. He's there now; I know because I called him—'

'Have you asked him what's wrong?' Stephanie asked.

'He won't tell me – he hardly talks to me at all. He doesn't come back 'til late, and I don't wait up for him. I'm afraid to, because he doesn't talk to me when he gets in. He makes me feel guilty just by looking at me, and I'd rather be asleep than face that. Then in the morning when I wake up he's leaving again.'

Yes, Stephanie thought, I know how it feels to be with someone who barely knows you're there.

'I don't know what's happening,' Gabrielle said, sounding

like a bewildered child: Penny, tearful and clinging when she was frightened.

'Would you like me to come over and stay with you tonight?' Stephanie asked. It was midnight, and she really wanted to stay home; she had been out to dinner with Max for the third time in a week and was tired and exhilarated at the same time. She wanted to think. But the panic in Gabrielle's voice brought a rush of anxiety and protectiveness she had not felt in a long while.

'No, don't. Sabrina, you're wonderful, and I love you, I don't know what I'd do without you. But if Brooks comes home early, I don't want him to know I've told you about us. I'll call you tomorrow.'

But the next day, instead of calling, she arrived on Stephanie's doorstep. 'He told me I had to leave. He said I was a spy; that I sold the secrets of Westermarck's new line to another company, I don't even remember which one—' She looked up helplessly, and then, as Stephanie put her arms around her, she began to sob.

They sat on the sofa. Stephanie rocked Gabrielle in her arms, feeling her breast become wet with tears. She put her cheek against Gabrielle's clustering curls. 'Hush, my dear Penny,' she said, and caught her breath. But Gabrielle had not heard, and Stephanie said, 'It will be all right, Gaby; we'll find out what happened, it will be all right,' while she ached for Penny and tears came to her eyes.

She blinked them away, 'Gaby, have you talked to *anybody* about Westermarck cosmetics?'

'No. I swear it. I don't know anything about them. I never even think about them except when I'm putting on makeup. Why should I? Anyway, I can't tell the difference between any of them. Westermarck, Revlon, Estee Lauder – they're all the same. Oh, God, don't tell Brooks I said that!'

Stephanie hid a smile. 'Did you bring any clothes with you?' Gabrielle shook her head. 'Well, we'll have to get your things.'

'I can't. I can't go there until he calls – he will call, won't he?'

'If he doesn't, I will.' Stephanie took Gabrielle upstairs to the pink and green bedroom she had used when she visited

Sabrina the year before. 'Take what you want from my closet, and then we'll talk about what comes next.'

The telephone rang and she took it quickly. But it was not Brooks; it was Alexandra. 'I have been asked to dine in splendor at a new Italian place in Soho, gracing it with my presence so it will become the new "in" restaurant.'

'A bit unsubtle of them. Does that happen often?'

'Honey? You all right?'

'Of course. Why?'

'Because either you are asleep or – oh, hell, are you in bed with someone?'

'No. What are you talking about?'

'I'm talking about us, you and me, getting these invites all the time. So what's bothering you?'

'Oh . . . we can talk about it later.'

'Uh huh, there is something. Okay, how about dinner with me tonight? This one I'm accepting because the owner did me a favor once.'

'What's the name of it?'

'Il Cocchio Oro. Could that possibly mean The Golden Cock?'

Stephanie laughed. 'The Golden Coach. Your Italian needs polishing. What time?'

'Eight? I'll pick you up.'

Before Stephanie could turn back to Gabrielle, the telephone rang again. This time it was Sabrina.

'I haven't got long, Stephanie, but I had to let you know.'

'What's wrong?'

'Nothing, everything is fine. But Naţ says he'll take X rays on the twenty-second.'

'The twenty-second? That's only a week away.'

'Ten days. Only?'

'I mean, it seems so soon. Does your wrist feel better?'

'You can't tell when it's inside a cast. Wait a minute.' Sabrina's voice turned from the telephone. 'Yes, Cliff, of course you're going to the airport with me. Yes, Penny, you too. We're all going.' Her voice came back, clear and exasperated. 'When do you get to be alone in a family?'

'Not often,' Stephanie said, remembering. 'Who are you meeting at the airport?'

'Garth. He's been in Berkeley all week. Stephanie, I have to go. There's some mayhem downstairs. I just wanted you to know about the date. October twenty-second. Call me soon so we can talk.'

Stephanie repeated it to herself. Ten more days. Sabrina had sounded so ... neutral. Not happy, not sad. How did she feel? How do *I* feel? she wondered. But there was no time to think about it; Gabrielle needed to talk, and she talked straight through to tea time.

By then Stephanie was so worried about her despair, and furious at the shabby way Brooks had treated her, that she called him and told him to meet her and Alexandra for dessert and coffee at Il Cocchio Oro. She did not wait for him to refuse.

'You don't mind?' she asked Alexandra later as they ate veal with almonds and raisins, baked mozarelle and scampi, while fending off a crew of waiters who had been ordered to make their meal memorable.

'Honey, after that story, I can't wait to see him. Do we use a horsewhip or hang him by his thumbs?'

'First we give him a chance. For Gaby's sake.'

They smiled at each other, and the mirrored walls multiplied their images in the white and gold room – two stunning women, simply dressed and attended as if they were royalty. When Brooks arrived at ten, he did not have to look for them; they glowed like jewels in the center of the room.

'Zabaglione and espresso for three,' Stephanie said to the waiter. She gazed, unsmiling, at Brooks. 'Gaby is staying with me. I'll be coming for her things tomorrow. Please have them packed and ready.'

He nodded. 'I'm not happy about this, you know.'

'Oh, my,' said Alexandra. 'I grieve to hear that.'

Brooks ignored her. 'I didn't act hastily. I have proof that she sold information to Rymer Cosmetics for a quarter of a million pounds.'

'Ridiculous,' Stephanie said automatically. 'Gaby would never betray you. And she doesn't need money.'

'She's in debt to everyone: dressmakers, shoemakers, beauty salons, a gymnasium. And she signed some notes in Monte Carlo a month ago that I knew nothing about until last week.'

'Everyone is in debt,' Alexandra said. 'I'll bet you are, too.'

'No.'

'Then you're unnatural,' she said flatly.

'What proof?' Stephanie asked.

'I was told by the man who bought the information. Rymer brought out its new line two weeks ago, beating ours by a full month, with identical brand names, colors and packaging. Not similar; identical. And all of it stolen. Do you know what it will cost us to formulate a new line? Do you know what we lose by coming in months behind Rymer and Revlon and the others?'

'No, but you're assuming that man is telling the—'

'Over a million pounds. Four times what Gabrielle got for her little job. If I'd know, I would have bought her off and saved three quarters of a million.'

'You bastard, Brooks,' said Alexandra.

Stephanie was silent as the waiter served their frothy zabaglione and espresso. Picking up the small lemon peel in her saucer, she dropped it in her coffee. 'If I were you,' she said to Brooks, 'I'd look at my employees. Your friendly informant is protecting someone by accusing Gaby.'

'For God's sake, this isn't a complicated spy story. Gaby has been acting guilty for a month, jumping every time I come near her, secretive about letters and phone calls. You would have acted exactly as I did if you had a million-pound loss and someone told you who was at fault. I love Gaby—'

'Oh, fuck,' Alexandra said disgustedly. 'My old-fashioned mommy always told me love means you trust somebody first and shoot second.'

'I love Gaby,' Brooks went on, less firmly. 'But we all know she's like a child. And a child can be tempted—'

'But that's what you want, isn't it?' Stephanie asked. 'For her to be like a little girl?'

Brooks gave her a startled glance. 'I never asked her to be a child,' he said, but he and Stephanie both knew they were remembering the night Gaby told him he spanked her with words.

'She wants to please you,' Stephanie said. 'That's all she wants.'

'She would please me by telling me about her debts.'

Stephanie shrugged slightly. 'Maybe she doesn't like to ask permission to spend money.'

'It has nothing to do with permission. I have to know what she is doing. In fact—'

'In fact,' Stephanie said, suddenly understanding, 'it's because you don't know for sure about Gaby that you're so angry.'

'I was told—' He hesitated. 'Perhaps I'll have a talk with her.'

'Isn't it beneath you,' asked Alexandra, 'to converse with a traitor who leaks information?'

'She's not a traitor,' he said coldly. 'She may be in trouble. And if I was hasty—'

'Hasty, the man says. In such a hurry you scared her speechless. And now you're going to do her a favor and have a talk with her. How about finding your real spy first, and then maybe you'd be fit to crawl over and apologize. She's better off now with Sabrina.'

'Sabrina,' said a new voice, and Stephanie turned to see Antonio standing beside her. 'How are you?' he said. 'I have not called you.'

She smiled. 'I know.' There was a brief silence. 'Will you join us for a drink?'

He swung around a chair from the next table and sat down, greeting Brooks and Alexandra and ordering cognac for all of them. 'If I am interrupting a personal talk—'

Again there was silence. 'Plumbing,' said Alexandra.

'I beg your pardon?' Antonio asked as Stephanie stifled a laugh.

'We were discussing leaks and evicting residents who are suspected of causing them. Do you know about such things?'

'Nothing. I have people to take care of them. Though lately I have been discussing them for the town I am building.'

285

'What does that mean: building a town?'

'What it says. Is it not clear?'

'You start with empty land and build a town? Houses, stores, everything?'

'Everything. Schools, hospitals—'

'Where will you get the people?'

'They are there, living in hovels. I am building them a new life.'

Alexandra's eyes gleamed. 'I always thought towns just . . . happened.'

'I make things happen.'

Stephanie watched as Antonio and Alexandra looked at each other, talking, listening, each beginning to consider what the other might offer. They were alike, Stephanie thought; both coming from poverty to luxury by their wits and determination, using whatever and whoever was at hand. And both now anxious to find a place with another person that would make it all seem worthwhile.

'Alexandra,' Stephanie said. 'I have to be home early to make a call to America. Will you forgive me?'

Alexandra winked, so quickly no one saw it but Stephanie. 'Call me whenever you want to talk about plumbing.'

'I'll come with you,' Brooks said. 'I want to ask you—'

Their eyes met, and Stephanie's lips curved in a reluctant smile. She liked him. Even now, they could share an unspoken decision to leave Alexandra and Antonio alone together. If only he hadn't hurt Gaby, she thought; what good friends we all could be.

At home, she told Gabrielle about the evening. Huddled in an armchair, wearing one of Sabrina's robes, her eyes red, Gabrielle began to brighten as Stephanie talked. 'I have to call him!' she cried. 'He hates to admit he's wrong. And it was my fault; I should have asked him what was happening so we could talk about it.'

'Gaby, that's not true.' Stephanie sat on the arm of her chair. 'Don't take the blame. You should have asked him, but his fault was worse; he heard a story and decided you were guilty without ever talking to you.'

Gabrielle sighed. 'I suppose. Sabrina, you know so much.'

Look who knows so much, Stephanie thought after Gabrielle went to bed. Look who's giving advice on living with a man. She thought of Garth, sitting in their kitchen, reading the paper, while she stood with her back to him and cooked dinner. I should have talked long ago about what was happening to us. I shouldn't have believed that ugly letter any more than Brooks should have believed the story about Gaby. It was my fault as much as Garth's that we drifted apart. It was my fault as much as his that we didn't make love very often. I wanted to punish him. For what? For being Garth Andersen; for having a career and recognition and success while all I had was a failed business. And a family. Yes, but he had the family, too. He had everything.

Well, I got back at him, didn't I? Played a first-class joke on him; left him without his even knowing it; found out I can make a life on my own.

Not true, she thought quickly. I need my family. I just don't have time to think about them right now.

Business was picking up at Ambassadors; Stephanie accepted three new commissions for November and December. I won't be able to do them, she thought regretfully; Sabrina will. She went to another auction with Nicholas, and once again he raised the question of a partnership. 'I'm thinking about it,' she said. 'I'll let you know soon.'

On Friday she supervised the placement of furniture on the top two floors of Max's house. Mrs Thirkell had packed a lunch, but she forgot about it until the movers were gone and she was alone, going from room to room with her checklist. It was almost five when she realized how hungry she was. The first meal in my new house, she thought, and, sitting cross-legged on the floor of the study, she opened the wicker basket.

She was eating scallop mousse from a plastic container when Max appeared in the doorway. 'An inaugural picnic. And I wasn't invited.'

Startled, she looked up. 'How did you get in?'

'With my key. Was I indiscreet?'

She laughed. 'Of course not. I'm sorry.'

He looked at her keenly. 'You forgot it was my house.'

'So it seems.' She kept her voice light. 'I let myself get carried away. But I promise I won't go so far as to move in.'

'The house would be lovelier if you did. May I sit down?'

'Of course.' Her face was warm, and she busied herself filling a small plate with water biscuits, paté and mousse. 'Your inaugural picnic. I'm sorry I have no wine.'

'One moment.' He left, returning with a bottle and corkscrew.

'Do you always carry a bottle of Beaujolais?' Stephanie asked as he pulled out the cork.

'Only today. A house is not furnished until it has a bed, a table and wine. You told me the first two would be delivered today. I provide the third. Now – do we have goblets?'

She held up her glass. 'I apologize again. It was to be a picnic for one.'

'Then we will share.'

As they ate and drank, he told her about his plans for an art gallery that would sell tapestries from eastern Europe. 'You must see them. Huge pieces, bold and vigorous. I'd like one in this house, on the long wall in the drawing room, if you approve.'

'But you don't need my approval. If you want something in your home, you should buy it.'

'Your judgment is important to me. Shall we have a guided tour of what you have done so far?'

'Certainly.' She repacked the picnic basket, moving slowly, trying to recapture the private pleasure he had shattered. His presence filled the space she had actually begun to feel was hers, and now it was his house, silent about them, his silence as he stood above her. She took a deep breath to slow the beating of her heart.

But the house was part of her, and, walking through the rooms, she almost forgot Max. She knew she had failed to achieve Sabrina's lightness of touch, her witty combinations and unexpected contrasts in fabric and line – but then, Stephanie told herself, I've been designing for Max Stuyvesant, who is not known for lightness of spirit. Give me an Alexandra, and then see what I can do.

Still, the rooms had an unmistakable elegance and

personality. Stephanie had made of each a separate setting with one or two massive pieces of furniture balanced by simpler ones, the walls covered in dark grasscloth or suede. The rooms blended together in dark woods and fabrics illuminated by recessed lights and occasional flashes of color to create an atmosphere both sensual and aloof, with a private, almost secretive air. Exactly like Max.

Standing in the center of each room, turning on lights against the October darkness, Stephanie hid her feelings of pride and possession as she described in dry phrases some finishing touches still to be done and the plans for completing the lower two floors. 'I won't be able to do it all,' she said quietly. 'I have only until Monday. But most of the work is done.'

Max was noncommittal, nodding as she spoke. When she finished, they were in the fourth-floor hallway, their shadows falling across the blocks of light from the bedroom doors. He took Stephanie's hands. 'It is superbly done. There is nothing I would change.' He kissed her palms, feeling with his lips the tremor that ran through her. Stephanie bent her head, resting it against his chest, and, with his arm around her, Max led her to his bedroom.

There was little time to think, but it did not matter. Max had been a shadow hovering over everything she had thought and done since she had danced with him at Annabel's, and she had known all afternoon, from the moment he appeared, that she was taking the last step away from the Stephanie Andersen who had come to London four weeks earlier. And why shouldn't I? she thought in a swift, defensive flash. Garth has Sabrina. It's crazy to pretend that by now they haven't . . . Max tightened his arms around her, one hand on the back of her head, and she met his open mouth in a triumph of desire over caution.

Mine! she exulted silently. Mine! My house that I made; my lover. Sabrina's life. And mine.

Max stripped off her clothes and lay her on his bed before he took off his own. He stood above her, looking down at her slender body. 'A long wait,' Stephanie heard him murmur, and then he lay beside her, his large body and frizzled red hair a silhouette lit dimly from behind, a shadow with hard, cool hands. She moved toward him, but he shook his head. Taking both her hands in one of his, he pinned them to the bed above her head and, with his other hand, stretched her taut, slowly tracing the curves of her body until her muscles rippled beneath his touch. He lowered his head to take her nipples between his teeth and flicked his tongue across them like a fine and rapid whip, then ran it in a fiery line along her stomach to the mound of hair and shrinking flesh that tried to deny him.

'No . . . ' Stephanie moaned. She tried to move away or pull him on top of her, but Max still held down her hands. She closed her eyes, shame and desire mixed, as he took her into his mouth, taking small bites in the soft flesh. She tried to lie as rigid as her thoughts, to separate herself from the sharp pain and pleasure of his relentless mouth, but her hips moved of themselves, her neck arched, and then she cried out with the sudden release, astonished at the pleasure of it.

Dimly, within her body's response, Stephanie recognized the calculated skill of Max's hands and mouth, but she ignored it. When at last he freed her hands and lay on her, she looked up and met his flat gray eyes, watching her. He moved deliberately, entering her slowly until she could not wait; lifting her hips, she put her hands on his buttocks and fiercely pulled him deep inside her. The room was loud with the cacophony of her thoughts and her lips formed his name. And Max smiled.

'Honey,' said Alexandra as Stephanie poured tea in her office on Monday morning, 'you look tired.'

Stephanie's lips curved. 'I didn't get much sleep over the weekend. *You* look wonderful. I haven't seen you since our Italian dinner.'

'I thought I'd talk to you about that. Can I talk to you about Antonio?'

'If it would please you.'

'It would please me to know whether you're still thinking about marrying him.'

'I'm not.'

'No doubts?'

'No doubts, Alexandra, he expects ... No, I shouldn't inflict my feelings on you.'

'Honey, how many times in the last year have you told me what he expects? And how many times have I told you what I'm looking for?'

Not knowing the answer, Stephanie looked at her in silence.

'I suppose you're thinking of my performance with Brooks last week.' She held out her cup for more tea and bit into a croissant. 'I did enjoy taking him apart, not because I like Gabrielle – actually, I think she's a fool – but because I get upset when I see self-satisfied men breaking their loyal little women in half. But the truth is, the whole time I knew he was the kind of man I wanted.'

'*Brooks?*'

'Parts of Brooks. Not the bastard who wants his little girl to adore him, but the other one – successful, sure of himself, building an empire and protecting it. That's what I want. I could trust a man like that to build my castle and help me run my life. I've done it alone long enough, you know; I'm tired of it. Antonio's rich enough to buy anything we could ever want, and he'll let me run part of his empire. I'll be more than a plaything; I'll be helping to *build towns* – how could I resist that? If he demands in return that I concentrate on him, stay at his side, that's a fair exchange. After all, how long will I be thirty-five? Or look it? What the hell, honey, I want a place to belong and be taken care of and have something of my own to do. I want the works. Isn't that what we all want?'

Stephanie swirled the tea in her cup. A few leaves at the bottom clustered like a four-petaled flower. Or a family. It's Monday, she thought. October twenty-second. Sabrina's X ray.

'Sabrina? You listening? You really do look tired.'

'I was wondering where love comes in the exchange.'

'Oh, love. Antonio says love comes later. It's an old Guarani legend. If we can be friends, I'll be satisfied. Maybe that's the best any of us can hope for.'

'Forgive me, my lady,' Brian interrupted, 'but Monsieur

Michel Bernard says it is important that he speak with you.'

Alexandra stood in a whirl of energy. 'I'll say goodbye, honey. We're off to Rio for a week.'

'Already?'

'Well, don't tell Antonio, but Alexandra thinks it's a good idea to see the lay of the land before getting knee-deep into coffee beans and Guarani Indians.'

'And what does Antonio think?'

'Antonio says he lost you because he was too patient. Forcefulness and speed are the order of the day, to sweep me into his arms. He told me a Guarani Indian legend to illustrate it. Too long to repeat. Come to think of it, too long to remember.'

They laughed. Impulsively, Stephanie hugged Alexandra and kissed her cheek, feeling her surprised, reflexive pulling back. A mistake, she thought; they don't do that. But what difference does it make? I won't be here when she gets back. I may never see her again.

'I'll call when we get back,' Alexandra said, and Stephanie nodded as she picked up the telephone.

'Michel? Weren't you going to call about four weeks ago?'

'I recall promising that and I apologize. I have been in Bonn and Jolie is in Turkey. I hear you had an accident at Lady Chasson's.'

'Yes. I was clumsy.'

'Truly amazing, for a graceful lady who knows fragile art so well. But then I heard also of a small contretemps with Rose Raddison.'

'You heard all that in Bonn?'

'No, Paris. Lady Chasson was visiting friends. It is a little world we live in, yes?'

'Yes.' With a rueful smile, Stephanie remembered how Sabrina's world had always seemed limitless compared to the narrowness of Evanston. 'What is Jolie doing in Turkey?'

'Photographing a cache of vases confiscated as they were being smuggled out of the country. I am calling to ask for your help. We are sure now that the forgeries are a sideline, not the main operation. The big money is in smuggling from countries where governments have banned the export of art and antiquities. Someone funds groups in these countries to rob museums and tombs and ancient temples, and then this someone smuggles the stuff out and sells it in Europe and America. You have heard of this?'

'Some . . . '

'Well, it does not affect you so much because you don't sell these things – art and jewelry from tombs in Turkey and Egypt, sculpture from temples in Cambodia, Thailand, Colombia; entire sections of the temples themselves – doorways, walls, altars.'

'But how can I help you if I don't sell them?'

'We think that Ivan Lazlo, who is listed as the owner of Westbridge Imports, and his salesman, Rory Carr, store the smuggled pieces in their warehouse. Some are smuggled out for specific buyers; others are sold along with legitimate antiques. But it seems Ivan and Rory wanted to make money on their own. So they dabble in forgeries.'

'But who really owns Westbridge?'

'Ah, that is our mysterious Mr Big Man whom we have not yet found. When we do, the last piece is in place. But now we hear rumblings that the little men and the big one may be quarreling over money and also over the risk of the smuggling being exposed if the forgeries are discovered and account books examined and questions asked. Thieves always fall out, yes? So we thought you might hear something. Gossip about salesmen suddenly being fired or quitting, dealers finding new partners, maybe many rare items dumped on the market all at once. If you do, will you call us here in Paris? In two weeks we will be in London. Save us a night and we will take you to dinner. Yes?'

'Yes.' I will be gone, she thought.

Brian brought in the mail. 'Gabrielle de Martel called, my lady. She asks that you return her call. And may I bring you some lunch?'

'No, thank you, Brian, I may go out.'

She leafed through the mail while dialing.

'Sabrina,' said Gabrielle. 'Brooks called.'

There was a letter from Sabrina; she tore it open.

'I didn't talk to him; I told Mrs Thirkell to say I was out.'

News from Evanston; news of the family. Chatty, nothing personal.

'But now I think I should call him back. He gets angry when—'

How could that be? Nothing personal in a letter about her own family?

'But I didn't want to do anything until I talked to you. What if I do the wrong thing?'

No mention of Garth.

'It's just that I'm not sure what to say.'

They hadn't talked for a week. Stephanie hadn't wanted to talk; her thoughts were too full of Max.

'Sabrina? Have you heard me?'

'Yes, Gaby.' Beneath her thoughts, she had been listening. 'I don't think you should call him back.'

'You think I should wait for him.'

'Don't you think you should? To make sure you both know what you're doing, and what you want to do? You shouldn't . . . deceive each other. Or yourself.'

Gabrielle sighed. 'I suppose so. God, I hate being sensible.'

It was not yet dawn in Evanston; hours before Sabrina's appointment with Nat Goldner, hours before she called to tell Stephanie what he had found. For awhile, then, Stephanie could think about Max. A weekend of Max, in his house, eating the food his butler brought from London's finest restaurants and served at the desk in the study. His maid had brought a suitcase for him and he wore a purple dressing gown, and Stephanie a blue velvet one that wrapped twice around her waist. She folded up the sleeves and tied them at her elbows with twine left by the movers. Her hair was tumbled, her eyes bright, every nerve alive to changes in temperature, a breath of air, the touch of sunlight on her skin and Max's hand on her breast, strong coffee in the morning and the dry bite of Burgundy wine at night, glowing darkly in the light of dying flames in the bedroom fireplace.

She glided on a fine edge of desire and excitement, flushed

with the triumph of discovery. 'Exquisite,' Max said. 'My stunning beauty.'

'High praise, from a connoisseur,' she said lightly, but the look of triumph was bright in her eyes.

But on Monday, sitting in her office – what triumph? she asked herself. Not the triumph of intimacy or affection, or even friendship. The triumph of passion. And that, she realized, was the last item on my checklist. I wanted to do all that Sabrina had done, experience her life in all the ways it was different from mine. And this was the last: the calculated sensuality of Max Stuyvesant.

She shivered. Her pride in Ambassadors, the decorating of Max's house, her caring for Gabrielle, her affection for Alexandra. It was all a dream.

But even if I could keep it, she thought, it still wouldn't be enough. I want love and cherishing and commitment. Otherwise, I wouldn't have a place to belong.

Where do I belong? Wherever I can be connected to other people. Once I had that, or thought I did, and then I lost it. And now I've discovered that Sabrina's life isn't the one I want, either.

But how will I know what I want until I go back to Garth and find out? Garth. Penny. Cliff. My home. 'I miss them,' she said aloud, startling herself in the silence. 'And I need them.'

Have they missed me and needed me?

Don't be ridiculous.

They don't even know I've been gone.

The telephone rang. Brian was out, so she answered it herself and heard the smooth tones of Max's voice.

'Without planning it, I seem to have moved into my new house over the weekend. Now I'm stumbling over workers. I think I should disappear for a few days.'

'Oh.' A stab of dismay; she heard it in her voice.

'I thought a cruise would be pleasant. The Mediterranean is magnificent this time of year. The workers could then finish without obstructions.'

'Yes.'

'Can they finish without your direction?'

She sighed. She had forgotten one more item on the list of

things she wanted to do: a cruise. Sabrina had had so many; all Stephanie wanted was one. Then I'll go back, she thought, to what is waiting for me. I'll go back to Garth and we'll find the love we used to have. I can do so much now. I've learned so much about myself. I will try. I promise.

But first I want one more dream. Only one.

'Brian can direct the construction crew,' she said.

'We'll sail from Monaco to the Italian Riviera; about four or five days. Will that suit you?'

'Yes.'

'Excellent. We'll take three other couples; you'll find them pleasant. We leave Wednesday morning, the 24th; can you be ready at nine?'

'Yes.'

Hanging up, she moved her chair to look through the office door, down the length of the showroom to the street beyond the paned window. The day was overcast but warm, the silvery air like a screen between Stephanie and the people hurrying past. She would call Sabrina and find out about the X ray; tell her she would be away for a few days. And then the adventure would end.

Everything was coming to a close. Mrs Thirkell would watch over Gaby, and it was only a matter of time before Brooks came for her. Alexandra was with Antonio. The forged Meissen stork was broken and she had told Rory Carr to stay away. Ambassadors had done well under her care: she had sold some large pieces, earned an impressive fee for Max's house, taken on new commissions for next month.

When Brian came in she stood up and slipped on her jacket. There were things she had to do: call Sabrina, rearrange drawers and closets on Cadogan Square that she had made her own, decide what to pack for the cruise. She stood in the middle of the showroom, memorizing it, and then made a last, silent farewell to Ambassadors.

Chapter 15

Sabrina stirred, half awake. October 6, she thought. Garth is going to California. But when she opened her eyes she saw it was barely dawn, the first pale light turning the windows pearl gray. In the maple tree, a bird sang. Sabrina stirred again and felt her hand in Garth's, their fingers entwined. Then the night rushed back, enveloping her – Garth's mouth whispering against her breasts, his body covering hers, the passion of her response. Not a dream; she had let it happen. *But, no, I couldn't help?—*

Garth's hand tightened in his sleep. Sabrina felt the warmth flowing between them and realized suddenly how changed the world could seem with a hand clasping hers in the darkness.

She was frightened. *Pull away. Your world has not changed.* But the thought faded as she slept again. When she woke, sunlight streamed through the clear, bright windows and she was alone in the bed.

She looked around the room. Garth's suitcase, packed but still open, was on the chair. I should get up, she thought, and see if he needs help. But she was afraid to face him. *Stephanie, please forgive me. I didn't mean it. Please understand* ... Unexpectedly, she remembered the terrible joy of feeling him inside her and the swift feelings of loss and guilt that followed.

I will never know what we might have had.

But she had no right to think that and, ashamed, she closed her eyes again, like a child hiding from herself. Because she could not deny that she had wanted to make love to Garth. And she would never know if that was why last night, for the first time, he had turned to her not with a question but with the assurance of a husband.

But he wouldn't have waited indefinitely, she thought; we were foolish to think he would. The risk was always there; it just finally caught up with me. It meant nothing.

She heard his quiet footsteps on the stairs and quickly shut her eyes. He came to the bed, kissed her, picked up his suitcase and left the room.

And then he was gone. An extraordinary feeling of lightness swept over Sabrina. Last night had been an accident. She hadn't really felt anything; no more than a brief response. It wasn't important.

You wanted him and he knew it. Your arms held him, and all night long your hand was in his.

One episode, she told herself firmly. I was tired and let down my guard. That was the risk. It was no more than that.

Liar.

There is nothing for Stephanie to worry about. Whatever I felt, I can easily forget. I have a job to do here, and a time to leave. I am not involved in any other way.

She avoided her reflection in the mirror. *I won't let it happen again.*

And Garth will be gone for a week.

Linda Talvia called, inviting Sabrina and the children to dinner.

'Not for a few days,' Sabrina said. 'Maybe the end of the week?'

'The lady wants some time alone,' said Linda. 'I know the feeling. When Marty is gone I feel three feet taller and a hundred pounds lighter. The house to myself. Paradise.'

That was my life in London, Sabrina thought. Responsible only to myself. What I wanted to get away from.

'But I want to see you,' said Linda. 'When does Garth get back?'

'Next Sunday.'

'Could you come on Wednesday, or even Tuesday? Early? I thought we could talk for awhile.'

She needs to talk, Sabrina thought. 'Why don't we come tonight? I'd love to have somebody else do the cooking for a change.'

'Would you really? Oh, Stephanie, what would I do without you? Come at four-thirty. Marty has an all-day seminar and won't be back 'til six. The kids can play in the yard.'

'We'll be there,' Sabrina said.

That afternoon she took Penny and Cliff shopping. She had put it off, hoping they could wait for Stephanie, but Cliff's shoes were falling apart, Penny was wailing that all the girls had something called Beene Jeans and she'd die if she didn't have some, too, and Sabrina finally ran out of excuses. I'm running out of excuses for everything, she thought; maybe I should break the other wrist.

At the shoe store the salesman measured Cliff's feet and brought out boxes of shoes. Cliff tried them on, looking from the shoes to Sabrina. What was he waiting for? 'Which one feels best?' she asked. 'Which do you like the best?' Hesitantly, Cliff picked up a heavy shoe, almost a hiking boot. 'You don't think they'll be too warm, sitting inside school all day?' He shook his head. 'All right, then. Let's go buy Penny some jeans.'

'Mom!' Cliff burst out. 'Can I really have these?'

Now what have I done? She picked up one of the heavy shoes, pretending to examine it. Evidently Stephanie would have said no, probably because they're for outside, not school, and maybe because of the price, but I don't know what boys' shoes cost. 'If you want them, they're yours. I've decided we should buy whatever will last the longest. But you'll have to take care of them. Can they be waterproofed?' The salesman brought a waterproofing spray and, as Sabrina searched for one of Stephanie's charge cards, Cliff put on the new boots, grinning with delight.

Outside the store, he turned to go meet his friends at the playing field, then hesitated. 'Mom? Thanks. A lot.' And he ran off, leaving Sabrina flushed with pleasure.

At the entrance to Marshall Field's they saw Vivian Goodman with Barbara. 'We are on the prowl for something called Beene Jeans,' Vivian said.

'Amazing,' Sabrina said dryly. 'Geoffrey Beene has hypnotized the entire sixth grade.'

'Mom,' said Penny, 'can I go with Barbara?'

'Why don't the two of you go alone while Vivian and I wander by ourselves? Here's the Field's charge card. But only buy one pair for now.'

Vivian looked at her curiously. 'Am I behind the times? I've never sent Barbara off with a credit card.'

'Penny's maiden voyage,' Sabrina said, noting Penny's wide-eyed wonder. 'I'm feeling reckless. But don't let me influence you—'

'On the contrary, I like it. Shall we have coffee?'

'If you don't mind, there's a new antique shop I'd like to see.'

'That's right; Garth told me you like antiques.'

It was a small shop called Collectibles, tucked between a high-priced luggage store and a restaurant specializing in crepes and homemade pastries. A perfect location, Sabrina thought; the owner knows what she's doing. Inside, dozens of small Oriental rugs overlapped to cover the floor of a square room crammed with furniture.

Vivian touched a leaded glass lamp shaped like a tulip. 'How can people afford a Tiffany lamp these days?'

Sabrina glanced at it. 'It's not Tiffany; it looks like Bohemian. They were wonderful imitators of Tiffany. If I were selling it, I wouldn't charge over fifty or sixty dollars.'

'Indeed,' said a new voice, and Sabrina saw a slender woman wending her way toward them. Her short hair was silver, brushed back from a thin, delicate face dominated by sharp, black eyes. With inexpensive clothes she achieved elegance and style, and Sabrina admired her; she does a lot, she thought, with not much money. And she owns the place. 'And how much have *I* charged for it?' the woman asked.

Vivian read the small sticker on the base of the lamp. 'Fifty-five dollars. That's amazing.'

'Not for someone who knows Bohemian glass.' The woman held out her hand to Sabrina. 'Madeline Kane. Do you work with antiques?'

'Sa – Stephanie Andersen.' They shook hands. 'I have, in the past.'

'Why don't you look around and tell me what you think. I've only been open for a week. Still getting organized.'

Sabrina was nervous as they began to maneuver around the furniture. It was the first time she had slipped on her name, and she knew why: she was caught in the spell of the shop, the pungent fragrance of furniture polish, musty velvets and brocades, dust dancing in sunbeams that turned the grains of well-worn woods to gold. *I want to go home. I want to walk through Ambassadors, and sit in my office; I want my own work.* It was a piercing homesickness and her eyes filled with tears.

Vivian looked at her in alarm. 'Stephanie? What is it?'

'Nothing.' She blinked, and a magnificently ugly couch, tufted in purple, wavered through her tears. 'An impossible thought.'

'Is there anything I can do?'

'No, it's—oh, once I had my own business, managing estate sales, and I handled furniture like this, art and antiques, collectibles. It didn't work out; I had to close it and get another job. And I miss all this. The smell and look and feel of my own shop—'

'You had a shop?'

'Oh, no. But I always wanted one.'

Madeline Kane had been following a little distance behind. There was something about this woman, she thought, that set her apart. The way she walked and held her head. The way she took in the shop with a swift glance, knowledgeable and certain. Her curiosity aroused, Madeline looked at her thoughtfully. 'Perhaps you can help me. I'm trying to find some background information on this Duncan Phyfe table. Do you know anything about it? I know it has to be about 1850—'

'It's not Phyfe,' Sabrina said bluntly. She ran her hand over it, bending to look at the feet. 'It's Belter. Very early, 1840s, but Phyfe never handled rosewood that way; look at the carvings on the claw feet.'

Madeline bent to look. 'Yes,' she mused. 'Of course.' She straightened up and pursed her mouth. 'Stephanie, why don't you get back into the estate business?'

Sabrina looked at her coolly.

'You're thinking it's none of my business,' Madeline said. 'But I need someone to work for me, occasionally with inventory and in the store, but mainly to run estate sales. I used to do it, and I didn't like it; I prefer puttering around here. But there's good money in those sales, and it's the easiest way to add to my inventory. So I'm offering you a job. Part-time, if you have to be home with children. Now is it my business? Or is it our business?'

No, you wonderful, wonderful woman, it's Stephanie's business. You just gave Stephanie a job. 'Our business,' Sabrina agreed with a smile. 'When would you like me to start?'

'Yesterday.'

'Then I'll be here Monday morning about ten.'

'Ten is for customers, my dear. Nine would be better.'

'Of course.' *I've forgotten what it's like to work for someone.* 'But I have to make a call first, to resign from another job. I'll be here as close to nine as I can make it.'

'Fine. I take it you're not interested in salary.'

'I beg your pardon?'

'You haven't asked about pay.'

Sabrina laughed. 'I'll be more practical when I manage estate sales. But it can wait until Monday, when we talk about how many hours I work and exactly what I'll be doing.'

Madeline gazed at her, clearly puzzled, and Sabrina knew she had to be more careful. She was behaving like Lady Longworth instead of a housewife who had to work to help make ends meet.

'If that is all right with you,' she added.

Madeline smiled faintly. 'Of course. I'll expect you on Monday.'

On their way to pick up Penny and Barbara, Vivian said, 'Garth didn't tell me you were an expert.'

'We don't talk about it much.' Sabrina felt like skipping down the street. A job for Stephanie. And for herself as long as she was here. But her homesickness had not gone away; she wanted Ambassadors. I'll call Nat, she thought, and try to push up the date for the X ray. If he can do it as soon as Garth gets back, I'll leave right away. She remembered waking up with her fingers twined in his. I have to leave right away.

'Mommy, look what I bought!' Penny cried. 'And guess what? The saleslady didn't want to wait on us, but I showed her the card – here it is – and then she treated us like she treats you; she called us Miss!'

The girls turned their shining faces from Vivian to Sabrina. 'What a wonderful thing you did for them,' Vivian said. 'I wish I'd thought of it. But eleven seems so young—'

I thought of it because I'm not a mother, Sabrina reflected. But when Penny hugged her and thanked her, she felt the same delight she had felt when Cliff thanked her for his shoes. She'd made them happy. And they loved her.

On the way home, Penny took her hand and held it tightly. And a thought chilled Sabrina: When I leave, I'll leave this behind.

Penny scuffed the brown and rust leaves on the sidewalk, talking happily about the puppet costumes she was making. 'I'll give you a fashion show in a few days,' she promised. 'And then I'll only have the last four to do. I need your help with those.'

I won't call Nat right away, Sabrina thought. I don't want to seem in too much of a hurry. He might get suspicious.

Penny and Cliff were on their way to bed when Garth called from Berkeley on Sunday night. Sabrina, fumbling with needle and thread and Cliff's torn jacket, and blaming her clumsiness on her cast instead of the fact that she never learned to sew, let them take over the kitchen and bedroom telephones. From her chair in the living room she could hear them chattering as if Garth had been gone a month instead of two days, and once Penny went into peals of laughter that rang through the house.

'Mom!' Cliff called. 'Dad wants to talk to you.'

She went into the breakfast room, and, in a moment, Garth's voice was there, astonishingly close, low and warm, familiar. And as Sabrina's heart leaped she knew how much she missed him.

'It's beautiful here,' he said. 'I wish you were with me to watch the sun burn through the fog. The world turns green and gold and the water changes from gray to a wonderful silver blue.'

'How do you see all that from a lecture hall?'

'The lectures begin tomorrow. All I've done so far is meet

with the other seminar leaders to organize the week. I understand you gave Cliff and Penny a day to remember.'

'Yesterday? We had a good time.'

'And where did you go while Penny and Barbara were trying on bean bags?'

'Jeans,' she said, laughing. What she missed was their companionship. Even as she had been pushing him away, they had become friends. She had happily looked forward to a week alone, to enjoy the family – *But it isn't a family without Garth*. 'Did you call them bean bags to Penny?'

'I did. She found it amusing. Where *did* you go while she was trying them on?'

'To a new antique shop on Sherman Avenue. Owned by a very attractive, very sharp lady who, I think, gave me a test on what she called a Duncan Phyfe table.'

'Did you pass?'

'With flying colors. And then she offered me a job. I start tomorrow morning.'

'You quit the university job?'

'I will first thing tomorrow.'

'Well. That's wonderful.'

'Is something wrong? You don't think I should quit?'

'Of course you should; you might recall the times I've urged you to find something you like better. And, as you took care to point out not so long ago, you help pay the mortgage, so I have no right to tell you where to work.'

'Garth, what is wrong?' She felt anxiety rising inside her. How had she made him angry? She tried to think of something to say, then caught herself. The job was for Stephanie; what did she care whether Garth was angry about it or not?

But I do care. Because when Garth is angry it usually means he's hurt. And I don't want him hurt.

'Garth, are you there?'

'Yes; I'm sorry I sounded—'

'No, I'm sorry. I should have talked to you about it, but I was so excited. . . . Do you know, I never even asked her what the job pays? I'll find out tomorrow, before I quit the other job, and then decide—'

'No, quit the job. If the new one doesn't work out, you'll find another.'

We're trying to make each other feel better, Sabrina thought.

Garth was still talking. 'What?' she asked.

'I asked how your dinner was, with Linda and Marty.'

'Oh. Sad.'

'Sad?'

'No, dinner was all right. But Linda asked me to come early so she could talk; she was so upset about . . . Garth, did Marty ever talk to you about having other women?'

After a moment, Garth said, 'If he did, it would have been in confidence.'

Oh, come on, nothing stays confidential for very long; everybody talks about these things.

But Garth isn't everybody.

'All right,' she said, 'but can you tell me if he thinks Linda is having affairs?'

'He's told her he thinks so.'

'She wants him to think that. She isn't, you know, but she scatters clues around to make him jealous so he'll stop having the affairs she thinks *he's* having and love her more, or guard her more carefully from temptations – something like that. Honestly, I've never known two people more at cross-purposes, absolutely incapable of talking about what they're thinking—'

'Never?'

Oh, damn.

She ignored it; he wasn't going to trap her into discussing their marriage. 'Garth, have you heard a rumor that some professors are giving passing grades to students they sleep with?'

This time the silence was longer. 'Where did you hear that?' he asked finally.

'Linda heard it at the university bookstore. *Have* you heard anything?'

'Nothing I would credit.'

'You've heard it, then. And Marty is one of the professors?'

'My God, no. Is that what Linda heard?'

'That's why she had to talk. Is it true?'

'The rumor? I think so. But I don't know who's involved. Accusations by themselves mean nothing; any student who's angry over a low grade could point a finger. But there's been some talk in the faculty club that sounds more serious. Have you talked about this to anyone else?'

'I am not in the habit of spreading rumors.'

'I know. I'm sorry. What did you tell Linda?'

'To keep quiet until I talked to you.'

'Did you really?'

'Well, why wouldn't I? I trust you more than anyone. And you understand better than anyone how to deal with the university. It's like all groups, isn't it? Everyone chewing on rumors for breakfast and dinner, as if they're the only real things in the world. I remember once Alexandra told me about a cruise—' She broke off.

'Alexandra?'

'Somebody at . . . on the China trip. She'd been on a cruise, and she said by the third day rumors were flying: sworn testimony about who was in whose bed and who was underneath taking notes. Something like the university, isn't it? Except I suppose at the university they use better grammar in their rumors.'

He chuckled. 'You're wonderful and I miss you. Why don't you fly out here for the end of the week?'

Oh, I'd like that. 'I can't just up and leave the children.'

'We could find someone.'

'And my new job?'

'Yes. Of course. Well, what else is happening in Evanston?'

They talked, Sabrina discovered later, for an hour. 'The university is paying for it,' Garth said the next night when he called and she asked him. 'But you're right; it is an unseemly extravagance. If you fly out here, we'd save the university hundreds of dollars.'

She laughed but didn't answer. She would stay where she was. She missed him, but she was relieved that he wasn't there. It was better for everyone if she and Garth stayed two thousand miles apart.

306

Each morning she woke to the sounds of the children and the neighborhood and looked forward to the day. And each evening, when Garth called, she wondered where the day had gone.

She raced through the housework in the mornings, doing as little as possible. She was irrationally angry at Stephanie for forcing her into it; she would have ignored it entirely between Juanita's appearances, but there was too much to do. Even with Penny and Cliff helping she felt a slave to dust balls and dirty clothes and out-of-place objects.

After housework, Collectibles was like a holiday. She and Madeline were organizing the merchandise, tagging pieces with their history and price and arranging them to show off the best and improve the appearance of the ordinary. Sabrina liked Madeline; and even though she chafed at working for someone else, she was building up the job so that Stephanie could step into it when she came back. But before she knew it, it was midafternoon and she had to hurry home to supervise the invasion of the house and the raiding of the refrigerator when Cliff and Penny arrived, usually with friends.

Later the three of them ate dinner picnic-style on the patio. After Penny and Cliff did the dishes, Sabrina joined in a three-way game of Scrabble or Boggle, usually ended by Garth's telephone call. And later, when the house was quiet, Sabrina curled up to read in the quiet living room or the armchair in the bedroom until she found herself nodding to sleep.

On Thursday she brought home a wok and a cookbook and they made a Chinese dinner. Penny added two dozen hot dried peppers to the chicken when no one was looking. 'You should have seen us, Daddy,' she said when Garth called. 'We were all crying. But Mommy said it was delicious anyway.' She held the telephone out to Sabrina. 'Daddy wants to talk to you and tell you he loves you.'

Sabrina's heart took a little skip. 'Is that what he said?'

'Not exactly, but isn't that what he tells you when he calls?'

Sabrina smiled and took the telephone.

'A corrosive dinner, I understand,' Garth said.

'We'll remember it for a long time.'

'I'm sorry I missed it.'

'So am I.'

'Will you make it on Sunday so I can share it? Peppers and all?'

'If you have the courage, and we don't grow faint of heart, we'll make it just for you.'

'I can't wait. By the way, Penny was right.'

'About what?'

'About my wanting to tell you I love you.'

She felt her heart skip again, and then again. She was short of breath. But it's just because I'm tired, she thought; it's been a long day. I'll settle down as soon as I have some time to myself.

'And that my plane arrives at two in the afternoon on Sunday. Can you meet me?'

'Yes, of course.'

'What are you doing tomorrow night? More Chinese food?'

'Dolores and Nat invited us for dinner.'

'Give them my love.'

'I will.'

After dinner on Friday night, when Penny and Cliff went upstairs with the Goldners' three children, Sabrina repeated for Dolores and Nat Garth's descriptions of his lectures and the people he was meeting. 'He won't say it outright, but it seems to me he must be the star of the show.'

She caught the quick glance between them. 'What's that all about?'

'Nothing,' Nat said quickly.

Sabrina pressed her fingers to her forehead. Now what had she done wrong?

'No, Stephanie has a right to know,' said Dolores. 'We were just thinking that usually when Garth has some kind of success you bring up that job he's been offered in Stamford. And this time you didn't.'

'Oh.' *I keep forgetting how much that job means to Stephanie. I've got to ask Garth about it before I leave. I promised Stephanie I would.*

Nat lit his pipe. 'You still getting headaches, Stephanie?'

'No,' she said, startled. And then an idea came to her. 'Well, yes, as a matter of fact. I wasn't going to say anything.'

'Why not?'

She shrugged. 'I knew I'd be seeing you soon to X ray my wrist and if they were still bad—'

'Are they bad?'

'Sometimes.'

'When?'

'Oh, evenings, mostly. It's probably just that I'm tired.'

'Where's the pain? Show me, on your head.'

She held her hand on the area where the headaches had been when she had her concussion. I'm sorry, Garth, she said silently. I wish I had a more creative way of refusing to make love to you. But this is the easiest lie I can think of. And it's only for a few days, until Stephanie is back. Then the headaches will end.

'—should have stopped by now,' Nat was saying. 'I think you should check it out with your internist. Aren't we going to look at that wrist, too, pretty soon? When did you break it?'

'September twenty-second.'

'I'd like to give it another ten days. Call the office and make an appointment for a week from Monday. If the X ray looks good, we'll take the cast off then.'

'All right.' Now she knew. She'd call Stephanie tomorrow morning. Ten days. A long time to get through with Garth.

But he's coming home on Sunday, she thought; how wonderful it will be to see him. Then she concentrated on what Dolores was saying and told herself she had not thought such a thing at all.

It was Wednesday before Garth caught up with his work at the university and had a chance to go through the mail that had accumulated while he was gone. He was restless and fed up with the nagging details of department administration that kept him at his desk. He'd come home from Berkeley like a schoolboy rushing to his first love, remembering Stephanie's warmth and laughter in their telephone calls, remembering that they had made love the night before he left. He'd come home looking forward to long hours with his family, and then, tied down at his office, the laboratory and classrooms, he'd barely seen them.

And his wife had almost encouraged him to stay away. He had found, with despair, her warmth muted, her wariness still intact.

It had not been that way at first. At the airport on Sunday her smile had welcomed him with such delight that he slowed as he walked toward her, stunned by her beauty. 'My God,' breathed a man behind him. 'Wouldn't I like to be the guy she's waiting for?'

His heart singing, Garth strode toward her, but as he came close her smile faded and her eyes grew shadowed, as if she had been as surprised as he by her open delight.

'Welcome home,' she said, her voice controlled.

He kissed her mouth, her cool lips soft beneath his, a small tremor at the corners. And then, casually, she moved away, and he did not see the delight again until, at dinner, he unpacked his gifts. For Penny and Cliff there were models, to be assembled, of the wagons used by miners in the California gold rush. And for his wife, from a shop in Ghirardelli Square, a suede blazer, as soft as butter, simple but rich in a deep hunter's green with antique gold buttons. Eyes shining, she put it on and spun around, modeling it. 'For *me*,' she murmured as if to herself.

She was touched and saddened by her surprise. 'For no one else.'

She put her cheek against his. 'Thank you. It's perfect.'

'I thought it was the right size,' he said, with only a touch of irony. 'I don't think you have anything like it, but it seems to go with the different way you've been dressing lately.'

'I'm dressing differently?'

'I think so. Aren't you?'

'How?'

'Brighter, it seems to me. Or different combinations of colors. Or maybe more casual. Didn't you used to button your blouses to the collar instead of leaving the top ones open?' She was laughing, and he shook his head. 'All those times you accused me of not noticing what you wear. You

310

were right; I'm sorry. However, I did notice the differences. And I like the new look, however you get it.'

A happy family evening at home. And then she told him about her headaches; that she'd talked to Nat about them. And gradually she withdrew to the friendly distance she had maintained since her return from China. If anything, she seemed even more nervous.

Doggedly, he went through the mail on his desk. Near the top, dated two days ago, was another invitation from Horace Kallen, president of Foster Laboratories, to visit Stamford on October 23. Next Tuesday. Impossible; he couldn't cancel classes again so soon. But – Foster and Stamford were Stephanie's dream. And he knew they would have sophisticated facilities for more advanced research than he could do here. He could ask Vivian to take his classes; he'd only miss two. Without debating it further, he scribbled a note of acceptance and put it with the outgoing mail. Maybe that would please her.

The truth was, he was so torn by his wife's changing moods that he was beginning to think it would be better to force a confrontation at the risk of destroying everything than to go on indefinitely tip-toeing around her. A life of scientific research had taught him patience and a tolerance for the unexpected, but it had also taught him to expect results from the clues and information he had or to look for new clues and new directions. Either they were married, and would work things out together, or they weren't. And if they weren't, they would have to find a new direction, because they were living a lie.

His telephone rang, and when he answered it the vice president's secretary asked him if he would come to Mr Strauss's office for a few minutes. It was a summons, not a request, and once again Garth put off going home early.

Lloyd Strauss was only a few years older than Garth, a tennis partner and a longtime friend. Small and compact, a dark bundle of energy always in motion, he had mastered the twists and turns of university politics to rise on a straight path to the vice presidency. Everyone knew that a majority of the board of trustees was ready to elect him president when the current president retired, and few challenged his decisions without careful thought.

'Well, the administrative board checked it all out,' he said, pacing while Garth sat on the edge of his desk. 'Went through your list of female rejects – sorry, lousy choice of words – your list of rejected female tenure-applicants. Looked into Webster's attitude toward women professors – actually, women in general – and interviewed other people in the sciences and on the tenure committee. No question, you were right; he's violated every equal-opportunity regulation on the books. Of course, we didn't have any until recently, so he's been a bastard, but a legal one, for most of his intolerant life.'

Garth stirred, and Strauss put out his hand. 'Hold on; let me finish. The administrative board is directing the tenure committee to review the application of Vivian Goodman. My prediction is she'll breeze through. The administrative board also, in its wisdom, has asked Dean Webster to take early retirement. He's sixty-two; we'll carry him for three years. Simplest way. He's been told that with the school year so young, we can hobble along if he leaves immediately. Since it would be crude to say he's been booted, I won't say it. So we're looking for a new Dean of Sciences.'

He sat at his desk and riffled through a stack of papers. Garth swiveled to watch him, knowing what was coming. It would please Stephanie, he thought. More money and prestige, regular hours, more time at home. But he would have to give up his research. And teaching. The Dean of Sciences was an administrator; he had no time for anything else. I can't sit in an office all day, he thought, while others are exploring the locked worlds I've begun to discover. If I have to make a change to please Stephanie, Foster Labs would be better.

Strauss was on his feet again. 'I don't need to tell you the first person we considered for the job was you. You have an international reputation for research and scholarship – good coverage, by the way, in *Newsweek*; amazing how your handsome puss in a popular magazine impresses the trustees more than a dozen scientific journals put together. So you'd bring prestige and dignity and fairness to the position. But I didn't think you'd want it.'

312

Garth looked at him sharply. It was one thing for him to decide he wouldn't take the job; it was another for Strauss to decide for him.

'Come on, Garth,' Strauss grinned. 'If I offered it, you'd thank me, shake my hand and tell me I could always count on you for help when I need it but you'd rather be in the lab and the classroom. You'd also offer to help find the new dean.'

Garth laughed. 'Agreed. But you're not going to give me the chance to make that handsome speech.'

'I'm going to give you the chance to make another one. What would you say to the Directorship of our new Institute of Genetic Engineering?'

Garth's head came up, alert, weighing new information. 'When was the decision made to build an Institute of Genetic Engineering?'

'Recently.'

'Lloyd, I've been trying to get that institute for five years, and the answer has always been that there's no money. That's one of the reasons—'

'That you're considering Foster Labs,' Strauss finished. 'Have you visited them yet?'

'Next week.'

'When they show you their stuff, you might compare it with this.' He unrolled a set of blueprints. 'Plus the director's salary, probably around sixty thousand, and any classes you want to teach.'

Garth spread the blueprints on the desk and pored over them. 'I see you've made a few changes. No auditorium.'

'Can't afford it. No cuts in lab facilities, however.'

'Where's the money coming from?'

'It was freed up.'

He looked at Strauss. 'It was always there? But not released?'

'There were other priorities—'

'Why wasn't it released?'

Strauss opened a file cabinet to reveal a small refrigerator. 'I always like a drink this time of day. What will you have?'

'Scotch. Lloyd, I asked you—'

313

'Hold on and listen. You'd convinced us we had to have the institute to keep in the running for federal research funds and to develop products that we could license. But every time we put out a feeler for a director, in this country and Europe, we got back the same answer: the best man was right under our nose and why were we looking elsewhere?'

'And why were you?'

'Drink your Scotch.'

'Well?'

'Garth, you couldn't have handled it. You're a brilliant researcher, but you were lousy with people. Impatient, bad-tempered – hell, we all knew how often you went to your office and swung your tennis racket at unseen fools or enemies ... more Scotch?'

'No.'

Strauss refilled both their glasses and added soda. 'You had a reputation as the pure scientist who would have been happy in a world uncluttered with people. I see that you wince. You've heard it before?'

'No.' But my wife used to hint as much, he thought, swirling the liquid in his glass. 'So you wouldn't put me in charge and you couldn't or wouldn't bring in someone else. Until now. Has the time suddenly become ripe for pure but bad-tempered scientists who whack unseen enemies with tennis rackets?'

'I think you've changed in the last year or so, especially in the last few months. You've done a top-notch job as department chairman – we do look kindly, you know, on chairmen who bring in government research grants; your support of Vivian has been admirable and your testimony to the administrative board on your charges against Webster was pithy and indisputable. And then there was the kid who messed up the lab work while you were in Berkeley. My God, Garth, a few months ago you would have torn him to pieces and banished him to the School of Agriculture to shovel out stables for the rest of his life. Instead, you only gave him sinks and beakers to scrub: the ones nobody has gotten clean in a hundred and fifty years. More Scotch?'

'If I'm as mellow as you say, I don't need it.'

'You don't. This one celebrates your new position.'

314

'Wait a minute. I haven't accepted it.'

'Garth, I have to report to the board of trustees—'

'Damn it, I told you I'm going to Stamford next week.'

'You don't want to go to Foster Labs. That was a gun at our heads.'

'Don't tell me what it was or wasn't. I'm going to Stamford next Tuesday. On Thursday or Friday I'll give you my answer.'

'And if I have to know before?'

Garth hesitated briefly. 'I want the position, Lloyd; you know how long I've cared about it. I hope I can take it. That's all I can tell you now. I have to visit Stamford.'

'Oh. Stephanie. But, Garth, there's money and prestige in the directorship—'

'I know. And she'll know that too. But this is something I owe her. And I owe it to myself to look at the great world out there now and then. I'll give you my answer next week, Lloyd. I hope that's good enough.'

'It's good enough. Can you let us know definitely by Friday?'

'Yes.'

Sabrina woke to the reverberating racket of Penny and Cliff bumping into each other in the kitchen and squabbling over burned toast. Saturday morning. No school. She burrowed into the pillow. They could manage; she'd sleep awhile longer.

But she could not relax. Something was wrong; there was something she had to think about. She heard Penny and Cliff talking about apple orchards. 'I'll pick a hundred bushels,' Cliff announced. 'They won't let you,' Penny said. 'There wouldn't be any left for the rest of the world.' And then Sabrina knew what she had to think about. *Penny and Cliff in the kitchen. Saturday. Apple-picking. Saturday, October 20. Monday would be the 22nd.*

'We'll X-ray it then,' Nat had said. 'And if everything looks good, we'll take the cast off at the same time.'

Time. There wasn't much more time. She opened her eyes. Garth was sleeping on his side, his face a few inches from hers. She gazed at him. He was so quiet, self-contained, sure of himself and where he was going. And even though he was not sure of her, often bewildered by the twists and turns of the past weeks, still he was gentle and loving even when she was cold, generous when she was stingy, giving her time, as he had promised he would, to find herself.

And who is that? she asked silently, and knew the answer before the question was finished. A woman in love with her sister's husband.

How long had she loved him? She didn't know; it was not important. She knew it now with a certainty so powerful it swept her up and she felt the absolute joy of loving him before it was pushed aside by despair. Impulsively she put out her hand and touched his face, the high strong cheekbone and the rough stubble on his skin, the little nerve below his eye that jumped as her finger accidentally pressed it. She pulled back her hand, but Garth had opened his eyes and was watching her.

He saw the love in her unguarded face, but before he could reach out and take her in his arms, her face became neutral and he was looking once again at a friendly companion.

'Good morning,' he said quietly, not moving.

She looked at him helplessly. Everything he did was right and whatever she did seemed wrong. Silently she said the words she wanted to say, *Good morning, my love*, when from the kitchen came a resounding crash and a ringing 'I told you so!' in Penny's triumphant voice.

Sabrina leaped out of bed. Her nightgown caught on the corner of the chair and she swore at it – she would have abandoned Stephanie's nightgowns entirely, but they made it easier to share the bed with Garth – then pulled on a robe and ran from the room.

In the kitchen, Cliff stood at the edge of a lake of orange juice dotted with islands of broken glass. Penny had thrown him a roll of paper towels and he held it in front of him, unrolling it in a long ribbon that folded back on itself in the middle of the lake, slowly turning orange. When Sabrina came in he looked up, frowning in solemn concentration exactly as Garth frowned when working on notes at his desk. 'How many *towels* do you think it will take,' he asked seriously, emphasizing key words as his father did, 'to *soak* this up so I can use the *wet* ones to pick up the pieces of *glass* and some of the *juice*, and then *dry* towels to get the *rest* of it?'

Sabrina burst out laughing. Penny was outraged. 'Why is it funny?' she demanded, and Sabrina knew Stephanie wouldn't have laughed. Stephanie would have been concerned about broken glass, cut fingers, children slipping on the floor, a sticky mess. But Sabrina saw a different scene: the warm bed upstairs, her hand on Garth's face, his eyes meeting hers, followed not by words of love but by the spectacular crash of a quart of orange juice, a trail of paper towels in the morning sun and Cliff's scientific study of the problem, his face the picture of Garth's.

She shook her head firmly, stopping her laughter. 'You're right, it's not funny. How did it happen?'

Cliff struggled a moment, then told the truth. 'I was balancing the bottle on my head.'

'The star forward of the hockey team doesn't know about balance?'

He shrugged glumly.

'Well, it's all yours. Use as many towels as it takes, wet and dry. If you run out, we have more. And I would say no apple-picking for you until the floor is washed clean.'

'Mom! Men don't wash kitchen floors! I'll pick up the glass and soak up the orange juice, but—'

'In this house,' said Sabrina calmly, 'men wash kitchen floors.' She started to leave, then turned back. 'Come on, Penny. Let's talk about what kind of apples we're going to pick.' She put her arm around Penny to urge her from the room, and over her shoulder she saw Cliff's swift look of gratitude for removing his sister so he could wash the floor without an audience.

As they walked upstairs, Penny looked at her curiously. 'What did you mean – what kind of apples? This late in October there's only one kind we can pick.'

Sabrina sighed. So many small details Stephanie hadn't told her. A lifetime of details.

'You're right,' she said. 'I guess I forgot.'

'What's the damage?' Garth asked from the bedroom, and Penny ran to tell him while Sabrina went to the end of the hallway. The house was rounded there, like a turret, and a bench had been built in the curved wall beneath a circular window that looked out over the side yard. It was one of Sabrina's favorite niches, isolated from the activity of the house by a folding screen Stephanie had placed there. She sat on the bench and looked through the window at the flaming orange leaves of the sugar maple in the yard. Apple-picking. Fall.

In London and Paris and Rome, everyone had returned from summer travel; the dinner parties and balls were beginning; clients would be coming in to Ambassadors. What was she doing planning a day in an apple orchard when her real world was stirring with a new season? She had so much to do – Mrs Pemberley would have finished her fall outfits by now; her hair needed shaping; clients were due in November to pick up items she hadn't even searched out.

I do not belong here. The words were harsh in the soft sunlit day. That other world across the ocean had not disappeared: Stephanie was living in it, and, no matter what news she told in letters and telephone calls, Sabrina knew now, better than ever, how many little details make up a life – more than could ever be covered from a distance. What was Stephanie doing in her world? What trail was she leaving as Sabrina Longworth that Sabrina would have to follow when she returned? *What is she doing with my life?*

She felt Garth sit down beside her, his arm around her waist. He pulled her to him and kissed her forehead, the corners of her eyes, the tip of her nose. 'Good morning,' he said again, his voice relaxed. 'Can one get into the kitchen to make breakfast?'

Her thoughts were still in Europe. 'I don't think we have any orange juice,' she said, and was surprised when he laughed and tightened his arm around her. Then it all came back: the orange lake, her laughter, Cliff's grateful look. Her family. This world. Garth. Loving him, wanting him, needing him. One world balanced against another.

Trembling, she leaned back against his arm, and he drew a line of small kisses along her forehead and down her cheek. Within her, a tight knot loosened, and desire flowed through her, insistent, warm and heavy. She raised her face and

318

opened her lips and kissed him for the first time as she wanted to kiss him, deeply, drinking him in, as she wanted to be kissed by him, as she knew now they were meant to kiss each other. He took his arm from her waist and encircled her shoulders, supporting her head as his mouth drove down on hers. With his other hand he pushed aside the film of her nightgown and cupped her full breast, drawing his fingers up along the curve to the nipple, taut beneath his touch.

Sabrina was dizzy, her thoughts spinning away from the hunger of her body. Tears stung her eyes and she pulled back, shaking uncontrollably. 'I can't do this!' she cried. *Stephanie, forgive me. I didn't mean to love him.* She shook her head. 'I can't. I can't.'

'What the hell is the matter with you?' Garth roared.

'Oh, don't!' Penny wailed and Sabrina looked up to see her standing in her bedroom doorway at the other end of the hall. *Too much is going on; how can I make sense of anything?* But Penny's face was twisted with fear and Sabrina went to her. She knelt and put her arms around her.

From below, Cliff shouted, 'Is Dad yelling at me? What did I do now?'

'Damn it!' Sabrina exploded. She was still shaking with desire and guilt. 'Does everyone have to get in on every act? Isn't anything private in this house?' Penny began to cry, and Sabrina felt the morning slide away from her as she ruined one thing after another. 'I'm sorry,' she said. She turned and called downstairs. 'Nobody's yelling at you, Cliff.' She turned back to Penny. 'I'm sorry, love. Don't be afraid. Everything is all right. It's all right,' she repeated, wondering whether she was reassuring Penny or herself or Garth. 'I'll bet we sounded like you and Cliff, didn't we?'

'Daddy sounded so *mad*,' Penny said, awed and fearful. 'He hardly ever yells at anybody.'

Sabrina waited for Garth to say something, but he was silent. He could help me, she thought, but he's too angry. She smiled at Penny. 'Well, sometimes you and Cliff sound like you could cheerfully pound each other to pulp.'

A small laugh escaped Penny. Sabrina knew she was thinking that parents aren't supposed to sound like their children, and perhaps she was even thinking of her friends whose parents fought and sometimes divorced.

'Yelling isn't a great thing to do,' she said lightly, 'but it does clear the lungs for cheering at soccer games.' Penny laughed again. 'Come on, now. You're n   even dressed yet. We have to check on Cliff's scrubbing talents and then eat and get out of here or all the Jonathans will be gone before we get to the orchard.'

'Golden Delicious,' said Penny automatically, 'I told you, that's all they let you pick by now. *You* knew that.'

'So far, there is nothing delicious about this morning,' Sabrina said, kissing Penny's cheek, 'except you. Go on, now; get some clothes on.'

After Penny went to her room she remained kneeling, waiting for Garth to tell her, as she had told Penny, that everything was all right. But he sat silently beside the window where she had run away from him. For a long moment they stayed that way, separated by the length of the house and a terrible gulf of misunderstanding. Sabrina looked up and met his eyes. 'I'm so sorry,' she said. Her words traveled down the hall and touched him with the same tender caution with which her fingers had touched his sleeping face less than an hour earlier.

Garth smiled then, a smile so loving she caught her breath. 'It's all right,' he said at last, and added, 'I thought you might have made up your mind.'

Sabrina heard him, but the words made no sense. Made up her mind to what? To make love to him? To tell him why she swung between coldness and warmth? To confess? If he knew or suspected something, why didn't he just say so? 'I must get dressed,' she said hurriedly and went to their room, closing the door behind her. *I won't think about it now; I'll think about it later. I don't want to know what he meant.* She pulled on a pair of Levi's, a pale yellow Oxford-cloth shirt and a russet boatnecked sweater that made her look, in the full-length mirror, only a few years older than Penny. For the briefest of moments she felt very young – untouched by time and the complicated maneuvering of adults.

She pulled back her heavy auburn hair, tying it at her neck with a brown velvet ribbon. Tendrils at the sides escaped, framing her face with wisps of curls that made her look more like a mischievous gamine than a grown woman.

She looked at the gamine in the mirror and recalled other mirrors, in palaces and estates, where she had dressed in gowns of tulle and lace and silk for Europe's most famous balls, and then had swept down staircases or through great doorways, bringing a hush to the most sophisticated of the world's beautiful people.

Where was she now, that stunning woman? In a three-story frame house in Evanston, Illinois, in faded Levi's and bare feet.

She went to breakfast in bare feet.

On the curved bench at the end of the hall, Garth watched his wife go into their bedroom and close the door; watched her ten minutes later leave the room and, without looking in his direction, go barefoot downstairs. He was amazed at her stubbornness; again and again she refused to let herself settle back comfortably into their marriage. For each step forward, she took half a step back into the hard shell she had worn since her trip.

And what did she expect of him while she huddled inside her shell, refusing to let him join her private debate over leaving him? Was she hoping he would force the issue, demand that they talk about it, make her face her own failures as well as his? Was she waiting for him to tell her, whether she wanted to hear it or not, that he was in love with her almost as if for the first time?

'Daddy!' Penny called, and he went downstairs to breakfast.

The kitchen floor was clean. In a corner, the wastebasket bulged with soggy orange paper towels. Cliff and Penny had set the table, poured glasses of grapefruit juice and piled a plate with doughnuts. The coffee was made. His family was sitting peacefully at the table, smiling at him.

'Have I walked into the wrong kitchen?' he asked. Penny giggled. He raised his juice glass. 'To a delicious day.'

Sabrina met his eyes. 'Thank you,' she said softly.

And in the car he felt her relax beside him. 'What a nice way to spend a Saturday,' she said. As if she had never done it before. And maybe, he thought, she hasn't. Not in this way, caught in her own arguments over her future. Our future, he added silently; I'll have to remind her of that.

In the back seat, Penny and Cliff were competing in identifying approaching cars. Garth was withdrawn in his thoughts. Left to herself, Sabrina watched the passing scene: neatly plowed fields stretching to the horizon; sleek cattle standing or lounging in small groups like guests she had seen at balls clustering with their friends; white farmhouses, cherry-red barns, bright yellow tractors, their colors burned into the blue sky. And around it all, the rich brown of the soil and the brilliance of autumn foliage.

European farms were smaller, older, more weathered. To Sabrina, these American farms radiated expansiveness and endless progress, dominion, from the road to the horizon and beyond. Everything seemed open and free, harmonious, settled, and she wanted to reach out and grasp it, to press it in a scrapbook, to remember.

The apple orchard lay in a countryside of small lakes. The larger ones were surrounded by homes, boat docks and parks, with week-end crowds spilling everywhere. Garth was cursing the traffic; the closer they came to the orchard the longer it took them to reach it. Cliff groaned. 'Can we get *out*? We'll race you there. And beat you.'

'Better yet,' Garth said. 'You drive. High time you did the work while I play. Your mother and I will stroll happily to the orchard while you and Penny fight traffic.'

'Do you mean it, Dad?' Cliff said eagerly. 'Will you let me drive?'

Garth shook his head. 'The law says no. When you're fifteen you'll learn in school.'

'They never teach anything,' Cliff said scornfully.

'If that's true, I'll teach you then, but not before. You'll be behind the wheel soon enough, and your mother and I will be waiting up fretting whenever you're ten minutes late getting home. Don't push time away – for us or yourself.'

Their voices seemed far away to Sabrina. *I won't be here when Cliff is fifteen. Garth and I will never stroll happily while Cliff and Penny fight traffic for us.* They'll go on, growing and changing, long after I leave. And – it struck her suddenly – *they won't even know I'm gone.* Garth's wife,

Penny and Cliff's mother, would still be part of their lives, their quarrels and jokes and family talks, their waking and sleeping. Their love. Only Sabrina would be gone.

As Garth pulled into the mass of cars in the parking lot, he glanced at her, smiling. Then his face changed. 'What is it?'

She shook her head quickly. 'Nothing. Shall we go?'

They picked up a bushel basket and walked into the orchard. The air was heavy with the scent of fallen ripe apples carpeting the trampled grass beneath the trees. Above them branches bowed down with the weight of hundreds more, perfect globes ranging from pale yellow-green to deep gold tinged with red. All around them, apple-pickers were filling baskets and plastic bags, but they walked on until they came to a quiet section. Cliff took one look at the gnarled trees and with a whoop of joy leaped up and climbed with sure hands and feet through the tangled leaves and branches. 'First cousin to a monkey,' said Garth with amusement.

Penny began to follow, but Cliff called down, 'Wait; I'll toss you the ones I pick, and then we'll trade places and I'll help you up.'

Sabrina was touched. They squabbled, but Stephanie had taught them to share, too. She and Garth watched as they found a rhythm of picking, throwing and catching. 'Can we walk awhile?' she asked.

'Nothing better.' He took her arm and waved to Cliff in the tree. 'We'll be back. If you fill a bushel, start another. The only limit is the number of apples you're willing to peel at home.'

Cliff paused, arm outstretched, then nodded. As they walked off, Sabrina heard him say to Penny in awe, 'Mom didn't even tell us to be careful.'

Garth and Sabrina walked down the path, the trees lush and heavy on either side, sounds of family groups a murmur in the air about them. Dark leaves and yellow apples shone against the deep blue sky; a breeze waved the tendrils of Sabrina's hair. She lifted her face to the sun and took a deep breath. Nothing had happened – nothing exciting, nothing glamorous, nothing that put her in the spotlight of attention among people of wealth and power. Nothing had happened except that she was in love with the man beside her. And she was happy.

The path intersected another that warned against trespassing. Here were rows of Jonathan, McIntosh and Red Delicious trees whose apples were being saved for sale in the orchard store and a final fate as cider and applesauce. 'Let's trespass,' said Garth. 'With respect for the flora and fauna.'

Their arms were linked and they walked slowly, warmed by the October sun, breathing the fragrance of apples and clover and cut grass from nearby fields. 'You make me wonderfully happy,' Garth said quietly. 'I don't tell you that often enough.'

She looked up at him.

'And,' he added, 'you are gloriously beautiful. I don't tell you that often enough, either.'

She continued to look at him in silence.

He turned her to him and held her face between his hands. He felt her stiffen. 'Don't run away, my love. I know what's bothering you and I'm trying not to force you into anything. But you must know that I won't sit by indefinitely – after all, I have a stake in bringing things into the open—'

He was stopped by the alarm in her eyes. Was she afraid of him – or of herself? 'Stephanie,' he said gently, his words oddly formal because he was being so careful, 'I will not hurt you. I would never hurt you. Whatever you decide, I suppose I would have to accept it. But I love you more now than I ever have, and I need you – as, of course, the children do – and it would mean everything to me if you stay with us.'

A late red apple fell with a soft plop on the ground near their feet. A dragonfly darted past, its translucent wings glinting in the sun; a chipmunk scattered a mound of dry leaves. Sabrina was silent. Garth's warm hands on her face kept her from turning away, and their eyes met, his probing, hers dark with uncertainty. She was bewildered by much of what he said, but one phrase echoed again and again – *more than I ever have; I love you more now than I ever have*. It reverberated with the desire he had aroused that morning, still pulsing through her body, beating strongly, steadily, glowing in her blood as the melting sun glowed through her eyelids when she closed them.

'Look at me,' Garth said roughly, but she shook her head. Whatever he knew, it was not the truth – could not be the truth or he would not have called her Stephanie – but somehow he had come to believe she might leave him and it was true, it was true, though he would never know why, or what it really meant. *My dear love, there is nothing I can tell you.*

He dropped his hands. Her face felt cold and naked, as cold as Garth's bleak look when she opened her eyes. She searched for words to recapture the harmony of a few minutes before, but there was nothing to say. 'We should turn back – the children—'

'Soon,' he said shortly, and turned onto another path. Sabrina kept pace with him. 'We owe each other some time,' he said casually. 'When did we last go away together?'

'I don't know,' she answered, grateful for the chance to tell a simple truth.

'This week, then. I meant to tell you, I finally accepted Kallen's invitation to visit Foster Labs. We'll fly out Tuesday morning, stay in New York that night and come back on Wednesday.'

Sabrina reacted automatically. 'No.' When he frowned, she fumbled for reasons. 'The children. My job. My wrist. The money.'

He ticked them off. 'The kids will stay with Vivian; I've already asked her. Your antiques got along without you for a hundred years; they'll manage another two days. You told me the cast comes off Monday. Foster is paying the whole tab, including the hotel in New York. Look, you've pushed me for months to take this job. That's why I said we'd go.'

Sabrina picked up an apple and polished it on her sleeve. It was perfect, without a bruise or soft spot. She bit into the flesh, its sharp tang crisp on her tongue. To travel with Garth, to be alone with him – *Oh, I'd love it*, she had thought when he asked her to join him in Berkeley. But how could she travel with Garth? How many intimacies could she share with him and keep on rejecting him?

But she could not tell him to forget the job when Stephanie so desperately wanted him to take it, and she'd even promised Stephanie she'd try to convince him to visit

Stamford. So, reluctantly, she nodded. She would go with him to Connecticut. He put his arm around her as they turned to go back to Penny and Cliff. 'It's about time we had a chance to be alone,' he said, 'and find out who we really are.'

Chapter 16

Nathan Goldner snapped the X ray into place on the illuminated panel and stood back so Sabrina could view it with him. 'Couldn't be better,' he said. 'You can go back to beating Garth and the kids and whipping up your famous cakes. Now let's get that cast off.'

He bent over Sabrina's arm, then looked up. 'No cries of joy at getting back your very own wrist?'

She smiled faintly, locked in her thoughts, seeing in her mind not her left wrist lying on the table, still encased in plaster, but two left wrists, healthy and identical: Stephanie's and Sabrina's wrists, once again interchangeable. 'Stephanie?' Nat said. 'Are you all right?'

I'm fine; that's the trouble. 'I'm sorry, Nat. I was thinking of three bushels of Golden Delicious apples at home. If you could leave the cast on for a few more weeks, I could delegate the pies and strudel and applesauce to the rest of the family.'

A joke: 'If you could leave the cast on for a few more weeks . . . ' Would she like that? As much as she missed London and wondered what was happening to her other life, would she like a few more weeks? She didn't know. That was the crazy part: she really didn't know. But what difference did it make? She had no choice.

But to Nat it was a joke. 'Condemned to strudel,' he said, and bent once again to cut open the cast.

When it was off, Sabrina saw her arm white and frail, newborn. 'Should I keep it bandaged? Or not use it too much?'

He shook his head. 'Can't get out of it, Stephanie. You can

peel apples from now until Christmas, or move all the furniture in that shop where you work. In fact, use the wrist as much as possible, to strengthen the muscles. The bone is even stronger now than before.'

I'm stronger than before, she said to herself as she went to her car. She thought of Garth. And more easily hurt.

She was taking the morning off from work, and, at home, she opened the patio door to let in the breeze and the spicy fragrance of late roses still blooming against the house. She gazed thoughtfully at the three heaping baskets standing in a row next to the back door where Garth had set them down the evening before. I should do something with them, she thought. Make a dent, at least.

Instead, she made a cup of coffee and sat at the table. Her wrist felt strange in the warm air. She flexed it – how weightless it was! – picked up her cup, pressed the bones, testing for pain. Nothing. She was cured. Sabrina Longworth, in one piece again, ready to take on the world. And then the telephone rang.

She knew it was Stephanie before she picked it up. 'Sabrina,' said Stephanie in a rush, her voice a little breathless. 'How are you? How are Penny and Cliff?'

'Wonderful.' Sabrina was puzzled. Not only breathless, she thought. Wary. As if she's afraid of what I might say. 'We went apple-picking, and they turned into a couple of harvesting machines. Stephanie, what do I do with three bushels of apples?'

Stephanie's laugh had a wistful note that Sabrina caught instantly. 'They always get carried away. How come you didn't tell them to stop?'

'We weren't there—'

'Weren't there?'

'We went for a walk. I . . . didn't feel like picking, the cast was clumsy, so we let them do the work.'

There was a brief silence. 'How is Garth?'

'Fine. He's . . . fine. I told you last week, he's spending more time at home, and that makes Penny and Cliff happy. We're all . . . fine.'

'And?'

Sabrina took a deep breath. 'And this morning I had—'

'No, I was asking about Garth. I was wondering if maybe, when he got back from California, he might have wanted to make love. Sort of a welcome home.'

Her voice was different again, as if she was trying to put distance between them. Sabrina was uneasy. 'Is that what he used to do?'

'Yes. And he did this time, didn't he? It's all right, you know. You can do what you want. It's too much to expect someone to live a whole life without doing . . . some things that are . . . different. After all, five weeks is a long time . . .'

Her voice trailed away, and suddenly Sabrina understood. Who's the man? she wondered. It must have happened very suddenly. 'It isn't so long,' she said cautiously. 'A lot has been going on—'

'He did want to, didn't he? Sabrina, how many times have you and Garth made love? Five? Ten? How many? *Don't lie to me.*'

'Once,' said Sabrina, stung, her guilt rushing back. She heard Stephanie take a sharp breath. 'The night before he went to California. I couldn't avoid it. But, Stephanie, it had no meaning. It – didn't mean anything at all.'

'It did to Garth.' Sabrina said nothing. Sighing, Stephanie curled up on the chaise in her bedroom, wishing she had someone to talk to. Gaby would be back soon, but she couldn't talk to her. Or anyone else. Not even her sister, who had made love to her husband.

'I hate this,' she said, but she didn't mean Garth and Sabrina as much as she meant her own wild swings of emotions. She had called to tell Sabrina about the cruise. Hearing about apple-picking, she wanted to be home. When Sabrina admitted making love to Garth, she wanted Max.

'I know you hate it,' Sabrina answered. 'But I didn't seduce him, you know. I just happen to sleep in a bed that happens to be his. I wouldn't even have told you—'

'Why not? Do you think it makes any difference to me? You can make love to Garth all you want.'

'I don't need to have you offer me your husband,' Sabrina said coldly. 'It only happened once, and I won't let it happen again. Not because of you, but so I can live with myself.'

'Sabrina, wait, don't be angry. I'm sorry; I didn't mean . . .
Sabrina, listen, I feel so far away; nothing I do here has
anything to do with that life, and I get confused. Sabrina?
Are you there?'

'Yes. I'm listening. What's wrong, Stephanie?'

Stephanie heard the love in Sabrina's voice and wanted to
tell her everything, but her thoughts were too tangled to sort
out. 'I don't know . . . Jitters, I guess, because sometimes I
don't know who I really want to be. No, that's not true – of
course I know. All this will pass as soon as I'm back where
I belong, but – it's hard to describe. So many odd feelings.'

In the noon sunlight of the breakfast room, Sabrina ran her
finger along a scratch in the round table and gazed at a dead
leaf dangling from an avocado plant that Penny refused to
throw away. As clearly as she could see the table and the
plant, she could picture each room at Cadogan Square; she
could feel their quiet serenity and privacy, the beauty she
had created.

Absentmindedly, she bent down and picked up a baseball
trading card Cliff had dropped. She put it on the sideboard,
thinking that she'd forgotten to take the pot roast out of the
freezer for dinner. 'I know,' she said. 'I'm going through the
same things you are.'

'In Evanston?' Stephanie asked, with such genuine surprise
that Sabrina laughed in a rush of love for her sister.

'Even in Evanston,' she said. 'A lot goes on here.'

'Yes, indeed,' Stephanie said flatly. 'You told me.'

All right, Sabrina thought. It's over. I don't know why she
hasn't asked about the X ray – she knew it was supposed to
be today – but I have to tell her and then get out. It doesn't
matter whether I want to or not; it's her family and I'm the
destructive outsider.

'Stephanie, I had an appointment with—'

'We've been busy at Ambassadors,' Stephanie interrupted.

'Oh, have you? What did you sell?'

'The Petuntse porcelain you bought in China.' Stephanie's
voice was elated. 'It arrived three days ago, and before Brian
and I even had it all unpacked a salesman from Bonn bought
it – Brooks sent him over. And a lawyer from Manchester

bought the Grendly day-bed, the mahogany one with scrolls. Oh, and Lady Stargrave came in – she wants a Chippendale lacquered cabinet for her new town house. I said I'd get it, but I don't know where.'

'Thomas Strang may have one in his shop. He bought two last year. If not, he'll probably have a Gillows, and Bettina would be satisfied with that; they're so similar in technique she'll never know the difference. But I can—'

'I'll call him,' Stephanie said, and raced on. 'Gabrielle is fine, though she moons around like a teenager about Brooks and won't go out with anyone else. I thought I'd ask her to help Brian in the shop while I'm away.'

Silence. 'While you're what?'

'Just for a few days. Sabrina, I've met someone – not the kind of man I'd want to be with for a long time, but exciting, and different from anyone I've ever known, and enormously wealthy.' She laughed lightly. 'The perfect fantasy. He wants me to go on a cruise in the Mediterranean for four or five days, on his yacht, and I've decided to go. It's just this once, this one chance, and I don't want to turn it down.'

That's why you forced me to say Garth and I had made love. You wanted to know, you wanted the excuse. And that's why you're not letting me tell you about my wrist. Quiet Stephanie, who had worried about being overshadowed; cautious Stephanie, afraid to take risks, who had met Garth so early and married and settled down – and now was having a daring romance. Sabrina smiled to herself at the twist their lives had taken. I'm having *my* daring romance, she thought, because I met Garth so late.

But – a cruise, a yacht, the Mediterranean. That was Sabrina's world, and thinking of it triggered her appetite as no other memory could. She knew those cruises: self-contained worlds of luxury and sensuality cut off from time and space. A blinding white yacht cutting through a blue-green sea, hazy islands like mirages on the horizon, molten sun, cool staterooms, and dark, dreamlike sex weaving through the days and nights. *Oh, I miss it, I miss it, I need it.*

'But you've done all that,' Stephanie said, as if she heard

Sabrina's thoughts. 'And you will again. This is my only chance.'

'A last fling?'

'A last fling.' It was a promise, made to both of them.

Sabrina took a deep breath. Another week. Another week with Garth. 'Who's the man?' she asked casually.

Stephanie hesitated. 'Max Stuyvesant.'

'No.'

'Don't be so quick. He's changed. Even Alexandra says so. Anyway, when did you see him last? He's been in New York for three years.'

'Alexandra says he's changed?'

'She says he's mellowed. Like a ripe pear.'

Sabrina laughed. 'That sounds like Alexandra. Stephanie, you can't know much about Max. Did you ask Alexandra about him?'

'I didn't need to. I decorated his house. Top to bottom. The way you did Alexandra's. I didn't tell you because I was afraid I'd fail and have to bring in someone to rescue me. But I didn't. Sabrina, I know all I need to know about Max. I'm not asking for permission, you know; I've already said I'd go with him. And you're hardly in a position to tell me to stay out of his bed.'

'I don't deserve that.' *Don't you? You're in love with her husband.*

'I suppose not,' said Stephanie carelessly. 'What's the real reason you don't want me to go? It can't be Max. Are you so bored you can't wait to get back? It's only a few more days, you know. And it's not as if I'm asking a favor; we don't have any choice. Do we, Sabrina? Nat hasn't taken the final X rays, has he?'

She wants me to lie. 'No. No, he hasn't. He changed it to the end of this week. About the time you get back from your fling.'

'Well, then, everything is fine, isn't it? I'm not making you wait any longer at all. I'll get my plane ticket for next Monday. Sabrina . . . don't be angry with me. I need you. I know I'm going back, and I'll live in my house and take care of my children and try to work things out with Garth, and everything will be all right. I just can't picture myself at

331

home yet. I'll be able to later, after the cruise. And I'll have your help, won't I? Because I guess by now there are things you can tell *me* about my family so I can take over again. I will have your help, won't I, Sabrina?'

Sabrina was crying. 'Yes. Any way I can.' She closed her eyes, blotting out the sun. She could hear the strain in Stephanie's voice and knew she was dreading coming back as much as she was anticipating it. But it didn't matter. Whatever happened between Stephanie and Garth, Sabrina would have disappeared and it would be Stephanie who was in Garth's arms, a world away from Max and his yacht. And Stephanie would have forgotten the fantasy of that yacht long before Sabrina had stopped aching for Garth.

Next Monday. But until then, let Stephanie have her cruise, her fling. I owe it to her. Let her go without knowing about the trip to Connecticut, without knowing that the cast is off. Let her go. There is plenty of time for the truth.

Sabrina watched Chicago tilt below them as the plane climbed through the early-morning haze and banked to the east. Lake Michigan glittered below, the skyscrapers of the city clustered on its shore. She could make out Evanston and the university campus, the green expanse and turning leaves of Lincoln Park, the wall of high-rise apartments along the pale ribbon of beaches lapped by long, slow waves. A few hardy sailors had their boats out, tall white sails snapping and billowing above the water striped blue and green beneath sunlight and shifting clouds.

'The end of the season,' Garth said, looking with her out the window. He put his arm around her. 'What a lovely autumn we've had.'

She held out her wrist, flexed the hand with its gold wedding band. 'A strange autumn.'

Her burnished hair curled against his shoulder; the perfect curve of her cheek, her clear skin and long curved eyelashes were inches from his lips as his arm held her. He thought back to last year when they had flown together to Amsterdam and she had gone on by herself to London to visit her sister. Had they spent any time together on that trip? He couldn't remember. Probably not. They hadn't done many things together in those days. Why not? He looked at the beautiful woman beside him and could not think of an answer.

They had climbed above the clouds. Below them, moving with them on the white landscape, was a perfect circle of a rainbow with the shadow of their plane in the center. 'It's called a pilot's halo,' Garth said when she pointed it out to him.

'Are we in the middle of a rainbow, too?'

'Not that I know of. Why?'

'I was wondering if our plane might look like a shadow inside a rainbow to the people in another plane, far above us.'

He chuckled. 'You think we might be only shadows, then?'

'If we were, I wonder if we'd know it.'

He put his lips to her hair. 'I wouldn't care, as long as you were this real to me.'

Sabrina was silent. Garth took his arm from her shoulders and opened his book to read, a minute later she did the same. When they had landed in New York and were in the limousine Foster Laboratories had sent to drive them to Stamford, he said wryly, 'My first trip with my wife in over a year, and I have to spend the day with a bunch of pharmaceutical executives. Doesn't make sense.'

'I have to spend it with their wives,' she countered. 'Does that make more sense?'

'No. Shall we run away? Go back to New York and have our own holiday and forget all about Stamford?'

'We can't.'

'No.' His voice changed. 'Of course not. I forgot how important this is to you.'

It's important to Stephanie. 'I meant that we'd accepted their invitation and they've made plans for us. Garth, what am I going to do with all those wives?'

'Nothing. Just follow them around. They're the ones with something to do – entertain you, I gather, and make you think Stamford is the earthly Garden of Eden so you can't wait to move there.'

'But I have no idea how to behave with them.'

'Any way you want.'

'Garth, what do *you* want? I can be wide-eyed and eager, or cold and disdainful, or cool but friendly – what would you like?'

'Look, my love, you're not playing a role. I just want you to be yourself.'

She looked at him, her lips slightly parted. 'I'll do my best.'

There were three of them waiting in the president's reception room when the limousine pulled up to the executive headquarters of Foster Laboratories in Stamford, a town much like Evanston, some thirty miles from New York. The steel and glass building rose from a marble plaza floating in a sea of grass with fountains, groves of pine trees and undulating chrysanthemum beds lining the half-mile-long driveway.

The women wore wool suits, blue and brown and green. They stood in a row in the huge, rosewood-paneled reception room, sinking slightly into the wool pile beneath their feet. Nearby, massive suede couches curved around a glass table resting on chromium scrolls. Here and there on the expanse of carpet stood illuminated lucite pillars with objects displayed inside them like rare jewels: hypodermic needles, time capsules, packets of pills, bottles of colored liquid.

The women gave Sabrina and Garth time to be awed by the dazzling scene. Garth said nothing. Sabrina knew he was unimpressed by carefully staged grandeur; in fact, he barely noticed it. He was more interested in a well-equipped laboratory, or even the inner workings of their new food processor, than in all the rosewood in Connecticut.

But she knew their hostesses expected the Andersens to be overwhelmed, so she turned her head to take in the entire room. 'Grand,' she murmured. 'Opulent.'

The women smiled and held out their hands to her, with sidelong glances at Garth, who turned out to be younger and far more handsome than expected. When he was whisked away by their dark-suited husbands, they concentrated on Sabrina. 'We meet again,' said one. 'Welcome to Stamford.'

It took Sabrina by surprise. Stephanie hadn't visited Stamford. This woman must have been in Evanston, then.

Why hadn't Garth mentioned it? 'We're glad to be here,' she said, but there had been a perceptible pause.

'Too many new faces,' said another of the women casually, coming to Sabrina's aid. 'Of course you remember Irma Kallen—'

'President,' Irma Kallen put in quickly.

'From the time she was passing through Chicago on her way to Los Angeles,' went on Sabrina's savior, supplying details. 'And I'm Freddie Payne, vice president, finance.'

'Angie Warner,' chimed the third, 'vice president, manufacturing.'

This time Sabrina was quicker, understanding that they were identifying themselves with their husband's titles. She smiled 'Stephanie Andersen, professor.' Freddie Payne grinned but shook her head slightly in warning. Bad beginning, Sabrina thought. Try again. 'We've been so looking forward to our visit.'

'Ah,' said Irma Kallen. 'We wondered. It has been postponed so many times.'

'We want you to love our town,' Angie Warner said quickly. Short and plump, she had the angelic face and rosebud mouth of a peacemaker. 'We want you to love us. We thought a short tour on the way to lunch at Irma's, and then a visit to the school and the Women's Club, if that seems all right ... if that pleases you ... '

Sabrina bowed her head in agreement. How could she disagree with Angie Warner? Or, at the moment, with any of them? Their husbands earned upwards of three hundred thousand dollars a year; her husband earned thirty-five thousand. On their home ground, using their yardsticks of power and prestige, Sabrina was at a distinct disadvantage. She told herself to remember it.

Irma Kallen led the way to her car, a Silver Shadow that glided through wide, peaceful streets past churches two centuries old and a village green where a battle of the Revolutionary War had been fought. She pulled into the driveway of a three-story brick mansion with newly added rooms jutting out on all sides – like a demented chicken flapping its wings, Sabrina thought. She had taken a strong dislike to Irma Kallen. But she's the president's wife, she told herself. Show respect.

Irma Kallen was tall and angular, long-chinned, with brown eyes that went in two directions, each unconcerned with what the other chose to look at. This caused difficulties for those around her who never knew which eye to meet in conversation. Sabrina chose the left and found herself in focus about half the time. Such a woman, whose looks made others nervous, and whose temper was short, would not take kindly to a visitor who was not only young and beautiful but also made light of her husband's title and, worse, forgot a previous meeting.

But Irma Kallen had a magnificent home, decorated with sophisticated imagination. Sabrina walked through the rooms impressed with the blend of two styles of simplicity: spare Shaker furniture and the more massive but still simple turn-of-the-century oak pieces of Philip Webb, stained with the green that was his trademark and decorated with lacquered leather or raised silver designs. She ran her hand over the delicate tracery on the piano. 'Webb,' she murmured. 'How marvelous.'

Irma looked startled and pleased. For a moment both eyes focused on Sabrina. 'How did you know that?'

'I know furniture,' said Sabrina. 'I work with antiques.'

'Oh,' cried Angie Warner, 'then you'll love Silvermine.' Sabrina looked a question. 'An artists' colony in Norwalk. Just a few miles away. We go there for shopping and lunch at least once a week.'

Freddie Payne chuckled. 'I have a feeling Stephanie is way ahead of Silvermine. She probably knows more than anyone there. Even more than you, Irma.'

Sabrina looked alert. A private war. She had seen a skirmish earlier, in the car. 'It's Frederique,' Freddie had said, explaining her name. She was tall and striking, with thick black hair cut bluntly and heavy-lidded hazel eyes beneath dark brows. 'Frederique, from some unknown French ancestor. But that doesn't go over big in Stamford. One does better as a Pilgrim. Irma is a Pilgrim, aren't you, Irma? Or rather, since even Irma is not that well preserved, more likely one of her pirate ancestors was.' Irma ignored her.

At lunch, angelic Angie worked at keeping the peace between Irma and Freddie. The women held the rank of their husbands, so Irma, as president, was clearly chief officer of the meal and of their entire social life; but she often allowed Angie to smooth edges made jagged by her temper.

Sabrina ate her broiled grapefruit and turkey Florentine and watched with amusement the same kind of small, swift, daggers-drawn drama she was used to among her circles in London. Of course, she thought, it exists everywhere, even in Evanston. But I never thought about it because I never thought of Evanston as anything but temporary.

Nothing with Garth is permanent.

She felt the familiar stab of pain at the thought. Irma's voice broke through. 'What?' Sabrina said. 'I'm sorry; I was thinking of something else.'

'I said,' Irma rapped out, 'we've planned a small dinner for this evening, at the club, so that you and your husband can meet all of us. You should know that we are a close-knit group. Many of the men in Stamford commute to New York, but we feel our duty is here. Foster is Stamford's most prestigious institution, and those of us who are its leaders are also leaders of the community. We strengthen Stamford; we do not take our money to New York. This is a responsibility we bear gladly, but it is effective only if we stay together. Freddie thinks this is foolish – she has a number of strange friends—'

'Whose husbands aren't executives,' Freddie said solemnly to Sabrina.

'But Freddie never wanders too far,' Irma continued. 'Because we all need each other, as you will discover when your husband joins us. And with our help you will learn quickly how to be one of us. The fact that you have much to learn need not embarrass you. Coming from the Midwest you could not be expected to know our ways.'

Sabrina listened, wide-eyed and silent, as Irma went on. 'Our way of life filters slowly to the rest of the country. Often, of course, by the time others pattern themselves after us, we have developed new styles.'

Angie looked embarrassed; Freddie winked at Sabrina. Sabrina looked steadily at Irma's precise mouth. 'We take as our model the cultured centers of Europe. We dine later, for example, than you do: eight o'clock; even, on occasion, nine. Six o'clock, of course, is proper for the children. We do not eat in backyards; we do not barbecue our food in clouds of foul smoke. We do not wear one-piece clothes such as jumpsuits and overalls. We support the public schools as essential to our town, but we do not send our children to them. You have children, of course.'

'Two,' Sabrina said automatically. She was fascinated, almost mesmerized, by Irma's chant. 'A boy and a girl.'

'And you are raising them as good Christians.'

'I think we are raising Cliff to be a soccer forward,' said Sabrina. 'We're not sure yet about Penny.'

Freddie burst into laughter; Angie giggled. Irma seemed frozen, coffee cup raised halfway to her mouth. 'Those of us who are blessed with material wealth take our responsibilities seriously.'

'It's all right, Stephanie,' Angie said brightly, aware that Irma was making a fool of herself. Angie didn't know exactly what it was – maybe the way Stephanie identified the Webb piano, or her steady, unimpressed gaze on Irma's face, or the regal way she held her head. Or her beauty, which Angie envied simply and good-naturedly, the way she envied one woman's cooking or another's needlepoint. Whatever it was, Angie knew Stephanie was no country girl, and she didn't want her to judge them by Irma's treating her like one. 'Irma's always serious with new people, but in our group she's lots of fun. She plays tennis, and I really have to work to keep up with her, and sometimes we get her on the volleyball court. Not often,' she added with sad honesty, 'but sometimes.'

'We don't play too much volleyball in the Midwest,' Sabrina said earnestly, leaning forward and addressing Irma's left eye. 'Though progress has brought tennis right to our doorstep. But we do work hard to learn how to be sophisticated. Some of us occasionally wear Karl Lagerfeld or Perry Ellis designs. Now and then we serve wine with dinner – Montrachet, or perhaps a Brouilly if red seems appropriate. And lately our more daring hostesses have begun serving the salad after the entrée rather than before. Of course we have to work very hard at it. But you may be sure we are grateful for all you allow us to learn from you.'

There was a long silence. Angie tried to smile, but her lips were trembling. Freddie said, 'Well, I'll be damned. Over to you, Irma. On second thought, never mind.' She turned to Sabrina. 'Irma told us you were a shy little housewife from the sticks. Irma, love, you must send your first impressions to bed without any dinner. They have failed you badly.' She pushed back her chair. 'Stephanie, let's look at the terrace.'

Sabrina sat still. *Damn. Oh, damn. What is wrong with me? Stephanie would have worried about Garth; she would have been quiet and sweet and let the president's wife feel superior. Now I've messed it up. Stephanie would have acted for Garth. I acted for myself. Why in heaven's name did I let this silly woman get to me?*

'Stephanie?' Freddie said. Sabrina excused herself and followed her though the folding doors. The two women sat on a low brick wall surrounding the flagstone terrace. Huge redwood planters with late roses and asters stood beside white wrought-iron furniture not yet stored for the winter. Beyond the wall a crew of gardeners raked fallen leaves and planted bulbs for next spring's tulips and hyacinths. Another crew was fitting a tarpaulin over the swimming pool while a third rolled up the nets in the tennis courts. It was a peaceful scene of abundance – so perfect, Sabrina thought, it might have been staged to illustrate the benefits of joining the Foster team.

'She can be harmful, but not really dangerous,' Freddie said. 'Unless you give her that power. The trick is to understand that she is a fool who must be taken seriously.'

Sabrina shrugged. 'I would only take her seriously if Garth asked me to.'

Freddie was surprised. 'Why else are you here?'

'To look around. To be looked at. Why do you all assume it's settled? Isn't there any room for doubt?'

'Look, sweetie, I don't know what your husband told you, but he is not here for an interview. This is a formal session

339

for the men to work out the details of the job, and for us to make sure your little heart flutters with delight at becoming one of us. From what I've heard, you're moving here when the current school quarter ends.'

Sabrina felt betrayed. Garth hadn't told her it was decided. Would he really take the job without talking it over with her? They always talked things over.

'Hey,' Freddie said. 'It's okay. Ignore Irma. She's a small piece of the scenery. Though I suggest, to make things easier when you move here, that you revive the act you put on for her in Chicago. You'll have a few required exercises: dinner parties with the correct guests, a few luncheons, sponsorship of a couple of charity affairs and some command appearances at Irma's parties – you do have to get along with her. But the rest of the time you can be yourself. As long as you're discreet, you can be anything you want, with anyone you want. It's not a bad way of life, you know.'

'I know.' Sabrina stood and brushed off her skirt. Stephanie could manage it; she could be what Irma expected, without getting angry but also without sinking into their little group as Angie, and even Freddie, had done. Stephanie could have a good time here.

She thanked Freddie. 'You rescued me twice; I'm very grateful. But now I think I'd better mend my own fences.' And returning to the dining room she made her apologies. 'So rude of me ... too many new impressions ... lunch was delicious ... the conversation so pleasant ...'

Irma put a hand to her perfectly smooth hair and smoothed it. 'We accept your apology. My husband thinks your husband will be a great asset to the Laboratories. Shall we have our little tour now?'

They drove through the town, inspected the new high school, visited the hospital where Irma was director of volunteers, parked along the shore of Long Island Sound and watched sailboats that made Sabrina think of home. Then they returned to the headquarters of Foster Laboratories and picked up Garth and the husbands of Sabrina's hostesses and went to dine at the club, so Sabrina and Garth could meet the people they were supposed to know.

340

Later, in the limousine taking them to the Plaza Hotel in New York, where they would spend the night before catching a morning plane to Chicago, Garth took Sabrina's hand. 'Wined and dined and flattered. Duck for lunch. What did you have?'

'Turkey. Dried out, then drowned in sauce.'

'And lobster for dinner. What was that we had for dessert?'

'Hazelnut mousse with raspberry puree.'

'Do you suppose professors eat this way whenever they come to Connecticut?'

'Do you suppose their wives get a lecture on how retarded Midwesterners can learn the high style of the East Coast whenever they come to Connecticut?'

'Intriguing. Who gave the lecture?'

She described the lunch, sparing herself nothing. 'I didn't do you any good at all. But if Freddie was right and you've already decided—'

'I haven't.' He was still holding her hand; he put his other hand over it and faced her. 'I agreed to come out here because I thought it was necessary for us. I would never make the decision without you. It occurs to me,' he went on carefully, 'that by letting Irma Kallen have it with both barrels, you may have been saying you didn't want me to take the job.'

Sabrina closed her eyes. All the lies, all the deceptions, all the guilt and tangled feelings of the past five weeks piled up between them in a wall she could not break down. *My love, I want to help you. I want you to be happy. But I owe this to Stephanie.* Her hand was warm between his. 'Garth, it's your decision. I can't make it for you.'

Tired and depressed, he took his hands from hers. If she no longer cared what he did, she was not planning a future with him. Yet she loved him. He had seen it in her face, heard it in her voice. She loved him.

But still she shut him out. So often they had come close to warmth, to love, to shared feelings – and she had pulled back, turned away. All those lost opportunities to talk. As if she were afraid that if she listened to him she might be swayed, by his arguments or her own feelings, and not be able to make her own decision to go or to stay.

341

How the hell did a man fight that? For, of course, he intended to fight. He had told her in the orchard he would accept her decision, but that was absurd. He would fight to keep her. But until he understood why she deliberately withdrew from him, why she refused to make love to him, why she had even relaxed her close vigilance of the children, he could not decide how to begin – or foresee how it would end.

They made the rest of the trip in silence, and in silence rode the hotel elevator to the suite that had been reserved for them. Sabrina stood at the window looking on either side of the leafy darkness of Central Park at the lighted windows of buildings that never slept.

Garth locked the door. 'I don't want the job,' he said abruptly. On a round table a bottle of champagne nestled in a bucket of ice; a card around its neck wished them a pleasant evening from the Kallens. Garth eased the cork out with his thumbs. 'Even if it means lobster every night and champagne at bedtime.'

'Why not?' she asked.

He filled two tall, slender glasses and handed one to her. 'How long has it been since you and I were in a hotel room?' he wondered aloud.

We have never been in a hotel room. She sat at one end of a striped silk couch. 'A long time. Why don't you want the job?'

'Because the only subjects my hosts talked about today were the market, the consumer, dollars-per-research-hour, return on investment. Because to them gene splicing means a product, as if I'd be directing a team of chefs inventing a new breakfast cereal. Because what they want to do is what they are supposed to do: make money. Because what I want to do is what the university expects me to do: research and teach. Because I don't want to have to explain why I'm following a promising new lead in research even though it might not result in a product for years – if ever. Because I can't look at the problems of genetics and see the bottom line of a corporate profit and loss statement. Because, damn it, I don't belong there. More champagne? It's on the house.'

She held out her glass. He refilled it and sat in a wing chair near the other end of the couch.

'Two other points,' he said. 'One, as I said before, I don't think you belong there, either. Maybe you did once, or thought you did, but not anymore. If this were two or three months ago you wouldn't have jumped on Irma Kallen; when she was in Chicago last spring you treated her like a first cousin to Queen Elizabeth. You've changed since then. You've changed since your trip.' He paused, waiting, but she ignored the opening he offered.

Garth could not bear to look at her. He had never been so aware of her nearness – or of how far from him she went when she withdrew into silence. He drained his glass. 'And one of the changes I like best is that you can put down a pompous, small-town queen mother like Irma Kallen without being afraid that she won't like you, or me, afterward. Which means one of two things. You have a lot more confidence than you've ever had before ... '

Sabrina watched the bubbles streaming upward in her glass. 'Or?'

'Or you've decided you don't give a damn what I do or what happens to me. Or us.'

The room was hushed. Soft light from the table lamp glinted off melting ice in the champagne bucket and the dark green bottle as Garth tilted it above their glasses. The rest of the room was in shadow. A doorway led to the bedroom where a single lamp illuminated the bed, turned down for the night by a maid who had left a gold-wrapped chocolate centered on each pillow. Nearby, their two overnight bags stood side by side, touching, like lovers.

They had not been alone, away from the children, in the five weeks Sabrina had been there. In the muffled quiet she was conscious of Garth's presence with such force that her skin felt his touch though he was a dozen feet away. She saw each detail of his face though she was not looking at him. Her mouth felt his mouth on hers though they had not kissed for three days, since the moment in the hallway at home when she had broken from his arms in a panic of love and guilt.

He has become a part of me.

'And finally,' he said when she did not answer, 'I have

been offered the directorship of the Institute of Genetic Engineering at Midwestern, to be built this spring and in operation by next year.'

'Garth!' She looked up, her eyes shining. 'But that's wonderful! It should have been your first reason – your only reason! Nothing else matters. Does it?'

'It might.'

'Why didn't you tell me? Oh, now I know what Vivian was talking about when I took Penny and Cliff over there yesterday. She said to give you her congratulations. I thought she was talking about your committee granting her tenure, that you'd won. But she wasn't; she knew about your appointment.'

'She knew I'd been offered the position. I haven't taken it.'

'But why not? Isn't it everything you want?'

'I don't know if it's what you want. The pay is about two-thirds of what Foster would pay, much less when you add bonuses, stock options, travel, company car, country club membership – all the perks that universities never heard of. I know how worried you've been about money – worried enough, probably, to make Irma Kallen tolerable.'

'But all those reasons you gave for not—'

'I said I don't want to take it. But if you want me to, if you would share it with me—'

'But you would hate it.'

He shrugged. 'A lot of it. I'd concentrate on the research and learn to deal with the rest of it.' He leaned forward in his chair. 'Stephanie. Listen to me. I love you. I can't imagine making a life without you. Nothing I do means a damn thing if I can't bring it home to you– if I can't say your name and hear you answer – if I can't go to sleep at night knowing that when I open my eyes in the morning I'll find you next to me. All the wonder of my work disappears when I look at the wonder of you. The discoveries are there, even the excitement is there, but it's empty, it doesn't mean a damn thing to me without you. I am not complete without you. Don't you understand that? Don't you understand that I would do anything to keep your life woven into mine? If you ask me to take this job—'

'I wouldn't. I don't want you to take it. Of course I don't want you to take it.'

He looked at her somberly. 'I don't know what that means.'

It means I love you. I love you. I want you to be happy. I want you to do what is best for you even if I'm gone, even if I'll never share it, never be with you when you wake up in the morning. He watched her lips move silently and tears fill her eyes. He stirred, wanting to go to her, but he forced himself to wait. 'I don't know what your tears mean, either,' he said harshly.

Sabrina put her hands over her face and let the tears come. She had been holding them back for so long that now they came with relief and a kind of exhilaration. *I can't help it, I'm sorry, I can't help it. I can only do so much. And I did try.* 'What do they mean?' he repeated. He went to her and pulled away her hands. Her face was wet with tears and her mouth trembled; her eyes were shining as they had been on that morning when he awakened and caught her in an unguarded moment.

'That I love you,' she said at last, the words finally freed, and his arms caught her up, enfolding her in an embrace so confident she felt she had at last come home.

He would have picked her up, but she shook her head. She would share this with him; her decision as well as his. They walked to the bedroom and undressed each other, hurrying, touching the skin they bared as children explore a new discovery to make sure it is real, and really theirs.

Garth removed the ivory combs in her hair and the heavy waves fell over her shoulders, bronze in the dim light. He looked at her slender body and passed his hands along the clear, silken skin as if he had never seen it before. Her ripe fullness lifted toward him, her head high and proud as he gazed at her. *I am a part of us,* her eyes said, *and my beauty is greater because you desire me.*

Once again he gathered her into his arms, her softness curving against the muscles of his arms and stomach and legs, the warmth of her body merging into his. They held each other, treasuring their desire, for now they knew it would be fulfilled. At last he bent his head to her uplifted face and kissed her, tasting the coolness of champagne in the warmth of her mouth.

'Dear love,' Sabrina whispered against his lips. They lay on the bed, Garth's full weight upon her. He raised his head and his eyes, dark and intense, met hers, deeper than he had ever imagined, with a blue flame in their depths.

'My love,' he murmured. 'My dearest, newfound love.' The room was bright from the luster of her body. He closed his eyes, but the brightness was still there and he knew then that it was everywhere, that in rediscovering his wife he had discovered light and life, and they were part of him as she was.

'Yes,' she said, and with the passion they had denied for so long he thrust into her. She moved against him, enclosing him, her bones against his, her skin against his, one body, one rush of blood.

This is where I belong, she thought, and then she let go of the solid room, let go of herself, and disappeared in the darkness of sensation, her mind finally stilled, nothing left but feeling and an overwhelming gratitude for what she was discovering of herself and of him in their flesh, the meeting of their mouths and the worlds they saw in each other's eyes.

The gilt-wrapped chocolate lay crushed on the pillow. Carefully, Garth unwrapped it, and Sabrina took it into her mouth from his hand. 'Where is yours?' she asked, and they hunted until they found the other on the floor where it had fallen.

'But I'm still hungry,' he said after nibbling it from her fingers. 'What shall we demand of room service?'

'Nectar. Robins' eggs. Rose petals with dew.'

Garth dialed. 'Champagne; omelet; salad. And grapefruit sorbet.'

Sabrina was laughing 'Grapefruit sorbet?'

'I forgot to tell you. A new passion I discovered in California. Robins' eggs take half an hour. I would like to make love to you again.'

'Yes.' *These are our years together; these hours. They are all we have.* Garth bent over her, kissing her mouth, but she put her hands on his chest, pushing him firmly until he lay back, and then she was kissing him, her lips trembling along his throat and through the dark hairs of his chest, slipping softly, lingeringly over his smooth flat stomach. She curled up beside him, her hands on his thighs, and raised her head for a moment, meeting the darkness of his gaze, telling him, with her eyes and her strong hands, to lie still and let her give him pleasure. Languidly, with her tongue, she caressed the tip of his penis extended before her, and then she brought him slowly into her mouth, along her tongue, into her throat. He filled her: smooth, firm, a strong, solid force pulsing with life, and Sabrina felt an exaltation, a freedom, a kind of love and giving she had never known before.

Garth groaned with the waves of pleasure that flowed through him in widening circles, thinking this was something else she brought him for the first time in so many years, thinking he could sink into her, drown himself in the tenderness and strength of her mouth. But finally he needed to give to her, and he pulled out of her mouth to bring her beside him.

He kissed her closed eyelids and followed with his lips the shape of her face, the long line of her slender throat, her rounded breasts, heavy against his cheek, and took into his mouth first one nipple and then the other, until they grew erect beneath his tongue.

Slowly, slowly, his lips moved along her body, drinking in her silken scent, brushing with light kisses the luminous skin, alive beneath his mouth, down her belly to the cluster of curling hair and within it the warm, pliant flesh that trembled as he reached it. Sabrina thrust her fingers into the thick black hair of his head and opened her legs as she felt him take her with his tongue and lips. All her senses were drawn to that one yielding place. Then suddenly, fiercely, he thrust his tongue deep inside her, possessing her throbbing dark center until it contracted, poised on a thin precipice, then leaped, pulsing wildly as she cried out and shuddered beneath his hands.

He was smiling at her when she opened her eyes. Her mouth formed a silent Oh and she smiled up at him. 'My love—' she began, when a knock came at the door and a hearty voice bellowed that room service had arrived.

Garth leaped from the bed. 'Dunce,' he muttered. 'If he's so energetic at three in the morning, why isn't he serenading us with Italian love songs? Do you know what? I forgot to pack a robe.'

He looked at Sabrina, sitting cross-legged on the bed, her face radiant, laughing at him. 'Here,' she said, holding out the quilt and as he made a toga from it he began to laugh with her, and their laughter filled the room.

Nothing was settled, but everything was changed. Sabrina sat beside an airplane window looking at a landscape of towering clouds as she had only twenty-four hours earlier and knew that the game was over. She would have to leave today. She had had her moment of love, and from now on everything in her life would be different because of it; but no matter how she relived the past twenty-four hours, they were not hers; they were Stephanie's.

What had begun in mid-September as a careless lark had grown by the end of October to a complex web of passion and need and commitment to a shared future. Which was impossible for Garth and Sabrina, but essential for Garth and his wife. And even if Sabrina had wanted to forget that, she could not. Because Garth's wife was the other half of herself.

Beside her, Garth shook his head as a stewardess offered him a magazine, and leaned back in his seat. 'It's hard to believe how much has happened since your trip.'

She clasped her hands in her lap and turned to him, letting herself look fully at him in the brilliant sunlight above the clouds, memorizing the tiny lines that radiated from the corners of his dark eyes, his strong cheekbones and wide mouth, the cleft in his chin, the gray hairs mixed with black at his forehead.

'A turning point,' he mused. 'Did you know it would be? Or did you just run away and then later realize it might be the first step of the final step out the door? I think that was it. And then you came back, trying in so many ways to be different, as if you were determined to remake our marriage, forcing me to see what happened to us. I've wanted for some time to tell you how grateful I am, though you must know. I want you to understand that I'm aware of what you've done, how hard it is to change, how hard you've tried. And you were the one to do it. I didn't know how. I didn't even know what had to be done.'

He took her hand. 'That was some of what I was trying to tell you last night. I suppose you knew most of it already. What I'm saying now is that I won't let you slip away again. You've taught me – Stephanie, what is it? What's wrong?'

She bent her head. 'I don't know. I'm so dizzy, all of a sudden. Could you get me a cup of tea?'

He rang for the stewardess, and Sabrina put her head back against the seat. 'Thank you.' Her voice was shaking; her body was shaking. What's wrong with me? she thought wildly. It's not Garth, it's something else. Something is wrong, something terrible, and I don't know what it is.

Reaching across to pull down the tray in front of her, Garth felt the violent trembling of her body. 'Good God, what is it? Stephanie, my love, what can I do—?'

'I don't know,' she whispered, and buried her face in his shoulder. Garth put his arms around her, holding her tightly until the stewardess came with a pot of tea.

'Is there anything I can do?' she asked. 'A blanket—?'

'I don't think so,' Garth said. Gently, he disengaged himself. 'Stephanie, can you manage some tea?'

She nodded and took the cup in both hands, sipping the scalding liquid.

Garth looked at his watch. 'Eleven-thirty; we'll be landing in half an hour. Penny and Cliff will be at the airport, you know, with Vivian.'

'Yes. Just give me a few minutes.'

Shivering, Sabrina drank the hot tea. As Garth refilled her cup, she saw through the window a plane, in the far distance, traveling in the opposite direction. Yesterday I was on that plane, she thought. Talking about shadows.

She forced herself to think of Garth and what he had been saying when the dizziness began. She understood now why he had not seen through the deception. Garth the trained scientist, the astute observer, who had been married to the same woman for twelve years, had not guessed he was living with his wife's twin sister because he convinced himself she was deliberately changing her behavior to save their marriage. If she and Stephanie had written a scenario to protect them, they could not have found a better one. How clever we were, she thought through her despair. And look where it got us.

She had to leave. Today. And that meant calling Stephanie, telling her to catch the first plane – but Stephanie wasn't there. Stephanie was on Max's yacht. Until Friday or Saturday.

I can't stay that long. I can't do that to any of us.

But I can't just disappear, either.

She closed her eyes. She would have to stay a few more days. Stephanie would call as soon as she got back to Cadogan Square, and on Monday they would meet at the aiport in Chicago and reverse the procedure they had gone through so lightheartedly in China: exchange clothes and purses, hand over a wedding ring, trade keys to their front doors. And it would be over.

It will be over. The words rang in her head. They echoed through the excited greetings of Penny and Cliff at the airport; echoed through the sounds of the house – a door slamming, Cliff dropping a tray of cookies and Penny shouting at him to clean up the mess, Garth walking from room to room talking of storm windows; echoed through the sizzling of the steaks Sabrina cooked for dinner, the burbling of the coffeepot, the tales that Penny and Cliff took turns relating: a stray cat, a school contest, plans for a Thanksgiving parade.

It will be over echoed through the rattling of dishes as the children cleaned the kitchen, echoed through the ringing of the telephone, echoed through Garth's words calling her to say that it was long distance; someone named Brooks Westermarck wanted to speak to her.

And then the echo stopped as Brooks's voice, from the

other side of the ocean, began heavily, 'Mrs Andersen ...
Stephanie ... ' and went on, crying, to tell her they had just
heard the news that Max Stuyvesant's yacht had exploded
and gone down in the Mediterranean about eleven-thirty
Chicago time. Everyone on board, including her sister, Lady
Sabrina Longworth, had been killed.

Part III

Chapter 17

The mourners came early to Kensington Cemetery. Some wept and others murmured together as they stood near the open grave. Sabrina heard them behind her, like rustling leaves, but she did not turn around; she was watching her sister's coffin, her own coffin, settle into the grave as the Vicar gave a short prayer and began to speak.

'Lady Sabrina Longworth, vivid with life, brought us love and joy—'

Heavy, pale clouds hung low over the earth and grass, draining their color, leaving them gray beneath the supplicating branches of bare trees. A light October mist drifted from the Thames, touching the mourners with chill fingers. Sabrina was numb, but still she shivered, and Garth tightened his arm around her shoulders.

'She was young and beautiful and awake to the beauty around her—'

In the circle of Garth's arm, Sabrina was very still, but a scream clawed in her throat. *Stephanie*.

'In the midst of life we are in death.'

Stephanie was dead.

She was cold, so cold, and her skin hurt, stretched across her bones: a thin, taut membrane holding in her pain and the invisible tears that would not stop, even when she slept.

Come back, Stephanie. We'll go back to the beginning, we'll do it all differently, and everything will be all right.

'The Lord is my shepherd, I shall not want ...'

But the only beginning she could think of was the phone call from Brooks, the beginning of the nightmare. His voice had come across the ocean, crying, and as he talked the room darkened around Sabrina, receded to a small pinpoint of light, then surged back, crushing her. She could not breathe.

353

The crash of the falling telephone brought Garth and the children running; she remembered Penny and Cliff, fearful and still, watching, as Garth cradled her and with his other hand picked up the telephone to talk to Brooks, his voice level, making arrangements. He was the steady center of that crazily spinning room, a whirlpool that would have sucked her down if Garth had not held her. She clung to him. *Garth, my love—*

But he didn't know, he didn't know what had happened. 'Wait.' She struggled to pull away from him. 'It wasn't Sabrina. It wasn't Sabrina. It wasn't Sabrina who died.'

'Sssh, dear love, just hold me; you don't have to face it yet.'

'But it wasn't Sabrina, it wasn't Sabrina—' And then the tears came, wrenching sobs that drowned her words while she struggled to tell them. 'Not ... Sabrina ... who died.' Until Nat came, with a hypodermic needle. 'No! Let me cry! Don't take that away from me, from both of us—!'

But the needle slid smoothly into her arm and slowly, shudderingly, she calmed, dimly hearing Nat's voice as she fell asleep. 'My God, my God, what a dreadful thing. Garth, what else can I do?'

Thursday was a blur of faces and voices. The telephone rang steadily. Doors opened and closed; people brought flowers and food. Why was everyone so busy when Stephanie was dead?

Garth took care of everything. He had called her parents; she heard him calling Brooks again. ' ... register the death at the American consulate in Marseilles and fly the body—'

Not 'the body,' you fools, it's Stephanie!

'—back to England ... at the undertaker's – yes, give me the address. T C Dryden and Sons, Regent Street, Mayfair—'

Near home; Stephanie will be near home.

'—leaving this afternoon; we'll see you tomorrow morning, Friday ... of course, at Sabrina's house; that's where Stephanie will want to be.'

Home. I'm going home.

She let Garth do everything. He drove the children to Vivian's house, packed for both of them and held her close when they reached the airport and walked through the echoing concourse to their plane.

Garth is the center of my world, she thought; all I have left. She tried to shake off her lethargy. I have to tell him; he still doesn't know. I'll tell him as soon as we settle down. Brooks just called; I can wait a few minutes until we're ... no, Brooks called – when? – I can't remember. Yesterday? A few minutes ago?

On the plane, Garth took the magazines the stewardess offered, giving Sabrina her privacy. She pushed back her seat and closed her eyes, trying to think, to go back to the beginning, while waves of sleepiness swept over her.

If I hadn't traded places, she thought, drifting in and out of sleep. Or broken my wrist. Then everything would be all right. Or if I'd insisted we end the deception then, tell the truth, instead of letting it go on. Or later, if I'd refused to give Stephanie another week, so she could have her cruise and I could stay a little longer with Garth.

If I hadn't fallen in love with Garth.

I caused my sister's death.

She was awake for the rest of the flight, her face turned from Garth. *Everything I did led to her death. But I didn't know—*

At the airport, she insisted on going straight to the undertaker's. 'I want to see my sister. I have to see my sister.'

She went in alone, to the small room at the back of T C Dryden and Sons, and knelt beside the coffin. 'Stephanie?'

Her sister slept, cold and remote, her beauty as fragile as parchment. Sabrina watched over her, at last going back to the beginning, all the way back – the cities where they had grown up, schools and rented houses, chauffeured limousines and servants, the sleek figures of Gordon and Laura leaving them alone, the two of them, alone, making their own family.

She remembered one summer vacation when they were seven or eight. She and Stephanie had run off to find a waterfall, and Stephanie had slipped on some rocks and broken her ankle. Sabrina had raced back to find Gordon and Laura, and while Gordon worked to free Stephanie's ankle from the rocks, Sabrina had gripped her hand, to help ease the pain. That night, in bed, Stephanie had said drowsily, 'We'll always help each other, won't we? Whenever we're hurt or lost, we'll always be there.'

'Yes,' Sabrina said.

'Promise.'

'I promise.'

'I promise, too,' Stephanie had said.

In T C Dryden's silent shadowed room, lit by candles and small lamps, heavy with the fragrance of tall bouquets of flowers, Sabrina watched her sister. 'We promised, Stephanie. We promised.'

She was crying, the tears cold on her cheeks, and she rested her forehead on the polished wood of the coffin. 'I love you, Stephanie. I never meant to hurt you. It didn't seem important – one more week. I wanted to love your family for a few more days and you could have your . . . one last fling . . .'

She closed her eyes. 'It's all my fault, and now I'm left alone to tell them. We didn't plan that; we were so careless, we never thought we might have to tell anyone, and now I don't know how to do it, or how I'll bear all their anger. I did try to tell them, but no one listened and I have no one to talk to about it. All these last weeks, when I didn't have anyone in Evanston, it didn't matter because I had you and we understood each other. But now . . . Stephanie, *there is no one who will understand*.'

Sabrina reached out to smooth her sister's hair and a gleam of gold caught her eye – the wedding band she wore, glinting against the dark strands. Swiftly she pulled it off. 'This is yours, Stephanie. I have no right to it.' She slipped it on Stephanie's finger, her warm hand holding her sister's marble one. 'It's always been yours. If I'd remembered that, you would have come home sooner and none of this—'

She clasped her hands in her lap, thinking. If I'd remembered that, I would have told everyone the truth by now. I never had any right to this family. And I have to tell them that. Alone. Without Stephanie's help when they turn their anger on me. Alone. I'd better get used to it.

She leaned forward again to say goodbye to her sister. She

felt drained, as lifeless as Stephanie. *Because part of me is gone. I am burying my sister, who is also myself.*

'No,' she said aloud. 'No, they can't bury us. I won't let them. No. No. No!'

'Stephanie,' said Garth. She had not heard him come in, but he was kneeling beside her, his arm around her shoulders. Huddled beside the coffin, Sabrina felt the life in his arm, the life in her body, and trembled. Who lay in the coffin? To this man she was Stephanie, she lived with him in Stephanie's house, caring for Stephanie's children, loving them, loving Stephanie's husband. And she was in London to bury Stephanie's sister. *What have I done?* she thought frantically. *I've caused us both to die.* A low cry tore from her throat, and then Garth was helping her into a taxi to take her to Sabrina's house.

'My love,' Garth said as they moved slowly through the afternoon traffic. 'I'll help you all I can, but in the end you have to face this yourself.' His voice was gentle but unsparing; he could not do it all for her. 'Are you sure you want to stay at Sabrina's house?' She nodded. 'Do you want to use a guest room instead of her bedroom?' She shook her head. 'It might be less painful for you.'

'No,' she said. 'It's my room; I'll stay in it.'

'Whatever you want,' he said. 'I'll do anything I can to help you.'

No, you won't. Not when I tell you. When we get home and we're alone and I tell you the truth.

At Cadogan Square, Mrs. Thirkell, crumpled with grief, met them at the door and gestured toward the upper floors. 'Mrs Andersen, your father arrived a few minutes ago; he's very ill, and your mother is—'

Sabrina flew past her up the stairs, leaving Garth to follow. She found Gordon and Laura in the third-floor study, her father sitting in a leather chair, his face gray and pinched, her mother at the telephone. 'Stephanie, thank goodness you're here. Do you know how to call an ambulance? I don't suppose you do, but—'

'Dial 999. I'll do it.' She dialed and turned to her father as Garth came into the room. 'What happened?'

He was bewildered. 'My chest and arm . . . thought it was indigestion. Airplane food.' His voice was shallow.

Laura paced angrily. 'His doctor said he shouldn't come to London. He's already had two of these—'

'An ambulance,' Sabrina said into the telephone. 'For St George's Hospital.' She gave the address on Cadogan Square. 'The home of Lady Longworth. Please hurry; her father may have had a heart attack.' She looked at her parents. 'You never told me about other attacks.'

'Incidents,' Gordon murmured. 'Not the real thing.' 'The doctors say they're warnings,' said Laura. 'What luck that you knew about the hospital. How did you know?'

'I've been here before.' Sabrina dialed on the house phone. 'Mrs Thirkell, an ambulance will come for Mr Hartwell. Please call us as soon as it arrives.'

Garth was watching her thoughtfully as she leaned over Gordon, who seemed small and frail, clinging to her hand like a child. Where was the tall powerful father of her childhood? She pushed aside her mourning and knelt before him. 'Is the pain bad?'

'Better. Would you bring me a shot of Scotch?'

'No.'

'Stephanie,' said Laura. 'What has happened to you?'

Gordon smiled palely. 'She is being as strong-willed as Sabrina. But an obedient daughter would not deny her father a small medicinal Scotch.'

'An obedient daughter would not kill her father,' Sabrina said, trying to keep her voice light. 'How do I know what Scotch would do to an uncooperative heart?'

Mrs Thirkell called to say the ambulance had arrived. 'They're bringing up the stretcher, my lady.' Her embarrassment came over the telephone. 'I'm sorry, I meant Mrs Andersen. I can't get used to—'

'It's all right,' Sabrina said. 'I understand.'

As the attendants came in, Gordon stood up, pushing his hands against the arms of the chair. 'I'll walk, Stephanie.' 'No,' she said. 'It's three flights.' As he hesitated she took his arm. 'Don't argue; we're trying to help you.'

He peered at her. 'How fierce you have become.' But he let them wrap him in a blanket and strap him down before carrying him out. 'We'll follow in a taxi,' Sabrina called after them, but as soon as they were gone her knees buckled. Garth was there in an instant, holding her. He sent Laura in a taxi to the hospital and settled Sabrina on a love seat in the drawing room.

Then people were everywhere, purposeful, bustling about. Everyone but Sabrina. Restless and confused, she followed them, watching, and now and then they moved her from one place to another, like a puppet, heavy and numb. Like Stephanie.

We're in the way, she thought wryly. No one needs us; they all have jobs to do. I have something to do, too. But I can't remember what it is.

She remembered it at the cemetery as the Vicar came to the end of the service. 'I will lift up mine eyes unto the hills from whence cometh my help.'

The crowd was still except for the rustle of its weeping. Behind Sabrina, Alexandra stood with Antonio, tears streaming down her face; next to her, in front of Brooks, Gabrielle sobbed into a handkerchief. Jolie held hands with a stony-faced Michel, and Nicholas Blackford bounced in agitation while Amelia tried to keep him still. Everyone was there: the American ambassador and his staff; a cluster of art dealers, some of whom had flown in from Paris and Rome; the nobility who had been clients and friends; servants, waiters and shop clerks who remembered a smile and a word of thanks. They were all there, even Mrs Pemberley, standing behind a stunned and motionless Brian, and Mrs Thirkell, clutching wet handkerchiefs to her crumpled face, and Olivia standing in a group that included the dim figures of Lady Iris Longworth and Denton Longworth. How strange that they had come, Sabrina thought. The Raddisons had not.

She felt the strength of Garth's arm around her shoulders. Standing at the edge of the grave, she heard the Vicar's cadenced voice.

'May we yet see the radiance of a new day.'

On this day she was burying her sister, her father was in the hospital and her mother stood beside her, clutching her hand.

'Earth to earth, ashes to ashes, dust to dust.' The Vicar looked at her, telling her with his sad eyes that it was time for her to throw the first handful of earth on the coffin. Everyone was waiting. All of them, waiting, and the Vicar looking at her. The first handful of earth on the coffin. The first handful of earth. And Sabrina remembered. *You haven't told them. This is your last chance. Tell them now. You can't put it off any longer. Tell them. TELL THEM!*

A long shudder ran through her body and Sabrina fell to her knees beside the grave. 'It's not Sabrina!' she cried. She heard gasps behind her, and a moan from Laura. She looked at the coffin and then pleadingly at the Vicar. 'It wasn't Sabrina who died, it was Stephanie! *Stephanie died!* Or perhaps it was both of us. sometimes it seems that ... Sometimes I *feel* like Stephanie but I'm not, I'm Sabrina, I've always been Sabrina. I've only been Stephanie since we—'

'Stop, my love.' Garth was raising her, his voice urgent, his arms holding her tightly against him. 'I'm going to take you home.'

'No, wait, listen.' She pushed against his arms. 'Listen to me—!'

Brooks was beside them and Garth met his eyes. 'You and the Vicar can finish the service?'

'Of course. We'll see you at the house. There's a Dr Farr, by the way—'

'Stop, please, stop!' Sabrina cried. 'Listen to me. Don't you understand, I'm trying to tell you—'

'—who could give her something; his number is in the book.'

Garth nodded and led his wife away. The Vicar's voice followed them. 'And may God have mercy on her soul.'

'I think we should call Dr Farr,' Garth said as they walked to the limousine. 'To help you through these first few days.'

Sabrina stumbled beside him, sick and empty, angry at herself. If it hadn't been for her confusion, when she wasn't sure who she was, they would have believed her. 'You didn't let me finish,' she said despairingly. 'I was trying to tell you the truth and you wouldn't listen.'

'Later.'

'You didn't believe me.'

'Later, my love.'

Garth remembered when his parents died, feeling anger and grief because they had left him. But his wife's mourning was more frantic: she was distraught, as if her whole being had been ripped from her. Even knowing that it was her twin sister who had died, he was puzzled that the strong woman he knew, who had taken command when her father was ill, could collapse into incoherence and overwhelming despair.

He knew that, in grief, people often took refuge in denial, refusing to acknowledge that a loved one had died. But if that were the case she would say her sister was alive, traveling, and they would be together soon. Instead she pretended to be her sister. Why? To make up to her for something? Or was it that, in spite of physical separation, the twins had been far closer, more innately parts of a whole, than he realized?

At Cadogan Square, Sabrina refused to see Dr Farr. 'He'll give me something to put me to sleep. Why can't you let me have my grief?'

'You should have grief. But not hysteria.'

'I'll try to avoid that,' she said with a trace of her own dry humor, and Garth let her have her way. She was right; it would be best if she could pull out of it herself.

Brooks and Olivia had arranged the funeral, and now the lunch guests they had invited were filling the house. Mrs Thirkell threw all the energies of her grief into directing the activities of the hired staff, and within a short time platters of meat and fish, cheeses, patés, breads, pastries and tortes covered long tables in the dining room and drawing room. Sabrina moved among the guests with Garth at her side, watching her. Pale and aloof, her head high, she moved easily through the rooms as if she belonged in them, or was taking Sabrina's place. Everyone commented on the resemblance between them and how natural it seemed to see her there, and she listened to them politely, as if trying to understand what they had to do with her.

Garth felt, painfully, that he had never loved her as much as now, when she seemed both lost and at home, needing him yet apart from him. Grief cloaked her in mystery and

361

vulnerability; he wanted to draw her close and kiss her despairing eyes, and listen closely to everything she said, whether it made sense or not, so that he could understand what it meant to lose someone who was so deeply a part of her.

But she said very little and so, while keeping watch over her, he listened to those around them talk about the accident. Brooks had told the story to a few, and it had spread rapidly. No one knew what caused the *Lafitte* to go down, but the rumor was that the fuel tanks had exploded just as it left the harbor at Monte Carlo. Denton Longworth had been gambling in the casino that week, and, when he heard it was Max Stuyvesant's yacht, he called the coast guard to offer his services. He was there when the first bodies were pulled from the water; one of them was Sabrina, and it was Denton who identified her.

The police had called London for the names of Lady Longworth's next-of-kin, but Gabrielle, who took the call, told them to call Brooks. And a good thing, Garth thought, for he had handled the complicated arrangements, involving Monaco police, the French coast guard and police, British Airways and British police, quietly and smoothly. Garth liked Brooks. Wary at first of his imperiousness, he soon found himself responding to his honesty. 'I'm going to miss Sabrina,' Brooks had said when the two men sat late over drinks the night before the funeral. 'I've got a problem on my hands – we needn't go into it – and Sabrina made me see that it might be partly my fault, or, rather that I might be looking at it the wrong way. She was a very whole person who knew what she believed in and was impatient with those who pretended they were something they weren't. I suppose she was as capable of pretending as the rest of us, but I always felt, when she told me something, that it was honest – it was the way she really felt.'

Garth had looked around the study and pictured the other rooms of the house with their quiet beauty and harmony, their interplay of serenity and wit. He had never been there before. If he had, he would have known much more about his sister-in-law, for the house was a reflection of a woman in many ways like his wife, not the woman he had imagined

Sabrina to be. 'I never really knew her,' he said to Brooks. 'I wish I had.'

And the next day, after the funeral, as he stood with his wife, listening to Sabrina's friends talk about her, he thought again how much he did not know.

'She worked very hard,' Olivia recalled, taking a bite of torte.

'For a long time she was afraid of failing,' said Alexandra.

'Nonsense. I never knew a woman more sure of herself. She had a way of listening to my ideas and nodding pleasantly, and then telling me just as pleasantly why I was wrong. I'm amazed when I think of how often she did that and how I took it from her.'

Jolie turned to Olivia. 'You don't think she was afraid of failure in the beginning? When everyone ignored her?'

'Why talk about bad times?' Nicholas interrupted. 'When she became successful and had her choice of clients, she worked for love – the love of beauty, the love of creating with her impeccable style, the love of—'

'Money,' Alexandra said with a small chuckle. 'Don't forget that. Unlike the rest of us, she had to earn her own living.'

Garth saw his wife listening with interest. 'I'm sorry,' he said to her softly. 'All the times I criticized her . . . I didn't really know her, which is exactly what you kept telling me.'

She nodded. 'Yes, but it doesn't matter, does it? Once I thought there was plenty of time for the truth, but I was wrong. Lies and mistakes keep growing, and it's so hard to stop them; and then it doesn't seem to matter so much.'

He had no idea what she was talking about, but before he could respond, a stranger came to them: tall, dark, with heavy brows in a thin face, and black, intense eyes. 'I'm sorry,' Sabrina said as he took her hand. 'I don't—'

'Dmitri Karras,' he said, smiling slightly. 'We met once a long time ago in—'

'Athens!' she cried, her face coming to life. 'When you hid us! But isn't this amazing! After all these years! Do you live in London? Are you working here? Wait until I tell Stephanie—' She stopped abruptly.

Garth saw sidelong glances on all sides – pity, embarrassment, curiosity. He held out his hand to Dmitri. 'Garth Andersen. Stephanie has told me about you.'

Dmitri took his hand in gratitude. 'Yes. We had an adventure, the three of us.' He turned to Sabrina. 'I remember your sister so clearly: her courage, and her eyes – so eager, demanding to see everything. I called her three days ago when I arrived, but she was away. Perhaps, before you leave, if you have time, we could have tea?'

'Perhaps,' Sabrina said, anxious to get away. He reminded her of a time when everything was simple. A dream time that was dead.

She was trembling. I can't tell Stephanie I met Dmitri, she thought. I can't tell Stephanie anything ever again. I can't even talk about her to anyone else. Because I'm still Stephanie. *And I can't find a way to tell the truth.*

'And how long are you here?' Dmitri asked. Sabrina turned, but he was speaking to Garth.

'I'm not sure.'

'Why not?' she asked abruptly. 'Your ticket is for tomorrow.'

'I won't leave if you need me.'

'I don't need you.'

'You may not be the best judge of that.'

Dmitri began to retreat. 'I will call, then, about tea – if you are still here—'

'I'll be here,' Sabrina said. 'My father is in the hospital, my mother is here and I have my own affairs to handle.'

'My dear,' urged Nicholas, coming close. 'I would like to talk to you about Ambassadors. Lady Longworth and I had talked about a partnership. How long will you stay in London?'

In an instant, Sidney Jones was at her elbow: Sabrina's solicitor, who had gotten her divorce from Denton, who had drawn up her will. 'I can arrange an appointment. I would, of course, be present. Lady Longworth would have wished that, since I drew up her will. And I have already spoken to Mrs Andersen about her inheritance of the estate.'

The whole thing, Sabrina thought. Left to Stephanie Andersen. I've left everything to myself. And the foolish, sad joke brought tears to her eyes.

But a spark of curiosity had been aroused. Stephanie had talked to Nicholas about a partnership? What else had she done, besides get involved with Max Stuyvesant? For the first time Sabrina realized that she knew almost nothing of what Stephanie had done in London. And now Stephanie could not tell her.

She looked at Antonio and Alexandra, standing nearby, the sexual pull between them so strong Sabrina could feel it. When did that begin? Stephanie had broken with him only a little while ago. But it was a good match. How clever of Stephanie, if she had encouraged it.

At the buffet Michel and Jolie were heaping a plate with chicken paté and cornichons. Stephanie hadn't mentioned them since the birthday party at Alexandra's. Sabrina would have to find out about their newspaper story without giving away her ignorance. More playacting. *There is no end to a deception once it begins.*

'My dear,' said Sidney Jones, 'may I get you a cup of tea?' He cocked a superior eyebrow at Garth to show him who knew best how to take care of fragile women.

'Not tea,' Sabrina said smoothly. 'Garth, would you get me a glass of wine?'

Garth smiled at her, his heart lifting as she came out of her grief to put this supercilious snob in his place. 'I love you,' he said, kissing her cheek, thanking her. 'I'll be right back.'

Sabrina saw Brooks come into the room and go to Gabrielle. Those nearby, their faces alert for a quarrel, inched closer to listen. Sabrina shook her head. Nothing changes, she thought. Some of them will miss me for awhile, but everything will go on just as it always has. Nothing changes.

But when I tell the truth, everything will change for Garth and the children.

Unless I don't. The thought whipped in so quickly it was a moment before she grasped it and realized she had thought it before. Unless I don't. If I told the truth today or tomorrow, or a month from now, or next year, what difference would it make? Or if I never did. We could just go on as we have been. What difference would it make to anyone?

But if I don't tell anyone the truth, how can I ever be Sabrina again?

Garth returned, followed by a waiter bearing a tray with canapés and wine. 'He wouldn't let me do my own serving. I gather he thinks of me as an outsider trying to bust his union.' Sabrina gave a small involuntary laugh, and he felt he had won a victory.

They sat together in quiet companionship, surrounded by noise. 'Nothing changes,' Garth murmured, eyeing the crowd.

Sabrina looked at him quickly. 'But you don't know them.'

'Do I need to? Look at them. They came here solemn and respectful, whispering, and within two hours they're thrashing around in their endless entanglements. Listen to them.'

Everything goes on, she thought again, listening to the high-pitched chatter of a cocktail party.

'Amazing resemblance; I could swear it was Sabrina.'

'No, it's quite superficial. The mouth is different, and the eyes; you just aren't very observant.'

'I'll ask her; she'll tell you I'm right – they're really identical.'

'Oh, for God's sake, you're not going to ask her! One more scene like the one at the grave and I'll take to my bed for a week. So chilling; my God, I couldn't bear another.'

Garth kept an eye on his wife, but she seemed indifferent to the chatter. She was very pale, but calm and alert; the look of the sleepwalker was gone. In fact, though she had let Brooks and Olivia arrange the funeral and buffet lunch, she behaved like the owner of the house with Mrs Thirkell and the staff. And, though she clung to him for support, she would still, at odd moments, suddenly and unexpectedly withdraw into her shell and look at him as if she was not sure who he was, or what she had to do with him.

'What I would like,' Garth said, 'is a Scotch.'

'I'll get you one,' Sabrina said, as if glad to have something to do, and before he could stop her she was gone.

'Restless,' said Nicholas Blackford knowingly. 'Usually

happens in mourning. Take her awhile to get over it. The two of them were so close in China that I can't imagine them apart.'

China? What the hell was the man talking about? They hadn't been together in China. But Blackford had been there; Garth remembered Stephanie saying she'd picked up British phrases from him. 'They did have that time together, though,' he said probingly.

'Right, exactly right; I hope you help Stephanie see it that way. Two whole weeks together, when otherwise Sabrina might have – oh, dear, how does one say it – died without their having been together for a year. Mysterious ways, the fates work. I was thinking of the pictures I took of them, in those identical silk dresses they bought in Shanghai. Do you know, I never saw those pictures. Did they come out?'

'Yes,' Garth said thoughtfully as his wife came up to them with a bottle and a glass with ice cubes.

'I foiled the union,' she said with a small smile. 'But I only brought one glass. Nicholas, if you'd like some—' She looked into Garth's face. 'What's wrong?'

'Nothing. Where did you locate the Scotch?'

'In the study upstairs. I . . . Sabrina kept a few bottles there. Something *is* wrong.'

Nicholas fidgeted, alarmed by hints of a domestic squabble. 'Perhaps I will get a drink. If you'll excuse me—'

Garth poured the amber liquid into his glass. 'Nicholas was telling me how close you and Sabrina were in China. He took pictures, he said.'

His face froze with a bleak emptiness. 'Yes,' she said finally. 'In Shanghai. Near the hotel. The day before he spilled his pastries all over the street, That isn't important, of course, I just remembered it. I meant to tell you all about it, everything, from the beginning, but so much has been happening, and I've been confused, and I kept putting it off . . . I was going to tell you tonight, when we were alone, so you'd know before you caught your plane tomorrow – at least, I think that's what I was going to do, but we can do it now if you want—'

Her voice was a monotone of such loneliness and despair that he was alarmed. 'No, not now. It can wait. In fact, you don't have to tell me at all. Whatever it was – were you afraid I'd be angry if I knew? You were right; I probably would have been. Because I didn't really know her. I only wish you hadn't been afraid of telling me, as if I was the ogre in the castle who had to be lied to or he'd eat everyone up. Was I really like that?'

She bent her head and shook it slowly back and forth, her hair hiding her face. 'No, don't say that. You're not an ogre. I love you.'

'Then nothing else matters. What the hell do I care if you were with Sabrina in China? Let's talk about something else. Can you tell me, for example, why these guests, who must collectively own half the wealth in England, are gorging themselves on lunch as if they are destitutes with no hope of dinner?'

She laughed, looking up at him. 'Maybe to remind themselves they're still alive.'

He brushed a lock of hair from her forehead. Even preoccupied with sorrow, he thought, her mind was quick. 'Or to make sure they haven't missed anything. Funerals remind them of the uncertainty of tomorrow.'

They smiled softly at each other, as if saying they were the lucky ones whose tomorrow was certain. And Garth began to believe they would soon find again what they had discovered in New York the night before Brooks called from London.

That night, as they lay in bed, he held her hand and offered again to stay with her for a few more days. But she refused to consider it. 'My mother is here, and all my . . . Sabrina's friends, and Mrs Thirkell – if I need company or help, they're all here. The children need you, and you shouldn't miss any more classes and lab work. And didn't you plan to meet with the architects for the Genetics Institute?'

'Yes, yes, and yes. But if you need me, I would stay here.'

She turned to him. Her eyes, in the soft light from the bedside lamp, studied him as if memorizing the lines of his face. 'I was going to tell you tonight about the China trip, the whole story—'

'I don't want to hear it. Unless you think it would help you

368

work out your feelings about your sister. But I can't tell you how to do that, you know. However you felt about her when she was alive, you have to be yourself now, separate from her and separate from her memory. You can't slide back and forth from one to the other—' She drew a sharp breath. 'What is it?'

'What you said – that's what I have to tell you. But every time I begin, I can't go on.'

'Then don't. Damn it, I don't want to hear it if it's so difficult for you.' He was afraid to hear it; afraid he would have no weapons against decisions she made in her grief. 'Wait until later, when we're home. Then you can tell me if you still think you must.'

'But it isn't—'

'Stephanie, I don't want to hear it. It can wait.' He raised himself on his elbow and kissed her. 'It's late and you're exhausted. Why don't you try to sleep?'

She hesitated. He was giving her time. Why not take it? She'd already decided it made no difference. Put it off a little longer. She touched his face. 'I thought you'd want to make love.'

'I want to do what you want,' he said. She moved toward him and he pulled her close; they lay still in each other's arms. Garth felt her stir and his hands caressed her. 'My love, shall I stay in London a while longer?'

'No. But make love to me now.'

She stirred against him and her breathing quickened; he lay on her, letting himself melt into the scent and touch of her body. As he was about to enter her he looked into her eyes and stopped abruptly. Without a word, he moved away and lay on his back beside her.

'Garth – what—?'

'You didn't want to make love. You were faking it, weren't you?'

After a moment, eyes closed, she nodded.

'Why? Do you think my pleasure is so important to me that I'd want to get it that way?'

'I wanted to make love to you.'

'That's not true.'

'*I* wanted to make love to you. My mind wanted to make

369

love to you. I don't know why I couldn't get my body to respond ... I tried, but it wouldn't, so I pretended. Because I wanted to make love to you. Don't you understand? I wanted to feel you inside me. I didn't care whether I had an orgasm or not. I wanted you inside me.'

'Then why not say that? Why fake it?'

She shuddered. 'I'm sorry. I don't know why I can't tell you everything.'

He took her hand. 'Go to sleep. When you get home, we'll talk; you can tell me anything you like.'

She burrowed her head into the pillow. 'You're going back tomorrow?'

'Yes.' He leaned over her and kissed the small corner of forehead he could see. 'Good night, my love.'

'Good night.'

He turned off the lamp. In the darkness, her voice reached him like a soft caress. 'I love you, Garth.'

On Sunday morning, Gordon lay propped up in his hospital bed reminiscing about the past. Sabrina kept her eyes on his thin face, but she was thinking of Garth, on his way back to America. Gordon's voice grew louder.

'Then in Algeria, there was so much to do ... of course, my heart was fine in those days – I could go eighteen hours at a stretch ... '

'And did,' Sabrina murmured. 'Leaving us with the servants.'

'Stephanie,' said Laura sharply.

Sabrina shrugged. 'It was a long time ago.'

'Then why bring it up? Your father always did the best he could, for his country and his family. I must say, I'm surprised. It wasn't you who complained in the past; it was always Sabrina.'

Her voice broke on Sabrina's name. 'I'm sorry,' Sabrina said.

Gordon's forehead creased as he looked at her. 'Your mother told me what happened at the cemetery. It's no good, you know, trying to be Sabrina. That won't bring her back.'

Sabrina met his eyes boldly, daring him to recognize her,

but she knew he would not; if he hadn't done so earlier, how could he now, when he was concentrating on the steady beating of his heart?

'And you don't owe her anything, either. She was different from you and lived a different life. I'm not saying it was good or bad . . .' He coughed, and immediately Laura was standing over him.

'Don't excite yourself. The doctors said you'd be all right if you kept quiet. We'll be here indefinitely if you don't do as they tell you.'

'I wasn't excited,' Gordon said mildly. 'I was simply pointing out that Stephanie needn't be ashamed to be herself.'

'You were implying that Sabrina's way of life had something to do with her death. You had no right – I'm sorry, Gordon, I shouldn't say that. Stephanie, what will you do about Ambassadors?'

'Your mother is changing the subject,' Gordon said to Sabrina. 'But I loved your sister, you know. Even when I thought her wild and reckless; even when she married that pompous ass what's-his-name duke—'

'Viscount,' Laura said. 'But I thought we weren't going to talk about Sabrina.'

'I always loved her. I just didn't feel as close to her as I do to you. Do you understand that?'

'Don't,' Sabrina said softly. 'Please don't.' Her face was hot and she wanted to run away.

'I was uncomfortable with her because I always felt she was about to spring out of her chair and go off and . . . *do* something. Run a race or explore some caves or shoot at a fox or be the belle of the ball. I loved her, there was no one like her, but I couldn't relax with her because I could never predict what she would do next.'

His voice was rising. Sabrina forced herself to sit still.

'I always worried about what she might do to the reputation of the embassy. We tried to tell both of you that we were symbols of America and my career depended on the image we presented to the world. I never had to worry about you, but Sabrina, with her high spirits, seemed uncontrollable. Do you understand why I was sometimes harsh with her, fearing she would do something foolish or dangerous? Why we decided to send you both to Juliette? Why I may have seemed not quite ... fatherly all the time?'

Sabrina was silent.

'But I loved her. She was fire and light and love. So much energy and curiosity. So much life. I regret that I never told her that.' Gordon's voice began to fade. 'Even when we settled in Washington, I didn't tell her. She was running about as much as ever, getting married and divorced, building up that shop of hers, going on hunts and cruises. She'd even taken up with some Brazilian at the end. But I loved her as much as I love you. And I wish I had told her so.'

Laura was crying, her head averted. Gordon's eyes were closed, his slight figure rising and falling with shallow breaths beneath the white coverlet. In the stillness, Sabrina heard footsteps and low voices of other Sunday afternoon visitors to the hospital.

Parents, she thought. She was thirty-two years old, and still they had the power to make her feel guilty about disappointing them. Gordon was trying to explain away a lifetime of neglect and, at the same time, tell her he didn't want her to act like Sabrina. And Laura, who had felt closest to Sabrina, was trying not to show that she resented his preference for Stephanie.

'She knew you loved her,' Sabrina said to Gordon's closed eyes, wishing she could find a way to convince him. 'Even when she knew she disappointed you.'

Gordon nodded. Absorbed in his own health, he was easily convinced that all was well. 'I'll take my nap now,' he said.

Laura took Sabrina's arm as they left the hospital. 'I feel I ought to apologize for what your father did just now.'

'What did he do?'

'Dismissed us as soon as he made his point and got some agreement. That's his way. It seems very effective in diplomacy, but it's not easy to live with.'

'Isn't it comforting, though, to know he's consistent? Even in grief?'

Laura looked sharply at her daughter. 'That's the kind of

double edged remark Sabrina would have made. It's not kind to your father.'

Sabrina sighed. 'Mother, you're as hard to deal with as he is.'

Parents, she thought again. But we keep loving them and wanting their approval, no matter how old we are. How was she going to have the courage to tell them the truth when Gordon recovered? Rejoice, Mother, Sabrina is not dead. Intensify your mourning, Father; it was your beloved Stephanie who died.

Neither of them would ever forgive her.

'I was hoping,' Laura said the next morning as Sabrina put her key into the door of Ambassadors, 'that you wouldn't sell it. Of course, it may not be fair to ask you that – I know you and Garth could use the money – but I was hoping you would keep it.'

Sabrina did not answer. She had been away so long, and now, walking through the dusky showroom, she breathed deeply, touching familiar pieces, and felt as she had when she walked into the house on Cadogan Square: she was back where she belonged. A shop, a home. Every inch of them hers; created by her, held together by her work. 'Of course I'll keep it,' she said.

'But what will you do with it? If you can't run it—'

'Of course I'll run it; what are you talking about, Mother?'

'Stephanie, I'm asking how you plan to run Ambassadors from Evanston. Unless – are you suggesting you might not be in Evanston? That you and Garth—?'

'No.' Standing with her mother at the door to her office, Sabrina came back to earth. 'I'd work something out with Nicholas Blackford. He's interested in a partnership.'

'Then you'd come over now and then. Well, that might work out. But, of course, Ambassadors really was Sabrina; it would take someone with her brilliance to keep its reputation. You could do it, though, if you study, or work in a small shop in Chicago to get some experience. And I would help you.' She put her arm around Sabrina. 'Oh, there is so much I could teach you! Wouldn't it be wonderful? Now my suggestion is—'

'Mother.'

Laura drew back at the coldness in her daughter's voice. 'If you don't want to talk about it now—'

'I don't want to talk about it now.' Sabrina felt the pressures building inside her. Last night she had not slept, thinking of Stephanie, and, alone in bed for the first time in weeks, she had felt lonely and vulnerable without the comfort of Garth's arms. But mostly she was angry at her mother: how dare she insult Stephanie by assuming she couldn't handle Ambassadors? All her life she'd favored Sabrina, and now she was doing it again, acting as if Stephanie would automatically fail if she were to take over the shop.

Wait, this doesn't make sense, she thought. Am I Sabrina, defending Stephanie, who is dead? Or am I Stephanie, angry because my mother doesn't believe in me?

'I don't want to talk about it now,' she said to Laura. 'I have to meet with Sidney Jones and Nicholas and Brian, and in a few days I'll know better what I'm going to do.' She was walking toward the front door, bringing Laura with her. The shop was closed for the week; she'd come back alone the next day and think about the future.

By the next day she had another reason for coming to Ambassadors: it was her only private place. Laura and Gabrielle both were living in her house, wanting to talk to her. Mrs Thirkell found little tasks on the upper floors so that she could find someone to talk to about Lady Longworth. The telephone rang constantly; everyone wanted to entertain Sabrina's American sister before she left London, and though she told Mrs Thirkell to refuse them all, more kept coming. Flowers, letters and telegrams arrived daily. Sabrina retreated to the dim quiet of Ambassadors.

Alone, she went through the account books and files, reading letters and scanning catalogues that had come while she was away. Stephanie had recorded the sale of the Grendly daybed, the French beaded bag and several other pieces. In a notebook on the shelf behind the cherry table, she had listed three interior decorating commissions she had accepted for November and December. Sabrina was about to put the notebook away when she saw a letter tucked in the back. 'Dearest Sabrina,' it began. Dated October 23. The day before the cruise.

'I've been wondering,' Stephanie had written, 'what present I can leave you when I go back to Chicago, to thank you for the most wonderful time of my life. I could buy you something, but I've just thought of a better gift than anything Harrods has to offer. It's a story I've kept secret, and I'm writing it now for you to discover when you return. I'll have such fun imagining your face when you read about it, and then your telephone call. . . .

'It began at a party at Olivia Chasson's some time ago. I was talking to Rose Raddison when a sad accident occurred. . . .'

How wonderful, Sabrina thought, reading about the broken stork. Such a simple solution. Why didn't it occur to me when I was trying to figure out what to do? Maybe now, after living with two rambustious kids, I would have thought of it. She picked up the letter to finish it.

'That's about all, except that Rory Carr did come in later, after I'd seen him at the Chilton auction, with a magnificent Sevres piece that it broke my heart to turn down. But by then you'd told me not to deal with him. He wasn't here to sell, anyway, not really. He'd heard about the stork and was fishing for information. When he kept prying, I did a small imitation of a police officer and said, "There isn't anything you can tell me that I don't already know." That shook him up – he kept adjusting his cravat with elegant nervousness, and speedily departed. Oh, there's the front bell. I'll try to finish this tomorrow.'

But tomorrow she was dead.

Alexandra walked in and found Sabrina carefully folding a handwritten letter. 'Mrs Thirkell gave away your hiding place; you don't mind if I invade your privacy?'

'Of course not. Please sit down. I'm not getting much done anyway.'

'Thinking about Sabrina.'

'Thinking about Sabrina and Stephanie.'

'Funny, I never realized how close you two were.'

There was a silence. 'Shall I make us some tea?' Alexandra asked.

'Oh, how rude of me. I'll make it.'

Sabrina put the kettle on the hot plate in Brian's office. 'I'm afraid we have only biscuits to eat.'

'Biscuits will be fine.' There was another silence. 'Are you still worried about your father?'

'No, he's much better. He'll go home Sunday.'

'And you with him?'

'I . . . think so. Probably.'

They sat in silence. 'I'm sorry, honey,' Alexandra burst out at last. 'I can't get used to it. Are you a ghost? Sabrina told me the two of you didn't look alike.'

'But – why would she say that?'

'How do I know? I thought she said it because it was true. Nicholas had played a little game, accusing her of being Stephanie – that you'd switched places in China, or something like that – and Sabrina was great; she frowned so seriously and told Nicholas to tell her who she was because he'd gotten her so confused she couldn't remember. You know, I loved that lady, though I don't think I ever actually told her so. Anyway, after Nicholas proclaimed her Sabrina, I asked if you two really were identical and she said, no, he just thought so because of his pastries or his diet or some such thing.'

Sabrina laughed. *Oh, Stephanie, good for you. You were saving that, weren't you, to tell me when we met in Chicago. So we could laugh about it together.* But they couldn't laugh about it together. She stood up quickly. 'I'll just see what's happening with the kettle.'

'Damn,' said Alexandra, following her into Brian's office. 'I'm a damn fool. Please forgive me, I don't mean to upset you. It's just that I can't get used to the resemblance; it's uncanny, you know – people must tell you that all the time. Oh, why can't I shut up and leave you in peace?'

'No, don't shut up. I'm fine.' The chatter helped; she made the tea with a steady hand and filled a plate with biscuits. She picked up the tray to carry it into his office. 'Napkins,' she said to Alexandra, tilting her head toward a cupboard in the corner.

'There! See? That's exactly what she did, only a week ago. See why I'm having trouble?'

Stephanie did that a week ago. But I've never done it before.

Sabrina poured the tea and spread jam on a biscuit, taking her time, thinking. Of all the people she knew in London, Alexandra was the most trustworthy, the one closest to her – and the toughest. There wasn't much that would shock Alexandra. But she was proud. Would she be such a close friend when she knew she'd been tricked?

It didn't matter. I have to tell someone, Sabrina thought. It's been so long since I had anyone to talk to – I have to tell someone. It will be my rehearsal for telling Garth. And everyone else.

'I'm going to tell you a story,' she said slowly, 'if you promise to listen to the whole thing without interrupting and not make a judgment until you've heard it all.'

'Intriguing. Possibly wicked. I can't wait.'

'Promise?'

'You want me to draw blood and sign my name?'

Sabrina smiled. 'No. I wouldn't be telling you if I didn't trust—' The bell over the front door rang as someone opened it. 'I'll be right back; I thought I had a *Closed* sign in the door.'

A tall man was silhouetted against the front window; Sabrina saw his graying hair, a slight stoop, the thin cane he carried. She could not make out his features. 'Mrs Andersen?' he asked.

'Yes. But the shop is closed. If you'll come back next week—'

'I'm from Scotland Yard, Mrs Andersen.' He showed his identification. 'Detective-Sergeant Thomas Phelps. I'd appreciate a few minutes of your time to talk to you about the death of your sister.'

'Scotland Yard?'

He walked past her. 'If we could sit down?'

Sabrina turned blindly and led the way into her office. Somehow they'd found out. They knew she was Sabrina. She wouldn't be able to tell the story in her own way after all. Everyone would learn about it in a jumble from the police, reporters, gossip columnists . . . and Garth would hear about it, too, from the police when they called – when they called to tell him his wife was dead. In London society it would be a scandal; at home in Evanston there would be pain and anger and tears. . . .

'My God,' cried Alexandra, looking at her face as she came into the office. 'What is it?' She looked at Phelps and stood up. 'If you think I should leave, honey – Stephanie—'

'No, would you mind staying? I'd like it if you stayed.'

'This is confidential, Mrs Andersen,' said Phelps.

'Then it will be confidential for Princess Martova,' Sabrina said coldly. 'I am asking her to stay.'

He hesitated, then shrugged. It would be all over London in no time, anyway; one more society gossip wouldn't make a difference. He sat down and opened a notebook. 'In the course of our investigations,' he began, 'we've learned that some of the people on Mr Stuyvesant's yacht were not what they seemed to be.'

Sabrina looked at him fixedly, waiting for his flat deliberate voice to call her Lady Longworth. 'How did you discover—?'

'Please, Mrs Andersen, let me begin at the beginning.'

Mrs Andersen. He had called her Mrs Andersen. She watched him, waiting for the moment when he would try to trap her.

'Let me tell you what we've learned so far. Lady Longworth flew with Max Stuyvesant and two other couples to Nice on October 24. From there they drove to Monaco. They spent some time in Monte Carlo while Mr Stuyvesant's yacht, the *Lafitte*, was being provisioned. At approximately 4:30 P.M. they boarded the yacht and left the harbor. When they were about two miles out – this would be at 5:30 P.M. – the yacht exploded and caught fire.'

As Sabrina shrank back, Alexandra moved over to sit on the arm of her chair. 'Are these details necessary?' she asked.

'I would not give them if I thought otherwise.' Phelps consulted his notes. 'By the time rescue boats got to the scene, the yacht was sinking. They concentrated on search-ing for survivors or bodies; they found three immediately, one of which was Lady Longworth. I'm sorry, ma'am; I know this gives you pain but I'm trying to explain why the yacht itself was not examined until a few days ago.'

'What difference does it make?' Sabrina asked, wondering why it was taking him so long to expose her. Was it something they found on the yacht? Something Stephanie had with her?

Phelps was reading from his notes. 'Positive identification, made by Lady Longworth's former husband, Viscount Longworth, was made at 1:00 A.M., and I'm told you were told the news about an hour later, around dinner time in America. By this time the yacht had sunk, and several of those aboard with it. It wasn't until two days ago that divers were able to raise it. What we found, Mrs Andersen – what the French police found, that is – was a large hole in the side of the *Lafitte* below the waterline in the area of the staterooms. They reported that—'

'The staterooms?' Sabrina leaned forward. 'The staterooms are nowhere near the fuel tanks. So they couldn't have been the cause of the explosion.'

Phelps was disconcerted. The revelation toward which he was building was being taken from him. 'That is precisely the point. We'd assumed it was a fuel tank. Now we know it was not. We think, in fact—'

'You think it was a bomb, set to go off in a stateroom.' Phelps sat back, defeated. He was a low-level investigator who did the preliminary work for higher-ups to evaluate; there was little excitement in his job and no glamour. His only enjoyment came when a gasp ran through his audience as he sprang an unexpected bit of information on them. Now, just when he was prepared to spring, this pale beauty, too smart for her own good, took his moment away from him.

'But that means they were murdered,' she was saying, and he looked at her with reluctant admiration.

'It seems likely, ma'am. So we're trying to discover if Mr Stuyvesant or his guests had any enemies. Now, I'm not suggesting that Lady Longworth had enemies, but we received information from two writers – Michel Bernard and Jolie Fantome – that they had recently learned Mr Stuyvesant was the owner of a company called Westbridge

Imports, and they also said that Lady Longworth occasionally bought – Mrs Andersen!'

But Alexandra held her and kept her from collapsing while Stephanie's letter echoed in her mind: I did a small imitation of a police officer, and said, 'There is nothing you can tell me that I don't already know.'

There is nothing you can tell me that I don't already know.

There is nothing you can tell me—

They were after me. They thought I knew about their forgeries.

Phelps was satisfied. He had achieved his effect. 'I have a few questions, Mrs Andersen,' he said gently.

Sabrina raised her head. They didn't know who she was. They were after something far worse. 'All right.'

Phelps was curious. There's something else on her mind, he thought. She's scared. Of what? Something about Westbridge. But what could it be? She lives in America; she has nothing to do with them. 'First,' he began, 'did Lady Longworth talk to you about Max Stuyvesant?'

'Only that she was going on a cruise with him.'

'And what did she say about the cruise? Anything about the other guests? Where they were going?'

'No. Nothing.'

'She didn't mention enemies that Stuyvesant might have had?'

'Mr Phelps, my sister never spoke to me about Max Stuyvesant's business or the people he dealt with.'

Phelps was puzzled. He would swear she was telling the truth. So what was she afraid of? He went on, using his notes. 'Michel Bernard came to us when he heard we suspected a bomb on the yacht. He told us there'd been a falling out between Stuyvesant and the people at Westbridge. Did Lady Longworth ever talk to you about Westbridge Imports or Rory Carr or Ivan Lazlo? Buying from them?'

There was a pause. 'She mentioned Carr occasionally, along with dozens of other salesmen and dealers. I don't think she had bought from him lately. At least not a major piece.'

They were silent. Well, Phelps thought, this time she's

lying about something. But damned if I know what. There's not a shred of evidence that this shop was involved in any smuggling or in collusion on forgeries. But something's bothering her. Trying to identify it, he continued to ask questions about people Sabrina knew and others she did not. He went on and on, pointlessly it seemed, and then at last closed his notebook.

'We're looking for Carr and Lazlo, and no doubt we'll know more when we find them. Do you have anything else you think might help us, ma'am?'

'No,' Sabrina said wearily. When they found Rory Carr, he probably would implicate her, but she couldn't do anything about it now. For the moment Ambassadors' reputation was safe, and so was her own secret. But she was so tired, as if she had run a race and finished barely a step ahead of everyone else. It was too late to tell Alexandra the truth; with Scotland Yard involved she could not make her a part of the half-lies she had told. She was more alone than ever. I want to go home, she thought. I want to be with Garth.

'Where can we reach you, Mrs Andersen?' Phelps asked, pocketing his notes. She gave them her number at Cadogan Square. 'And in America?'

'I'll let you know when I return. I plan to be here for a while.'

Alexandra saw him out. She held in her questions while Sabrina pulled the shades on the front windows and locked the door. 'Do you want to talk, honey?' she asked, as they flagged down a taxi. Sabrina shook her head. 'No. But thank you. Maybe later . . . ' At Cadogan Square she got out alone, still holding Stephanie's letter. As she unlocked her door and went inside, she was still repeating one line of it, over and over, in her mind.

The nights were the hardest times – the slow quiet hours when Sabrina was alone, thinking of Stephanie, aching for Garth, her thoughts skipping wildly between her two worlds. The days were better; she kept busy and thought only about what she was doing from one minute to the next.

Each morning, she visited Gordon and then had lunch with Laura at Grenadier, a pub tucked away among mews houses behind the hospital. Afterward, Sabrina walked to Ambassadors to plan the decorating jobs Stephanie had accepted and to study auction catalogues. But she never stayed long; restless and impatient, she would escape as soon as she could to be alone in the crowds of the city. All week she took long, solitary walks through the villages that make up London's neighborhoods. At tea time she returned home to Mrs Thirkell and Gabrielle and listened to Gabrielle talk from tea time through dinner about London gossip and Brooks. Without knowing it, she filled Sabrina in on everything that had happened while she was in America.

'I don't suppose you're interested, Stephanie, since you don't know most of these people. But you're so much like Sabrina—'

'It's all right. Of course I'm interested. They're your friends, and Sabrina's. Of course I'm interested.'

'I feel so odd talking to you. Eerie. It's so amazing, how you look ... as if Sabrina hadn't died. The last few weeks, you know, she was the only one who really cared about me. And now – I know it's not fair to you, but you're all I have. And not even you, really, because you've got a family to worry about and you've lost Sabrina, too—'

When Gabrielle's eyes filled with tears, she looked like Penny, small and disconsolate. Sabrina led her to the couch in the drawing room and put her arms around her, and by the way Gabrielle relaxed against her, she knew that was what Stephanie had done.

Would she have held Gaby this way a few months ago? Probably not, or at least not so easily. She would have been self-conscious about displays of affection and nurturing, as were her friends. But here sat Sabrina Longworth, comforting Gabrielle de Martel without embarrassment or discomfort; in fact, feeling perfectly natural.

It was Penny and Cliff, Sabrina thought; living with them changed me so that this seems right. And important. She could close her eyes and see them: Penny sitting quietly in a corner, drawing and humming to herself, or sitting close, touching, confiding something special; Cliff chanting words for a spelling test, or sitting with her, eyes bright as they joked together. Oh, she missed them; she missed their trust and love and even the chaos they brought into a house. Her arms felt empty. Holding Gabrielle, they still felt empty.

On most nights Gabrielle was restless and soon would find a party to fill her evening while Sabrina went upstairs to the quiet of her room. Mrs Thirkell would have lit a fire, laid out her robe and left a snack of cake and a silver thermos of tea. Sabrina would sit beside a small lamp, reading and thinking – about Stephanie, about Garth, about the children, about a future she could not predict. And each night, almost exactly at ten, Garth called. In Evanston it was four o'clock; he was home from the university and Penny and Cliff were with him in the breakfast room, clamoring for the telephone so they could talk for a few precious minutes.

'When are you coming home?' they asked each night, and finally, when Gordon had been told he could leave the hospital, Sabrina had an answer.

'We're leaving on Saturday,' she told Garth. 'I'll fly to Washington with my parents and then to Chicago on Monday.'

'Monday,' he said, passing the news to Penny and Cliff, and Sabrina heard their shouts of delight.

But it won't last, she thought, watching the flames in the fireplace and the long, distorted shadows they threw on the walls and ceiling. Because she was going back to tell them the truth. For a week she had been acting as Stephanie in Sabrina's world, and by now she felt she was no one. Garth had been right: she could not drift back and forth; she had to be one or the other; she had to be Sabrina. So she would tell them the truth, and then they would hate her. When Garth knew his wife was dead, when Penny and Cliff knew their mother was dead, that Sabrina had deceived them for weeks, they would turn away from her. She couldn't even tell them she loved them. They wouldn't want her love. She would be left with no one to give it to.

When they said goodbye and she had put down the telephone, Sabrina sat in the silent room until she was tired enough to fall asleep before the longing for Garth began to pulse through her. It was not making love that she craved – she didn't let herself think of that at all – but just his presence, close beside her, sharing the small space that was theirs alone.

But she was too tired even to reach out to touch the warm dream that was not there. She turned off her light and went to sleep.

'Are you coming back?' Alexandra asked when she stopped in at Ambassadors on Friday. She had brought a stack of photographs and fanned them out on the table. 'These were taken at a new restaurant where Sabrina and I had dinner one night. Brooks joined us there later. So did Antonio, in fact – the launching of our passionate romance. I thought you'd like a set. *Are* you coming back, do you think?'

'Yes, of course,' said Sabrina, studying the photographs in silent amazement. How had Stephanie done it? In the tilt of her head, her posture and cool, public smile, she had become Sabrina. And what about me? Sabrina asked herself. What did I become? 'Yes, of course I'm coming back,' she said absently. 'This is home.'

'Home? What about America?'

'I meant, this is Sabrina's home and I haven't decided what I'll do about it. So I'll be back soon. What about you? Will you be here or chatting in Portuguese with contractors and jungle-clearers?'

Alexandra gave her a swift glance. 'Sounded like your sister there, honey. Looks like I may be chatting. But not in Portuguese. It took me a long time to learn proper English, and I'm not going to start another language for anybody. I can make Antonio understand that.'

'Why don't you find a Guarani legend that says the home tongue is the best and quote it whenever he asks you to learn Portuguese?'

'Now that is a brilliant ... What do I do if there isn't one?'

'Make one up. He'll be ashamed to admit he's never heard of it.' Alexandra burst into laughter. 'God damn, honey, I'll do it. You're wonderful, you're as sharp as Sabrina. Do they ever let you out of Chicago? Come visit us. In our lavish hut in the middle of nowhere, or our condominium in Rio. Or here, when we're in London. Will you come? You and your husband, of course. If he's interested.'

'I might.'

'We'd make you welcome. For your sister's sake, as well as your own.' She pulled on her coat and stood in the doorway. 'She was a very special lady, and you are, too. I think we'd get along fine.'

'So do I. Will you write and tell me about yourself? I'll miss ... I'll miss having a chance to get to know you.'

'Honey, I never write. The words pile up in my head and won't come out. They get so crowded they give me a headache and I give up. But I'm terrific with a telephone; what's your number in Evanston?'

Sabrina hesitated. 'I may be here. You should call Ambassadors first, or at Cadogan Square.'

Alexandra looked at her keenly, began to say something, then changed direction. 'Whatever you say. Take care of yourself, Stephanie.'

'Goodbye, Alexandra.'

On Friday afternoon she told Nicholas and Sidney Jones she was going to America for a few days. 'I'll be back as soon as I get my father settled in Washington and spend a few days with my family. I'm keeping the shop closed, and I've told Brian the same thing I'm telling you; I won't make any decisions until I talk to both of you. Until then, nothing is to be done with Ambassadors or my house. Is that clear?'

What would they say, she wondered, when she came back and told them the truth? They wouldn't care much; their lives would not change.

But she was gentler that night when she told Gabrielle and Mrs Thirkell. 'I'll be back soon, so neither of you should think of leaving. This is your home, Gaby, as long as you want it, and yours, too, Mrs Thirkell. I want you to keep it in good order until I come back. I'll let you know when to expect me.'

They will care, she thought, when I tell them the truth. Because they have relied on me in different ways.

And who else would care? Scotland Yard. Because someone blew up Max's yacht to kill her and would probably try again when it became public that it was her sister, not Sabrina Longworth, who had been killed.

Maybe I won't come back, she thought. It's safer in Chicago.

Flying at thirty-five thousand feet through bright Saturday sunlight, a week after Stephanie's funeral, Gordon sat between his daughter and his wife, planning the future. He and Laura talked about selling their house, buying a smaller one without stairs and hiring an assistant to help him research and write his book on American foreign policy in Europe. How much they've aged, Sabrina reflected; arranging their time to do less, have more help, smooth their days. And she realized she could not tell her story to both of them at the same time. She would tell her mother first; Laura would know how to tell Gordon.

But first she had to tell Garth. She would stay with her parents in Washington over Saturday and Sunday night, and fly to Chicago on Monday. Monday noon, while Penny and Cliff were in school. She couldn't bear to see them, and she couldn't talk to Garth while they were there. So, at noon, when they were safely in school, Garth would meet her plane and they would go – where? Not home. Not that wonderful, protective shabby house that was home. A restaurant. Some place where Garth need never go again and hear echoes of that terrible moment when she looked at him and finally told him the truth.

Then, that same afternoon, she would go back to Washington to tell her parents, and the next day she would return to London. And it would be truly over. She would never see Penny and Cliff again. Never see Garth again. Never see Dolores and Nat, Vivian, Madeline Kane, Linda and Martin, Garth, Garth, Garth . . .

'Stephanie, what is it?'

She wiped her eyes and leaned over to kiss her father. 'Just thinking.' Gordon peered at her. 'You're sure you're all right?'

'I'm fine,' Sabrina said, pleasing him. 'Don't worry about me; I'll do my thinking less damply.'

You'd think I'd be dried up by now, she thought. How can

386

one person have so many tears? But she knew there would be more when she confessed to everyone. And anger. But only then, when it was all out, would it be time to put this life behind her and pick up the pieces in London where she had left them in September.

If you can. Her eyes flew open at the thought. What makes you so sure you can simply pick up the pieces? Things have happened since you left. Will your London friends be overjoyed when they hear how you and Stephanie made fools of them, even letting them weep at a funeral for the wrong woman? Will they laugh in high good humor at such a jolly prank? Or will they walk away from you and Ambassadors because they don't like to be the butt of someone's joke? Especially in public.

Alexandra wouldn't do that.

Alexandra will be in South America most of the time.

Gaby wouldn't do that.

But Gaby and Brooks will get back together soon, or she'll find someone else. And how much time will she have for an ostracized Sabrina Longworth?

Olivia – but, of course, Olivia would do just that.

And how pleased will Scotland Yard be when they discover you lied about who was killed on that yacht near Monte Carlo? An international incident – Monaco, France, England.

No one will want to have anything to do with you.

You can't live in Evanston and you can't live in London.

I'll have to live somewhere else, she thought. Start again somewhere else. New York. I could open a shop in New York.

And who will you be?

Not Stephanie Andersen. You're going to tell everyone Stephanie is dead.

Sabrina Longworth.

Yes. Sabrina Longworth, starting a new life in New York, opening a new shop called – what will you call it?

No Deceptions.

Very amusing. Any other ideas?

No.

The plane followed the sun across the ocean. In the cabin,

stewards cleared lunch trays, brought pillows, poured drinks. Laura read. Gordon closed his eyes and slept. Sabrina moved to an empty seat and rested her head against the cool window, looking at the pale merging of water and sky. *Stephanie, I miss you.*

Garth, dear love . . .

Any other ideas?

No.

Chapter 18

Sunlight glinted off the Potomac River as Sabrina's plane banked and climbed for its flight to Chicago. Early November: the trees of Virginia flamed with yellow, russet and orange across the river from Washington's clustered stone and marble monuments.

She caught a glimpse of Georgetown before the plane finished its turn. Laura and Gordon would be in the study, thinking of lunch. By nightfall I'll be back, she thought, shattering their tranquility with my story. Garth is first.

I have something to tell you; could we go somewhere for a cup of coffee?

No, not home. A restaurant.

These last few weeks, since September, I haven't been what you think—

These last weeks, when you thought I was . . . I have something to tell you . . . in a restaurant . . . You see, last September, in China, Stephanie and I decided for a lark—

No, that wasn't a mistake. I meant to say Stephanie. That's what I want to tell you. When we were in China, Stephanie and I decided to change places for a week.

Far below, the black tangle of Indiana's steel mills moved into view. And then there was the curved shore of Lake Michigan. *I have something to tell you; can we go to a restaurant?*

When they had landed, she walked with the other

passengers from the plane to the waiting area and paused, scanning the crowd.

'Mom! Here we are!'

'Mommy!' Penny flung her arms around Sabrina. 'I'm glad you're back, I'm glad you're back, I don't *like* it when you're gone.' Cliff reached up to plant a vigorous kiss on her cheek. Stunned, Sabrina stared at them and over their heads at Garth.

'Why aren't you in school?'

Cliff grinned. 'Dad said we could stay out to meet your plane. Aren't you glad to see us?'

Slowly Sabrina nodded. With Penny's arms tight around her and the imprint of Cliff's warm kiss on her cheek – oh, yes, she was glad to see them. But this wasn't the way she had rehearsed it; it had never occurred to her that Garth would bring them. Which shows, she thought, how much I know about being a mother. 'Speechless with delight,' she said, kissing them. 'And surprise.'

'Make some room, you two,' said Garth. He took her in his arms, holding her close, and Sabrina felt the shape of her bones fit into his. 'Hello,' he said quietly. 'Welcome home.'

She looked at the strong lines of his face and the glow in his dark eyes. *Oh, I've missed you, I've missed you.* She rested her head against him.

Enclosed in his arms, her face against his chest, she heard his heartbeat and felt his lips touch her hair. And in that moment, she knew, with absolute certainty, that she could never tell him the truth.

She could never tell him he had been tricked into loving and cherishing a woman who was a fraud. She would not fling her lies in the face of his tenderness.

Then stay. Live with him and his family – my family. Stay. This is home.

But the thought did not make it so, and neither did the desire. This was not her place; her home and life were elsewhere. And even though she had seen her London world all too clearly after Stephanie's funeral, with its gossip and jealousies and idle entanglements, it was a world she knew, where she moved with confidence. And Ambassadors and

Cadogan Square – built by her, maintained by her efforts and her own social and business contacts – were where she belonged.

But as Garth's arms held her she knew there was another reason she could not stay: the most important reason. They could not build a life together based on a deception. He had been honest and open with her, trusting her with the self he kept hidden from others. In return she had lied and kept her private self hidden from him. She could not see any way out of that, except deeper into lies. *And I can't do that – to either of us.*

She would have to find a reason, any reason, tell it to him and leave, just as she'd planned, right away, before their love drew her into their life again. 'I have to tell you something, but not with the children—'

'And I have a great deal to tell you, but not with the children. Shall we pack them off somewhere?' With his arm around her they were walking through the terminal, and he scanned the airline gates. 'Denver. Seattle. Fairbanks ... how about Fairbanks? They can explore Alaska while we explore each other.'

'Garth, I'm serious.'

'So am I. We need to be alone. I thought we'd go to Wisconsin this weekend, just the two of us, find a lodge, do some hiking, sit in front of the fire. Sound all right?'

She shook her head.

'Think about it, we have all week to decide.'

Chattering steadily, Penny and Cliff skipped beside them to the car. Then, as Garth drove, Penny asked a question about London and Cliff hushed her sharply. Sabrina turned around.

'It's all right. You can ask about London. And anything else.'

'Daddy told us about the funeral,' said Penny. 'It sounded very impressive.'

'Indeed it was.'

'All those noble people.'

'The nobility, Penny. To be noble takes more than a title.'

Garth chuckled and relaxed, no longer worried that the

questions would upset her. They talked about the Vicar and the people who came to Cadogan Square, Gordon's heart attack and the ambulance, Mrs Thirkell, Alexandra and the Guarani Indians, Ambassadors. And, through it all, Sabrina listened in disbelief.

Two months ago, when she arrived from China, Garth wanted to have a serious talk and she would not give him a chance. Today, when she arrived from London and wanted to have a serious talk, no one would give her a chance.

But soon they would be home. Not home, she thought quickly. The Andersens' home. Then Penny and Cliff would go off somewhere and she would tell Garth she was leaving. She wouldn't even sit down or take off her coat; she would tell him immediately, take a cab back to the airport and still be in Washington before her parents went to bed.

'You're very quiet,' Garth said, as he parked the car. Sabrina was looking at the house.

'It looks so different – all the leaves are gone.'

'We had a spectacular thunderstorm one night that sent both kids scurrying to our room – pretending they wanted to watch the lightning with me – and it stripped the trees clean. Autumn came to a crashing end.'

I've never seen it look so bare. And unprotected.

Garth carried in her suitcase and put on a pot of coffee. Penny and Cliff took cookies from the jar. 'Five-thirty, Mom?' Cliff asked.

I won't be here. 'Yes. Can I have a quick hug?'

They held her tightly. 'It's *awful* when you're not here,' Penny said. 'I *hate* it. The house is so *empty*.' She looked quickly at Garth. 'I'm sorry, Daddy, I didn't mean . . . '

Garth chuckled and kissed her. 'I know what you meant, my sweet. It seemed empty to me, too. Are you off somewhere?'

'I told Barbara I'd come over when we got back from the airport.'

'Go on, then. Five-thirty for you, too.'

And in one swift moment, Sabrina and Garth were alone in the breakfast room.

Sabrina did not sit down. 'Garth, I have to leave. I wanted to tell you at the airport and not come home at all, but I

391

couldn't with Penny and Cliff there. I'm going back to London, to be alone, to find out what I really want, I can't stay here—'

'Wait.' Incredulous, Garth had swung his head to look at her, and now he put out his hand – a barrier to stop her voice. 'I'll see if our coffee is ready, I think you should sit down.'

Sabrina was shaking. She pulled out a chair and fell into it, gripping her hands and staring through the window at the bare, wintry backyard. Empty; the way she felt. Garth came back with the coffeepot. 'I don't think that's a good idea,' he said carefully. Sabrina saw the stiffness of his movements; he was holding himself in. He sat beside her and took her cold hands between his, warming them. 'You can't run away from yourself. You can't live Sabrina's life. Nothing would be solved by leaving; Penny and Cliff and I would always be here, waiting, like an unfinished story. You'd have two half-finished lives instead of one.'

The front doorbell broke into his words. 'Goddamn it, there aren't five quiet minutes . . . I'd better see who it is. Don't go away, I'll be right back. You won't go away? You'll wait?'

'Yes.' Alone, Sabrina looked around the honey-colored room. Home. An unfinished story. A half-finished life. She couldn't argue with him because he was right, but he only knew part of the story and she couldn't tell him the rest. She would just have to get up and walk out. And whatever pain he felt when she left would be far less than the pain of the truth.

Faintly she heard Dolores's voice from the front porch. Don't let her in, she prayed silently to Garth; I can't face her. On the sideboard was a stack of mail addressed to Stephanie. Mechanically she began to tear open the envelopes. A condolence card from Vivian. Another from Linda and Martin. A note from Juanita. Three cards from people she'd never heard of. A pink envelope with no return address, and inside a short, typed note.

How come those stories about students fucking profs for passing grades leave out Garth Andersen – the fuckingest of them all? A regular gene-ius at fucking students, that's our Professor Garth!

She read it twice and then again, frozen in the cold wave of fury that swept through her. How dare someone—! This filth, these obscene lies – how dare anyone accuse Garth of them! Who would do this – try to destroy a man who was more honorable than anyone she had ever known?

Everything else dropped away; the past week receded, and all she saw was the letter and what it could do to Garth. Energy surged through her, buoying her up from the despair that had dragged at her since Stephanie's death. Someone was trying to ruin Garth, viciously, anonymously ... and whoever it was would succeed; he could be irreparably damaged if they didn't fight. They had to find out who—

Wait, wait, she thought. What about leaving? I've told Garth I'm leaving.

She brushed it aside. Yes, of course, of course I have to leave. Nothing has changed that. But I can't right now, not this minute, because there's something I have to do first. I owe it to Stephanie; I owe it to Garth, because I deceived him. Nothing has changed; I'll still leave – I'm just putting it off for a little while until this is cleared up. Because it's obvious that—

'I told Dolores you'd call tomorrow,' said Garth, coming in. 'I'm sorry I was so long; I feel as if I'd been in combat with a tornado. You haven't poured the coffee.' He sat down and filled their mugs. 'Now maybe we can – my God, Stephanie, what is it?'

Wordlessly, she handed him the letter. He scanned it, the lines in his face hardening as he read it a second time. 'I didn't know they'd drag me into it.' A thought struck him. 'Unless ... you've gotten one of these damned things before, haven't you? This is what you were talking about when we quarreled just before you went to China. Why didn't you show it to me? All that anguish, when I didn't know what the hell you meant—'

'I don't want to talk about the past,' Sabrina broke in impatiently. 'We have to think about what we're going to do now to stop it before it goes any further.' She was thinking quickly. 'If copies were sent to the trustees or officers of the university, and they believe it, or even if they don't but they're afraid of a scandal, you could be hurt; couldn't it even affect your appointment as director of the Genetics Institute?'

'Yes. But wait a minute.' Events were whipping past Garth, and he tried to slow them down. A few minutes ago, answering the doorbell, he left behind a drooping, anxious figure determined to run away. He came back to a vividly alive woman sitting on the edge of her chair, a warrior charging to his defense, recognizing with perfect insight what damage the letter could do. Six months ago, concerned with herself and less interested in the politics of the university, she would not have been so quick. He was stirred by the bright anger in her eyes, the taut line of her slender neck as she held her head high, ready for battle. For him. 'You don't believe the letter,' he said.

'*Believe it?* Garth, you can't be serious. No one who knows you would believe this trash. Someone wants to destroy you; we have to find out who it is.'

He looked at her thoughtfully. She had believed it in September. Now she didn't. 'I'm a little slow today,' he ventured. 'I thought I heard you say you were leaving, going back to London.'

'You're not slow and you know it; don't play games with me.'

'And if I ask the same of you?'

'I'm not playing games! What is the matter with you? Can't you see how things have changed? If other people get this letter and I'm not here, they'll assume I've left you because what it says is true. No one will believe I left for other reasons; if I leave now, you would be condemned no matter what you said.'

So she had seen that, too, Garth thought. She had seen it all. He went to her and took her face between his hands. 'I thought of that when I saw the letter. Thank you.'

'You didn't say anything.'

'Such as?'

'Asking me to stay because of the harm that would be done if I left.'

'If you left. My dear love, if you left, the wreckage would extend far beyond a campus scandal. It would destroy this house, this family, three hearts and minds and spirits—'

'Don't, please don't—'

He kissed the tears from her eyes. But her body was tense, as if she was clamping down the possibility of desire, and he moved away. They had time now. As long as she was staying, they had time. Her grief and despair in London had been so terrible, and her loneliness for her sister so much more than he could imagine, that he felt demands on her would be intrusions in a healing process he could support but not direct.

But now he asked for one more assurance. He took her hands in his. 'You are staying? Whatever your reasons were for wanting to leave, I don't have to wonder each morning if I'll find you here at the end of the day?'

'I'll help you get through this,' she promised.

'That isn't what I asked.'

'Garth, can't we take one step at a time? So much has happened in such a little while . . . I'm trying to do what is right for everyone.'

'You can't make that decision alone. It involves all of us.'

She bent her head. Garth began to say something, then stopped. In the silence, she felt him turn over the hand he was holding. Her left hand. 'You aren't wearing your ring.'

A chill touched her. 'No.'

'Where is it?'

She hesitated, swinging between lies and the truth. 'In London.'

'Damn it, who are you to take all these steps on your own? You decide you won't have a family anymore, so you take off your ring and that makes it official. Then all you have to do is say a quick goodbye?'

She felt relief and guilt. One lie or another, she thought, but better this than the truth; that she'd returned the ring to Stephanie. 'I thought it would be—'

'A symbol,' he said. 'And it is. But I happen to believe in symbols. Where is it now?'

'I suppose . . . in the house on Cadogan Square.'

'Then Mrs Thirkell can send it back.'

'If she can find it.'

'Write to her.'

'All right.'

'And if she can't find it, we'll buy another.'

I won't be here long enough.

'And I'm asking you, Stephanie – are you listening to me?' She nodded. 'I'm asking you to let me help you at the same time you're helping me. Damn it, we're part of each other and we'll help each other. Agreed?'

'Agreed,' she said, wishing he could, knowing he could not. She picked up the letter. 'What does this mean – "those stories about students—"?'

'I'll show you.' He left the room and brought back the university newspaper. 'Last Wednesday's *Standard*. Our journalism students outdid themselves.'

Sabrina read the banner headline, 'Sex for Grades', and beneath it, 'Or Vice Versa.'

'The *Standard* doesn't know who makes the first offer,' she read. 'But three professors and a passel of fair female students have been summoned to VP Lloyd Strauss's office for an airing of charges that they've been trading favors, with payment in grades – the only thing more valuable than money hereabouts. It may have been going on since last spring quarter; a nasty tale that could affect class standing and even graduation in some cases. Not to mention the academic future of the professors.'

'Written like a gossip column,' Garth muttered. 'Somebody ought to teach those kids that journalism is serious business. They're dealing with people's lives.'

'Which people?' Sabrina asked.

'Melvin Blake, someone named Millburn and Marty Talvia—'

'Not Marty. You mean those rumors were—? I don't believe it. Oh, poor Linda.'

'—and now, it seems, Garth Andersen.'

'But it's all absurd. You and Marty wouldn't—'

'And Blake and Millburn?'

'I don't know them. I suppose if any of the rumors are true—'

'The problem is, my love, that if you admit the possibility of one, you admit the possibility of all.'

396

'But Garth, I know you wouldn't, and Marty ... *would* Marty?'

'I think he and Linda had a bad time a few months ago. He didn't confide in me; I think he tried to once or twice and then backed off.'

'When you were in California I asked you once on the telephone—'

'He's had other women. He talks about them, long after the fact, ashamed of himself for behaving like a kid who sneaks candies even when he's not hungry. But I would have thought he'd keep away from students.'

'What did he tell Lloyd Strauss?'

'All of them denied it.'

'And then?'

'That's as much as I know. I assume Lloyd is doing some checking; I haven't talked to him lately. I will now. Would you like more coffee?'

'No, I ought to be thinking about dinner.' How naturally she said it; how natural it was to slip back. Sabrina looked at Garth, close to her in the warm room. How natural it was to love him.

He met her look. 'And I love you,' he said. 'As for dinner, we'll go out. The larder is bare. We didn't want to function too successfully without you. But there is wine.'

Sabrina watched him open a bottle and fill two glasses. 'I think we should make some waves on the social scene,' she mused. 'I think we should be highly visible. Garth and ... Stephanie Andersen, in the open, with nothing to hide.'

He handed her a glass. 'Who is it you're trying to convince?'

'Whoever wonders about our marriage and what you do with your free time.'

He laughed. 'If you think it will help. I'd rather find the letter-writer.'

'Oh, yes,' she said calmly. 'We'll do that, too. We should make a list of students you've failed in the past year. Or any who got a lower grade than expected. Or anyone you yelled at. Why are you laughing?'

'The list is getting very long.'

'How long? You think of names and I'll start writing.'

Half an hour later, when Penny and Cliff came in, they found their parents still at the breakfast room table, talking. Dad was relaxed in his chair, legs stretched out before him, a quiet smile on his face. Mom sat straight, writing, her eyes bright. Penny sighed and touched Cliff's arm. 'Right,' he said, and they both knew what he meant: their home was back together again.

When Sabrina unpacked that night, she discovered Mrs Thirkell had filled the suitcase with Lady Longworth's clothes. Her closet in Evanston was now a mixture of Stephanie and Sabrina – like our lives, she thought. I wonder how much longer I'll be able to tell them apart. Putting everything away, she slid into the familiar four-poster bed, feeling the weariness of a day that had gone through a dozen transformations since she left Washington in the morning.

She saw Garth's silhouette in the doorway before he disappeared into the bathroom. There was something special about that; she tried to think what it was. And in a moment she had it; this was their first night together in a routine of family life since the night in New York when she had acknowledged her love for him. Since then they had been separated, first by her grief and then by the ocean. Now, she had agreed to stay. As his wife. And she could not pretend that night in New York had never happened.

She lay still, waiting for him, remembering the hours of longing that had filled her nights in London. And then he was beside her, silently gathering her to him.

'My sweet love,' he murmured. 'This bed grew emptier and wider each night you were not in it.'

She laughed, a low, contented laugh, moving her lips against his. 'So did mine. If we had waited long enough, they might have met in the middle of the Atlantic.'

'No. We waited long enough. Too long.'

His hands moved over her slender form, and hers answered along the harder lines of his body. Their lips spoke against each other, murmuring, laughing, making small wordless sounds, while their eyes met. When they came together, it was with the incandescence they remembered: joy and delight, the intensity of pleasure given and received, a sense of belonging, of coming home. They were strong in what they could give each other; they were both vulnerable, without shame, in what they needed from each other.

Wonderingly, Garth gazed at her beauty, at the brightness it cast. 'You fill the room with light,' he said.

'And life and love,' Sabrina said softly. She traced the lines of his face with tender fingers. 'I remember a poem: "Love makes one little room an everywhere." That's what I've found with you.' 'What we have found,' he said. They lay still in the lamplight, holding hands, Garth's arm cradling her, Sabrina's head on his shoulder as she drifted in the pleasure of the last hour and the comfort of his flesh, so much a part of hers there seemed no division between them.

She gazed at the reflection of the moon in the mirror, a clear white crescent caught in the black branches of an oak tree. As I am caught, she thought drowsily, in my love for this man, and his for me. She remembered with a smile one of Antonio's Indian tales. It was not important, he had said, if she did not love him before she married him. 'The Guarani gods say love is the last thing, not the first. It grows slowly through sharing and creating. When you live together and build a family, love will come.'

'Do you know,' Garth said ruefully, 'reluctant as I am to admit it—'

'—You're hungry,' Sabrina finished, laughing. 'Well, come on. Let's see what we can find in the bare larder. It won't be the first time you and I have made something from nothing.'

Garth handed Lloyd Strauss the letter, in its envelope. 'Add it to my official biography for university press releases: BA, MA, PhD, director of the Genetics Institute and lecher.'

Strauss took a similar envelope from his desk drawer and held it out to Garth. 'Came yesterday.'

Garth felt a stab of helplessness: an invisible presence, vindictive and persevering, on a campus of thirty thousand students – assuming it was a student who was behind it. He pulled out the letter, identical to his. 'Are there others?'

'Not that I know of. The president didn't get one.'

'How come you got the honor?'

399

Strauss shrugged. 'The story in the *Standard*? My strong arm summoning Talvia and Blake? Somebody wants you summoned. And lo and behold, here you are.'

'Not through a summons.'

'You beat me to it.'

'Lloyd, you're not taking this seriously.'

'I take all accusations seriously.'

Garth gave him a long look. 'Something else is new, I gather.'

'Talvia and Blake resigned from the faculty today.'

Garth swore softly and began to pace the office. 'Forced out? To make it look as if the university was cleaning house?'

'They confessed, Garth. I had weeping girls in here, outraged parents, remorseful professors . . . more drama than Shakespeare. The guy who started it – called the president, bellowing about his little girl being corrupted – happens to be a big contributor to the new football stadium. It would be football, wouldn't it? Can't ignore football. So the stink spread, and the president ordered me to clear it up before word got out. Word, of course, got out; the *Standard*, damn its industrious student hide, got the details into last week's paper before I'd even arranged my Shakespearean session. By the time I did, I was getting telephone calls from, as they say, the media.'

Sitting on the edge of the window seat, arms folded, Garth shook his head. 'Poor Marty. You think you know someone, you think you've built trust, and then, when it's too late, you find there are still gaps. I hardly know Blake; wasn't there another one?'

'Millburn. I'll have his resignation tomorrow. And— you.'

'Oh, for God's sake, Lloyd – an anonymous letter. You know me well enough to know what shit that is—'

'Right. I know you; I know what shit it is. Does the *Chicago Tribune* know it? Does *Time*? Does *Newsweek*?'

'What the hell—' Garth stopped in disbelief. '*That* media?'

'That media. This is juicy stuff, my friend. "What dark doings really go on behind those ivy-covered walls? Tune in

400

tomorrow, or buy tomorrow's paper or next week's magazine." We set ourselves up for this, you know, acting as if we're above the crowd: scholars, researchers, keepers of the truth. So, of course, the public loves to hear that we're as fucked up as the rest of them, and out of the woodwork come the reporters, to tell them all about it. So even though I'd like to burn anonymous letters, I can't do it. How do I know who else got them? How do I know who's blabbing all kinds of crap to reporters? You're my friend and colleague, and I trust you, but my first responsibility is to the university.'

'Which means an investigation.'

'That's what it means. It's already started. I hired a top-notch firm this morning.'

'And just what are they going to investigate?'

Strauss jumped up and paced the length of his office. 'You, other professors, students. Maybe we have it all, maybe this is only the tip of an iceberg. But when someone makes a specific charge, we have to look into it. They'll find out who wrote the letter, talk to people about your reputation and character...'

'My reputation and character!' Garth swept up his briefcase and strode to the door. 'Listen, you son of a bitch, I don't have to defend my reputation and character to you or anyone else. You know me well enough to handle this yourself without bringing in professional spies. If you don't, you shouldn't be announcing my appointment to the Genetics Institute next week.'

Strauss looked at him in silence. Garth held the door half open. 'You *are* announcing it next week.'

'It's been postponed. Garth, *I've got to cover my ass*. And you know it. It's not just money for a goddamn football stadium; it's the whole university. We have to be pure as a virgin when we apply for government research grants or ask donors to fund a new theater, a music building, the library addition, an international studies center . . . I have to show that I am doing my damnedest to keep this a safe place for people to send their kids or give money to so their name can be on a building. That's my job. If it means hiring a detective to ask people if Garth Andersen screws between seminars, I'll do it. And, since your job is to teach and do research, *and be the director of a new Genetics Institute*, you'll answer every one of their fucking questions. What do you have to hide? You'll be here a lot longer than they will.'

'Has it occurred to you that it might affect my reputation just to have those fucking questions asked at all?'

'It has. I considered it. The university's reputation comes first. Yours will survive. Garth, for Christ's sake, you were a hero in *Newsweek* not so long ago; that's your reputation. You don't need to be in the same magazine again under a cloud of suspicion.'

Helplessness swept Garth again. First an invisible foe, now a stranger investigating him. He opened the door. 'I can't stop you from playing hide-and-seek with your detective. But you could have asked us first. My wife, who believes in me without the guidance of a top-notch agency, is helping me look for the person responsible—'

'Garth, I'd rather you didn't do anything. We'll take care of it, swiftly and discreetly.'

'That sounds like the motto of your detective friends.'

Strauss looked sheepish. 'I think it is. But they know what they're doing, and they won't frighten anyone off. You and Stephanie might. Just hold on until we see what they come up with. We're on your side, Garth. We want to clear you.'

'You can't clear me if I haven't been charged with anything. But that's the difference between us. We're looking for a vicious liar who writes letters; you're looking for proof of my virtue. If we discover that I am of moral and upright character before you do, we'll be sure to let you know.'

'Oh, fuck it, Garth,' Strauss said wearily. 'You know I have complete faith in you.'

'Good. So does my wife. So do my children. Can your Dick Tracy and the media be far behind? But I still think we'll try to see what we can do on our own. I'll talk to you soon, Lloyd; I'm off to buy a magnifying glass.'

Madeline Kane had managed to create disarray in every corner of Collectibles in the two weeks Sabrina had been gone. 'I'm not sure exactly how it happened, Stephanie,' she said on Wednesday morning with a perplexed air. 'I just turned around one day and everything was out of place. Do you think I was trying to show how much I missed you?'

'I would have believed you if you'd just told me,' Sabrina said dryly. 'Shall we start with the breakfront and move outward from there?'

They worked silently, saving their energy for moving the heavy furniture. 'Coffee,' Madeline gasped finally, and they walked to the back of the shop. 'Has it been a very bad time for you?' she asked as they sat at her small desk.

'Yes.'

'Is there anything I can do?'

'You did it. You messed up Collectibles. Physical labor is good therapy for someone in mourning.'

'Tell me when you need it again. I seem to do it with no trouble at all. What will you do about your sister's shop in London?'

'Keep it going, at least for now. There's an assistant manager who's been there for some time and an antique dealer who wants to buy into it. I've told them to open the shop, and I've set a limit on what they can spend at auction.'

'But surely, without supervision—'

'They're both highly professional and competent. And my solicitor keeps an eye on the funds and handles the accounts for my housekeeper as well.'

'But how can he? I mean, I don't mean to pry, but if he has no authority—'

'I've sent him my power of attorney.'

'I see,' Madeline said.

Sabrina stood up. 'Back to work, I think.'

'And your sister's house?' Madeline asked. 'Will your solicitor sell it?'

'No. The housekeeper will maintain it. A friend is living there until she gets her own affairs in order.'

'Ah. It's all yours now – the shop and the house?'

'Yes.'

'Ah. Valuable furnishings and property, I gather.'

'Yes.'

'I don't mean to pry.'

'Of course you do, Madeline; you want to know everything about my affairs in London. Why?'

'No reason. I just ... oh, the truth is, it all sounds quite glamorous and – forgive me, Stephanie, but you seem to belong in that kind of life. I've never quite believed that *you* work for *me*.'

Sabrina looked at her quizzically. 'I haven't done a good job?'

'You know that's not what I mean. *Are* you going back?'

'Of course I am.' She chose her words carefully. 'To see my solicitor, and Nicholas, who's running Ambassadors, and my housekeeper.'

Madeline sighed. 'You see, I've come to depend on you. You're very special, and I don't want to lose you. In fact, while you were away, I contracted for five major estate sales, which will probably require an assistant anyway. If you're gone—'

'Right now, I'm going only as far as lunch. Five estate sales? What a businesswoman you are, Madeline! Tell me about them after lunch. Shall we lock the shop or are you staying in?'

'Staying; I brought a sandwich. Will you be long?'

'I don't know. It's a solace session for a friend whose husband just resigned from the university.'

'Talvia or Blake?'

Pulling on her coat, Sabrina sighed. 'Does everyone know everything—?'

'I read the *Standard*. What a marvelous coat. Real leather?'

'The real thing. I brought it back from London. It was my sister's.' She settled on her shoulder the strap of the matching bag she also had brought back. 'Do you hear campus rumors, too?'

'No. Am I missing much?'

'Not much. I'm late; I'd better run.'

She was meeting Dolores and Linda at Café Provençal, and she walked there quickly in the brisk wind whipping off the lake. She found them at a table in the back. Linda was wearing dark glasses.

'I've been crying a lot.'

'I don't mind your looks, Linda; I can't talk to dark glasses.'

She took them off and, looking at her swollen eyelids and blotched cheeks, Sabrina ached for her, not so much for her unhappiness as for the cowed look of shame in her eyes. 'It's not your fault,' she said, taking Linda's hand. 'You didn't know anything about it.'

The waitress took their order and Dolores leaned forward. 'Exactly what I told her.'

Linda shook her head. 'He wouldn't have done it if I'd been nicer to him, if we weren't always fighting, if I didn't tell him ... ' Her mouth worked for a moment. 'He doesn't always satisfy me. He says it isn't his fault, that I'm too busy criticizing his performance to relax. And he's probably right, he's always right about everything; but I still blame him and make him feel like he isn't really a man. So I guess he goes to young girls who tell him what he wants to hear.'

'That's absurd,' Sabrina said flatly. 'You can't blame yourself because Marty got taken in by a couple of young girls who set him up and then blackmailed him into giving them passing grades.'

'Who said it was only a couple?'

'Garth.'

'Did he really? Marty refused to tell me. But it doesn't make any difference, does it? Even one means I'm a failure. I've always known I'd be a failure with Marty. I don't have a college degree, you know. I haven't read half the books he has, and I keep wondering if he wouldn't rather have someone who's smarter than me. And I can't talk to him about it, I wish I could, but I keep putting it off and the longer I wait the harder it gets, because I don't know where to begin. Marty says if you really want to talk about something you'll do it, not make up excuses. He's always right, so I guess I don't really want to talk. But now he's found college women to make him happy, so I know I'm a failure.'

Sabrina was looking at her intently. 'You're nothing of the kind. Give Marty credit for being a unique individual with his own problems and his own ways of working them out. Are you so powerful you're responsible for everything he does?'

Linda finished her salad, her lips pouting in thought. 'It sounds different when you say it that way.'

Dolores ordered dessert. 'What you need, Linda, is something to do. You'll need an income until Marty finds a job, and it will occupy your mind. You come with me to the next meeting of the garden club; those women know when their husbands need secretaries.'

'I don't want to be a—'

'You don't have so many choices, Linda; you'll do what you have to do. You'll hear about a number of openings at the meeting, and I'll help you put together a résumé – all those secretarial jobs you held in the past – and I can go with you to your interviews, to bolster you up—'

'Dolores, *please stop arranging my life!*'

Heads swiveled at other tables. Dolores flushed. 'I'm sorry, I thought you needed a friend.'

'I do, I do, I don't mean to sound ungrateful . . . '

'I'm going to order coffee,' Sabrina said. 'For all of us.'

Dolores straightened in her chair. 'I always go a little too far, don't I? I never know I'm doing it until it's too late.'

'We'll be glad to tell you,' Sabrina offered, easing the tension, and they laughed.

Dolores frowned. 'You've changed, Stephanie. You never used to be the one to take charge.'

'Oh, we're all mixed up by everything that's happened . . .' Sabrina said vaguely. 'Linda,' she added. 'We need an assistant at Collectibles, to help with estate sales. Why don't you try it?'

'I don't even know what an estate sale is.'

'We organize the sale of homes and their furnishings, everything from oil paintings to paring knives. You'd learn how to price items, how to make up a catalogue, how to advertise the sale and then how to run it – which means you have to be there the whole time, hovering over customers who try to sneak off with silver and snuffboxes and anything else portable.'

Linda's eyes brightened. 'It sounds like fun.'

'It is. Exciting, dusty, aggravating, and always different. Interested?'

'If you're offering it just because we're in trouble—'

'I'm offering it because less than two hours ago Madeline told me she's got five estate sales lined up, and we can't handle them without an assistant.'

'Somebody without a college degree?'

'Linda, I'm asking you if you want to try it. I didn't ask you anything else.'

'Yes, yes, yes, it sounds wonderful! Oh, Stephanie, how can I repay you?'

'By becoming better at it than I am. Then, if I ever have to leave, you'll keep it going.'

'Leave? What are you talking about? Are you and Garth moving? You're not going away, Stephanie!'

'No, I didn't mean—' *What is the matter with me?* 'I meant if I ever get another job. But that's a long way off. Now I've got to get back to work or I won't even have this job.'

'Should I come too?' Linda asked.

'Not today. I'll talk to Madeline and call you later. Dolores, is ten dollars enough for lunch? I really have to run.'

'No, lunch is my treat; it was my idea.'

Sabrina leaned over and kissed her on the cheek. 'Next time I'm buying.'

She looked back at them from the door: Dolores talking and Linda looking dreamily at a picture on the wall. She thought of Alexandra and Gabrielle. How strange, the many ways we help each other, she thought. And for a moment she wondered who would help her when she finally left for good. They would all be so busy. Oh, but there was one. She smiled faintly as she opened the door to Collectibles. There was always Mrs Thirkell.

On Friday afternoon Sabrina left the shop early to take Linda a stack of books on the history of furniture and decorative arts.

'You don't need to memorize them,' she said when she saw the dismay on Linda's face. 'But you have to know how to use them to look up a piece. And you ought to have an idea of the way furniture styles have changed and how fads affect the market in collectibles. Right now it's political posters and lacquerware; I have a feeling dolls will be next. Anyway, read through these, and we'll talk on Monday.'

Walking up the front steps of the house, she sighed with anticipation. An hour alone before Penny and Cliff arrived; a little time to herself without the demands of family and friends and work. But the door was unlocked. No time after all, she thought; which one of them had come home early?

The living room was empty. 'Cliff?' she called. 'Penny?' There was no answer. Curious, Sabrina went upstairs and found Cliff sitting on his bed, desperately shoving into a plastic bag a jumble of pocket calculators, FM radios, pen-and-pencil sets, wallets, tie clips, cuff links and gloves.

'You look like a pirate with his loot,' she said lightly from the doorway.

Cliff spun round. 'I thought you got home at four.'

'I thought you got home at four-thirty.'

'Well, I came home early—'

'So did I. Did you plan to hide everything before I got here?'

He looked up with such fear and shame that Sabrina wanted to rush to him and tell him not to be afraid, she would help him, everything would be all right. But it was clear that something was very wrong, and she stayed across the room. Pulling out his desk chair, she sat down. 'I think you'd better start at the beginning and tell me about it.'

'But I told Dad. When you were in China. Didn't he tell you?'

No one told me anything, she thought. But Stephanie did talk about problems with Cliff.

'It seems he decided to keep it between the two of you. I wonder if you appreciate that. From the evidence, I doubt it.'

Cliff looked at his shoes.

'Well?' Sabrina pressed. 'Did you promise him then that you'd stop whatever you were up to? I suppose you did. What happened next? Cliff, you're going to have to answer me sooner or later; why not save time and do it now? Before Penny gets home.'

His eyes brimming with tears, Cliff looked up. 'I did stop. I told them my dad knew about it and I couldn't hide any more stuff for them. But last week, when you were in England, they brought over this whole load and told me I had to keep it, and I didn't know what to do.'

'Where was Garth – your dad?'

'At a meeting, and Penny was at school working on her puppet show, and they came over—'

'Cliff, who are "they"?'

'These kids, they're in eighth grade, and they sort of, you know, run the school. They choose the teams and they're always the captains and they go through the cafeteria first even if the rest of us are ahead of them in line . . . you know. And they rip off stores. They'll say, "I'm going over to Radio Shack to rip off a calculator." Like that. They used to do it just for themselves, but then they started selling the stuff to kids in Chicago when they were down there dealing drugs. So they needed a place to keep things before they sold them, and one day they asked me if I'd help out. I thought they liked me . . . I mean, I felt . . . good about it . . . '

Flattered, Sabrina thought. The little tin dictators ask for your help. Join the elite. 'You thought then *you'd* be able to go first through the cafeteria,' she said.

Cliff looked startled. 'How did you know that?'

She smiled at him. 'When I was in high school most of the girls were very rich, looking way down their noses at St – at Sabrina and me. We always felt they were doing us a favor by asking us to help them with their homework. Then, later, when we began to win prizes for classwork and trophies in fencing and sailing, they started looking up to us and suddenly they weren't special or awesome at all. Pretty ordinary, in fact. What did this gang promise you for helping them?'

'I could take something for myself once a month, or they'd pay me fifteen dollars a week. I took the money. I was going to buy a stereo for my room.'

'Expensive. It sounds like a lot of fifteen-dollar weeks. Are you sure you were a reluctant partner?'

Cliff studied his shoes again. 'Sometimes I was, and then I guess sometimes I wasn't.' Sabrina's careful mildness had reassured him and he talked with relief and growing confidence. 'It's better to be friends with those guys than against them. You never win if you're against them. And I thought, when they asked me, I'd be part of their group . . . and I'd get money, too and . . . so that's what happened.'

'Did it ever occur to you that you were aiding and abetting criminals?'

'Mom! They're not criminals! They just rip off stores. It's not like murder or robbing a bank or something. Anyway, they said the stores make so much money they don't even notice when a few things are missing.'

'Oh, don't they? Cliff, stealing is wrong, wherever it's done, and whether it's noticed or not. But it usually is discovered. Did you ever hear of taking inventory?'

'No.'

'That's when stores count their stock and check it against what they bought and sold. When the figures don't match, they know what's been stolen. It's called shrinkage. And then, to make up their losses, they raise the price of everything else in the store. So the rest of us, who don't believe in stealing, end up paying for your pals' thievery.'

There was a pause. 'I never thought of that.'

'And your friends never told you.'

'They're not really my friends.'

'I thought you said you'd be part of their group.'

'I did. But . . . they don't really want me, Mom. They don't like me at all. Oh, shit.' The tears had come back and he brushed them away fiercely. 'I'm sorry, I know you don't like me to say that, but nothing's the way I thought it would be. They never talk to me like friends; they make fun of me.'

'For what?' Sabrina asked gently.

'Liking books and getting good grades.'

'Well, we're proud of you for that. But why did you stay with them if they made fun of you? Was it the money?'

'No, it was . . . If you really want to know, I'm scared of them. They said they'd beat me up if I told on them, and last week they said if I didn't hide this stuff they'd tell the principal I'd stolen it. Dad wanted to go to the police, but I asked him not to and I wouldn't tell him their names. I can't tell anybody. And I can't stop helping them, either, because even if they don't beat me up they'd keep me off the teams. They'd keep people from talking to me, even my friends, and

I'd be out of everything and *alone*. They can do that, Mom, and I'm sorry, but I'm scared of them, and whatever I do, things will be bad. I know you can't understand that, because you always know what to do, but I don't. I don't know *what* to do.'

Sabrina went to sit beside him as he slumped on the bed. I *understand exactly how you feel*. She put her arms around him, and after a minute he put his head on her shoulder. 'I'm sorry, Mom.'

'For what?'

'Crying.'

'We all cry when we're sad and afraid; you shouldn't apologize. I'd rather you were sorry for not telling us when this mess started again. Are you more afraid of us than these bullies?'

Cliff ducked his head. 'I *wanted* to.'

'And?'

'Dad trusted me.'

'And you didn't want him to know you had failed him?'

'I didn't want him to know I'd lied. Every once in a while he asks if they ever tried to get me in with them again, and I always say no. So I let him down and then I lied. Now I guess you'll tell him, but there still isn't anything anybody can do.'

'Oh, I think there is.'

'What? Mom, they'll beat me up or oster . . . ostra . . . '

'Ostracize. They won't do either one. I'm going to ground you for a month.'

'Ground me! Mom!' He pulled back and glared at her through reddened eyes. 'That's not fair!'

'Is it fair to work for these bullies? Or to get beat up and ignored? Or to be accused of shoplifting to the principal?'

'But—'

'If your parents say that for one month you have to come straight home from school every day, you can't have friends over and you can't go out at night, what better excuse do you have for not working with these fellows? You can tell them honestly that you have no choice. And, after a month, you'll say your parents are suspicious and you don't want to get grounded again so you have to stay away from them. But that may not be necessary. Because while you're grounded, I think we'll alert the police to put some detectives in Radio Shack and other places you'll tell us about. That way, you won't have to give us any names. It shouldn't take long to spot them and break up their ring; they sound fairly stupid to me.'

Cliff's eyes were round with admiration. 'Mom that's not bad! That's pretty clever!'

'Yes, I thought so. Considering I've never done anything like it before.'

'Sure you have. You grounded me—'

'I try to forget past punishments.'

'Mom? I've got an idea. If you help me get rid of this stuff now, we wouldn't have to tell Dad. He'd never have to know.'

'You mean you'd lie to him again.'

'No, I just wouldn't say anything at all.'

'But hiding the truth is just a different kind of lie. If you let him believe something that you know isn't true—' She stopped and stared into space. *Who am I to give advice.*

'Mom?'

Slowly Sabrina turned back to him. 'Cliff, there are some empty cartons in the storeroom. If you'll get a couple of them, we'll pack everything up and your Dad and I will deliver them to the police when we talk to them.'

'But then they'll know I had it all here.'

'We'll find a way to keep you out of it.' As he stood uncertainly, she lost her patience. 'You'll just have to trust us. Now go get those boxes!'

Mumbling, Cliff went off, and Sabrina stood up, trying to slow the beating of her heart. She started to go to her room – maybe now she could have a few minutes alone – just as the front door slammed and Penny's voice danced ahead of her into the house.

Garth had gone through his records and listed eleven students who had complained in the last year about low or failing grades.

'What about this one?' Sabrina asked. 'The one with a question mark after her name.'

'Rita McMillan,' said Garth. 'Only a possibility. Didn't I tell you about her last June?'

'I don't think so.'

'I thought I did. She offered her charms in return for a passing grade, and I chased her out with my tennis racket. Something like that. I believe I may have called her a whore. It was the week Vivian had been turned down by the tenure committee, and I was not favorably impressed with young women trading on their anatomy. I didn't flunk her, though; she took an incomplete and I gave her permission to take Vivian's class this quarter so she could graduate. But it was all six months ago; I can't believe she'd be involved now.'

Sabrina repeated the name. 'Young women have long memories. Especially when their crown jewels are rejected.'

He smiled. 'Rita might think of it that way. Well, now, what shall we do with this list? I must say it makes me feel ridiculous – as if someone handed me a toy gun and told me to play cops and robbers. I'm better at hunting an elusive bacterium.'

'And I'd rather look for a lost Wedgwood.'

He chuckled. 'Bacteria and Wedgwood. Cops and robbers. What a couple we are.'

They were a couple. Sabrina made sure of that. They were seen everywhere. Wednesday night, two days after she returned, they attended a film preview and a reception for the director. On Thursday they went to a cocktail party, where the president of the university was attentive and admiring. 'Rightfully so,' said Garth. 'You've never been so beautiful.'

She was vividly beautiful, dressing all that week, for the first time, with the brilliance of Sabrina Longworth. In vibrant greens and blues, in wine velvet, in striped silk, her heavy hair falling in waves of shimmering bronze below her shoulders, poised and quick, she was a beacon, drawing others to stand in her orbit. And she was never far from Garth. On Saturday night they appeared at the opening of the new university art museum, where Sabrina talked to artists and sculptors and collectors in their language, drawing on all her years of experience. She was exhilarated by the surroundings and the people, and Lloyd Strauss, finding her for a rare moment alone, was effusive.

'You're magnificent, Stephanie; it's wonderful that you can do it, so soon after your loss.'

'I am doing it for Garth,' she said clearly, and met Strauss's gaze, daring him to doubt Garth's innocence or call her naive. He did neither; instead he invited them to dinner the following night.

'You're never home!' Penny wailed as Sabrina brushed her hair at her dressing table on Sunday evening.

'Our social season,' Garth said wryly, adjusting his tie and talking to Penny's reflection in the full-length mirror. 'In the line of duty, my sweet.'

A tag end of memory caught Sabrina, and she turned to see Penny's woebegone face. 'We hardly have a family anymore – we never even see you!'

The bedroom faded. Sabrina and Stephanie Hartwell stood before a triple mirror in a bedroom in Athens, watching their parents dress for an embassy ball. 'Everybody gets to be with you but us! The only family we have is Stephanie and me – we're our whole family.'

She remembered it so clearly. But for a week she had forgotten it. For a week, with Garth, she had filled the calendar, going out each night after working each day, just as she had done in London: hours crammed with dinners and conversation and new faces. She hadn't realized how much she missed it. And sometimes, standing in a group beneath bright lights, talking, holding a glass of wine, hearing music and laughter on all sides, she forgot for a brief moment who she was; her worlds merged, and she would touch Garth's arm as he stood beside her, loving him, loving the way others looked at them, as a couple, as husband and wife.

But the crowded calendar was not fair to Penny and Cliff, and Sabrina knew it. They need a family, she thought, and I should help them have one. I'll be gone soon enough.

'You're right, Penny,' she said. 'We should slow down and stay home more.'

Bemused, Garth looked at her. 'I thought this was your campaign.'

'But you only do it because I think we should.'

'On the contrary. I'm having a good time.'

'Daddy!' Penny cried, and Sabrina looked at him in surprise.

'It's true, we've overdone it a bit,' he said, enjoying his wife's startled silence. 'But after years of telling me we didn't go out enough, you've shown me how much I've been missing. I might,' he said, seeing the shadow in her eyes, 'stay home four or five nights out of seven, but no more.'

She laughed softly. 'Not excessive; we could arrange that.'

'But what about tonight?' Penny asked.

'Tonight we go out; we are expected. Tomorrow we stay home. Can we manage that, Stephanie?'

'Yes.' She smiled as Penny ran out of the room and Garth put his arms around her. 'Tomorrow we stay home.'

She canceled the party they were to attend on Monday, and the four of them spent a slow, quiet evening together. After Penny and Cliff had gone to bed, Sabrina and Garth sat in the living room, talking, reading, thinking separate thoughts. How had she done it, Sabrina wondered – slipped so comfortably back into the life of the family? It had not been effortless; each morning she woke to the shattering realization of Stephanie's death and the precariousness of her life with Garth. But then, as the hours passed in a web of people and activities, she was pulled away from guilt and sadness over Stephanie toward the life of the family and community around her. And each day the pull of life became stronger. For the first time she could remember, she felt she had found the place where she belonged.

But then she would be pulled up short. This was not where she belonged; it was based on a lie, it all depended on a lie. She sat in the living room with Garth and reminded herself of that, repeating it to keep it real. Because beneath the touch of his hand, the weight of his body, the love in his eyes, she knew she could lose sight of what she had to do, or the strength to do it.

She turned back to her book just as the doorbell rang. Garth answered it and brought into the living room a small, middle-aged man who introduced himself as Karl Jenks, the special investigator hired by Lloyd Strauss to look into anonymous charges against Professor Andersen.

'I've been talking to some folks,' he began, settling into an armchair in the living room and looking around. 'Nice room.' His small features, tucked beneath a high forehead, gave him a permanently suspicious look, and when he wrote in his notebook he puckered his mouth in concentration, like a child having trouble with spelling. 'Anybody mad at you, professor? You take somebody's job, or flunk somebody, or borrow a lawnmower and forget to return it?'

'No.'

'Nobody's mad at you? Nobody at all in the whole very wide world? You are universally loved?'

Garth looked steadily at Jenks until the small eyes slid sideways. 'We've made a list of students who may have felt badly treated by me. I'll get it for you.'

'In a minute. You help with the list, Stephanie?'

Sabrina raised her eyebrows. 'Have we met before?'

'What? Before tonight? I don't think so; why?'

'Because, Mr Jenks, only my friends use my first name.'

There was a pause. 'Oh, ho,' Jenks said finally. 'Excuse me, madam. Or perhaps you prefer *my lady*.'

Sabrina smiled and said nothing.

'Well, then, how about this list, my lady? You help make it up?'

'No.'

'You believe it?'

'Believe what? It's simply a list.'

'Might be you think your hubby didn't include everybody.'

'That is absurd.'

'Ah.' He wrote. Sabrina and Garth exchanged glances. Nothing they had said seemed worth recording.

'You play tennis, professor?'

Garth looked up from his thoughts. 'Yes. Does that apply to your investigation?'

'Might. Do you, Mrs Andersen?'

'Yes.'

'Played together lately?'

416

'No,' said Garth. 'My wife's sister died recently, and she is in mourning.'

'My condolences. Busy life you have – parties and museum openings and such. That part of your mourning?'

'What a busy bee you've been, Mr Jenks,' Sabrina said pleasantly. 'Investigating our social life. Garth, do you think we should discuss our social life with Mr Jenks?'

'I think if Mr Jenks doesn't talk about anonymous letters, there is no reason for him to be here.'

'Nice little rugs,' Jenks said, swiveling his head. 'From China?'

'Yes,' said Sabrina.

'You get them in China?'

'No.'

'The professor go with you to China?'

'That's enough,' Garth said, standing up. 'I'll show you out.'

'Professor, I'm conducting an investigation. Under orders from your boss.'

'You're not investigating; you're fishing.'

'That's what an investigation is, professor. We toss out a bunch of worms and see who bites. You'll just have to be patient with me. You were in Stamford lately. Connecticut.'

Garth stood beside a bookcase, resting his arm on a shelf. 'That's right.'

'Didn't take the job, though, right?'

'Evidently you know the answer already.'

'Right. Professor Andersen go with you to China, Mrs Andersen?'

'No. I traveled with an association of antique dealers, and my husband generously made the trip possible by taking care of our children while I was away.'

Jenks wrote, puckering his mouth. 'This Talvia – you've been friends for a long time?'

'A long time,' Garth said evenly.

'They fight a lot, he and the little lady?'

Garth and Sabrina were silent.

Jenks wrote. 'Too bad about marital discord. Makes for wanderings. And all those young lovelies you teach.'

417

Sabrina caught Garth's eye and shook her head slightly.

'You don't agree, Mrs Andersen? About wandering, or about those young lovelies?'

'I don't agree that you're a fool.'

Jenks was thrown off his stride. He pulled a stick of chewing gum from his pocket and folded it into his mouth. 'Blake now. How well d'you know him?'

'He and I have met,' Garth said. 'Briefly. My wife doesn't know him.'

'Now, there's a reputation for you. He likes 'em all ages and sizes, from what I hear.'

Sabrina looked at him pensively. 'What an unpleasant job you have, Mr Jenks.'

'Then there's Millburn.'

They were silent.

'You don't know him at all, I gather. Someone wrote a letter – there you are, professor, I'm talking about anonymous letters – and I checked him out for your boss. Mathematician. Fools with numbers. When he's not fooling with young lovelies.'

'Is that based on the anonymous letter?' Sabrina asked coldly.

'No, ma'am, it's based on his confession. He says it only happened once, but who knows? His wife was his student when he married her. He likes the young ones. And I must say' – a wistful note entered his voice – 'they are indeed lovely. So tempting.'

The room was still. From upstairs, Sabrina heard Cliff's radio. 'You have office hours, professor.'

'Of course.'

'You see one student at a time or a group?'

'One at a time. We discuss confidential matters – grades, the quality of their work, their plans for the future.'

'One at a time. With the door closed?'

'Sometimes.' Sabrina could see rage building in him from being forced to treat seriously Karl Jenks and his slithering questions.

'Mrs Andersen, you have many dinner guests?'

'Occasionally.'

'Ever invite any of the professor's students?'

I have no idea. Sabrina looked at Garth.

'No,' he answered for her. 'We have an open house in June for all my students and lab assistants.'

'Mrs Andersen couldn't say that herself?'

'Mrs Andersen does not have to answer anything she doesn't want to. Especially if she thinks you are trying to trap her.'

Jenks chewed his gum. 'Professor, I've just come from Talvia's house. Everything hunky-dory, lovey-dovey; you'd never guess they have a reputation for fighting at parties. I come here, there's a houseful of sweetness and light, but the wife has been running off to China and England and the husband dashes to California whenever he gets a chance, and there's a very specific letter accusing the professor of screwing those tempting lovelies and making payment with grades, and I have a strong suspicion, professor, that you did not look the other way when the treats were offered.'

Swiftly Sabrina crossed the room and stood beside Garth, putting her arm around the rigid muscles of his waist. Her breast was against his arm, and she could feel him gradually relax.

'I could throw you out,' he said conversationally. 'But that would take more energy than you deserve. Lloyd Strauss told me you were brought in to find an anonymous letter-writer and get a confession, or whatever is required, to clear my name. Instead, in your own mind, you have tried and convicted me, on what information I have no idea. You did not come here to investigate, as you claimed, but to entrap. Therefore, you are here under false pretenses; you are impersonating an investigator and that is a crime under statute 44-C-1 of the City of Evanston, for which you can lose your license. I will decide whether to call the police or the university, or both, in the morning. It will depend in part on how quickly you leave my house. I will give you sixty seconds. Beginning now'. He put his arm around Sabrina and brought up his other wrist to look at his watch.

'You can't intimidate me, professor.'

'I'm sure I can't. Forty-five seconds.'

'Your wife knows that an innocent man would not try to kick me out of his house.'

'Thirty seconds.'

'Bluffing. That's all you're doing—'

'Twenty seconds.'

Jenks shot out of his chair and bolted to the front door. 'I'll be back; your boss will be very interested to know that you kicked me out. An innocent man wouldn't—'

'Out!' roared Garth, and Jenks yanked open the door and was gone.

Sabrina's laughter rang out. 'Garth, how ridiculous.'

'I know.' Laughing with her, he took her in his arms. 'You were wonderful.'

'There's no Evanston law against impersonating yourself.'

'Of course not. The man is stupid. You were right—he's too sly to be a fool, but he is most certainly stupid.'

She stopped laughing. 'You're worried about him.'

'Yes. Aren't you?'

'Yes.'

The next morning Garth called Lloyd Strauss. 'You've put my career in the hands of a stupid son of a bitch who's already decided I'm guilty. I warn you, Lloyd—'

'Garth, don't warn me. I'm taking enough heat from the president on this, I'll be damned if I'll take it from you. Has it occurred to you that you aren't the only one with a job and a future on the line? I want this whole fucking mess out of the way so we can get back to normal, and if you think I'm going to call off an investigator just because he rubbed you the wrong way ... Oh, shit. Listen, I don't like him either. But I needed an agency in a hurry, and his was recommended by someone who'd used it. I'll call to see if they can put someone else on the case. Good enough?'

'Good enough.' And he hung up before Strauss could tell him again not to do anything on his own. Because they had decided, after Jenks had gone, that they would begin to talk to the students on Garth's list. Someone, they thought, would give away something. And even if not, it was intolerable to sit by and do nothing.

He called his wife at Collectibles. 'I just wanted to hear your voice. And tell you I love you. I talked to Lloyd, who will try to replace our stupid friend. And Marty Talvia finally called, full of apologies, saying he let us all down. I told him to take care of Linda; we'd survive. Is she there with you?'

'Yes, we're planning a sale. And Thanksgiving dinner. Marty has a new job.'

'He told me. That was the reason he finally called. He didn't feel he could face us until he was earning a living again. So Thanksgiving will be a celebration.'

'For them. Not for us, yet. What time will you be home?'

'About five. You'll be there?'

'Of course.'

Sabrina went home for an hour at noon to call London. 'Nicholas, it's Stephanie Andersen. I haven't heard from you about Ambassadors.'

'Ah, my dear Stephanie, I meant to write; your dear sister would be so pleased, everything is so excellent.'

'What does that mean, Nicholas?'

'We bought at auction the chaise and ormolu clock you mentioned before; we bought the Regency chiffonier from—'

'Nicholas.'

'Yes, Stephanie.'

'What have you sold?'

'Ah, sold. There is a slowing down this time of year—'

'There is no slowing down this time of year, Nicholas; what do you take me for? This should be the height of the season for our customers. What about your own shop?'

'We are doing – well.'

'Is that because – of Amelia?'

'My dear Stephanie, you sound exactly like Sabrina. How sad you make me feel, remembering.'

'Nicholas, perhaps you will call Brian to the telephone.'

'No, no, Stephanie, there is no need. In fact, we sold the French clock, the one with the angels, you recall, and both pieces you bought at the Chilton auction. And I believe I will put the George V secretary in Lady Stargrave's new country house.'

'How much for the clock?'

'Three thousand.'

'It might have brought four. And the Chilton pieces?'

'Twenty-three thousand for both.'

'Excellent. I can't believe you were going to keep that from me.'

'No, no, my dear, of course not. It was to be a surprise. But you dragged it out of me. How could I keep things from you, even if it entered my mind? Sidney Jones looks over my shoulder every day. By the by, he asks when you'll be here again.'

'Soon. Am I needed now?'

'Of course, dear Stephanie, since final decisions at Ambassadors still depend on you. Olivia was saying the other day that you reminded her so much of Sabrina she wishes you would move here and we could all pretend . . . oh dear, how crude that sounds; somehow it didn't seem that way when Olivia—'

'Yes, Nicholas, I know. Olivia has a way of making outrageous statements in the most ordinary way.'

'Goodness, did Sabrina really tell you such small details about us?'

'Often.' I can stop this pretending, she thought, as soon as I get back and tell them the truth. She and Nicholas talked about her December decorating commission, and she gave instructions on two auctions and the sale to Bettina Stargrave. Nicholas listened to her now; he no longer treated her like an ignorant provincial who could be disdainfully brushed aside. Finally she hung up, but before she could leave the breakfast room a new thought came to her and she sat down again. *As soon as I get back and tell them the truth.* But how can I do that? How can I tell my parents or anyone else that I'm Sabrina if I don't want Garth to know? If anyone knows, even one person, eventually it would get back to him.

She got up and began to walk around the kitchen, arms crossed, nervously running her hands up to her shoulders and down again.

I can't tell Garth the truth.

I can't tell anyone.

But if I don't, I'll be Stephanie Andersen for the rest of my life.

Sabrina Longworth will be dead.
As, of course she is. We were all at her funeral.
Oh, Stephanie, look what we've done.

Chapter 19

Snow fell on the morning of November 20, a light dusting like
a whispered warning of what lay ahead. The sky was steel
gray, hanging low over the yard, over black tree limbs furred
with snow and bushes as delicate as spider webs. Garth
turned up the furnace, Sabrina helped locate missing gloves
and Penny and Cliff took careful steps on their way down the
front walk, admiring their footprints.

When they were gone, Sabrina stood at the front window,
finishing her coffee. The yard was a tapestry of grass and
chrysanthemum stalks jutting through the snow; the white
street was striped with dark automobile tracks. Powdery
snow clung to roofs, chimneys and windowsills. A light wind
caught the branches of trees, and now and then, with a soft
sigh, snow fell in a spray to the ground.

Winter. The seasons were changing, and they were no
nearer to clearing Garth's name. She had helped by standing
by him and being seen with him in a social whirl that was
now bringing invitations in each day's mail to rival the
number she used to receive in London: but they hadn't yet
begun talking to the students on his list. They'd been too
happy. Loving, living together with no holding back for the
first time since she returned from China. Trusting, joyful,
alive.

Because my sister is dead.

She turned from the white world outside and walked back
through the house to the kitchen. There it was again. She
would let the truth slip to the back of her mind and begin to
think, in small snatches, of perhaps finding a way to stay
with Garth, as if somehow the truth could become part of a
past that had nothing to do with the present.

Deceiving herself. She had promised never to do that. *Because I will not profit from my sister's death.*

She could not change that even if she could forget it for small bits of time. *Someday, when we least expect it, it would catch up with us. And destroy us.*

The telephone rang; Garth calling from the university. 'My calendar reminds me I have a meeting in New York in December. Can you arrange with Madeline to get away? I want you with me.'

'When in December?'

'The third. For three days. I'll ask Vivian if Penny and Cliff can stay at her house. We're going to have to board her kids for six months to make up for all the times she's done it for us. You will come?'

'Yes, I'd love to.' How strange that he should call, just now, when she was reminding herself why she had to leave. 'Would you mind if I went on to London from there to take care of some business?'

There was a barely perceptible pause. 'Of course not. Would you want me to come along?'

'No. I want to go by myself.' *Because I won't be coming back.*

'If you want to go alone, of course you should. How long will your business take?'

'I don't know. But I'll probably stay on for a bit, once I'm there, in the house . . . '

This time the pause was longer. Garth had almost convinced himself she no longer thought about living in her sister's house, following in her sister's footsteps. But now, suddenly, she was talking again of leaving them to playact in another life. It seemed when things were best between them she thought of running away. He considered reminding her that she had promised to stay at least until the letter-writer was found. But he would not whine or beg. 'We can talk about it later,' he said. 'But you will arrange to come with me to New York?'

'Yes. And I'm having lunch with Vivian, so I'll talk to her about Penny and Cliff.'

'You look so somber,' said Vivian, joining her in the

restaurant at noon. 'Like our premature winter. Is there anything I can do?'

'Talk about cheerful subjects. Your tenure, for one. Garth says the committee vote was unanimous. Have I thoroughly congratulated you?'

'You should thoroughly congratulate your husband. He outwitted our former dean, outmaneuvered a timid committee and turned a century-old policy on its head. And that was just on campus. He also made it possible for the Goodman family to stay put, since I don't have to look for another job. That's called security. First time I ever had it. Did he tell you I have dubbed him Saint Garth?'

Sabrina shook her head, laughing. 'No doubt modesty prevented him.'

'He is modest, isn't that amazing? Anyone with his reputation and popularity has a right to take a bow now and then. His students are so proud of him, you know. Oh, let me tell you what one of them said – a girl in my genetics class. We were talking about Garth's work, and she said – here, let me write it, it's more amusing that way.' On a paper napkin, Vivian wrote a single word and showed it to Sabrina.

'Gene-ius,' Sabrina read, and reread it. *Bingo*.

'Clever,' she said casually. 'What's her name?'

'Rita McMillan. And clever describes her. Not a good student, not at all interested in learning, but clever. The kind who finds shortcuts to get where she wants to go. Wherever that is. Now, tell me, does your somber face have anything to do with an anonymous letter about Garth?'

Sabrina was caught off guard. 'Have you seen it?'

'I wasn't even sure it existed until this minute. There are rumors all through the department. And some pasty-faced fellow is going around asking determinedly rude questions, which all of us are determinedly not answering. No one believes Garth is involved in that mess; he's not only too ethical, he's too smart. Tell me what's happening.'

Sabrina described Jenks's visit and the way Garth got rid of him. They laughed together and went on to talk about their jobs and the books they were reading.

'I'm due back at work,' Sabrina said at last. 'Oh, I almost forgot. Can we prevail on you once more to take Penny and

Cliff, for three days this time? Garth has a meeting in New York on December third, and he wants me to go along.'

'Of course I'll take them; they're wonderful to have around, and our kids love them. I think Barbara's secret wish is to be Penny Andersen. When will you leave?'

'I'll let you know. You're a good friend, Vivian.'

'I *have* good friends. I'm off to class. See you soon.'

'Vivian?'

'Yes?'

'Is that the class with Rita McMillan?'

'Yes; why?'

'Just curious. I enjoyed our lunch.'

Sabrina called Madeline and told her she would not be in for the rest of the day. 'Too bad,' Madeline said. 'You'd enjoy watching Linda – she's been following me around, examining different woods and carvings and memorizing shapes and construction techniques. She's a quick learner, and she's beginning to believe in herself. That was your good deed, bringing her here.' Yes, Sabrina agreed silently. And it will go on long after I've left.

She debated stopping at Garth's office to tell him about Rita, but she knew he would want to talk to the girl himself. *I* want to handle it, she thought. This is what I stayed here for – to do this for him, and for Stephanie.

Outside Vivian's classroom, at the end of the hour, Sabrina stopped a boy and asked him to point out Rita McMillan. When he did, she went directly to her.

'Stephanie Andersen.' She held out her hand. The girl, blonde and lithe, with pale blue eyes, reluctantly touched Sabrina's hand with limp fingers. 'I want to talk to you. The faculty club is across the street; we can be private there.'

'I don't think—'

'This is very important.' Smoothly, she steered Rita down the hall. 'I understand you studied genetics with my husband last year.'

She felt the quick alarm that brought a flush to the girl's face. Neither of them spoke again until they were in the faculty club. Sabrina had been there before with Garth, and the receptionist leaped up to greet her.

'Mrs. Andersen! How nice to see you again.' After a brief

426

glance at Rita, he turned to Sabrina with admiring eyes. 'Coffee hour begins in the living room in a few minutes; would you care for fruit or dessert?'

'Would it be possible to have tea?'

'Tea! Of course. There is no one upstairs now,' he added. 'You'll have it to yourself.'

Sabrina smiled at him, offering no clues to satisfy his curiosity. Upstairs, she led Rita to a corner of the long, high-ceilinged room, crowded with desks, couches and chairs. They sat in two wing chairs, almost touching. Sabrina, folding her hands in her lap, gazed steadily at Rita, taking her measure, noting the puzzlement in her round eyes. Not used to being ignored by men, she thought, while an older woman is admired. And how old I must seem to her, at thirty-two! It would be amusing if she hadn't tried to destroy Garth.

The girl was beginning to fidget under Sabrina's steady gaze. 'Well?' she demanded truculently. 'I'm here; what do you want?'

'I thought it would be a good idea for us to get acquainted. You're about to graduate, aren't you?'

'Yes,' Rita said, perched on the edge of the chair.

'But weren't you supposed to graduate last June?'

'I . . . changed my plans.'

'And what will you do after graduation?'

'I don't know. Travel, maybe get a job.'

'What kind of job?'

'I don't know. Something exciting. Designing clothes, maybe. Interior decorating. Something like that.'

'And become famous?'

'Sure; why not?'

'Your tea, Mrs Andersen.' The headwaiter from the dining room appeared with a rolling cart. Every afternoon the faculty club served rolls and coffee, but for Sabrina they had worked a miracle. 'Sliced jelly roll,' said the waiter, lifting a napkin with a flourish. 'Torte. Cookies. If there is something else you would prefer—'

'This is perfect,' Sabrina said, smiling at him. 'And very special. Thank you.'

He returned the smile, lingering a moment before crossing

the room to set up the coffee urn. Nat Goldner, walking through from the library on the third floor, stared in amazement at the cart as he greeted Sabrina with a kiss. 'Did you mesmerize the kitchen staff?'

'The magic word seems to be tea.'

'Not if I'm the one who says it. May I join you?'

'Not this time, Nat. Will you forgive us? This is a private talk.'

'Another time, then, if you promise to work your magic for me. And I gather we'll see you at Thanksgiving. Your house or ours?'

'I've convinced Dolores to make it ours.'

'I'll bring the wine.' He nodded to Rita and kissed Sabrina's cheek. 'See you soon.'

Rita had slid back in her chair, watching with undisguised envy. 'You sure wind them around your finger.'

'I treat people with respect,' Sabrina said gently, handing her a cup of tea. 'So,' she went on thoughtfully, 'you want to become famous. You'll make a lot of friends if you do.'

Rita nodded with satisfaction. 'I know.'

'But probably a few enemies, too. It seems that the more people you know, the more chances you have of making someone angry or jealous – without even realizing you're doing it.'

'I don't know anything about that.'

'Of course, I'm sure you'll have many more friends than enemies, but you have to be prepared for both. Because when you're famous, you never know how people feel about you, or how they talk about you to others. You're prepared for that, of course.'

'What?'

'For the fact that people might say things about you that aren't true.' Sabrina was relaxed now, her anger controlled. 'When that happens, we call it a rumor. You know about rumors; they're found everywhere. Did you ever wonder why they start? Sometimes for excitement or on a dare, sometimes for someone to feel important, sometimes just to see how people react, but probably most often for revenge. More tea?'

Rita's blue eyes were fixed on her. 'No.'

She filled her own cup. 'Of course, anyone interested in a career like dress designing or interior decoration would never take a chance of starting a rumor. After all, you know from your history classes that rumors have started wars and panics and revolutions ... who could ever trust someone who had started even one rumor? A dangerous person, careless with a whisper or a little joke – or an anonymous letter.'

The pale eyes blinked. 'Are you trying to scare me?'

'Why would I do that?'

'Because you don't like me.'

'I don't know you; I neither like nor dislike you.' Sabrina reached over to fill Rita's cup and met her wary eyes through the tendrils of steam rising between them. 'But it is true that our interests and loyalties have clashed.'

Rita looked uncomprehending.

'Your interest is what pleases you; your loyalty is to yourself. Ordinarily that would not concern me, since I find self-centered people boring and easily forgettable. But when your self-interest threatens my husband, in whom I have a strong interest and loyalty, that puts us on a collision course.'

'I don't know what you're talking about.' The pouting lips had turned sullen. 'You're crazy.'

'That was a mistake,' Sabrina said softly. 'You should not be antagonizing me, but trying to gain my sympathy.'

'I don't care about your—'

'Yes, you do. Or you should.' She leaned forward, holding the girl's eyes with her own. Her voice was low, but her words whipped like steel between them. 'Because I am going to expose you for what you are, and I am going to make it impossible for you to graduate.'

'You can't do that! There's no way you can do that! Just because your husband hates me—!'

'My husband hates you? Why?'

'Because ... because I wouldn't go to bed with him,' Rita said defiantly.

Sabrina shook her head slowly. 'You little fool. Couldn't you just once use your head instead of what you have between your legs? How long do you think you can buy your way by being a woman? How good a bargain can you get? And

429

how many friends will you have, when every time you sell yourself you make it harder for women who are relying on their brains?'

'He told you to say that; that's what he said to me last June.'

Sabrina pushed aside her cup. 'Now, you listen to me. My husband does not know I am talking to you. You are dealing with me, and we will settle this between us. But even if he knew I was here, he would not tell me what to say. *No one* tells me what to say. *I* decide what I will say, and I ask no one's permission. You would understand that if you believed in yourself as a person instead of a motorized sex machine.' She paused. 'But we were talking about other things, weren't we? Your graduation. Anonymous letters. And the kind of gene-ius who writes them.'

There was a long silence. Sabrina watched expressions move across Rita's face as the girl tried to think of a response and then slowly crumpled.

'Are you going to tell on me?'

Tell on me. As if she were three years old, Sabrina thought. 'What did you think I meant when I said I was going to expose you?'

'I didn't know. I didn't know you knew about the letters.' She waited. 'But you can't tell on me! They'd suspend me, or even expel me, and then I couldn't graduate!'

Exasperated, Sabrina said. 'Of course you can't graduate! I told you I would make it impossible.'

'But I have to graduate! My parents told me they wouldn't give me any more money if I didn't graduate this time. And I haven't got any of my own, so I have to graduate.'

Perfect logic, Sabrina thought. 'And how do you intend to graduate?'

'I have a C in my class, and that's all I need.'

'No, you also need to have me on your side.'

Nibbling a fingernail, Rita looked bewildered. 'But there's nothing I can do for you.'

'Think about it,' Sabrina suggested. 'Since I have no desire to go to bed with you, what might you offer that would interest me?'

Rita nibbled, glancing vaguely around the room, then

looked at Sabrina in dismay. 'You want me to tell them what I wrote isn't true! But then I'd have to say I wrote the letters! I can't do that! They'll kick me out! I won't graduate!'

'Well, I think that's negotiable,' Sabrina said with a sigh. 'I'll go with you to the vice president's office; if you confess the whole story, I'm sure the three of us can work something out.' She pushed the tea cart away and leaned closer to Rita. 'Now. Why don't we go over exactly what it is you are going to say?'

Snow fell again on Thanksgiving morning and continued all day. 'It's all right,' Dolores said briskly. 'We need the moisture. It was a dry summer and fall.'

'How grateful the snow must be,' Nat said, putting an affectionate arm around her shoulders. 'For your permission to keep on falling.'

Dolores smiled calmly. 'You'll notice I don't ask it to stop.' She winked at Linda as she went back to grinding cranberries.

Linda clutched Sabrina's arm. 'Did you see that?' she asked in an audible whisper. Her cheeks were crimson from the heat of the oven, and her black eyes were sparkling. 'Have you ever seen Dolores wink before?'

'No,' answered Sabrina honestly. She was cutting oranges and handing them to Dolores to be ground with the cranberries, while Linda grated nutmeg for the sweet potatoes. The pungent odors filled the warm kitchen, mingling with the pervasive smell of the stuffed turkey roasting in the oven and the spicy fragrance of cooling pumpkin pies. At the other end of the counter, Garth and Marty were making corn pudding from a recipe of Garth's great-grandmother's that he was trying to recall from memory as they went along, debating proportions and the scientific properties of baking soda and sour milk. Nat decanted wine and basted the turkey and circled the room, tasting everything.

Sabrina listened to the talk and laughter and breathed deeply, as if she could draw in the scents and sounds with her happiness and store them for the future. Since Gordon's doctor had ruled against his traveling, Sabrina was spared the sharp eye of her mother and could relax in a celebration of her first Thanksgiving dinner since she was fifteen. It was the first time she had spent such a day with a group of friends: cooking together, decorating the rooms with the flowers and Indian corn Dolores had brought, listening to the giggles and chatter of all their children setting the table while, outside, snowflakes fell, dark against the gray sky, piling in soft drifts on the ground. My first and my last, she thought, and it shouldn't even be mine; it should be Stephanie's day. Sadness slid through her happiness and a tear splashed on the orange she was cutting.

'I thought only onions did that,' Nat said, beside her. 'First time I ever saw oranges have that effect. Shall I take over?'

Sabrina shook her head. 'It will pass.'

'Mourning always does, though memories don't. You haven't had much time. And then you had this business with Garth to worry about. Which reminds me.' Picking up an open bottle of wine, he filled six glasses and handed them around the room. 'Ladies and gentlemen, I propose the first toast of the holiday, no doubt the first of many. We hope the first of many.' He paused as they turned to him. 'We have, of course, countless blessings, but at the moment three special ones, and so I offer a toast. To Marty Talvia, the new senior editor at Fairbanks Publishers, who will revolutionize textbooks by ensuring that they are written in English instead of jargon; and to Garth Andersen, for his victory over scurrilous lies that only a heteromorphic pinch-mouthed, dim-witted, imbecilic investigator would believe.'

'It means unnatural,' Marty said as Linda and Dolores demanded a definition. Looking up, Sabrina saw the six of them reflected in the dark window, close together in the honey-colored kitchen as the early winter night closed in. She held the picture with her eyes, fixing it in her mind. *Mourning passes; memories don't. I'll have my memories. Of Stephanie. And of her friends and family. Because, for a little while, they were my friends and family, too.*

'But what's the third blessing?' Dolores asked.

Nat turned to Garth. 'Your turn.'

'My wife,' Garth said, and took Sabrina's hand. 'Who discovered our anonymous letter-writer and, through a

432

conversation she will not describe to me, cowed the young woman into accompanying her quite meekly to Lloyd Strauss's office, where a full confession was written in ink and signed. And who kept her promise to the letter-writer by convincing Lloyd he should allow her to graduate. And who then, after the young woman departed – Lloyd told me this himself – gave him a scolding he will not soon forget and stood over him while he read a statement to his secretary to be telephoned to the media. And who finally, as Lloyd also told me, refused to leave until he set the date for the announcement of my appointment as director of the Genetics Institute.'

He touched his glass to Sabrina's. 'My wife. My dearest love.'

Linda's eyes brimmed with tears. 'Stephanie, you never said a word. That's the most wonderful story I ever heard.'

'Poor Lloyd,' Nat said wryly. 'Facing Stephanie's wrath. He must have been terrified.'

'He deserved it,' said Dolores scornfully.

'I wish,' Linda said to Marty, her voice low, 'I wish I'd done something that wonderful for you.'

'You did,' he said. 'You stayed with me.'

In the golden, fragrant room, Sabrina lay her palm against Garth's cheek. 'I love you.'

He put his arms around her, his mouth close to hers. 'My life, my world, my whole being.'

She closed her eyes. *I can't, I can't; don't make me leave him.*

In a moment, she opened her eyes. 'I have a toast, too.'

'I should hope so,' said Nat. 'My glass is empty.' Her tears were gone, he saw; she looked magnificent. Stunningly beautiful – strange how they all got used to it and then suddenly would see her as if for the first time and be taken aback by her beauty. Today, flushed from the heat of the kitchen, her hair casually held back by a gold band, she was at once a lovely woman and a young girl radiantly in love. And why not, after Garth's words? Looking at her, it was hard to believe in the confused, incoherent, grieving woman Garth had described after the funeral. But Nat still heard her stumble occasionally, thinking of herself as Sabrina, and he knew she had not yet resolved her confusion – though at the moment she seemed to know exactly who she was.

Thinking about her, he had missed her toast. To Garth, he gathered, for being elected to the National Genetics Research Advisory Council. A high honor for a man not yet forty; no wonder they were pleased.

'—Council meeting next week in New York,' Garth was saying.

'Stephanie, too?' Linda asked. 'But the estate sale—'

'Madeline will help you,' Sabrina said. 'And I'll work with you this week, before I leave. You've learned so much; you'll be wonderful and you know it. Madeline thinks you're amazing. And so do I.'

'Mom, we're starved!' Cliff said, coming into the kitchen. 'When do we eat?'

'My God, the bird!' Nat cried. 'I've abandoned my duties as a baster.' He opened the oven. 'When *do* we eat?'

'One hour,' Dolores said. 'If Garth and Marty get that corn concoction in the oven right away.'

'Can we have some pretzels?' Cliff asked.

'Go easy,' said Sabrina. 'There's a feast ahead of us.'

As everyone moved about the kitchen to different tasks, she took a quick glance at the window. It was smooth and dark; all the reflections were gone.

After dinner the next night Sabrina climbed the stairs to the third floor and sat at Stephanie's desk. The room was bare but no longer dusty; Juanita's determined hand had been at work. And its sad air of defeat was gone, too; it was just a room where projects had been stored and now were about to be revived. She emptied the drawers of the records and photographs Stephanie had kept from her estate business and slipped them into large envelopes for Linda. In the years to come, she would continue the business that Stephanie had begun.

In the strange quiet, so rare in that house, Sabrina looked at the pile of envelopes. One by one she was completing the unfinished pieces of Stephanie's life. Cliff was free of his gang and so relieved about it that he was tolerating almost cheerfully a month of restrictions. He had gone to Garth with the whole story, and the two of them had reached their own understanding; all Sabrina knew about it was Garth's comment later, in bed. 'Someday Cliff will appreciate what you've done for the two of us, helping us to be friends. I appreciate it now. I appreciate *you*.'

She had seen Garth through the ugliness of the anonymous letters; the story already was fading and he was deep in discussions with architects and contractors on the new Genetics Institute. She had helped Linda when she needed it, as Stephanie would have done. Soon Penny's art classes would begin, and next month the costumes she had designed and made would be seen in the class puppet show—

I won't see it. And I promised—

'Mom? You coming down?' 'In a few minutes, Cliff,' she called. Opening the desk drawers to make sure nothing was left behind, she ran her hand to the back of each one. They were all empty. Picking up the envelopes, she reached for the light to turn it off.

'Mom!'

'Yes, Cliff, right—'

'Telephone, Mom! From London!'

London? At this hour? Something must have happened; it was three in the morning there; who would call—?

She swept up the envelopes and ran downstairs to the telephone in the bedroom.

'Mrs Andersen, this is Michel Barnard; we met at Sabrina's funeral, if you remember.'

'Of course, I remember. What is it? Ambassadors? Has something happened—?'

'No, it's something else. We wanted you to know as soon as we did. We heard today from Scotland Yard that Ivan Lazlo and Rory Carr have been arrested for placing a bomb on Max Stuyvesant's yacht. It seems they—'

'Wait. Please, wait a minute.'

'Oh damnation – forgive me – Jolie told me not to rush into – hey!'

'Mrs Andersen, this is Jolie Fantome. Michel is a boor and I apologize for him. This not the way to tell you.'

Sabrina sat on the edge of the bed. 'It's all right; I knew

there had been a bomb; it was just suddenly hearing it. It all seems so far away from here. What else have they found?'

'This is what we know. It will all be in our story when it is published in December. You know about Max Stuyvesant's smuggling? And that Lazlo and Carr stored his smuggled goods and also had a little sideline of selling forged art mixed in with the real thing? You know all that from Sabrina?'

'Yes. But what about Ambassadors?'

'Almost nothing. It is listed in the books at Westbridge as a customer; but reporters want drama, and a few forged art works are not dramatic. The reporters are interested in Lazlo and Carr because they put a bomb on Stuyvesant's yacht. *That* is dramatic. And it has nothing to do with Ambassadors.'

'But it does. If Sabrina was killed because of what she knew—'

'No, that is not correct. We thought you feared that, but we could not say for sure you were wrong. Now we can. Carr and Lazlo are babbling on and on, blaming each other for everything, but it all comes down to a quarrel with Stuyvesant over the forgeries; he said they could be discovered, which would open the door to exposing his smuggling operation. Carr and Lazlo thought he was planning to get rid of them, so they simply beat him to it.'

'It wasn't Sabrina – it was Max they were after?'

'That is what I'm telling you. Years ago, Lazlo spent some time on the *Lafitte* as Stuyvesant's secretary and also doing a little smuggling for him, making deliveries along the Italian Riviera.'

A boat, Sabrina remembered, near dawn, when she had gone on deck for some air and to get away from Denton. Ivan Lazlo in a motorboat, helped on board by a crew member, disappearing down the stairs to the crew's quarters without seeing her.

'So,' Jolie went on, 'he knew some of the crew members still there from those days, and he went aboard to see them in the Monte Carlo harbor. At some time while he was there he put a bomb in the stateroom. It went off too soon, he had not set it properly, which is why the boat was only two miles out and the French divers were able to raise it so quickly.

Otherwise, we might never have known it was not an accident.'

'They killed all those people—'

'They didn't care. They wanted it to look like an accident.' There was a pause. 'Stephanie, does this make you feel better or worse?'

'A little of each.'

'I thought it might. They were an unpleasant bunch, but Stuyvesant had great charm and knew the art world better than anyone. He and Sabrina had known each other for years; she decorated his London house; and we think she may have gone on the cruise on legitimate business, perhaps to buy for her gallery. He had been at Chilton and all the major fall auctions; he would have had a good selection for her to choose from. Honestly come by.'

She is defending Sabrina Longworth to her American sister, thought Sabrina. Explaining her presence on that yacht. 'Thank you,' she said. 'I'm grateful for that.'

Jolie talked on, mentioning casually that Sabrina's little friend Gabrielle had been seen several times at dinner with Brooks Westermarck; Sabrina was grateful for that, too. Life goes on, Jolie was saying, and yours will, too. 'Goodbye, then,' Jolie said.

'Thank you,' said Sabrina. 'And thank Michel.'

'Oh, Michel I shall strike on the rump for being so abrupt with you.'

A small laugh broke from Sabrina. Those two, she thought affectionately, as she used to think when she was Sabrina and lived in London. She wondered if the three of them could be as close now that she was Stephanie as they had been when she was Sabrina.

The pile of envelopes lay on the bed beside her. Tomorrow she would give it to Linda. And that would mean there was nothing left for her to do. There was not even an obstacle to her returning to London anymore: the forgery story was public and Ambassadors was not part of it; she needn't fear damage to its reputation or to Sabrina's memory. Nor was she in any personal danger; in fact, she never had been.

Nothing was left for her to do; there was no longer any reason for her to stay.

'Mom? Is everything all right?'

She steadied her voice. 'Yes, Cliff. Everything is all right.'

'Could we have a quick game of Monopoly then?'

'There is no such thing as a quick game of Monopoly. That's a ploy to stay up until midnight. How about Scrabble?'

'Sure. Are you coming now?'

'Right away.'

No reason for her to stay. She sat on the bed and felt time slow down, everything slow down, coming gradually to an end. Around her, every object was clear and sharp; ordinary pieces of furniture seemed to glow and burn themselves into her memory, joining the pictures from Thanksgiving. One last chance to memorize them so that when she closed her eyes she could see them still and know she would for a long time to come. In three days, on Monday, she would leave. First to New York with Garth and then, alone, to London. Stephanie Andersen going home to Sabrina Longworth's life.

We'll always be here, Garth had said; an unfinished story.

The one part of Stephanie's life, and my life, that I cannot finish.

Two half-finished lives, Garth had said.

Yes. But still better than wounding you with the truth. Or living a lie with you, founded on my sister's death.

'Mom!'

Don't think about it. Enjoy these last few days. 'Yes, Cliff,' she said, and went downstairs.

Later Sabrina would remember those three days as a haze of voices and gestures. She would try to recall single moments, but they slipped from her. All she had was the blurred memory of a time when her feelings swung wildly from piercing happiness to dark despair, and the hours escaped her as she tried to hold them back.

On Friday night Lloyd Strauss hosted a dinner for university trustees, faculty members and scientists from around the country. Penny and Cliff were there, sitting near the front, awed by the talk about their father and the glowing elegance of their mother in an antique gold full-skirted dress with a matching short embroidered jacket. The room was brightly lit and crowded. 'Lloyd's apology,' Garth said, amused but touched. 'For our investigative friend.'

Watching, saying little, Sabrina let the evening carry her along, loving Garth for his quiet acceptance of praise from scientists older and more famous than he and congratulations from trustees and faculty members. After dinner, sitting at the head table, she listened to the president describe Garth's background – telling her much she never knew about him – and then make the formal announcement of his appointment as director of the new Genetics Institute.

Keeping her face serene through the applause and flashes from reporters' cameras, Sabrina thought, I helped this happen. It all may have happened without me, but I helped. He will always have that to remember.

Beside her, Garth stood and made a brief speech on his goals for the Institute and its staff and thanked those who were helping make it a reality. 'But in my smaller, personal sphere,' he added, 'I want to thank two people who helped me reach this night. Lloyd Strauss, who has balanced friendship and his responsibility to the university as few others could, and my wife, who has never failed me in love and encouragement and in challenging me to look as far and as high as possible without losing sight of the wonders of our family and our life together.' He looked down at Sabrina's shining eyes. 'Stephanie Andersen.'

Everyone stood, applauding, as Garth sat down and took Sabrina's hand. 'Who is also,' he added to her alone, beneath the applause, 'the most desirable woman I have ever known, and whom I would much rather be in bed with than in this large and very public room.'

She laughed, buoyant with joy and love. 'Soon,' she promised. 'As soon as I can seduce you from all your other admirers.' Nothing was real but Garth's eyes on hers, his hand holding hers, his lips lightly on hers before the university president took him away to talk to a local businessman who wanted to contribute to the Institute building fund.

That was all she remembered of that night, though she talked to dozens of people, and later, when the children were in bed, she and Garth made love. They made love as they had learned to in these last weeks; slowly, leisurely, as if all the time in the world was theirs, savouring each urgent moment as they came wondrously alive, still exploring, still learning what they could give and share and take from each other.

But she only remembered the rightness of it, the sense of completeness, not the individual moments when they filled each other's vision and nothing else mattered. Those moments were blurred, part of the darkness of the night and the glaring brightness of the morning when Penny and Cliff woke them with a reminder of the weekend's plans.

'You didn't forget! We're going cross-country skiing at the Goldners'!'

'There is a difference,' Garth said sternly from his pillow, his hand, beneath the covers, on Sabrina's breast, 'between forgetting and beginning one's weekend at a civilized hour.' But, urged on by the children, they bestirred themselves, and within a short time were on their way to Michigan.

Dolores and Nat had been inviting them to their country house at Lakeside in the dunes since Thanksgiving. When the time came, Sabrina had not wanted to go. *I want it to be just the four of us; it's the last weekend we'll ever have together.* But she could not say that, and Penny and Cliff were so excited that she gave in.

The weekend was as blurred as the rest of those last few days. Her memory could recapture the whiteness: snow-covered dunes against a pale sky, the lake shining like pewter under the slanting rays of the sun, the white shadows of their ski tracks snaking up and down the low slopes. She could recall Garth's face close to hers when the children had pulled ahead and they were alone, her mouth opening beneath his and his whispered 'I love you' before Nat and Dolores caught up to them. She remembered a lazy dinner before the Goldners' huge fireplace and quiet talk late into the night, the four of them watching the flames die to glowing, shimmering coals. And she could remember the freezing bedroom where she and Garth undressed quickly and slipped into the icy bed, shivering, until the two of them, clasped in each other's arms, grew warm, and, almost without moving, Garth was inside her.

But that was all, except for the sharp pain of happiness and the dull despair that lay just beneath it.

Early Monday morning, they packed for the New York trip and said goodbye to Penny and Cliff at breakfast. 'Don't forget,' Sabrina said. 'After school you go to the Goodmans' house.'

'Mom,' said Cliff, 'you've told us that fifty times. That's what we did when you went to Connecticut, so how come you think we'll forget?'

'I don't like the idea of your coming home to an empty house.'

'We won't, I told you. We're not babies.'

'I know.' She smoothed Penny's curls and straightened the strap of her jumper. 'It's just that I'm going to miss you—' Her voice broke, and she turned abruptly away.

'Mom?' Cliff was alarmed; she could hear it in his voice as Garth came into the kitchen.

'Something wrong?' he asked.

'I think Mom's sick.'

Garth moved quickly toward her, but Sabrina stood up before he reached her. 'Small upset stomach,' she said lightly. 'Nothing that breakfast won't cure.'

He studied her face. 'Nothing else?'

'Nothing else.'

They bustled about. 'You'll remember—'

'—to go to the Goodmans',' Cliff and Penny said together, and they all laughed.

'Mom,' said Cliff, 'could you get me a suit of armor in England?'

'A suit of—Cliff, do you know what they weigh?'

'No, how much?'

'Over a hundred pounds. Knights had to be lifted onto their horses with a crane.'

'How come the horse didn't fall down under them?' Penny asked.

'That would have been a knightmare,' said Cliff and collapsed, laughing, on the floor.

'Not bad,' said Garth, chuckling. 'Now get yourself together before you're late for school. And we have a plane to catch, Stephanie. Are you almost ready?'

'Yes. Just these dishes—'

Garth was upstairs and Penny and Cliff were in their coats when she found them at the living room door. Penny gripped her with both arms. 'Don't stay in England long.' She dropped her voice to a whisper. 'Daddy said not to nag you, there are things you have to do, but you have things here, too. You won't stay long, will you?'

Sabrina kissed Penny's smooth cheek and held her close. 'I don't want to. I don't want to leave you at all. I love you, my Penny. Don't ever forget that. I love you and I'm proud of you. You are my very special girl.'

'Mom,' Cliff said. 'We're late. Can I kiss you goodbye?'

She tried to let Penny go, but her arms would not move. *Don't go. Please don't go.*

'Mommy, don't cry,' said Penny. Her hand began to pat Sabrina's shoulder. 'You'll be back soon. Don't cry.'

'I didn't mean to. I guess trips sometimes do that to people. Your turn, Cliff.'

He gave her a quick hug. 'If you can't bring me some armor, could you get me a sword like King Arthur's?'

She laughed shakily. 'I'll find you something. Does it have to be destructive?'

'Well, since I'm reading about King Arthur . . . '

'I'll see what I can do. Cliff, take . . . take care of Penny and yourself, will you?'

'Sure. I always do. You'll bring her something, too, won't you?'

'I'll send presents as soon as I get there. How will that be?'

'Okay. 'Bye, Mom. Have a good trip.' He kissed her cheek. Sabrina put her arms around him and kissed him on both cheeks. 'The French do it that way,' he said.

'I do, too,' said Sabrina, kissing him again. 'I'm going to miss you, my star soccer-player. Especially your awful puns. And your dear face and smile—'

'Come on, Mom!'

'Sorry,' she said, wiping her eyes. 'I didn't mean to start up again. Off with you now, or you really will be late. Have a good time at the Goodmans' and give my love to Vivian.'

They ran down the walk. Sabrina watched them. At the corner they turned and waved. She raised her arm and waved back and watched them disappear through the mist of tears in her eyes.

Chapter 20

The streets of New York were slick with rain. Lunchtime crowds scurried under black umbrellas that bobbed and bumped against each other like an awning whipped by the wind. Young boys and old men sat in doorways selling umbrellas for those who had left home unprepared, and messengers on bicycles were almost hidden in ballooning yellow slickers that dripped rain onto the puddles in the street.

Sitting in the taxicab with Garth, Sabrina thought of winter tears, cold and gray, dropping from the dark clouds that had settled on the tops of skyscrapers. Windows shone as if it were night. In front of every hotel a doorman raised his arm, as if saluting a parade, and blew his whistle to stop a cab in flight, but none stopped; they all had passengers.

'Don't matter, though,' their driver grumbled as they sat in the middle of a crosstown street, immobilized by a mass of traffic. 'Sun shines, nobody rides. It rains, everybody rides but nobody moves.'

'Shall we buy an umbrella and walk?' Garth asked Sabrina.

'Helluva long walk, mister,' the driver answered.

'I know. I used to teach there.'

'You hold on and keep dry. We get to the corner we're all right. Uptown is faster than crosstown.'

'I know.'

'Right. You useta teach there. My kid teaches third grade. She likes it, but she don't make much.'

Garth looked at Sabrina, but she was gazing out the window on her side. She had barely spoken since they had left home. On the plane, he had asked what she would like to do in New York, but she had answered briefly and absently, and he knew she was barely aware of him. Thinking of London, of her sister's life. Of adopting that life? He had no idea and would not ask her. If it came to that, he would find her wherever she was and try to bring her back, but he would not anticipate a crisis where, so far, none existed. If the bond with her sister was so strong it withstood death, he would not try to break it, even if he thought he could, unless he saw it destroying his marriage.

'Have you bought your ticket?' he asked as lunch was being served, and she looked surprised.

'No. I've ... been so busy. I will in New York.'

When they reached the Plaza, Garth watched her face. 'Oh,' she said. 'I didn't know, you didn't tell me—'

'We had a very special night here about six weeks ago. I liked the idea of coming back.'

'Yes.' She looked at him, her eyes so lonely he cried out. 'My love, what is it?'

He watched the effort she made to push her thoughts aside, and he marveled at her strength, even more because at other times he had seen it fail her. She took his arm as the bellhop unlocked the door of their room. 'What are you going to do now?' she asked.

'You and I are going for a quick visit to Columbia. I want to poke my nose into my first lab and have a moment of nostalgia. For both of us.' When she made no response, he said, 'Do you want to unpack? Hang some things in the closet?'

'Not now.'

Garth surveyed the room. 'Not the suite the Kallens provided, but it will do very well. I'm looking forward to crushing chocolates on the pillow again.'

'And losing one on the floor,' she murmured, remembering with a small smile. 'Shall we go?'

In the rain, it took them an hour to get to Columbia, but

they still had time to visit the lab before Garth's lecture to a graduate seminar. 'A favor to an old friend,' he said as they entered the building. 'Since my meeting isn't until tomorrow, he asked if I'd mind dispensing wisdom to his students for a couple of hours this afternoon. You can sit in, or would you rather shop?'

'Shop, I think. There are some antique dealers I'd like to meet.'

'Then I'll meet you at the hotel about five-thirty or six.'

They rode the elevator to the fourth floor. 'Quieter than the last time you were here,' said Garth.

Sabrina had no idea what he was talking about. A month ago, a week ago, she would have tried to cover her ignorance, but now it seemed unimportant. She had said goodbye to the children and had taken a last walk through the house; now she could feel herself withdrawing steadily from Garth. In an hour she would buy her ticket for London and tomorrow she would tell him she would not be coming back.

She walked ahead of him into the laboratory, a large room partitioned down the center by tall steel cabinets. They went to one side, and Garth looked at the bare soapstone bench. 'Gone are the Tinkertoys. Ah, but look there. They don't get rid of me so easily.'

Still not understanding him, Sabrina followed his gaze and saw on the wall framed drawings that did indeed look like Tinkertoy constructions. Now she knew what he meant: models of molecules. She had seen others like them in his lab at Midwestern.

'I did those just before I left,' he said. 'They still look pretty good. But how little we knew then; what incredible miles we've traveled in twelve years! Let's see what Bill's successor is up to.'

On the other side of the cabinets, Sabrina saw cages of scampering white mice stacked on a wall beside a large window. 'Not a bit different,' Garth said, smiling. 'I think Bill may still be on the premises. He may even still have a stock of tweezers and gauze bandages for unexpected wounds.'

Sabrina was looking at the mice. 'I wonder if that window

seems like protection, or a view of a world they can't ever touch.'

'Give me your hand,' Garth said roughly.

Puzzled, she held it out to him. 'Why?'

'To see if I can jog your memory.'

'Jog my—' Mentally, she shook herself. 'I'm sorry, please forgive me; I'm being absentminded and rude.' Her hand, held out to him, was trembling. 'Shall we reenact the scene? *I'll do the best I can; just give me some clues.*

'No, we don't need to relive the past. I do remember, though, how you looked when I told you I wanted to marry you and make love to you.'

'How?' she asked faintly.

'As if I'd given you a gift. Your eyes were red and swollen from that damn tear gas, but they shone so brightly that I remember wondering how a pair of midnight-blue eyes could look as if they held the sun within them. And then you frowned, as if you were wondering what gift to give me in return.'

'And what did I give you?'

'Yourself. The most I have ever wanted. And what incredible miles *we've* traveled since that day.' He drew her to him and kissed her. 'Stephanie, whatever is troubling you, I promise you we'll remedy it. Two such fine gift-givers have no place in their life for troubles.'

'Good God, would you believe it?' A tall gray-bearded man with horn-rimmed glasses came into the lab. 'It isn't enough they have their own bedroom; they still make out in the lab. What an example for the younger generation!' He stretched out his hands to Sabrina. 'Rolf Taggart. I thought Garth was exaggerating when he described you in his letters. Now I find he didn't do you justice. Welcome.' He shook Garth's hand. 'And welcome home.'

Garth smiled. 'Rolf does not admit I could have another home, even after twelve years.'

'I still miss you, even after twelve years; best researcher I ever worked with. Are you prepared to face the sharp questioning of my sharpest students?'

'Probably not, but I'll do my best. Stephanie, five-thirty at the hotel? Six at the latest.'

'I'll be there. I hope it goes well.'

As she took the elevator to the cabstand, Rolf said, 'Garth, she's stunning, but that pallor . . . is she ill?'

'She's troubled about going to London. I'm not sure why.' In their correspondence over the years, Garth had written to Rolf about matters he could not discuss with Nat or Marty, simply because it often was easier to confide in a friend one did not see every day. But he could not tell Rolf, any more than anyone else, that his wife might still be thinking of leaving him. 'She's always identified strongly with her sister; as long as I've known her she's had fantasies about being Sabrina, or at least living her kind of life. Now, since Sabrina's death, she's been confused, off and on, about whether she's Stephanie or Sabrina. As if she feels a compulsion to live both their lives or choose between them. But lately, in the most extraordinary way, we'd finally come together, found each other for the first time in the way all of us dream of—'

Garth rubbed his forehead. They had reached the door of the seminar room, and he looked apologetically at his friend. 'I didn't come here for a therapy session, Father Rolf. Why didn't you stop me?'

'Because you needed to talk and I wanted to hear. But now there's this damn seminar. Can you face these young animals whose favorite sport is trying to show professors youth knows more than middle age?'

Garth squared his shoulders. 'Let's show them our tricks.'

The room was full; Garth's name was a magnet. He looked at the sixty faces before him, alert and expectant, and felt renewed. However unsure he felt about his future with Stephanie, here in this room he was absolutely confident and excited about the contact with students. Pacing back and forth, he talked easily, relaxed and humorous, but technical; he did not talk down to students. At the same time, he made them feel they were part of a community of scientists, free to ask questions or make comments as he talked.

It was almost four-thirty when he paused and then said, casually, 'I want to talk now about immortal antibodies.' A stir went through the class; the phrase caught their imagination, and the inflection in Garth's voice told them it was something big. He let the suspense build, enjoying it.

'What we are working on,' he said, leaning on the desk with both hands, 'is the ability to make the human immune system immortal. That implies exactly what you think it does: perpetual production of antibodies. We are looking at the potential for fusing two human cells – one that produces antibodies and one that reproduces itself forever. The result is a hybrid that will produce an endless supply of antibodies, vastly strengthening the body's natural defense system, which, by itself, often is not effective. In other words, an immortal immune system. In addition, the antibodies would be used to make a broad spectrum of vaccines against disease.'

A hand went up. 'Sir, hasn't this kind of cell fusion been done in mice?'

Garth nodded. 'For about ten years. But you know that when we treat human disease with vaccines made from animal antibodies, there are drastic side effects. Those of you who've had the vaccine for rabies, which is made from horse antibodies, know how painful it is. But humans can accept human antibodies, as they do in blood transfusions, without those side effects. When we perfect the technology, we expect to produce unlimited amounts of them, specific to various diseases.'

'Which ones, sir?'

'At the moment, tetanus, erythroblastosis – a cause of jaundice in babies – and malignancy of the white blood cells in children, or childhood leukemia. We're probably seven or eight years away from availability of these vaccines for treatment, but clinical tests may begin within a couple of years.'

'Professor, what chemical is used to fuse the cells?'

'Ethylene glycol, inexpensive and readily available.'

'Sir, have you compared actual nucleotide sequences between the original hybrid and succeeding ones to determine that they are truly identical? How many generations have you followed, and what methods do you use to keep track of the original hybrid cell?'

There's always a show-off, Garth thought, trying to

448

impress the professor and the class. 'We've compared a number of the DNA nucleotide sequences through several generations, and so far they've been found to be identical in every respect. With identical cells, there is, as you point out, the problem of distinguishing the original from the copy. We've found the most efficient method is to use a radioactive tracer to give the original cell a special identification. This is sufficient, even when all other aspects are identical, to distinguish it from a copy—'

He stopped. The words echoed in his mind: Distinguish it from a copy. Original. Identical. Copy. Distinguish the original from – Identical. Copy. Identical. Original. Copy...

A blank look in the laboratory; no recollection of tear gas and a cut hand. Wine before dinner. 'I don't want you to take the job at Foster Labs.' Deflating Irma Kallen. Intimidating Mrs Casey and Rita McMillan. Hiring a maid, taking a new job, without discussion. 'It wasn't Sabrina who died . . . ' A funeral: 'I'm Sabrina . . . ' China. *China*.

The copy can be determined from the original.

'Professor Andersen has another appointment.' Rolf was at his side – where had he come from? – completing the answer to the question, bringing the seminar smoothly to a close. The students were standing, applauding. A few came up with questions poised on their lips, but Rolf turned them away. 'A tight schedule, not this time, perhaps a return visit . . . ' And then they were alone in the empty room.

'Come on. I'll get you to a doctor.'

Slowly, Garth focused on him. 'Do I look that bad?'

'Like you'll pass out any moment. Where's the pain? Chest? Arm?'

He laughed shortly. 'Head and heart. But not a heart attack, Rolf. Just an attack of reality; enough to wake me up.' He looked at the high dark windows, raindrops running crazily down their length, and heard his voice go on and on. He could not stop it. 'Amazing, isn't it, how we keep ourselves deluded long past the time when we should have forced our eyes open? We see things, we hear them, and they don't fit, but we force them to make sense, we push them into the shapes we want, we don't even allow ideas to reach the

449

surface of our minds because they're impossible to accept, too awful to contemplate. I sound like a psychologist. Maybe I'm in the wrong profession. God knows I'm in the wrong marriage.'

'Garth, what the hell—!'

'Oh, fuck it, don't pay any attention to my ravings, Rolf. I have no right to burden you with a delayed awakening. I'm going for a walk; think some things out.'

'In this rain? And aren't we meeting later, for dinner?'

'Not tonight. Rolf, I let you down. I'm sorry. The seminar—'

'The seminar was terrific. An abrupt ending, but that wasn't important. You can't tell me about your waking up? Sometimes it's easier to have the eyes forced open if a friend shares the view.'

'I can't. I'm not even sure I'm right. But there may be a time ... I'll let you know.' They shook hands. 'I owe you another seminar.' 'Forget it. Let me get you a cab.'

'I'll find one.'

But there were no cabs. The rain was as steady as before, and, after walking a few blocks, he gave up and ran down the subway stairs. He stood on the platform, jostled by riders positioning themselves to leap through the train doors when they opened. The air smelled of wet wool. He was in no hurry; he stepped back.

He could be wrong. He had no proof. Scientists insist on proof or overwhelming evidence. Observation, controlled experiments, documentation, replication. All he had was the sudden flood of light that had blinded him in the seminar room, as if a curtain had been ripped aside. Everything fit together; he was certain she was Sabrina.

There were no empty seats on the train. He stood in the packed aisle, swaying, grasping the steel loop above his head, shaped like a hangman's noose, he noted, or a teardrop. Fooled him. How well she had fooled him. The scientist, the careful observer, with an international reputation for the purity of his experiments and the thoroughness of his documentation. Couldn't even tell he was living with his wife's twin sister. Sleeping with his wife's twin sister. Excused her mistakes; convinced himself she was trying to

450

improve their marriage; gave her the benefit of every doubt; helped her make a fool of him. Again and again, helped her make a fool of him, *helped her* and loved her while doing it.

Fool.

In the hotel lobby he slowed his steps. But it was only when he was in the crowded elevator, stopping at every floor, that the full impact hit him and he doubled over as if struck in the stomach.

His wife was dead.

'You getting off here?'

Garth looked up. The elevator doors had opened at his floor and a young girl was holding them back with her hand.

'Yes,' he said hoarsely. He cleared his throat. 'Thank you.'

She watched him shuffle along the flowered carpet. 'You got somebody to take care of you?'

'Yes. Thank you.' No. No one. But it doesn't concern anyone else. Only Sabrina and me.

Outside the door of their room, he leaned against the wall. Cold tremors ran down his legs and arms and crushed his chest; his breath came in gasps. He stood there, in that frozen vise, waiting for the tremors to stop. Guests passed with curious glances. A waiter pushed a cart loaded with drinks and hors d'oeuvres to a room down the hall. And from the other side of the door beside him, Garth heard the telephone ring, and heard it answered. So she was there. Waiting for him.

He stood away from the wall. He had to face her. He might, after all, be wrong. An infinitesimal, unscientific hope. He put his key in the door and went in.

Sabrina was curled up in a chair beside the window. Lamplight turned her hair red-gold and her skin a pale translucence; she looked fragile and vulnerable, and reflexively Garth's arms began to reach out to her. *No!* he cried silently, and stayed beside the door as Sabrina said, 'Rolf called, wondering how you—'

She stopped as she saw the set of his mouth and the deep lines of his face. And she knew that he knew the truth. Briefly she wondered how he had discovered it. Her stupidity in the lab that afternoon, some other mistake or, at last, his analytical mind putting everything together? What difference did it make? It was too late to make a difference.

She was frightened, but she also felt a strange sense of relief. It was out of her hands. She had not been able to tell him herself, but *she had wanted him to find out;* she wanted to leave with the truth between them, not layer upon layer of lies . . .

The silence stretched like a fuse between them. They were hesitating, each reluctant to say the words that would alter their lives forever. At last Garth walked stiffly to a floor lamp and turned it on. 'No shadows. We've had enough shadows, haven't we, Sabrina?'

She did not recognize her name on his lips; it was a stranger's name.

No, not a stranger's. Her own. A stranger to Garth.

'Well?' he asked, and she heard in his voice the desperate thread of hope that perhaps he was wrong.

'No,' she said, so quietly he had to strain to hear her. 'You aren't wrong.'

'Sabrina.'

'Yes.'

His body spun about, as if flung by an explosion, and he strode the length of the room and back, not looking at her. 'What was it, a game? You wanted to play housewife for awhile and needed an instant family, some simpletons who would lie back and play dumb and let you walk all over them? Life was dull in London, so you told your rich friends to hold the fort while you dabbled in genteel poverty? Nothing like a little diversion, is there, to make the time pass more—'

'Garth, stop it, stop, please stop, it isn't true, none of it—'

'And the professor, the stuffy professor, does tricks, sits up and begs for Lady Sabrina Longworth while she plays him for a fool. The greatest fool of all time.'

'Please, that isn't—'

He kicked his suitcase aside. 'Now why would the Lady Sabrina do that? What did she want? Just to play housewife? Probably not. She wanted something more. What could that

452

be?' He perched on the arm of a sofa near Sabrina. 'Could it be, could it possibly be, that she wanted to show up her sister at being a housewife? Was that it? Lady Longworth, bored with her rich friends, decided to show her sister there was nothing she couldn't do. She'd already beat her at everything else – money, success, freedom, lovers ... oh, my God ...' His voice trailed away and he stared vacantly at his hands, opening and closing them as if reminding himself they had nothing to hold. 'Stephanie is dead. My wife is dead. *You knew that.* You stood beside me at her funeral. *You let me bury my wife and never told me what I was doing.*' He stood over her, and she shrank back in her chair. 'You damn bitch, how could you stand there while they put that coffin in its grave and *not tell us who was in it?*'

'I told you! I tried to tell you! You wouldn't listen to me, I told you I was Sabrina—!'

He began to pace again. 'You did. Now that is true. How hard did you try? How many times? *How soon after the news came of her death?*'

As he heard himself say it, he flinched and his body froze, while a jumble of images tore through his mind: Penny and Cliff laughing, their upturned faces filled with trust; his family at dinner, listening as he talked about his work; Thanksgiving and a kitchen crowded with friends; a cemetery, a coffin, Stephanie trembling within the curve of his arm ... no, damn it, no – not Stephanie; Stephanie was dead; he had comforted Sabrina and watched the Vicar bury his wife. 'My God, you took that telephone call, you flew with us to London, you spent two days before the funeral weeping prettily and never told us, *never told us* who was dead.'

'That's enough! How dare you!' She leaped up and stood beside the window, her head high. 'Whatever else happened, how dare you imply I was not really mourning my sister? How dare you accuse me of taking her place to show her I was better than she was? I wasn't better, I never thought I was; we were the same, we were part of each other and I loved her more than anyone in the world. I loved her more than you did – at least I cared about her as a person and not just as *a wife;* I wanted her to have love and attention, and you gave her neither; you were so wrapped up in yourself you barely looked at her for years, you didn't listen to her . . . oh, Garth, I'm sorry, I'm sorry, I don't mean that. I know it was more complicated than that, things are never so simple between two people. . . . But I loved her so, and I miss her, and we never intended any of this, we thought it would just be a week—'

'We? What are you talking about?' Pacing the room, he touched each piece of furniture as if they were the only solid supports in his shifting world. 'Stephanie would never be a part of a filthy trick—'

'Of course she was; how else would we change places? I'm sorry, I didn't want you to know, I didn't want you hurt—'

'Hurt! Are you mad? After weeks of lying to me, playing me for a fool, you didn't want me hurt?'

'I know how it sounds.' She looked through the cold window at the lights of the city, distorted by the rain. 'But I told you, we never expected it to last more than a week. Stephanie felt she had to get away for a few days, to think about problems with Cliff, and with you, worries about money, about the job in Stamford—'

'Did she broadcast all our intimacies?'

'Of course not. She didn't even go into details. But I knew she needed to get away, and so did I; there were pressures in my life, too – problems I had to think about. And then we had the idea of spending a week in each other's lives—'

'Who had the idea?'

'I did,' she said swiftly. Too swiftly.

'You're lying. It was her idea, wasn't it?'

'I don't remember. What difference does it make?'

'Can't you for once in this whole stinking mess tell the simple truth?'

'It was Stephanie's idea. But I agreed.'

'To change places. And then?'

'We thought we could look at our lives from a different angle, understand ourselves better – where we were and where we wanted to go. And then we'd change back. No one would have known. I told Stephanie I wouldn't make love to you, and she said it happened so seldom—'

His face darkened, the lines deep and harsh about his mouth. 'But you did, didn't you? And my God, weren't you good at it? That was quite an act you put on; I even brought us back here, like a damned romantic fool. ... You had a good time, didn't you, night after night, and I believed it all, fell for it—'

'It wasn't a lie. Don't you understand? Garth, please try to understand. *I fell in love with you.* I didn't want to; I tried not to, but I loved you for a long time before I even admitted it to myself. And then, when I realized it, I wanted to go back to London right away, but Stephanie wanted to go on a – but my wrist wasn't healed, and we were afraid if we changed then you'd discover—'

'Where did Stephanie want to go?'

'She wanted to come home to you. But until my wrist—'

'Where did she want to go before she came home to me and her children?'

'It doesn't matter.'

'Goddamn it, don't treat me like a child who can't be told the truth. That's what you've done from the beginning. It's a little late for that now. *Where did she want to go?*'

'On a cruise. Because I'd been on so many and she never had.'

'With whom?'

'A group of people.'

'In other words, she'd found someone else.'

'Garth, what difference does it make? She's dead. She loved you and the children, she wanted to come back and stay with you and make your marriage a good one, and then she was killed. Nothing else matters.'

'Nothing else matters. Isn't that convenient? Is that how you live with yourself? I'll tell you what matters: three goddamned months. Three months of lying to two children who loved you and trusted you. Three months of lying to friends who worried about you and helped you when you broke your damned wrist. Three months of lying while I explained away your behavior and believed you were trying to reshape our marriage. Three months of smiles and kisses and some remarkably passionate lovemaking. Three months of a deception – and you did it well, I must say, I congratulate you on a remarkable—'

'Stop, stop, don't you see, *I wasn't always sure who I was.*'

He was arrested in his pacing. His face took on a look of curiosity – the scientist hearing something new and intriguing – but he shoved it aside; he even made a movement with his hands, pushing it away and letting his anger return, as if she had not spoken. 'And how much longer were you going to play your little deception? Until the novelty wore off? Until the kids and I got on your nerves? Until you decided it was time to get back to your glamorous friends and the social whirl?'

'That's not fair,' she whispered. She turned back to the window and said aloud, 'It was over.' Her breath misted the glass, and she watched the circle of moisture shrink and disappear.

'What does that mean?' He swung a chair around and straddled it. 'Turn around, damn it; look at me when you talk to me.'

The pain in his voice knifed into her, and Sabrina felt she was bleeding from his anger and grief. Her knees gave way; she moved shakily to the sofa. 'You knew I was flying to London from here. I bought my ticket this afternoon while you were giving your lecture. I was going to tell you tomorrow that I couldn't live with you anymore, that I didn't think we could make our marriage—'

'Not ours, lady!'

'I'm trying to tell you what I was going to say. That I didn't think we could make our marriage work and I was going to stay in London permanently.'

'After that remarkable faked loving, in bed and out, after tackling Rita McMillan, after such a good job of acting that you really succeeded in making us a family—' His voice caught and he had to stop for a minute. 'After all that,' he went on huskily, 'and carrying on as if we did indeed have a marriage, you were going to say it wouldn't work.'

Her hands were cold and stiff, and, crossing her arms, she tucked them into her armpits. 'I never faked anything, or acted with you and Penny and Cliff. I wasn't carrying on. I love all of you so much I hurt from it. But it was over.' Her voice grew stronger. 'After the funeral I came back to tell you

456

the truth, to end all the deceptions, and then I was going to tell my parents, and then go back to London. But you brought the children to the airport, and I couldn't tell you in front of them, and later, at home, I saw the letter, and I knew I had to stay and help you.'

'I didn't ask for your help. I didn't need it or want it.'

'Yes you did. You were worried, and it didn't matter what name you called me, you loved me and wanted me to stand with you. Garth, my love—'

'Don't call me that!'

She flinched as if he had struck her. 'No, of course, I have no right. But I'm trying to tell you that by then the only deception was my name. Everything I felt for you was the truth. I love you, and we had a wonderful marriage—'

'We had no marriage at all! *What kind of monster are you that you would profit from your sister's death?'*

Sabrina broke. Sobs racked her body, and she curled into a ball on the couch, her face in her hands. Garth tensed in his chair, torn apart, wanting to hold her and comfort her, remembering her body, her laughter, the love in her eyes – and despising her, despising himself.

'Get up,' he said, his voice empty. 'And get out of here. I can't bear to look at you. Go back to your own kind; that's where you belong.'

'No. Not anymore.' She walked blindly to the bathroom, and Garth heard the splashing of water. In a few minutes she came back, her face washed, the deadly pallor of her skin looking like wax. Tendrils of damp hair curled about her forehead. 'Sabrina Longworth is dead. She died when the *Lafitte* went down. I'm someone different now; I don't even know who. I was going to London as Stephanie, so no one would ever know what had happened; that way, I knew the truth wouldn't accidentally get back to you and the children. I was going to keep it a secret, and I will, for the children, unless you decide to tell the truth. But that would be your decision. Because, either way, I've become someone else.'

She put on the green suede blazer Garth had bought her in San Francisco and pulled on her coat. 'I want you to know that I love Penny and Cliff. They are so dear to me, their love

457

meant so much to me . . . I never had children, and I didn't pretend with them; it was so wonderful to love them and know they loved me—' She bent her head and waited until she could control her voice. 'And I love you, my darling, with all my heart, more than I can ever tell you. I know you don't want to hear it, but you are my life and all my dreams, all I ever hoped I might someday find, and I wanted to make you happy. It was all wrong, I know; I did a terrible thing to you, and I knew from the beginning it could never end well, but before I left I wanted to be able to help you one last time, to do what I could—'

Garth's head was averted, his forehead resting on his hand. 'Get out,' he said, and he was crying.

Sabrina reached for her suitcase, then straightened. Most of what it contained was Stephanie's. She left it on the floor beside Garth's, picked up her shoulder bag and opened the door. She stood there a moment, looking at the back of his head, the thick dark hair mixed with gray, seeing in her mind the lock that fell over his forehead when he leaned forward that way. . . . *My love, my love, forgive me.*

Garth thought she was gone and turned to find her watching him. 'Goddamn it, get out!' he cried through his tears. 'And let me mourn my wife!'

Swiftly she left and pulled the door shut behind her, leaning against it, her heart pounding. It was over. She touched the door with her fingertips. 'I love you,' she said softly, and turned to walk down the flowered carpet to the elevator. She forced herself to stand straight, her head high, as she left the hotel in the rain.

Chapter 21

Mrs Thirkell was just returning from the market, maneuvering her dripping umbrella and damp packages through the front door, when the cab from the airport pulled up. 'Mrs Andersen!' she cried, and stood in the pouring rain, holding the door while Sabrina paid the driver and ran into the house. 'Come in, come in, oh, I am so glad to see you! And won't Miss de Martel be pleased! Let me take your coat and hat; there's a fire laid in the drawing room and one in my lady's ... in your bedroom, and I'll bring you tea. Where would you like to go first?'

'My room, Mrs Thirkell. And muffins and jelly with the tea, please. Is Miss de Martel in?'

'No, my lady, you just missed her.' Mrs Thirkell's forehead creased in confusion. 'I'm sorry, I meant Mrs Andersen. You're so alike—'

'It's all right; you needn't apologize.' Stephanie turned to the stairway. 'Many others have been unable to tell us apart.'

'But, Mrs Andersen! Where is your luggage?'

'I have none. When you bring the tea, Mrs Thirkell, please bring the mail and today's *Times*.'

'Yes, my lady.'

Sabrina smiled faintly and climbed the stairs to her room, pausing on the third floor to examine a bouquet of pink and red carnations on the piano. 'Until tonight,' the card read. Gabrielle had an admirer. Brooks? Jolie had said they'd been dining together. Well, Gabrielle would soon tell her. In detail. She looked about the quiet drawing room, gleaming in soft lamplight. Mrs Thirkell had not been idle; everything was exactly as it should be.

Except that it was empty, without the laughter of children and the caressing voice of a husband.

In the fourth-floor bedroom, she knelt to light the fire and then found she could not get up. She was so tired, her limbs dragging her down, that she stayed where she was, leaning against an ottoman and watching the leaping flames through half-closed eyes. Her thoughts were heavy and slow, creeping away from a hotel room in New York and slowly fastening on today and tomorrow and all the weeks to come, barren weeks without her family, long hours of making a new life that was neither hers nor Stephanie's. *How do I make a life for a person who never existed before?*

When Mrs Thirkell knocked and brought in the tea tray, she got up and sat at the round table beside the window. She glanced at the small stack of mail. 'Has Sidney Jones taken care of the rest of it?'

'He collects it every few days.' She stood uncertainly. 'Mrs Andersen, may I ask ... will you be staying long? Or entertaining? Or have you come back to sell this house? I don't know what plans I should make, do you see—'

Sabrina looked at her curved reflection in the silver teapot and the teapot's reflection in the rain-streaked window. There were two of everything. *Once there were two of me.* 'I'll be staying permanently, Mrs Thirkell.' It was the first time she had said the words aloud; they were sharp blows, hammering down a lid. 'I hope you will stay with me as you did with my sister.'

'Oh, I will, of course I will, there's nothing I'd like better. But – your husband, ma'am? Your children? Your home in America?'

'This is my home,' Sabrina said dismissively. 'The children are with their father and in school, where they belong.' *I have to say more; I can't let people think I've just abandoned them.* 'Perhaps this summer they'll join me here. I don't see the *Times* on the tray.'

'Oh, dear, I forgot, there seem to be so many things, all at once. I'll bring it, ma'am, and then I'll go back to the market, since I didn't buy enough for – will you be entertaining?'

'Not at first. But I'll be eating in.'

Mrs Thirkell left, returned with the newspaper and left again, admirably subduing her curiosity. When she returned an hour later to remove the tea tray, Sabrina had changed into a soft wool robe and was lying on the chaise in front of the fire. 'Mrs Andersen, it would be an honor for me to stay with you. I had the highest esteem and affection for Lady Longworth, and I miss her deeply. If I can stay with you, it will be almost as if I had not lost her.'

'Thank you,' Sabrina said. 'I appreciate that more than I can say.'

And neither of them ever again touched on the strangeness of Stephanie Andersen's unheralded arrival from America, without luggage, to make her permanent home in London and live her sister's life.

Yet there was another home, with shadowy rooms,

footsteps and voices, that clung to the edges of her thoughts whatever she did. All night, restless between the silken sheets, she reached for Garth's hand or turned toward the remembered warmth of his body and the sheltering circle of his arms whenever she began to doze. But there was nothing, nothing, and each time she would come awake with a start of realization and remembrance, and a sinking emptiness within her that matched the emptiness of the bed and her silent, dark house.

But in the morning, on her way to work, she planned the first day of her new life: Nicholas and Brian at Ambassadors, a conference with Sidney about finances, lunch with Gabrielle and shopping. And in a few days she would begin to call her friends to let them know she was here.

At Ambassadors, Nicholas and Brian were discussing a small crack in a red-painted tulipwood cabinet and chest dated 1766. The drawers of the chest were decorated with square, Sevres porcelain plaques; the cabinet above it had round plaques centered in its doors; and atop the chest was a gilded clock with gold candelabra extending on each side, like arms in prayer, and two ebony figures perched on top. From the doorway Sabrina gazed in amusement at the absurd beauty of the piece. 'Wherever did you find it?' she asked, walking in. 'I haven't seen a Carlin for years.'

Nicholas scrambled up, his hand on his chest. 'My dear Stephanie! What a start you gave us! We had no idea ... you should have let us know ... '

'Brian,' said Sabrina, 'are you having trouble with your heart, too?'

'No,' he said, smiling as he took her hand. 'I'm glad to see you.'

She nodded thoughtfully. 'Nicholas, please come into my office. Brian, you'll take care of the showroom?'

'Of course.'

'And I'd like to talk to you in a few minutes.'

'Of course.'

'Amiable fellow,' said Nicholas, following her. 'But tell me, dear Stephanie, however do you know the furniture of Martin Carlin? Sabrina never told us your knowledge was so

461

extensive. I *am* impressed; it seems there is much about you we don't know.'

She sat at the cherry table, running her fingers over its polished surface. 'Nicholas, I understand your concern. You're afraid I'll interfere with your running of Ambassadors or sell it to someone else. Let me clarify things for you. First, Ambassadors is not for sale, to you or anyone else. Second, I intend to manage it, as Sabrina did, but with your participation. So you see, you need have been only half as worried as you were.'

'My dear lady—'

'Excuse me.' She went to the door. 'Brian, could we have tea, please? And croissants.' She returned to her chair and gazed at Nicholas. 'In our recent telephone calls I had the impression you might be planning to conceal some inventory and financial matters from me.'

'My dear Stephanie!'

'Of course, since Brian keeps the books and Sidney keeps an eye on Brian, you would have to be clever. But we both know you are clever. I thought a private discussion might make it unnecessary for me to speak to Brian or Sidney.'

There was a pause. Nicholas's bouncing energy was stilled. 'You understand, Stephanie, we had no idea when you would be back, or for how long,or, indeed, if at all. Even now, though you say you will manage the shop, I fail to see how you can do that from America. We are the ones with the day-to-day responsibility for—'

'I am here to stay, Nicholas. Living in my house on Cadogan Square and running Ambassadors.'

'You have left your husband? And your children?'

'I am here to stay. We need not discuss it further. As for the partnership you wanted with Sabrina, I suggest this arrangement: you will supervise Ambassadors and Blackford's and buy from dealers. I will buy at auction for both shops and handle all home decorating and restoration. Brian will run the office – invoices, bank statements, correspondence, and so on – for Ambassadors, as Amelia does for Blackford's. Division of finances between us will be worked out with Sidney Jones. Does that meet with your approval?'

462

Speechless, Nicholas nodded.

'I will retain an auditor to check Brian's and Amelia's bookkeeping, since our finances will be intertwined. You and Brian and I will consult regularly on buying and selling, combining operations where possible for economy. Does this seem feasible to you?'

'Stephanie.' Nicholas cleared his throat. 'In China you were so quiet. Have you changed because Sabrina did not trust me?'

'On the contrary. She did trust you. But in the last few weeks, on the telephone, I found you evasive. I will not tolerate that.'

'I assure you, Stephanie—'

'I'll have Sidney begin work on the partnership papers tomorrow. Will that be satisfactory?'

'Quite uncanny, you know – you are so like Sabrina. Uncanny. Did the two of you often think alike?'

'Often.' She stood and held out her hand. 'Nicholas, will we be friends?'

He jumped up. 'Yes, yes indeed. Haven't we always been friends? In fact, I could not agree so readily to a partnership with anyone else. But you are quite extraordinary, my dear. And then, I must tell you, these last weeks I have discovered what a remarkable reputation Sabrina built for Ambassadors. If your skill is like hers, as your self-confidence seems to be, we have an amazing future. Indeed, there is no telling how far we can go.'

'Yes, I thought you felt that way.' She smiled so pleasantly that it was several minutes before Nicholas realized how well she had understood his hunger for a share in Ambassadors. 'Now, before I talk to Brian, what would you suggest for his salary? Perhaps a small percentage of ownership?'

Nicholas was confused. After taking the initiative, as Sabrina would, she asked his advice, as Stephanie would. Or, he realized, as if they already were partners. He made a suggestion. When she encouraged him, he made another, and soon they had worked out an arrangement that pleased them both. 'I'll bring him in,' Nicholas said, and then swiftly stood on tiptoe and kissed her cheek. 'Remarkable,' he said, and left the office.

Waiting for the two of them, Sabrina stood beside the table, feeling the blood course through her veins. She had taken a chance, guessing that Nicholas, in keeping back information, was preparing to try to wrest Ambassadors from her. And, because she'd been right, she was now fully in control, her energy, determination, and knowledge intact. With the security of two shops and Nicholas and Brian sharing the work, she would specialize in restoration and decorating and fill her evenings with a selective social life, seeing only those people she really wanted to see, not everyone who might be good for business.

And if she concentrated on all that, she could build a new life and keep hidden in a small corner of her thoughts the laughter of two children and the caressing voice of a husband.

'Lunch?' Gabrielle said, interrupting her thoughts. 'I'm sorry to interrupt your work Stephanie, but I thought you might have forgotten. And I've been looking forward to it all morning.'

'It's all right, Gaby. We can go now.'

They walked to Le Suquet because Gabrielle wanted fish. 'We'll split the *fruits de mer* platter, shall we? It's too much for me but so beautiful I can't resist it. Oh, you don't know how happy I am you're here. You don't know how awful it is with no one to talk to. Oh, damn, of course you know, what am I saying? Stephanie, do you want to banish me or shall I just shut up and eat?'

'Neither.' Sabrina found herself laughing. Gabrielle's mixture of cultivated childishness and genuine vulnerability was just what she needed. It's good for me, she thought, to have someone besides myself to worry about. 'Tell me about Brooks,' she said.

Gabrielle divided the seafood platter between them and buttered a second roll. 'I'm amazingly hungry. For weeks I didn't eat, and now I eat all the time. He wants to marry me. I told him I had to talk to you first.'

'Why?'

'Because to me you're the same as Sabrina, and of course she must have told you about me, and I don't have anyone else. There's Alexandra, but she's in Rio, and she never liked me anyway. I was going to call you in America, but now here you are. Don't you miss your children?'

'Yes.'

'And your husband?'

'You were going to tell me about Brooks.'

'That's right, I was. Well, he found his spies. One in the London office sold trade names and marketing strategy to Rymer Cosmetics, and another one in the Bern plant sold them chemical formulas. That's why it took Brooks so long to find them; he knew one person wouldn't have both kinds of information – except for me.'

'But why did he believe you did it?'

'The one in Bern, the spy, told somebody I was selling information to Rymer. When the rumor spread, someone wrote to Brooks. Then Rymer came out with Brooks's fall line of cosmetics and he lost millions and he blamed me because I had access to his personal files. He put it all together and kicked me out. I don't know what I would have done without Sabrina. I never had the confidence in myself that she had, or your strength. The two of you always could get through bad times, I suppose because you had each other. I never had any – oh, damn, I'm sorry, Stephanie, I did it again. You must miss her terribly.'

Sabrina was silent, waiting for the rush of pain and loneliness to subside. The maître d' approached and bent to her. 'Mrs Anderson, we wish to convey to you our condolences. We all admired Lady Longworth; she was gracious and unfailingly kind to everyone.'

Sabrina bowed her head in acknowledgment. The pain had settled back to the dull ache she carried all the time – Stephanie, Garth, Penny, Cliff, a thousand might-have-beens. 'Would you like to be married at Cadogan Square?' she asked Gabrielle.

'Oh, Stephanie, may we? How wonderful! I thought of it, but, of course, it was impossible without you, but now that you're here, it would be perfect.'

'Come to dinner with Brooks on Friday, and we'll plan your wedding. Mrs Thirkell will need to know the number of guests.'

'And you'll stand up with me in the ceremony? I always

wanted to do it . . . Stephanie, do you mind if I think of you as Sabrina? The two of you – it's very confusing, you know.'

'I know.'

After lunch, Sabrina had one more promise to keep. At Peter Dale, in the Royal Opera Arcade in Pall Mall, she browsed among antique suits of armor. 'Not an entire suit,' she explained to the proprietor. 'Something smaller—'

'One moment. I have it.' He had known Sabrina, and, after offering his sympathies in a voice that creaked like the armor he sold, he vanished into the back of the tiny shop to bring out a small shield brilliantly decorated with a griffin protecting a castle keep. 'Used by one of the Cecils in practice jousts when he was about ten.' It was perfect, Sabrina thought, and, as she wrote a check, she imagined Cliff showing it off and then hanging it on his bedroom wall to remind him he once had a mother who loved him.

At Falkiner's she put together a collection of artist's papers for Penny – Japanese parchment, watercolor, marbled sheets in fantastic designs and vellum with fine deckle edges. At Winsor and Newton she bought one of their largest boxes of oil paints, then, caught up in her vision of Penny's delight, she stopped at Collett's for a set of Oriental brushes and ink sticks.

'Brian,' she said, when she returned to Ambassadors, 'how does one ship this unwieldy mass to America?'

'The same way we ship unwieldy art. Leave it to me, Mrs Andersen.'

'Wait. One thing more.' She disappeared into her office and returned in a moment with a sealed envelope. 'It all goes to this address.'

A shield, art supplies, a letter.

'My dearest Penny and Cliff: I think of you and I miss you, and every time I close my eyes I see you very clearly. I can't reach across the ocean to hug you, so instead I'm sending you the presents I promised, for now and an early Christmas. I love you both. I love you both.'

And a note for Garth.

'Whatever you decide to tell Penny and Cliff, please let them have these gifts. I won't write to them again, or send them anything else, unless you tell me I may, but I promised to send them presents as soon as I arrived in London. Please let me keep my promise. It is the last favor I will ask of you.'

She had nothing more to do for her family now except long for them and wait for the pain of her longing to diminish. But she had forgotten her mother.

Laura called on Saturday noon as Sabrina and Gabrielle were going out to buy a wedding dress. 'Stephanie, what in heaven's name is going on? Garth says you're staying in London indefinitely. Just what does that mean?'

'What it sounds like, Mother. I'm living here now.'

'And Garth and your children?'

'Mother, you know the answer to that. They're in Evanston.'

'You've left your children?'

'I left . . . Yes. They're with Garth.'

'And you've left him?'

'Yes.'

'For how long?'

'For . . . as long as necessary.'

'Necessary! To do what? To destroy a wonderful marriage, a fine home, the lives of two—'

'Please, Mother, don't . . . '

'Why shouldn't I? Do you know what you've thrown away? The best—'

'Mother, stop it. Please. Garth and I both decided I should leave. We have more than enough pain without your making it worse. Someday I may be able to tell you the whole story, but I can't now. You'll just have to trust me, that I'm doing what I have to do.'

'Stephanie,' Gordon said on the extension phone, his voice like a frail thread. 'You don't love Garth anymore?'

I love him with all my heart. I love him more with every memory that haunts me and clings to me through the long endless nights. 'There are problems I can't talk about,' she answered. 'You'll have to believe that. And trust me. I'm sorry I've caused you unhappiness—'

467

'So soon after Sabrina!' Laura cried. 'You might have waited and dealt us just one blow at a time.'

'Yes, Mother. It was thoughtless of me. I apologize.'

'I don't need your sarcasm—'

'What will you do?' Gordon interrupted. 'Alone in London.'

'I've formed a partnership with Nicholas Blackford to run Ambassadors. I'll keep Sabrina's house, make friends, make a life for myself.'

'Terrible,' Laura moaned. 'Terrible. The last thing we ever would have expected. We were so sure of you.'

'Yes. I'm sorry. I let you down.'

'But you'll go back, of course. You'll think things over and then go back to your family. Women are doing that these days; you read about it all the time: someone who seems perfectly happy suddenly ups and decides she needs space, whatever that is. I don't understand what these women mean when they say they need space. Most of them mean they want a lover. Is that what you want?'

'No.'

'Well, if it is, have one and get it out of your system and then go back to your family. If you're not looking for a lover, what are you looking for? A career? You had one, that little place, what was it, Collectibles. Are you looking for a new career?'

'No.'

'Then what are you looking for? What do you expect to find by living in Sabrina's house and running her shop?' Sabrina did not answer. 'Stephanie? Stephanie, are you trying to pretend you're Sabrina? I remember you always talked about her glamorous life in London, her successes . . . and I suppose I encouraged you . . . is that what you're trying to do? Finally, after all these years, to turn yourself into Sabrina?'

'Mother.' Sabrina's voice caught between an involuntary laugh and a sob. 'I am trying to be myself.'

'Do you know who that is?' Gordon asked.

'Not always,' she said. 'But I'm finding out.'

How simple that sounded: *Finding out.* And I will, she told herself the next day as she took a taxi to Kensington Cemetery. It will just take a little while.

She walked slowly toward the small rise in the ground where they all had stood not so long ago. The cemetery was gray and damp, as she remembered it, wavering in a mist that made the stones seem to soften and change shape. The trees wept clear drops, and puddles on the walks were small flat mirrors reflecting the scudding clouds, gray on gray.

She stood beside the grave, letting her memories weave in and out – childhood, school days, Juliette, visits to New York, visits in London, childhood again, servants packing, the strangeness of new schools, two sisters always holding hands. But soon the dampness cut through her coat and the suit beneath it, and, shivering, she turned and left.

Near the gate, a tall man got out of a waiting car. 'Your housekeeper told me you were here,' Dmitri said. 'May I drive you home?'

She looked at his thin face, dark eyes beneath fierce brows, deep lines on either side of his firm mouth. His arm was extended to help her into the car. She remembered a young boy forcing himself to be brave while men in heavy boots searched his room and clomped above the cellar where he was hiding two American girls. He wants to protect me, she thought. But his eyes were gentle and undemanding. He was offering friendship. 'Yes,' she said. 'I'd like a ride home.'

Chapter 22

No one met Garth's plane from New York; no one expected him for two more days. He had left the hotel early Tuesday, phoning Rolf from La Guardia to say he would not be at the executive committee meeting, and flew back on the first plane leaving for Chicago. He had not slept, and in his fatigue everything seemed exaggerated: too loud, too bright, voices clattering off hard walls and floors. But at home, when he unlocked his door and stepped inside, the silence overwhelmed him. An empty house. Penny and Cliff at school. His wife dead. Her impostor in London. A silent, empty house.

He stood in the center of the kitchen and wondered what to do. Nothing that he could think of seemed worth doing. He looked about at the neat kitchen, at the couch and low table where Penny's sketches lay beside a book Stephanie had been reading, at the breakfast-room table. A picture sprang to Garth's memory: night-time, very late, the house dark and hushed. Penny and Cliff were asleep, and he and Stephanie sat together at the round table, eating pumpkin pie from a single plate. Only it hadn't been Stephanie. That had been—

'*NO!*' he cried, a long anguished note that echoed through the empty rooms. Snatching her book from the table, he hurled it at the wall. Its page fluttered as it fell to the floor, and Garth sank to the couch, weeping for his wife and the shattered pieces of his world.

Exhausted, he fell asleep, and when he woke it was dark. Confused, he fumbled for the light and looked at his watch to discover it was only five o'clock. He shivered; they had turned the furnace down when they left, and the house was cold. Then he remembered everything that had happened, and he could feel his anger settling, spreading through his body in a cold viscous mass, inseparable from the flow of his blood and the pumping of his heart and the roar in his ears.

He had to move, act, occupy his mind, 'At least be practical,' he said aloud, and called Vivian to tell her the meeting had been shorter than expected; he would pick up Penny and Cliff in an hour.

'Come for dinner,' she urged. 'And tell us about New York.'

'Not this time. Give me a rain check.'

'Then let your offspring eat before you pick them up. They helped make the food; I think they should be compelled to eat it.'

'All right. Eight o'clock?'

'Eight o'clock. Garth, whatever it is, eat something. You'll feel better.'

So it was in his voice. Well, why not? How much anger could one person contain before it spilled over into public view? He unpacked, washed his face, changed his shirt and downed two quick Scotches. Refilling the ice tray, he saw that the refrigerator was full. How thoughtful; the bitch had left them well taken care of before she flew the coop to go back to her European playground.

He paced the house, his thoughts flying wildly like debris from an explosion; nothing was whole, nothing was solid. Why hadn't he suspected her? He'd been over it time and time again, trying to understand how he had been so thoroughly taken in. Looking back, remembering slips of the tongue and quick recoveries, atypical behavior, lapses in memory, he could not understand it. He was a trained observer, a man who collected facts and analyzed them. Why had he been so easily deceived? He didn't know. Nothing made sense; he had nothing to hold onto except his house and his children, and that was why he had to see them as soon as possible; they were all he could be sure of.

He left early for the Goodmans' house, driving slowly on snow-packed side streets. He was rehearsing.

I have something to tell the two of you; it's not easy, it's not very nice—

Sit down, both of you, I want to talk to you about your mother—

I have to tell you, some time ago your mother was in an accident – no, not on the bicycle, another accident, on a yacht, in Europe; you see, the woman who's been living here, the one who had the accident on the bicycle—

The woman who's been living here, making fools of us, laughing at us for loving her and needing her while she was playing a game—

How the hell did a man tell that to his children?

He brought Penny and Cliff home, and the three of them sat in the breakfast room, eating ice cream and pretzels.

'Mom doesn't think this a great combination,' said Cliff. 'But I like it.'

'It's ice cream and dill pickles she really doesn't like,' Penny said. 'And I think she's right.'

'I do, too,' Cliff admitted. 'Dad, can we call her in London?'

'No.'

'Why not? You called every night when she was there after Aunt Sabrina's funeral.'

'That was different.'

'Why?'

'She was very unhappy then . . . '

'Well, maybe she's unhappy now, missing us.'

'No, Cliff.'

'But why? Does it cost a lot?'

'More than a dollar a minute. Are you willing to pay for it?'

'Yeah, if you won't. If that's the only way I can talk to Mom.'

'Daddy?' Penny said. 'Why are you mad? Are you mad at Mommy? Is that why you came home early? Is she mad at you?'

Through the coldness that gripped him, Garth felt a flash of wry humour. We take pride in our intelligent children, and then we have to live with the fact that they see through us.

But why didn't these intelligent children see through that woman and know she was not their mother?

Because they are innocent and trusting and she took advantage of them.

'Daddy?'

'It's true, Penny, I am angry. I'll tell you why.' He searched for a way to begin. His children watched him, their bright, curious faces just beginning to be apprehensive. Garth let the moment drag on, unable to say the first word. Finally, he opened his hands and dropped them in resignation. He could not do it. Later, perhaps, when the time was right. But not now. 'I'm angry because your mother is off in London instead of being here with us. And because she thinks she has to stay there for awhile, to think about her life away from everything here.'

'But she already did that,' said Penny, biting her lip. 'In China.'

'That's right, she did. And remember, when we talked about it, I said that often people need to get away from their everyday lives to think about themselves in different ways.

472

But sometimes they have to do it more than once, or for a longer time.'

'But when we talked you said you weren't going to get a divorce.'

Garth felt a wave of nausea and clenched his teeth. No divorce; a surgical operation: cut her out of our lives. 'We're not talking about divorce, Penny. Look, it's late; don't you two have homework?'

'We did it this afternoon,' said Cliff. 'Is Mom coming back?'

'I don't know.'

'She is!' Penny screamed. 'She is! I know she is! You're lying!'

'I'm not lying!' Garth said, more sharply than he intended. He lowered his voice; he had to make them understand. 'Penny, sometimes people do things that may not seem right or sensible to you, but that doesn't mean they're wrong. Your mother and I had a ... disagreement about something, and she thought she'd go back to London for awhile. You knew she was going anyway, to take care of her sister's business. The only change is that she's going to stay longer than she thought—'

'How long?'

'I don't know.'

'You do! You and Mommy decided and you're lying about it! It's not fair, nobody asked Cliff and me what we wanted and we live here, too, and she's our mother, and I'm going to tell her we're waiting for her to come home and you can't stop me!'

She dashed from the room and up the stairs. Cliff looked at his father and spoke carefully, trying to be more grown up than his sister. 'She is coming back, isn't she? I mean, you said you don't know, but isn't that what scientists always say when they don't know exactly what's going to happen?'

Garth nodded. 'That's what scientists say.'

'Dad.' Cliff squirmed in his chair. 'Dad, you want her to come back, don't you?'

'It's ... complicated, Cliff. I can't give you a simple answer.'

Cliff squeezed his eyes shut. 'Bullshit.'

'Now, that's enough! I don't talk to you that way, and I expect the same courtesy from you. Do you think I like this? Damn it, things are happening that I can't help. Can you begin to understand that? If you're old enough to tell your father he's talking bullshit, you're old enough to listen when I tell you that I *can't control everything that happens to me.*'

'Well, you can't blame us if you screw up your life!' Shocked at his own words, Cliff drew back. 'I'm sorry, Dad I'm sorry. I didn't mean it.'

Garth felt the ground pull out from beneath him. His children never spoke to him like this; Stephanie wouldn't allow it. Stephanie held them all together. Now things fell apart – the center did not hold. He started to say something, then let it go. He pushed back his chair, wanting a drink.

'Dad?'

'Yes, Cliff.'

'Do you love Mom?'

In the silence they could hear the humming of the electric clock and the refrigerator. 'Do you know,' Garth said, 'when we were married, your mother was so beautiful everyone stared at her; they thought I was the luckiest guy in the world. And when we moved here and you were born—'

'Why won't you answer?' Cliff shouted. '*We* love her; how come you don't? She loves you too. What's wrong with you? Oh, shit.' He rubbed his eyes. 'I guess I don't want to talk about it. I'm going to write to Mom. I suppose you don't like *that*, either.'

We're going to cut her out of our lives, Garth thought. That means no communication. He kept his voice even. 'Maybe we should leave her alone, let her have some time without any contact from us. Maybe that's what she wants.'

'How do you know? You don't care what she wants. Anyway, you told me scientists shouldn't make decisions until they have as many facts as possible. Shouldn't Mom have facts, too?'

'What facts?'

'That we love her,' Cliff said reprovingly. 'And we want her to come back. And,' he added in a burst of inspiration, 'if she doesn't come back, we'll go to London and *get* her!'

474

Crushed between his anger and love for his children, Garth tried to speak, and no words came out.

'Well,' Cliff said, emboldened by his father's silence. 'I don't get this whole thing, but I'm writing to Mom. Penny and I can mail our letters together. I might even call her one of these days. Out of my allowance.'

'We'll talk about it again tomorrow, Cliff. All right?'

'Yeah, but we're still going to write to her tonight.'

Garth nodded. 'I'll be up to say good night to both of you later.'

Bitch, he thought, and repeated it, the vicious word like a hammer blow as he sat alone and poured himself a drink. Look what you've done to them. They'd be better off if they knew you were dead.

If *who* was dead? he asked himself. And answered unclearly: I don't know.

Nat called him in his office the next day. 'Just heard you were back. Good meeting?'

'I didn't go. A change in schedule.'

'And Stephanie? Did her schedule change, too?'

'No'.

'So she's in London now?'

'Yes.'

'When does she get back?'

'She doesn't.'

'She—What does that mean?'

'She's staying there. Nat, I don't want to talk about it.'

'So I gather. Dolores will ask me questions.'

'If you'll forgive my saying it, Dolores's questions are your problem, not mine.'

'An indisputable fact. I have a couple of days off next week; we could go ice-fishing.'

'You are inventing a couple of days off.'

'So I am. But my patients will survive. Shall we take some time in the wilds and perhaps get a new perspective on the world?'

'I don't want to leave Penny and Cliff.'

'For a day or two?'

'Nat, let me get used to being a single parent.'

There was a pause. 'Right. Then how about dinner with us? Dolores will ask that, too.'

'You come here. I'll cook something in a wok. Did you know that almost any idiot can make an acceptable meal in a wok?'

'Dolores would prefer cooking for you.'

'And I prefer cooking for her. Tell her I'll call soon. And Nat – thank you.'

Others called as the days passed, asking when Stephanie would be home, and they asked, too, in the faculty club, the library, even in the grocery store. 'She must feel lost in London,' said Linda, inviting Garth and the children to dinner. 'And I'm lost without her. We have an estate sale coming up just after the first of the year and I need her. She'll be home soon, won't she? After all, it's getting close to Christmas.'

To everyone, he answered that he did not know.

Liar, he lashed out at himself at night, in the silence of his bedroom. Coward. Perpetuating the lie. How much longer will you keep it up? Who are you to talk about deception when you're as guilty of it as they were?

He heard Penny and Cliff talking in Cliff's room as they wrote another letter to London.

The three of us – Sabrina, Stephanie and I – caught in their damned deception, entangled in it as the days pass, until there seems no way to end it without inflicting pain on those we would protect.

He understood that now.

At night he lay alone in the four-poster bed in a room filled with ghosts: the fragrance of her clothes, the sound of her laughter, memories of a woman who had become his light and life. He held himself carefully still along the edge of the bed, for every movement sent ripples of longing through his muscles and set his blood pounding until he forgot his anger and reached out unthinkingly to pull her warm body to his. He could feel her against him, hear himself tell her he loved her and feel the warm whisper of her breath as she answered him, again and again: I *love* you.

But his arm found empty space, the sheets cold and taut, and with a cry of fury he flung the blanket away and left the

476

bed, pulled on a robe and sat for hours before the dead coals in the living room fireplace. He would read until a memory touched him: the two of them sitting here, reading, looking up to share a glance in a quiet so deep it seemed they were the only two people alive in the world. Then, sick with loneliness, he would close his book and stare at the gray landscape of the cold fireplace, brooding and growing fearful of something that was happening to him.

He was having trouble separating his wife from the woman who had lived with him for the past three months.

His wife of twelve years was dead, but how did he mourn her when he had only lost her a few days ago?

Who are you mourning? he asked his reflection in the dark living room window a week after his return. My dead wife. Who died twice. Once off the Mediterranean coast and once in a hotel in New York.

Two separate women. One left him; the other casually took her place, toyed with their lives and kept her secret long past the time when she should have revealed it.

But she had said she wanted to end the deception. All the deceptions, she had said.

Then why hadn't she?

Garth stood at his front window, gazing at the ghostly sphere of the Victorian streetlight through his transparent reflection. He was not able to tell his children the truth. Had she faced the same indecision, trying and failing, saying, as he did, 'Later, when the time is right?'

He didn't know. But one thing he now believed. His wife of twelve years had wanted more than a brief trip to the Orient. Oh, yes, he believed that now. She had wanted to be on her own, loose and free, shed of her husband and family. For as long as it pleased her. There was no rush to return. After all, her sister was filling in.

Why hadn't she come to him, to talk, to see what they could salvage together instead of planting her sister and taking off on an experiment that shut him out completely?

Because he would have chalked it up as another example of her dissatisfaction – with him, with his job and salary, with Evanston, with the life she led, especially when compared with the glittering star of Sabrina's London life. He would have accused her of wanting to be Sabrina.

And he would have been right. Because that was exactly what she did want. And finally got. Sabrina's life, ready-made, a home, wealth, social life, status, friends – and lovers.

His mourning for her was subtly shifting to anger, and at the same time his thoughts were turning to Sabrina. It had been Stephanie's idea to change places. Did Sabrina come to Evanston as a game – or as a favour to Stephanie? It was the first time he had asked that question.

On Monday, he came home from the university just as Penny and Cliff arrived, and together they all saw the strange-shaped package from London on the porch. He watched as they excitedly untied knots, ripped off heavy tape and tore open the layers of protective wrapping paper.

'Oh, Dad,' Cliff breathed as he lifted the shield. He studied it from all angles, then slipped it on his arm, positioning it to cover his body. 'I'll hang it on the wall in my room, okay?'

'Look, look,' Penny bubbled, setting out the packages of colored papers in a circle around her, with the box of oil paints in the center beside a bundle of Japanese brushes and ink sticks. 'Mommy knew, she knew exactly what I wanted, I never told her I wanted the ink sticks, but she knew, oh, Daddy, look how many kinds of paper, here, feel the edges of these . . . Oh, look, this is for you.'

Garth touched the envelope. His name was on it. Penny pushed it into his fingers and slowly he opened it and read the brief message.

' . . . Please let me keep my promise. It is the last favor I will ask of you.'

The words wavered before his eyes. He could hear her voice and see her mouth; he could see the light in her eyes when she looked at the children.

She loves them.

Chapter 23

Alexandra flew in from Rio and came for tea, unashamedly curious. 'I heard you were here for good, that you dealt smartly with Nicholas and are now doing business with him and that you have had dinner twice in a row with a handsome, unknown male of distinguished bearing.'

Sabrina laughed with a delight that cut through the numbness of the past two weeks. She may have thought her life lay in pieces, but some things stayed the same; here was Alexandra to prove it. 'His name is Dmitri Karras and he hid me in a cellar when I was eleven.'

Alexandra's eyes gleamed. 'You told part of that story at your birthday party. Do I get the rest of it some time? Or will it be like the one you never finished the day Scotland Yard intruded?'

'This one I promise to finish. How long will you be in London?'

'Long enough to close Antonio's flat, catch up on gossip—'

'Which you are doing admirably.'

'And buy out Harrods, Zandra Rhodes and Fortnum and Mason.'

'Are there no stores in Rio?'

'Honey, you wouldn't believe the stores in Rio. Everything anyone could want. But I want London, and London it isn't. I suppose I'll get used to it after awhile, but until then, if I can buy out a few stores and ship everything across the ocean, why not? Do you have time to shop with me, or are you too busy marrying off Gaby and Brooks?'

'Is there anything about me you haven't heard?'

'I haven't heard how you feel about leaving a couple of kids back in the States with their father.'

Sabrina put down her cup with a shaking hand. Everyone mentioned it, obliquely or carefully – you must miss them, my dear; it must be difficult for you – but no one spoke out with Alexandra's bluntness; no one had challenged her to a direct answer. And no one knew that Penny's and Cliff's letters lay on her bedside table, read and reread each night and answered in her thoughts but never on paper, not until Garth gave her permission to write to them. 'I don't discuss my feelings,' she said.

'I know, honey, or I would have heard about it. But I thought you might like a sympathetic ear. Sabrina and I never talked about feelings much, but when we said goodbye, just before that damned cruise, she kissed me. Surprised me – it wasn't like her, and I pulled away. I think it hurt her; she was being honest about her feelings and I didn't let her. I thought about that after she died. That's why I'm keeping my house for when we visit London. Antonio wanted to keep his apartment, but I won't sell my house; it's Sabrina's, too. Which reminds me – while I'm here I could introduce you to some people for business and pleasure, get you started, help take your mind off your kids.'

'I really just want to be quiet and alone.'

'Brooding. An unhealthy pastime. Are you going to see them soon?'

'You don't give up, do you?'

'Come on, lady, you must miss them. And also your handsome if slightly stuffy husband. Don't you want to unburden?'

'I can't. It hurts to talk. It hurts all the time, I miss them so much, and if I had any tears left I'd walk around in a pool of my own making. What good does it do to talk? I want them close to me, I want the feel of a place with people who love me and need me ... oh, damn, look what I've done, I've started and now I can't stop. Have some more tea; I'll be back in a minute.'

'No, stay. My God, I'm sorry, I didn't know it was that bad. But then why did you leave?'

'I had to.'

'He kicked you out?'

'I had to leave. I had no choice. I can't go back, and I can't talk about it.'

A shudder swept her, like the trembling of a leaf, and Alexandra said quickly, 'Honey, I didn't know. I won't bring it up again. I don't know anybody who feels that way about families; most of them leave it all to servants and boarding schools. I find it pretty scary, if you want to know. I'm not sure I want a family of my own if there's so much . . . *emotion* involved.'

In spite of herself, Sabrina laughed. 'There is if you want it.'

They sat together in friendly silence. 'Well,' Alexandra said, 'what about Dmitri of the cellar? How do you have dinners with him and still be quiet and alone?'

'Dmitri is a friend.'

'So am I.'

'Then I'll have dinner with you, too.'

'I'd like that. I wish we had more time; I have this crazy feeling I've known you for years, because of Sabrina, but then I want to get to know you better. What the hell am I going to do in the middle of Brazil without you? Come to my wedding! Will you? You've got to come; I won't consider it legitimate unless you're there.'

'When is it?'

'Christmas Eve or Christmas Day, whichever suits the Guaranis. Can you imagine waiting for permission to get married from a bunch of Indians who have to consult the stars or the moon or the shape of ant hills, or some such thing? Do you think I'm crazy?'

'No. I think you're doing what you want to do.'

'You're the only one with sense enough to say that and not ask me if I'm in love. Say you'll come to the wedding.'

'I can't, Alexandra. I have to stay in one place for awhile until I get straightened out.'

Alexandra nodded. 'I thought you'd say that. But you'll be here, whenever I'm in London?'

'Where would I go?'

'Back to America, to your husband and children.'

The smile faded from Sabrina's face. 'No. I'll be here. And I'll be glad to see you. I hope you come often.'

'As often as I can. If you change your mind, you can just show up at the wedding, you know, without warning.'

Sabrina shook her head. 'I won't change my mind. But I'll

481

give you my blessing and kiss you. And this time you won't pull back.'

They looked at each other. 'You know, honey, if I walked in here right now, for the life of me I couldn't say whether you were Sabrina or Stephanie.'

'I know,' Sabrina said. 'That's the way it should be.'

Others said the same; invitations poured in from hostesses who declared Stephanie the sensation of the season for taking Sabrina's place with such panache. And then a new story obliterated all others. On December 17, the *Times* of London featured a front-page article on art thefts and forgeries written by Michel Bernard, with photographs by Jolie Fantome. The article appeared simultaneously in the international edition of the *Herald Tribune* published in Paris, *Die Welt* in Germany and *The New York Times*. Within hours of its appearance, a tempest of whispers and telephone calls swept it through restaurants, clubs, boutiques and every art and antique gallery in London. Sabrina was awakened with the news by a frantic early-morning call from Nicholas, who remembered seeing Westbridge Imports and Rory Carr listed in Ambassadors' ledgers.

'All I ask, dear Stephanie, is are we involved? Blackford's is not. I recall meeting this Carr several times, but I never bought from him. Sabrina did; there were several porcelains listed—'

'Which porcelains, Nicholas?'

He read the descriptions. Dancers, animals, figures, birds. No Meissen stork. Of course not; the record and invoice had been destroyed soon after the stork was broken. Somewhere in the books at Westbridge, Ambassadors would be listed with dozens of other galleries, but Michel and Jolie's story did not mention Ambassadors at all and there was no reason to connect them. No one would even be interested in such a small detail when the story was already splashed in sensational headlines: multi-millionaire Max Stuyvesant, his personal art collection, his smuggling network and dealings with forgers, murder on the Mediterranean and so many dead, among them the beautiful Lady Sabrina Longworth.

'We are not involved,' Sabrina said. 'The porcelains

Sabrina bought from Westbridge were genuine; she told me she checked their provenance.'

'But are you sure?' Nicholas persisted. 'I don't like to press you, Stephanie, I know this brings back dreadful memories—'

'Nicholas, I will say it once more. We are not involved. There is no danger. But rumors can be deadly and if I ever hear you question Ambassadors' reputation or integrity, I will not hesitate to dissolve our partnership and purchase your half. That should set your mind at rest.'

'Good heavens, Stephanie, I never meant to imply ... I trusted Sabrina; I admired her. But she was on that yacht; I had to make sure—'

'And now you have. So there is no need for further discussion.'

'None. Of course, none. Will you be in the shop today?'

'Of course.'

She was in her office every day, catching up on the past three months, poring over auction records, preparing for the time when she would begin buying and decorating again. She felt she was wandering in an unmarked land between past and future, building a barrier between her work and life of today and her memories of a sister, a husband, children, a home. She lived one day at a time. To plan ahead was to admit that the door was locked on the past. She knew it was, but, still, it was easier to live in the present.

Olivia Chasson was part of the present and she called, inviting her to dinner. 'Just a small party; I was Sabrina's friend and patron, and I want to get to know you as well as I knew her.'

'I'm sorry, I'm having dinner with a friend—'

'Bring him, my dear. I assume he would be comfortable with us?'

Is he our kind? Sabrina translated silently. 'His name is Dmitri Karras—'

'Oh, international banking. We met at lunch after Sabrina's funeral; we have several friends in common. Do bring him.'

Fourteen people sat down to dinner in Olivia's house near Belgrave Square. They greeted Sabrina eagerly, getting through their condolences as quickly as possible so they could ask her for inside information on the smuggling and forgery scandal; the second installment had appeared in that morning's paper.

They discussed it with the relish reserved for the downfall of the powerful but also with wariness, since they all were collectors investing in art and antiques and no one knew what revelations lay in future installments.

Over the consommé, they asked Sabrina about detecting forgeries. She answered briefly, describing types of clay, glazes, paints and designs. She explained how ultraviolet light could sometimes detect false or double glazing but not always, and less reliably with improved glazes. 'Much of it is instinct,' she said. 'If you study details, you begin to get a feel for style and treatment that often makes it possible to distinguish an original from a copy' – she hesitated for a fraction of a minute, and then went smoothly on – 'by examining them. Usually, though, we first check the provenance of an object, looking for clues that help us tell our clients whether a work is an original or a forgery. In my experience, few forgeries go undetected in the long run.'

Her low, clear voice had captured the guests' attention. 'Fascinating', someone said as she listened to the echo of her words. 'But that wasn't Max's line, was it?'

Dmitri put his hand on her arm, but Sabrina did not need him. She raised her chin and looked coolly down the length of the table. 'I do not discuss Max Stuyvesant or any of his activities.'

'Well, really!' said the same voice, but whispers cut across it.

'Don't be so stupid; her sister—'

'Just a few weeks ago—'

'Really quite idiotic of you to bring it up.'

Olivia's strong voice overrode the whispers. 'Stephanie is my guest, not a hired art expert. We are welcoming her to London.' She turned to Sabrina, on her right. 'My dear, you will answer no more questions. Will you have more wine?'

Sabrina and Dmitri exchanged a smile. 'You have forbidden me to answer you,' she said to Olivia. Laughter rippled around the table; someone asked about a new game in Monte

Carlo, and Dmitri began to tell Sabrina about the villa he had just bought outside Athens, near the villas of his sisters and their families. She listened in silence, relaxed and grateful for his presence. He reminded her of Garth in his quiet way, ready to help her if she needed it but not forcing himself upon her. Even the light in his eyes ... But no, nothing was the same as the light in Garth's eyes. 'It is quite lovely,' Dmitri said of his villa. 'The air smells of flowers, thyme and oregano. No one gossips and we do not discuss business. There is music, and stories of gods and goddesses and the glories of the past. We pretend the present does not exist. Will you come one day and see it for yourself?'

She smiled. 'Perhaps, one day.'

After coffee and cognac, Olivia invited Sabrina and Dmitri to view her art gallery. 'I want it enlarged and redecorated,' she said. 'With better lighting. And I want you to do it, Stephanie.'

They stood in the doorway, looking down the long, arched room.

'Sabrina was after me for years to modernize it, but I never cared until now. It won't do for my new sculptures.'

'What kind are they?' Dmitri asked.

'Modern. Ten, fifteen, twenty feet high. Frankly, they look like plumbers' nightmares and carpenters' drunken binges, but I only say that privately. Experts call them art and good investments. Some museum in Boston has already offered to call them the Chasson collection if I leave it to them in my will. What would you do with them?'

'Forget the museum,' Dmitri suggested. 'Build the Olivia Chasson playground. Children can climb on them.'

Olivia laughed and clapped him on the shoulder. 'You finance it; Stephanie will design it.'

'And name it,' Sabrina said, '*Cacher et chasser.*'

Dmitri chuckled at the pun on Olivia's last name. 'Hide-and-seek,' he said, as Olivia laughed delightedly. 'Wonderful,' she said.

'Wonderful. I feel I haven't lost Sabrina at all. You can begin remodeling the gallery after the new year, my dear Stephanie.' And she returned to her guests, happily repeating the French words.

Dmitri took Sabrina's hand. 'A callous woman. *She* does not feel she has lost your sister.'

'But she hasn't,' Sabrina said, moving away as she began to walk the length of the gallery. 'With only a brief interruption, she has before her a woman who looks the same, treats her as an equal and will help redecorate her house. What more could she want?'

'A real person.'

'Really? Most people are satisfied with the surface.'

Dmitri followed her, and they gazed at the Chasson collection of French and German oil paintings. 'I would like to get to know you better, if you would let me. You are a remarkable woman.'

Sabrina turned from a brooding portrait of a long-dead wool merchant and looked into the living warmth of Dmitri's eyes.

'We've had dinner together three times,' he said, 'and we are no closer than when I first saw you.'

'I hope we're friends,'she said quietly.

'Friends. Of course. I want much more than that, you know. But I am in no hurry.'

'How thoughtful,' she murmured dryly. 'Since I am still married.'

'It is not necessary to remind me. You are also still in love with your husband.'

She froze, then turned to walk back the way they had come. 'I think we need not discuss that.'

'Please.' He put his hand on her arm. 'I apologize. There is such a difference between us, in the way we see each other. In a way, you know, I've spent a lifetime thinking about you. One memorable afternoon, and you have been clear in my mind ever since; I never forgot you or your sister.'

They strolled on, and Sabrina relaxed as Dmitri talked about himself, especially about the reporter who had 'adopted' him and his sisters after photographing them at the embassy. 'He had no children, and we became his family. He got my father a new job, sent us to school, helped me get a scholarship to Cambridge, even tried to find me a wife.' He smiled. 'There he failed.'

They neared the end of the gallery. 'I know I stayed in your past,' Dmitri said. 'But you must understand that you and your sister have been in my dreams since I was a child, weaving through my life, appearing at odd times when I least expected you – sometimes, you will forgive me, at awkward times.'

'You mean when you were with other women.'

'Even then.' He continued talking, but Sabrina was no longer listening. He had described her dream of Garth, and his words brought the dream back: Garth's touch on her hand, his mouth covering hers, his quiet voice, his eyes desiring her, the warmth of their bodies when they lay together after making love. Loneliness swept her; she felt lost. *Oh, my love, my dear love, I miss you so, I need you, I can't bear* . . . and then she clamped down her silent cry and listened again to Dmitri.

' . . . your beauty and courage,' he was saying. 'And your joy in being alive. I suppose I have always loved you because you showed me those things when I was young, and from then on no one else ever showed them to me in the same way. I always hoped I would find you some day and give you a dream to match mine. I never thought I would find you through a tragedy.'

Suddenly she felt smothered by his insistence on bringing back the past. *I have to get away, I can't breathe, I can't think* . . . *I want my sister. I want my family. I want Garth.*

'Stephanie, what is it? What have I said?'

Breathing quickly, she tried to smile. 'Too much talk of the past when I'm supposed to be building a new life. Shall we go back to the others?'

'But wait, we are friends? If I promise not to talk about the past, we will be friends?'

'Yes. Of course.' Why did everyone push her so? Why did they try to shape her to their own desires? Couldn't they leave her alone to be herself? *I would have shaped myself to Garth's desire because he never demanded it. He did not even ask. And never will.*

'Of course we are friends,' she said, returning to the party. But she forgot him as Gabrielle's wedding day approached and, to keep from thinking about Garth, she forced herself to concentrate on details that Mrs Thirkell could have handled admirably. And when the guests began to arrive, she knew she had succeeded in creating a setting Gabrielle would love, even if she had failed in pushing Garth from her thoughts.

In the drawing room, bouquets of violet orchids and white roses from Olivia's greenhouses glowed softly in the light from white candles in silver candelabra as fifty guests sat on velvet chairs listening to duets played on a harp and piano. 'Exactly the way Sabrina would have done it,' the guests said again and again. 'How wonderfully well you have kept her spirit alive.'

Gabrielle wore ivory peau de soie with a satin cape trimmed in ivory and gold braid. She admired herself in the tall mirror in Sabrina's bedroom. 'It's as close as I can come to white without pretending I'm a virgin. But I feel virginal. Silly, isn't it?'

'No,' said Sabrina beside her, wearing coral velvet. 'You look lovely. As if you're standing at the beginning of the world.'

'But that's exactly how I feel! How on earth did you—Oh, how stupid, forgive me, Stephanie. You shouldn't have to listen to my sentimental ravings when your own marriage is—'

'Gaby, I'll listen to your ravings if you promise not to talk about my marriage.'

'That's fair. But now I feel guilty about raving.'

'Then I'll run downstairs for a word with Mrs Thirkell. We should start in about five minutes, I think.'

In the drawing room, Brooks stood before the fireplace with its bower of white and lilac, calmly surveying the room; a friend from Paris stood at his side. Alexandra sat in the first row; she was leaving the next day to join Antonio in Rio, and three days later, on Christmas Eve, they would be married.

I am surrounded by romance, Sabrina thought. For years no one got married; everyone was getting divorced. Now my house is filled with love and marriage. The words echoed within her and she wanted to send everyone home, to curl up in the silence of her room and spread out her memories, one by one, like photographs that could not be taken away. *Soon enough. They'll all be gone soon enough.*

She stood beside Gabrielle during the ceremony, listening to the traditional words and responses and thinking of Garth. I took this from you, she said to him silently. The ceremony, its dignity and mystery and faith, I took from you. I made it a joke in your eyes. That was one of the worst things I did to you. And I never knew it until now. I wish you and I were standing here, saying these words. I would promise you that what I would build with you is marriage – not a game, not a diversion, not a brief adventure. I would pledge to you my heart and my hand and my love, but you are so far and so angry—

'Stephanie,' Alexandra said. 'Are you all right?'

She turned. Brooks and Gabrielle, arm in arm, married, were greeting their guests. She apologized. 'I seem to have let my thoughts get the better of me.'

Alexandra put her arm around her. 'You're so pale. What can I do?'

'Help me feed everyone and keep the gossip light and pleasant.'

'I meant, what can I do to make you happier?'

For the briefest of moments, Sabrina rested her forehead on Alexandra's shoulder. Then she stood straight and smiled. 'Come back to London often. It will be good to have that to look forward to.'

And they went downstairs to supervise the wedding feast.

Chapter 24

Garth was in the university library when the headline of the December 17 *New York Times* caught his eye. Snatching it from the librarian's neat arrangement, he took it to an armchair in a corner of the periodical room and sped through the story, then went back to the beginning and read more slowly. His heart was pounding. Here in Michel Bernard's precise words was the whole story of the conniving and maneuvering, the rivalries and vast sums of money, the art thefts and forgeries that had led to the murder of Max Stuyvesant.

And of his wife.

He went through it a third time, and still it did not seem real. He was reading about the death of his wife, but her name was not mentioned. He was learning about her lover, who had not even known her true identity. He was reading about the life and death of a woman he was no longer sure he knew.

The other night he had told Cliff how she had looked at their wedding. That was clear in his mind. And he remembered their early years when the children were young and they were becoming a family. But when he tried to recall the last year, everything slid away from him. The only image in his mind was of the woman he had known for the past three months.

And he could not ignore the truth about that woman any longer. He loved her with a passion he could not eradicate or contain, though he still fought to destroy it, night after night, pacing alone and exhausted in his cold living room.

Which woman was he mourning? Both. Both. He no longer tried to deny it.

But he tried to forget. So many people were asking when Stephanie would return that he withdrew from the social contacts she had so carefully built and buried himself in work and activities with his children. He was supervising three new research projects in the laboratory, meeting daily with architects and contractors for the Genetics Institute, making preliminary plans with Lloyd Strauss for the groundbreaking ceremony scheduled for March, teaching an extra graduate seminar and gathering material for his paper on an immortal immune system in humans. He drove himself through the hours of each day, barely pausing to eat, never allowing himself to think about anything but the work he was doing.

And at home he drove himself with Penny and Cliff: cross-country skiing in the lakefront parks in Evanston and Chicago, going to movies and hockey games, playing word games at the dining room table, helping them with homework and working together on projects around the house that had been neglected for years. He refused to talk about their mother. 'We'll talk about her soon. It isn't time yet. I'm sorry; I'm not any happier than you are; you'll just have to trust me on this.'

What was he waiting for? He didn't know. But as each day passed and he did not expose the deception, he knew that the deeper its roots, the more real it became.

Which, he now understood, was exactly what Sabrina had discovered.

An air of quiet sadness clung to Penny and Cliff, even when they were praised at school or brought home a paper with a high grade. Even their squabbling was subdued. They fell into it automatically now and then but always stopped quickly, as if afraid of losing each other as they had lost their mother. They no longer rushed to see each day's mail in the hopes of finding a letter from her, but Garth knew they had written to her at least twice and he was not surprised when, at dinner on the same day he had seen the story in the *New York Times*, Cliff told him they were going shopping the next day for presents. 'If we mail them tomorrow, will they be in London in time for Christmas?'

'It's possible. If they're small we can send them airmail and a week might be enough. But it will be close.'

'Why didn't you tell us earlier how long it would take?' Penny demanded. 'You know more about it than we do! You don't want us to buy presents for her!'

'Maybe not,' he said, trying to be honest before their accusing eyes. 'Maybe I think we should only have Christmas here.'

'That's mean,' Penny said flatly. 'I think you're awful.'

But, later, when he came to say good night and found Cliff in her room, they both put their arms around him. 'We don't think you're awful,' Penny said. 'We think you're crying inside just like us. Daddy?'

'Yes, sweetheart.'

'Cliff said we shouldn't bug you, but why won't Mommy write to us? Or come home?'

'She's doing what we both think is best, Penny.'

'But if you think that, too, why are you crying inside?'

'Because often we can't have what we want.'

491

'If you want it bad enough, you can,' Cliff said.

'Look, both of you—' Garth heard the angry impatience in his voice and stopped. Leave me alone, he pleaded silently to his two children, who had done nothing wrong and needed reassurance as much as he did. I can't talk about it, I can hardly bear to think about it. I love her, I love her; not a moment goes by that I don't cry out for her. But more than an ocean lies between us, and I don't see any way in the world that we can cross it.

But he could say none of that aloud. 'Listen, now,' he said gently. 'Your mother and I have problems that I still can't talk about. You have a right to know, as soon as I sort things out, but for now, all I can tell you is that they keep us apart, like a broken bridge. How we feel isn't as important as the destruction between us. Can you understand that?'

'No,' they said together.

Garth sighed. 'I'm not surprised.' He put his arms around them and held them close, feeling them burrow against him as if looking for a hiding place. He bent his head and his voice was low and strained. 'I know I'm not doing a very good job at this, and I'm sorry for the mistakes I make, and for the times I seem cruel but, my dear ones, I don't know what to do. I know I make it harder for you by not telling you everything, but I can't do it, not yet. Can you trust me on that? Can you believe that I'll tell you as much as I can, as soon as I can? Please believe that, please believe in me. I need that. And I need your love. Because I love you, you know. More than anyone in the world—'

'More than Mom?' Cliff demanded.

'Oh, Cliff,' Penny scolded, and put her hand on Garth's cheek, for a brief moment becoming a woman, comforting a man. 'Don't cry, Daddy. We'll wait until you tell us. But—' And she was a little girl again. 'I just wish Mommy would come home.'

Garth kissed them and stood up. 'Get to sleep now, it's late. I love you both.'

The next day Penny and Cliff went shopping, and when Garth got home they handed him two small wrapped packages, asking him to mail them right away. He did not ask what was in them and they did not tell him.

On the last day of school Penny's puppet show was presented in the lunchroom and Garth left the university early so he could be there. In the front of the room, students from other classes sat cross-legged on the floor; in the back, parents sat on folding chairs, Garth and Vivian among them. Penny and Barbara Goodman were behind the stage with Mrs Casey, supervising the puppets before their classmates put them in action. Afterward, while Cliff stocked up on punch and cookies served by the sixth-grade food committee, Penny stood beside Garth, gravely accepting compliments from the audience. 'My mother can't be here,' she said to everyone. 'Her twin sister died in London and she has to be there to take care of the grave and things like that. She wanted to be here, but she couldn't. She helped me with the costumes. I didn't do them myself. She helped me.'

Vivian brought Garth a paper cup of punch. 'It tastes awful, but it's wet. Is Stephanie coming back?'

'No.'

Silently she looked at Penny, in earnest conversation with another parent about her mother's twin sister.

'It's not enough,' Garth said angrily. 'You can't rebuild a ruined marriage just because your children are unhappy.'

'Is it a ruined marriage?' Vivian asked. 'I never saw any signs of it, or got any clues.'

'It isn't even a marriage.' He looked at her worried face. 'I'm sorry, Vivian; I can't talk about it. Thank you for the punch.'

He counted the passage of each day, not knowing what he was waiting for. He and the children bought a Christmas tree, smaller than usual – 'since our family is smaller this year,' Penny said – and decorated it, putting their wrapped packages beneath it. Dolores invited them to their country house for cross-country skiing, but Penny and Cliff refused to go. 'I won't do it again without Mom,' Cliff declared. When school and the university closed for the holidays, the three of them spent a day painting the upstairs bedrooms. 'Won't Mommy be amazed?' Penny exclaimed again and again. 'Everything looks so *bright*. Won't she be amazed?'

And finally, though he had turned down every other invitation to holiday parties, Garth gave in to Nat and

493

Dolores's insistence that he join their annual gathering three days before Christmas. He sat with Penny and Cliff while they ate dinner, saw them settled in the living room with books, television and popcorn and walked alone to the Goldners' house.

It was always a large party. Dolores was determined to combine the university and the town into one happy community, and when Garth arrived he saw her steering local lawyers, insurance agents, store owners and physicians to small groups of faculty members. 'They complain they have nothing to say to each other,' she confided to Garth as she brought him a glass of wine. 'But after half an hour they're all talking about sewage problems and schools and Dutch elm disease. They have a wonderful time, thank me for introducing them to everyone and then go their own ways and never cross paths again until next year in this room. Can you explain it?'

Garth laughed with her. 'How often do most of us want to be in unpredictable situations? Once a year is plenty. The rest of the time we stay with comfortable places and people. Fewer surprises.'

'Surprises are lovely,' she protested.

'Only when they don't shatter everything that is familiar,' he said with such gravity that she stared, for once speechless.

Nat appeared. 'I've enlarged my library. Come have a look.'

Garth turned to apologize to Dolores for leaving, but as she exchanged a look with Nat he realized they had planned this: Nat was to have a talk with him. The conspiracies of happily married couples, he thought, to solve problems of their friends.

'You're in one of those unpredictable situations, aren't you?' Nat said, switching on the light in his upstairs library. 'But uncommunicative as a double agent. Is she or is she not coming back?'

'She's not.'

'So you said. So others have said. I didn't believe it.' He pulled two leather armchairs together. 'Have a seat. There's wine and Scotch in that cabinet. You two were closer than

I've ever seen you the last couple of months. So what happened so suddenly?'

'I thought we came here to see your enlarged library.'

'So we did. You're looking at it. What happened so suddenly?'

'Nat, do I ask you about your marriage?'

'No. You're more polite than I am. Also, you aren't a doctor. I am; therefore, I am accustomed to prying.'

'Into bones and ligaments, not—'

'Despair.'

'Do I seem to be in despair?'

'Why the hell do you think I'm prying? I'm worried about you; we're all worried about you. For God's sake, Garth, what happened between you and Stephanie?'

'I found out she wasn't the woman I thought she was.'

'Well, what does that mean? If you're saying that after twelve years you've discovered things about your wife you hadn't suspected, I wouldn't be surprised. Stephanie is in many ways a private person. I would be surprised if you had discovered depravity or criminal behavior, but, knowing Stephanie as a friend and patient, I'd say the chances of that are nonexistent. So is it *what* you have discovered, or simply the fact that there was something you hadn't known that has hurt you?'

Garth sat back in the leather chair and watched the wavering reflection of lamplight in the deep red of his wine. He was very tired, and Nat's words drifted to him from far away.

After twelve years you've discovered things about your wife you hadn't suspected.

A little more serious than that. But still, something to think about. 'Nat,' he said. 'Would you do me a favor?'

'Ask.'

'Let me sit here alone for awhile. No interruptions. I'll join the festivities later.'

'Whenever you're ready.' Nat opened the cabinet and brought out a bottle of wine and a box of crackers. 'Everything you need for profound thoughts. Dinner is at ten-thirty.'

Garth barely heard him leave. *Is it* what *you have*

discovered—? What had he discovered besides the fact that he'd been deceived for three months into thinking he was living with his wife? He refilled his glass, and for the first time in weeks relaxed the rigid control he had kept over his thoughts. Images poured in: pictures, memories, recollections – a kaleidoscope revolving before his eyes.

He saw the woman who led the family to talk about his research at the dinner table and who encouraged him to turn down Foster Labs and stay where he would be most happy. He saw the woman who tore into Mrs Casey for damaging Penny's belief in herself and later found a way to ease Cliff out of his gang of thieves. He saw the woman who got Linda a job at Collectibles to give her a way to succeed on her own. He saw the woman who cowed Rita McMillan, marching her off to Lloyd Strauss's office to clear Garth Andersen's name and pave the way for his formal appointment as director of the Genetics Institute.

Why? Because she was having fun playing a role? Or because she cared about the people she was helping? Because she had fallen in love?

She loved his children. He knew that now.

The door opened, and Garth looked up to see Madeline Kane. 'Excuse me,' she said. 'Dolores wonders if you will join us for dinner.'

'I don't think so. I have some . . . work to do at home. Dolores will understand.'

'Before you go, could you tell me – I don't mean to pry, but – could you tell me when Stephanie will be back?'

Garth hesitated. 'I don't know. I can't tell you. Would you make my apologies to Dolores?'

He found his coat and left by the side door. The night was brittle with cold, and in the silent streets his footsteps crunched on hard-packed snow. He plunged his hands into his pockets and turned into the park along the lake, lengthening his stride across the unbroken white expanse shimmering beneath a full moon.

His wife of twelve years had cared about people, loved them, worried about them. But, no matter how involved she became in their lives, when there was a crisis she became fearful and withdrew. She could not have backed Mrs Casey

496

into a corner or frightened Rita McMillan into a confession or even confronted Cliff when she thought he had been shoplifting.

And I knew that, Garth thought; I knew it but I let myself think that was one of the ways she was changing to help us rebuild our marriage.

But Sabrina, Lady Sabrina Longworth, who had no family and no responsibilities, who lived a life of extravagance that skimmed the surface of friendships and love affairs and even marriage ... she could dominate, she could confront, she could speak out. In fact, Stephanie had envied Sabrina for the courage to speak out and take the offensive when a wrong needed correcting. But was Lady Longworth the kind of woman who would have cared enough to take the trouble? Would she have loved Penny and Cliff? Would she have loved Garth Andersen?

His face felt frozen and his fingers in his coat pockets were numb. Garth turned toward home, slipping sideways on patches of ice as he broke into a run on the last block. The house was quiet; Penny and Cliff had left him half a bowl of cold popcorn and gone to sleep. Shivering, he laid a fire and lit it, then ran upstairs and changed into an old pair of jeans and a turtleneck sweater. In the kitchen, he fixed a tray of corned-beef sandwiches and beer, put on a pot of coffee and carried it all into the living room where the fire crackled and leaped up the chimney. Pulling up an armchair, he sat down with his tray on a table beside him, looking at the flames, letting the warmth seep into his skin. He realized suddenly that he felt extraordinarily good.

Why? he wondered. And knew the answer even as he asked it. Because, as a scientist, he was making progress, making discoveries, and spiraling in on the central one, the heart of the puzzle. The woman he had lived with for the last three months was neither his wife nor her sister, but a different person, just as she had said she was in New York – a woman with the caring and loving of Stephanie and the independence and strength of Sabrina. *That was why he had not seen through the deception.*

There had been far more to his blindness than the explanations he clutched in order to avoid disquieting suspicions; trying to believe she wanted to renew their marriage, or was in shock after the accident, or was mourning and identifying with her sister. The fact was, Sabrina Longworth had not lived with them very long before she began to act as much like her sister as herself. Twins, Garth thought. In each other's homes, in each other's thoughts. Within a few weeks the best of Sabrina merged with the best of her sister; she was Stephanie Andersen in so many important ways that the suggestion that she was someone else would have seemed absurd.

And as that happened to her, she became as much a victim of the deception as he – loving him and unable to tell him so until she was sure it was over. She had been caught, and neither of them had realized it.

And then, of course, there was one more reason why he was content to believe this woman was his wife; he had fallen in love with her. She had deceived him for three months, yet for almost every moment of that time she was more than he had ever dreamed of finding and loving and making a part of his life. And even now, knowing what he did, he thought of her as his wife.

The sandwich plate was empty; the beer was gone. More than I've eaten in three weeks, Garth thought. He poked the fire, adding more wood, and then poured a cup of coffee. Holding it between his hands, he watched the orange flames, tinged with yellow and blue, as they licked the cherry logs and sputtered and hissed when they reached a hidden drop of sap. There was no one left to hate, no more room for anger. He mourned the woman he had married years ago, who had fled their house to find something of herself, only to find death. He remembered the love they once had, and he thought with sorrow of the misunderstandings and failures they had brought to each other in their years together.

But out of the tangle that she and her sister had created when they took each other's place, Garth found a single strand: a new beginning. We might have found it anyway, he thought. After twelve years, both of us were changing; perhaps we were almost at the place where we could have built a new kind of love and marriage.

498

Instead, her sister came and stayed and became both of them. My dearest love. My wife.

In the quiet room, he smiled at the softly whispering flames. We'll have to get married, he thought.

Chapter 25

Each morning, Dmitri called. Two days after the wedding, as Sabrina was closing Ambassadors for the holidays, he came to take her to lunch. 'I thought you might be melancholy, seeing your friend married and being without your family at Christmas.'

In the pub, a group was singing a French carol. 'I know that song,' Sabrina said. 'We sang it at Juliette, my sister and I.'

'I want to talk about you,' he said. 'How can I give you what you want if you won't tell me what it is?'

'I told you, Dmitri. Friendship.'

'And that means someone to share feelings as well as talk and a lunch. All right,' he went on as she was silent, 'I will talk about my villa in Athens. As it is near the homes of my sisters and their husbands and their children, too numerous to count, it is a good place to spend Christmas.' He took her hand. 'We could be private and see no one, or be part of a large family with much noise and kissing and music. We would do whatever you wish. Come with me, Stephanie. I would make no demands on you; only that you enjoy friends and family instead of being alone.'

The group ended its Christmas carol on a soft chord and began another. Dmitri smiled. 'We would teach you our Greek songs.'

Temptation tugged at her. To be with a family, even one that was not hers; to have a change of scene with no reminders of a sister who was gone ... But it was not fair to Dmitri. She was not a whole person. And though she had told him that many times, if she went with him to Athens he would think it a first step, not a single time shared by friends.

She shook her head. 'Someday I might, Dmitri, but not yet.'

'You should not be alone,' he insisted.

'Sometimes being alone is important. How else do we have conversations with ourselves to make decisions about the future?'

'Friends can help you make decisions. Stephanie, I would make no demands on you.'

She took her hand from his to pick up her glass of ale. She wanted very much to believe him. 'May I let you know tomorrow?'

His face lit up. 'I'll call you in the morning. We would leave in the afternoon of the twenty-fourth. Would that suit you? Never mind,' he added hastily. 'You can tell me tomorrow.' And, as they finished lunch, he talked about his family and Greek friends and neighbors. 'And you could help me decorate my villa,' he said as they left the pub, as if looking for one last incentive for her to come with him.

'Perhaps,' she answered, smiling, and they talked about the brilliant white sunlight of southern Greece, so different from the light of other countries, while walking through London's damp gray afternoon, brightened only by Christmas lights.

Christmas lights: even the December mist could not dim them. They walked along Oxford Street, past Selfridges, where crowds stood at the windows, watching the story of Pinocchio acted out by puppets in miniature villages; and through Piccadilly Circus to Trafalgar Square, where the huge spruce, given each year to London by the city of Oslo, glittered as if stars had settled on its dark branches. Farther on, past Hyde Park Corner, every lintel, archway and window of Harrods, even its high dome, was outlined in pale gold lights like hundreds of small moons in the misty air.

Dmitri was silent, leaving Sabrina with her thoughts. She told herself the holiday meant nothing to her, that the lights and songs of carolers left her unaffected; but each time she saw a family group, with two children looking up and talking eagerly to the adults beside them, she turned quickly away, fixing her gaze elsewhere. It was then that she was grateful for Dmitri's undemanding companionship and his graceful withdrawal at her door on Cadogan Square.

Inside, she found Mrs Thirkell gazing happily at a small tree in the drawing room. 'I thought it might cheer you up, my lady, but I'll put it in my apartment upstairs if it brings back too many memories.'

'No, leave it,' Sabrina said. 'Will you decorate it?'

'I will, my lady, but I thought we might do it together.'

My lady. She no longer corrected Mrs Thirkell; often she barely heard it. Nor did it seem important; it made Mrs Thirkell happy, and they were both used to it.

The telephone rang. Sabrina's hands clenched. Each time it rang she thought . . . but it never was. 'Another invitation,' Mrs Thirkell predicted.

'If so, another refusal,' Sabrina responded, and they smiled at each other. It was curious, she thought, as Mrs Thirkell went to answer it, how close they had become. Lady Longworth could not have done it; too many social barriers lay between them. But now, even though Mrs Thirkell called her 'my lady,' she also thought of her as an American who had never been married to a viscount. They still were not quite friends, but they were two women sharing a home, and Sabrina felt less isolated than she had feared she would.

It was Mrs Thirkell who handled the torrent of invitations that came in the week before Christmas – for house parties, trips to the south of France, skiing at St Moritz, New Year's Eve balls – telling everyone that Mrs Andersen was accepting no invitations for the holidays.

The calls were still coming the day before Christmas. 'You're the rage of the season,' said Mrs Thirkell with satisfaction as the telephone rang in the late morning. 'Because you're something of a mystery. Not quite real, if you know what I mean.'

Yes, Sabrina thought as Mrs Thirkell left the room. I know what you mean. But she was listening. Each time the telephone rang, she could not help herself; her body grew still, waiting.

'It's Mr Karras, my lady,' Mrs Thirkell said, returning. 'And if you don't mind my saying so, I think you should go to Greece with him. It would do you good.'

501

Sabrina touched the needles of the small spruce tree they had decorated. It smelled of forests and mountains; of serene, private places. 'Perhaps I will,' she said, and went to talk to him.

But her face was clouded when she hung up; his delighted, eager voice, saying he would pick her up at four o'clock, made her feel guilty. It was not fair, it was not fair. I only want Garth, she thought; how will I talk and laugh with other people when I keep turning to the telephone to see if Garth is calling?

Mrs Thirkell found her a while later in the study. 'The post, my lady. Mostly cards, but also these packages.'

Sabrina knew what they were before she opened them. Two. One from Cliff, one from Penny. Nothing from Garth. Nothing. Not even a note. She unwrapped the packages, each colorfully wrapped, each with its own note. 'Mom, have a Happy Christmas,' Cliff wrote. 'With lots of food and presents. I hope you find what you're looking for. I wish I knew what it was. I love you. Your loving son, Cliff.'

'Dearest Mommy,' wrote Penny. 'I hope you like this and it makes you happy. I'd rather give it to you but I can't so Daddy will mail it. We're all fine but sad and Cliff and I talk about you a lot. I love you, I miss you, I love you. Love, Penny.'

I will not cry. I knew this might happen and I was prepared for it. I will not cry. Gently, she refolded the notes, pressing the creases with her fingertips, and then she opened the boxes. Cliff had sent a pin: a pair of yellow enameled birds on an enameled branch with two small leaves of green jade. A note inside the box said, 'These are you and Dad.'

Penny's box, long and narrow, held a silver pen and pencil set engraved with the letters *S A*. A small note beneath them read, 'For writing letters.'

The best extortionists, Sabrina thought, are children. She picked up the house phone. 'I'll have lunch in my room, Mrs Thirkell.' Carrying her presents, she climbed the stairs. Rain drummed against the windows, and her room was dark and chilly. She lit a fire, curling up before it on the chaise with an angora afghan over her lap, and looked at the enameled birds and the pen and pencil set and at the bright, dancing flames.

She should be packing for Athens, but, instead, she sat still, seeing in the flames all the dreams that haunted her days and nights.

They had been so careless, she and her sister, so incredibly careless of others. But what if it had ended differently; what if, somehow, there had been a way for her to love Garth and receive his love without guilt, a way to live with him and build a life with him? We could have had a child, she thought. A surprise for Penny and Cliff. A small smile curved the corners of her mouth as she pictured the two of them tossing a coin to see who got to feed the baby.

She could have gone into partnership with Madeline, decorating and restoring old buildings, while Linda handled estate sales. What a team the three of them would have made, especially if they joined Collectibles to Ambassadors and had the best art and antiques of two continents to choose from.

She and Garth would have the money from her sale of the Cadogan Square house and she would lure Mrs Thirkell to America. Then they could travel – to London, to Paris, where Gaby and Brooks would be living part of the time; even to Rio, to see Alexandra and finally meet some Guarani Indians. They could combine the whirl of her London social life with the home and community life she loved in Evanston. They could afford it all. They could even fix up the house. At least, they could finally paint the bedrooms. And she could buy Garth the leather jacket he'd been eyeing at Mark Shale one day when they were browsing together.

Jacket. Packing. She had to get ready. Taking her small suitcase and makeup case from the closet, she began to look through her clothes to choose what she would pack for Athens. But each dress meant gaiety and people, laughter and lights, and as she ran her fingers across them she knew she could not do it. Not yet; not when Garth was still a part of her, so real she felt she could reach out and touch his face and put her lips to his; so much a part of her deepest self that all she longed for was to tell him she loved him and wanted to be with him for the rest of her life – only him, no one else.

She called Dmitri and told him she could not go. Perhaps another time; perhaps they had a future. She did not know. It was not fair; she heard the disappointment in his voice and knew it was not fair. Whatever she did caused pain. Perhaps she would just sit in her room, alone, and eventually fade away. Then they would both be gone. Sabrina and Stephanie Hartwell: grew up together; later traded places; still later, disappeared.

She poked the fire, putting on another log, and went back to the chaise, the afghan on her lap. Her dreams were still there, in the flames, brighter than ever. They don't go away, she thought; they don't even fade. The days and weeks pass, the telephone rings and presents come from two loving children; the days go by and people come and go in our lives, and the dreams remain, vivid and alive.

She heard Mrs Thirkell climbing the stairs. Lunchtime, she thought. Then I'll do some work; I brought so much with me from Ambassadors – catalogues to read, books to study, letters to answer. Enough work to fill all the holidays. If I concentrate, I can forget everything else, at least for a while.

Mrs Thirkell knocked and appeared in the doorway, breathless, red-faced and beaming. 'My lady, there's a visitor to see—'

But before she could finish, following closely behind and overtaking her, Garth strode into the room, his face alight with love.

With a cry, Sabrina leaped up, but Garth had stopped, hesitant and watchful halfway across the room, the memory of their violent words echoing between them. Sabrina held out her hands, her voice barely a whisper. 'I dreamed of you ... all the time ... '

As if her words had released him he was suddenly beside her, catching her up, enfolding her tightly in his arms, her cheek against his heart. Dimly, she heard Mrs Thirkell leave the room, and then she heard only Garth's wild heartbeat and his voice, murmuring as his lips moved against her hair.

504

'My love, my dearest love, all the empty days without you—'

She stirred within his arms, turning up her face, and her mouth met his. Through closed eyes she saw the orange glow from the fireplace; she smelled the damp wool of his coat and felt with her fingertips the raindrops clinging to his hair. *These are real; no longer a dream; not ever again.* Garth felt her slender bones beneath his hands and breathed the silken fragrance that had haunted him for weeks. In the deepest part of him he felt his aching restlessness subside; he had come home.

'Yes,' she breathed, as if he had spoken, and opened her eyes to meet his, dark and intense. 'A place to belong ... '

But not yet. We haven't ... She put her hands on his chest, between them. 'Garth, we haven't talked ... so much is unfinished ... '

'No, my love.' He kissed her eyes, her mouth, the hollow of her throat. 'Not unfinished. Begun. And not with lies; with the truths you've told.'

'Truth! I deceived you—'

'Shamefully. But did you deceive me in the way you felt about Penny and Cliff? Or me? Or our life together?'

She shook her head. 'But beneath it all—'

'Beneath it all was love. Dear one, you made a marriage, you made us a family, and that is the truth you gave us. Except—' He laughed slightly. 'It is not quite the truth. My dearest love, I want to marry you, I want to take you home, to make the past and the present one life, our life together ... '

She took his face between her hands and searched his eyes for traces of the bitterness and hurt of their last meeting. But they were gone; he had resolved them, and there was only the warm caress of the times they had loved without restraint. She kissed him then, a long, slow kiss, pledging her heart and hand and love. Garth's arm tightened around her; his hand held her breast. 'Dear heart—' she said, a low sigh deep in her throat, and her body curved to his as if already taking him inside her. Together, they turned to the bed.

'Oh ... wait.' She held him back. 'We forgot ... What did you tell Penny and Cliff?'

Garth looked at her radiant face, her eyes bright with anticipation, and knew they mirrored his own. All the dreams were coming together at once. 'That I would try to bring you home,' he said.

'Are they at Vivian's?'

He nodded, his love for her so powerful it made him tremble, stopping the words in his throat.

She picked up the telephone and dialed and when Vivian answered, she settled back in the curve of Garth's arm. 'Vivian,' she said, 'it's Stephanie. Could I talk to my children, to tell them I'm coming home?'